TALES
OF
THE
DEAD

TALES
OF
THE
DEAD

Edited by
BILL PRONZINI

BONANZA BOOKS
New York

This book was originally published, in a slightly different form, as *The Arbor House Necropolis*.

This 1986 edition is published by Bonanza Books, distributed by Crown Publishers, Inc., by arrangement with Arbor House Publishing Company.

Printed and Bound in the United States of America

LIBRARY OF CONGRESS CATALOGING-IN-PUBLICATION DATA

Tales of the dead.

  Rev. ed. of: The Arbor House necropolis/edited by Bill Pronzini. 1981.
    1. Horror tales, American.   2. Horror tales, English.
3. Voodooism—Fiction. 4. Mummies—Fiction. 5. Ghouls
and ogres—Fiction. I. Pronzini, Bill. II. Arbor House
necropolis.
PS648.H6A7 1986   813′.0872′08   86-11694
ISBN 0-517-61818-4

h g f e d c b a

ACKNOWLEDGMENTS

PAPA BENJAMIN, by Cornell Woolrich. Copyright © 1935 by Popular Publications, Inc.; copyright renewed © 1962 by Cornell Woolrich. Originally published in *Dime Mystery* as "Dark Melody of Madness." Reprinted by permission of The Chase Manhattan Bank, N.A., Executor of the Estate of Cornell Woolrich.

". . . DEAD MEN WORKING IN THE CANE FIELDS," by W.B. Seabrook. From *The Magic Island*, copyright © 1929 by Harcourt, Brace & Company, Inc. Reprinted by permission of A. Watkins, Inc., Agents for the Estate of W.B. Seabrook.

MOTHER OF SERPENTS, by Robert Bloch. Copyright © 1936 by Weird Tales, Inc. First published in *Weird Tales*. Reprinted by permission of the author and the author's agents, Scott Meredith Literary Agency, Inc., 845 Third Avenue, New York, New York 10022.

THE DIGGING AT PISTOL KEY, by Carl Jacobi. Copyright © 1947 by Weird Tales, Inc. First published in *Weird Tales*. Reprinted by permission of Arkham House Publishers, Inc., Sauk City, Wisconsin 53583.

THE WEEKEND MAGUS, by Edward D. Hoch. Copyright ©
1980 by Edward D. Hoch. An original story published by
permission of the author.

THE PRINCESS, by Joe R. Lansdale. Copyright © 1980 by Joe
R. Lansdale. An original story published by permission of the
author.

THE EAGLE-CLAW RATTLE, by Ardath Mayhar. Copyright
© 1980 by Ardath Mayhar. An original story published by
permission of the author.

THE OTHER ROOM, by Charles L. Grant. Copyright © 1980
by Charles L. Grant. An original story published by permission of the author.

REVELATION IN SEVEN STAGES, by Barry N. Malzberg.
Copyright © 1980 by Barry N. Malzberg. An original story
published by permission of the author.

THE EDINBURGH LANDLADY, by Aubrey Davidson. Copyright © 1980 by Aubrey Davidson. First published in *Ellery
Queen's Mystery Magazine.* Reprinted by permission of the author.

INDIGESTION, by Barry N. Malzberg. Copyright © 1977 by
Ultimate Publications, Inc. First published in *Fantastic.* Reprinted by permission of the author.

THE CHADBOURNE EPISODE, by Henry S. Whitehead.
Copyright © 1933 by The Popular Fiction Publishing Company. First published in *Weird Tales.* Reprinted by permission of Arkham House Publishers, Inc., Sauk City, WI
53583.

DISTURB NOT MY SLUMBERING FAIR, by Chelsea Quinn
Yarbro. Copyright © 1978 by Chelsea Quinn Yarbro. First
published in *Cautionary Tales.* Reprinted by permission of the
author.

QUIETLY NOW, by Charles L. Grant. Copyright © 1981 by
Charles L. Grant. An original story published by permission
of the author.

THE SPHERICAL GHOUL, by Fredric Brown. Copyright ©
1942 by Better Publications, Inc. First published in *Thrilling
Mystery.* Reprinted by permission of Scott Meredith Literary

8   ACKNOWLEDGMENTS

Agency, Inc., 845 Third Avenue, New York, New York 10022, agents for the estate of Fredric Brown.

CORPUS DELECTABLE, by L. Sprague de Camp and Fletcher Pratt. Copyright © 1953 by Twayne Publishers. From *Tales of Gavagan's Bar*. Reprinted by permission of L. Sprague de Camp.

MEMENTO MORI, by Bill Pronzini. Copyright © 1974 by H.S.D. Publications, Inc.; revised version copyright © 1981 by Bill Pronzini. First published in *Alfred Hitchcock's Mystery Magazine*. Reprinted by permission of the author.

GRAY MATTER, by Stephen King. Copyright © 1973 by Cavalier, Inc. First published in *Cavalier;* from the book *Night Shift* by Stephen King. Reprinted by permission of Doubleday & Company, Inc.

PREFACE

THE WORD "necropolis," which derives from the Greek, means "city of the dead." *Tales of the Dead* presents not one but three complete "cities of the dead" in literary form—a compendium of fact and fiction about beings real and supernatural, alive and long buried. In the pages that follow, you will find a wealth of graveyard plots dealing with zombies, voodoo curses, resurrected mummies, and ravening ghouls, all calculated to chill your blood and disturb your sleep.

The first two books, *Voodoo!* and *Mummy!*, appeared previously in separate volumes; if you missed either or both, *Tales of the Dead* contains the full text of each title. The third book, *Ghoul!*, has not been published separately prior to its inclusion here. *Ghoul!* not only offers some of the finest tales ever penned on that theme, by such masters of the macabre as Stephen King, Fredric Brown, and Chelsea Quinn Yarbro, but makes *Tales of the Dead* one of the most complete excursions into the realm of horror ever published.

Pleasant dreams....

—Bill Pronzini

CONTENTS

BOOK ONE: VOODOO!

PART II: VOODOO ELSEWHERE AND OTHERWISE

PART III: THE "ULTIMATE" VOODOO

BOOK TWO: MUMMY!

PART I: EGYPTIAN MUMMIES

PART II: OTHER LANDS, OTHER CULTURES

PART III: IN THE FAR FUTURE

BOOK THREE: GHOUL!

PART I: TRADITIONAL GHOULS

PART II: VARIATIONS ON THE THEME

Book One

VOODOO!
A Chrestomathy
of Necromancy

INTRODUCTION

IT BEGINS with the drums.

In a hidden clearing, by firelight under a moonless sky, the small band of worshipers stands waiting and listening to the steady throbbing beat of hands on the *rada* skins. The young goat tied near the *vodun* altar, already washed and anointed with perfume and wearing brightly colored bits of cloth, makes frightened bleats; no one notices. The two priests, the *papaloi* and the *mamaloi*, take their places on the altar next to an ornamented box containing the holy serpent known as Damballah.

Soon the *papaloi* starts chanting the words *"Papa Legba, ouvri barrie pou nous passer"*—asking Legba, master of the barrier which divides men from the world of spirits, to open the gate so that he and his followers may pass through and become one with the *loa,* the gods of voodoo. Then, one by one, the other believers approach to swear their devotion and ask their private favors.

The rhythm of the drums quickens. The *papaloi* touches the serpent box with one hand, clutches the *mamaloi*'s hand with the other; their bodies begin to tremble, to undulate in time to the thudding beat. It is not long before he lifts his queen atop the box, where her writhings become more intense, spasmodic, arms and legs thrusting out at acute angles, head lolling as if broken on the stem of her neck. She screams, then cries out a sacred invocation to Baron Samedi, the ruler of the cemetery, the symbol of death—and the worshipers know that she is possessed and the words she speaks are no longer her own but those of the serpent within the box.

A sharp knife flashes; the goat makes its final bleating cry. Earthenware bowls are quickly placed to catch the blood from its slit throat.

Now the *papaloi* commences the ancient *afro-americaine* chant, and the others can feel the power of the *loa* seizing control of their bodies too. They enter into a series of convulsions, moaning and shrieking with the ecstasy of their possession. Hands are clasped to increase the flow of power, like electrical current, from one twitching body to another; the chant rises and falls to the staccato pulse of the drums.

> *Eh! Eh! Bomba hen hen!*
> *Canga bafie te*
> *Danga moune de te*
> *Canga do ki li!*
> *Canga li!*

The *papaloi* takes up a bowl of the kid's blood, hands it to the *mamaloi*. She drinks, passes the bowl on. Other bowls are lifted; dark fluid stains the lips and chins of the believers.

Both the chant and the rhythm of the drums increase to a feverish tempo. The movements of those in the clearing grow frenzied: they spin, leap, bend and twist, spread-eagle themselves on the earth, slither along it on their bellies in emulation of the serpent Damballah; they tear off their clothing, and the women clutch their breasts and lift them high, present them as offerings to the *loa*. Hands and bodies touch, blood-wet mouths fuse and slide apart; they bite, claw, scratch, fondle one another. For some, the intensity of the experience is too great, and they fall unconscious and are carried away into the shadows behind the fires. But the others go on, driven to ever greater paroxysms, naked flesh gleaming eerily in the firelight.

And the drums and the chant go on, too—*Eh! Eh! Bomba hen hen!*—far into the night.

It is only when dawn approaches, and but a few worshipers are left who have not succumbed to exhaustion, that the *loa* have been satisfied and the ceremony reaches its completion. Only then that the *rada* skins are still. For it ends as it begins—with the drums. This is always so.

And it is always so, too, that somewhere between the beginning and the ending there is a flashing knife, and a final bleating cry, and bowls placed quickly to catch blood from a slit throat.

But it is not always so that the cry and the blood come from a goat or other animal. Sometimes, in other clearings on other dark nights, the voodoo gods receive a different and more powerful form of sacrifice.

Sometimes the victim is human. . . .

There is some disagreement as to the origin of voodoo, both as a word and as a religion in the Americas. The most widely accepted version is that it originated in the West African province of Dahomey, from which most slaves were imported to the New World more than two hundred years ago. Among the Fon and other tribes of this region, there was a widespread belief in *vodu* or *vodun*—a word which translates as "something apart and holy" or, simply, as "god." And the god they worshiped was the serpent (traditionally, a python) because they believed that the first man and woman who came into the world were blind and it was the snake who bestowed sight upon the human race.

The second theory is that voodoo is of French origin and can be traced to the followers of Peter Valdo, also known as Father Valdesius, a member of the Catholic clergy in the twelfth century who founded a sect known as Vaudois. This sect was said to have practiced both witchcraft and human sacrifice, and thus the word *vaudois* eventually became a generic term for sorcerers and servants of black magic. Early French colonists, according to this theory, brought the practice of vaudois to Haiti, where the word was corrupted to *voudou.*

In either case, voodoo came to the "brave new world" in the early 1700s and spread rapidly among the oppressed slaves. Life for them under the yoke of French and Spanish settlers was appalling: they were "tamed" in slave camps upon arrival, then worked in chains from dawn to dusk, frequently whipped and branded with the fleur-de-lis, locked in guarded quarters at night, and forbidden by law to assemble for any purpose. On some plantations, atrocities against blacks almost exceed belief: slaves turned loose and hunted down for sport; slaves buried alive in vertical positions so that only their heads remained above ground, after which heavy balls were bowled at them for sport by the colonists—the object being to split open or knock off as many as possible. Less sadistic masters made superficial attempts to convert their slaves to Catholicism, but in the main blacks were allowed no religion at all. The consensus was that they had no souls.

The fact that voodoo nonetheless managed to flourish frightened the plantation owners, who considered it to be a "terrible weapon" which might one day rally the slaves to revolt. (Part of their fear, too, lay in their own deep-rooted European beliefs in the powers of black magic and the supernatural, and in such voodoo-related beings as werewolves, witches and demons.) Those blacks who were discovered to practice this "unholy" religion were beaten, imprisoned or executed. A number of restrictions on slave traffic were put into effect as well. Louisiana governor Gálvez, for example, forbade the importation of blacks from Martinique in 1782 because their voodooism "would make the lives of the citizens unsafe"; a similar ban on slaves from Santo Domingo occurred ten years later.

One of the reasons voodoo thrived in spite of all efforts to suppress it was that the slaves came from many classes of African society, including that of priests and magicians. Once arrived in the Americas, all classes were forced to live, work, and even die together, and voodoo was the only common bond; its teachings, therefore, were carefully handed down from one generation to the next. By the time most of the cruel laws and restrictions were abolished by American authorities in Louisiana after the Purchase of 1803, voodoo was a powerful and organized force both in this country and throughout the Caribbean.

Its greatest strength, of course, was in Haiti, the "Magic Island," where it still flourishes today. On such West Indian islands as Jamaica and Trinidad, it took shallower roots and evolved somewhat differently into the form known as Obeah. Other variations, called Macumba and Santería, were and still are practiced in Latin America. And there are examples of primitive magic, of spiritism (sometimes combined with Christianity), in such divers places as Hawaii, the islands of the South Seas and New Guinea.

In the West Indies the early voodoo ceremonies were those primitive ones which were born in Dahomey, Senegal and other African provinces. But as time passed, certain Roman Catholic features were incorporated into them to create the curious mixture which exists today. God is considered the ruler of the universe and the creator and sustainer of all life; but it is the *loa,* or lesser gods, who serve to give men and women direct contact with God and His supernatural forces, and who are concerned with the existence of humans and with their fate after death. Sacrifice and the drinking of blood are justified as offerings to the *loa,* rather than to God Himself, for favors, good fortune and good health.

But some voodoo was and is of a darker and more pagan variety. For one, there is the Sect Rouge (or *cochons gris*—gray pigs or hairless pigs) of Haiti. Although the Red Sect has a long tradition on the Magic Island, few people will discuss it and little has been written about it. Some believe it is only a myth, another of Haiti's many voodoo legends; but there are others who will swear otherwise, and infrequent but documented evidence to corroborate their belief.

Members of the Sect Rouge are said to dress in red robes and headwear in the shape of horns or straw hats with sharp tall witches' crowns; to carry candles and whips. They meet late at night in the countryside and then move in a column to the nearest cemetery. There they make offerings of food, drink and money to Papa Legba, Baron Samedi and other *loa*—imploring help in obtaining a "goat without horns," a human being who can be sacrificed.

The *houngan* or priest dances chanting around the cemetery graves; candles and bowls of animal blood are placed on top of them. Then the sect leaves, again in a column, and goes to the nearest crossroads, which is considered the best place to find a victim. Once an unwary traveler has been taken—once rags have been stuffed into his mouth and a cord of intestines wound around his neck—he is transported to a secluded clearing and immediately killed with a ceremonial knife. After the killing, the corpse is carved into several pieces and his flesh eaten and his blood drunk. (The belief in Haiti is widespread that these victims are first turned into beasts ready for slaughter. Some of the animals brought to slaughterhouses are thought to be human beings who escaped from the Sect Rouge after being magically transformed; according to the superstition, these creatures are recognizable by the sad expression in their eyes.)

There are other voodoo sects reputed to believe in human sacrifice, both in the Caribbean and in the United States. Some of these also believe, as do many other voodoo followers, in the use of the voodoo fetish called the devil doll to destroy an enemy. These dolls are small, usually six inches or so in height, and made of earth or clay or wax and bits of rags; resemblance to the victim is unnecessary, but in order for the dolls to work they must contain nail parings, strands of hair or something else from the victim's body. Magical incantations are then said over the fetish, after which sharp things are jabbed into it, or string is tied around its neck, or its limbs are squeezed into odd shapes or pulled off entirely—a simulation of whatever it is the believer wishes to happen, fatally or otherwise, to his enemy. In some instances, depending on the type of magic used, the victim is to feel pain the instant the doll is savaged; in other cases, where an even more torturous vengeance is desired, the victim may not feel pain for weeks or months, but is given the doll immediately so he will know well in advance of what lies in store for him.

Universal among all voodoo sects is belief in the living dead. In Haiti and other places, the fear of zombies is severe; people are not only afraid that they themselves will become zombies after death, but that a member of their family will become one, or that a zombie might harm them while they are alive. Some families go to great lengths to protect their dead: a thirty-six hour watch after burial in a cemetery, so that there can be no possibility of revival; burial at a well-traveled crossroads; bodies cut open and the hearts damaged to assure absolute death; a knife placed in the right hand of the corpse, in the hope that it will stab anyone who tries to disturb it. When someone dies suddenly, young people in particular, and if a body stays warm after death, chances are the person expired from unnatural causes and a plot is afoot to turn him or her into a zombie. Special care is always taken in these cases.

A Haitian legend about zombies, recounted by Kyle Kristos in his book *Voodoo*, concerns a rich farmer who needs cheap labor for his farm and who makes an arrangement with a voodoo magician or *bocor*. The *bocor*, after performing a certain ritual once the sun has set, mounts a horse facing the tail and rides to the victim's house. Once there, he puts his lips to the crack of the door and sucks out the soul of his prey. Before long the victim dies; and following the funeral the *bocor* watches the cemetery interment without facing anyone in the mourning party. Later, after midnight, he returns to claim the body by unearthing it or opening its crypt, calling out the victim's name to awaken it, then chaining the corpse and beating it about the head to make it respond.

On the way to his voodoo temple, the *bocor* takes the zombie past the house where it lived in order to gain complete control of it; otherwise the zombie might one day pass the house and remember it. At the temple the corpse is given a drop of special liquid—and from then on it will do the *bocor*'s (and the farmer's) bidding, without question and without being conscious of who it once was. Nor will it ever speak, unless by accident it is given salt to eat.

But this is, of course, a legend. There is really no such thing as a corpse resurrected from the grave, mindless and soulless, capable of carrying out the orders of a voodoo priest; those purportedly documented zombie cases in Haiti may almost always be explained as living men and women who fell under a *bocor*'s spell, cast through hypnosis and the use of drugs. (Similarly, it is not supernatural forces which cause the victim of a devil-doll curse to succumb according to what was done to the doll; it is the power of suggestion, the victim's own mind, which leads him into self-destruction.) Necromancy may be at the core of voodoo, but there is nothing magical in the effects of its ceremonies.

And yet . . .

There are, after all, some cases which seem to defy logical explanation. Is that illusion or is it truth? *Is* it possible that sometimes, in certain instances, the power of voodoo really does work?

Perhaps.

Yes, perhaps. For there *are* more things in heaven and earth, you know, than are dreamt of in our philosophy.

The first significant writing on the subject of voodoo was published in 1884 and authored by Spencer St. John, a former British consul in Haiti (or Hayti, as it was then spelled). The book, entitled *Hayti; or the Black Republic,* included a number of lavish descriptions of voodoo ceremonies, as well as accounts of such atrocities as cannibalism and the sacrificing of children, and was thus the basis for much of the early horror fiction on the voodoo theme. Unfortunately, there is as much romanticized fact and outright fiction in the book as there is valid material (and not a little racism to boot).

The same is true, although to a far less exaggerated and less offensive degree, of perhaps the most well-known "nonfiction" work on voodoo, W.B. Seabrook's *The Magic Island.* Published in 1929 and widely read, it relates Seabrook's own adventures in Haiti with voodoo and offers native accounts of such legendary figures as werewolves and fire-hags. One of the book's most provocative chapters, dealing with zombies, appears later in these pages—and it is left to the reader to determine how much of the information recounted therein is nonfiction and how much pure storytelling.

Of the dozens of works about West Indian voodoo, perhaps the most authoritative and objective are Hugh B. Cave's *Haiti: Highroad to Adventure* (1952), Alfred Metraux's *Voodoo in Haiti*

(1959), and Kyle Kristos' *Voodoo* (1976). Robert Tallant's *Voodoo in New Orleans* (1946) is a superior history of *vodun* practices in that city and its outlying areas. And on the subjects of primitive magic and spiritism elsewhere, both Migene Gonzalez-Wippler's *Santería: African Magic in Latin America* (1973) and A.J. Langguth's *Macumba: White and Black Magic in Brazil* (1975) are fascinating and informative.

There are no works of fiction which may be termed "voodoo classics"; however, a number of novels and collections of short stories are quite good and deserve to reach a wider audience than they have thus far.

Charles G. Chesnutt (1858–1932), a black lawyer from North Carolina, was the first American to publish fiction dealing with the "conjuring practices" of slaves. His short stories, some humorous and some weird, appeared in *The Atlantic* in the 1880s and 1890s—the first, "The Goophered Grapevine," in 1887—and were collected in 1899 under the title *The Conjure Woman;* all are post–Civil War plantation tales narrated by a white Northerner but for the most part told in a North Carolina black dialect. Although they were popular at first, it is a sad comment on the times to note that their popularity underwent a rapid decline when it was revealed Chesnutt was a black, not a white, author. As a result of this prejudicial rejection, he wrote no more fiction during the last thirty-three years of his life.

A pair of Haitian writers, Philippe Thoby-Marcelin and Pierre Marcelin, authored three novels between 1944 and 1951—*Canapé Vert, The Beast of the Haitian Hills,* and *The Pencil of God*—which were lavishly praised by such critics as Edmund Wilson and Waldo Frank, the latter commenting that they "capture the profound rhythms of Haitian life." *Canapé Vert,* which deals with the voodoo religion in depth, was judged by John Dos Passos to be the best Latin American novel of 1944.

Hugh B. Cave's 1959 novel, *The Cross on the Drum,* is a first-rate study of the conflicts between Christianity and voodoo on the mythical Caribbean island of St. Joseph; the book contains a considerable amount of voodoo lore (as does Cave's recent macabre tale of voodoo and zombieism, *Legion of the Dead,* published in 1979). Other noteworthy novels include bestselling author Morris West's second book, *Kundu* (1956)—a searing account of primitive magic on New Guinea, excerpts from which are included here; Robert Tallant's meticulously researched *Voodoo Queen* (1956), a fictionalized biography of New Orleans's famous nineteenth-century voodoo priestess, Marie Laveau; Sax Rohmer's Fu Manchu adventure, *The Island of Fu Manchu* (1941); and a 1930 mystery entitled *Voodoo* by John Esteven—a pseudonym of historical novelist Samuel Shellabarger—which has several well-portrayed and chilling voodoo scenes (although the book is marred by certain fantastic and foolish notions about blacks).

Two excellent volumes of West Indian voodoo stories by Henry S. Whitehead, *Jumbee and Other Uncanny Tales* and *West India Lights,* were published in the 1940s by Arkham House. Several of the stories are considered by aficionados to be superior examples of the literature of the weird and macabre; one of these, "Seven Turns in a Hangman's Rope," appears in these pages.

As for voodoo films, there are only a few, and but two of those are of any quality. The best is Val Lewton's masterful *I Walked with a Zombie* (1943), starring Frances Dee and Tom Conway and set in Haiti. Although it was released as a "B" horror movie, it had fine production values, atmospheric direction by Jacques Tourneur, and a superior script by Curt Siodmak (his plot was freely adapted from *Jane Eyre* and made liberal use of authentic voodoo practices as described in a series of newspaper articles of the time; it also vividly expressed one of Lewton's obsessive themes—the conflict between the powers of reason and the powers of the unknown).

Another unusual film was the 1932 *White Zombie,* with Bela Lugosi and Madge Bellamy as stars and Haiti again as the setting. Despite almost uniform bad acting, which makes for giggles instead of shudders at certain moments when viewed today, there are some well-done scenes of ritualized death and brooding horror. One, the best in the film, takes place in a sugar mill owned by Lugosi and depicts a horde of black zombies operating a cane-crushing machine; one of the zombies accidentally falls into the crusher and is ground up with the sugar cane, while the others continue about their methodical and mindless duties.

With the exceptions of *The Ghost Breakers*, a 1940 comedy vehicle for Bob Hope in which zombies play a minor role, and *The Devil's Own* (1966), a mildly interesting British screech-and-shudder vehicle for Joan Fontaine, the remaining voodoo films are what Hollywood itself calls "drek"—godawful melodramas which mostly seem to star Bela Lugosi and John Carradine and which mostly seem to deal with a bastardized form of the zombie legend. Even their titles are more or less interchangeable: *Revenge of the Zombies, Revolt of the Zombies, Zombies on Broadway; The Voodoo Man, Voodoo Woman, Voodoo Tiger*.

There are as few short stories on the voodoo theme as films, but among them are several outstanding works; all of the best are presented in the pages which follow. Joining Henry S. Whitehead's "Seven Turns in a Hangman's Rope" are such tales of traditional voodoo (that is, the West Indian variety) as Cornell Woolrich's "Papa Benjamin," Robert Bloch's "Mother of Serpents" and Carl Jacobi's "The Digging at Pistol Key." Locales include Haiti, New Orleans, Trinidad and the Virgin Islands.

Unusual examples of voodoo elsewhere and otherwise, in addition to the excerpt from Morris West's *Kundu,* are Robert Louis Stevenson's "The Isle of Voices," John Russell's "Powers of Darkness," Edward D. Hoch's "Exú," Mary Elizabeth Counselman's "Seventh Sister" and Bryce Walton's "The Devil Doll." The settings here are as diverse as the thematic approaches: Hawaii, Papua, Brazil, Alabama, New York City, New Guinea.

And for a proper finale, there is Henry Slesar's "The Candidate"—a story of the "ultimate" voodoo adapted to contemporary society.

Twelve stories in all, and all written by past and present masters of the bizarre and the special.

With pens dipped in blood. . . .

The time has come; only a matter of seconds remain before the first ceremony begins.

So prepare yourself. Turn up the lights; lay another log on the fire. For some of the rituals you're about to witness are truly strange and truly terrifying, and they are best viewed from within a shadowless room.

Listen, now.

Listen.

There. Can you hear it?

There—the first throbbing beat of the voodoo drums. . . .

—BILL PRONZINI

PART I
TRADITIONAL VOODOO

PAPA BENJAMIN

by CORNELL WOOLRICH

Think of New Orleans and any number of things come immediately to mind: gutbucket jazz, the Mardi Gras, the French Quarter, Storyville, riverboat gamblers and Creole beauties and gentlemen fighting duels over a lady's honor. Yes, and of course voodoo. For close to two centuries New Orleans has been the center of voodoo practice in this country; for close to two centuries thousands have worshiped and hundreds have died at shrines hidden among its cemetery gravestones, inside its decaying buildings, along its backwater canals. The beat of voodoo drums is as much a part of the city's rhythms as the throbbing notes from a jazzman's horn.

Only a few works of fiction, however, capture both the mystery of voodoo and the unique flavor of New Orleans. The two novels which best accomplish that difficult feat are Robert Tallant's Voodoo Queen *and Kenneth Perkins's* Voodoo'd. *The best short story by far is Cornell Woolrich's "Papa Benjamin."*

First published in 1936 in Dime Mystery, *a "shudder pulp" magazine, "Papa Benjamin" is the tale of what happens to a successful band leader named Eddie Bloch when he makes a commercial musical number of the voodoo rhythm and thus "mocks the spirits with the chant that summons them." Its brooding atmosphere, its feelings of cosmic malevolence and palpably mounting terror, make it not only a classic of voodoo*

33

fiction but one of Woolrich's most powerful stories.

The ability to create that sense of palpable dread was the primary reason Cornell Woolrich achieved his considerable reputation as a master of the suspense story. No writer past or present rivals him in the art of expressing the kind of pure terror found in such stories as "Papa Benjamin" and "Rear Window" and such novels as The Bride Wore Black, Phantom Lady *(as by William Irish), and* The Night Has a Thousand Eyes *(written under the pseudonym George Hopley). The cinematic quality of his work is another reason for its success, and accounts for the remarkable total of twenty-eight feature films and twenty-five teleplays based on his novels and stories. ("Papa Benjamin," in fact, was adapted for the screen in 1961 as a segment of the TV series* Thriller.*) A tragic figure who lived most of his life in New York City hotel rooms, both alone and with his domineering mother, Woolrich died in 1968 at the age of sixty-five.*

AT FOUR in the morning, a scarecrow of a man staggers dazedly into the New Orleans police headquarters building. Behind him at the curb a lacquered Bugatti purrs like a drowsy cat, the finest car that ever stood out there. He weaves his way through the anteroom, deserted at that early hour, and goes in through the open doorway beyond. The sleepy desk sergeant looks up; an idle detective scanning yesterday's *Times-Picayune* on the two hind legs of a chair tipped back against the wall raises his head; and as the funnel of light from the cone-shaped reflector overhead plays up their visitor like flashlight powder, their mouths drop open and their eyes bat a couple of times. The two front legs of the detective's chair come down with a thump. The sergeant braces himself, eager, friendly, with the heels of both hands on his desk top and his elbows up in the air. A patrolman comes in from the back room, wiping a drink of water from his mouth. His jaw also hangs when he sees who's there. He sidles nearer the detective and says behind the back of his hand, "That's Eddie Bloch, ain't it?"

The detective doesn't take the trouble to answer. It's like telling him what his own name is. The three stare at the figure under the light, interested, respectful, almost admiring. There is nothing professional in their scrutiny, they are not the police studying a suspect; they are nobodies looking at a celebrity. They take in the rumpled tuxedo, the twig of gardenia that has shed its petals, the tie hanging open in two loose ends. His topcoat was slung across his arm originally; now it trails along the dusty station-house floor behind him. He gives his hat the final, tortured push that dislodges it. It drops and rolls away behind him. The policeman picks it up and brushes it off—he never was a bootlicker in his life, but this man is Eddie Bloch.

Still it's his face, more than who he is or how he's dressed, that would draw stares anywhere. It's the face of a dead man—the face of a dead man on a living body. The shadowy shape of the skull seems to peer through the transparent skin; you can make out its bone structure as though an X-ray were outlining it. The eyes are stunned, shocked, haunted gleams, set in a vast purple hollow that bisects the face like a mask. No amount of drink or dissipation could do this to anyone, only long illness and the foreknowledge of death. You see faces like that looking up at you from hospital cots when all hope has been abandoned— when the grave is already waiting.

Yet, strangely enough, they knew who he was just now. Instant recognition of who he was came first—realization of the shape he's in comes after that, more slowly. Possibly it's because all three of them have been called on to identify corpses in the morgue in their day. Their minds are trained along those lines. And this man's face is known to hundreds of people. Not that he has ever broken or even fractured the most trivial law, but he has spread happiness around him, set a million feet to dancing in his time.

The desk sergeant's expression changes. The patrolman mutters under his breath to the detective, "Looks like he just came out of a bad smashup with his car." "More like a drinking bout, to me," answers the detective. They are simple men, capable within their limitations, but those are the only explanations they can find for what they now see before them.

The desk sergeant speaks. "Mr. Eddie Bloch, am I right?" He extends his hand across the desk in greeting.

The man can hardly stand up. He nods, he doesn't take the hand.

"Is there anything wrong, Mr. Bloch? Is there anything we can do for you?" The detective and the patrolman come over closer. "Run in and get him a drink of water, Latour," the sergeant says anxiously. "Have an accident, Mr. Bloch? Been held up?"

The man steadies himself with one arm against the edge of the sergeant's desk. The detective extends an arm behind him, in case he should fall backward. He keeps fumbling, continually fumbling in his clothes. The tuxedo jacket swims on him as his movements shift it around. He is down to about a hundred pounds in weight, they notice. Out comes a gun, and he doesn't even have the strength to lift it up. He pushes it and it skids across the desk top, then spins around and points back at him.

He speaks, and if the unburied dead ever spoke, this is the voice they'd use. "I've killed a man. Just now. A little while ago. At half-past three."

They're completely floored. They almost don't know how to handle the situation for a minute. They deal with killers every day, but killers have to be gone out after and dragged in. And when fame and wealth enter into it, as they do once in a great while, fancy lawyers and protective barriers spring up to hedge the killers in on all sides. This man is one of the ten idols of America, or was until just lately. People like him don't kill people. They don't come in out of nowhere at four in the morning and stand before a simple desk sergeant and a simple detective, stripped to their naked souls, shorn of all resemblance to humanity, almost.

There's silence in the room for a minute, a silence you could cut with a knife. Then he speaks again, in agony. "I tell you I've killed a man! Don't stand there looking at me like that! I've killed a man!"

The sergeant speaks, gently, sympathetically. "What's the matter, Mr. Bloch, been working too hard?" He comes out from

behind the desk. "Come on inside with us. You stay here, Latour, and look after the telephone."

And when they've accompanied him into the back room: "Get
him a chair, Humphries. Here, drink some of this water, Mr.
Bloch. Now what's it all about?" The sergeant has brought the
gun along with him. He passes it before his nose, then breaks
it open. He looks at the detective. "He's used it all right."

"Was it an accident, Mr. Bloch?" the detective suggests re-
spectfully. The man in the chair shakes his head. He's started to
shiver all over, although the New Orleans night is warm and
mellow. "Who'd you do it to? Who was it?" the sergeant puts
in.

"I don't know his name," Bloch mumbles. "I never have.
They call him Papa Benjamin."

His two interrogators exchange a puzzled look. "Sounds
like—" The detective doesn't finish it. Instead he turns to the
seated figure and asks almost perfunctorily: "He was a white
man, of course?"

"He was colored," is the unexpected answer.

The thing gets more crazy, more inexplicable, at every step.
How should a man like Eddie Bloch, one of the country's best-
known band leaders, who used to earn a thousand dollars every
week for playing at Maxim's, come to kill a nameless colored
man—and then be put into this condition by it? These two men
have never seen anything like it in their time; they have subjected suspects to forty-eight-hour grillings and yet compared to
him now those suspects were fresh as daisies when they got
through with them.

He has said it was no accident and he has said it was no
hold-up. They shower questions at him, not to confuse him but
rather to try to help him pull himself together. "What did he do,
forget his place? Talk back to you? Become insolent?" This is
the South, remember.

The man's head goes from side to side like a pendulum.

"Did you go out of your mind for a minute? Is that how it
was?"

Again a nodded no.

The man's condition has suggested one explanation to the detective's mind. He looks around to make sure the patrolman outside isn't listening. Then very discreetly: "Are you a needle-user, Mr. Bloch? Was he your source?"

The man looks up at them. "I've never touched a thing I shouldn't. A doctor will tell you that in a minute."

"Did he have something on you? Was it blackmail?"

Bloch fumbles some more in his clothes; again they dance around on his skeletonized frame. Suddenly he takes out a cube of money, as thick as it is wide, more money than these two men have ever seen before in their lives. "There's three thousand dollars there," he says simply and tosses it down like he did the gun. "I took it with me tonight, tried to give it to him. He could have had twice as much, three times as much, if he'd said the word, if he'd only let up on me. He wouldn't take it. That was when I had to kill him. That was all there was left for me to do."

"What was he doing to you?" They both say it together.

"He was killing me." He holds out his arm and shoots his cuff. The wristbone is about the size of the sergeant's own thumb joint. The expensive platinum wristwatch that encircles it has been pulled in to the last possible notch and yet it still hangs almost like a bracelet. "See? I'm down to one hundred and two. When my shirt's off, my heart's so close to the surface you can see the skin right over it move like a pulse with each beat."

They draw back a little, almost they wish he hadn't come in here. That he had headed for some other precinct instead. From the very beginning they have sensed something here that is over their heads, that isn't to be found in any of the instruction books. Now they come out with it. "How?" Humphries asks. "How was he killing you?"

There's a flare of torment from the man. "Don't you suppose I would have told you long ago, if I could? Don't you suppose I would have come in here weeks ago, months ago, and demanded protection, asked to be saved—if I could have told you what it was? If you would have believed me?"

"We'll believe you, Mr. Bloch," the sergeant says soothingly. "We'll believe anything. Just tell us—"

But Bloch in turn shoots a question at them, for the first time since he has come in. "Answer me! Do you believe in anything you can't see, can't hear, can't touch—?"

"Radio," the sergeant suggests not very brightly, but Humphries answers more frankly, "No."

The man slumps down again in his chair, shrugs apathetically. "If you don't, how can I expect you to believe me? I've been to the biggest doctors, biggest scientists in the world—they wouldn't believe me. How can I expect you to? You'll simply say I'm cracked, and let it go at that. I don't want to spend the rest of my life in an asylum—" He breaks off and sobs. "And yet it's true, it's true!"

They've gotten into such a maze that Humphries decides it's about time to snap out of it. He asks the one simple question that should have been asked long ago, and the hell with all this mumbo-jumbo. "Are you sure you killed him?" The man is broken physically and he's about ready to crack mentally too. The whole thing may be a hallucination.

"I know I did. I'm sure of it," the man answers calmly. "I'm already beginning to feel a little better. I felt it the minute he was gone."

If he is, he doesn't show it. The sergeant catches Humphries' eye and meaningfully taps his forehead in a sly gesture.

"Suppose you take us there and show us," Humphries suggests. "Can you do that? Where'd it happen, at Maxim's?"

"I told you he was colored," Bloch answers reproachfully. Maxim's is tony. "It was in the Vieux Carré. I can show you where, but I can't drive anymore. It was all I could do to get down here with my car."

"I'll put Desjardins on it with you," the sergeant says and calls through the door to the patrolman, "Ring Dij and tell him to meet Humphries at the corner of Canal and Royal right away!" He turns and looks at the huddle on the chair. "Buy him a bracer on the way. It doesn't look like he'll last till he gets there."

The man flushes a little—it would be a blush if he had any blood left in him. "I can't touch alcohol any more. I'm on my last legs. It goes right through me like—" He hangs his head, then raises it again. "But I'll get better now, little by little, now that he's—"

The sergeant takes Humphries out of earshot. "Pushover for a padded cell. If it's on the up-and-up, and not just a pipe dream, call me right back. I'll get the commissioner on the wire."

"At this hour of the night?"

The sergeant motions toward the chair with his head. "He's Eddie Bloch, isn't he?"

Humphries takes him under the elbow, pries him up from the chair. Not roughly, but just briskly, energetically. Now that things are at last getting under way, he knows where he's at; he can handle them. He'll still be considerate, but he's businesslike now; he's into his routine. "All right, come on Mr. Bloch, let's get up there."

"Not a scratch goes down on the blotter until I'm sure what I'm doing," the sergeant calls after Humphries. "I don't want this whole town down on my neck tomorrow morning."

Humphries almost has to hold him up on the way out and into the car. "This it?" he says. "Wow!" He just touches it with his nail and they're off like velvet. "How'd you ever get this into the Vieux Carré without knocking over the houses?"

Two gleams deep in the skull jogging against the upholstery, dimmer than the dashboard lights, are the only sign that there's life beside him. "Used to park it blocks away—go on foot."

"Oh, you went there more than once?"

"Wouldn't you—to beg for your life?"

More of that screwy stuff, Humphries thinks disgustedly. Why should a man like Eddie Bloch, star of the mike and the dance floor, go to some colored man in the slums and beg for his life?

Royal Street comes whistling along. He swerves in toward the curb, shoves the door out, sees Desjardins land on the running board with one foot. Then he veers out into the middle again without even having stopped. Desjardins moves in on the other side of Bloch, finishes dressing by knotting his necktie and buttoning his vest. "Where'd you get the Aquitania?" he wants to know, and then, with a look beside him, "Holy Kreisler, Eddie Bloch! We used to hear you every night on my Emerson—"

"Matter?" Humphries squelches. "Got a talking jag?"

"Turn," says a hollow sound between them and three wheels take the Bugatti around into North Rampart Street. "Have to leave it here," he says a little later, and they get out. "Congo Square," the old stamping ground of the slaves.

"Help him," Humphries tells his mate tersely, and they each brace him by an elbow.

Staggering between them with the uneven gait of a punch-drunk pug, quick and then slow by turns, he leads them down a ways, and then suddenly cuts left into an alley that isn't there at all until you're smack in front of it. It's just a crack between two houses, noisome as a sewer. They have to break into Indian file to get through at all. But Bloch can't fall down; the walls almost scrape both his shoulders at once. One's in front, one behind him.

"You packed?" Humphries calls over his head to Desjardins, up front.

"Catch cold without it," the other's voice comes back out of the gloom.

A slit of orange shows up suddenly from under a window sill and a shapely coffee-colored elbow scrapes the ribs of the three as they squirm by. "This far 'nough, honey," a liquid voice murmurs.

"Bad girl, wash y'mouth out with soap," the unromantic Humphries warns over his shoulder without even looking around. The sliver of light vanishes as quickly as it came.

The passage widens out in places into moldering courtyards dating back to French or Spanish colonial days, and once it goes under an archway and becomes a tunnel for a short distance. Desjardins cracks his head and swears with talent and abandon.

"Y'left out—" the rearguard remarks dryly.

"Here," pants Bloch weakly, and stops suddenly at a patch of blackness in the wall. Humphries washes it with his torch and crumbling mildewed stone steps show up inside it. Then he motions Bloch in, but the man hangs back, slips a notch or two lower down against the opposite wall that supports him. "Let me stay down here! Don't make me go up there again," he pleads.

"I don't think I can make it anymore. I'm afraid to go back in there."

"Oh, no!" Humphries says with quiet determination. "You're showing us," and scoops him away from the wall with his arm. Again, as before, he isn't rough about it, just businesslike. Dij keeps the lead, watering the place with his own torch. Humphries trains his on the band leader's forty-dollar custom-made patent-leather shoes jerking frightenedly upward before him. The stone steps turn to wood ones splintered with usage. They have to step over a huddled black drunk, empty bottle cradled in his arms. "Don't light a match," Dij warns, pinching his nose, "or there'll be an explosion."

"Grow up," snaps Humphries. The Cajun's a good dick, but can't he realize the man in the middle is roasting in hell-fire? This is no time—

"In here is where I did it. I closed the door again after me." Bloch's skull face is all silver with his life sweat as one of their torches flicks past it.

Humphries shoves open the sagging mahogany panel that was first hung up when a Louis was still king of France and owned this town. The light of a lamp far across a still, dim room flares up and dances crazily in the draft. They come in and look.

There's an old broken-down bed, filthy with rags. Across it there's a motionless figure, head hanging down toward the floor. Dij cups his hand under it and lifts it. It comes up limply toward him, like a small basketball. It bounces down again when he lets it go—even seems to bob slightly for a second or two after. It's an old, old colored man, up in his eighties, even beyond. There's a dark spot, darker than the weazened skin, just under one bleared eye and another in the thin fringe of white wool that circles the back of the skull.

Humphries doesn't wait to see any more. He turns, flips out and down, and all the way back to wherever the nearest telephone can be found, to let headquarters know that it's true after all and they can rouse the police commissioner. "Keep him there with you, Dij," his voice trails back from the inky stairwell, "and no quizzing. Pull in your horns till we get our orders!" The scarecrow with them tries to stumble after him and get out of the place, groaning, "Don't leave me here! Don't make me stay here—!"

"I wouldn't quiz you on my own, Mr. Bloch," Dij tries to reassure him, nonchalantly sitting down on the edge of the bed next to the corpse and retying his shoelace. "I'll never forget it was your playing 'Love in Bloom' on the air one night in Baton Rouge two years ago gave me the courage to propose to my wife—"

But the commissioner would, and does, in his office a couple hours later. He's anything but eager about it, too. They've tried to shunt him, Bloch, off their hands in every possible legal way open to them. No go. He sticks to them like flypaper. The old colored man *didn't* try to attack him, or rob him, or blackmail him, or kidnap him, or anything else. The gun didn't go off accidentally, and he didn't fire it on the spur of the moment either, without thinking twice, or in a flare of anger. The commissioner almost beats his own head against the desk in his exasperation as he reiterates over and over: "But why? Why? Why?" And for the steenth time, he gets the same indigestible answer, "Because he was killing me."

"Then you admit he did lay hands on you?" The first time the poor commissioner asked this, he said it with a spark of hope. But this is the tenth or twelfth and the spark died out long ago.

"He never once came near me. I was the one looked him up each time to plead with him. Commissioner Oliver, tonight I went down on my knees to that old man and dragged myself around the floor of that dirty room after him, on my *bended knees,* like a sick cat—begging, crawling to him, offering him three thousand, ten, any amount, finally offering him my own gun, asking him to shoot me with it, to get it over with quickly, to be kind to me, not to drag it out by inches any longer! No, not even that little bit of mercy! Then I shot—and now I'm going to get better, now I'm going to live—"

He's too weak to cry; crying takes strength. The commissioner's hair is about ready to stand on end. "Stop it, Mr. Bloch, stop it!" he shouts, and he steps over and grabs him by the shoulder in defense of his own nerves, and can almost feel the shoulder bone cutting his hand. He takes his hand away again in a hurry. "I'm going to have you examined by an alienist!"

The bundle of bones rears from the chair. "You can't do that! You can't take my mind from me! Send to my hotel—I've got a trunkful of reports on my condition! I've been to the biggest minds in Europe! Can you produce anyone that would dare go against the findings of Buckholtz in Vienna, Reynolds in London? They had me under observation for months at a time! I'm not even on the borderline of insanity, not even a genius or musically talented. I don't even write my own numbers, I'm mediocre, uninspired—in other words completely normal. I'm saner than you are at this minute, Mr. Oliver. My body's gone, my soul's gone, and all I've got left is my mind, but you can't take that from me!"

The commissioner's face is beet red. He's about ready for a stroke, but he speaks softly, persuasively. "An eighty-odd-year-old colored man who is so feeble he can't even go upstairs half the time, who has to have his food pulleyed up to him through the window in a basket, is killing—whom? A white stumblebum his own age? No-o-o, Mr. Eddie Bloch, the premier bandsman of America, who can name his own price in any town, who's heard every night in all our homes, who has about everything a man can want—that's who!"

He peers close, until their eyes are on a level. His voice is just a silky whisper. "Tell me just one thing, Mr. Bloch." Then like the explosion of a giant firecracker, "How?" He roars it out, booms it out.

There's a long-drawn intake of breath from Eddie Bloch. "By thinking thought-waves of death that reach me through the air."

The poor commissioner practically goes all to pieces on his own rug. "And you don't need a medical exam!" he wheezes weakly.

There's a flutter, the popping of buttons, and Eddie Bloch's coat, his vest, his shirt, undershirt, land one after another on the floor around his chair. He turns. "Look at my back! You can count every vertebra through the skin!" He turns back again.

"Look at my ribs. Look at the pulsing where there's not enough skin left to cover my heart!"

Oliver shuts his eyes and turns toward the window. He's in a particularly unpleasant spot. New Orleans, out there, is stirring, and when it hears about this, he's going to be the most unpopular man in town. On the other hand, if he doesn't see the thing through now that it's gone this far he's guilty of a dereliction of duty, malfeasance in office.

Bloch, slowly dressing, knows what he's thinking. "You want to get rid of me, don't you? You're trying to think of a way of covering this thing up. You're afraid to bring me up before the grand jury on account of your own reputation, aren't you?" His voice rises to a scream of panic. "Well, I want protection! I don't want to go out there again—to my death! I won't accept bail! If you turn me loose now, even on my own recognizance, you may be as guilty of my death as he is. How do I know my bullet stopped the thing? How does any of us know what becomes of the mind after death? Maybe his thoughts will still reach me, still try to get me. I tell you I want to be locked up, I want people around me day and night, I want to be where I'm safe—!"

"Shh, for God's sake, Mr. Bloch! They'll think I'm beating you up—" The commissioner drops his arms to his sides and heaves a gigantic sigh. "That settles it! I'll book you all right. You want that and you're going to get it! I'll book you for the murder of one Papa Benjamin, even if they laugh me out of office for it!"

For the first time since the whole thing has started, he casts a look of real anger, ill-will, at Eddie Bloch. He seizes a chair, swirls it around, and bangs it down in front of the man. He puts his foot on it and pokes his finger almost in Bloch's eye. "I'm not two-faced. I'm not going to lock you up nice and cozy and then soft-pedal the whole thing. If it's coming out at all, then all of it's coming out. Now start in! Tell me everything I want to know, and what I want to know is—everything!"

The strains of "Good Night Ladies" die away; the dancers leave the floor, the lights start going out, and Eddie Bloch throws down his baton and mops the back of his neck with a handkerchief. He weighs about two hundred pounds, is in the pink, and is a good-looking brute. But his face is sour right now, dissatisfied. His outfit starts to case its instruments right and left, and Judy Jarvis steps up on the platform, in her street clothes, ready to go home. She's Eddie's torch singer, and also his wife. "Coming, Eddie? Let's get out of here." She looks a little disgusted herself. "I didn't get a hand tonight, not even after my rumba number. Must be staling. If I wasn't your wife, I'd be out of a job I guess."

Eddie pats her shoulder. "It isn't you, honey. It's us, we're beginning to stink. Notice how the attendance has been dropping the past few weeks? There were more waiters than customers tonight. I'll be hearing from the owner any minute now. He has the right to cancel my contract if the intake drops below five grand."

A waiter comes up to the edge of the platform. "Mr. Graham'd like to see you in his office before you go home, Mr. Bloch."

Eddie and Judy look at each other. "This is it now, Judy. You go back to the hotel. Don't wait for me. G'night, boys." Eddie Bloch calls for his hat and knocks at the manager's office.

Graham rustles a lot of accounts together. "We took in forty-five hundred this week, Eddie. They can get the same ginger ale and sandwiches any place, but they'll go where the band has something to give 'em. I notice the few that do come in don't even get up from the table any more when you tap your baton. Now, what's wrong?"

Eddie punches his hat a couple of times. "Don't ask me. I'm getting the latest orchestrations from Broadway sent to me hot off the griddle. We sweat our bald heads off rehearsing—"

Graham swivels his cigar. "Don't forget that jazz originated here in the South, you can't show this town anything. They want something new."

"When do I scram?" Eddie asks, smiling with the southwest corner of his mouth.

"Finish the week out. See if you can do something about it by Monday. If not, I'll have to wire St. Louis to get Kruger's crew. I'm sorry, Eddie."

"That's all right," broad-minded Eddie says. "You're not running a charity bazaar."

Eddie goes out into the dark dance room. His crew has gone. The tables are stacked. A couple of old colored crones are down on hands and knees slopping water around on the parquet. Eddie steps up on the platform a minute to get some orchestrations he left on the piano. He feels something crunch under his shoe, reaches down, picks up a severed chicken's claw lying there with a strip of red-tag tied around it. How the hell did it get up there? If it had been under one of the tables, he'd have thought some diner had dropped it. He flushes a little. D'ye mean to say he and the boys were so rotten tonight that somebody deliberately threw it at them while they were playing?

One of the scrubwomen looks up. The next moment, she and her mate are on their feet, edging nearer, eyes big as saucers, until they get close enough to see what it is he's holding. Then there's a double yowl of animal fright, a tin pail goes rolling across the floor, and no two stout people, white or colored, ever got out of a place in such a hurry before. The door nearly comes off its hinges, and Eddie can hear their cackling all the way down the quiet street outside until it fades away into the night. "For gosh sake!" thinks the bewildered Eddie, "they must be using the wrong brand of gin." He tosses the object out onto the floor and goes back to the piano for his music scores. A sheet or two has slipped down behind it and he squats to collect them. That way the piano hides him.

The door opens again and he sees Johnny Staats (traps and percussion) come in in quite a hurry. He thought Staats was home in bed by now. Staats is feeling himself all over like he was rehearsing the shim-sham and he's scanning the ground as he goes along. Then suddenly he pounces—and it's on the very scrap of garbage Eddie just now threw away! And as he straightens up with it, his breath comes out in such a sign of relief that Eddie can hear it all the way across the still room. All this keeps him from hailing Staats as he was going to a minute ago and suggesting a cup of java. But, "Superstitious," thinks broadminded Eddie. "It's his good-luck charm, that's all, like some people carry a rabbit's foot. I'm a little that way myself, never walk under a ladder—"

Then again, why should those two mammies go into hysterics when they lamp the same object? And Eddie recalls now that some of the boys have always suspected Staats has colored blood, and tried to tell him so years ago when Staats first came in with them, but he wouldn't listen to them.

Staats slinks out again as noiselessly as he came in, and Eddie decides he'll catch up with him and kid him about his chicken claw on their way home together. (They all roost in the same hotel.) So he takes his music sheets, some of which are blank, and he leaves. Staats is way down the street—in the *wrong direction,* away from the hotel! Eddie hesitates for just a minute, and then he starts after Staats on a vague impulse, just to see where he's going, just to see what he's up to. Maybe the fright of the scrubwomen and the way Staats pounced on that chicken claw just now have built up to this, without Eddie's really knowing it.

And how many times afterward he's going to pray to his God that he'd never turned down that other way this night—away from his hotel, his Judy, his boys—away from the sunlight and the white man's world. Such a little thing to decide to do, and afterward no turning back—ever.

He keeps Staats in sight, and they hit the Vieux Carré. That's all right. There are a lot of quaint places here a guy might like to drop in. Or maybe he has some Creole sweetie tucked away, and Eddie thinks, I'm lower than a ditch to spy like this. But then suddenly right before his eyes, half way up the narrow lane he's turned into—there isn't any Staats any more! And no door opened and closed again either. Then when Eddie gets up to where it was, he sees the crevice between the old houses, hidden by an angle in the walls. So that's where he went! Eddie almost has a peeve on by now at all this hocus-pocus. He slips in himself and feels his way along. He stops every once in a while and can hear Staats' quiet footfall somewhere way up in front. Then he goes on again. Once or twice the passage spreads out a little and lets a little green-blue moonlight partway down the walls. Then later, there's a little flare of orange light from under a window and an elbow jogs him in the appendix. "You'd be happier here. Doan go the rest of the way," a soft voice breathes. A prophecy if he only knew it!

But hardboiled Eddie just says, "G'wan to bed, y' dirty stay-up!" out of the corner of his mouth, and the light vanishes. Next a tunnel and he bangs the top of his head and his eyes water. But at the other end of it, Staats has finally come to a halt in a patch of clear light and seems to be looking up at a window or something, so Eddie stays where he is, inside the tunnel, and folds the lapels of his black jacket up over his white shirt front so it won't show.

Staats just stands there for a spell, with Eddie holding his breath inside the tunnel, and then finally he gives a peculiar, dismal whistle. There's nothing carefree or casual about it. It's a hollow swampland sound, not easy to get without practice. Then he just stands there waiting, until without warning another figure joins him in the gloom. Eddie strains his eyes. A gorilla-like, Negro roustabout. Something passes from Staats' hand to his—the chicken claw possibly—then they go in, into the house Staats has been facing. Eddie can hear the soft shuffle of feet going upstairs on the inside, and the groaning, squeaking of an old decayed door—and then silence.

He edges forward to the mouth of the tunnel and peers up. No light shows from any window, the house appears to be untenanted, deserted.

Eddie hangs onto his coat collar with one hand and strokes his chin with the other. He doesn't know just what to do. The vague impulse that has brought him this far after Staats begins to peter out now. Staats has some funny associates—something funny is going on in this out-of-the-way place at this unearthly hour of the morning—but after all, a man's private life is his own. He wonders what made him do this; he wouldn't want anyone to know he did it. He'll turn around and go back to his hotel now and get some shut-eye; he's got to think up some novelty for his routine at Maxim's between now and Monday or he'll be out on his ear.

Then just as one heel is off the ground to take the turn that will start him back, a vague, muffled wailing starts from somewhere inside that house. It's toned down to a mere echo. It has to go through thick doors and wide, empty rooms and down a deep, hollow stairwell before it gets to him. Oh, some sort of a revival meeting, is it? So Staats has got religion, has he? But what a place to come and get it in!

A throbbing like a faraway engine in a machine shop underscores the wailing, and every once in a while a *boom* like distant thunder across the bayou tops the whole works. It goes *boom-putta-putta-boom-putta-putta-boom!* And the wailing, way up high at the moon: *Eeyah-eeyah-eeyah—!*

Eddie's professional instincts suddenly come alive. He tries it out, beats time to it with his arm as if he were holding a baton. His fingers snap like a whip. "My God, that's grand! That's gorgeous! Just what I need! I gotta get up there!" So a chicken foot does it, eh?

He turns and runs back, through the tunnel, through the courtyards, all the way back where he came from, stooping here, stooping there, lighting matches recklessly and throwing them away as he goes. Out in the Vieux Carré again, the refuse hasn't been collected. He spots a can at the corner of two lanes, topples it over. The smell rises to heaven, but he wades into it ankle-deep like any levee-rat, digs into the stuff with both forearms, scattering it right and left. He's lucky, finds a verminous carcass, tears off a claw, wipes it on some newspaper. Then he starts back. Wait a minute! The red rag, red strip around it! He feels himself all over, digs into all his pockets. Nothing that color. Have to do without it, but maybe it won't work without it. He turns and hurries back through the slit between the old houses, doesn't care how much noise he makes. The flash of light from Old Faithful, the jogging elbow. Eddie stoops, he suddenly snatches in at the red kimono sleeve, his hand comes away with a strip of it. Bad language, words that even Eddie doesn't know. A five-spot stops it on the syllable, and Eddie's already way down the passage. If only they haven't quit until he can get back there!

They haven't. It was vague, smothered when he went away; it's louder, more persistent, more frenzied now. He doesn't bother about giving the whistle, probably couldn't imitate it exactly anyhow. He dives into the black smudge that is the entrance to the house, feels greasy stone steps under him, takes one or two and then suddenly his collar is four sizes too small for him, gripped by a big ham of a hand at the back. A sharp something that might be anything from a pocket-knife blade to the business edge of a razor is creasing his throat just below the apple and drawing a preliminary drop or two of blood.

"Here it is, I've got it here!" gasps Eddie. What kind of religion is this, anyway? The sharp thing stays, but the hand lets go his collar and feels for the chicken claw. Then the sharp thing goes away too, but probably not very far away.

"Whyfor you didn't give the signal?"

Eddie's windpipe gives him the answer. "Sick here, couldn't."

"Light up, lemme see yo' face." Eddie strikes a match and holds it. "Yo' face has never been here before."

Eddie gestures upward. "My friend—up there—he'll tell you!"

"Mr. Johnny yo' friend? He ax you to come?"

Eddie thinks quickly. The chicken claw might carry more weight than Staats. "That told me to come."

"Papa Benjamin sen' you that?"

"Certainly," says Eddie stoutly. Probably their deacon, but it's a hell of a way to—The match stings his fingers and he whips it out. Blackness and a moment's uncertainty that might end either way. But a lot of savoir faire, a thousand years of civilization, are backing Eddie up. "You'll make me late, Papa Benjamin wouldn't like that!"

He gropes his way on up in the pitch blackness, thinking any minute he'll feel his back slashed to ribbons. But it's better than standing still and having it happen, and to back out now would bring it on twice as quickly. However, it works, nothing happens.

"Fust thing y'know, all N'yorleans be comin' by," growls the African watchdog sulkily, and flounders down on the staircase with a sound like a tired seal. There is some other crack about "darkies lookin' lak pinks," and then a long period of scratching.

But Eddie's already up on the landing above and so close to

the *boom-putta-boom* now it drowns out every other sound. The whole framework of the decrepit house seems to shake with it. The door's closed but the thread of orange that outlines it shows it up to him. Behind there. He leans against it, shoves a little. It gives. The squealings and the grindings it emits are lost in the torrent of noise that comes rushing out. He sees plenty, and what he sees only makes him want to see all the more. Something tells him the best thing to do is slip in quietly and close it behind him before he's noticed, rather than stay there peeping in from the outside. Little Snowdrop might always come upstairs in back of him and catch him there. So he widens it just a little more, oozes in, and kicks it shut behind him with his heel—and immediately gets as far away from it as he can. Evidently no one has seen him.

Now, it's a big shadowy room and it's choked with people. It's lit by a single oil lamp and a hell of a whole lot of candles, which may have shone out brightly against the darkness outside but are pretty dim once you get inside with them. The long flickering shadows thrown on all the walls by those cavorting in the center are almost as much of a protection to Eddie, as he crouches back amidst them, as the darkness outside would be. He's been around, and a single look is enough to tell him that whatever else it is, it's no revival meeting. At first, he takes it for just a gin or rent party with the lid off, but it isn't that either. There's no gin there, and there's no pairing off of couples in the dancing —rather it's a roomful of devils lifted bodily up out of hell. Plenty of them have passed out cold on the floor all around him and the others keep stepping over them as they prance back and forth, only they don't always step over but sometimes *on*—on prostrate faces and chests and outstretched arms and hands. Then there are others who have gone off into a sort of still trance, seated on the floor with their backs to the wall, some of them rocking back and forth, some just staring glassy-eyed, foam drooling from their mouths. Eddie quickly slips down among them on his haunches and gets busy. He too starts rocking back and forth and pounding the floor beside him with his knuckles, but he's not in any trance, he's getting a swell new number for his repertoire at Maxim's. A sheet of blank score paper is partly hidden under his body, and he keeps dropping one hand down to it every minute jotting down musical notes with the stub of pencil in his fingers. "Key of A," he guesses. "I can decide that when I instrument it. Mi-re-do, mi-re-do. Then over again. Hope I didn't miss any of it."

Boom-putta-putta-boom! Young and old, black and tawny, fat and thin, naked and clothed, they pass from right to left, from left to right, in two concentric circles, while the candle flames dance crazily and the shadows leap up and down on the walls. The hub of it all, within the innermost circle of dancers, is an old, old man, black skin and bones, only glimpsed now and then in a space between the packed bodies that surround him. An animal pelt is banded about his middle; he wears a horrible juju mask over his face—a death's head. On one side of him, a squatting woman clacks two gourds together endlessly, that's the "putta" of Eddie's rhythm; on the other, another beats a drum, that's the "boom." In one upraised hand he holds a squalling fowl, wings beating the air; in the other a sharp-bladed knife. Something flashes in the air, but the dancers mercifully get between Eddie and the sight of it. Next glimpse he has, the fowl isn't flapping any more. It's hanging limply down and veins of blood are trickling down the old man's shriveled forearm.

"That part don't go into my show," Eddie thinks facetiously. The horrible old man has dropped the knife; he squeezes the lifeblood from the dead bird with both hands now, still holding it in midair. He sprinkles the drops on those that cavort around him, flexing and unflexing his bony fingers in a nauseating travesty of the ceremony of baptism.

Drops spatter here and there about the room, on the walls. One lands near Eddie and he edges back. Revolting things go on all around him. He sees some of the crazed dancers drop to their hands and knees and bend low over these red polka dots, licking them up from the floor with their tongues. Then they go about the room on all fours like animals, looking for others.

"Think I'll go," Eddie says to himself, tasting last night's supper all over again. "They ought to have the cops on them."

He maneuvers the score sheet, filled now, out from under him and into his side pocket; then he starts drawing his feet in toward him preparatory to standing up and slipping out of this hell hole. Meanwhile a second fowl, black this time (the first was white), a squeaking suckling pig, and a puppy dog have gone the way of the first fowl. Nor do the carcasses go to waste when the old man has dropped them. Eddie sees things happening on the floor, in between the stomping feet of the dancers, and he guesses enough not to look twice.

Then suddenly, already reared a half-inch above the floor on his way up, he wonders where the wailing went. And the clacking of the gourds and the boom of the drum and the shuffling of the feet. He blinks, and everything has frozen still in the room around him. Not a move, not a sound. Straight out from the old man's gnarled shoulder stretches a bony arm, the end dipped in red, pointing like an arrow at Eddie. Eddie sinks down again that half-inch. He couldn't hold that position very long, and something tells him he's not leaving right away after all.

"White man," says a bated breath, and they all start moving in on him. A gesture of the old man sweeps them into motion-lessness again.

A cracked voice comes through the grinning mouth of the juju mask, rimmed with canine teeth. "Whut you do here?"

Eddie taps his pockets mentally. He has about fifty on him. Will that be enough to buy his way out? He has an uneasy feeling, however, that none of this lot is as interested in money as they should be—at least not right now. Before he has a chance to try it out, another voice speaks up. "I know this man, *papaloi*. Let me find out."

Johnny Staats came in here tuxedoed, hair slicked back, a cog in New Orleans' nightlife. Now he's barefooted, coatless, shirtless—a tousled scarecrow. A drop of blood has caught him squarely on the forehead and been traced, by his own finger or someone else's, into a red line from temple to temple. A chicken feather or two clings to his upper lip. Eddie saw him dancing with the rest, groveling on the floor. His scalp crawls with repugnance as the man comes over and squats down before him. The rest of them hold back, tense, poised, ready to pounce.

The two men talk in low, hoarse voices. "It's your only way, Eddie. I can't save you—"

"Why, I'm in the very heart of New Orleans! They wouldn't dare!" But sweat oozes out on Eddie's face just the same. He's no fool. Sure the police will come and sure they'll mop this place up. But what will they find? His own remains along with that of the fowls, the pig and the dog.

"You'd better hurry up, Eddie. I can't hold them back much longer. Unless you do, you'll never get out of this place alive and you may as well know it! If I tried to stop them, I'd go too. You know what this is, don't you? This is voodoo!"

"I knew that five minutes after I was in the room." And Eddie thinks to himself, "You son-of-a-so-and-so! You better ask Mombo-jombo to get you a new job starting in tomorrow night!" Then he grins internally and, clown to the very end, says with a straight face, "Sure I'll join. What d'ye suppose I came here for anyway?"

Knowing what he knows now, Staats is the last one he'd tell about the glorious new number he's going to get out of this, the notes for which are nestled in his inside pocket right now. And he might even get more dope out of the initiation ceremonies if he pretends to go through with them. A song or dance for Judy to do with maybe a green spot focused on her. Lastly, there's no use denying there *are* too many razors, knives and the like, in the room to hope to get out and all the way back where he started from without a scratch.

Staats' face is grave, though. "Now don't kid about this thing. If you knew what I know about it, there's a lot more to it than there seems to be. If you're sincere, honest about it, all right. If not, it might be better to get cut to pieces right now than to tamper with it."

"Never more serious in my life," says Eddie. And deep down inside he's braying like a jackass.

Staats turns to the old man. "His spirit wishes to join our spirits."

The *papaloi* burns some feathers and entrails at one of the candle flames. Not a sound in the room. The majority of them squat down all at once. "It came out all right," Staats breathes. "He reads them. The spirits are willing."

"So far so good," Eddie thinks. "I've fooled the guts and feathers."

The *papaloi* is pointing at him now. "Let him go now and be silent," the voice behind the mask cackles. Then a second time he says it, and a third, with a long pause between.

Eddie looks hopefully at Staats. "Then I can go after all, as long as I don't tell anyone what I've seen?"

Staats shakes his head grimly. "Just part of the ritual. If you went now, you'd eat something that disagreed with you tomorrow and be dead before the day was over."

More sacrificial slaughtering, and the drum and gourds and wailing start over again, but very low and subdued now as at the beginning. A bowl of blood is prepared and Eddie is raised to his feet and led forward, Staats on one side of him, an anonymous colored man on the other. The *papaloi* dips his already caked hand into the bowl and traces a mark on Eddie's forehead. The chanting and wailing grow louder behind him. The dancing begins again. He's in the middle of all of them. He's an island of sanity in a sea of jungle frenzy. The bowl is being held up before his face. He tries to draw back, his sponsors grip him firmly by the arms. "Drink!" whispers Staats. "Drink—or they'll kill you where you stand!"

Even at this stage of the game, there's still a wisecrack left in Eddie, though he keeps it to himself. He takes a deep breath. "Here's where I get my vitamin A for today!"

Staats shows up at orchestra rehearsal next A.M. to find somebody else at drums and percussion. He doesn't say much when Eddie shoves a two-week check at him, spits on the floor at his feet and growls: "Beat it, you filthy—"

Staats only murmurs, "So you're crossing them? I wouldn't want to be in your shoes for all the fame and money in this world, guy!"

"If you mean that bad dream the other night," says Eddie, "I haven't told anybody and I don't intend to. Why, I'd be laughed at. I'm only remembering what I can use of it. I'm a white man, see? The jungle is just trees to me; the Congo just a river; the nighttime just a time for electric lights." He whips out a couple of C's. "Hand 'em these for me, will ya, and tell 'em I've paid up my dues from now until doomsday and I don't want any receipt. And if they try putting rough-on-rats in my orange juice, they'll find themselves stomping in a chain gang!"

The C's fall where Eddie spat. "You're one of us. You think you're pink? Blood tells. You wouldn't have gone there—you couldn't have stood that induction—if you were. Look at your fingernails sometime, look in a mirror at the whites of your eyes. Good-bye, dead man."

Eddie says good-bye to him, too. He knocks out three of his teeth, breaks the bridge of his nose, and rolls all over the floor on top of him. But he can't wipe out that wise, knowing smile that shows even through the gush of blood.

They pull Eddie off, pull him up, pull him together. Staats staggers away, smiling at what he knows. Eddie, heaving like a bellows, turns to his crew. "All right, boys. All together now!" *Boom-putta-putta-boom-putta-putta-boom!*

Graham shoots five C's on promotion and all New Orleans jams its way into Maxim's that Saturday night. They're standing on each other's shoulders and hanging from the chandeliers to get a look. "First time in America, the original VOODOO CHANT," yowl the three-sheets on every billboard in town. And when Eddie taps his baton, the lights go down and a nasty green flood lights the platform from below and you can hear a pin drop. "Good evening, folks. This is Eddie Bloch and his Five Chips, playing to you from Maxim's. You're about to hear for the first time on the air the Voodoo Chant, the age-old ceremonial rhythm no white man has ever been permitted to listen to before. I can assure you this is an accurate transcription, not a note has been changed." Then very softly and faraway it begins: *Boom-putta-putta-boom!*

Judy's going to dance and wail to it, she's standing there on the steps leading up to the platform, waiting to go on. She's powdered orange, dressed in feathers, and has a small artificial bird fastened to one wrist and a thin knife in her other hand. She catches his eye, he looks over at her, and he sees she wants to tell him something. Still waving his baton he edges sideways until he's within earshot.

"Eddie, don't! Stop them! Call it off, will you? I'm worried about you!"

"Too late now," he answers under cover of the music. "We've started already. What're you scared of?"

She passes him a crumpled piece of paper. "I found this under your dressing-room door when I came out just now. It sounds like a warning. There's somebody doesn't want you to play that number!"

Still swinging with his right hand, Eddie unrolls the thing under his left thumb and reads it:

> *You can summon the spirits but can you dismiss them again? Think well.*

He crumples it up and tosses it away. "Staats trying to scare me because I canned him."

"It was tied to a little bunch of black feathers," she tries to tell him. "I wouldn't have paid any attention, but my maid pleaded with me not to dance this when she saw it. Then she ran out on me—"

"We're on the air," he reminds her between his teeth. "Are you with me or aren't you?" And he eases back center again. Louder and louder the beat grows, just like it did two nights ago. Judy swirls on in a green spot and begins the unearthly wail Eddie's coached her to do.

A waiter drops a tray of drinks in the silence of the room out there, and when the headwaiter goes to bawl him out he's no-where to be found. He has quit cold and a whole row of tables has been left without their orders. "Well, I'll be—!" says the captain and scratches his head.

Eddie's facing the crew, his back to Judy, and as he vibrates to the rhythm, some pin or other that he's forgotten to take out of his shirt suddenly catches him and strikes into him. It's a little below the collar, just between the shoulder blades. He jumps a little, but doesn't feel it any more after that.

Judy squalls, tears her tonsils out, screeches words that neither he nor she know the meaning of but that he managed to set down on paper phonetically the other night. Her little body goes through all the contortions, tamed down of course, that that brownskin she-devil greased with lard and wearing only earrings performed that night. She stabs the bird with her fake knife and sprinkles imaginary blood in the air. Nothing like this has ever been seen before. And in the silence that suddenly lands when it's through, you can count twenty. That's how it's gotten under everyone's skin.

Then the noise begins. It goes over like an avalanche. But just the same, more people are ordering strong drinks all at once than has ever happened before in the place, and the matron in the women's restroom has her hands full of hysterical sob-sisters.

"Try to get away from me, just try!" Graham tells Eddie at curfew time. "I'll have a new contract, gilt-edged, ready for you in the morning. We've already got six-grand worth of reservations on our hands for the coming week—one of 'em by telegram all the way from Shreveport!"

Success! Eddie and Judy taxi back to their rooms at the hotel, tired but happy. "It'll be good for years. We can use it for our signature on the air, like Whiteman does the Rhapsody."

She goes into the bedroom first, snaps on the lights, calls to him a minute later: "Come here and look at this—the cutest little souvenir!" He finds her holding a wax doll, finger high, in her hands. "Why, it's you, Eddie, look! Small as it is it has your features! Well isn't that the clev—!"

He takes it away from her and squints at it. It's himself all right. It's rigged out in two tiny patches of black cloth for a tuxedo, and the eyes and hair and features are inked onto the wax.

"Where'd you find it?"

"It was in your bed, up against the pillow."

He's fixing to grin about it, until he happens to turn it over. In the back, just a little below the collar, between the shoulder blades, a short but venomous-looking black pin is sticking.

He goes a little white for a minute. He knows who it's from now and what it's trying to tell him. But that isn't what makes him change color. He's just remembered something. He throws off his coat, yanks at his collar, turns his back to her. "Judy, look down there, will you? I felt a pin stick me while we were doing that number. Put your hand down. Feel anything?"

"No, there's nothing there," she tells him.

"Musta dropped out."

"It couldn't have," she says. "Your belt line's so tight it almost cuts into you. There couldn't have been anything there or it'd still be there now. You must have imagined it."

"Listen, I know a pin when I feel one. Any mark on my back, any scratch between the shoulders?"

"Not a thing."

"Tired, I guess. Nervous." He goes over to the open window and pitches the little doll out into the night with all his strength. Damn coincidence, that's all it was. To think otherwise would be to give them their inning. But he wonders what makes him feel so tired just the same—Judy did all the exercising, not he—yet he's felt all in ever since that number tonight.

Out go the lights and she drops off to sleep right with them. He lies very quiet for a while. A little later he gets up, goes into the bathroom where the lights are whitest of all, and stands there looking at himself close to the glass. "Look at your finger-nails sometime; look at the whites of your eyes," Staats had said. Eddie does. There's a bluish, purplish tinge to his nails that he never noticed before. The whites of his eyes are faintly yellow.

It's warm in New Orleans that night but he shivers a little as he stands there. He doesn't sleep any more that night. . . .

In the morning, his back aches as if he were sixty. But he knows that's from not closing his eyes all night, and not from any magic pins.

"Oh, my God!" Judy says, from the other side of the bed;

"look what you've done to him!" She shows him the second page of the *Picayune*. "John Staats, until recently a member of Eddie Bloch's orchestra, committed suicide late yesterday afternoon in full view of dozens of people by rowing himself out into Lake Pontchartrain and jumping overboard. He was alone in the boat at the time. The body was recovered half an hour later."

"I didn't do that," says Eddie grimly. "I've got a rough idea what did, though." Late yesterday afternoon. The night was coming on, and he couldn't face what was coming to him for sponsoring Eddie, for giving them all away. Late yesterday afternoon—that meant *he* hadn't left that warning at the dressing room or left that death sentence on the bed. He'd been dead himself by then—not white, not black, just yellow.

Eddie waits until Judy's in her shower, then he phones the morgue. "About Johnny Staats. He worked for me until yesterday, so if nobody's claimed the body send it to a funeral parlor at my exp—"

"Somebody's already claimed the remains, Mr. Bloch. First thing this morning. Just waited until the examiner had established suicide beyond a doubt. Some colored organization, old friends of his it seems—"

Judy comes in and remarks: "You look all green in the face."

Eddie thinks: "I wouldn't care if he was my worst enemy, I can't let that happen to him! What horrors are going to take place tonight somewhere under the moon?" He wouldn't even put cannibalism beyond them. The phone's right at his fingertips, and yet he can't denounce them to the police without involving himself, admitting that he was there, took part at least once. Once that comes out, bang! goes his reputation. He'll never be able to live it down—especially now that he's played the Voodoo Chant and identified himself with it in the minds of the public.

So instead, alone in the room again, he calls the best-known private agency in New Orleans. "I want a bodyguard. Just for tonight. Have him meet me at closing time at Maxim's. Armed, of course."

It's Sunday and the banks are closed, but his credit's good

anywhere. He raises a G in cash. He arranges with a reliable crematorium for a body to be taken charge of late tonight or early in the morning. He'll notify them just where to call for it. Yes, of course! He'll produce the proper authorization from the police. Poor Johnny Staats couldn't get away from "them" in life, but he's going to get away from them in death, all right. That's the least anyone could do for him.

Graham slaps a sawbuck-cover on that night, more to give the waiters room to move around in than anything else, and still the place is choked to the roof. This voodoo number is a natural, a wow.

But Eddie's back is ready to cave in, while he stands there jogging with his stick. It's all he can do to hold himself straight.

When the racket and the shuffling are over for the night, the private dick is there waiting for him. "Lee is the name."

"Okay, Lee, come with me." They go outside and get in Eddie's Bugatti. They whizz down to the Vieux, scrounge to a stop in the middle of Congo Square, which will still be Congo Square when its official name of Beauregard is forgotten.

"This way," says Eddie, and his bodyguard squirms through the alley after him.

" 'Lo, suga' pie," says the elbow-pusher, and for once, to her own surprise as much as anyone else's, gets a tumble.

" 'Lo, Eglantine," Eddie's bodyguard remarks in passing. "So you moved?"

They stop in front of the house on the other side of the tunnel. "Now here's what," says Eddie. "We're going to be stopped halfway up these stairs in here by a big orangutan. Your job is to clean him, tap him if you want, I don't care. I'm going into a room up there, you're going to wait for me at the door. You're here to see that I get out of that room again. We may have to carry the body of a friend of mine down to the street between us. I don't know. It depends on whether it's in the house or not. Got it?"

"Got it."

"Light up. Keep your torch trained over my shoulder."

A big, lowering figure looms over them, blocking the narrow

stairs, apelike arms and legs spread-eagled in a gesture of malignant embrace, receding skull, teeth showing, flashing steel in hand. Lee jams Eddie roughly to one side and shoves up past him. "Drop that, boy!" Lee says with slurring indifference, but then he doesn't wait to see if the order's carried out or not. After all, a weapon was raised to two white men. He fires three times, from two feet away and considerably below the obstacle, hits where he aimed to. The bullets shatter both kneecaps and the elbow joint of the arm holding the knife.

"Be a cripple for life now," he remarks with quiet satisfaction. "I'll put him out of his pain." So he crashes the butt of gun down on the skull of the writhing colossus, in a long arc like the overhand pitch of a baseball. The noise of the shots goes booming up the narrow stairwell to the roof, to mushroom out there in a vast rolling echo.

"Come on, hurry up," says Eddie, "before they have a chance to do away with—"

He lopes on up past the prostrate form, Lee at his heels. "Stand there. Better reload while you're waiting. If I call your name, for Pete's sake don't count ten before you come in to me!"

There's a scurrying back and forth and an excited but subdued jabbering going on on the other side of the door. Eddie swings it wide and crashes it closed behind him, leaving Lee on the outside. They all stand rooted to the spot when they see him. The *papaloi* is there and about six others, not so many as on the night of Eddie's initiation. Probably the rest are waiting outside the city somewhere, in some secret spot, wherever the actual burial, or burning, or—feasting—is to take place.

Papa Benjamin has no juju mask on this time, no animal pelt. There are no gourds in the room, no drum, no transfixed figures ranged against the wall. They were about to move on elsewhere, he just got here in time. Maybe they were waiting for the dark of the moon. The ordinary kitchen chairs on which the *papaloi* was to be carried on their shoulders stands prepared, padded with rags. A row of baskets covered with sacking are ranged along the back wall.

"Where is the body of John Staats?" raps out Eddie. "You claimed it, took it away from the morgue this morning." His eyes are on those baskets, on the bleared razor he catches sight of lying on the floor near them.

"Better far," cackles the old man, "that you had followed him. The mark of doom is on yo' even now—" A growl goes up all around.

"Lee," grates Eddie, "in here!" Lee stands next to him, gun in hand. "Cover me while I take a look around."

"All of you over in that corner there," growls Lee, and kicks viciously at one who is too slow in moving. They huddle there, cower there, glaring, spitting like a band of apes. Eddie makes straight for those baskets, whips the covering off the first one. Charcoal. The next. Coffee beans. The next. Rice. And so on.

Just small baskets that Negro women balance on their heads to sell at the marketplace. He looks at Papa Benjamin, takes out the wad of money he's brought with him. "Where've you got him? Where's he buried? Take us there, show us where it is."

Not a sound, just burning, shriveling hate in waves that you can almost feel. He looks at that razor blade lying there, bleared, not bloody, just matted, dulled, with shreds and threads of something clinging to it. Kicks it away with his foot. "Not here, I guess," he mutters to Lee and moves toward the door.

"What do we do now, boss?" his henchman wants to know.

"Get the hell out of here I guess, where we can breathe some air," Eddie says, and moves on out to the stairs.

Lee is the sort of man who will get what he can out of any situation, no matter what it is. Before he follows Eddie out, he goes over to one of the baskets, stuffs an orange in each coat pocket, and then prods and pries among them to select a particularly nice one for eating on the spot. There's a thud and the orange goes rolling across the floor like a volleyball. "Mr. Bloch!" he shouts hoarsely, "I've found—him!" And he looks pretty sick.

A deep breath goes up from the corner where the Negroes are. Eddie just stands and stares, and leans back weakly for a minute against the doorpost. From out of the layers of oranges in the basket, the five fingers of a hand thrust upward, a hand that ends abruptly, cleanly at the wrist.

"His signet," says Eddie weakly, "there on the little finger— I know it."

"Say the word! Should I shoot?" Lee wants to know.

Eddie shakes his head. "They didn't—he committed suicide. Let's do what we have to—and get out of here!"

Lee turns over one basket after the other. The stuff in them spills and sifts and rolls out upon the floor. But in each there's something else. Bloodless, pallid as fish flesh. That razor, those shreds clinging to it, Eddie knows now what it was used for. They take one basket, they line it with a verminous blanket from the bed. Then with their bare hands they fill it with what they have found, and close the ends of the blanket over the top of it, and carry it between them out of the room and down the pitch-black stairs, Lee going down backward with his gun in one hand to cover them from the rear. Lee's swearing like a fiend. Eddie's trying not to think what the purpose, the destination of all those baskets was. The watchdog is still out on the stairs, with a concussion.

Back through the lane they struggle and finally put their burden down in the before-dawn stillness of Congo Square. Eddie goes up against a wall and is heartily sick. Then he comes back again and says: "The head—did you notice—?"

"No, we didn't," Lee answers. "Stay here, I'll go back for it. I'm armed. I could stand anything now, after what I just been through."

Lee's gone about five minutes. When he comes back, he's in his shirt, coatless. His coat's rolled up under one arm in a bulky bulge. He bends over the basket, lifts the blanket, replaces it again, and when he straightens up, the bulge in his folded coat is gone. Then he throws the coat away, kicks it away on the ground. "Hidden away in a cupboard," he mutters. "Had to shoot one of 'em through the palm of the hand before they'd come clean. What were they up to?"

"Practice cannibalism maybe, I don't know. I'd rather not think."

"I brought your money back. It didn't seem to square you with them."

Eddie shoves it back at him. "Pay for your suit and your time."

"Aren't you going to tip off the squareheads?"

"I told you he jumped in the lake. I have a copy of the examiner's report in my pocket."

"I know, but isn't there some ordinance against dissecting a body without permission?"

"I can't afford to get mixed up with them, Lee. It would kill my career. We've got what we went there for. Now just forget everything you saw."

The hearse from the crematorium contacts them there in Congo Square. The covered basket's taken on, and what's left of Johnny Staats heads away for a better finish than was coming to him.

"G'night, boss," says Lee. "Any time you need any other little thing—"

"No," says Eddie, "I'm getting out of New Orleans." His hand is like ice when they shake.

He does. He hands Graham back his contract, and a split week later he's playing New York's newest, in the frantic Fifties. With a white valet. The chant, of course, is still featured. He has to; it's his chief asset, his biggest draw. It introduces him and signs him off, and in between Judy always dances it for a high spot. But he can't get rid of that backache that started the night he first played it. First he goes and tries having his back baked for a couple of hours a day under a violet-ray lamp. No improvement.

Then he has himself examined by the biggest specialist in New York. "Nothing there," says the big shot. "Absolutely nothing the matter with you: liver, kidneys, blood—everything perfect. It must be all in your own mind."

"You're losing weight, Eddie," Judy says, "you look bad, darling." His bathroom scales tell him the same thing. Down five pounds a week, sometimes seven, never up an ounce. More experts. X-rays this time, blood analysis, gland treatments, everything from soup to nuts. Nothing doing. And the dull ache, the lassitude, spreads slowly, first to one arm, then to the other.

He takes specimens of everything he eats, not just one day, but every day for weeks, and has them chemically analyzed. Nothing. And he doesn't have to be told that anyway. He knows that even in New Orleans, way back in the beginning, nothing was ever put into his food. Judy ate from the same tray, drank from the same coffeepot he did. Nightly she dances herself into a lather, and yet she's the picture of health.

So that leaves nothing but his mind, just as they all say. "But I don't believe it!" he tells himself. "I don't believe that just sticking pins into a wax doll can hurt me—me or anyone!"

So it isn't his mind at all, but some other mind back there in New Orleans, some other mind *thinking,* wishing, ordering him dead, night and day.

"But it can't be done!" says Eddie. "There's no such thing!"

And yet it's being done; it's happening right under his own eyes. Which leaves only one answer. If going three thousand miles away on dry land didn't help, then going three thousand miles away across the ocean will do the trick. So London next, and the Kit-Kat Club. Down, down, down go the bathroom scales, a little bit each week. The pains spread downward into his thighs. His ribs start showing up here and there. He's dying on his feet. He finds it more comfortable now to walk with a stick —not to be swanky, not to be English—to rest as he goes along. His shoulders ache each night just from waving that lightweight baton at his crew. He has a music stand built for himself to lean on, keeps it in front of his body, out of sight of the audience while he's conducting, and droops over it. Sometimes he finishes up a number with his head lower than his shoulders, as though he had a rubber spine.

Finally he goes to Reynolds, famous the world over, the biggest alienist in England. "I want to know whether I'm sane or insane." He's under observation for weeks, months; they put him through every known test, and plenty of unknown ones, mental, physical, metabolic. They flash lights in front of his face and watch the pupils of his eyes; they contract to pinheads. They touch the back of his throat with sandpaper; he nearly chokes. They strap him to a chair that goes around and around and does somersaults at so many revolutions per minute, then ask him to walk across the room; he staggers.

Reynolds takes plenty of pounds, hands him a report thick as a telephone book, sums it up for him. "You are as normal, Mr. Bloch, as anyone I have ever handled. You're so well-balanced you haven't even got the extra little touch of imagination most actors and musicians have." So it's not his own mind, it's coming from the outside, is it?

The whole thing from beginning to end has taken eighteen months. Trying to outdistance death, with death gaining on him slowly but surely all the time. He's emaciated. There's only one thing left to do now, while he's still able to crawl aboard a ship —that's to get back to where the whole thing started. New York, London, Paris, haven't been able to save him. His only salvation, now, lies in the hands of a decrepit colored man skulking in the Vieux Carré of New Orleans.

He drags himself there, to that same half-ruined house, without a bodyguard, not caring now whether they kill him or not, almost wishing they would and get it over with. But that would be too easy an out, it seems. The gorilla that Lee crippled that night shuffles out to him between two sticks, recognizes him, breathes undying hate into his face, but doesn't lift a finger to harm him. The spirits are doing the job better than he could ever hope to. Their mark is on this man, woe betide anyone who comes between them and their hellish satisfaction. Eddie Bloch totters up the stairs unopposed, his back as safe from a knife as if he wore steel armor. Behind him the Negro sprawls upon the stairs to lubricate his long-awaited hour of satisfaction with rum —and oblivion.

He finds the old man alone there in the room. The Stone Age and the twentieth century face each other, and the Stone Age has won out.

"Take it off me," says Eddie brokenly. "Give me my life back —I'll do anything, anything you say!"

"What has been done cannot be undone. Do you think the

spirits of the earth and of the air, of fire and water, know the meaning of forgiveness?"

"Intercede for me, then. You brought it about. Here's money, I'll give you twice as much, all I earn, all I ever hope to earn—"

"You have desecrated the *obiah*. Death has been on you from that night. All over the world and in the air above the earth you have mocked the spirits with the chant that summons them. Nightly your wife dances it. The only reason she has not shared your doom is because she does not know the meaning of what she does. You do. You were here among us."

Eddie goes down on his knees, scrapes along the floor after the old man, tries to tug at the garments he wears. "Kill me right now, then, and be done with it. I can't stand any more—" He bought the gun only that day, was going to do it himself at first, but found he couldn't. A minute ago he pleaded for his life, now he's pleading for death. "It's loaded, all you have to do is shoot. Look! I'll close my eyes—I'll write a note and sign it, that I did it myself—"

He tries to thrust it into the witch doctor's hand, tries to close the bony, shriveled fingers around it, tries to point it at himself. The old man throws it down, away from him. Cackles gleefully, "Death will come, but differently—slowly, oh, so slowly!"

Eddie just lies there flat on his face, sobbing dryly. The old man spits, kicks at him weakly. He pulls himself up somehow, stumbles toward the door. He isn't even strong enough to get it open at the first try. It's that little thing that brings it on. Something touches his foot, he looks, stoops for the gun, turns. Thought is quick but the old man's mind is even quicker. Almost before the thought is there, the old man knows what's coming. In a flash, scuttling like a crab, he has shifted around to the other side of the bed, to put something between them. Instantly the situation's reversed, the fear has left Eddie and is on the old man now. He's lost the aggression. For a minute only, but that minute is all Eddie needs. His mind beams out like a diamond, like a lighthouse through a fog. The gun roars, jolting his weakened body down to his shoes. The old man falls flat across the bed, his head too far over, dangling down over the side of it like an overripe pear. The bed frame sways gently with his weight for a minute, and then it's over.

Eddie stands there, still off-balance from the kickback. So it was as easy as all that! Where's all his magic now? Strength, willpower flood back through him as if a faucet was suddenly turned on. The little smoke there was can't get out of the sealed-up room, it hangs there in thin layers. Suddenly he's shaking his fist at the dead thing on the bed. "I'm gonna live now! I'm gonna live, see?" He gets the door open, sways with it for a minute. Then he's feeling his way down the stairs, past the unconscious watchdog, mumbling it over and over but low, "Gonna live now, gonna live!"

The commissioner mops his face as if he were in the steam room of a Turkish bath. He exhales like an oxygen tank. "Judas, Joseph and Mary, Mr. Bloch, what a story! Wish I hadn't asked you; I won't sleep tonight." Even after the accused has been led from the room, it takes him some time to get over it. The upper right-hand drawer of his desk helps some—just two fingers. So does opening the windows and letting in a lot of sunshine.

Finally he picks up the phone and gets down to business. "Who've you got out there that's absolutely without a nerve in his body? I mean a guy with so little feeling he could sit on a hatpin and turn it into a paper clip. Oh, yeah, that Cajun, Desjardins, I know him. He's the one goes around striking parlor matches off the soles of stiffs. Well, send him in here."

"No, stay outside," wheezes Papa Benjamin through the partly open door to his envoy. "I'se communin' with the *obiah* and yo' unclean, been drunk all last night and today. Deliver the summons. Reach yo' hand in to me, once fo' every token, yo' knows how many to take."

The crippled Negro thrusts his huge paw through the aperture, and from behind the door the *papaloi* places a severed chicken claw in his upturned palm. A claw bound with a red rag. The messenger disposes of it about his tattered clothing, thrusts his hand in for another. Twenty times the act is repeated, then he lets his arm hang stiffly at his side. The door starts closing slowly.

"*Papaloi,*" whines the figure on the outside of it, "why you hide yo' face from me, is the spirits angry?"

There's a flicker of suspicion in his yellow eyeballs in the dimness, however. Instantly the opening of the door widens. Papa Benjamin's familiar wrinkled face thrusts out at him, malignant eyes crackling like fuses. "Go!" shrills the old man, " 'liver my summons. Is you want me to bring a spirit down on you?" The messenger totters back. The door slams.

The sun goes down and it's nighttime in New Orleans. The moon rises, midnight chimes from St. Louis Cathedral, and hardly has the last note died away when a gruesome swampland whistle sounds outside the deathly still house. A fat Negress, basket on arm, comes trudging up the stairs a moment later, opens the door, goes in to the *papaloi,* closes it again, traces an invisible mark on it with her forefinger and kisses it. Then she turns and her eyes widen with surprise. Papa Benjamin is in bed, covered up to the neck with filthy rags. The familiar candles are all lit, the bowl for the blood, the sacrificial knife, the magic powders, all the paraphernalia of the ritual are laid out in readiness, but they are ranged about the bed instead of at the opposite end of the room as usual.

The old man's head, however, is held high above the encumbering rags, his beady eyes gaze-back at her unflinchingly, the familiar semicircle of white wool rings his crown, his ceremonial mask is at his side. "I am a little tired, my daughter," he tells her. His eyes stray to the tiny wax image of Eddie Bloch under the candles, hairy with pins, and hers follow them. "A doomed one, nearing his end, came here last night thinking I could be killed like other men. He shot a bullet from a gun at me. I blew my breath at it, it stopped in the air, turned around, and went back in the gun again. But it tired me to blow so hard, strained my voice a little."

A revengeful gleam lights up the woman's broad face. "And he'll die soon, *papaloi?*"

"Soon," cackles the weazened figure in the bed. The woman

gnashes her teeth and hugs herself delightedly. She opens the top of her basket and allows a black hen to escape and flutter about the room.

When all twenty have assembled, men and women, old and young, the drum and the gourds begin to beat, the low wailing starts, the orgy gets under way. Slowly they dance around the three sides of the bed at first, then faster, faster, lashing themselves to a frenzy, tearing at their own and each other's clothes, drawing blood with knives and fingernails, eyes rolling in an ecstasy that colder races cannot know. The sacrifices, feathered and furred, that have been fastened to the two lower posts of the bed, squawk and flutter and fly vertically up and down in a barnyard panic. There is a small monkey among them tonight, clawing, biting, hiding his face in his hands like a frightened child. A bearded Negro, nude torso glistening like patent leather, seizes one of the frantic fowls, yanks it loose from its moorings, and holds it out toward the witch doctor with both hands. "We'se thirsty, *papaloi*, we'se thirsty fo' the blood of ou' enemies."

The others take up the cry. "We'se hung'y, *papaloi*, fo' the bones of ou' enemies!"

Papa Benjamin nods his head in time to the rhythm.

"Sac'fice, *papaloi*, sac'fice!"

Papa Benjamin doesn't seem to hear them.

Then back go the rags in a gray wave and out comes the arm at last. Not the gnarled brown toothpick arm of Papa Benjamin, but a bulging arm thick as a piano leg, cuffed in serge, white at the wrist, ending in a regulation police revolver with the clip off. The erstwhile witch doctor's on his feet at a bound, standing erect atop the bed, back to the wall, slowly fanning his score of human devils with the mouth of his gun, left to right, then right to left again, evenly, unhurriedly. The resonant bellow of a bull comes from his weazened slit of a mouth instead of *papaloi*'s cracked falsetto. "Back against that wall there, all of you! Throw down them knives and jiggers!"

But they're slow to react; the swift drop from ecstasy to stupefaction can't register right away. None of them are over bright anyway or they wouldn't be here. Mouths hang open, the wailing stops, the drums and gourds fall still, but they're still packed close about this sudden changeling in their midst, with the familiar shriveled face of Papa Benjamin and the thickset body, business suit, of a white man—too close for comfort. Blood lust and religious mania don't know fear of a gun. It takes a cool head for that, and the only cool head in the room is the withered cocoanut atop the broad shoulders behind that gun. So he shoots twice, and a woman at one end of the semicircle, the drum beater, and a man at the other end, the one still holding the sacrificial fowl, drop in their tracks with a double moan. Those in the middle slowly draw back step by step across the room, all eyes on the figure reared up on the bed. An instant's carelessness, the wavering of an eye, and they'll be in on him in a body. He reaches up with his free hand and rips the dead witch-doctor's features from his face, to breathe better, see better. They dissolve into a crumpled rag before the blacks' terrified eyes, like a stocking cap coming off someone's head—a mixture of paraffin and fiber, called moulage—a death mask taken from the corpse's own face, reproducing even the fine lines of the skin and its natural color. Moulage. So the twentieth century has won out after all. And behind them is the grinning, slightly perspiring, lantern-jawed face of Detective Jacques Desjardins, who doesn't believe in spirits unless they're under a neat little label. And outside the house sounds the twenty-first whistle of the evening, but not a swampland sound this time; a long, cold, keen blast to bring figures out of the shadows and doorways that have waited there patiently all night.

Then the door bursts inward and the police are in the room. The prisoners, two of them dangerously wounded, are pushed and carried downstairs to join the crippled doorguard, who has been in custody for the past hour, and single file, tied together with ropes, they make their way through the long tortuous alley out into Congo Square.

In the early hours of that same morning, just a little more than twenty-four hours after Eddie Bloch first staggered into police headquarters with his strange story, the whole thing is cooked, washed and bottled. The commissioner sits in his office listening attentively to Desjardins. And spread out on his desk as strange an array of amulets, wax images, bunches of feathers, balsam leaves, *ouangas* (charms of nail parings, hair clippings, dried blood, powdered roots), green mildewed coins dug up from coffins in graveyards, as that room has ever seen before. All this is state's evidence now, to be carefully labeled and docketed for the use of the prosecuting attorney when the proper time comes. "And this," explains Desjardins, indicating a small dusty bottle, "is methylene blue, the chemist tells me. It's the only modern thing we got out of the place, found it lying forgotten with a lot of rubbish in a corner that looked like it hadn't been disturbed for years. What it was doing there or what they wanted with it I don't—"

"Wait a minute," interrupts the commissioner eagerly. "That fits in with something poor Bloch told me last night. He noticed a bluish color under his fingernails and a yellowness to his eyeballs, but *only* after he'd been initiated that first night. This stuff probably had something to do with it, an injection of it must have been given him that night in some way without his knowing it. Don't you get the idea? It floored him just the way they wanted it to. He mistook the signs of it for a giveaway that he had colored blood. It was the opening wedge. It broke down his disbelief, started his mental resistance to crumbling. That was all they needed, just to get a foothold in his mind. Mental suggestion did the rest, has been doing it ever since. If you ask me, they pulled the same stunt on Staats originally. I don't believe he had colored blood any more than Bloch has. And as a matter of fact the theory that it shows up in that way generations later is all the bunk anyway, they tell me."

"Well," says Dij, looking at his own grimy nails, "if you're just going to judge by appearances that way, I'm full-blooded Zulu."

His overlord just looks at him, and if he didn't have such a poker face, one might be tempted to read admiration or at least approval into the look. "Must have been a pretty tight spot for a minute with all of them around while you put on your act!"

"Nah, I didn't mind," answered Dij. "The only thing that bothered me was the smell."

Eddie Bloch, the murder charge against him quashed two months ago, and the population of the state penitentiary increased only this past week by the admission of twenty-three ex-voodoo-worshipers for terms varying from two to ten years, steps up on the platform at Maxim's for a return engagement. Eddie's pale and washed-out looking, but climbing slowly back up through the hundred-and-twenties again to his former weight. The ovation he gets ought to do anyone's heart good, the way they clap and stamp and stand up and cheer. And at that, his name was kept out of the recently concluded trial. Desjardins and his mates did all the states-witnessing necessary.

The theme he comes in on now is something sweet and harmless. Then a waiter comes up and hands him a request. Eddie shakes his head. "No, not in our repertoire any more." He goes on leading. Another request comes, and another. Suddenly someone shouts it out at him, and in a second the whole place has taken up the cry. "The Voodoo Chant! Give us the Voodoo Chant!"

His face gets whiter than it is already, but he turns and tries to smile at them and shake his head. They won't quit, the music can't be heard, and he has to tap a lay-off. From all over the place, like a cheering section at a football game, "We want the Voodoo Chant! We want—!"

Judy's at his side. "What's the matter with 'em anyway?" he asks. "Don't they know what that thing's done to me?"

"Play it, Eddie, don't be foolish," she urges. "Now's the time, break the spell once and for all, prove to yourself that it can't hurt you. If you don't do it now, you'll never get over the idea. It'll stay with you all your life. Go ahead. I'll dance it just like I am."

"Okay," he says.

He taps. It's been quite some time, but he can rely on his outfit. Slow and low like thunder far away, coming nearer. *Boom-*

putta-putta-boom! Judy whirls out behind him, lets out the first preliminary screech, *Eeyaeeya!*

She hears a commotion in back of her, and stops as suddenly as she began. Eddie Bloch's fallen flat on his face and doesn't move again after that.

They all know, somehow. There's an inertness, a finality about it that tells them. The dancers wait a minute, mill about, then melt away in a hush. Judy Jarvis doesn't scream, doesn't cry, just stands there staring, wondering. That last thought—did it come from inside his own mind just now—or outside? Was it two months on its way, from the other side of the grave, looking for him, looking for him, until it found him tonight when he played the chant once more and laid his mind open to Africa? No policeman, no detective, no doctor, no scientist, will ever be able to tell her. Did it come from inside or from outside? All she says is, "Stand close to me, boys—real close to me, I'm afraid of the dark."

" . . . DEAD MEN WORKING IN THE CANE FIELDS"

by W.B. SEABROOK

As noted in the Introduction, " '. . . Dead Men Working in the Cane Fields' " is a chapter from W.B. Seabrook's The Magic Island, *a flamboyant and exaggerated firsthand account of voodoo in Haiti in the 1920s. (Other chapters in the book have even more lurid titles: "Goat-Cry, Girl-Cry," "The Altar of Skulls," "The God Incarnate," "A Nymph in Bronze." And the several illustrations by one Alexander King, most of which are stereotypical black caricatures, also add to the book's sensationalism.)*

Nevertheless, no matter what percentage is factual and what percentage fictional, Seabrook's account of zombies and zombieism offers more than a few shudders. Take, for example, this passage:

But the zombies shuffled through the marketplace, recognizing neither father nor wife nor mother, and as they turned leftward up the path leading to the graveyard, a woman whose daughter was in the procession of the dead threw herself screaming before the girl's . . . feet and begged her

77

to stay; but the grave-cold feet of the daughter and the feet of the other dead shuffled over her and onward; and as they approached the graveyard, they began to shuffle faster and rushed among the graves, and each before his own empty grave began clawing at the stones and earth to enter it again; and as their cold hands touched the earth of their own graves, they fell and lay there, rotting carrion.

A well-known explorer and author during the early years of this century, William B. Seabrook produced a number of (supposedly) authentic records of black magic, spiritualism, and witchcraft throughout the world. Another of his books, Witchcraft, *received as much attention in its day as did* The Magic Island *and is a prized item among students and collectors of the occult. Although he wrote relatively little fiction per se, two excellent short stories, "The Salamander" and "The Witch's Vengeance," often appear in anthologies of the supernatural and the macabre. He died during World War II, not long after the publication of his autobiography,* No Hiding Place, *in 1942.*

PRETTY MULATTO Julie had taken baby Marianne to bed. Constant Polynice and I sat late before the doorway of his *caille,* talking of fire-hags, demons, werewolves and vampires, while a full moon, rising slowly, flooded his sloping cotton fields and the dark rolling hills beyond.

Polynice was a Haitian farmer, but he was no common jungle peasant. He lived on the island of La Gonave. He seldom went over to the Haitian mainland, but he knew what was going on in Port-au-Prince, and spoke sometimes of installing a radio.

A countryman, half peasant born and bred, he was familiar with every superstition of the mountains and the plain, yet too intelligent to believe them literally true—or at least so I gathered from his talk.

He was interested in helping me toward an understanding of the tangled Haitian folklore. It was only by chance that we came presently to a subject which—though I refused for a long time to admit it—lies in a baffling category on the ragged edge of things which are beyond either superstition or reason. He had been telling me of fire-hags who left their skins at home and set the cane fields blazing; of the vampire, a woman sometimes living, sometimes dead, who sucked the blood of children and who could be distinguished because her hair always turned an ugly red; of the werewolf—*chauché*, in Creole—a man or woman who took the form of some animal, usually a dog, and went killing lambs, young goats, sometimes babies.

All this, I gathered, he considered to be pure superstition, as he told me with tolerant scorn how his friend and neighbor Osmann had one night seen a gray dog slinking with bloody jaws from his sheep-pen, and who, after having shot and exorcised and buried it, was so convinced he had killed a certain girl named Liane who was generally reputed to be a *chauché* that when he met her two days later on the path to Grande Source, he believed she was a ghost come back for vengeance, and fled howling.

As Polynice talked on, I reflected that these tales ran closely parallel not only with those of the Negroes in Georgia and the Carolinas, but with the medieval folklore of white Europe. Werewolves, vampires and demons were certainly no novelty. But I recalled one creature I had been hearing about in Haiti, which sounded exclusively local—the zombie.

It seemed (or so I had been assured by Negroes more credulous than Polynice) that while the zombie came from the grave, it was neither a ghost, nor yet a person who had been raised like Lazarus from the dead. The zombie, they say, is a soulless human corpse, still dead, but taken from the grave and endowed by sorcery with a mechanical semblance of life—it is a dead body which is made to walk and act and move as if it were alive. People who have the power to do this go to a fresh grave, dig up the body before it has had time to rot, galvanize it into movement, and then make of it a servant or slave, occasionally for the commission of some crime, more often simply as a drudge around the habitation or the farm, setting it dull heavy tasks, and beating it like a dumb beast if it slackens.

As this was revolving in my mind, I said to Polynice: "It seems to me that these werewolves and vampires are first cousins to those we have at home, but I have never, except in Haiti, heard of anything like zombies. Let us talk of them for a little while. I wonder if you can tell me something of this zombie superstition. I should like to get at some idea of how it originated."

My rational friend Polynice was deeply astonished. He leaned over and put his hand in protest on my knee.

"Superstition? But I assure you that this of which you now speak is not a matter of superstition. Alas, these things—and other evil practices connected with the dead—exist. They exist to an extent that you whites do not dream of, though evidences are everywhere under your eyes.

"Why do you suppose that even the poorest peasants, when they can, bury their dead beneath solid tombs of masonry?

"Why do they bury them so often in their own yards, close to the doorway?

"Why, so often, do you see a tomb or grave set close beside a busy road or footpath where people are always passing?

"It is to assure the poor unhappy dead such protection as we can.

"I will take you in the morning to see the grave of my brother, who was killed in the way you know. It is over there on the little ridge which you can see clearly now in the moonlight, open space all around it, close beside the trail which everybody passes going to and from Grande Source. Through four nights we watched yonder, in the peristyle, Osmann and I, with shotguns —for at that time both my dead brother and I had bitter enemies —until we were sure the body had begun to rot.

"No, my friend, no, no. There are only too many true cases. At this very moment, in the moonlight, there are zombies working on this island, less than two hours' ride from my own habitation. We know about them, but we do not dare to interfere so long as our own dead are left unmolested. If you will ride with me tomorrow night, yes, I will show you dead men working in the cane fields. Close even to the cities, there are sometimes zombies. Perhaps you have already heard of those that were at Hasco. . . ."

"What about Hasco?" I interrupted him, for in the whole of Haiti, Hasco is perhaps the last name anybody would think of connecting with either sorcery or superstition.

The word is American-commercial-synthetic, like Nabisco, Delco, Socony. It stands for the Haitian-American Sugar Company—an immense factory plant, dominated by a huge chimney, with clanging machinery, steam whistles, freight cars. It is like a chunk of Hoboken. It lies in the eastern suburbs of Port-au-Prince, and beyond it stretch the cane fields of the Cul-de-Sac. Hasco makes rum when the sugar market is off, pays low wages, twenty or thirty cents a day, and gives steady work. It is modern big business, and it sounds it, looks it, smells it.

Such, then, was the incongruous background for the weird tale Constant Polynice now told me.

The spring of 1918 was a big cane season, and the factory, which had its own plantations, offered a bonus on the wages of new workers. Soon heads of families and villages from the mountain and the plain came trailing their ragtag little armies, men, women, children, trooping to the registration bureau and thence into the fields.

One morning an old black headman, Ti Joseph of Colombier, appeared leading a band of ragged creatures who shuffled along behind him, staring dumbly, like people walking in a daze. As Joseph lined them up for registration, they still stared, vacant-eyed like cattle, and made no reply when asked to give their names.

Joseph said they were ignorant people from the slopes of Morne-au-Diable, a roadless mountain district near the Dominican border, and that they did not understand the Creole of the plains. They were frightened, he said, by the din and smoke of the great factory, but under his direction they would work hard in the fields. The farther they were sent away from the factory, from the noise and bustle of the railroad yards, the better it would be.

Better indeed, for these were not living men and women but poor unhappy zombies whom Joseph and his wife Croyance had dragged from their peaceful graves to slave for him in the sun —and if by chance a brother or father of the dead should see and recognize them, Joseph knew that it would be a very bad affair for him.

So they were assigned to distant fields beyond the crossroads, and camped there, keeping to themselves like any proper family or village group; but in the evening when other little companies, encamped apart as they were, gathered each around its one big common pot of savory millet or plantains, generously seasoned with dried fish and garlic, Croyance would tend *two* pots upon the fire, for as everyone knows, the zombies must never be permitted to taste salt or meat. So the food prepared for them was tasteless and unseasoned.

As the zombies toiled day after day dumbly in the sun, Joseph sometimes beat them to make them move faster, but Croyance began to pity the poor dead creatures who should be at rest— and pitied them in the evenings when she dished out their flat, tasteless *bouillie*.

Each Saturday afternoon, Joseph went to collect the wages for them all, and what division he made was no concern of Hasco, so long as the work went forward. Sometimes Joseph alone, and sometimes Croyance alone, went to Croix de Bouquet for the Saturday night *bamboche* or the Sunday cockfight, but always one of them remained with the zombies to prepare their food and see that they did not stray away.

Through February this continued, until Fête Dieu approached, with a Saturday-Sunday-Monday holiday for all the workers. Joseph, with his pockets full of money, went to Port-au-Prince and left Croyance behind, cautioning her as usual; and she agreed to remain and tend the zombies, for he promised her that at the Mardi Gras she should visit the city.

But when Sunday morning dawned, it was lonely in the fields, and her kind old woman's heart was filled with pity for the zombies, and she thought, "Perhaps it will cheer them a little to see the gay crowds and the processions at Croix de Bouquet, and since all the Morne-au-Diable people will have gone back to the mountain to celebrate Fête Dieu at home, no one will recognize them, and no harm can come of it." And it is the truth that Croyance also wished to see the gay procession.

So she tied a new bright-colored handkerchief around her head, aroused the zombies from the sleep that was scarcely different from their waking, gave them their morning bowl of cold, unsalted plantains boiled in water, which they ate dumbly uncomplaining, and set out with them for the town, single file, as the country people always walk. Croyance, in her bright kerchief, leading the nine dead men and women behind her, past the railroad crossing, where she murmured a prayer to Legba, past the great white-painted wooden Christ, who hung life-sized in the glaring sun, where she stopped to kneel and cross herself —but the poor zombies prayed neither to Papa Legba nor to Brother Jesus, for they were dead bodies walking, without souls or minds.

They followed her to the market square, before the church where hundreds of little thatched, open shelters, used on weekdays for buying and selling, were empty of trade, but crowded here and there by gossiping groups in the grateful shade.

To the shade of one of these market booths, which was still unoccupied, she led the zombies, and they sat like people asleep with their eyes open, staring, but seeing nothing, as the bells in the church began to ring, and the procession came from the priest's house—red-purple robes, golden crucifix held aloft, tinkling bells and swinging incense pots, followed by little black boys in white lace robes, little black girls in starched white dresses, with shoes and stockings, from the parish school, with colored ribbons in their kinky hair, a nun beneath a big umbrella leading them.

Croyance knelt with the throng as the procession passed, and wished she might follow it across the square to the church steps, but the zombies just sat and stared, seeing nothing.

When noontime came, women with baskets passed to and fro in the crowd, or sat selling bonbons (which were not candy but little sweet cakes), figs (which were not figs but sweet bananas), oranges, dried herring, biscuit, casava bread, and *clairin* poured from a bottle at a penny a glass.

As Croyance sat with her savory dried herring and biscuit baked with salt and soda, and provision of *clairin* in the tin cup by her side, she pitied the zombies who had worked so faithfully for Joseph in the cane fields, and who now had nothing, while all the other groups around were feasting, and as she pitied them, a woman passed, crying,

"*Tablettes! Tablettes pistaches! T'ois pour dix cobs!*"

Tablettes are a sort of candy, in shape and size like cookies, made of brown cane sugar (*rapadou*); sometimes with *pistaches*, which in Haiti are peanuts, or with coriander seed.

And Croyance thought, "These *tablettes* are not salted or seasoned, they are sweet, and can do no harm to the zombies just this once."

So she untied the corner of her kerchief, took out a coin, a gourdon, the quarter of a gourde, and bought some of the *tablettes*, which she broke in halves and divided among the zombies, who began sucking and mumbling them in their mouths.

But the baker of the *tablettes* had salted the *pistache* nuts before stirring them into the *rapadou*, and as the zombies tasted the salt, they knew that they were dead and made a dreadful outcry and arose and turned their faces toward the mountain.

No one dared stop them, for they were corpses walking in the sunlight, and they themselves and all the people knew that they were corpses. And they disappeared toward the mountain.

When later they drew near their own village on the slopes of Morne-au-Diable, these dead men and women walking single file in the twilight, with no soul leading them or daring to follow, the people of their village, who were also holding *bamboche* in the marketplace, saw them drawing closer, recognized among them fathers, brothers, wives and daughters whom they had buried months before.

Most of them knew at once the truth, that these were zombies who had been dragged dead from their graves, but others hoped that a blessed miracle had taken place on this Fête Dieu, and rushed forward to take them in their arms and welcome them.

But the zombies shuffled through the marketplace, recognizing neither father nor wife nor mother, and as they turned leftward up the path leading to the graveyard, a woman whose daughter was in the procession of the dead threw herself screaming before the girl's shuffling feet and begged her to stay; but the grave-cold feet of the daughter and the feet of the other dead shuffled over her and onward; and as they approached the graveyard, they began to shuffle faster and rushed among the graves, and each before his own empty grave began clawing at the stones and earth to enter it again; and as their cold hands touched the earth of their own graves, they fell and lay there, rotting carrion.

That night the fathers, sons and brothers of the zombies, after restoring the bodies to their graves, sent a messenger on muleback down the mountain, who returned next day with the name of Ti Joseph and with a stolen shirt of Ti Joseph's which had been worn next his skin and was steeped in the grease-sweat of his body.

They collected silver in the village and went with the name of Ti Joseph and the shirt of Ti Joseph to a *bocor* beyond Trou Caiman, who made a deadly needle *ouanga,* a black bag *ouanga,* pierced all through with pins and needles, filled with dry goat dung, circled with cock's feathers dipped in blood.

And lest the needle *ouanga* be slow in working or be rendered weak by Joseph's counter-magic, they sent men down to the plain, who lay in wait patiently for Joseph, and one night hacked off his head with a machete. . . .

When Polynice had finished this recital, I said to him, after a moment of silence, "You are not a peasant like those of the Cul-de-Sac; you are a reasonable man, or at least it seems to me you are. Now how much of that story, honestly, do you believe?"

He replied earnestly: "I did not see these special things, but there were many witnesses, and why should I not believe them when I myself have also seen zombies? When you also have seen them, with their faces and their eyes in which there is no life, you will not only believe in these zombies who should be resting in their graves, you will pity them from the bottom of your heart."

Before finally taking leave of La Gonave, I did see these "walking dead men," and I did, in a sense, believe in them and pitied them, indeed, from the bottom of my heart. It was not the next night, though Polynice, true to his promise, rode with me across the Plaine Mapou to the deserted, silent cane fields where he had hoped to show me zombies laboring. It was not on any night. It was in broad daylight one afternoon, when we passed that way again, on the lower trail to Picmy. Polynice reined in his horse and pointed to a rough, stony, terraced slope—on which four laborers, three men and a woman, were chopping the earth with machetes, among straggling cotton stalks, a hundred yards distant from the trail.

"Wait while I go up there," he said, excited because a chance had come to fulfill his promise. "I think it is Lamercie with the zombies. If I wave to you, leave your horse and come." Starting up the slope, he shouted to the woman, "It is I, Polynice," and when he waved later, I followed.

As I clambered up, Polynice was talking to the woman. She had stopped work—a big-boned, hard-faced black girl, who regarded us with surly unfriendliness. My first impression of the three supposed zombies, who continued dumbly at work, was that there was something about them unnatural and strange. They were plodding like brutes, like automatons. Without stooping down, I could not fully see their faces, which were bent expressionless over their work. Polynice touched one of them on the shoulder, motioned him to get up. Obediently, like an animal, he slowly stood erect—and what I saw then, coupled with what I had heard previously, or despite it, came as a rather sickening shock. The eyes were the worst. It was not my imagination. They were in truth like the eyes of a dead man, not blind, but staring, unfocused, unseeing. The whole face, for that matter, was bad enough. It was vacant, as if there was nothing behind it. It seemed not only expressionless, but incapable of expression. I had seen so much previously in Haiti that was outside ordinary normal experience that for the flash of a second I had a sickening, almost panicky lapse in which I thought, or rather felt, "Great God, maybe this stuff is really true, and if it is true, it is rather awful, for it upsets everything." By "everything" I meant the natural fixed laws and processes on which all modern human thought and actions are based. Then suddenly I remembered—and my mind seized the memory as a man sinking in water clutches a solid plank—the face of a dog I had once seen in the histological laboratory at Columbia. Its entire front brain had been removed in an experimental operation weeks before; it moved about, it was alive, but its eyes were like the eyes I now saw staring.

I recovered from my mental panic. I reached out and grasped one of the dangling hands. It was calloused, solid, human. Holding it, I said, *"Bonjour, compère."* The zombie stared without responding. The black wench, Lamercie, who was their keeper, now more sullen than ever, pushed me away—*"Z'affai' nèg' pas z'affai' blanc"* (Negroes' affairs are not for whites). But I had seen enough. "Keeper" was the key to it. "Keeper" was the word that had leapt naturally into my mind as she protested, and just as naturally the zombies were nothing but poor, ordinary demented human beings, idiots, forced to toil in the fields.

It was a good rational explanation, but it is far from being the end of this story. It satisfied me then, and I said as much to Polynice as we went down the slope. At first he did not contradict me, even said doubtfully, "Perhaps"; but as we reached the horses, before mounting, he stopped and said, "Look here, I respect your distrust of what you call superstition and your desire to find out the truth, but if what you were saying now were the whole truth, how could it be that over and over again, people who have stood by and seen their own relatives buried have, sometimes soon, sometimes months or years afterward, found those relatives working as zombies, and have sometimes killed the man who held them in servitude?"

"Polynice," I said, "that's just the part of it that I can't believe. The zombies in such cases may have resembled the dead persons, or even been 'doubles'—you know what doubles are, how two people resemble each other to a startling degree. But it is a fixed rule of reasoning in America that we will never accept the possibility of a thing's being 'supernatural' so long as any natural explanation, even farfetched, seems adequate."

"Well," said he, "if you spent many years in Haiti, you would have a very hard time to fit this American reasoning into some of the things you encountered here."

As I have said, there is more to this story—and I think it is best to tell it very simply.

In all Haiti, there is no clearer scientifically trained mind, no sounder pragmatic rationalist, than Dr. Antoine Villiers. When I sat later with him in his study, surrounded by hundreds of scientific books in French, German and English, and told him of what I had seen and of my conversations with Polynice, he said:

"My dear sir, I do not believe in miracles nor in supernatural events, and I do not want to shock your Anglo-Saxon intelligence, but this Polynice of yours, with all his superstition, may have been closer to the partial truth than you were. Understand me clearly. I do not believe that anyone has ever been raised literally from the dead—neither Lazarus, nor the daughter of Jairus, nor Jesus Christ himself—yet I am not sure, paradoxical as it may sound, that there is not something frightful, something in the nature of criminal sorcery if you like, in some cases at least, in this matter of zombies. I am by no means sure that some of them who now toil in the fields were not dragged from the actual graves in which they lay in their coffins, buried by their mourning families!"

"It is then something like suspended animation?" I asked.

"I will show you," he replied, "a thing which may supply the key to what you are seeking," and standing on a chair, he pulled down a paper-bound book from a top shelf. It was nothing mysterious or esoteric. It was the current official *Code Pénal* (Criminal Code) of the Republic of Haiti. He thumbed through it and pointed to a paragraph which read:

"*Article 249.* Also shall be qualified as attempted murder the employment which may be made against any person of substances which, without causing actual death, produce a lethargic coma more or less prolonged. If, after the administering of such substances, the person has been buried, the act shall be considered murder no matter what result follows."

MOTHER OF SERPENTS

by ROBERT BLOCH

Like the Seabrook piece, "Mother of Serpents" tells of dark voodoo rites on the island of Haiti; but there all similarity ends. Robert Bloch's story is pure fiction (although it is based on factual material), and recounts the saga of a certain "educated man" who rose to become president of the republic after Toussaint l'Ouverture, Dessalines, and King Christophe freed it from its French oppressors in the 1800s. It is also one of the most chilling horror stories ever to use the voodoo theme.

The quality and the gooseflesh are not surprising, of course, considering that Robert Bloch has long been recognized as the premier contemporary writer of horror fiction. But what is remarkable is that "Mother of Serpents" was published in the great fantasy pulp Weird Tales *in 1936 —when Bloch was just nineteen years old. (His first professional sale, also to* Weird Tales, *was made two years previous, at the even more precocious age of seventeen.) That a teenager—even one of Bloch's talent— should produce a story of this craftsmanship is as unusual as its subject matter.*

In his forty-six year career Robert Bloch ("I have the heart of a little boy; I keep it in a jar on my desk") has published hundreds of fantasy/hor-

ror, science fiction, and mystery stories, a dozen or so collections, some twenty novels (among them the classic Psycho *and the near-classic* The Scarf)*, scores of television and movie scripts, and countless articles and essays. His most recent books are a pair of novels—*Strange Eons, *a horror tale built around H.P. Lovecraft's Cthulhu mythos;* There is a Serpent in Eden, *a suspense story—and a collection entitled* Out of the Mouths of Graves.

VOODOOISM IS a queer thing. Forty years ago it was an unknown subject, save in certain esoteric circles. Today there is a surprising amount of information about it, due to research—and an even more surprising amount of misinformation.

Recent popular books on the subject are, for the most part, sheer romantic fancy; elaborated with the incomplete theorizings of ignoramuses.

Perhaps, though, this is for the best. For the truth about voodoo is such that no writer would care, or dare, to print it. Some of it is worse than their wildest fancies. I myself have seen certain things I do not dare to discuss. It would be useless to tell people anyway, for they would not believe me. And once again, this may be for the best. Knowledge can be a thousand times more terrifying than ignorance.

I know, though, for I have lived in Haiti, the dark island. I have learned much from legend, stumbled on many things through accident, and the bulk of my knowledge comes from the one really authentic source—the statements of the blacks. They're not talkative people, as a rule, those old natives of the back hill country. It took patience and long familiarity with them before they unbent and told me their secrets.

That's why so many of the travel books are so palpably false —no writer who visits Haiti for six months or a year could possibly ingratiate himself into the confidence of those who know the facts. There are so few who really do know; so few who are not afraid to tell.

But I have learned. Let me tell you of the olden days; the old times, when Haiti rose to an empire, borne on a wave of blood.

It was many years ago, soon after the slaves had revolted. Toussaint l'Ouverture, Dessalines and King Christophe freed them from their French masters, freed them after uprisings and massacres and set up a kingdom founded on cruelty more fantastic than the despotism that reigned before.

There were no happy blacks in Haiti then. They had known too much of torture and death; the carefree life of their West Indian neighbors was utterly alien to these slaves and descendants of slaves. A strange mixture of races flourished: fierce tribesmen from Ashanti, Damballah and the Guinea Coast; sullen Caribs; dusky offspring of renegade Frenchmen; bastard admixtures of Spanish, Negro and Indian blood. Sly, treacherous half-breeds and mulattos ruled the coast, but there were even worse dwellers in the hills behind.

There were jungles in Haiti, impassable jungles, mountain-ringed and swamp-scourged forests filled with poisonous insects and pestilential fevers. White men dared not enter them, for they were worse than death. Blood-sucking plants, venomous reptiles, diseased orchids filled the forests, forests that hid horrors Africa had never known.

For that is where the real voodoo flourished, back there in the hills. Men lived there, it is said, descendants of escaped slaves, and outlaw factions that had been hunted from the coast. Furtive rumors told of isolated villages that practiced cannibalism, mixed in with dark religious rites more dreadful and perverted than anything spawned in the Congo itself. Necrophilism, phallic worship, anthropomancy and distorted versions of the Black Mass were commonplace. The shadow of Obeah was everywhere. Human sacrifice was common, the offering up of roosters and goats an accepted thing. There were orgies around the voodoo altars, and blood was drunk in honor of Baron Samedi and the old black gods brought from ancient lands.

Everybody knew about it. Each night the *rada*-drums boomed out from the hills, and fires flared over the forests. Many known *papalois* and conjure-doctors resided on the edge of the coast itself, but they were never disturbed. Nearly all the "civilized" blacks still believed in charms and philtres; even the churchgoers reverted to talismans and incantations in time of need. So-called "educated" Negroes in Port-au-Prince society were admittedly emissaries from the barbarian tribes of the interior, and despite the outward show of civilization the bloody priests still ruled behind the throne.

Of course there were scandals, mysterious disappearances, and occasional protests from emancipated citizens. But it was not wise to meddle with those who bowed to the Black Mother, or incur the anger of the terrible old men who dwelt in the shadow of the Snake.

Such was the status of sorcery when Haiti became a republic. People often wonder why there is still sorcery existent there today; more secretive, perhaps, but still surviving. They ask why the ghastly zombies are not destroyed, and why the government has not stepped in to stamp out the fiendish blood-cults that still lurk in the jungle gloom.

Perchance this tale will provide an answer; this old, secret tale of the new republic. Officials, remembering the story, are still afraid to interfere too strongly, and the laws that have been passed are very loosely enforced.

Because the Serpent Cult of Obeah will never die in Haiti— in Haiti, that fantastic island whose sinuous shoreline resembles the yawning jaws of a monstrous *snake.*

One of the earliest presidents of Haiti was an educated man. Although born on the island, he was schooled in France, and studied extensively while abroad. His accession to the highest office of the land found him an enlightened, sophisticated cosmopolite of the modern type. Of course he still liked to remove his shoes in the privacy of his office, but he never displayed his naked toes in an official capacity. Don't misunderstand—the man was no Emperor Jones; he was merely a polished ebony gentleman whose natural barbarity occasionally broke through its veneer of civilization.

He was, in fact, a very shrewd man. He had to be in order to become president in those early days; only extremely shrewd men ever attained that dignity. Perhaps it would enlighten you a bit to say that in those times the term "shrewd" was a polite Haitian synonym for "crooked." It is therefore easy to realize the president's character when you know that he was regarded as one of the most successful politicians the republic ever produced.

In his short reign he was opposed by very few enemies; and those that did work against him usually disappeared. The tall, coal-black man with the physical skull-conformation of a gorilla harbored a remarkably crafty brain beneath his beetling brow.

His ability was phenomenal. He had an insight into finance which profited him greatly; profited him, that is, in both his official and unofficial capacity. Whenever he saw fit to increase the taxes he increased the army as well, and sent it out to escort the state tax-collectors. His treaties with foreign countries were masterpieces of legal lawlessness. This black Machiavelli knew that he must work fast, since presidents had a peculiar way of dying in Haiti. They seemed peculiarly susceptible to disease—"lead poisoning," as our modern gangster friends might say. So the president worked very fast indeed, and he did a masterful job.

This was truly remarkable, in view of his humble background. For his was a success saga in the good old Horatio Alger manner. His father was unknown. His mother was a conjure woman in the hills, and though quite well-known, she had been very poor. The president had been born in a log cabin; quite the classic setting for a future distinguished career. His early years had been most uneventful, until his adoption, at thirteen, by a benevolent Protestant minister. For a year he lived with this kind man, serving as houseboy in his home. Suddenly the poor minister died of an obscure ailment; this was most unfortunate, for he had been quite wealthy and his money was alleviating much of the suffering in this particular section. At any rate, this rich minister died, and the poor conjure woman's son sailed to France for a university education.

As for the conjure woman, she bought herself a new mule and said nothing. Her skill at herbs had given her son a chance in the world, and she was satisfied.

It was eight years before the boy returned. He had changed a great deal since his departure; he preferred the society of whites and the octoroon society people of Port-au-Prince. It is recorded that he rather ignored his old mother, too. His newly acquired fastidiousness made him painfully aware of the woman's ignorant simplicity. Besides, he was ambitious, and he did not care to publicize his relationship with such a notorious witch.

For she was quite famous in her way. Where she had come from and what her original history was, nobody knew. But for many years her hut in the mountains had been the rendezvous of strange worshipers and even stranger emissaries. The dark powers of Obeah were evoked in her shadowy altar-place amidst the hills, and a furtive group of acolytes resided there with her. Her ritual fires always flared on moonless nights, and bullocks were given in bloody baptism to the Crawler of Midnight. For she was a Priestess of the Serpent.

The Snake-God, you know, is the real deity of the Obeah cults. The blacks worshiped the Serpent in Dahomey and Senegal from time immemorial. They venerate the reptiles in a curious way, and there is some obscure linkage between the snake and the crescent moon. Curious, isn't it—this serpent superstition? The Garden of Eden had its tempter, you know, and the Bible tells of Moses and his staff of snakes. The Egyptians revered Set, and the ancient Hindus had a cobra god. It seems to be general throughout the world—the kindred hatred and reverence of serpents. Always they seem to be worshiped as creatures of evil. American Indians believed in Yig, and Aztec myths follow the pattern. And of course the Hopi ceremonial dances are of the same order.

But the African Serpent legends are particularly dreadful, and the Haitian adaptations of the sacrificial rites are worse.

At the time of which I speak some of the voodoo groups were believed to actually breed snakes; they smuggled the reptiles over from the Ivory Coast to use in their secret practices. There were tall tales current about twenty-foot pythons which swallowed infants offered up to them on the Black Altar, and about *sendings* of poisonous serpents which killed enemies of the voodoo-masters. It is a known fact that several anthropoid apes had been smuggled into the country by a peculiar cult that worshiped gorillas; so the serpent legends may have been equally true.

At any rate, the president's mother was a priestess, and equally as famous, in a way, as her distinguished son. He, just after his return, had slowly climbed to power. First he had been a tax-gatherer, then treasurer, and finally president. Several of his rivals died, and those who opposed him soon found it expedient to dissemble their hatred; for he was still a savage at heart, and savages like to torment their enemies. It was rumored that he had constructed a secret torture chamber beneath the palace, and that its instruments were rusty, though not from disuse.

The breach between the young statesman and his mother began to widen just prior to his presidential incumbency. The immediate cause was his marriage to the daughter of a rich octoroon planter from the coast. Not only was the old woman humiliated because her son contaminated the family stock (she was pure Negro, and descendant of a Niger slave-king), but she was further indignant because she had not been invited to the wedding.

It was held in Port-au-Prince. The foreign consuls were there, and the cream of Haitian society was present. The lovely bride had been convent-bred, and her antecedents were held in the highest esteem. The groom wisely did not deign to desecrate the nuptial celebration by including his rather unsavory parent.

She came, though, and watched the affair through the kitchen doorway. It was just as well that she did not make her presence known, as it would have embarrassed not only her son, but several others as well—official dignitaries who sometimes consulted her in their unofficial capacity.

What she saw of her son and his bride was not pleasing. The man was an affected dandy now, and his wife was a silly flirt. The atmosphere of the pomp and ostentation did not impress her; behind their debonair masks of polite sophistication she knew that most of those present were superstitious Negroes who would have run to her for charms or oracular advice the moment they were in trouble. Nevertheless, she took no action; she merely smiled rather bitterly and hobbled home. After all, she still loved her son.

The next affront, however, she could not overlook. This was the inauguration of the new president. She was not invited to this affair either, yet she came. And this time she did not skulk in the shadows. After the oath of office was administered she marched boldly up to the new ruler of Haiti and accosted him before the very eyes of the German consul himself. She was a grotesque figure; an ungainly little harridan barely five feet tall, black, barefooted, and clad in rags.

Her son quite naturally ignored her presence. The withered crone licked her toothless gums in terrible silence. Then, quite calmly, she began to curse him—not in French, but in native patois of the hills. She called down the wrath of her bloody gods upon his ungrateful head, and threatened both him and his wife with vengeance for their smug ingratitude. The assembled guests were shocked.

So was the new president. However, he did not forget himself. Calmly he motioned to his guards, who led the now hysterical witch-woman away. He would deal with her later.

The next night when he saw fit to go into the dungeon and reason with his mother, she was gone. Disappeared, the guards told him, rolling their eyes mysteriously. He had the jailer shot, and went back to his official chambers.

He was a little worried about that curse business. You see, he knew what the woman was capable of. He did not like those threats against his wife, either. The next day he had some silver bullets moulded, like King Henry in the old days. He also bought an *ouanga* charm from a devil-doctor of his own acquaintance. Magic would fight magic.

That night a serpent came to him in dreams; a serpent with

Meanwhile he sat in the palace with the embers of slow insanity in his eyes—embers that flared into fiendish flame when the guards brought in the withered crone, who had been captured near that awful grove of idols in the swamp.

They took her downstairs, although she fought and clawed like a wildcat, and then the guards went away and left her son with her alone. Alone, in a torture chamber, with a mother who cursed him from the rack. Alone, with frantic fires in his eyes, and a great silver knife in his hand. . . .

The president spent many hours in his secret torture chamber during the next few days. He seldom was seen around the palace, and his servants were given orders that he must not be disturbed. On the fourth day he came up the hidden stairway for the last time, and the flickering madness in his eyes was gone. Just what occurred in the dungeon below will never be rightly known. No doubt that is for the best. The president was a savage at heart, and to the brute, prolongation of pain always brings ecstasy. . . .

It is recorded, though, that the old witch-woman cursed her son with the Serpent's Curse in her dying breath, and that is the most terrible curse of all.

Some idea of what happened may be gained by the knowledge of the president's revenge; for he had a grim sense of humor, and a barbarian's idea of retribution. His wife had been killed by his mother, who fashioned a waxen image. He decided to do what would be exquisitely appropriate.

When he came up the stairs that last time, his servants saw that he bore with him a great candle, fashioned of corpse-fat. And since nobody ever saw his mother's body again, there were curious surmises as to where the corpse-fat was obtained. But then, the president's mind leaned toward grisly jests. . . .

The rest of the story is very simple. The president went directly to his chambers in the palace, where he placed the candle in a holder on his desk. He had neglected his work in the last few days, and there was much official business for him to transact. For a while he sat in silence, staring at the candle with a

green eyes that whispered in the way of r
with shrill and mocking laughter as he st
There was a reptilian odor in his bedroo
and a nauseous slime upon his pillow tha
stench. And the president knew that only
him.

That afternoon his wife missed one of her
president questioned his servants in his priv
below. He learned some facts he dared no
thereafter he seemed very sad. He had see
with wax images before—little mannikins re
women, dressed in parts of their stolen gar
she stuck pins into them or roasted them over
the real people sickened and died. This kno
president quite unhappy, and he was still n
when messengers returned and said that his
from her old hut in the hills.

Three days later his wife died, of a painful v
which no doctors could explain. She was in ag
and just before her passing it was rumored that
blue and bloated up to twice its normal size. H
eaten away as if with leprosy, and her swollen l
those of an elephantiasis victim. Loathsome t
abound in Haiti, but none of them kill in three

After this the president went mad.

Like Cotton Mather of old, he started on a
crusade. Soldiers and police were sent out to con
side. Spies rode up to hovels on the mountain pe
patrols crouched in far-off fields where the liv
work, their glazed and glassy eyes staring ceas
moon. *Mamalois* were put to the question over s
possessors of forbidden books were roasted over
the very tomes they harbored. Bloodhounds yam
hills, and priests died on altars where they were wor
Only one order had been specially given: the presid
was to be captured alive and unharmed.

curious satisfied smile. Then he called for his papers and announced that he would attend to them immediately.

He worked all that night, with two guards stationed outside his door. Sitting at his desk, he pored over his task in the candlelight—the candlelight from the corpse-fat taper.

Evidently his mother's dying curse did not bother him at all. Once satisfied, his blood-lust abated, he discounted all possibility of revenge. Even he was not superstitious enough to believe that the sorceress could return from her grave. He was quite calm as he sat there, quite the civilized gentleman. The candle cast ominous shadows over the darkened room, but he did not notice—until it was too late. Then he looked up to see the corpse-fat candle wriggle into monstrous life.

His mother's curse. . . .

The candle—the corpse-fat candle—was *alive!* It was a sinuous, twisting thing, weaving in its holder with sinister purpose.

The flame-tipped end seemed to glow strongly into a sudden terrible semblance. The president, amazed, saw the fiery face— his mother's; a tiny wrinkled face of flame, with a corpse-fat body that darted out toward the man with hideous ease. The candle was lengthening as if the tallow were melting; lengthening, and reaching out towards him in a terrible way.

The president of Haiti screamed, but it was too late. The glowing flame on the end snuffed out, breaking the hypnotic spell that had held the man betranced. And at that moment the candle leapt, while the room faded into dreadful darkness. It was a ghastly darkness, filled with moans, and the sound of a thrashing body that grew fainter, and fainter. . . .

It was quite still by the time the guards had entered and turned up the lights once more. They knew about the corpse-fat candle and the witch-mother's curse. That is why they were the first to announce the president's death; the first to fire a bullet into his temple and claim he committed suicide.

They told the president's successor the story, and he gave orders that the crusade against voodoo be abandoned. It was better so, for the new man did not wish to die. The guards had explained why they shot the president and called it suicide, and his successor did not wish to risk the Serpent Curse.

For the president of Haiti had been strangled to death by his mother's corpse-fat candle—*a corpse-fat candle that was wound around his neck like a giant snake.*

THE DIGGING AT PISTOL KEY

by CARL JACOBI

The form of voodoo known as Obeah is practiced on such West Indian islands as Jamaica and Trinidad, chiefly by peasants who have been observed "speaking incantations over broken eggshells, bones, tufts of hair and other disagreeable objects." It is said that some Obeahs—those in whom the Power is strongest—are even able to reach from beyond the grave to destroy a hated enemy. This may only be superstition, of course. Then again, it may be something more.

"The Digging at Pistol Key," which first appeared in **Weird Tales** in 1947, makes a strong case for the mystical (and deadly) qualities of Obeah. At the same time it tells a suspenseful tale of murder, greed, vengeance and the search for buried treasure on the narrow promontory near Port-of-Spain, Trinidad, known as Pistol Key. The chills it offers may be of the rippling rather than hair-raising variety, but those ripples do tend to linger a while . . .

A native of Minneapolis, where he was born in 1908, Carl Jacobi published his first stories while a student at the University of Minnesota. After graduation in 1931 he became a news reporter and book and play reviewer for the Minneapolis **Star** and remained with that paper for *several years, leaving finally to edit an advertising and radio trade journal and to devote more time to his fiction writing. His stories have appeared in such diverse magazines as* MacLean's, Weird Tales, Galaxy Science Fiction, The Toronto Star, Thrilling Mystery *and* Railroad Stories. *The best of his fantasy/horror tales appear in three Arkham House collections:* Revelations in Black *(recently reprinted in paperback),* Portraits in Moonlight, *and* Disclosures in Scarlet.

ALTHOUGH HE had lived in Trinidad for more than fifteen years, Jason Cunard might as well have remained in Devonshire, his original home, for all the local background he had absorbed. He read only British newspapers, the *Times* and the *Daily Mail,* which he received by weekly post, and he even had his tea sent him from a shop in Southampton, unmindful of the fact that he could have obtained the same brand, minus the heavy tax, at the local importer in Port-of-Spain.

Of course, Cunard got into town only once a month, and then his time was pretty well occupied with business matters concerning his sugar plantation. He had a house on a narrow promontory midway between Port-of-Spain and San Fernando which was known as Pistol Key. But his plantation sprawled over a large tract in the center of the island.

Cunard frankly admitted there was nothing about Trinidad he liked. He thought the climate insufferable, the people—the Britishers, that is—provincial, and the rest of the population, a polyglot of races that could be grouped collectively as "natives and foreigners." He dreamed constantly of Devonshire, though he knew of course he would never go back.

Whether it was due to this brooding or his savage temper, the fact remained that he had the greatest difficulty in keeping house servants. Since his wife had died two years ago, he had had no less than seven: Caribs, quadroons, and Creoles of one sort or another. His latest, a lean, gangly black boy, went by the name of Christopher, and was undoubtedly the worst of the lot.

As Cunard entered the house now, he was in a distinctly bad frame of mind. Coming down the coast highway, he had had the misfortune to have a flat tire and had damaged his clothes considerably in changing it. He rang the antiquated bell-pull savagely.

Presently Christopher shambled through the connecting doorway.

"Put the car in the garage," Cunard said tersely. "And after dinner repair the spare tire. Some fool left a broken bottle on the road."

The Negro remained standing where he was, and Cunard saw then that he was trembling with fear.

"Well, what the devil's the matter?"

Christopher ran his tongue over his upper lip. "Can't go out dere, sar," he said.

"Can't . . . Why not?"

"De holes in de yard. Der Dere again."

For the first time in more than an hour Cunard permitted himself to smile. While he was totally without sympathy for the superstitions of these blacks, he found the intermittent recurrence of these holes in his property amusing. For he knew quite well that superstition had nothing to do with them.

It all went back to that most diabolical of buccaneers, Francis L'Ollonais and his voyage to the Gulf of Venezuela in the middle of the seventeenth century. After sacking Maracaibo, L'Ollonais sailed with his murderous crew for Tortuga. He ran into heavy storms and was forced to put back in here at Trinidad.

Three or four years ago some idiot by the idiotic name of Arlanpeel had written and published a pamphlet entitled *Fifty Thousand Pieces of Eight* in which he sought to prove by various references that L'Ollonais had buried a portion of his pirate booty on Pistol Key. The pamphlet had sold out its small edition, and Cunard was aware that copies had now become a collector's item. As a result, Pistol Key had come into considerable fame. Tourists stopping off at Port-of-Spain frequently telephoned Cunard, asking permission to visit his property, a request which of course he always refused.

And the holes! From time to time during the night Cunard would be awakened by the sound of a spade grating against gravel, and looking out his bedroom window, he would see a carefully shielded lantern down among the cabbage palms. In the morning there would be a shallow excavation several feet across with the dirt heaped hastily on all four sides.

The thought of persons less fortunate than himself making clandestine efforts to capture a mythical fortune dating to the seventeenth century touched Cunard's sense of humor.

"You heard me, Christopher," he snapped to the houseboy, "put the car in the garage."

But the black remained cowering by the door until Cunard, his patience exhausted, dealt him a sharp slap across the face with the flat of his hand. The boy's eyes kindled, and he went out silently.

Cunard went up to his bathroom and washed the road grime from his hands. Then he proceeded to dress for his solitary dinner, a custom which he never neglected. Downstairs, he got to thinking again about those holes in his yard and decided to have a look at them. He took a flashlight and went out the rear entrance and under the cabbage palms. Fireflies in the darkness and a belated *Qu'-est-ce-qu'il-dit* bird asked its eternal question.

Forty yards from the house he came upon the diggings Christopher had reported. That they were the work of some ambitious fortune hunter was made doubly apparent by the discarded tape-measure and the cheap compass which lay beside the newly turned earth.

Again Cunard smiled. It would be "forty paces from this point to the north end of a shadow cast by a man fifteen hands high," or some such fiddle faddle. Even if L'Ollonais had ever buried money here—and there was no direct evidence that he had—it had probably been carted away long years ago.

He saw Christopher returning from the garage then. The houseboy was walking swiftly, mumbling a low litany to himself. In his right hand he held a small cross fashioned of two bent twigs.

Back in the house, Cunard told himself irritably that Christopher was a fool. After all, he had seen his mother come into plenty of trouble because of her insistence on practicing Obeah. She had professed to be an Obeah-woman and was forever speaking incantations over broken eggshells, bones, tufts of hair and other disagreeable objects. Employed as a laundress by Cunard, he had discovered her one day dropping a white powder into his teacup, and unmindful of her plea that it was merely a good-health charm designed to cure his recurrent spells of malaria, he had turned her over to the Constabulary. He had pressed charges too, testifying that the woman had attempted to poison him. Largely because of his influence, she had been convicted and sent to the Convict Depot at Tobago. Christopher had stayed on because he had no other place to go.

The meal over, Cunard went into the library with the intention of reading for several hours. Although the *Times* and the *Daily Mail* reached him in bundles of six copies a fortnight or so after they were published, he made it a practice to read only Monday's copy on Monday and so on through the week, thus preserving the impression that he was still in England.

But this night as he strode across to his favorite chair, he drew up short with a gasp. The complete week's bundle of newspapers had been torn open and their contents scattered about in a wild and disorganized pile. To add to this sacrilege, one of the sheets had a ragged hole in it where an entire column had been torn out. For an instant Cunard was speechless. Then he wheeled on Christopher.

"Come here," he roared. "Did you do this?"

The houseboy looked puzzled.

"No, sar," he said.

"Don't lie to me. How dare you open my papers?"

But Christopher insisted he knew nothing of the matter. He had placed the papers on their arrival in the library and had not touched them since.

Cunard's rage was mounting steadily. A mistake he might have excused, but an out-and-out lie. . . .

"Come with me," he said in a cold voice.

Deliberately he led the way into the kitchen, looked about him carefully. Nothing there. He went back across the little corridor to the houseboy's small room under the stairway. While Christopher stood protesting in the doorway, Cunard marched across to the table and silently picked up a torn section of a newspaper.

"So you did lie!" he snarled.

The sight of the houseboy with his perpetual grin there in the doorway was too much for the planter. His rage beyond control, he seized the first object within reach—a heavy length of wood resting on a little bracket mounted on the wall—and threw it with all his strength.

The missile struck Christopher squarely on the temple. He uttered no cry, but remained motionless a moment, the grin frozen on his face. Then his legs buckled and he slumped slowly to the floor.

Cunard's fists clenched. "That'll teach you to respect other people's property," he said. His anger, swift to come, was receding as quickly, and noting that the houseboy lay utterly still, he stepped forward and stirred him with his foot.

Christopher's head rolled horribly.

Quickly Cunard stooped and felt for a pulse. None was discernible. With trembling fingers he drew out a pocket mirror and placed it by the boy's lips. For a long moment he held it there, but there was no resultant cloud of moisture. Christopher was dead!

Cunard staggered across to the chair and sat down. Christopher's death was one thing and one thing only—murder! The fact that he was a man of color and Cunard an influential planter would mean nothing in Crown court of law. He could see the bewigged magistrate now; he could hear the evidence of island witnesses, testifying as to his uncontrollable temper, his savage treatment of servants.

Even if there were not actual danger of incarceration—and he knew there was—it would mean the loss of his social position and prestige.

And then Cunard happened to think of the holes in his yard. A new one—a grave for the dead houseboy—would never be noticed, and he could always improvise some sort of story that the boy had run off. As far as Cunard knew, other than the old crone who was his mother, Christopher had no other kin, having come originally from Jamaica.

The planter was quite calm now. He went to his room, changed to a suit of old clothes and a pair of rubber-soled shoes. Then, returning to the little room under the stairs, he rolled the body of the houseboy into a piece of sailcloth and carried it out into the yard.

He chose a spot near the far corner of his property where a clump of bamboo grew wild and would effectually shield him from any prying eyes. But there were no prying eyes, and half an hour later Cunard returned to the house. Then he carefully cleaned the clinging loam from the garden spade, washed his shoes and brushed his trousers.

It was when he went again to the room under the stairs to gather together Christopher's few possessions that he saw the piece of wood that had served as the death missile. Cunard picked it up and frowned. The thing was an Obeah fetish apparently, an ugly little carving with a crude likeness of an animal head and a squat human body. The lower half of the image ended in a flat panel, the surface of which was covered with wavy lines, so that the prostrate figure looked as if it were partially immersed in water. Out of that carved water two arms extended upward, as in supplication, and they were arms that were strangely reminiscent for Cunard. Christopher's mother had had arms like that, smooth and strangely youthful for a person of her age. There was even a chip of white coral on one of the fingers like the coral ring the old woman always wore.

Cunard threw the thing into the pile of other objects he had gathered: spare clothes, several bright-colored scarves, a sack of cheap tobacco, made a bundle of them and burned them in the old-fashioned cook stove with which the kitchen was equipped.

The last object to go into the fire was the newspaper clipping, and the planter saw then with a kind of grim horror that Christopher had not lied at all, that the top of the paper in fact bore a dateline several months old and was one of a lot he had given to the houseboy "to look at de pictures."

For several days after that Cunard did not leave his house. He

felt nervous and ill-at-ease, and he caught himself looking out
the window toward the bamboo thicket on more than one occasion. Curiously too, there was an odd murmuring in his ears like
the sound of distant water flowing.

On the third day, however, he was sufficiently himself to make
a trip to town. He drove the car at a fast clip to Port-of-Spain,
parked on Marine Square and went about his business. He was
walking down Frederick Street half an hour later when he suddenly became aware that an aged Negro woman with head tied
in a red kerchief was following him.

Cunard didn't have a direct view of her until just as he turned
a corner, and then only a glance, but his heart stopped dead still
for an instant. Surely that black woman was Christopher's
mother whom he had sent to prison. True, her face was almost
hidden by the folds of the loosely draped kerchief, but he had
seen her hand, and there was the coral ring on it. Wild thoughts
rushed to Cunard's head. Had the woman been released then?
Had she missed her son, and did she suspect what had happened?

Cunard drew up in a doorway, but the old crone did not pass
him, and when he looked back down the street, she was nowhere
in sight.

Nevertheless the incident unnerved him. When, later in the
day, he met Inspector Bainley of the Constabulary, he seized the
opportunity to ask several questions that would ease his mind.

"Where have you been keeping yourself?" Bainley asked. "I
haven't seen much of you lately."

Cunard lit a cigar with what he hoped was a certain amount
of casualness.

"I've been pretty busy," he replied. "My houseboy skipped,
you know. The blighter simply packed off without warning."

"So?" said Bainley. "I thought Christopher was a pretty
steady chap."

"In a way," said Cunard. "And in a way he wasn't." And then:
"By the way, do you remember his mother? I was wondering
whether she had been released. I thought I saw her a moment
ago on the street."

The inspector smiled a thin smile. "Then you were seeing things," he said. "She committed suicide over at the Convict Depot at Tobago two months ago."

Cunard stared.

"At least we called it suicide," Inspector Bainley went on. "She took some sort of an Obeah potion when she found we weren't going to let her go, and simply lay back and died. It was rather odd that the medico couldn't find any trace of poison though."

Cunard was rather vague about the rest of the day's events. He recalled making some trifling purchases, but his mind was wandering, and twice he had to be reminded to pick up his change. At four o'clock he abruptly found himself thinking of his old friend, Hugh Donay, and the fact that Donay had employed Christopher's mother a year or so before she had entered Cunard's services. Donay had a villa just outside of town, and it would take only a few moments to see him. Of course there was no reason to see him. If Bainley said the old woman had committed suicide, that settled it. Yet Cunard told himself the inspector might have been mistaken or perhaps joking. He himself was a strong believer in his powers of observation, and it bothered him to have doubts cast upon them.

The planter drove through the St. Clair district and turned into a driveway before a sprawling house with roof of red tile. Donay, a thin waspish man, was lounging in a hammock and greeted Cunard effusively.

"Tried to get you by phone the other day," he said, "but you weren't at home. Had something I wanted to tell you. About that L'Ollonais treasure that's supposed to be buried on your property."

Cunard frowned. "Have you started believing that too?"

"This was an article in the *Daily Mail,* and it had some new angles that were rather interesting. I get my paper here in town before you do out there on Pistol Key, you know."

Cunard attempted to swing the conversation into other channels, but Donay was persistent.

"Funny thing about that article," he said. "I read it the same day the burglar was here."

"Burglar?" Cunard lifted his eyes.

"Well," Donay said, "Jim Barrett was over here, and I showed him the paper. Barrett said it was the first description he had read that sounded logical and that the directions given for locating the treasure were very clear and concise. Just at that moment there was a sound in the corridor, and Barrett leaped up and made a dash for the kitchen.

"I might tell you that for several days I thought prowlers were about. The lock on the cellar door was found broken, and several times I'd heard footsteps in the laundry room. Several things were out of place in the laundry room too, though what anyone would want there is more than I can see.

"Anyway, Barrett shouted that someone was in the house. We followed the sounds down into the cellar, and just as we entered the door into the laundry room, there was a crash and the sound of glass breaking."

Donay smiled sheepishly as if to excuse all these details.

"It was only a bottle of bluing," he went on, "but what I can't figure out is how the prowler got in and out of that room without our seeing anyone pass. There's only one door, you know, and the windows are all high up."

"Was anything stolen?" Cunard asked.

"Nothing that I'm aware of. That bluing though was running across the floor toward a hamper of clean linen, and without thinking I used the first thing handy to wipe it up. It happened to be the newspaper with that treasure article in it. So I'm afraid . . ."

"It doesn't matter. I can read it in my copy," Cunard said. But even as he spoke, a vision of his own torn paper flashed to him.

"That isn't quite all," Donay said. "The next day I found every blessed wastebasket in the house turned upside down and their contents scattered about. Queer, isn't it?"

The conversation changed after that, and they talked of idle things. But just before he left Cunard said casually:

"By the way, my houseboy, Christopher's run off. Didn't his

mother work for you as a laundress or something?"

"That's right," Donay said, "I turned her over to you when I took a trip up to the States. Don't you remember?"

Cunard drove through town again, heading for the highway to Pistol Key. He had just turned off Marine Square when he suddenly slammed down hard on the brakes. The woman darted from the curb directly into his path, and with the lowering sun in his eyes, he did not see her until it was too late. Cunard got out of the car, shaking like a leaf, fully expecting to find a crumpled body on the bumper.

But there was no one there, and a group of Portuguese street laborers eyed him curiously as he peered around and under the car. He was almost overcome with relief, but at the same time he was disturbed. For in that flash he had seen of the woman against the sun, he was almost sure he had seen the youthful dark-skinned arms of Christopher's mother.

Back at Pistol Key Cunard spent the night. The sensation of distant running water was stronger in his ears now. "Too much quinine," he told himself. "I'll have to cut down on the stuff."

He lay awake for some time, thinking of the day's events. But as his brain went over the major details in retrospection, he found himself supplying the missing minor details and so fell into a haze of peaceful drowsiness.

At two o'clock by the radium clock on the chiffonier, he awoke abruptly. The house was utterly still, but through the open window came an intermittent metallic sound. It died away, returned after an interval of several minutes. Cunard got out of bed, put on his brocaded dressing robe and strode to the window. A full moon illuminated the grounds save where the palmistes cast their darker shadow, and there was no living person in evidence.

Below him and slightly to the left there was a freshly dug hole. But it was not that that caused Cunard to pass his hands before his eyes as if he had been dreaming. It was the sight of a spade alternately disappearing in the hole and reappearing to pile the loosened soil on the growing mound. A spade that moved slowly, controlled by aged yet youthful-appearing arms and hands, but arms unattached to any human body.

In the morning Cunard called the Port-of-Spain *Journal,* instructing them to run an advertisement for a houseboy, a task which he had neglected the day before. Then he went out to his post box to get the mail.

The morning mist had not yet cleared. It hung over the hibiscus hedges like an endless line of white shrouds. As he reached the end of the lane, Cunard thought he saw a figure turn from the post box and move quickly toward a grove of ceiba trees. He thought nothing of it at first, for those trees flanked the main road which was traveled by residents of the little native settlement at the far end of Pistol Key. But then he realized that the figure had moved away from the road, in a direction leading obliquely toward his own house.

Still the matter did not concern him particularly until he opened the post box. There was a single letter there, and it had not come by regular mail; the dirty brown envelope bore neither stamp nor cancellation mark. Inside was a torn piece of newspaper.

Cunard realized at once that it was the missing piece from his *Daily Mail.* But who besides Christopher could have had access to the house and who would steal a newspaper column and return it in the post box?

It was like him that he made no attempt to read the paper until he had returned to the library. Then he matched it with the torn sheet still on his desk. The two pieces fitted exactly. He sat back and began to read.

The first part was a commonplace enough account of the opening of new auction parlors in Southwick Street, London, and a description of some of the more unusual articles that had been placed for sale there. Cunard, reading swiftly, found his eye attracted to the following:

Among the afternoon offerings was the library of the late Sir Adrian Fell of Queen Anne's Court, which included an authentic first edition of McNair's *Bottle of Heliotrope* and a rare quarto volume of *Lucri Causa.* There was also a curious volume which purported to be the diary of the Caribbean buccaneer, Francis L'Ollonais, written while under the protection of the French West India Company at Tortuga.

This correspondent had opportunity to examine the latter book and found some interesting passages. According to the executors of the estate, it had been obtained by Sir Adrian on his trip to Kingston in 1904, and so far as is known, is the only copy in existence.

Under the heading, "The Maracaibo Voyage," L'Ollonais describes his destruction of that town, of his escape with an enormous booty, and of the storms which beset him on his return trip to Tortuga. It is here that the diary ceases to be a chronological date-book and becomes instead a romantic narrative.

L'Ollonais, driven southward, managed to land on Trinidad, on a promontory known as Pistol Key. There "By a greate pile of stones whiche looked fair like two horses running," he buried the equivalent of fifty thousand pieces of eight. His directions for locating the treasure are worth quoting:

"Sixty paces from the south forward angle of the horse rock to the crossing of a line west by south west by the compass from a black pointed stone shaped like a broken needle near the shore. At this point if a man will stand in the light of a full moon at the eleventh hour, the shadow of his head will fall upon the place."

Cunard lowered the paper and thoughtfully got a cigar out of the silver humidor on the table. So there was truth in that story of hidden treasure after all. Perhaps the money was still there, and he had been a fool to ridicule the motive behind those holes in his yard. He smoked in silence.

How many persons, he wondered, had seen that newspaper story. There was Hugh Donay and Jim Barrett, of course, but they didn't count. Few others here subscribed to the *Daily Mail.* Of those that did, the odds were against any of them wading through such a dull account. The fact remained, however, that someone had read it in his own copy and had been sufficiently interested to tear it from the sheet. Who was that person? And why had they seen fit to return it by way of his post box?

The landmarks he knew only too well. He had often remarked that that stone near the end of his property resembled two galloping horses. And the black stone "like a broken needle" was still there, a rod or two from shore.

Suddenly fear struck Cunard—fear that he might already be too late. He leaped from his chair and ran out into the grounds.

There were four holes and the beginning of a fifth in evidence. But, moving quickly from one to another, the planter saw with relief that all were shallow and showed no traces of any object having been taken from them.

Cunard hastened back to the house where he procured a small but accurate compass and a ball of twine. Then he went into the toolhouse and brought out a pair of oars for the dory that was moored at the water's edge on a little spit of sand.

An hour later his work was finished. He had rowed the dory out to the needle point of rock and fastened one end of the twine to it. The other end he stretched across to the horse rock in the corner of his property. Then he counted off the required sixty paces and planted a stick in the ground to mark the spot. After that there was nothing he could do until night. He hoped there would be no clouds to obstruct the moon.

Still there was the possibility someone might blunder here while he was in the house, and after a moment's thought Cunard returned to the toolhouse and rummaged through the mass of odds and ends that had collected there through the years. He found an old doorbell that had been discarded when the more musical chimes had been installed in the house, also several batteries and a coil of wire.

During the war Cunard had made a superficial study of electricity and wireless as part of what he considered his patriotic duties, and he now proceeded to wire a crude but efficient alarm system around the general area where he conceived the treasure to be.

Back in the house, he settled himself to wait the long hours until moonrise. In the quiet of inactivity he was conscious again of that sound of distant water flowing. He made a round of all taps in the house, but none was leaking.

During his solitary dinner he caught himself glancing out the window into the grounds, and once he thought he saw a shadow move across the lawn and into the trees. But it must have been a passing cloud, for he didn't see it again.

At two P.M. a knock sounded on the door. Cunard was surprised and somewhat disconcerted to see Inspector Bainley standing on the veranda.

"Just passing by," Bainley said, smiling genially. "Had a sudden call from the native village out on the Key. Seems a black boy got into some trouble out there. Thought it might be your Christopher."

"But that's impos—" Cunard checked himself. "I hardly think it likely," he amended. "Christopher would probably go as far as he could, once he started."

They drank rum. The inspector seemed in no hurry to leave, and Cunard was torn between two desires, not to be alone and to be free from Bainley's gimlet eyes which always seemed to be moving about restlessly.

Finally he did go, however. The throb of his car was just dying off down the road when Cunard heard a new sound which electrified him to attention. The alarm bell!

Yet there was no one in the grounds. The wires were undisturbed, and the makeshift switch he had fashioned was still open. The bell was silent when he reached it.

With the moon high over his shoulder Cunard wielded his spade rapidly. The spot where the shadow of his head fell was disagreeably close to the bamboo thicket where he had buried Christopher, but as a matter of fact, he wasn't quite sure where that grave was, so cleverly had he hidden all traces of his work.

The hole had now been dug to a depth of four feet, but there was no indication anything had been buried there. Cunard toiled strenuously another half hour. And then quite suddenly his spade struck something hard and metallic. A wave of excitement swept over him. He switched on his flashlight and turned it in the hole. Yes, there it was, the rusted top of a large iron chest—the treasure of L'Ollonais.

He resumed digging, but as he dug, he became aware that the sand, at first dry and hard, had grown moist and soggy. The spade became increasingly heavy with each scoop, and presently water was running off it, glistening in the moonlight. Water began to fill the bottom of the hole, too, making it difficult for Cunard to work.

But it was not until ten minutes later that he saw something protruding from the water. In the moonlight two slender dark objects were reaching outward, a pair of Negro feminine arms gently weaving to and fro.

Cunard stiffened while a wave of horror swept over him. They were dark-skinned arms of an aged Negress, yet somehow they were smooth and youthful. The middle finger of the left hand bore a ring of white coral.

Cunard screamed and lunged backward. Too late, one of those grasping hands encircled his ankle and jerked him forward. And as he fell across the hole, those hands wrapped themselves about his throat and drew his head slowly but deliberately downward. . . .

"Yes, it's a queer case," Inspector Bainley said, tamping tobacco into his pipe. "But then of course no more queer than a lot of things that happen here in the islands."

"You say this fellow, Cunard, murdered his houseboy, Christopher?" the warrant-officer said.

Bainley nodded. "I knew his savage temper would get the better of him some day. He buried the body in the yard and apparently rigged up that alarm arrangement to warn him of any trespassers. Then he contrived that story which he told me, that Christopher had run off.

"Of course we know now that Cunard was trying to find that buried treasure by following the directions given in that newspaper clipping. But that doesn't explain why he disregarded those directions and attempted to dig open the houseboy's grave again. Or why, before he had finished, he thrust his head into the shallow hole and lay in the little pool of seepage water until he drowned."

SEVEN TURNS IN A HANGMAN'S ROPE

by HENRY S. WHITEHEAD

The Spanish Main in the 1820s, a cutthroat pirate named Captain Fawcett and a dashing rogue known as Saul Macartney, a woman called Camilla who has mastered the art of voodoo as well as any slave, and a century-old painting of a gallows execution, in which one of the condemned men bleeds fresh blood . . . these are just some of the ingredients to be found in "Seven Turns in a Hangman's Rope." Blended together by the artful hand of Henry S. Whitehead, they form a savory and unusual brew of swashbuckling adventure, historical romance, and shivery horror.

Although the story's initial publication was in the pulp Adventure *in 1932, it reached its most appreciative audience—aficionados of the macabre—only when it was included in Whitehead's first posthumous collection,* Jumbee and Other Uncanny Tales, *in 1944. This book, and a second collection which appeared two years later,* West India Lights, *contain a total of thirty-one of his best stories of voodoo and the supernatural; among them are the oft-reprinted and highly acclaimed "Cassius," "Jumbee," "The Lips," "The Ravel Pavane," and "Sea Change."*

Born in New Jersey in 1882, Henry St. Clair Whitehead wrote and sold his first story the year after graduating from Harvard in the same class with Franklin Delano Roosevelt. In 1909 he entered divinity school, was ordained minister in the Episcopal Church three years later, and subsequently did missionary work in the West Indies. In addition to macabre, adventure, and juvenile fiction for such magazines as Weird Tales, Strange Tales, Adventure, *and* Outdoors, *he wrote extensively for church papers and published* The Invitations of Our Lord, Neighbors of the Early Church, *and other religious books until his death in Florida in 1932.*

I

I FIRST became acutely aware of the dreadful tragedy of Saul Macartney one sunny morning early in the month of November of the year 1927. On that occasion, instead of walking across the hall from my bathroom after shaving and the early morning shower, I turned to the left upon emerging and, in my bathrobe and slippers, went along the upstairs hallway to my workroom on the northwest corner of the house into which I had just moved, in the west coast town of Frederiksted on the island of Santa Cruz.

This pleasant room gave a view through its several windows directly down from the hill on which the house was located, across the pretty town with its red roofs and varicolored houses, directly upon the indigo Caribbean. This workroom of mine had a north light from its two windows on that side and, as I used it only during the mornings, I thus escaped the terrific sun drenching to which, in the absence of any shade without, the room was subjected during the long West Indian afternoon.

The occasion for going in there was my desire to see, in the clear morning light, what that ancient oil painting looked like; the canvas which, without its frame, I had tacked up on the south wall the evening before.

This trophy, along with various other items of household flotsam and jetsam, had been taken the previous afternoon, which was a day after my arrival on the island, out of a kind of lumber room wherein the owners of the house had plainly been storing for the best part of a century the kinds of things which accumulate in a family. Of the considerable amount of material which my houseman, Stephen Penn, had taken out and stacked and piled in the upper hallway, there happened to be nothing of interest except this good-sized painting—which was about three feet by five in size. Stephen had paused to examine it curiously and it was this which drew my attention to it.

Under my first cursory examination, which was little more than a glance, I had supposed the thing to be one of those ubiquitous Victorian horrors of reproduction which fifty years ago might have been observed on the walls of most middle-class front parlors, and which were known as chromos. But later that evening, on picking it up and looking at it under the electric light, I found that it was honest paint, and I examined it more closely and with a constantly increasing interest.

The painting was obviously the work of a fairly clever amateur. The frame of very old and dry wood had been riddled through and through by woodworms; it literally fell apart in my hands. I left it there on the floor for Stephen to brush up the next morning and took the canvas into my bedroom where there was a better light. The accumulations of many years' dust and grime had served to obscure its once crudely bright coloration. I carried it into my bathroom, made a lather of soap and warm water, and gave it a careful and much needed cleansing, after which the scene delineated before me assumed a surprising freshness and clarity.

After I had dried it off with a hand towel, using great care lest I crack the ancient pigment, I went over it with an oiled cloth. This process really brought it out, and although the canvas was something more than a century old, the long obscured and numerous figures with which it had been almost completely covered seemed once more as bright and clear—and quite as crude—as upon the long distant day when that rather clever amateur artist had laid down his (or perhaps her) brush after putting on the very last dab of vermilion paint.

The subject of the old painting, as I recognized quite soon, was an almost forgotten incident in the history of the old Danish West Indies. It had, quite obviously, been done from the viewpoint of a person on board a ship. Before me, as the setting of the scene, was the well-known harbor of St. Thomas with its dull red fort at my right—looking exactly as it does today. At the left-hand margin were the edges of various public buildings which have long since been replaced. In the midst, and occupying nearly the entire spread of the canvas, with Government Hill and its fine houses sketched in for background, was shown the execution of Fawcett, the pirate, with his two lieutenants; an occasion which had constituted a general holiday for the citizens of St. Thomas, and which had taken place, as I happened to be aware, on the eleventh of September, 1825. If the picture had been painted at that time, and it seemed apparent that such was the case, the canvas would be just one hundred and two years old.

My interest now thoroughly aroused, I bent over it and examined it with close attention. Then I went into my workroom and brought back my large magnifying glass.

My somewhat clever amateur artist had left nothing to the imagination. The picture contained no less than two hundred and three human figures. Of these only those in the remoter backgrounds were sketched in roughly in the modern manner. The actual majority were very carefully depicted with a laborious infinitude of detail; and I suspected then, and since have found every reason to believe, that many, if not most of them, were portraits! There before my eyes were portly Danish worthies of a century ago, with their ladyfolk, all of whom had come out to see Captain Fawcett die. There were the officers of the garrison. There were the *gendarmes* of the period, in their stiff-looking uniforms after the manner of Frederick the Great.

There were Negroes, some with large gold rings hanging from one ear; Negresses in their bebustled gingham dresses and bare feet, their foulards or varicolored head handkerchiefs topped by the broad-brimmed plaited straw hats which are still to be seen along modern St. Thomas's concrete drives and sidewalks. There was the executioner, a huge, burly, fierce-looking black man; with the policemaster standing beside and a little behind him, gorgeous in his glistening white drill uniform with its gilt decorations. The two stood on the central and largest of the three scaffolds.

The executioner was naked to the waist and had his woolly head bound up in a tight-fitting scarlet kerchief. He had only that moment sprung the drop, and there at the end of the manila rope (upon which the artist had carefully painted in the seven turns of the traditional hangman's knot placed precisely under the left ear of the miscreant now receiving the just reward of his innumerable villainies) hung Captain Fawcett himself, the gruesome central figure of this holiday pageant—wearing top boots and a fine plum-colored laced coat.

On either side, and from the ropes of the two smaller gibbets, dangled those two lesser miscreants, Fawcett's mates. Obviously their several executions, like the preliminary bouts of a modern boxing program, had preceded the main event of the day.

The three gibbets had been erected well to the left of the central space which I have described. The main bulk of the spectators was consequently to the right as one looked at the picture, on the fort side.

After more than a fascinating hour with my magnifying glass, it being then eleven o'clock and time to turn in, I carried the brittle old canvas into my workroom and by the rather dim light of a shaded reading lamp fastened it carefully at a convenient height against the south wall with thumbtacks. The last tack went through the arm of the hanging man nearest the picture's extreme left-hand margin. After accomplishing this I went to bed.

The next morning, as I have mentioned, being curious to see how the thing looked in a suitable light, I walked into the workroom and looked at it.

I received a devastating shock.

My eye settled after a moment or two upon that dangling mate whose body hung from its rope near the extreme left-hand margin of the picture. I found it difficult to believe my eyes. In this clear morning light the expression of the fellow's face had changed startlingly from what I remembered after looking at it closely through my magnifying glass. Last night it had been merely the face of a man just hanged; I had noted it particularly because, of all the more prominent figures, that face had been most obviously an attempt at exact portraiture.

Now it wore a new and unmistakable expression of acute agony.

And down the dangling arm, from the point which that last thumbtack had incontinently transfixed, there ran, and dripped off the fellow's fingers, a stream of bright, fresh red blood. . . .

II

Between the time when the clipper schooner, which had easily overhauled the Macartney trading vessel *Hope*—coming north across the Caribbean and heavily laden with sacked coffee from Barranquilla—had sent a challenging shot from its swivel-gun across the *Hope*'s bows, and his accomplishing the maneuver of coming about in obedience to that unmistakable summons, Captain Saul Macartney had definitely decided what policy he should follow.

He had made numerous voyages in the *Hope* among the bustling trade ports of the Caribbean and to and from his own home port of St. Thomas, and never before, by the Grace of God and the Macartney luck, had any freetrader called up on him to stand and deliver on the high seas. But, like all seafaring men of Captain Macartney's generation, plying their trade in those latitudes in the early 1820s, he was well aware of what was now in store for him, his father's ship and the members of his crew. The *Hope* would be looted; then probably scuttled, in accordance with the freetraders' well nigh universal policy of destroying every scrap of evidence against them. As for himself and his men, they would be confronted with the formula—

"Join, or go over the side!"

A pirate's recruit was a pirate, at once involved in a status which was without the law. His evidence, even if he were attempting the dangerous double game of merely pretending to join his captor, was worthless.

There was no possible ray of hope, direct resistance being plainly out of the question. This might be one of the better established freebooters, a piratical captain and following whose notoriety was already so widespread, who was already so well known, that he would not take the trouble to destroy the *Hope*; or, beyond the usual offer made to all volunteers for a piratical crew—constantly in need of such replacements—to put the captured vessel, officers and crew through the mill; once they were satisfied that there was nothing aboard this latest prize to repay them for the trouble and risk of capture and destruction.

The *Hope*, laden almost to her gunwales with sacked coffee, would provide lean pickings for a freetrader, despite the value of her bulk cargo in a legitimate port of trade like Savannah or Norfolk. There were cases, known to Captain Macartney, where a piratical outfit under the command of some notable such as Edward Thatch—often called Teach, or Blackbeard—or England, or Fawcett, or Jacob Brenner, had merely sheered off and sailed away in search of more desirable game as soon as it was plain that the loot was neither easily portable nor of the type of value represented by bullion, silks, or the strong box of some interisland trading supercargo.

It was plain enough to Captain Saul Macartney, whose vessel had been stopped here about a day's sail south-southwest of his home port of St. Thomas, capital of the Danish West Indies, and whose cargo was intended for delivery to several ship's brokerage houses in that clearinghouse port for the vast West Indian shipping trade, that this marauder of the high seas could do nothing with his coffee. These ideas were prominent in his mind in the interval between his shouted orders and the subsequent period during which the *Hope*, her way slacking rapidly, hung in the wind, her jibs, booms, and loose rigging slapping angrily while the many boats from the freetrading vessel were slung outboard in a very brisk and workmanlike manner and dropped one after the other into the water alongside until every one— seven in all—had been launched.

These boats were so heavily manned as to leave them very low in the water. Now the oars moved with an almost delicate precision as though the rowers feared some mischance even in that placid sea. The *Hope*'s officers and crew—all of the latter Negroes—crowded along their vessel's starboard rail, the mates quiet and collected as men taking their cue from their superior officer; the crew goggle-eyed, chattering in low tones among themselves in groups and knots, motivated by the sudden looming terror which showed in a gray tinge upon their black skins.

Then, in a strident whisper from the first mate, a shrewd and experienced bucko, hailing originally from Portsmouth, New Hampshire, wise in the ways of these tropical latitudes from twenty years' continuous seafaring:

"God! It's Fawcett himself!"

Slowly, deliberately, as though entirely disdainful of any possible resistance, the seven boats drew toward the doomed *Hope*. The two foremost edged in close alongside her starboard quarter and threw small grapples handily from bow and stern and so hung in under the *Hope*'s lee.

Captain Saul Macartney, cupping his hands, addressed over the heads of the intervening six boatloads the man seated in the sternsheets of the outermost boat:

"Cargo of sacked Brazil coffee, captain, and nothing else to make it worth your while to come aboard me—if you'll take my word for it. That's the facts, sir, so help me God!"

In silence from all hands in the boats and without any immediate reply from Fawcett, this piece of information was received. Captain Fawcett sat there at the sternsheets of his longboat, erect, silent, presumably pondering what Captain Saul Macartney had told him. He sat there calm and unruffled, a fine gold-laced tricorn hat on his head, which, together with the elegance of his wine-colored English broadcloth coat, threw into sharp relief his brutal, unshaven face with its sinister, shining white scar—the result of an old cutlass wound—which ran diagonally from the upper corner of his left ear forward down the cheek, across both lips, clear to the edge of his prominent chin.

Fawcett, the pirate, ended his reflective interval. He raised his head, rubbed a soiled hand through his beard's stubble, and spat outboard.

"Any ship's biscuit left aboard ye?" he inquired, turning his eye along the *Hope*'s freeboard and thence contemplatively about her masts and rigging. "We're short."

"I have plenty, captain. Will it answer if I have it passed over the side to ye?"

The two vessels and the seven heavily laden boats lay tossing silently in the gentle swell. Not a sound broke the tension while Captain Fawcett appeared to deliberate.

Then a second time he spat over the side of his longboat and rubbed his black stubbly chin with his hand, reflectively. Then he looked across his boats directly at Captain Saul Macartney. The ghost of a sour grin broke momentarily the grim straight line of his maimed and cruel mouth.

"I'll be comin' aboard ye, captain," he said very slowly, "if ye have no objection to make."

A bellow of laughter at this sally of their captain's rose from the huddled pirate crew in the boats and broke the mounting tension. A Negro at the *Hope*'s rail cackled hysterically, and a chorus of gibes at this arose from the motley crews of the boats grappled alongside.

In the silence which followed Captain Fawcett muttered a curt, monosyllabic order. The other five boats closed in with haste, two of them passing around the *Hope*'s stern and another around her bow. It was only a matter of a few seconds before the entire seven hung along the *Hope*'s sides like feasting wolves upon the flanks of a stricken deer. Then at a second brief order their crews came over the rails quietly and in good order, Fawcett himself arriving last upon the *Hope*'s deck. No resistance of any kind was offered. Captain Macartney had had the word passed quietly on that score while the pirates' boats were being slung into the water.

After the bustling scramble involved in nearly a hundred men climbing over the *Hope*'s rail from the seven boats and which was, despite the excellent order maintained, a maneuver involving considerable noisy activity, another and even a more ominous silence settled down upon the beleaguered *Hope*.

Supported by his two mates, one of whom was a small, neat, carefully dressed fellow, and the other an enormous German who sported a cavalryman's moustache and walked truculently, Captain Fawcett proceeded directly aft, where he turned and faced forward, a mate on either side of him, and leaned against the superstructure of Captain Macartney's cabin.

Macartney's mates, taking pattern from this procedure, walked over from the rail and flanked him where he stood just aft of the *Hope*'s foremast. The rest of the freebooters, having apparently been left free by their officers to do as they pleased for the time being, strolled about the deck looking over the vessel's superficial equipment, and then gathered in little knots and groups about the eleven Negro members of the *Hope*'s crew.

Through this intermingling the comparative silence which had followed their coming aboard began to be dissipated with raillery, various low-voiced sallies of crude wit at the Negroes' expense, and an occasional burst of nervous or raucous laughter. All this, however, was carried on, as Captain Macartney took it in, in what was to him an unexpectedly restrained and quiet manner, utterly at variance with the reputed conduct of such a group of abandoned villains at sea, and to him, at least, convincing evidence that something sinister was in the wind.

This expectation had its fulfillment at a harsh blast from the whistle which, at Fawcett's nod, the huge German mate had taken from his pocket and blown.

Instantly the pirates closed in and seized those members of the *Hope*'s Negro crew who stood nearest them; several, sometimes five or six, men crowding in to overpower each individual. Five or six of the pirates who had been as though without purpose near the forward hatchway which led below decks began forthwith to knock out the wedges. The *Hope*'s Negroes, with a unanimity which bespoke the excellent discipline and strategy which Fawcett was generally understood to maintain, were hustled forward and thrust into the forecastle; the hatch of which, as soon as they were all inside, was forthwith closed tight and

at once nailed fast by the undersized little Englishman who was
Fawcett's ship's carpenter.

None of the *Hope*'s crew had been armed. None seemed to
Captain Macartney to have been even slightly injured in the
course of this rough and effective handling. Captain Macartney
surmised, and rightly, that the pirates' intention was to preserve
them alive either for ultimate sale into slavery, which was of
course then extant throughout the West India Islands, or, perhaps, to convey them as shore servants to Fawcett's settlement
which, it was generally believed, was well in the interior of the
island of Andros in the Bahama group, where a network of
interlacing creeks, rendering anything like pursuit and capture
well nigh out of the question, had made this private fastness a
stronghold.

But Captain Macartney had little time to waste thinking over
the fate of his crew. With perhaps a shade less of the roughness
with which the Negroes had been seized he and his mates were
almost simultaneously surrounded and marched aft to face their
captors. It seemed plain that the usual choice was to be given
only to the three of them.

Fawcett did not hesitate this time. He looked at the three men
standing before him, lowered his head, relaxed his burly figure
and barked out—

"Ye'll join me or go over the side."

He pointed a dirty finger almost directly into the face of the
older mate, who stood at his captain's right hand.

"You first," he barked again. "Name yer ch'ice, and name it
now."

The hardbitten New Hampshire Yankee stood true to the
traditions of an honest sailorman.

"To hell with ye, ye damned scalawag," he drawled, and spat
on the deck between Captain Fawcett's feet.

There could be but one reply on the part of a man of Fawcett's
heady character to such an insult as this. With a speed that
baffled the eye the great pistol which hung from the right side
of his belt beneath the flap of his fine broadcloth coat was
snatched free, and to the accompaniment of its tearing roar, its

huge ounce ball smote through the luckless Yankee's forehead. As the acrid cloud of smoke from this detonation blew away Captain Macartney observed the huge German mate lifting the limp body which, as though it had been that of a child, he carried in great strides to the nearer rail and heaved overboard.

Fawcett pointed with his smoking weapon at Macartney's other mate, a small-built fellow, originally a British subject from the Island of Antigua. The mate merely nodded comprehendingly. Then—

"The same as Elias Perkins told ye, ye blasted swab, and may ye rot deep in hell."

But Fawcett's surly humor appeared to have evaporated, to have discharged itself in the pistoling of the other man whose scattered brains had left an ugly smear on the *Hope*'s clean deck. He merely laughed and, with a comprehensive motion of his left hand, addressed the larger of his mates, who had resumed his position at his left.

"Take him, Franz," he ordered.

The huge mate launched himself upon the Antiguan like a ravening beast. With lightninglike rapidity his enormous left arm coiled crushingly about the doomed man's neck. Simultaneously, his open right hand against his victim's forehead, he pushed mightily. The little Antiguan's spine yielded with an audible crack and his limp body slithered loosely to the deck. Then with a sweeping, contemptuous motion the huge mate grasped the limp form in one hand, lifting it by the front of the waistcoat and, whirling about, hurled it with a mighty pitch far outboard.

The German mate had not yet resumed his place beside Fawcett when Captain Saul Macartney addressed the pirate leader.

"I'm joining you, captain," he said quietly.

And while the surprised Fawcett stared at him the newly enlisted freebooter, who had been Captain Saul Macartney of the schooner *Hope,* with a motion which did not suffer by comparison with Fawcett's for its swiftness, had produced a long dirk, taken the two lightning strides necessary for an effective stroke, and had plunged his weapon with a mighty upward thrust from under the ribs through the German mate's heart.

Withdrawing it instantly, he stooped over the sprawled body and wiped the dirk's blade in a nonchalant and leisurely manner on the dead ruffian's fine cambric shirt frill. As he proceeded to this task he turned his head upward and slightly to the left and looked squarely in the eye the stultified pirate captain who stood motionless and staring in his surprise at this totally unexpected feat of his newest recruit. From his crouching position Saul Macartney spoke, quietly and without emphasis—

"Ye see, sir, I disliked this larrikin from the minute I clapped eyes on him and I'll call your attention to the fact that I'm a sound navigator, and—" Saul Macartney smiled and showed his handsome teeth—"I'll ask your notice preliminary to my acting with you aft that it might equally well have been yourself that I scragged, and perhaps that'll serve to teach ye the manner of man that you're now taking on as an active lieutenant!"

Then Saul Macartney, his bantering smile gone now, his Macartney mouth set in a grim line, his cleansed dirk held ready in his sound right hand, stood menacingly before Captain Fawcett, their breasts almost touching, and in a quarterdeck voice inquired:

"And will ye be taking it or leaving it, Captain Fawcett?"

III

It was more than two months later when the *Hope,* her hull now painted a shining black, her topmasts lengthened all round by six feet, her spread of canvas vastly increased, eight carronade ports newly cut along her sides, and renamed the *Swallow,* entered the harbor of St. Thomas, dropped her anchor and sent over her side a narrow longboat.

Into this boat, immediately after its crew of six oarsmen had settled down upon their thwarts and laid their six long sweeps out upon the harbor water, interested onlookers observed two officers descend over the *Swallow*'s side, where they occupied the sternsheets together. As the boat, rowed man-o'-war style, rapidly approached the wharves it was observed by those on shore that the two men seated astern were rather more than handsomely dressed.

The shorter and heavier man wore a fine sprigged long coat of English broadcloth with lapels, and a laced tricorn hat. His companion, whose appearance had about it something vaguely familiar, was arrayed in an equally rich and very well tailored, though somewhat plainer, coat of a medium blue which set off his handsome figure admirably. This person wore no hat at all, nor any shade for his head against the glare of the eleven o'clock sun save a heavy crop of carefully arranged and naturally curly hair as black as a crow's wing.

So interesting, indeed, to the loungers along the wharves had been the entrance of this previously unknown vessel into the harbor and the subsequent coming ashore of these two fine gentlemen, that a considerable knot of sightseers was already assembled on the particular jetty toward which the longboat, smartly rowed, came steadily closer and closer. The hatless gentleman, who was by far the taller and handsomer of the two, appeared to be steering, the taut tiller ropes held firmly in his large and very shapely hands.

It was the Herr Rudolph Bernn, who had observed the crowd collecting on the jetty through the open windows of his airy shipping office close at hand, and who had clapped on his pith sun helmet and hastened to join the group, who was the first to recognize this taller officer.

"Gude Gott! If id iss nod der Herr Captain Saul Macartney. Gude Gott, how dey will be rejoiced—Oldt Macartney andt de Miss Camilla!"

Within five minutes the rapidly approaching longboat had been laid aside the pier head in navy style. Without any delay the two gentlemen, whose advent had so greatly interested the St. Thomas harbor watchers, stepped ashore with an air and mounted the jetty steps side by side. At once Saul Macartney, whose fine clothes so well became him, forged ahead of his well-dressed, shaved and curled companion. He wore the dazzling smile which revealed his magnificent teeth and which had served to disarm every woman upon whom it had been consciously turned since his eighth year or thereabouts.

Like a conquering hero this handsome young man—who had taken clearance from the South American port of Barranquilla nearly three months before and subsequently disappeared into thin air along with his vessel and all hands off the face of the water—now stepped jauntily across the jetty toward the welcoming group whose numbers were, now that the news of his homecoming was beginning to trickle through the town, constantly increasing. He was instantaneously surrounded by these welcoming acquaintances who sought each to outdo his neighbor in the enthusiastic fervency of his congratulatory greetings.

During this demonstration the redoubtable and notorious Captain Fawcett stood quietly looking on through its milling course, a sardonic smile faintly relieving the crass repulsiveness of his maimed countenance. The pirate had been "shaved to the blood" that morning; dressed for the occasion with the greatest care. His carefully arranged locks were redolent of the oil of Bergamot, filched a week before out of the accessories of a lady passenger taken from the luckless vessel on which she had been coming out to the West Indies to join her planter husband. This lady had, after certain passing attentions from Saul Macartney, gone over the *Swallow*'s side in plain sight of the volcanic cone of Nevis, the island of her destination.

That Macartney had brought Captain Fawcett ashore with him here in St. Thomas was a piece of judgment so lamentably bad as to need no comment of any kind. His doing so initiated that swift course of events which brought down upon his handsome head that ruinous doom which stands, probably, as unique among the annals of retribution; that devasting doom which, for its horror and its strangeness, transcends and surpasses, in all human probability, even the direst fate, which, in this old world's long history, may have overtaken any other of the sons of men.

But the sheer effrontery of that act was utterly characteristic of Saul Macartney.

In the course of the long, painstaking, and probably exhaustive research which I, Gerald Canevin, set in motion in order to secure the whole range of facts forming the basis of this narrative—an investigation which has extended through more than three years and has taken me down some very curious bypaths of antique West Indian history as well as into contact with various strange characters and around a few very alluring corners of research—one aspect of the whole affair stands out in my mind most prominently. This is the fact that—as those many who nowadays increasingly rely for guidance upon the once discredited but now reviving science of astrology would phrase it—Saul Macartney was in all ways "a typical Sagittarian!"

One of the more readily accessible facts which I looked up out of ancient, musty records in the course of this strange affair was the date of his birth. He had been born in the city of St. Thomas on the twenty-eighth of November, in the year 1795. He was thus twenty-nine—in his thirtieth year and the full vigor of his manhood—at the time when Captain Fawcett had captured the *Hope* and, having lightened that vessel by emptying her hold of her cargo which he consigned to the sea, and having scuttled his own disabled vessel, had sailed for his home base among the Andros creeks.

From there a month later the transformed *Swallow* had emerged to maraud upon the Spanish Main. He was not yet out of his twenties when he had chosen to tempt fate by coming ashore with Fawcett in St. Thomas. He was still short of thirty when a certain fateful day dawned in the month of September, 1825.

True to this hypothetical horoscope of his and to every sidereal circumstance accompanying it, Saul Macartney was an entirely self-centered person. With him the "main chance" had always been paramount. It was this addiction to the main chance which had caused him to join Fawcett. A similar motive had actuated him in the notable coup which had at once, because of its sheer directness and the courage involved in it, established him in the high esteem of the pirate captain. There had been no sentiment in his killing of the gigantic mate, Franz. He was not thinking of avenging his own faithful lieutenant whom that hulking beast had slain with his bare hands before his eyes a moment before he had knifed the murderer.

His calculating sense of self-interest had been the sole motive behind that act. He could quite as easily have destroyed Fawcett himself, as he characteristically pointed out to that ruffian. He would have done so with equal ruthlessness save for his knowledge of the fact that he would have been overwhelmed immediately thereafter by Fawcett's underlings.

There is very little question but what he would have before very long succeeded to the command of the *Swallow* and the control of the considerable commerce in the slave trade and other similar illegitimate sources of revenue which went with the command of this piratical enterprise. He had already inaugurated the replacement of Captain Fawcett by himself in the esteem of that freebooter's numerous following well before the refurbished *Swallow* had sailed proudly out upon her current voyage. His unquestionable courage and enormous gift of personality had already been for some time combining actively to impress the pirate crew. Among them he was already a dominating figure.

Since well before he had attained manly maturity he had been irresistible to women. He was a natural fighter who loved conflict for its own sake. His skill with weapons was well nigh phenomenal. In the prosecution of every affair which concerned his own benefit, he had always habituated himself to going straight to the mark. He was, in short, as it might be expressed, both with respect to women and the securing of his own advantage in general affairs, thoroughly spoiled by an unbroken course of getting precisely what he wanted.

This steady impact of continuous success and the sustained parallel effect of unceasing feminine adulation had entrenched in his character the fatal conviction that he could do as he pleased in every imaginable set of conditions.

The first reversal suffered in this unbroken course of selfish domination inaugurated itself not very long after he had stepped ashore with Captain Fawcett beside him. After ten minutes or so, Macartney gradually got himself free from the crowd of friends congratulating him there on the jetty.

Stimulated as he always was by such adulation, highly animated, his Irish blue eyes flashing, his smile unabated, his selfish heart full to repletion of his accustomed self-confidence, he disentangled himself from the still-increasing crowd and, with several bows and various wavings of his left hand as he backed away from them, he rejoined Fawcett, linked his right arm through the crook of the pirate captain's left elbow and proceeded to conduct him into the town. Those fellows on the wharf were small fry! He would, as he smilingly mentioned in Fawcett's ear, prefer to introduce the captain at once into a gathering place where he would meet a group of gentlemen of greater importance.

They walked up into the town and turned to the left through the bustling traffic of its chief thoroughfare and, proceeding to the westward for a couple of hundred feet or so, turned in through a wide arched doorway above which, on its bracket, perched guardianlike a small gilded rooster. This was Le Coq d'Or, rendezvous of the more prosperous merchants of the flourishing city of St. Thomas.

A considerable number of these prosperous worthies were already assembled at the time of their arrival in Le Coq d'Or. Several Negroes under the direction of the steward of this clublike clearinghouse were already bringing in and placing on the huge polished mahogany table the planter's punch, swizzles of brandy or rum, and sangaree such as always accompanied this late-morning assembly. It lacked only a minute or two of eleven, and the stroke of that hour was sacred at Le Coq d'Or and similar foregathering places as the swizzle hour. No less a personage than M. Daniell, some years before a refugee from the Haitian revolution and now a merchant prince here in the Danish colonial capital, was already twirling a carved swizzle stick in the fragrant iced interior of an enormous silver jug.

But this hospitable activity, as well as the innumerable conversations current about that board, ceased abruptly when these city burghers had recognized the tall, handsome gentleman in blue broadcloth who had just stepped in among them. It was, indeed, practically a repetition of what had occurred on the jetty, save that here the corporate and individual greetings were, if anything, more intimate and more vociferous.

Here were the natural associates, the intimates, the social equals of the Macartneys themselves—a well-to-do clan of proud, self-respecting personages deriving from the class of Irish Protestant high gentry which had come into these islands three generations before upon the invitation of the Danish Colonial Government.

Among those who rose out of their chairs to surround Saul Macartney with hilarious greetings was Denis Macartney, his father. He had suspected that the Old Man would be there. The two clasped each other in a long and affectionate embrace, Denis Macartney agitated and tearful, his son smiling with an unforced whimsicality throughout the intensive contact of this reunion. At last the Old Man, his tears of happiness still flowing, held off and gazed fondly at his handsome, strapping son, a pair of still trembling hands upon the shoulders of the beautiful new broadcloth coat.

"An' where, in God's own name, have ye been hidin' yourself away, me boy?" he asked solicitously.

The others grouped about, and now fallen silent, hovered about the edge of this demonstration, the universal West Indian courtesy only restraining their common enthusiasm to clasp the Macartney prodigal by his bronzed and shapely hands, to thump his back, to place kindly arms about his broad shoulders, later to thrust brimming goblets of cut crystal upon him that they might drink his health and generously toast his safe and unexpected return.

"I'll tell ye all about that later, sir," said Saul Macartney, his dazzling smile lighting up his bronzed face. "Ye'll understand, sir, my anxiety to see Camilla; though, of course, I looked in upon ye first off."

And thereupon, in his sustained bravado, in the buoyancy of his fatal conviction that he, Saul Macartney, could get away with anything whatever he might choose to do, and taking full advantage of the disconcerting effect of his announcement that he must run off, he turned to Captain Fawcett, who had been standing close behind him and, an arm about the captain's shoulders, presented him formally to his father, to M. Daniell and, with a comprehensive wave of his disengaged arm, to the company at large; and, forthwith, well before the inevitable effect of this act could record itself upon the corporate mind of such a group, Saul Macartney had whirled about, reached the arched doorway almost at a run, and disappeared in the blinding glare, on his way to call upon his cousin Camilla.

The group of gentlemen assembled in Le Coq d'Or that morning, intensely preoccupied as they had been with the unexpected restoration to their midst of the missing mariner, Macartney, had barely observed the person who had accompanied him. They were now rather abruptly left facing their new guest, and their immediate reaction after Macartney's hasty departure was to stage a greeting for this very evil-looking but highly dandified fellow whom they found in their midst. To this they proceeded forthwith, actuated primarily by the unfailing and highly developed courtesy which has always been the outstanding characteristic of the Lesser Antilles.

There was not a man present who had not winced at the name which Saul Macartney had so clearly pronounced in the course of his threefold introduction of Captain Fawcett. For this name, as that of one of the principal maritime scourges of the day, was indeed very familiar to these men, attuned as they were to seafaring matters. Several of them, in fact, vessel owners, had actually been sufferers at the hands of this man who now sat among them.

Courtesy, however—and to a guest in this central sanctum—came first. Despite their initial suspicion, by no single overt act, nor by so much as a single glance, did any member of that polished company allow it to be suspected that he had at least given harborage to the idea that Saul Macartney had brought Fawcett the pirate here to Le Coq d'Or and left him among them as a guest.

Besides, doubtless, it occurred to each and every one of these excellent gentlemen, apart from the impossibility of such a situation being precipitated by anyone named Macartney—which was an additional loophole for them—the name of Fawcett was by no means an uncommon one; there might well be half a dozen Fawcetts on Lloyd's List who were or had been commanders of ships. It was, of course, possible that this overdressed, tough-looking seahawk had fooled the usually astute Saul.

As for Fawcett himself, the wolf among these domestic cattle, he was enjoying the situation vastly. The man was intelligent and shrewd, still capable of drawing about him the remnants of a genteel deportment; and, as the details of his projected coming ashore here had been quite fully discussed with Saul Macartney, he had anticipated and was quite well prepared to meet the reaction released at the first mention of that hated and dreaded name of his, and which he now plainly sensed all about him. There was probably even a touch of pride over what his nefarious reputation could evoke in a group like this to nerve him for the curious ordeal which had now begun for him.

It was, of course, his policy to play quietly a conservative—an almost negative—role. He busied now his always alert mind with this, returning courtesy for courtesy as his hosts toasted him formally, assured him of their welcome, exchanged with him those general remarks which precede any real breaking of the ice between an established group and some unknown and untried newcomer.

It was Old Macartney who gave him his chief stimulation by inquiring:

"An' what of me dear son, captain? Ye will have been in his company for some time, it may be. It would be more than gracious of ye to relate to us—if so be ye're aware of it, perchance —what occurred to him on that last voyage of his from Sout' America."

At this really unexpected query the entire room fell silent. Every gentleman present restrained his own speech as though a signal had been given. Only the Negro servants, intent upon their duties, continued to speak to each other under their breaths and to move soft-footedly about the room.

Captain Fawcett recognized at once that Mr. Denis Macartney's question contained no challenge. He had even anticipated it, with a thin yarn of shipwreck, which he and Saul had concocted together. In a sudden access of whimsical bravado he abandoned this cooked-up tale. He would give them a story. . . .

He turned with an elaborate show of courtesy to Old Macartney. He set down his half-emptied goblet, paused, wiped his maimed mouth with a fine cambric handkerchief and set himself, in the breathless silence all about him, to reply.

"The freetraders took him, sir," said Captain Fawcett. Then he nodded twice, deprecatingly; next he waved a hand, took up his goblet again, drank off its remaining contents in the sustained, pregnant silence, and again turned to Saul's father.

Settling himself somewhat more comfortably in his chair, he then proceeded to relate, with precise circumstantial detail, exactly what had actually taken place, only substituting for himself as the captor the name of the dreaded Jacob Brenner, who, like himself, had a place of refuge among the Andros creeks, and whom Captain Fawcett regarded with profound and bitter detestation as his principal rival.

He told his story through in the atmosphere of intense interest all about him. He made Captain Saul Macartney pretend to join the cutthroat Brenner and, the wish greatly father to the thought, brought his long yarn to a successful conclusion with the doughty Saul staging a desperate hand-to-hand encounter with his captor after going ashore with him on Andros Island, together with a really artistic sketching-in of his escape from the pirate settlement in a dinghy through the intricacies of the mosquito-infested creeks; and his ultimate harborage—"well nigh by chance, or a trace of what he names 'the Macartney luck,' sir"—with himself.

"I've a very pleasant little spot there on Andros," added Captain Fawcett.

Then, satisfying another accession of his whimsicality:

"I'm certain any of you would be pleased with it, gentlemen. It's been good—very good and pleasurable, I do assure you—to have had Captain Macartney with me."

And Fawcett, the pirate, whose own longboat had fetched him

ashore here from that very vessel whose capture by freetraders
on the high seas he had just been so graphically recounting, with
a concluding short bow and a flourish of the left hand, took up
his recently replenished crystal goblet and, again facing the
senior Macartney, toasted him roundly on this, the glad occasion
of his seafaring son's prosperous return.

Saul Macartney walked rapidly across the crowded main thoroughfare so as to avoid being recognized and stopped. He
turned up a precipitous, winding and abruptly cornered street
of varying width, and, following it between the many closely
walled residences among which it wound, mounted at a rapid
stride to a point two-thirds of the way up the hill. Here he
paused to readjust his clothes and finally to wipe the sweat
induced by his pace from his bronzed face with another fine
cambric handkerchief like that being used by his colleague about
this time down there at Le Coq d'Or. The two of them had
divided evenly four dozen of these handkerchiefs not long before from the effects of a dandified French supercargo now
feeding the fishes.

It was a very sultry day in the middle of the month of May, in
that spring period when the *rada* drums of the Negroes may be
heard booming nightly from the wooded hills in the interior of
the islands; when the annual shift in the direction of the trade
wind between the points east and west of north seems to hang
a curtain of sultriness over St. Thomas on its three hillsides. It
was one of those days when the burros' tongues hang out of dry
mouths as they proceed along dusty roads; when centipedes
leave their native dust and boldly cross the floors of houses;
when ownerless dogs slink along the inner edges of the baking,
narrow sidewalks in the slits of house shade away from the sun.

Saul Macartney had paused near the entrance to the spacious
mansion of his uncle, Thomas Lanigan Macartney, which stood
behind a stately grille of wrought iron eleven feet high, in its
own grounds, and was approached through a wide gateway
above which the cut stone arch supported a plaque on which had
been carved the Macartney arms. Through this imposing en-

trance, his face now comfortably dry and his fine broadcloth coat readjusted to his entire satisfaction, Saul Macartney now entered and proceeded along the broad, shell-strewn path with its two borders of cemented pink conch shells toward the mansion.

Through the accident of being his father's first-born son and the rigid application of the principle of primogeniture which had always prevailed among the Macartney clan in the matter of inheritances, old T. L. Macartney possessed the bulk of the solid Macartney family fortune. He had married the only daughter of a retired Danish general who had been governor of the colony. Dying in office, the general had left behind him the memory of a sound administration and another substantial fortune which found its way through that connection into the Macartney coffers.

The only reason why Saul Macartney had not led his heavenly endowed cousin, Camilla, to the altar long before, was merely because he knew he could marry her any time. Camilla's lips had parted and her blue eyes become mysterious, soft and melting, at every sight of him since about the time she was eight and he ten. As for Saul Macartney, he could not remember the time when it had not been his settled intention to marry his cousin Camilla when he got ready. He was as sure of her as of the rising and setting of the sun; as that failure was a word without meaning to him; as that the Santa Cruz rum was and always would be the natural drink of gentlemen and sailors.

Jens Sorensen, the black butler, who had witnessed his arrival, had the door open with a flourish when Saul was halfway between the gate and the gallery. His bow as this favored guest entered the house was profound enough to strain the seams of his green broadcloth livery coat.

But black Jens received no reward for his assiduousness from the returned prodigal, beyond a nod. This was not like Saul in the least, but black Jens understood perfectly why Captain Macartney had not quizzed him, paused to slap mightily his broad back under his green coat, or to tweak the lobe of his right ear ornamented with its heavy ring of virgin gold, all of which attentions black Jens could ordinarily expect from this fine gentleman of his family's close kinfolk. There had been no time for such persiflage.

For, hardly had black Jens's huge, soft right hand begun the motion of closing the great door, when Camilla Macartney, apprised by some subtlety of "the grapevine route" of her cousin's arrival, appeared on the threshold of the mansion's great drawing room, her lips parted, her eyes suffused with an inescapable emotion. Only momentarily she paused there. Then she was running toward him across the polished mahogany flooring of the wide hallway, and had melted into the firm clasp of Saul Macartney's brawny arms. Raising her head, she looked up into his face adoringly and Saul, responding, bent and kissed her long and tenderly. No sound save that occasioned by the soft-footed retirement of black Jens to his pantry broke the cool silence of the dignified hall. Then at last in a voice from Camilla Macartney that was little above a whisper:

"Saul—Saul, my darling! I am so glad, so glad! You will tell me all that transpired—later, Saul, my dear. Oh, it has been a dreadful time for me."

Withdrawing herself very gently from his embrace, she turned and, before the great Copenhagen mirror against the hallway's south wall, made a small readjustment in her coiffure—her hair was of the purest, clearest Scandinavian gold, of a spun-silk fineness. Beckoning her lover to follow, she then led the way into the mansion's drawing room.

As they entered, Camilla a step in advance of Macartney, there arose from a mahogany and rose-satin davenport the thickset figure of a handsome young man of about twenty-four, arrayed in the scarlet coat of His Britannic Majesty's line regiments of infantry. This was Captain the Honorable William McMillin, who, as a freshly commissioned coronet-of-horse, had actually fought under Wellington at Waterloo ten years before. Recently he had attained his captaincy, and sold out to undertake here in the Danish West Indies the resident management of a group of Santa Cruzian sugar estates, the property of his Scottish kinsfolk, the Comyns.

These two personable captains, one so-called because of his

courtesy title, and the other with that honorable seafaring title really forfeited, were duly presented to each other by Camilla Macartney; and thereby was consummated another long stride forward in the rapid march of Saul Macartney's hovering doom.

The Scottish officer, sensing Saul's claim upon that household, retired ere long with precisely the correct degree of formality.

As soon as he was safely out of earshot Camilla Macartney rose and, seizing a small hassock, placed it near her cousin's feet. Seating herself on this, she looked up adoringly into his face and, her whole soul in her eyes, begged him to tell her what had happened since the day when he had cleared the *Hope* from Barranquilla.

Again Saul Macartney rushed forward upon his fate.

He told her, with circumstantial detail, the cooked-up story of shipwreck, including a touching piece of invention about three days and nights in the *Hope*'s boats and his timely rescue by his new friend, Fawcett, master of the *Swallow*—a very charitable gentleman, proprietor of a kind of trading station on Andros in the Bahamas. Captain Fawcett, who had considerately brought the prodigal back to St. Thomas, was at the moment being entertained in Le Coq d'Or.

Camilla Macartney's eyes grew wide at the name of Saul's rescuer. The first intimation of her subsequent change of attitude began with her exclamation:

"Saul! Not—not Captain Fawcett, the pirate! Not that dreadful man! I had always understood that *his* lying-up place was on the Island of Andros, among the creeks!"

Saul Macartney lied easily, reassuringly. He turned upon his cousin—anxious, now, as he could see, and troubled—the full battery of his engaging personality. He showed those beautiful teeth of his in a smile that would have melted the heart of a Galatea.

Camilla dropped the subject, entered upon a long explication of her happiness, her delight at having him back. He must remain for breakfast. Was his friend and benefactor, Captain Fawcett, suitably housed? He might, of course, stay here—her father would be so delighted at having him . . .

It was as though she were attempting, subconsciously, to anni-
hilate her first faint doubt of her cousin Saul, in this enthusiasm
for his rescuer. She rose and ran across the room, and jerked
violently upon the ornamental bell rope. In almost immediate
response to her ring black Jens entered the room softly, bowed
before his mistress with a suggestion of prostrating himself.

"A place for Captain Macartney at the breakfast table. Champagne; two bottles—no, four—of the 1801 Chablis—Is Miranda
well along with the shell-crustadas?"

Again Camilla Macartney was reassured. All these commands
would be precisely carried out.

Thereafter for a space, indeed, until the noon breakfast was
announced, conversation languished between the cousins. For
the first time in his life, had Saul Macartney been to the slightest
degree critically observant, he would have detected in Camilla's
bearing a vague hint that her mind toward him was not wholly
at rest; but of this he noticed nothing. As always, and especially
now under the stimulation of this curious game of bravado he
and Fawcett were playing here in St. Thomas, no warning, no
sort of premonition, had penetrated the thick veneer of his
selfishness, his fatuous conviction that any undertaking of his
must necessarily proceed to a successful outcome.

He sat there thinking of how well he had managed things; of
the chances of the *Swallow*'s next venture on the Main; of the
ripe physical beauty of Camilla; of various women here in the
town.

And Camilla Macartney, beautiful, strangely composed, exquisitely dressed, as always, sat straight upright across from him,
and looked steadily at her cousin, Saul Macartney. It was as
though she envisaged vaguely how he was to transform her love
into black hatred. A thin shadow of pain lay across her own
Irish-blue eyes.

Captain the Honorable William McMillin, like many other
personable young gentlemen before him, had been very deeply
impressed with the quality of Camilla Macartney. But it was not

only that West Indian gentlewoman's social graces and cool blond beauty that were responsible for this favorable impression. The young captain, a thoroughly hard-headed Scot with very much more behind his handsome forehead than the necessary knowledge of military tactics possessed by the ordinary line regiment officer, had been even more deeply impressed by other qualities obviously possessed by his West Indian hostess. Among these was her intellect; unusual, he thought, in a colonial lady not yet quite twenty-eight. Nothing like Miss Macartney's control of the many servants of the household had ever seemed possible to the captain.

From black Jens, the butler, to the third scullery maid, all of them, as they came severally under the notice of this guest, appeared to accord her a reverence hardly distinguishable from acts of worship. In going about the town with her, either walking for early evening exercise or in her father's barouche to make or return formal calls, the trained and observant eye of the young Scotsman had not failed to notice her effect upon the swarming Negro population of the town.

Obeisances from these marked her passage among them. The gay stridency of their street conversations lulled itself and was still at her passing.

Doffed hats, bows, veritable obeisances in rows and by companies swayed these street loiterers as her moving about among them left them hushed and worshipful in her wake.

Captain McMillin noted the very general respectful attitude of these blacks toward their white overlords, but, his eyes told him plainly, they appeared to regard Camilla Macartney as a kind of divinity.

In the reasonable desire to satisfy his mounting curiosity Captain McMillin had broached the matter to his hostess. A canny Scot, he had approached this matter indirectly. His initial questions had had to do with native manners and customs, always a safe general topic in a colony.

Camilla's direct answers had at once surprised him with their clarity and the exactitude of their information. It was unusual and—as the subject broadened out between them and Camilla told him more and more about the Negroes, their beliefs, their manner of life, their customs and practices—it began to be plain to Captain McMillin that it was more than unusual; if someone entitled to do so had asked him his opinion on Camilla Macartney's grasp of this rather esoteric subject, and the captain had answered freely and frankly, he would have been obliged to admit that it seemed to him uncanny.

For behind those social graces of hers which made Camilla Macartney a notable figure in the polite society of this Danish colonial capital, apart from the distinction of her family connection, her commanding position as the richest heiress in the colony, her acknowledged intellectual attainments, and the distinguished beauty of face and form which lent a pervading graciousness to her every act, Camilla Macartney was almost wholly occupied by two consuming interests.

Of these, the first, generally known by every man, woman and child in St. Thomas, was her preoccupation with her cousin, Saul Macartney. The other, unsuspected by any white person in or out of Camilla Macartney's wide acquaintance, was her knowledge of the magic of the Negroes.

The subject had been virtually an obsession with her since childhood. Upon it she had centered her attention, concentrated her fine mind and, using every possible opportunity which her independent position and the enormous amount of material at hand afforded, had mastered it in theory and practice throughout its almost innumerable ramifications.

There was, first, the Obeah. This, deriving originally from the Ashanti slaves, had come into the West Indies through the gate of Jamaica. It was a combined system of magical formulas and the use of drugs. Through it a skillful practitioner could obtain extraordinary results. It involved a very complete *materia medica*, and a background setting for the usage and practice thereof, which reached back through uncounted centuries into rituals that were the very heart of primitive savagery.

The much more greatly extended affair called voodoo, an extraordinary complex fabric of "black," "white," and revelatory occultism, had made its way through the islands chiefly through the Haitian doorway from its proximate source, Dahomey, whence the early French colonists of Hispaniola had brought their original quotas of black slaves.

Voodoo, an infinitely broader and more stratified system than the medicinal Obeah, involved much that appeared to the average white person mere superficial Negro "stupidity." But in its deeper and more basic aspects it included many very terrible things, which Camilla Macartney had encountered, succeeded in understanding, and appropriated into this terrific fund of black learning which was hers as this fell subject took her through the dim backgrounds of its origin to the unspeakable snake worship of Africa's blackest and deadliest interior.

The considerable Negro population of the island, from the most fanatical *hougan* presiding in the high hills over the dire periodic rites of the "baptism" and the slaughter of goats and bullocks and willingly offered human victims whose blood, mingled with red rum, made that unholy communion out of which grew the unnameable orgies of the deep interior heights, down to the lowliest pickaninny gathering fruits or stealing yams for the sustenance of his emaciated body—every one of these blacks was aware of this singular preoccupation; acknowledged the supremacy of this extraordinarily gifted white lady; paid her reverence; feared her acknowledged powers; would as soon have lopped off a foot as to cross her lightest wish.

Captain the Honorable William McMillin made up his mind that her grasp of these matters was extraordinary. His questionings and Camilla's informative replies had barely touched upon the edge of what she knew.

And the former captain, her cousin, Saul Macartney, did not know that his heiress cousin cherished any interest except that which she had always demonstrated so plainly in his own direction.

Going in to breakfast, Saul Macartney was nearly knocked off his feet by the physical impact of his uncle's greeting. Camilla's father had been spending the morning overlooking a property of his east of the town, in the direction of Smith's Bay. He had thus missed meeting Saul at Le Coq d'Or, but had learned of his nephew's arrival on his way home. The town, indeed, was agog with it.

So sustained was his enthusiasm, the more especially after imbibing his share of the unusually large provision of wine for a midday meal which his daughter's desire to honor the occasion had provided, that he monopolized most of his nephew's attention throughout breakfast and later in the drawing room after the conclusion of that meal. It was perhaps because of this joviality on his uncle's part that Saul Macartney failed to observe the totally new expression which had rested like a very small cloud on Camilla Macartney's face ever since a short time before going into the dining room.

His uncle even insisted upon sending the prodigal home in the English barouche, and in this elegant equipage—with its sleek, Danish coach horses and the liveried Negroes on its box with cockades at the sides of their glistening silk toppers—he made the brief journey down one hill, a short distance through the town, and up another one to his father's house.

Here, it being well after two o'clock in the afternoon, and siesta hour, he found Fawcett, whom the Old Man had taken under his hospitable wing. The two had no private conversation together. Both were in high spirits and these Old Macartney fostered with his cordials, his French brandy and a carafe of very ancient rum. The three men sat together over their liquor during the siesta hour, and during the session Old Macartney did most of the talking. He did not once refer to his son's capture by Brenner, the freebooter.

He confined himself in his desire to be entertaining to his son's benefactor, Captain Fawcett, to a joyous succession of merry tales and ripe, antique quips. Saul Macartney had therefore no reason to suspect, nor did it happen to occur to Fawcett to inform him, that the latter's account of Macartney's adventures since the time he had last been heard from until the present was in any wise different from the tale of shipwreck upon which they had agreed and which Macartney had told out in full to his cousin, Camilla.

The three had not finished their jovial session before various strange matters affecting them very nearly, odd rumors, now being discussed avidly in various offices, residences and gathering places about St. Thomas, were gathering headway, taking on various characteristic exaggerations and, indeed, running like wildfire through the town.

In a place like St. Thomas, crossroads and clearinghouse of the vast West Indian trade which came and went through that port and whose prosperity was dependent almost wholly upon shipping, even the town's riffraff was accustomed to think and express itself in terms of ships.

It was an unimportant, loquacious Negro youth who started the ball a-rolling. This fellow, a professional diver, came up to one of the wharves in his slab-sided, homemade rowboat where he lounged aft, submitting to the propulsion of his coal-black younger brother, a scrawny lad of twelve. This wharf rat had had himself rowed out to the vessel from which the two notables he had observed had come ashore that morning. It was from the lips of this black ne'er-do-well that various other wharfside loiterers learned that the beautiful clipper vessel lying out there at anchor was provided with eight carronade ports.

Out of the idle curiosity thus initially aroused there proceeded various other harbor excursions in small boats. The black diver had somehow managed to miss the stanchion of the "long tom" which Fawcett, in an interval of prudence, had had dismounted the night before. The fact that the *Swallow* carried such an armament, however, very soon trickled ashore.

This nucleus of interesting information was soon followed up and almost eclipsed in interest by the various discussions and arguments which were soon running rife among the shipping interests of the town over the extraordinary numbers of the *Swallow*'s crew.

A round dozen, together with the usual pair of mates to supplement the captain, as all these experts on ships were well aware, would ordinarily suffice for a vessel of this tonnage. Accounts and the terms of the various arguments varied between estimates ranging from seventy-five to a hundred men on board the *Swallow*.

A side issue within this category was also warmly discussed. Crews of vessels with home ports in the islands were commonly Negro crews. This unprecedented gathering of men was a white group. Only two—certain of the debaters held out firmly that they had observed three—Negroes were to be perceived aboard the *Swallow,* and one of these, a gigantic brown man who wore nothing but earrings and a pair of faded dungaree trousers, was plainly the cook in charge of the *Swallow*'s galley, and the other, or others, were this fellow's assistants.

But the town got its real fillip from the quite definite statement of a small-fry worthy, one Jeems Pelman, who really gave them something to wrangle about when he came ashore after a visit of scrutiny and stated flatly that this rakish, shining, black-hulled clipper was none other vessel than the Macartney's *Hope,* upon both hull and rigging of which he had worked steadily for three months in his own shipyard when the *Hope* was built during the winter of 1819.

All these items of easily authenticated information bulked together and indicated to the comparatively unsophisticated, as well as to the wiseacres, only one possible conclusion. This was that the Macartney vessel, in command of which Captain Saul Macartney was known to have cleared from a South American port three months earlier, had in some as yet unexplained fashion been changed over into a freetrading ship and that the harsh-featured seadog in his fine clothes who had accompanied Captain Macartney ashore that morning could very well be none other than its commander.

A certain lapse of time is ordinarily requisite for the loquacious stage of drunkenness to overtake the average hard-headed seafaring man. The crew of Fawcett's longboat, after three weeks' continuous duty at sea, had bestowed the boat safely, engaged the services of an elderly Negro to watch it in their absence, and drifted into the low rum shop nearest their landing place; and there not long after their arrival Fawcett's boatswain, a Dutch island bruiser, had been recognized by several former acquaintances as a sailorman who had gone out of the harbor of St. Eustasia in a small trading schooner which had disappeared off the face of the wide Caribbean three years previously.

The rum-induced garrulity of this gentleman, as the report of it went forth and flared through the town, corroborated the as yet tentative conclusion that a fully manned pirate ship lay for the time being at anchor in the peaceful harbor of St. Thomas; and that its master, whose identity as a certain Captain Fawcett had spread downward through the social strata from Le Coq d'Or itself, was here ashore, hobnobbing with the town's high gentry, and actually a guest of the Macartneys.

By three o'clock in the afternoon the town was seething with the news. There had been no such choice morsel to roll on the tongue since Henry Morgan had sacked the city of Panama.

The first corroboration of that vague, distressing, but as yet unformed suspicion which had lodged itself in Camilla Macartney's mind came to her through Jens Sorensen, the butler. The "grapevine route," so-called—that curious door-to-door and mouth-to-ear method of communication among the Negroes of the community—is very rapid as well as very mysterious. Black Jens had heard this devastating story relayed up to him from the lowest black riffraff of the town's waterfront a matter of minutes after the name of their guest, seeping downward from Le Coq d'Or, had met, mingled with, and crowned the damnatory group of successive details from the wharves.

To anyone familiar with the effect of voodoo upon the Negro mentality there would be nothing surprising in the fact that black Jens proceeded straight to his mistress to whisper the story without any delay. For fear is the dominant note of the voodoo-ist. The St. Thomas Negroes were actuated in their attitude toward Camilla Macartney by something infinitely deeper than that superficial respect which Captain McMillin had noted. They feared her and her proven powers as they feared the dread demigod Damballah, tutelary manifestation of the unnamed Guinea-Snake himself.

For it was not as one who only inquires and studies that Camilla Macartney commanded awe and reverence from the St. Thomas Negroes. She had *practiced* this extraordinary art and it was her results as something quite tangible, definite and unmistakable which formed the background of that vast respect, and which had brought black Jens cringing and trembling into her presence on this particular occasion.

And black Jens had not failed to include in his report the drunken sailorman's leering account of that captive lady's treatment by Saul Macartney—how an innocent young wife, off Nevis, had been outrageously forced into Saul's cabin, and when he had tired of her, how he had sent her back to the deck to go across the plank of death.

What desolation penetrated deep and lodged itself there in Camilla Macartney's soul can hardly be guessed at. From that moment she was convinced of the deep infamy of that entrancing lover-cousin of hers whom she had adored with her whole heart since the remoteness of her early childhood.

But, however poignantly indescribable, however extremely devastating, may have been her private feelings, it is certain that she did not retire as the typical gentlewoman of the period would have done to eat out her heart in solitary desolation.

Within ten minutes, on the contrary, in response to her immediately issued orders, the English barouche with its sleek Danish horses, its cockaded servants on the box, was carrying her down the hill, rapidly along through the town, and then the heavy coach horses were sweating up the other hill toward her uncle's house. If the seed of hatred, planted by Saul's duplicity, were already sprouting, nevertheless she would warn him. She dreaded meeting him.

Saul Macartney, summoned away from the somewhat drowsy end of that afternoon's convivial session with Fawcett and the Old Man, found his cousin awaiting him near the drawing room door. She was standing, and her appearance was calm and collected. She addressed him directly, without preamble:

"Saul, it is known in the town. I came to warn you. It is running about the streets that this Captain Fawcett of yours is the pirate. One of his men has been recognized. He talked in one of the rum shops. They say that this ship is the *Hope*, altered into a different appearance. I advise you to go, Saul—go at once, while it is safe!"

Saul Macartney turned his old disarming smile upon his cousin. He could feel the liquor he had drunk warming him, but his hard Irish head was reasonably clear. He was not befuddled. He stepped toward her as though impulsively, his bronzed face flushed from his recent potations, his arms extended and spread in a carefree gesture as though he were about to take her in his embrace.

"Camilla, *allana,* ye should not sadden your sweet face over the likes of me. I know well what I'm about, me darling. And as for Fawcett—well, as ye're aware of his identity, ye'll know that he can care for himself. Very suitably, very suitably indeed."

He had advanced very close upon her now, but she stood unmoving, the serious expression of her face not changed. She only held up a hand in a slight gesture against him, as though to warn him to pause and think. Again Saul Macartney stepped lightly toward his doom.

"And may I not be having a kiss, Camilla?" His smiling face was unperturbed, his self-confidence unimpaired even now. Then, fatally, he added. "And now that ye're here, *acushla,* why should ye not have me present my friend, the captain? 'Twas he, ye'll remember, that brought me back to ye. I could be fetching him within the moment."

But Camilla Macartney merely looked at him with a level gaze.

"I am going now," she said, ignoring his suggestion and the crass insult to her gentility involved in it, and which beneath her calm exterior had outraged her and seared her very soul. The seed was growing apace. "I have warned you, Saul."

She turned and walked out of the room and out of the house: then across the tiled gallery and down the black marble steps, and out to her carriage.

Saul Macartney hastened back to his father and Fawcett. Despite his incurable bravado, motivated as always by his deep-seated selfishness, he had simply accepted the warning just given him at its face value. He addressed his drowsing father after a swift, meaningful glance at Fawcett:

"We shall be needing the carriage, sir, if so be it's agreeable to ye. We must be getting back on board, it appears, and I'll be hoping to look in on ye again in the morning, sir."

And without waiting for any permission, and ignoring his father's liquor-muffled protests against this abrupt departure, Saul Macartney rang the bell, ordered the family carriage to be waiting in the shortest possible time, and pressed a rix-dollar into the Negro butler's hand as an incentive to hasten the process.

Within a quarter of an hour, after hasty farewells to the tearful and now well-befuddled Old Man, these two precious scoundrels were well on their way through the town toward the jetty where they had landed, and where, upon arrival, they collected their boat's crew out of the rum shop with vigorous revilings and not a few hearty clouts, and were shortly speeding across the turquoise and indigo waters of St. Thomas harbor toward the anchored *Swallow.*

Inside half an hour from their going up over her side and the hoisting of the longboat, the *Swallow,* without reference to the harbormaster, clearance, or any other formality, was picking her lordly way daintily out past Colwell's Battery at the harbor mouth, and was soon lost to the sight of all curious watchers in the welcoming swell of the Caribbean.

This extraordinary visit of the supposedly long-drowned Captain Macartney to his native town, and the circumstances accompanying it, was a nine-days' wonder in St. Thomas. The widespread discussion it provoked died down after awhile, it being supplanted in current interest by the many occurrences in so busy a port-of-call. It was not, of course, forgotten, although it dropped out of mind as a subject for acute debate.

Such opinion as remained after the arguments had been abandoned was divided opinion. Could the vessel possibly have been the Macartneys' *Hope?* Was this Captain Fawcett who had brought Saul Macartney ashore Captain Fawcett, the pirate? Had Captain Saul Macartney really thrown in his lot with free-traders, or was such a course unthinkable on his part?

The yarn which Captain Fawcett had spun in Le Coq d'Or seemed the reasonable explanation—if it were true. In the face of the fact that no other counter-explanation had been definitely put forward by anybody, this version was tacitly accepted by St. Thomas society; but with the proviso, very generally made and very widely held, that this fellow must have been *the* Captain Fawcett after all. Saul Macartney had either been fooled by him, or else Saul's natural gratitude had served to cover, in his estimation of the fellow, any observed shortcomings on the part of this rescuer and friend-in-need.

Camilla Macartney made no allusion whatever, even within the family circle, to the story Saul had told *her*. She was not, of course, called upon to express any opinion outside. She was quite well aware that both versions were falsehoods.

She faced bravely, though with a sorely empty and broken heart, all her manifold social obligations in the town. Indeed, somewhat to distract her tortured mind, wherein that seed of hate was by now growing into a lusty plant, the heiress of the Macartney fortune engaged herself rather more fully than usual that summer season in the various current activities. She forced herself to a greater preoccupation than ever in her attention to her occult pursuits. She even took up afresh the oil painting, long ago abandoned by her, which had been one of her early "accomplishments."

It was during this period—a very dreadful one for her, succeeding as it did, abruptly upon her momentary happiness at her cousin Saul's restoration to the land of the living which had dissipated her acute and sustained grief over his presumptive loss at sea in the *Hope*—that she undertook, with what obscure premonitory motive derived from curious skill in the strange and terrible arts of the black people can only be darkly surmised —another and very definite task.

This was the painting of a panoramic view of the town as seen from the harbor. At this she toiled day after day from the awninged afterdeck of one of the smaller Macartney packet vessels. This boat had been anchored to serve her purpose at the point of vantage she had selected. She worked at her panorama in the clear, pure light of many early summer mornings. Before her on the rather large canvas she had chosen for this purpose there gradually grew into objectivity the wharves, the public buildings, the fort, the three hills with their red-roofed mansions, set amid decorative trees. Her almost incredible industry was, really, a symptom of the strange obsession now beginning to invade her reason. Camilla Macartney had suffered a definite mental lesion.

The scrupulous courtesy of the St. Thomians, that graceful mantle of manners which has never been allowed to wear thin, was unobtrusively interposed between the respected Macartneys and the dreadful scandal which had reached out and touched their impeccable family garment of respectability. By no word spoken, by no overt act, by not so much as a breath were they reminded of Captain Macartney's recent visit ashore or his hasty and irregular departure. Captain McMillin, therefore, as a guest of Camilla's father, heard nothing of it. He sensed, however, a certain indefinite undercurrent of family trouble and, yielding to this sure instinct, ended his visit with all the niceties of high breeding and departed for Santa Cruz.

Just before he left, on the morning after the farewell dinner which had been given as a final gesture in his honor, the captain managed to convey to Camilla the measure of his appreciation. He placed, as it were, his sword at her disposal! It was very nicely made—that gesture of gallantry. It was not to be mistaken for the preliminary to a possible later offer of marriage. It was anything but braggadocio. And it was somehow entirely appropriate to the situation. The handsome, upstanding captain left with his hostess precisely the impression he intended; that is, he left her the feeling that he was an adequate person to depend upon in a pinch, and that she had been invited to depend upon him should the pinch come.

A third of the way up one of the low mountains northward and behind the three gentle hills on the southern slopes of which the ancient city of St. Thomas is built, there stood—and still stands —a small stone gentry residence originally built in the middle of the eighteenth century by an exiled French family which had taken refuge in this kindly Danish colony and played at raising vanilla up there on their airy little estate overlooking the town and the sea.

This place was still known by its original name of Ma Folie—a title early bestowed upon it by Mme. la Marquise, who had looked up at it through a window in her temporary apartment in the Hôtel du Commerce, in the town, while the roofing was being placed upon her new house, there and then assuring herself that only perched upon the back of one of those diminutive burros which cluttered up the town streets could anyone like herself possibly manage the ascent to such a site.

Ma Folie was now one of the many Macartney properties. It belonged to Camilla, having come to her as a portion of her maternal inheritance, and upon it she had reestablished the vanilla planting, helped out by several freshly cleared acres in cocoa. No donkey was required nowadays to convey a lady up the tortuous, steep, little trail from the town to Ma Folie. A carriage road led past its unpretentious square entrance posts of whitewashed, cemented stone, and when Camilla Macartney visited her hillside estate the English barouche carried her there, the long climb causing the heavy coach horses to sweat mightily and helping, as the coal-black coachman said, to keep them in condition.

It was up here that she had long ago established what might be called her laboratory. It was at Ma Folie, whose village housed only Negroes selected by herself as her tenant-laborers, that she had, in the course of years, brought the practice of the "strange art" to its perfection. She had for some time now confined her practice to meeting what might be called charitable demands upon her.

Talismans to protect; amulets to attract or repel; potent *ouangas*—only such modest products of the fine art of voodoo as these went out from that occult workshop of hers at Ma Folie—went out into the eager, outstretched hands of the afflicted whose manifold plights had engaged Camilla Macartney's sympathy; to the relief of those abject ones who called upon her, in fear and trembling, as their last resort against who knows what obscure devilish attacks, what outrageous charmings, wrought by that inimical ruthlessness of one Negro to another which Caucasians hardly suspect.

No vanilla pod, no single cocoa bean, had been stolen from Ma Folie estate since Camilla Macartney had planted it afresh nine years before. . . .

It was at about ten o'clock in the morning of a day near the middle of August that a kind of tremor of emotion ran through the town of St. Thomas, a matter of minutes after a report of the official watcher and the many other persons in the town and along the wharves whose sustained interest in shipping matters caused their eyes to turn ever and anon toward the wide harbor mouth. The *Swallow*, which three months before had literally run away, ignoring all the niceties of a ship's departure from any port and even the official leavetaking, was coming in brazenly, lilting daintily along under the stiff trade, her decks visibly swarming with the many members of her efficient and numerous crew.

She came up into the wind like a little man-o'-war, jauntily, her sails coming down simultaneously with a precision to warm the hearts of those ship-wise watchers, her rigging slatting with reports like musket shots, the furling and stowing of canvas a truly marvelous demonstration of the efficiency which now reigned aft.

These details of rapid-fire seamanship, swiftly as they were being handled, were as yet incomplete when the longboat went straight down from its davits into the water and Saul Macartney followed his boat's crew over the side and picked up his tiller ropes.

The *Swallow*'s anchorage this time was closer in, and it seemed no time at all to the thronging, gaping watchers on the jetty before he sprang ashore and was up the steps. There was no rum shop for the boat's crew this time. Without their officer's even looking back at them over his shoulder the oarsmen pushed off, turned about and rowed back to the *Swallow*.

Saul Macartney was, if possible, even more debonair than ever. His self-confident smile adorned his even more heavily bronzed face. He was hatless, as usual, and his handsome figure was mightily set off by a gaily sprigged waistcoat and a ruffled shirt of fine cambric which showed between the silver braided lapels of the maroon-colored coat of French cloth with a deep velvet collar, the pantaloons of which, matching the coat's cloth, were strapped under a pair of low boots of very shining black leather.

The throng on the jetty was plainly in a different mood as compared to the vociferous, welcoming mob of three months before. They stayed close together in a little phalanx this time and from them came fewer welcoming smiles.

Plainly sensing this, Saul Macartney bestowed on this riffraff of the wharves no more than a passing glance of smiling raillery. He passed them and entered the town with rapid, purposeful strides as though intent on some very definite business and, utterly ignoring the hum of released though muted conversation which rose behind him as though from an aroused swarm of bees, entered the main thoroughfare, turned sharply to his left along it, proceeded in this direction some forty feet, and turned into the small office of one Axel Petersen, a purveyor of ships' stores.

Blond, stout, genial Axel Petersen stared from his broad, comfortable desk at this entrance and allowed his lower jaw to sag. Then he rose uncertainly to his feet and his four neatly garbed mulatto clerks rose from their four respective high stools with him and, in precise conformity with their employer's facial reaction, their four pairs of mottled-iris eyes rounded out altogether like saucers, and their four lower jaws sagged in unison.

Saul Macartney threw back his head and laughed aloud. Then, addressing Petersen:

"Axel, Axel! I couldn't've thought it of ye! 'Tis but stores I'm after, man—vast stores, the likes of which ye might be selling in the course of a week to five vessels, if so be ye had the fortune to get that many all in one week!" Then, a shade more seriously, " 'Tis pork I want; beans, coffee in sacks, limes by the gunny sack —a hundred and one things, all of them written down to save ye trouble, ye great, feckless porker! And here—beside the list which I'm handing ye now—is the reassurance—"

And Saul Macartney, thrusting his list of ship's supplies neatly printed on a long slip of paper under the nose of the stultified

Petersen, slapped down upon the desktop beside it the bulging purse which he had hauled out of the tail pocket of his beautiful, maroon-colored French coat.

"There's two hundred and fifty English sovereigns there forninst ye, Axel. Ye can have it counted out or do it yourself, and if that does not suffice to cover the list, why, there's another shot in the locker behind it, ye *omadhoun*—ye fat robber of pettifogging ships' stewards!"

And before the protruding, bemused blue eyes of portly Axel Petersen, Saul Macartney shook banteringly a thick sheaf of Bank of England ten-pound notes. By the time he had returned these to the same capacious pocket, he was at the door, had paused, turned and, leaning for an instant nonchalantly against its jamb, remarked—

"Ye're to have the stores piled on your wharf not an instant later than two o'clock this day." Then, the bantering smile again to the fore, and shaking a long, shapely forefinger toward the goggling dealer in ships' stores, he added, "Ye'll observe, Axel. I'm not taking your stores by force and arms. I'm not sacking the town—this time!"

Then Saul Macartney was gone, and Axel Petersen, muttering unintelligibly as he assembled his scattered wits and those of his four clerks, the heavy purse clutched tightly by its middle in one pudgy hand, and the long list of the *Swallow*'s required stores held a little unsteadily before his nearsighted blue eyes, methodically began the process of getting this enormous order assembled.

It was with a perfectly calm exterior that Camilla Macartney received her cousin Saul a quarter of an hour later. The turmoil beneath this prideful reserve might, perhaps, be guessed at; but as the art of guessing had never formed any part of Saul Macartney's mental equipment, he made no effort in that direction.

He began at once with his usual self-confident directness upon what he had come to say.

"Camilla, *acushla,* I've come to ye in haste, 'tis true, and I'm asking your indulgence for that. 'Twas gracious of ye, as always, to be here at home when I chanced to arrive.

"I'll go straight to the point, if so be ye have no objections to make, and say in plain words what I well know to have been in the hearts of the two of us this many a year. I'm askin' ye now, Camilla—I'm begging ye with my whole soul to say that ye'll drive down with me now, Camilla, to the English Church, and the two of us be married, and then sail with me for the truly magnificent home I've been establishing for ye over on Andros."

Camilla Macartney continued to sit, outwardly unmoved, where she had received him when black Jens had shown him into the drawing room. She had not been looking at her cousin during this characteristically confident and even impulsive declaration of his. Her eyes were upon her hands which lay, lightly clasped, in her lap, and she did not raise them to reply. She did not, however, keep him waiting. She said in a perfectly level voice in which there was apparently no single trace or indication of the tearing, internal emotion which surged through her outraged heart at this last and unforgivable insult—

"I shall not become your wife, Saul—now or ever."

Then, as he stood before her, his buoyant self-confidence for once checked, his face suddenly configured into something like the momentary grotesqueness of Axel Petersen's, she added, in that same level tone, which had about it now, however, the smallest suggestion of a rising inflection:

"Do not come to me again. Go now—at once."

This final interview with her cousin Saul was unquestionably the element which served to crystallize into an active and sustained hatred the successive emotional crises and their consequent abnormal states of mind which the events here recorded had stirred up within this woman so terribly equipped for vengeance. The seed of hatred was now a full-grown plant.

Upon a woman of Camilla Macartney's depth and emotional capacity the felonious behavior of Saul Macartney had had a very terrible, and a very deep-reaching, mental effect. She had adored and worshiped him for as long as she could remember. He had torn down and riven apart and left lying about her in brutally shattered fragments the whole structure of her life. He had smashed the solid pride of her family into shreds. He had

disgraced himself blatantly, deliberately, with a ruthless abandon. He had piled insult to her upon insult. He had taken her
pure love for him, crushed and defiled it.

And now these irresistible blows had had the terrible effect of
breaking down the serene composure of this gentlewoman. All
her love for her cousin and all her pride in him were transformed into one definite, flaming and consuming purpose: She
must wipe out those dreadful stains!

Arrived in the empty library, Camilla Macartney went straight
to the great rosewood desk, and without any delay wrote a letter.
The black footman who hurried with this missive down the hill
actually passed Saul Macartney, likewise descending it. Within
a very short time after its reception the captain of the little
packet-vessel—upon which, anchored quite close to shore,
Camilla Macartney had been painting her nearly finished panorama of the town—had gone ashore to round up his full crew.
The packet itself, with Camilla Macartney on board, sailed out
of St. Thomas harbor that afternoon in plain sight of the re-
stocked *Swallow,* whose great spread of gleaming white canvas
showed gloriously under the afternoon's sun as she laid her
course due southwest. The packet, laying hers to the southward,
rolled and tossed at a steady eight-knot clip under the spanking
trade, straight for the Island of Santa Cruz.

Captain the Honorable William McMillin was summoned
from his seven o'clock dinner in his estate house up in the gentle
hills of the island's north side, and only his phlegmatic Scottish
temperament, working together with his aristocratic self-con-
trol, prevented *his* shapely jaw from sagging and his blue eyes
from becoming saucerlike when they had recorded for him the
identity of this wholly unexpected visitor. Camilla Macartney
wasted none of the captain's time, nor was her arrival cause for
any cooling of the excellent repast from which he had arisen to
receive her.

"I have not," said she downrightly in response to the astonished captain's initial inquiry as to whether she had dined.
"And," she added, "I should be glad to sit down with you at
once, if that meets your convenience, sir. It is, as you may very

well have surmised, a very deep and pressing matter upon which I have ventured to come to you. That, I should imagine, would best be discussed while we sit at table, and so without delay."

Again the captain demonstrated his admirable manners. He merely bowed and led the way to the door of his dining room.

Once seated opposite Captain McMillin, Camilla Macartney again went straight to her point. The captain quite definitely forgot to eat in the amazing and immediate interest of what she proceeded to say.

"I am offering the reward of a thousand English sovereigns for the apprehension at sea and the bringing to St. Thomas for their trials of the freetrader, Fawcett, and his mates. It may very well be no secret to you, sir, that a member of our family is one of these men. I think that any comment between us upon that subject will be a superfluity. You will take note, if you please, that it is I, a member of our family, who offer the reward I have named for his apprehension. You will understand—everything that is involved.

"Earlier this day it was proposed to me that I should sail away upon a ship without very much notice. I have come here to you, sir, on one of my father's vessels—Captain Stewart, her commander, a trusted man in our employ, has accompanied me all the way to your door. He is here now, waiting in the hired *calèche* which I secured in Frederiksted for the drive here to your house. Perhaps you will be good enough to have some food taken to him.

"I have come, Captain McMillin, in all this haste, actually to request you to do the same thing that I mentioned—you made me see, when you were our guest, that I could wholly rely upon you, sir. I am here to ask you, as a military man, to command the expedition which I am sending out. I am asking you to sail back with Captain Stewart and me for St. Thomas—tonight."

Captain McMillin looked at Camilla Macartney across the length of his glistening mahogany dining table. He had been listening very carefully to her speech. He rang his table bell now that he was sure she was finished, and when his serving man answered this summons, ordered him to prepare a repast for the waiting ship's captain, and to send in to him his groom. Then, with a bow to his guest, and pushing back his chair and rising, he said:

"You will excuse me, Miss Macartney, I trust, for the little time I shall require to pack. It will not occupy me very long."

IV

The story of how the *Hyperion,* newest and swiftest of all the Macartney vessels, was outfitted and armed for the pursuit and capture of Captain Fawcett is a little epic in itself. It would include among many details extant the intensive search among the shipping resources of St. Thomas, for the swivelgun which, two days after Captain McMillin's arrival on the scene, was being securely bolted through the oak timbers of the *Hyperion's* after-deck.

A surprisingly complete record of this extraordinary piece of activity survives among the ancient colonial archives. Perhaps the recording clerk of the period, in his Government House office, was, like everyone else in St. Thomas, fascinated by the ruthless swiftness with which that job, under the impact of Camilla Macartney's eye, was pushed through to a successful conclusion in precisely forty-eight hours. Nothing like this rate of speed had ever been heard of, even in St. Thomas. The many men engaged in this herculean task at Pelman's Shipyard worked day and night continuously in three eight-hour shifts.

It is significant that these shipwrights and other skilled artisans were all Negroes. They had assembled in their scores and dozens from every quarter of the widespread town, irrespective of age or the exactions of their current employment, from the instant that the grapevine route spread through the black population of the town the summons to this task which Camilla Macartney had quietly uttered in the ear of her butler, Jens Sorensen.

The *Hyperion,* under the command of her own officers but with the understanding that Captain McMillin was in sole charge of the expedition, came up with the *Swallow* a little under four days from the hour of her sailing out of St. Thomas harbor.

Captain McMillin caught Fawcett at a vast disadvantage. The *Swallow,* very lightly manned at the moment, hung in stays, her riding sails flapping with reports like pistol shots as her graceful head was held into the wind. She lay some ten shiplengths away to the leeward of an American merchant vessel about which the *Swallow*'s boats—now nine in number—were grouped, a single member of the crew in each. Fawcett and his two lieutenants, and nine-tenths of his crew of cutthroats, were ransacking their prize, whose officers, crew and passengers had been disposed of under nailed hatches. They appeared, indeed, to be so thoroughly occupied in this nefarious work as to have ignored entirely any preparations for meeting the *Hyperion*'s attack—a circumstance sufficiently strange to have impressed Captain McMillin profoundly.

The *Hyperion*'s officers, unable to account for this singular quiescence on the part of the pirates, attributed it to their probably failing to suspect that the *Hyperion* was anything but another trading vessel which had happened to blunder along on her course into this proximity. With a strange, quick gripping at the heart, quite new in his experience, Captain McMillin permitted himself to suspect, though for a brief instant only, that something of the strange power which he had glimpsed in his contacts with Camilla Macartney, might in some extraordinary fashion be somehow responsible for this phenomenon.

But this thought, as too utterly ridiculous for harborage in a normal man's mind, he put away from him instanter.

The strategy of the situation appeared to be simple. And Captain McMillin formulated his plan of attack accordingly, after a brief consultation with his officers.

Realizing that there could be no effective gunnery from the handful of men in charge of the *Swallow,* Captain McMillin ordered a dozen men in charge of the *Hyperion*'s second mate over the side in the largest of the boats. The maneuver of dropping an already manned boat from the davits—a risky undertaking in any event—was handled successfully, an exceptionally quiet sea contributing to the management of this piece of seamanship.

This boat's crew, all Negroes and all armed with the pistols and cutlasses which had been hastily served out to them, had no difficulty whatever in getting over the *Swallow*'s side and making themselves masters of the pirate vessel. The dozen Negroes had butchered the seven members of the pirate crew left on board the *Swallow* within forty seconds of their landing upon her deck, and Mr. Matthews, the officer in charge of them, hauled down with his own hand the Jolly Roger which, true to the freetrading traditions of the Main, flaunted at the *Swallow*'s main peak.

The magnificent cooperation of the fifteen Negroes constituting the *Hyperion*'s deck crew made possible the next daring piece of seamanship which the *Hyperion*'s captain had agreed to attempt. This was Captain McMillin's plan.

The *Hyperion* should lay alongside the American vessel, grapple to her and board—with all hands—from deck to deck. This idea, almost unheard of in modern sea warfare, had suggested itself as practicable in this instance to Captain McMillin, from his reading. Such had been the tactics of the antique Mediterranean galleys.

For the purpose of retaining the outward appearance of a simple trader, Captain McMillin had concealed the thirty-three additional members of his heavily armed crew, and these had not been brought on deck until he was almost ready to have the grapples thrown. These reserves now swarmed upon the *Hyperion*'s deck in the midst of a bedlam of shouts, yells and curses, punctuated by pistol shots, from the pirate crew on board their prize.

These were taken at a vast disadvantage. Their prize vessel was immobile. They had, for what appeared to Captain McMillin some inexplicable reason, apparently failed until the very last moment to realize the *Hyperion*'s intentions. Most of them were busily engaged in looting their prize. Under this process five of the *Swallow*'s nine boats had already been laden gunwale deep with the miscellaneous plunder already taken out of the American ship. Two of these laden small boats and two others of the *Swallow*'s nine were crushed like eggshells as the *Hyperion* closed in and threw her grappling hooks.

Then, in a silence new and strange in Captain McMillin's previous experience in hand-to-hand fighting, his forty-eight black fighting men followed him over the rails and fell upon the pirates.

Within three minutes the American vessel's deck was a shambles. Camilla Macartney's black myrmidons, like militant fiends from some strange hell of their own, their eyeballs rolling, their white teeth flashing as they bared their lips in the ecstasy of this mission of wholesale slaughter, spread irresistibly with grunts and low mutterings and strange cries about that deck.

Not a member of the pirate crew escaped their ruthless onslaught. Hard skulls were split asunder and lopped arms strewed the deck, and tough bodies were transfixed, and the gasping wounded were trampled lifeless in the terrible energy of these black fighting men.

Then abruptly, save for a harsh sobbing sound from laboring panting lungs after their terrific exertion, a strange silence fell, and toward Captain McMillin, who stood well nigh aghast over the utter strangeness of this unprecedented carnage which had just taken place under his eye and under his command, there came a huge, black, diffidently smiling Negro, his feet scarlet as he slouched along that moist and slippery deck, a crimson cutlass dangling loosely now from the red hand at the end of a red arm. This one, addressing the captain in a low, humble and deprecating voice, said—

"Come, now, please, me marster—come, please sar, see de t'ree gentlemahn you is tell us to sabe alive!"

And Captain McMillin, bemused, followed this guide along that deck slashed and scarlet with the lifeblood of those pulped heaps which had been Captain Fawcett's pirate crew, stepped aft to where, behind the main deckhouse, three trussed and helpless white men lay upon a cleaner section of that vessel's deck, under the baleful eye of another strapping black man with red feet and a naked red cutlass brandished in a red hand.

The *Swallow*, her own somewhat bloodsoiled deck now shining spotless under the mighty holystonings it had received at the hands of its prize crew of twelve under command of the *Hype-rion*'s second mate, the Danish flag now flying gaily from her masthead, followed the *Hyperion* into St. Thomas harbor on the second day of September, 1825. The two vessels came up to their designated anchorages smartly, and shortly thereafter, and for the last time, Saul Macartney, accompanied by his crony, Captain Fawcett, and his colleague, the other pirate mate, was rowed ashore in the familiar longboat.

But during this short and rapid trip these three gentlemen did not, for once, occupy the sternsheets. They sat forward, their hands and feet in irons, the six oarsmen between them and Mr. Matthews, the *Hyperion*'s mate, who held the tiller rope, and Captain the Honorable William McMillin, who sat erect beside him.

V

I have already recorded my first horrified reaction to the appearance of the handsome black-haired piratical mate whose painted arm my innocent thumbtack had penetrated. My next reaction, rather curiously, was the pressing, insistent, sudden impulse to withdraw that tack. I did so forthwith—with trembling fingers. I here openly confess.

My third and final reaction which came to me not long afterward and when I had somewhat succeeded in pulling myself together, was once more to get out my magnifying glass and take another good look through it. After all, I told myself, I was here confronted with nothing more in the way of material facts than a large-sized, somewhat crudely done and very old oil painting.

I got the glass and reassured myself. The "blood" was, of course—as now critically examined, magnified by sixteen diameters—merely a few spattered drops of the very same vermilion pigment which my somewhat clever amateur artist had used for the red roofs of the houses, the foulards of the Negresses and those many gloriously flaming flower blossoms.

Quite obviously these particular spatters of red paint had not been in the liquid state for more than a century. Having ascertained these facts beyond the shadow of any lingering doubt in the field of everyday material fact, my one remaining bit of surviving wonderment settled itself about the minor puzzle of just why I had failed to observe these spots of ancient, dry and brittle paint during the long and careful scrutiny to which I had subjected the picture the evening before. A curious coincidence, this—that the tiny red spots should happen to be precisely in the place where blood would be showing if it *had* flowed from my tack wound in that dangled painted arm.

I looked next, curiously, through my glass at the fellow's face. I could perceive now none of that acutely agonized expression which had accentuated my first startled horror at the sight of the blood.

And so, pretty well reassured, I went back to my bedroom and finished dressing. And thereafter, as the course of affairs proceeded, I could not get the thing out of my mind. I will pass over any attempt at describing the psychological processes involved and say here merely that by the end of a couple of weeks or so I was in that state of obsession which made it impossible for me to do my regular work, or, indeed, to think of anything else. And then, chiefly to relieve my mind of this vastly annoying preoccupation, I began upon that course of investigatory research to which I have already alluded.

When I had finished this, had gone down to the end of the last bypath which it involved, it was well on in the year 1930. It had taken three years, and—it was worth it.

I was in St. Thomas that season and St. Thomas was still operating under the régime which had prevailed since the spring of 1917, at which time the United States had purchased the old Danish West Indies from Denmark as a war measure, during the presidency of Woodrow Wilson.

In 1930 our naval forces had not yet withdrawn from our Virgin Island Colony. The administration was still actively under the direction of his Excellency Captain Waldo Evans, USN Retired, and the heads of the major departments were still the efficient and personable gentlemen assigned to those duties by the Secretary of the Navy.

My intimate friend, Dr. Pelletier, the pride of the USN Medical Corps, was still in active charge of the Naval Hospital, and I could rely upon Dr. Pelletier, whose interest in and knowledge of the strange and outré beliefs, customs and practices of numerous strange corners of this partly civilized world of ours were both deep and, as it seemed to me, virtually exhaustive.

To this good friend of mine, this walking encyclopedia of strange knowledge, I took, naturally, my findings in this very strange and utterly fascinating story of old St. Thomas. We spent several long evenings together over it, and when I had imparted all the facts while my surgeon friend listened, as is his custom, for hours on end without a single interruption, we proceeded to spend many more evenings discussing it, sometimes at the hospitable doctor's bachelor dinner table and afterward far into those tropic nights of spice and balm, and sometimes at my house which is quite near the old T.L. Macartney mansion on Denmark Hill.

In the course of these many evenings I added to the account of the affair which had emerged out of my long investigation two additional phases of this matter which I have not included in my account as written out here because, in the form which these took in my mind, they were almost wholly conjectural.

Of these, the first took its point of departure from the depiction of the rope, as shown in the painting, with which Saul Macartney had been hanged. I have mentioned the painstaking particularity with which the artist had put in the minor details of the composition. I have illustrated this by stating that the seven traditional turns of the hangman's knot were to be seen showing plainly under Captain Fawcett's left ear. The same type of knot, I may add here, was also painted in laboriously upon the noose which had done to death Fawcett's other mate.

But Saul Macartney's rope did not show such a knot. In fact, it showed virtually no knot at all. Even under the magnifying glass a knot expert would have been unable to name in any category of knots the inconspicuous slight enlargement at the place where Saul Macartney's noose was joined. Another point about this rope which might or might not have any significance, was the fact that it was of a color slightly but yet distinctly different from the hemp color of the other two. Saul Macartney's rope was of a faint greenish-blue color.

Upon this rather slight basis for conjecture I hazarded the following enlargement:

That Camilla Macartney, just after the verdict of the Danish Colonial High Court had become known to her—and I ventured to express the belief that she had known it before any other white person—had said in her quiet voice to her black butler, Jens Sorensen:

"I am going to Ma Folie. Tonight, at nine o'clock precisely, Ajax Mendoza is to come to me there."

And—this is merely my imaginative supplement, it will be remembered, based on my own knowledge of the dark ways of voodoo—burly black Ajax Mendoza, capital executioner in the honorable employ of the Danish Colonial Administration, whose father, Jupiter Mendoza, had held that office before him, and whose grandfather, Achilles Mendoza (whose most notable performance had been the racking of the insurrectionist leader, Black Tancrède, who had been brought back to the capital in chains after the perpetration of his many atrocities in the St. Jan Uprising of the slaves in 1733), had been the first of the line; that Ajax Mendoza, not fierce and truculent as he looked standing there beside the policemaster on Captain Fawcett's gallow platform, but trembling, and cringing, had kept that appointment to which he had been summoned.

Having received his orders, he had then hastened to bring to Camilla Macartney the particular length of thin manila rope which was later to be strung from the arm of Saul Macartney's gallows and had left it with her until she returned it to him before the hour of the execution; and that he had received it back and reeved it through its pulley with even more fear and trembling and cringings at being obliged to handle this transmuted thing whose very color was a terror and a distress to him, now that it had passed through that fearsome laboratory of "white missy who knew the Snake. . . ."

And my second conjectural hypothesis I based upon the fact which my research had revealed to me that all the members of the honorable clan of Macartney resident in St. Thomas had, with obvious propriety, kept to their closely shuttered several residences during the entire day of that public execution. That is, all of the Macartneys except the heiress of the great Macartney fortune, Camilla.

Half an hour before high noon on that public holiday the English barouche had deposited Camilla Macartney at one of the wharves a little away from the center of the town where that great throng had gathered to see the pirates hanged, and from there she had been rowed out to the small vessel which had that morning gone back to its old anchorage near the shore.

There, in her old place under the awning of the afterdeck, she had very calmly and deliberately set up her easel and placed before her the all-but-finished panorama upon which she had been working, and had thereupon begun to paint, and so had continued quietly painting until the three bodies of those pirates which had been left dangling "for the space of a whole hour," according to the sentence, "as a salutary example," and had then ended her work and gone back to the wharf carrying carefully the now finished panorama to where the English barouche awaited her.

By conjecture, on the basis of these facts, I managed somehow to convey to Dr. Pelletier, a man whose mind is attuned to such matters, the tentative, uncertain idea—I should not dare to name it a conviction—that Camilla Macartney, by some application of that uncanny skill of hers in the arts of darkness, had, as it were, caught the life principle of her cousin, Saul Macartney, as it escaped from his splendid body there at the end of that slightly discolored and curiously knotted rope, *and fastened it down upon her canvas within the simulacrum of that little painted figure through the arm of which I had thrust a thumbtack!*

These two queer ideas of mine, which had been knocking about inside my head, strangely enough did not provoke the retort, "Outrageous!" from Dr. Pelletier, a man of the highest scientific attainments. I had hesitated to put such thoughts into words, and I confess that I was surprised that his response in the form of a series of nods of the head did not seem to indicate the indulgence of a normal mind toward the drivelings of some imbecile.

Dr. Pelletier deferred any verbal reply to this imaginative climax of mine, placed as it was at the very end of our discussion. When he did shift his mighty bulk where it reclined in my Chinese rattan lounge chair on my airy west gallery—a sure preliminary to any remarks from him—his first words surprised me a little.

"Is there any doubt, Canevin, in your mind about the identity of this painted portrait figure of the mate with Saul Macartney himself?"

"No," said I. "I was able to secure two faded old ambrotypes of Saul Macartney—at least, I was given a good look at them. There can, I think, be no question on that score."

For the space of several minutes Pelletier remained silent. Then he slightly shifted his leonine head to look at me.

"Canevin," said he, "people like you and me who have *seen* this kind of thing working under our very eyes, all around us, among people like these West Indian blacks, well—we *know.*"

Then, more animatedly, and sitting up a little in his chair, the doctor said:

"On that basis, Canevin—on the pragmatic basis, if you will, and that, God knows, is scientific, based on observation—the only thing that we can do is to give this queer, devilish thing the benefit of the doubt. Our doubt, to say nothing of what the general public would think of such ideas!"

"Should you say that there is anything that can be done about it?" I inquired. "I have the picture, you know, and you have heard the—well, the *facts* as they have come under my observation. Is there any—what shall I say?—any *responsibility* involved on the basis of those facts and any conjectural additions that you and I may choose to make?"

"That," said Pelletier, "is what I meant by the benefit of the doubt. Thinking about this for the moment in terms of the limitations, the incompleteness, of human knowledge and the short distance we have managed to travel along the road to civilization, I should say that there is—a responsibility."

"What shall I do—if anything?" said I, a little taken aback at this downrightness.

Again Dr. Pelletier looked at me for a long moment, and nodded his head several times. Then:

"Burn the thing, Canevin. Fire—the solvent. Do you comprehend me? Have I said enough?"

I thought over this through the space of several silent minutes. Then, a trifle hesitantly because I was not at all sure that I had grasped the implications which lay below this very simple suggestion—

"You mean—?"

"That if there is anything in it, Canevin—that benefit of the doubt again, you see—if, to put such an outrageous hypothesis into a sane phrase, the life, the soul, the personality remains unreleased, and that because of Camilla Macartney's use of a pragmatic 'magical' skill such as is operative today over there in the hills of Haiti; to name only one focus of this particular *cultus* —well, then . . ."

This time it was I who nodded; slowly, several times. After that I sat quietly in my chair for long minutes in the little silence which lay between us. We had said, it seemed to me, everything that was to be said. I—we—had gone as far as human limitations permitted in the long investigation of this strange affair. Then I summoned my houseman, Stephen Penn.

"Stephen," said I, "go and find out if the charcoal pots in the kitchen have burned out since breakfast. I imagine that about this time there would be a little charcoal left to burn out in each of them. If so, put all the charcoal into one pot and bring it out here on the gallery. If not, fix me a new charcoal fire in the largest pot. Fill it about half full."

"Yes, sar," said Stephen, and departed on this errand.

Within three minutes the excellent Stephen was back. He set down on the tile floor beside my chair the largest of my four kitchen charcoal pots. It was half full of brightly glowing embers.

I sent him away before I went into the house to fetch the painting. It is a curious fact that this faithful servitor of mine, a *zambo* or medium-brown Negro, and a native of St. Thomas, had manifested an increasing aversion to anything like contact with or even sight of the old picture, an aversion dating from that afternoon when he had discovered it, three years before, in the lumber room of my Santa Cruzian hired residence.

Then I brought it out and laid it flat, after clearing a place for it, on the large plain table which stands against the wall of the house on my gallery. Pelletier came over and stood beside me, and in silence we looked long and searchingly at Camilla Macartney's panorama for the last time.

Then, with the sharp, small blade of my pocketknife, I cut it cleanly through again and again until it was in seven or eight strips. A little of the brittle old paint cracked and flaked off in this process. Having piled the strips one on top of another, I picked up the topmost of the three or four spread newspapers which I had placed under the canvas to save the table top from my knife point, and these flakes and chips I poured first off the newspaper's edge upon the glowing embers. These bits of dry, ancient pigment hissed, flared up, and then quickly melted away. Then I burned the strips very carefully until all but one were consumed.

This, perhaps because of some latent dramatic instinct whose existence until that moment I had never really suspected, was the one containing the figure of Saul Macartney. I paused, the strip in my hand, and looked at Pelletier. His face was inscrutable. He nodded his head at me, however, as though to encourage me to proceed and finish my task.

With perhaps a trifle of extra care I inserted the end of this last strip into the charcoal pot.

It caught fire and began to burn through precisely as its predecessors had caught and burned, and finally disintegrated into a light grayish ash. Then a very strange thing happened—

There was no slightest breath of air moving in that sheltered corner of the gallery. The entire solid bulk of the house sheltered it from the steady northeast trade—now at three in the afternoon at its lowest daily ebb, a mere wavering, tenuous pulsing.

And yet, at the precise instant when the solid material of that last strip had been transmuted by the power of the fire into the whitish, wavering ghost of material objects which we name ash —from the very center of the still brightly glowing charcoal embers there arose a thin, delicate wisp of greenish-blue smoke which spiraled before our eyes under the impact of some obscure pulsation in the quiet air about us, then stiffened, as yet unbroken, into a taut vertical line, the upper end of which abruptly turned, curving down upon itself, completing the representation of the hangman's noose; and then, instantly, this contour wavered and broke and ceased to be, and all that remained there before our fascinated eyes was a kitchen charcoal pot containing a now rapidly dulling mass of rose-colored embers.

PART II
VOODOO ELSEWHERE AND OTHERWISE

THE ISLE OF VOICES

by ROBERT LOUIS STEVENSON

Voodoo magic elsewhere and otherwise takes a variety of forms. One of the most fascinating is that of the early natives of the Hawaiian Islands, who believed that their sorcerers could read the stars, divine by the bodies of the dead and by the means of evil creatures, go alone into the highest parts of the volcanic mountains where the hobgoblins dwell and lay snares to entrap the spirits of the ancients. One such sorcerer is Kalamake, the wise man of the island of Molokai, who can make himself grow to such massive size that he is able to wade across the ocean and who can magically transport himself to the place called the Isle of Voices, where there is great wealth to be found—and the most fearful of all deaths as well.

Although it is not nearly as well known as **The Strange Case of Dr. Jekyll and Mr. Hyde** *and other macabre classics from the pen of Robert Louis Stevenson, "The Isle of Voices" ranks as one of his finest tales of this type. Not only is it beautifully and evocatively told, it also captures the voice and the spirit of Hawaii before the turn of the century with such deftness that it reads like native folklore. You'll not soon forget Kalamake, Keola, and the things that happen on the Isle of Voices. . . .*

Scottish novelist, essayist and poet Robert Louis Stevenson was born in Edinburgh in 1850 and studied both engineering and law before taking up writing in his middle twenties. Because he suffered from a respiratory

179

illness, he traveled often in search of healthier climates; it was these travels, most notably those in America and in the South Seas, which led to such romantic adventure novels as Treasure Island, Kidnapped, The Master of the Ballantrae, *and* David Balfour, *and to such nonfiction travel and autobiographical works as* The Silverado Squatters, Across the Plains, *and* In the South Seas. *He also published collections of short stories* (The New Arabian Nights, Island Nights' Entertainments), *collections of essays and critical studies* (Virginibus Puerisque, Familiar Studies of Men and Books), *collections of poetry* (A Child's Garden of Verses, Underwoods, Ballads), *and novels in collaboration with his American stepson, Lloyd Osbourne* (The Wrong Box, The Wrecker). *He was only forty-four at the time of his death from tuberculosis in Samoa, where he had settled with his American wife five years before.*

KEOLA WAS married with Lehua, daughter of Kalamake, the wise man of Molokai, and he kept his dwelling with the father of his wife. There was no man more cunning than that prophet; he read the stars, he could divine by the bodies of the dead, and by the means of evil creatures: he could go alone into the highest parts of the mountain, into the region of the hobgoblins, and there he would lay snares to entrap the spirits of the ancients.

For this reason no man was more consulted in all the kingdom of Hawaii. Prudent people bought, and sold, and married, and laid out their lives by his counsels; and the king had him twice to Kona to seek the treasures of Kamehameha. Neither was any man more feared: of his enemies, some had dwindled in sickness by the virtue of his incantations, and some had been spirited away, the life and the clay both, so that folk looked in vain for so much as a bone of their bodies. It was rumored that he had the art or the gift of the old heroes. Men had seen him at night upon the mountains, stepping from one cliff to the next; they had seen him walking in the high forest, and his head and shoulders were above the trees.

This Kalamake was a strange man to see. He was come of the best blood in Molokai and Maui, of a pure descent; and yet he was more white to look upon than any foreigner; his hair the color of dry grass, and his eyes red and very blind, so that "Blind as Kalamake that can see across tomorrow," was a byword in the islands.

Of all these doings of his father-in-law, Keola knew a little by the common repute, a little more he suspected, and the rest he ignored. But there was one thing troubled him. Kalamake was a man that spared for nothing, whether to eat or to drink, or to wear; and for all he paid in bright new dollars. "Bright as Kalamake's dollars," was another saying in the Eight Isles. Yet he neither sold, nor planted, nor took hire—only now and then from his sorceries—and there was no source conceivable for so much silver.

It chanced one day Keola's wife was gone upon a visit to Kaunakakai on the lee side of the island, and the men were forth at the sea-fishing. But Keola was an idle dog, and he lay in the verandah and watched the surf beat on the shore and the birds fly about the cliff. It was a chief thought with him always—the thought of the bright dollars. When he lay down to bed he would be wondering why they were so many, and when he woke at morn he would be wondering why they were all new; and the thing was never absent from his mind. But this day of all days he made sure in his heart of some discovery. For it seems he had observed the place where Kalamake kept his treasure, which was a lock-fast desk against the parlor wall, under the print of Kamehameha the fifth, and a photograph of Queen Victoria with her crown; and it seems again that, no later than the night before, he found occasion to look in, and behold! the bag lay there empty. And this was the day of the steamer; he could see her smoke off Kalaupapa; and she must soon arrive with a month's goods, tinned salmon and gin, and all manner of rare luxuries for Kalamake.

"Now if he can pay for his goods today," Keola thought, "I shall know for certain that the man is a warlock, and the dollars come out of the devil's pocket."

While he was so thinking, there was his father-in-law behind him, looking vexed.

"Is that the steamer?" he asked.

"Yes," said Keola. "She has but to call at Pelekunu, and then she will be here."

"There is no help for it then," returned Kalamake, "and I must take you in my confidence, Keola, for the lack of anyone better. Come here within the house."

So they stepped together into the parlor, which was a very fine room, papered and hung with prints, and furnished with a rocking-chair, and a table and a sofa in the European style. There was a shelf of books besides, and a family Bible in the midst of the table, and the lock-fast writing-desk against the wall; so that anyone could see it was the house of a man of substance.

Kalamake made Keola close the shutters of the windows, while he himself locked all the doors and set open the lid of the desk. From this he brought forth a pair of necklaces hung with charms and shells, a bundle of dried herbs, and the dried leaves of trees, and a green branch of palm.

"What I am about," said he, "is a thing beyond wonder. The men of old were wise; they wrought marvels, and this among the rest: but that was at night, in the dark, under the fit stars and in the desert. The same will I do here in my own house, and under the plain eye of day." So saying, he put the Bible under the cushion of the sofa so that it was all covered, brought out from the same place a mat of a wonderfully fine texture, and heaped the herbs and leaves on sand in a tin pan. And then he and Keola put on the necklaces and took their stand upon the opposite corners of the mat.

"The time comes," said the warlock, "be not afraid."

With that he set flame to the herbs, and began to mutter and wave the branch of palm. At first the light was dim because of the closed shutters; but the herbs caught strongly afire, and the flames beat upon Keola, and the room glowed with the burning; and next the smoke rose and made his head swim and his eyes darken, and the sound of Kalamake muttering ran in his ears. And suddenly, to the mat on which they were standing came a snatch or twitch, that seemed to be more swift than lightning. In the same wink the room was gone, and the house, the breath all beaten from Keola's body. Volumes of sun rolled upon his eyes and head, and he found himself transported to a beach of the sea, under a strong sun, with a great surf roaring: he and the warlock standing there on the same mat, speechless, gasping and grasping at one another, and passing their hands before their eyes.

"What was this?" cried Keola, who came to himself the first, because he was the younger. "The pang of it was like death."

"It matters not," panted Kalamake. "It is now done."

"And, in the name of God, where are we?" cried Keola.

"That is not the question," replied the sorcerer. "Being here, we have matter in our hands, and that we must attend to. Go, while I recover my breath, into the borders of the wood, and bring me the leaves of such and such an herb, and such and such a tree, which you will find to grow there plentifully—three handfuls of each. And be speedy. We must be home again before the steamer comes; it would seem strange if we had disappeared." And he sat on the sand and panted.

Keola went up the beach, which was of shining sand and coral, strewn with singular shells; and he thought in his heart:

"How do I not know this beach? I will come here again and gather shells."

In front of him was a line of palms against the sky; not like the palms of the Eight Islands, but tall and fresh and beautiful and hanging out withered fans like gold among the green, and he thought in his heart:

"It is strange I should not have found this grove. I will come here again, when it is warm, to sleep." And he thought, "How warm it has grown suddenly!" For it was winter in Hawaii, and the day had been chill. And he thought also, "Where are the gray mountains? And where is the high cliff with the hanging forests and the wheeling birds?" And the more he considered, the less he might conceive in what quarter of the islands he was fallen.

In the border of the grove, where it met the beach, the herb was growing, but the tree farther back. Now, as Keola went towards the tree, he was aware of a young woman who had nothing on her body but a belt of leaves.

"Well!" thought Keola, "they are not very particular about their dress in this part of the country." And he paused, supposing she would observe him and escape; and seeing that she still looked before her, he stood and hummed aloud. Up she leaped at the sound. Her face was ashen; she looked this way and that, and her mouth gaped with the terror of her soul. But it was a strange thing that her eyes did not rest upon Keola.

"Good day," said he. "You need not be so frightened, I will not eat you." And he had scarce opened his mouth before the young woman fled into the bush.

"These are strange manners," thought Keola, and, not thinking what he did, ran after her.

As she ran, the girl kept crying in some speech that was not practiced in Hawaii, yet some of the words were the same, and she knew she kept calling and warning others. And presently he saw more people running—men, women and children, one with another, all running and crying like people at a fire. And with that he began to grow afraid himself, and returned to Kalamake bringing the leaves. Him he told just what he had seen.

"You must pay no heed," said Kalamake. "All this is like a dream and shadows. All will disappear and be forgotten."

"It seemed none saw me," said Keola.

"And none did," replied the sorcerer. "We walk here in the broad sun invisible by reason of these charms. Yet they hear us; and therefore it is well to speak softly, as I do."

With that he made a circle round the mat with stones, and in the midst he set the leaves.

"It will be your part," he said, "to keep the leaves alight, and feed the fire slowly. While they blaze (which is but for a little moment) I must do my errand; and before the ashes blacken, the same power that brought us carries us away. Be ready now with the match; and do you call me in good time lest the flames burn out and I be left."

As soon as the leaves caught, the sorcerer leaped like a deer out of the circle, and began to race along the beach like a hound that has been bathing. As he ran, he kept stooping to snatch shells; and it seemed to Keola that they glittered as he took them. The leaves blazed with a clear flame that consumed them swiftly; and presently Keola had but a handful left, and the sorcerer was far off, running and stopping.

"Back!" cried Keola. "Back! The leaves are near done."

At that Kalamake turned, and if he had run before, now he flew. But fast as he ran, the leaves burned faster. The flame was ready to expire when, with a great leap, he bounded on the mat. The wind of his leaping blew it out; and with that the beach was gone, and the sun and the sea; and they stood once more in the dimness of the shuttered parlor, and were once more shaken and blinded; and on the mat betwixt them lay a pile of shining dollars. Keola ran to the shutters; and there was the steamer tossing in the swell close in.

The same night Kalamake took his son-in-law apart, and gave him five dollars in his hand.

"Keola," said he; "if you are a wise man (which I am doubtful of) you will think you slept this afternoon on the verandah, and dreamed as you were sleeping. I am a man of few words, and I have for my helpers people of short memories."

Never a word more said Kalamake, nor referred again to that affair. But it ran all the while in Keola's head—if he were lazy before, he would now do nothing.

"Why should I work," thought he, "when I have a father-in-law who makes dollars of seashells?"

Presently his share was spent. He spent it all upon fine clothes. And then he was sorry:

"For," thought he, "I had done better to have bought a concertina, with which I might have entertained myself all day long." And then he began to grow vexed with Kalamake.

"This man has the soul of a dog," thought he. "He can gather dollars when he pleases on the beach, and he leaves me to pine for a concertina! Let him beware: I am no child, I am as cunning as he, and hold his secret." With that he spoke to his wife Lehua, and complained of her father's manners.

"I would let my father be," said Lehua. "He is a dangerous man to cross."

"I care that for him!" cried Keola; and snapped his fingers. "I have him by the nose. I can make him do what I please." And he told Lehua the story. But she shook her head.

"You may do what you like," said she; "but as sure as you thwart my father, you will be no more heard of. Think of this person, and that person; think of Hua, who was a noble of the House of Representatives, and went to Honolulu every year: and not a bone or a hair of him was found. Remember Kamau, and how he wasted to a thread, so that his wife lifted him with one hand. Keola, you are a baby in my father's hands; he will take you with his thumb and finger and eat you like a shrimp."

Now Keola was truly afraid of Kalamake, but he was vain too; and these words of his wife's incensed him.

"Very well," said he, "if that is what you think of me, I will show how much you are deceived." And he went straight to his father-in-law.

"Kalamake," said he, "I want a concertina."

"Do you, indeed?" said Kalamake.

"Yes," said he, "and I may as well tell you plainly, I mean to have it. A man who picks up dollars on the beach can certainly afford a concertina."

"I had no idea you had so much spirit," replied the sorcerer. "I thought you were a timid, useless lad, and I cannot describe how much pleased I am to find I was mistaken. Now I begin to think I may have found an assistant and successor in my difficult business. A concertina? You shall have the best in Honolulu. And tonight, as soon as it is dark, you and I will go and find the money."

"Shall we return to the beach?" asked Keola.

"No, no!" replied Kalamake; "you must begin to learn more of my secrets. Last time I taught you to pick shells; this time I shall teach you to catch fish. Are you strong enough to launch Pili's boat?"

"I think I am," returned Keola. "But why should we not take your own?"

"I have a reason which you will understand thoroughly before tomorrow," said Kalamake. "Pili's boat is the better suited for my purpose. So, if you please, let us meet there as soon as it is dark; and in the meanwhile, let us keep our own counsel, for there is no cause to let the family into our business."

Honey is not more sweet than was the voice of Kalamake, and Keola could scarce contain his satisfaction.

"I might have had my concertina weeks ago," thought he, "and there is nothing needed in this world but a little courage." Presently after he spied Lehua weeping, and was half in a mind to tell her all was well.

"But no," thinks he; "I shall wait till I can show her the concertina; we shall see what the chit will do then. Perhaps she will understand in the future that her husband is a man of some intelligence."

As soon as it was dark father and son-in-law launched Pili's boat and set the sail. There was a great sea, and it blew strong from the leeward; but the boat was swift and light and dry, and skimmed the waves. The wizard had a lantern, which he lit and held with his finger through the ring, and the two sat in the stern and smoked cigars, of which Kalamake had always a provision, and spoke like friends of magic and the great sums of money which they could make by its exercise, and what they should buy first, and what second; and Kalamake talked like a father.

Presently he looked all about, and above him at the stars, and back at the island, which was already three parts sunk under the sea, and he seemed to consider ripely his position.

"Look!" says he, "there is Molokai already far behind us, and Maui like a cloud; and by the bearing of these three stars I know I am come to where I desire. This part of the sea is called the Sea of the Dead. It is in this place extraordinarily deep, and the floor is all covered with the bones of men, and in the holes of this part gods and goblins keep their habitation. The flow of the sea is to the north, stronger than a shark can swim, and any man who shall here be thrown out of a ship it bears away like a wild horse into the uttermost ocean. Presently he is spent and goes down, and his bones are scattered with the rest, and the gods devour his spirit."

Fear came on Keola at the words, and he looked, and by the light of the stars and the lantern, the warlock seemed to change.

"What ails you?" cried Keola, quick and sharp.

"It is not I who am ailing," said the wizard; "but there is one here sick."

With that he changed his grasp upon the lantern, and, behold —as he drew his finger from the ring, the finger stuck and the ring was burst, and his hand was grown to be the bigness of three.

At that sight Keola screamed and covered his face.

But Kalamake held up the lantern. "Look rather at my face!" said he—and his head was huge as a barrel; and still he grew and grew as a cloud grows on a mountain, and Keola sat before him screaming, and the boat raced on the great seas.

"And now," said the wizard, "what do you think about that concertina? and are you sure you would not rather have a flute? No?" says he; "that is well, for I do not like my family to be changeable of purpose. But I begin to think I had better get out of this paltry boat, for my bulk swells to a very unusual degree, and if we are not the more careful, she will presently be swamped."

With that he threw his legs over the side. Even as he did so, the greatness of the man grew thirty-fold and forty-fold as swift as sight or thinking, so that he stood in the deep sea to the armpits, and his head and shoulders rose like the high isle, and the swell beat and burst upon his bosom, as it beats and breaks against a cliff. The boat ran still to the north, but he reached out his hand, and took the gunwale by the finger and thumb, and broke the side like a biscuit, and Keola was spilled into the sea. And the pieces of the boat the sorcerer crushed in the hollow of his hand and flung miles away into the night.

"Excuse me taking the lantern," said he; "for I have a long wade before me, and the land is far, and the bottom of the sea uneven, and I feel the bones under my toes."

And he turned and went off walking with great strides; and as soon as Keola sank in the trough he could see him no longer; but as often as he was heaved upon the crest, there he was striding and dwindling, and he held the lamp high over his head, and the waves broke white about him.

Since first the islands were fished out of the sea, there was never a man so terrified as this Keola. He swam indeed, but he swam as puppies swim when they are cast in to drown, and knew not wherefore. He could but think of the hugeness of the swelling of the warlock, of that face which was great as a mountain, of those shoulders that were broad as an isle, and of the seas that beat on them in vain. He thought, too, of the concertina, and shame took hold upon him; and of the dead men's bones, and fear shook him.

Of a sudden he was aware of something dark against the stars that tossed, and a light below, and a brightness of the cloven sea; and he heard speech of men. He cried out aloud and a voice answered; and in a twinkling the bows of a ship hung above him on a wave like a thing balanced, and swooped down. He caught with his two hands in the chains of her, and the next moment was buried in the rushing seas, and the next hauled on board by seamen.

They gave him gin and biscuit and dry clothes, and asked him how he came where they found him, and whether the light which they had seen was the lighthouse, Lae o Ka Laau. But Keola knew white men are like children and only believe their own stories; so about himself he told them what he pleased, and as for the light (which was Kalamake's lantern) he vowed he had seen none.

This ship was a schooner bound for Honolulu, and then to trade in the low islands; and by a very good chance for Keola she had lost a man off the bowsprit in a squall. It was no use talking. Keola durst not stay in the Eight Islands. Word goes so quickly, and all men are so fond to talk and carry news, that if he hid in the north end of Kauai or in the south end of Kaü, the wizard would have wind of it before a month, and he must perish. So he did what seemed the most prudent, and shipped sailor in the place of the man who had been drowned.

In some ways the ship was a good place. The food was extraordinarily rich and plenty, with biscuits and salt beef every day, and pea soup and puddings made of flour and suet twice a week, so that Keola grew fat. The captain also was a good man, and the crew no worse than other whites. The trouble was the mate, who was the most difficult man to please Keola had ever met with, and beat and cursed him daily, both for what he did and what he did not. The blows that he dealt were very sure, for he was strong; and the words he used were very unpalatable, for Keola was come of a good family and accustomed to respect. And what was the worst of all, whenever Keola found a chance to sleep, there was the mate awake and stirring him up with a rope's end. Keola saw it would never do; and he made up his mind to run away.

They were about a month out from Honolulu when they made the land. It was a fine starry night, the sea was smooth as well as the sky fair; it blew a steady trade; and there was the island on their weather bow, a ribbon of palm trees lying flat along the sea. The captain and the mate looked at it with the night glass, and named the name of it, and talked of it, beside the wheel where Keola was steering. It seemed it was an isle where no traders came. By the captain's way, it was an isle besides where no man dwelt; but the mate thought otherwise.

"I don't give a cent for the directory," said he. "I've been past here one night in the schooner *Eugenie:* it was just such a night as this; they were fishing with torches, and the beach was thick with lights like a town."

"Well, well," says the captain, "it's steep-to, that's the great point; and there ain't any outlying dangers by the chart, so we'll just hug the lee side of it. Keep her ramping full, don't I tell you!" he cried to Keola, who was listening so hard that he forgot to steer.

And the mate cursed him, and swore that Kanaka was for no use in the world, and if he got started after him with a belaying-pin, it would be a cold day for Keola. And so the captain and mate lay down on the house together, and Keola was left to himself.

"This island will do very well for me," he thought, "if no traders deal there, the mate will never come. And as for Kalamake, it is not possible he can ever get as far as this."

With that he kept edging the schooner nearer in. He had to do this quietly, for it was the trouble with these white men, and above all with the mate, that you could never be sure of them; they would all be sleeping sound, or else pretending, and if a sail shook, they would jump to their feet and fall on you with a rope's end. So Keola edged her up little by little, and kept all drawing. And presently the land was close on board.

With that, the mate sat up suddenly upon the house.

"What are you doing?" he roars. "You'll have the ship ashore!"

And he made one bound for Keola, and Keola made another clean over the rail and plump into the starry sea. When he came up again, the schooner had payed off on her true course and the mate stood by the wheel himself, and Keola heard him cursing. The sea was smooth under the lee of the island; it was warm besides, and Keola had his sailor's knife, so he had no fear of sharks. A little way before him the trees stopped; there was a break in the line of the land like the mouth of a harbor; and the tide, which was then flowing, took him up and carried him through. One minute he was without, and the next within, had floated there in a wide shallow water, bright with ten thousand stars, and all about him was the ring of the land with its string of palm trees.

The time of Keola in that place was in two periods—the period when he was alone, and the period when he was there with the tribe. At first he sought everywhere and found no man; only some houses standing in a hamlet, and the marks of fires. But the ashes of the fires were cold and the rains had washed them away; and the winds had blown, and some of the huts were overthrown. It was here he took his dwelling; and he made a fire drill, and a shell hook, and fished and cooked his fish, and climbed after green cocoanuts, the juice of which he drank, for in all the isle there was no water. The days were long for him, and the nights terrifying. He made a lamp of cocoa-shell, and drew the oil off the ripe nuts, and made a wick of fiber; and when evening came he closed up his hut, and lit his lamp, and lay and trembled till morning. Many a time he thought in his heart he would have been better in the bottom of the sea, his bones rolling there with the others.

All this while he kept by the inside of the island, for the huts were on the shore of the lagoon, and it was there the palms grew best, and the lagoon itself abounded with good fish. And to the outer side he went once only, and he looked but once at the beach of the ocean, and came away shaking. For the look of it, with its bright sand, and strewn shells, and strong sun and surf, went sore against his inclination.

"It cannot be," he thought, "and yet it is very like. And how do I know? These white men, although they pretend to know where they are sailing, must take their chances like other people. So that after all we have sailed in a circle, and I may be quite near to Molokai, and this may be the very beach where my father-in-law gathers his dollars."

It was perhaps a month later, when the people of the place arrived—the fill of six great boats. They were a fine race of men, and spoke a tongue that sounded very different from the tongue of Hawaii, but so many of the words were the same that it was not difficult to understand. The men besides were very courteous, and the women very towardly; and they made Keola welcome, and built him a house, and gave him a wife; and what surprised him the most, he was never sent to work with the young men.

And now Keola had three periods. First he had a period of being very sad, and then he had a period when he was pretty merry. Last of all, came the third, when he was the most terrified man in the four oceans.

The cause of the first period was the girl he had to wife. He was in doubt about the island, and he might have been in doubt about the speech, of which he had heard so little when he came there with the wizard on the mat. But about his wife there was no mistake conceivable, for she was the same girl that ran from him crying in the wood. So he had sailed all this way, and might as well have stayed in Molokai; and had left home and wife and all his friends for no other cause but to escape his enemy, and the place he had come to was that wizard's hunting ground, and the place where he walked invisible. It was at this period when he kept the most close to the lagoon side, and as far as he dared, abode in the cover of his hut.

The cause of the second period was talk he had heard from his wife and the chief islanders. Keola himself said little. He was never so sure of his new friends, for he judged they were too civil to be wholesome, and since he had grown better acquainted with his father-in-law the man had grown more cautious. So he told them nothing of himself, but only his name and descent, and that he came from the Eight Islands, and what fine islands they were; and about the king's palace in Honolulu, and how he was a chief friend of the king and the missionaries. But he put many questions and learned much. The island where he was was called the Isle of Voices; it belonged to the tribe, but they made their home upon another, three hours' sail to the southward. There they lived and had their permanent houses, and it was a rich island, where were eggs and chickens and pigs, and ships came trading with rum and tobacco. It was there the schooner had gone after Keola deserted; there, too, the mate had died, like the fool of a white man he was. It seems, when the ship came, it was the beginning of the sickly season in that isle, when the fish of the lagoon are poisonous, and all who eat of them swell up and die. The mate was told of it; he saw the boats preparing, because in that season the people leave that island and sail to the Isle of Voices; but he was a fool of a white man, who would believe no stories but his own, and he caught one of these fish, cooked it and ate it, and swelled up and died, which was good news to Keola. As for the Isle of Voices, it lay solitary the most of the year, only now and then a boat's crew came for copra, and in the bad season, when the fish at the main isle were poisonous, the tribe dwelt there in a body. It had its name from a marvel, for it seemed the seaside of it was all beset with invisible devils; day and night you heard them talking with one another in strange tongues; day and night little fires blazed up and were extinguished on the beach; and what was the cause of these doings no man might conceive. Keola asked them if it were the same in their own island where they stayed, and they told him no, not there; nor yet in any other of some hundred isles that lay all about them in that sea; but it was a thing peculiar to the Isle of Voices. They told him also that these fires and voices were ever on the seaside and in the seaward fringes of the wood, and a man might dwell by the lagoon two thousand years (if he could live so long) and never be any way troubled; and even on the seaside the devils did no harm if let alone. Only once a chief had cast a spear at one of the voices, and the same night he fell out of a cocoanut palm and was killed.

Keola thought a good bit with himself. He saw he would be all right when the tribe returned to the main island, and right enough where he was, if he kept by the lagoon, yet he had a mind to make things righter if he could. So he told the high chief he had once been in an isle that was pestered the same way, and the folk had found a means to cure that trouble.

"There was a tree growing in the bush there," says he, "and it seems these devils came to get the leaves of it. So the people of the isle cut down the tree wherever it was found, and the devils came no more."

They asked what kind of a tree this was, and he showed them the tree of which Kalamake burned the leaves. They found it hard to believe, yet the idea tickled them. Night after night the old men debated it in their councils, but the high chief (though he was a brave man) was afraid of the matter, and reminded them daily of the chief who cast a spear against the voices and was killed, and the thought of that brought all to a stand again.

Though he could not yet bring about the destruction of the trees, Keola was well enough pleased, and began to look about him and take pleasure in his days; and, among other things, he was the kinder to his wife, so that the girl began to love him greatly. One day he came to the hut, and she lay on the ground lamenting.

"Why," said Keola, "what is wrong with you now?"

She declared it was nothing.

The same night she woke him, and he saw by her face she was in sorrow.

"Keola," she said, "put your ear to my mouth that I may whisper, for no one must hear us. Two days before the boats begin to be got ready, go you to the seaside of the isle and lie in a thicket. We shall choose that place beforehand, you and I; and hide food; and every night I shall come near by there singing. So when a night comes and you do not hear me, you may know we are clean gone out of the island, and you may come forth again."

The soul of Keola died within him.

"What is this?" he cried. "I cannot live among devils. I will not be left behind upon this isle. I am dying to leave it."

"You will never leave it alive, my poor Keola," said the girl; "for to tell you the truth, my people are eaters of men; but this they keep secret. And the reason they will kill you before we leave is because in our island ships come, and Donat-Kimaran comes and talks for the French, and there is a white trader there in a house with a verandah, and a catechist. Oh, that is a fine place indeed! The trader has barrels filled with flour; and a French warship once came in the lagoon and gave everybody wine and biscuit. Ah, my poor Keola, I wish I could take you there, for great is my love to you, and it is the finest place in the seas except Papeete."

So now Keola was the most terrified man in the four oceans. He had heard tell of eaters of men in the south islands, and the thing had always been a fear to him; and here it was knocking at his door. He had heard besides, by travelers, of their practices, and how when they are in a mind to eat a man, they cherish and fondle him like a mother with a favorite baby. And he saw this must be his own case; and that was why he had been housed, and fed, and wived, and liberated from all work; and why the old men and the chiefs discoursed with him like a person of weight. So he lay on his bed and railed upon his destiny; and the flesh curdled on his bones.

The next day the people of the tribe were very civil, as their way was. They were elegant speakers, and they made beautiful poetry, and jested at meals, so that a missionary must have died laughing. It was little enough Keola cared for their fine ways: all he saw was the white teeth shining in their mouths, and his gorge rose at the sight; and when they were done eating, he went and lay in the bush like a dead man.

The next day it was the same, and then his wife followed him.

"Keola," she said, "if you do not eat, I tell you plainly you will be killed and cooked tomorrow. Some of the old chiefs are murmuring already. They think you are fallen sick and must lose flesh."

With that Keola got to his feet, and anger burned in him.

"It is little I care one way or the other," said he. "I am between the devil and the deep sea. Since die I must, let me die the quickest way; and since I must be eaten at the best of it, let me rather be eaten by hobgoblins than by men. Farewell," said he, and walked to the seaside of that island.

It was all bare in the strong sun; there was no sign of man, only the beach was trodden, and all about him as he went, the voices talked and whispered, and the little fires sprang up and burned down. All tongues of the earth were spoken there: the French, the Dutch, the Russian, the Tamil, the Chinese. Whatever land knew sorcery, there were some of its people whispering in Keola's ear. That beach was thick as a cried fair, yet no man seen; and as he walked he saw the shells vanish before him, and no man to pick them up. I think the devil would have been afraid to be alone in such a company; but Keola was past fear and courted death. When the fires sprang up, he charged for them like a bull. Bodiless voices called to and fro; unseen hands poured sand upon the flames; and they were gone from the beach before he reached them.

"It is plain Kalamake is not here," he thought, "as I must have been killed long since."

With that he sat him down in the margin of the wood, for he was tired, and put his chin upon his hands. The business before his eyes continued; the beach babbled with voices, and the fires sprang up and sank, and the shells vanished and were renewed again even while he looked.

"It was a by-day when I was here before," he thought, "for it was nothing to this."

And his head was dizzy with the thought of these millions and millions of dollars, and all these hundreds and hundreds of persons culling them upon the beach, and flying in the air higher and swifter than eagles.

"And to think how they have fooled me with their talk of mints," says he, "and that money was made there, when it is clear that all the new coin in all the world is gathered on these sands! But I will know better the next time!" said he. And at last, he knew not very well how or when, sleep fell on Keola, and he forgot the island and all his sorrows.

Early the next day, before the sun was yet up, a bustle woke him. He awoke in fear, for he thought the tribe had caught him napping; but it was no such matter. Only, on the beach in front of him, the bodiless voices called and shouted one upon another, and it seemed they all passed and swept beside him up the coast of the island.

"What is afoot now?" thinks Keola. And it was plain to him it was something beyond ordinary, for the fires were not lighted nor the shells taken, but the bodiless voices kept posting up the beach, and hailing and dying away; and by the sound of them these wizards should be angry.

"It is not me they are angry at," thought Keola, "for they pass me close."

As when hounds go by, or horses in a race, or city folk coursing to a fire, and all men join and follow after, so it was now with Keola; and he knew not what he did, nor why he did it, but there, lo and behold! he was running with the voices.

So he turned one point of the island, and this brought him in view of a second; and there he remembered the wizard trees to have been growing by the score together in a wood. From this

point there went up a hubbub of men crying not to be described;
and by the sound of them, those that he ran with shaped their
course for the same quarter. A little nearer, and there began to
mingle with the outcry the crash of many axes. And at this a
thought came at last into his mind that the high chief had consented; that the men of the tribe had set to cutting down these
trees; that word had gone about the isle from sorcerer to sorcerer, and these were all now assembling to defend their trees.
Desire of strange things swept him on. He posted with the
voices, crossed the beach, and came into the borders of the
wood, and stood astonished. One tree had fallen, others were
part hewed away. There was the tribe clustered. They were back
to back, and bodies lay, and blood flowed among their feet. The
hue of fear was on all their faces; their voices went up to heaven
shrill as a weasel's cry.

Have you seen a child when he is all alone and has a wooden
sword, and fights, leaping and hewing with the empty air? Even
so the man-eaters huddled back to back and heaved up their
axes and laid on, and screamed as they laid on, and behold! no
man to contend with them! only here and there Keola saw an axe
swinging over against them without hands; and time and again
a man of the tribe would fall before it, clove in twain or burst
asunder, and his soul sped howling.

For a while Keola looked upon this prodigy like one that
dreams, and then fear took him by the midst as sharp as death,
that he should behold such doings. Even in that same flash the
high chief of the clan espied him standing, and pointed and
called out his name. Thereat the whole tribe saw him also, and
their eyes flashed, and their teeth clashed.

"I am too long here," thought Keola, and ran farther out of
the wood and down the beach, not caring whither.

"Keola!" said a voice close by upon the empty sand.

"Lehua! is that you!" he cried, and gasped, and looked in vain
for her; but by the eyesight he was stark alone.

"I saw you pass before," the voice answered; "but you would
not hear me. Quick! get the leaves and the herbs, and let us
flee."

"You are there with the mat?" he asked.

"Here, at your side," said she. And felt her arms about him. "Quick! the leaves and the herbs, before my father can get back!"

So Keola ran for his life, and fetched the wizard fuel; and Lehua guided him back, and set his feet upon the mat, and made the fire. All the time of its burning, the sound of the battle towered out of the wood; the wizards and the man-eaters hard at fight; the wizards, the viewless ones, roaring out aloud like bulls upon a mountain, and the men of the tribe replying shrill and savage out of the terror of their souls. And all the time of the burning, Keola stood there and listened, and shook, and watched how the unseen hands of Lehua poured the leaves. She poured them fast, and the flame burned high, and scorched Keola's hands, and she speeded and blew the burning with her breath. The last leaf was eaten, the flame fell, and the shock followed, and there were Keola and Lehua in the room at home.

Now, when Keola could see his wife at last he was mighty pleased, and he was mighty pleased to be home again in Molokai and sit down beside a bowl of poi—for they made no poi on board ships, and there was none in the Isle of Voices—and he was out of the body with pleasure to be clean escaped out of the hands of the eaters of men. But there was another matter not so clear, and Lehua and Keola talked of it all night and were troubled. There was Kalamake left upon the isle. If, by the blessing of God, he could but stick there, all were well: but should he escape and return to Molokai, it would be an ill day for his daughter and her husband. They spoke of his gift of swelling and whether he could wade that distance in the seas. But Keola knew by this time where that island was—and that is to say, in the Low or Dangerous Archipelago. So they fetched the atlas and looked upon the distance in the map, and by what they could make of it, it seemed a far way for an old gentleman to walk. Still, it would not do to make too sure of a warlock like Kalamake, and they determined at last to take counsel of a white missionary.

So the first one that came by Keola told him everything. And the missionary was very sharp on him for taking the second wife in the low island; but for all the rest, he vowed he could make neither head nor tail of it.

"However," says he, "if you think this money of your father's ill-gotten, my advice to you would be to give some of it to the lepers and some to the missionary fund. And as for this extraordinary rigmarole, you cannot do better than keep it to yourselves." But he warned the police at Honolulu that, by all he could make out, Kalamake and Keola had been coining false money, and it would not be amiss to watch them.

Keola and Lehua took his advice, and gave many dollars to the lepers and the fund. And no doubt the advice must have been good, for from that day to this, Kalamake has never more been heard of. But whether he was slain in the battle by the trees, or whether he is still kicking his heels upon the Isle of Voices, who shall say?

POWERS
OF DARKNESS

by JOHN RUSSELL

Some men never learn, it seems. This seems especially true of those who travel far from their "civilized" homelands to take up residence among primitive cultures, usually for the purpose of exploitation; men who strip away their own veneer of civilization and revert to attitudes and actions far more atavistic than those of the natives. The antagonist in "Powers of Darkness," Dobel, is such a man, and Papua, New Guinea, in the early 1900s is such a place.

But Dobel makes the mistake of underestimating a certain native sorcerer at Warange Station. The sorcerer's magic is great: he can turn pandanus seeds into yellow and crimson moths and then make them melt away into the shadows; he can bring a dead crocodile back to life merely by stroking it from head to tail. And even greater are the powers of darkness, particularly when a brutish nonbeliever like Dobel makes it necessary to call on them. The result is as satisfying as it is strange.

John Russell was a master of the wry, suspenseful and unusual adventure tale, of which "Powers of Darkness" is a fine example. (He also wrote excellent popular and crime fiction.) Born in Iowa in 1885, he wandered the world during the first few decades of this century and spent a considera-

ble amount of time in the South Seas, where many of his staggering total of sixteen hundred short stories are set. The best of his work has been favorably compared to that of Kipling and O. Henry and can be found in such collections as The Red Mark *(a.k.a.* Where the Pavement Ends*),* Cops 'n Robbers, In Dark Places, *and* Far Wandering Men. *During and after World War II he wrote and adapted scripts for several Hollywood film companies, and continued writing until his death in 1956.*

NICKERSON, R.M., failed in judgment concerning his guest Dobel. This was the reason of his ordeal that night at Warange Station: a black night and a bitter ordeal. If Dobel had been a cannibal or a headhunter—wandering thief or fugitive murderer—Nickerson would have made no mistake. But himself he was a gentle soul, trained merely in all forms of conceivable wickedness, and although he disliked the gross stranger with the sly and slitted red eyes he had no intimation of the fellow's real nature. Not until Dobel showed such an utterly brutal manner of disbelief.

At the very first demonstration of the native Sorcerer—at the very first piece of native magic which Nickerson had been at diplomatic pains to stage and arrange for him—Dobel grabbed an empty beer bottle. "You black-faced swine. Dried shark liver!" he rumbled. "Try and fool me with your dam' faking tricks, will you?"

He made a motion as if to crown the Sorcerer, kneeling quietly there on the mat beside them, when Nickerson let out a cry, involuntary. "For God's sake, stop it, Dobel. Stop it—I say, you drunken idiot. . . . The man's my friend!"

Evidently Dobel had not really meant it just then: it was rather his line of humor, his revealing gesture. For he stopped and put down the bottle and leaned back in his chair again, with a grunt.

The two white men were sitting at dinner in Nickerson's palisaded station at the far end of the world. By way of information,

the far end of the world is Papua. This is not only geographic,
it is also entirely authentic, being well known to everybody who
has survived it in person. Papua remains the last mystery on this
big round globe. It remains largely impenetrable and unpene-
trated beyond a coastal strip and a few gold mines. It remains
an active hell of heat, fever, violence and sudden death. In fact,
it remains . . . Whenever a hard-working explorer casts about for
some place to get lost and to write his next book, he considers
Papua on the map and then goes somewhere else.

However: Nickerson was used to it. For some years he had
been what is called a "Resident Magistrate" in the nominal
government thereabouts. This meant that he personated the
whole British Empire over a theoretical "District" of monstrous
mountains and reeking jungles. It also meant that he was supposed to control various unconquered tribes of large, muscular
and extremely serious-minded black gentlemen who have been
cannibals and headhunters from time immemorial and who see
no particular reason why they should change their habits at the
behest of strange armed intruders. As if messengers from Mars
should suddenly descend upon us and make us all eat grass. But
Nickerson had done very well. With his handful of native police
he had won his wilder charges to a moderate righteousness. He
liked his work: yes, and he liked his black folk, because he respected them as lost ancestors of ours left over from the Stone
Age, with many singular gifts and virtues of their own. So they
in turn respected him, and even obeyed him sometimes.

Dobel. . . . Well, Dobel was quite a different person. Nickerson
had received him as he did all dispensations, with the same
kindly simplicity, and with no more than a vague suspicion that
there occurs from time to time such sort of commercial adventurer for the chastening of every colonial administrator—inevitable as the worm in a walnut. Arriving from nowhere, equipped
with credentials, a brazen assurance and an unholy familiarity
with the waterfront dives and lingos of a dozen tropical ports,
Dobel had announced himself a coffee planter proposing to
develop the country. In which capacity, of course, he could claim
aid, hospitality and protection at Nickerson's station of Wa-

range. This he managed off-hand, and meanwhile conveyed without too much subtlety an opinion of his host, his host's ideas, methods and general worth that might have provoked the mildest man. But Nickerson—poor chap!—he was the mildest man. And thus one word leading to another, and because after all they were the only two whites (outside the Brothers at Warange Mission) in a howling wilderness together, the little R.M. had finally invited his uninvited guest to the private proof and demonstration as hereinbefore stated.

He was already sorry for it. He was due to be a great deal sorrier. . . .

"Make him do it again."

"That's not quite fair, is it?" protested Nickerson.

"Didn't you say you'd show me some native stuff I couldn't explain?"

"I did. And you couldn't. And many others have tried—and couldn't."

"Well, you called him a friend," sneered Dobel. "Is he afraid to try it over?"

All this while the Sorcerer had stayed resting on his mat beside the table. Certainly there never was a sorcerer less under implication that he should roll up his sleeves. Naked except for a bark strip about his middle, he resembled some image in polished basalt from before the days of Egypt. Anywhere else he would have been amazing: here he was magnificent, with the features of an ancient Assyrian king—the hooked nose of power and the mouth of imperious pride. He stayed motionless and inscrutable, as becomes a high chief and a master of magic in Papua, until at Nickerson's quiet word again he proceeded to oblige.

Now, his magic was this:

Taking in his hands a few loose seeds of pandanus, with appropriate incantation he tossed them sharply into the lamplight. There they hung suspended an instant, when they took miraculous life of their own, spreading the wings of yellow and crimson moths that fluttered and circled as a brilliant flake-storm—melting away at last with the shadows.

At least, so it seemed, and the seeming was a gracious and a harmless fancy.

Perhaps such qualities were especially irritating to Dobel. Perhaps one of those synthetic insects flipped past and made him jump. Or perhaps the true animus of the man lay bedded in something deeper, of which his skepticism was merely the fat layer. At any rate, he liked it no better than the first time: once more he flushed with evil anger.

"Dam' blasted faker! Pig-snout—" he began to growl. But once more he checked abruptly: and this time for a very special reason.

A new and surprising figure had just glided in between the bead curtains of the inner verandah, carrying a tray with their next relay of drink.

Through their meal together the two white men had been waited upon by Nickerson's houseboys: rough-handed and half-tamed products of the cannibal frontier. But this was a girl! A girl, and the like of a girl to draw the bloodshot gaze of any Dobel, East or West. "What—ho!" he gurgled.

A native girl in a white man's house?

What made it better (or worse), she was attractive by any standard: slim and lithe. She wore a single white garment of the sort supplied by missionary enterprise for the suppression, one supposes, of the female form divine. But this garment had been often laundered, and if its effect was not displeasing the young lady herself seemed not unaware. No. If old Mother Hubbard had garbed her, old Mother Eve had endowed this copper-bronze child of hers with something much more elemental. It showed in the provocative face with sweeping lashes. It showed in the willing grace with which she leaned over to pour Dobel's glass. Timidly. Yet not too timidly, either. . . .

Well, of course there are things that merely happen, and there are other things that merely are not done. All depends upon how you look at them and how much you know. And who should know better than Dobel, who seemed to know everything?

"Well, *well*—!" he murmured, very softly, for him. He looked with great favor. He looked with very particular favor. Nickerson was paying the girl no attention whatsoever. Neither was the Sorcerer. Which left Dobel her sole appreciator.

He was highly appreciative. He watched while she filled the drinks. He watched and let his slow gaze run along the smoothly perfect contour of cheek and arm. He continued to watch when she moved noiselessly away to the bead curtains, and there paused to flash back a look at the gross white man that made him wet his thick lips and chuckle in his thick throat. . . . Nevertheless it was his further humor to say nothing about her—to make no comment. Not yet. When he did speak, he was grinning.

"Ah. Very pretty. But it's only tricks."

"You saw what he did?"

"I saw something. But I hate to be fooled by a nigger. No—nor anybody else!" added Dobel, with a red glint. "Nobody fools me much!"

"Dobel—" Nickerson was almost pathetic. "It's my job to steer you through and make you successful, and all that. But if you're going to stay in this country you'll have to change your way with these people. One thing: you must never use that word. They're not—what you said. They're not a subject race at all. And we hold them none too safe, if you know what that means. . . . Heavens, man—you can't hit a native!"

"No?" drawled the other. "You can't hit 'em. And you can't love 'em either, maybe?"

"That's true."

"I've heard a lot of such talk. . . . It don't mean a blasted thing."

"It means we're dealing with one of the most powerful chiefs —a gentleman in his own fashion. It means he has to be treated properly."

Dobel gave a bark of amusement. "Listen: I've dealt with all shades of natives, black to pea-green—for twenty years. D'you think you can teach me anything? If you do—carry on with the show!"

Nickerson hesitated. He had lived too long in the unaccountable spaces of the earth: he had forgotten how to account for a type like Dobel. He served a friendless Service, devil-ridden by political amateurs (Papua is not a Crown Colony, worse luck!). But, poor pay and all, he needed his place for his family back home. What if this annoying, accredited guest should start up complaints at headquarters? The mere thought gave him a shiver familiar to every empire-builder. Did people really act so? As a matter of fact, he could not tell: any more than he could judge just how drunk Dobel might be: any more than he could gauge the precise peril behind those sly and slitted eyes. At the present moment the fellow seemed not too awfully drunken— he was keeping a grin quite amiable with his gaze fixed over yonder toward the curtains somewhere. . . .

All of which will indicate the perplexity of Nickerson, R.M., and the reason of his mistake, as aforesaid. For presently he consulted again with the Sorcerer. (It was curious how he gained ease and confidence with that language.)

"I'm sorry, Dobel," he announced at last. "The old boy doesn't much fancy you."

"No?"

"No. He says if men like you had been the only white men in Papua, he would own a lot of fine smoked heads. . . . I'm quoting his drift."

"Yes?"

"Yes. And for that reason, as nearly as I can make out, he is willing to show you just one more thing you *can't* explain."

"Carry on," repeated Dobel.

Now, the only visible possessions of the Sorcerer were these: on one side of him his keen little belt-axe, and on the other his grass-woven sack. The weapon he had discarded in courtesy. The sack he kept for his oddments and conjuring stuff—his bag o' tricks, so to speak.

From out of that bag he dragged forth next an object which he threw with a limp flop on the mat before them. Not a pleasing object. It was a baby crocodile about ten inches long, and quite evidently it had passed some time ago from this crocodile vale of tears. It was already blue, the scales loosening from it. "He wants you to be sure this creature is dead," explained Nickerson.

"Faugh! . . . Guess I know a dead croc!"

"You're sure?"

"Of course," growled Dobel.

"Then hold tight," said Nickerson.

The Sorcerer exhibited a fragment of ordinary greenstone, delicately shaped, about the size of an arrowhead. Taking it between finger and thumb like a pencil, he began carefully to stroke the point. Then very gently, very slowly, he stroked the crocodile from head to tail. Some way, but in the way of an artist, he brought to that fantastic employ a silent suspense that grew and grew almost tangibly. Kneeling there in the aura of light, the big black man stroked gently—gently. And slowly—slowly, the result appeared on the dead animal. A pulsation ran through its flanks. Its scales brightened to a pallid green, firmed and quivered. All at once its sunken lids lifted on two gleaming, pinpricked nodules. It stood propped on its four legs. And at the final touch—impossibly, unbelievably—with a flirt and a whisk it rattled over the mattings and was gone! The thump of its escape outside made an end to that manifestation—also an end to Dobel's restraint.

He rose with a roar. He wanted no bottle this time. All he used was his fist, and a fist cruel as a knotted club, and he swung it with scientific impact squarely to the jaw.

Like a cloud across the moon, like the dark wind that slashes some sunny beach, so quickly they turned from comedy to tragedy—never far apart anywhere, it may be, but surely never as close as in this strange, deep and untamed land: tragicomedy and tragedy not very comic in Papua. . . .

"Good God!" Nickerson whispered.

As if stricken by the same foul blow he dropped on one knee by the victim who lay limp and helpless as any crocodile, an inert heap. "You beast. . . . You unspeakable beast!"

Dobel stayed straddled. "That's a' right. 'S only a sleep punch."

"How—*how* could you!"

"Time enough, too. I told you nobody was making a fool of me."

"Fool—? Have you any sense of what you've done? All his

fighting men are camped outside the gates. Enough to swamp us, and the whole district! . . . Death is out there. *Death!*"

True, in the hush they might have been aware of Papua around them, stirring in the night. From the savage camp came the soft throb of a tom-tom, like the beating of a heart. A sigh passed in the jungle, stealthy and sinister—a hot breath that is like nothing except a tiger's throat.

But it meant nothing to Dobel—he only stayed grinning—and the sight of his hateful, impervious sneer was more than Nickerson could stand: it drove him near to madness. "Besides—when I—when I said he was my friend!" he half-sobbed, and simply threw himself at the fellow. Another mistake and about the worst possible, of course, though doubtless the sort Dobel had been playing for. Gleefully he took the little R.M., twisted him easily as a banana stalk, slammed him against the wall.

Appalled—almost stunned—still Nickerson made the proper official effort. "That stops it, Dobel. You're going out of here. I'll have you deported. On the coasting-steamer tomorrow. . . . Consider yourself under arrest, sir!" With a shaking hand he felt for the police whistle on a cord about his neck.

Before he could touch it, Dobel ripped it away and bulked over him, the whole brutal assurance of the man projected like a cliff.

"*Me* going out? Y' sop and weakling—why, that's exactly what I come to do for *you!* . . .

"You didn't guess it yet? Why, I knew all about you, Mister Resident Magistrate, before I ever started here. Sure. Your record at headquarters: y'r silly reports on native habits and customs and such. Ho!" He gave his bark of laughter. " 'Habits an' customs.' Soon as I saw that, I knew where I'd catch you. Says I, 'Leave him to me. I'll get that dam' nigger-loving R.M. out of there!' "

Dazed—bewildered—still Nickerson was able to ask the proper official question.

" 'Order'?" echoed Dobel. "Order be blowed. No—I ain't in your service. I represent a company that gives their orders to any service. We hold a concession for this distric'. But first we reckoned to be rid of you. And how easy you made it! What? Did you never hear of laws and regulations—Section 89—against 'witchcraft or sorcery, or pretense to same'? And don't I find you promoting sorcery your own silly self, Mister Magistrate Nickerson?"

"You—you wanted it."

"Sure, did I. I wanted to see how much I could pin onto you. And if I needed any more—" Dobel's voice rose to a virtuous bellow. "If that ain't enough—don't I find you here in your own house with a good-lookin' brown girl?"

"Girl? . . . That girl?" stammered the unfortunate R.M. "Why, she's a Mission girl. From Warange Mission. She came over tonight because her father was here. The chief—the Sorcerer—he's her father!"

"Eyewash. D' you think I can't tell that kind? With her free-for-all ways? . . . Another one of your 'native habits,' I suppose!"

Poor Nickerson. "You're wrong. . . . On my honor!" This was what he gasped, and it deserves to live as a tribute to the female persuasion at large: "They only act so. It's—it's nothing against them. Only they can't help themselves—some of 'em!"

Whereat Dobel did laugh.

"My colonial oath. Of all the soft sops! Wait till I tell that for headquarters!"

True enough, it was naïve comedy close to grim tragedy again. True enough, it was Dobel's entire triumph. He laughed. He straddled there, the hateful and conquering fellow, with his red grin directed over Nickerson's shoulder toward the bead curtains. He finished his last drink. He stretched his great arms. "Well, that'll do for entertainment. I'll just be mooching along to my bungalow. . . . I'm taking that steamer tomorrow, you know. . . . Oh. I'll be back. Yes, yes! Only I got to file my report, you see—the report that's going to scupper y'r job for you, Mister Nonresident! Meanwhile, many thanks for the show."

And he swaggered out.

Poor R.M. He was like a man overtaken in a nightmare. It was not so much the insult, the humiliation that had been put upon him. It was not even the inevitable loss of post and pay. What wrung him was his mistake—his failure to judge and to understand the given crisis: as every empire-builder should and must. Did such things really happen? They seemed incredible—far beyond any magic.

This was the ordeal of Nickerson, R.M., when he turned mechanically to attend again on his stricken performer—and found the place empty. The Sorcerer had vanished. . . .

Outside lay Papua, primitive and incalculable: Papua, where mystery and death wait on every move. What could he do? To be sure, he had two armed sentries at the station gate. To be sure, he might rouse the rest of his police from their barrack. What good would his handful be, against Papua? . . . A wind sighed in the swamps and the trees—heady as the essence of vitality—heavy as the scent of a slaughterhouse. From the cannibal camp just beyond his flimsy palisade the tom-tom kept throbbing: and his own pulse kept time with it. Nobody else could have listened with such agony for another sound—like the gather and snarl of a breaking wave. Nobody else could have visioned so vividly the horror that has overwhelmed and blotted in blood so many outposts. (In Papua.)

It was rather with some vague idea of finishing more or less on his own feet with his face in front that he reeled over toward the bead curtains of the verandah and peered through.

A dim glint of moonshine slanted across the parade ground and made visible its sandy strip. And more besides. Something curious, and curiously illuminated and illuminating. Over yonder, by the clump of croton bushes. Over yonder, near the guest bungalow: two figures, interlaced. One a great hulking white man who held clipped in his arms a native woman: the other the slim, thin-garmented native woman who clung quite willingly to the white man. . . .

Well, there are things which happen and there are things which are not done: the burden is in judging them aright even among strange and dark spaces. But in that flash that burden was lifted from Nickerson, R.M. For then he understood, at last. Then it dawned upon him—the real nature of his guest and enemy. Then it came clear, what he had failed to conceive: the wickedness rejecting all belief and all decency—the only actual power of darkness.

A gentle chap, kindly and mild and earnest to the verge of simplicity, so indeed he was, as hereinbefore stated. But then he remembered that he was the administrator responsible for Warange Station. Then he also remembered that he represented in his own person on the pay of a chimney-sweep the whole British Empire. And further, for the first time that night, he remembered the pistol strapped on his thigh! His hand fell to it. As if released with a steel spring in all his slight frame, he took a single jump over the verandah and out onto the parade-ground.

He was just too late. At the same instant Papua had chosen her own tragedy once more. An inky shape rose out of the croton bushes. A polished belt-axe gleamed in the moonlight. . . . A sweeping gesture—a choking cry—and a cloud closing swiftly as a wink.

When Nickerson reached them, the two figures were still interlaced more or less, though rather differently. The man could scarcely hold the woman, sinking from his paralyzed arms. It was Nickerson who received her as she fell, limp and voiceless. It was Nickerson unaided who carried her back the entire distance. Finally it was Nickerson who brought her into his house and laid her carefully on the mat beside his table.

She looked quite handsome, the good-looking native girl—under the lamp. But her fringed lashes were lowered with no provocation now, and her graceful copper-bronze body was now neither timid nor bold, only pitiful and elemental. . . . Nickerson knelt beside it. His hands never shook. His face never altered. He had the deft detachment of any trained surgeon as he made his examination, and straightened up.

"She's dead."

"Good God—!" stammered Dobel.

"I suggest you had better make sure of that fact yourself. . . ."

"How could—how could she be—?"

"Instantaneous, I think. A blow at the base of the skull. But I would ask you to verify."

Dobel? . . . Dobel could verify nothing. The big, gross and

swaggering fellow had gone like a punctured bladder of lard. He was all of a sop of terror: his joints sagging under him, the sweat steaming from his flabby cheeks and the eyes starting in his head. He tried to speak and made no more than whimpering noises in his thick throat.

Nickerson considered him, gauged him with one contemptuous scalpel glance and dismissed him from immediate mind. Nickerson had never been calmer in all his years of work. Icy and aloof, he stayed thinking, with the images and the measures of all his knowledge running clear—everything he had ever learned about his people—everything that had given him his control of cannibal and headhunter, wandering thief and fugitive murderer. And his thoughts followed somewhat along this line:

How had the Sorcerer escaped? To the right, into the crotons. What lay behind him? The palisade, surmountable, but sharp with spikes. What lay in front? The open parade-ground. And to the left—? The gate, and the only exit from Warange. . . . Meanwhile there had been no alarm, and the tom-tom was still drumming quietly outside. . . .

He shifted his pistol to his left hand. He edged with infinite precaution toward the verandah entrance. He poised silently by the curtains. From there, on a venture desperate as the last gasp of a swimmer—necessary as the last leap from under an avalanche—from there he launched himself into outer shadow. And . . . simply plucked forth the black crouching bulk he found in that exact concealment!

The Sorcerer had nothing much to remark: there is little even a Sorcerer can say with the muzzle of eternity pressing against his ear. He had nothing much to do except precisely as he was told: there is little else for anybody when he feels the oiled click of a large-sized automatic pistol jarring into his bones. Besides, as Nickerson explained to him (it was interesting how explicit and convincing the R.M. could be with that language)—besides, the plain choice was between one corpse and two corpses: life or death: just an ordinary matter for adjustment any hour and any minute in Papua.

So presently the Sorcerer was kneeling on the mat again, in

the same spot under the lamplight, as before. And presently he had opened his bag of oddments and conjuring stuff, and had brought out a fragment of greenstone shaped like an arrowhead —as before. And presently, with the subject of his demonstration in proper position—very gently, very slowly—he began to stroke—precisely as before. . . . And thereafter the souls of two white men—watching—were drawn from their roots and whirled upward . . . were tossed and torn in a suspense almost intolerable . . . waiting . . . while they glimpsed the depths of lost and forgotten fantasies in the backward abysm of time. . . .

The garrison of Warange Station are a very smart drill. They have often proved it, and it does them credit, and they are rather swanky about it. They are only a handful of native police. But they have practiced the call to arms, even at midnight, until they can do it generally—starting on the unannounced toot of the whistle—in something close to two minutes. (Nickerson's weekly reports are always meticulous in stating such details.) On this particular occasion it could hardly have been more than a few seconds over the two minutes when the little command stood ready.

The gates had been closed and the sentries doubled. Corporals Arigita and Sione had arrived one pace to the front. Behind them clicked to attention a rank of six privates—kilts, rifles and bandoliers complete. While Sergeant Bio, a prince of noncoms, stepped forward on the verandah before the wide-opened curtains in the lamplight, and saluted.

"Company under arms, *Tabauda!*"

The R.M. inspected them for a moment. They noticed nothing unusual about him. Except perhaps a certain added ring in his tone and a certain stiffening of his parade-ground manner as he snapped his orders.

What he said to the corporals was:

"Sione and Arigita—you see this fella black girl? You walk along with her one time to Mission House. You escort her safe and leave her there!" Whereat the corporals saluted, received their charge and tramped away, stolidly.

What he said to the sergeant was:

"Bio—you see this fella white man here? You take him and lock him in the lock-up. With irons if necessary. Tomorrow he goes by the coast-steamer. And he does not come back!" Whereat Bio saluted, fell in the prisoner between two guards, and started, smartly.

What the prisoner said, as he was led off nearly weeping, was: "Oh God—get me out of here! Take me away from this dam' country. . . . Oh, take me away!"

What Nickerson said to the Sorcerer was little more than a formal apology, ceremoniously delivered, for events that had happened. But what the Sorcerer said to Nickerson in reply deserves to be recorded.

They were alone there in Nickerson's house. The Sorcerer stood proud and inscrutable as a carven Assyrian statue—dignified as becomes a high chief and a master of magic and a gentleman in his own fashion, in Papua. And his answer substantially was this:

"*Tabauda:* nothing has happened. It has been a pleasant evening between friends. I am much honored by my visit. I am gratified if I have entertained you with my poor art. It is my hope that your days may be long in this land—and I would ask your lordly permission to depart!"

From outside in Papua somewhere there sounded the peaceful throbbing of a tom-tom. . . .

EXÚ

by EDWARD D. HOCH

*In Rio de Janeiro and other parts of Brazil, application of the voodoo
form called Macumba is widespread. Spirit cults such as Umbanda, Quimbanda and Candomblé have large followings and even hold black magic
ceremonies on Copacabana beach in the heart of Rio, with thousands of
candles aglow, cabalistic signs drawn in the sand, worshipers gyrating in
circles to the beat of drums and praying to Saravá, Yemanjá, the Old Black
Slave and the devil Exú.*

*This story, brief though it is, vividly portrays the spiritist movement in
modern Brazil—and serves up more than its fair share of goosebumps in
the bargain. But "Exú" is also a thinking person's horror story: what you
are witness to and what you are told in the final few hundred words may
or may not be taken literally, and is open to more than one interpretation.
In voodoo, as in other aspects of life, the answers are not always easy and
obvious.*

*Born a half-century ago in upstate New York, Edward D. Hoch toiled
in an advertising agency before and after beginning his literary career in
the mid-1950s. In the past twenty-five years he has published more than
five hundred and fifty short stories in the mystery, fantasy/horror, science
fiction and Western categories; four novels, three of which are science
fiction mysteries; and four collections of stories, including two—*City of

Brass *and* The Judges of Hades—*about Simon Ark, a man who claims to be 2,000 years old. Hoch has also edited one anthology for the Mystery Writers of America (who awarded his "The Oblong Room" an Edgar as the best short story of 1968) and the last five volumes of the annual* Best Detective Stories of the Year. *He lives with his wife in Rochester, New York, where at present he supports himself solely by writing short fiction.*

ALMOST FROM the moment he arrived in Rio de Janeiro, Jennings knew he had come to the right place. There was something garish about the sights and sounds of the great city—something exotic and just a bit dangerous. He saw it in the paintings displayed at news kiosks, where pictures of Christ and Saint Sebastian vied for space with the spiritist divinities such as Yemanjá and the Old Black Slave.

And he heard it in the voices of the people, and in their music. That December a decade-old song of Rio, *Garôta de Ipanema*—"Girl from Ipanema"—was popular again and he heard it sung in Portuguese in the bars and cafes of the city.

He listened, and felt the old excitement building within him. On his second night in Rio he approached a singer at the conclusion of her act and invited her to join him for a drink. She stared at him, apparently sizing him up, and then accepted.

"Are you new to the city?" she asked, sipping at the tall glass before her. "You speak the language very well."

"New, yes. I am only here on a visit." He laid a one-hundred-cruzeiros banknote on the table between them. "I need some excitement."

"I do not—" she began, looking frightened.

"Where can I find voodoo?" he asked quietly, and the sound of his voice was almost obscured by the beat of the music.

She pushed the banknote away. "There is no voodoo in Rio. Only the spirit cults. Rio is a Catholic city."

"Then tell me of the spirit cults. Tell me of Quimbanda."

She shook her head. "I know nothing of this," she insisted.

Jennings grew impatient. He added a second banknote to the first. "I listened while you sang. I heard it in the lyrics of your song—the mention of Saravá and Yemanjá and the other spirit gods. Tell me where I can worship them."

She cast her dark eyes down at the table, studying the money. Finally she said, "Quimbanda is a cult of black magic. They worship the devil Exú."

"Where?" he asked again.

Her reply was so soft he barely heard it. "The cemetery of Inhaúma. Go there any night. Close to midnight." She scooped up the banknotes and was gone from his table.

Outside the cemetery a young woman with coal-black hair sat against a wall selling candles. Jennings was struck by the beauty of her face as he dropped a few coins in her cup and accepted a candle in return. A number of expensive cars were drawn up at the cemetery gates, and he could see the light of a hundred candles flickering in the blackness among the tombstones.

"Are you here every night?" he asked the young woman.

"Every night. They come to make an offering to Exú."

"The devil."

She shrugged. "If you wish."

He gestured toward the flickering lights. "Do you believe?"

"I only sell candles."

He left her and walked among the gravestones then, passing a black man eating fire as a circus entertainer might. There were bowls of food on the tombstones, offerings to the devil. Cigars were scattered about, and bottles of some strong-smelling alcoholic drink. There were black chickens with their throats cut, and the head of a goat resting in a bowl of its own blood.

And always the people, just beyond the edge of shadow, watching him.

Suddenly his arm was gripped from the side, and he saw a man all in black pull him away. It took him an instant to realize the man was a priest.

"You do not belong here," the priest said to him. "Come with me!"

Jennings followed him into the darkness, more curious than anything else. "I hardly expected to meet a priest here," he said at last. "These people are worshiping the devil."

"Not worshiping," the priest corrected, his pale face reflecting the candlelight. "Only making their foolish sacrifices to a deity who does not listen. My name is Father Aaral, and I have a parish church near here. I saw at once that you were not one of them, from the way you boldly walked among the tombstones. The cemetery at midnight is not a safe place for outsiders."

"I have come here to study the spirit cults," Jennings said.

"To study or to worship? This is not a new religion, my friend. It is, in fact, a very old religion. Come back to the rectory with me and I will give you some coffee while we talk."

The December night was warm and Jennings had to remind himself it was only two days until New Year's Eve. He had never gotten used to the Southern Hemisphere with its seasonal reverses. But he went with Father Aaral, because he had seen enough for the moment of dead chickens and beheaded goats.

"The spirit cults of Rio," the priest began when they were settled in his rectory study, "are very closely allied with the Catholic Church. That is not surprising in a country that is ninety-three percent Catholic. Like the more traditional voodoo cults of the West Indies, they are a combination of African cult worship and elements borrowed from the Catholic religion. The cult of Candomblé climaxes its month-long initiation ceremony by taking new members—their heads shaven and bodies painted —to hear a Catholic mass in a church or cathedral. I have had them in my church on occasion."

"But the people in the cemetery tonight were not merely natives. Some were well-dressed white families."

"Quimbanda is a black magic subsidiary of the Umbanda cult. It is very dangerous because in worshiping the devil one attracts all sorts. I go to the cemetery because I have heard rumors of human sacrifice, though I have never seen any."

"I have come a long way to study these things," Jennings said.

"Be careful you do not study them too well."

"Where would you suggest I go?"

Father Aaral sighed. "In two nights it will be New Year's Eve. Go to the Copacabana beach and see the Umbanda pay special homage to the ruling divinity of the sea, Yemanjá."

"Yemanjá," Jennings repeated. "Yes, I have seen the pictures. A beautiful dark-haired goddess coming from the water."

"That is Yemanjá, and the coming of the new year is her night. Go there, and perhaps you will find what you seek."

"Thank you, father," Jennings said.

But in two nights' time he went instead to the cemetery once more, because the place held a strange fascination for him. He saw again the lovely dark-haired girl who sold candles by the entrance and wondered if she might be the sea goddess Yemanjá. "We must go to the beach later," he told her, but she only smiled.

Inside the gates the candles flickered once more, and the silent worshipers waited with their offerings. One young woman scattered popcorn, because that was said to be the devil's favorite delicacy. Another broke a bottle of liquor, scattering blue flame over the flickering candles.

He walked among them as he had two nights ago, turning occasionally from side to side. He saw the blood of the chickens, and came at last to the large bowl that had held the goat's head.

Tonight it held something else.

Tonight it held the head of Father Aaral.

He was running then, terrified, wanting only to get away. He had gone some distance before he realized that the dark-haired young woman was running with him. He held her hand, and they might have been lovers off on a spree.

"Where are we going?" she asked him once.

"To the beach. It's almost midnight."

"I am not Yemanjá," she told him. "That is all a dream."

But he ran on, dragging her along. "Did you see that back there?" he asked after a time, when they'd paused for breath. "In the cemetery?"

"I have seen many things in the cemetery. Sometimes it is better not to see too much."

They crossed the serpentine mosaic of Copacabana's promenade and hurried across the beach. There were more candles here—thousands of candles—and magical signs drawn in the sand. There were pictures of the blue-clad Yemanjá, and a virginal statue of her. And always the worshipers, moving in their circles. Occasionally some would venture into the surf, casting a bouquet of flowers or an offering of jewelry to the goddess of the sea.

"She will come at midnight," Jennings said.

"She will never come," the woman at his side said.

They moved further along the beach where all was frenzy and the worshipers beat their drums while others whirled and gyrated to the music. Here a medium with a ritual cigar told a fortune, while another lit a final row of candles in the form of a cross.

It was midnight at last, and Jennings fell to his knees before the young woman. "Behold, Yemanjá has come!" he shouted.

But the worshipers paid him no heed, because they knew this was only the poor girl who sold candles at the cemetery.

"She did not come," the young woman said, helping him to his feet. "There is no Yemanjá."

"There must be!" he insisted. "She must be here! She must be real!"

"Why?"

"Because I am Exú," he said at last. "I am Exú and I am real."

"The devil." She said it simply, neither believing nor disbelieving.

"I am the one they worship back there, with their candles and popcorn and orgies at midnight. I walked among them and they did not recognize me. Even the priest did not recognize me."

"I recognize you, Exú," she told him.

The chanting grew louder all around them, and he reached out his arm to her. "How can I tell them? How can I tell them that I have no use for their blood and chickens and heads of priests? There is more evil in the mind of man than even I would have thought possible."

"I will tell them for you," she said. "I will tell them tomorrow."

"By tomorrow I will be elsewhere."

Presently they slept there on the beach together, and at the first light of dawn when the young woman awakened she saw that the man named Jennings was no longer beside her. As far as she could see down the beach there was no sign of him.

She waded into the surf to wash herself, and as she emerged a young girl brought her flowers, thinking she was Yemanjá.

SEVENTH SISTER

by MARY ELIZABETH COUNSELMAN

There were many superstitions involved in the voodoo and conjuring practices of blacks in the Old South. But perhaps the most unusual is that of the Seventh Sister—the seventh girl baby in a family, born on a night when the squinch-owl hollers and a dog howls three times and a martin gets into the house and batters its brains out against the walls before anyone can set it free. For she has the Power: she can touch warts and make them disappear; she can make bullbats fly out of the dusk; she can cause birds to die with blood on their feathers by pointing a chicken bone at them and shouting, "Bang, bang! Boom!"

The "Seventh Sister" here, however, is even stranger than most: she was born an albino. Her translucent pink eyes and cotton-colored hair frighten her brothers and sisters as much as her Power, and make her even more of an outcast; yet she wants desperately to belong, so desperately that she'll do almost anything for a little affection. Her tragic and poignant story, told in the plantation-black dialect of the pre-Depression years, has been hailed as a superior work in the field of weird fantasy.

Mary Elizabeth Counselman is an Alabaman by birth (in 1911) and still makes her home in that state. Shortly after attending the University of Alabama and Montevallo University, she began writing and selling stories to Collier's, The Saturday Evening Post, Good

Housekeeping, Ladies' Home Journal, Weird Tales *and other magazines. She is considered by many to be the foremost woman writer of macabre fiction at work today; her recent Arkham House collection,* Half in Shadow, *which contains fourteen of her finest stories, gives strong support to that claim.*

THE NIGHT Seven Sisters was born, a squinch-owl hollered outside the cabin from sundown until the moment of her birth. Then it stopped its quavering cry. Everything stopped—the whippoorwills in the loblollies; the katydids in the fig tree beside the well; even the tree-frogs, burring their promise of rain as "sheet lightning" flickered across the black sky.

The row of slave cabins behind the Old Place looked ramshackle and deserted; had been deserted, for a fact, ever since Grant took Richmond. Daylight or a moon would have shown their shingle roofs fallen in and their sagging porches overgrown with jimson weed and honeysuckle. Only one cabin was livable now and inhabited. Dody, grandson of a Saunders slave, had wandered back to the Old Place, with a wife and a flock of emaciated little pickaninnies.

They had not thrived on odd-job fare in the city. So Dody had come home, the first year of the Depression, serenely certain of his welcome. He knew Cap'm Jim and Miss Addie would give them a cabin with a truck garden, in return for whatever sporadic labor was needed on the old rundown plantation smack on the Alabama-Georgia line.

That was in '29, six years ago. Miss Addie was dead now and buried in the family cemetery on the south hill. Most of the land had been sold to meet taxes. Miss Addie's grandson, Cap'm Jim, alone was left. Cap'm Jim was a baby doctor in Chattanooga. He kept the Old Place closed up except for weekend trips down with his wife and two young sons.

The red clay fields lay fallow and uncultivated. The rail fences had fallen, and even the white-columned Place itself was leaky and in need of paint. Whenever Dody or Mattie Sue thought of it, they had one of the young-uns sweep the leaves and chicken-sign from the bare sanded clay of the front yard. But aside from that weekly chore, they had the deserted plantation all to themselves, and lived accordingly. The children grew fat and sassy on yams and chitterlings. Dody drank more homebrew and slept all day in the barrel-slat hammock. And Mattie cooked, quarreled and bore another pickaninny every year. . . .

That is, until Seven Sisters was born.

That night a squinch-owl hollered. And somewhere beyond the state highway, a dog howled three times. More than that, one of the martins, nesting in the gourd-pole in front of the cabin, got into the house and beat its brains out against the walls before anyone could set it free.

Three Signs! Small wonder that at sundown Mattie Sue was writhing in agony of premature childbirth. Not even the two greased axes, which Ressie and Clarabelle—her oldest unmarried daughters; aged fifteen and seventeen—had placed under her bed to cut the pain, did any good.

"Oh, Lawsy—Mammy done took bad!" Ressie whimpered.

She hovered over the fat groaning black woman on the bed, eyewhites large and frightened in her pretty Negro face. Ressie had seen many of her brothers and sisters come into the world. But always before, Mattie Sue had borne as easily and naturally as a cat.

"Do, my Savior!" Clarabelle whispered. "We got to git somebody to midwife her! Aunt Fan. . . . Go 'long and fotch her, quick! Oh, Lawsy. . . ." she wailed, holding high the kerosene lamp and peering down at the woman in pain. "I . . . I'se sho skeered. . . . What you waitin' on, fool? Run! . . . Oh, Lawsy, mammy . . . mammy?"

Ressie plunged out into the night. The *slap-slap* of her bare feet trailed into silence.

The cabin's front room was very still. Save for the regular moaning of Dody's wife—and an occasional snore from Dody himself, drunk and asleep on the kitchen floor—there was no sound within. The other children were clustered in one corner, silent as young foxes. Only the whites of their eyes were visible against the dark. Clarabelle tiptoed about in her mail-order print dress, her chemically straightened hair rolled up on curlers for the church social tomorrow.

Light from the sooty lamp threw stunted shadows. The reek of its kerosene and the smell of Negro bodies blended with the pungent odor of peaches hung in a string to dry beside the window. Hot summer scents drifted in: sun-baked earth, guano from the garden, the cloying perfume of a clematis vine running along the porch rafters.

It was all so familiar—the smells, the night-sounds. The broken and mended furniture, discarded by four generations of Saunderses. The pictures tacked on the plank walls—of a snow-scene, of a Spanish dancer, of the president—torn from old magazines Cap'm Jim and Miss Ruth had cast aside. The last year's feed-store calendar, dated January 1934. The gilded wreath, saved from Miss Addie's funeral, now decorating the mantel with its purple and gilt ribbon rain-marred to read: ABID WI H MF.

Even the childbirth scene was familiar to all of Mattie's children except the youngest. And yet. . . .

There was an eerie quality about the night, throwing the familiar out of focus. The young-uns felt it, huddled, supperless, in the corner while Clarabelle fluttered ineffectually about the bed and its burden. It was so hot and oppressive, with a curious air of waiting. Even a rumble of thunder along the horizon sounded hushed and furtive.

And the screech-owl's cry drifted nearer.

The woman on the bed writhed and moaned again. Clarabelle twisted her black hands together, bright with pink nail polish— relic of the winters spent in Chattanooga as nurse for Cap'm Jim's youngest. She went to the open door for a fourth time, listening for the sound of approaching footsteps.

Aunt Fan had a cabin down the road about half a mile, and had washed for the Andrews as far back as anyone remembered. She was a church woman; in fact, one of her three husbands had been a preacher before he knifed a man and got sent away to prison. If anyone could help Mattie Sue in her extremity, it would be Aunt Fan. . . .

The squinch-owl wailed again. Clarabelle drew a quick circle on the cabin floor and spat in it. But the moaning of her mother went on and on, incoherent, rising and falling as though in imitation of the owl's ill-omened call.

Clarabelle stiffened, listening. The hurried *crunch-crunch* of shod feet came to her ears at last. With a gasp of relief she ran out to meet the pair—Ressie, returning, and a tiny wizened old Negress with a wen in the center of her forehead, jutting out like a blunt horn.

"Aunt Fan, what I tell you? Listen yonder!" Ressie whimpered. "Dat ole squinch-owl been holl'in' fit to be tied ever since sundown!"

The old midwife poised on the porch step, head cocked. She grunted, and with a slow, precise gesture took off her apron, to don it again wrong-side out.

"Dah. Dat oughta fix 'im. What-at Mattie Sue? My land o' Goshen, dat young-un don't b'long to get borned for two month yet! She been workin' in de garden?"

"Well'm. . . ." Clarabelle started to lie, then nodded, contrite. "Seem like she did do a little weedin' yestiddy. . . ."

"Uh-huh! So dat's hit! I done tole her! Dat low-down triflin' Dody. . . ." Aunt Fan, with a snort that included all men, switched into the cabin.

Outside, the screech-owl chuckled mockingly, as though it possessed a deeper knowledge of the mystery of birth and death.

Ressie and Clarabelle hunched together on the front stoop. Through the door they could hear Aunt Fan's sharp voice ordering the pickaninnies out of her way into the kitchen. Mattie Sue's regular moaning had risen in timbre to a shrill cry. Clarabelle, squatting on the log step of the porch, whispered under her breath.

"Huh!" Ressie muttered. "Ain't no use prayin' wid dat ole squinch-owl holl'in' his fool head off! Oh, Lawsy, Clary, you reckon Aunt Fan can . . . ?"

The older girl shivered but did not reply. Her eyes, wide and shining from the window's glow, swept across the flat terrain. Fireflies twinkled in the scrub pines beyond the cornfield. A muffled roar from above caught her ear once. She raised her head. Wing lights on a transport plane, racing the storm from Birmingham to Atlanta, winked down at her, then vanished in the clouds.

" 'Leb'm-thirty," she murmured. "Less hit's late tonight. . . . Daggone! If'n dat ole fool don't shet up his screechin'. . . ." She hushed herself, sheepishly fearful of her own blasphemy.

Of course there was nothing to all that stuff her mammy and Aunt Fan had passed down to them, huddling before the fire on rainy nights. Signs! Omens! Juju . . . Cap'm Jim had laughed and told them, often enough, that. . . .

The girl started violently. From the cabin a scream shattered the night. High-pitched. Final.

Then everything was still. The tree-frogs. The quarreling katydids. The whippoorwills. The muttering thunder. A trick of wind even carried away the sound of the transport plane.

And the screech-owl stopped hollering, like an evil spirit swallowed up by the darkness.

A few minutes later Aunt Fan came to the door, a tiny bundle in her arms swaddled in an old dress of Mattie's. The girls leaped to their feet, wordless, eager.

But the old Negress in the doorway did not speak. She was murmuring something under her breath that sounded like a prayer—or an incantation. There was a sinister poise to her tiny form framed in the lighted doorway, silent, staring out into the night.

Suddenly she spoke.

"Clary honey . . . Ressie. You' mammy done daid. Wan't nothin' I could do. But . . . my soul to Glory! Hit's somep'm funny about dis gal-baby! She white as cotton! I reckon yo' mammy musta had a sin on she soul, how come de Lawd taken her. . . ."

Clarabelle gasped a warning. A broad hulk had blotted out the lamplight behind Aunt Fan—Dody, awake, still drunk, and mean. A tall sepia Negro, wearing only his overalls, he swayed against the door for support, glowering down at the bundle in Aunt Fan's arms.

"Woods-colt!" Dody growled. "I ain't gwine feed no woods-colt. . . . Git hit on out'n my cabin! I got eight young-uns o' my own to feed, workin' myself down to a frazzle. . . . Git hit on out, I done tole you!" he snarled, aiming a side swipe at Aunt Fan that would have knocked her sprawling if it had landed.

But the old Negress ducked nimbly, hopped out onto the porch, and glared back at Dody. Her tiny black eyes glittered with anger and outrage, more for herself than for the squirming handful of life in her embrace.

"You Dody Saunders!" Aunt Fan shrilled. "You big low-down triflin' piece o' trash! I gwine tell Cap'm Jim on you! Jes' wait and see don't I tell 'im! Th'owin' Mattie's own baby out'n de house like she want nothin' but a mess o' corn shucks! And Mattie layin' daid in yonder. . . ."

Dody swayed, bleary eyes trying to separate the speaker from her alcoholic image.

"Daid? M-mattie Sue . . . my Mattie Sue done daid? Oh, Lawsy —why'n you tell me . . . ?"

His blunt, brutal features crumpled all at once, childlike in grief. He whirled back into the cabin toward the quilt-covered bed. "Mattie?" the three on the porch heard his voice. "Mattie honey? Hit's your Dody—say somep'm, honey. . . . Don't sull up like dat and be mad at Dody! What I done now? . . . Mattie . . . ?"

Clarabelle and Ressie clung together, weeping.

Only Aunt Fan was dry-eyed, practical. In the dark she looked down at the mewling newborn baby. And slowly her eyes widened.

With a gesture almost of repugnance the old woman held the infant at arm's length, peering at it in the pale glow from the open cabin door.

"My Lawd a-mercy!" she whispered. "No wonder Mattie Sue died a-birthin' dis-heah one! Makes no diff'rence if'n hit's a woods-colt or not, dis heah chile. . . ."

She stopped, staring now at Clarabelle and Ressie. They

paused in their grieving, caught by Aunt Fan's queer tone. The old woman was mumbling under her breath, counting on her black fingers; nodding.

"Dat ole squinch-owl!" Ressie sobbed. "I knowed it! If'n hit hadn't a-hollered, mammy wouldn't. . . ."

"Squinch-owl don't mean nothin' tonight," Aunt Fan cut in with an odd intensity. "Eh, Lawd, hit's jes' stomp-down nachel dat a squinch-owl'd come around to holler at dis-heah birthin'. Nor neither hit wouldn't do no good to put no axes under Mattie's bed, nor do no prayin'. You know why? Dis-heah young-un got six sisters, ain't she? Dat makes she a seb'm-sister! *She gwine have de Power!*"

Like a solemn period to her words, a clap of thunder boomed in the west, scattering ten-pin echoes all over the sky.

"Yessirree, a seb'm-sister," Aunt Fan repeated, rubbing the wen on her wrinkled forehead for good luck. "Y'all gwine have trouble wid dis chile! Hit's a pyore pity she didn't die alongside she mammy."

Ressie and Clarabelle, saucer-eyed, peered at their motherless newborn sister, at her tiny puckered face that resembled nothing so much as a small monkey. But she was *white,* abnormally white! Paler than any "high yaller" pickaninny they had ever seen; paler even than a white baby. Her little eyes were a translucent watery pink. Her faint fuzz of hair was like cotton.

"De Lawd he'p us to git right!" Clarabelle whispered in awe. "What us gwine do wid her? Pappy won't leave her stay here— not no woods-colt, and *sho* not no seb'm-sister! Will you keep care of her, Aunt Fan? Anyways, till after de funeral?"

The old Negress shook her head. With flat emphasis she thrust the wailing bundle into Ressie's arms, and stumped down the porch step.

"Nawsuh, honey! Not me! Hit say in de Good Book not to have no truck wid no conjure 'oman. And dat little seb'm-sister of yourn gwine be a plain-out, hard down conjure 'oman, sho as you born! . . . Jes' keep her out in de corncrib; Dody won't take no notice of her. Feed her on goat's milk. . . . Mm-mmm!" Aunt Fan shook her head in wonder. "She sho is a funny color!"

It was a month after Mattie's funeral before Cap'm Jim came down to the Old Place again with the boys and Miss Ruth. When he heard, by neighborhood grapevine, that Dody's new baby was being hidden out in the corncrib like an infant Moses, he stormed down to the cabin with proper indignation.

He took one startled look at the baby, white as a slug that has spent its life in darkness under a rock. Pink eyes blinked up at him painfully. The little thing seemed to be thriving very well on goat's milk, but the corncrib was draughty and full of rats. Cap'm Jim attacked Dody with the good-natured tyranny of all Deep-Southerners toward the darkies who trust and depend upon them.

"I'm ashamed of you, boy!"—Dody was over ten years older than Dr. Saunders. "Making your own baby sleep out in a corn-crib, just for some damn-fool notion that she's a hoodoo! And of course she is your own baby. She's just an albino; that's why she's so white."

Dody bobbed and scratched his head. "Yassuh, cap'm? Sho nuff?"

"Yes. It's a lack of pigment in the skin . . . er. . . ." Dr. Saunders floundered, faced by the childlike bewilderment in the big Negro's face. "I mean, she's black, but her skin is white. She . . . Oh, the devil! You take that child into your cabin and treat her right, or I'll turn you out so quick it'll make your head swim!"

"Yassuh . . ." Dody grinned and bobbed again, turning his frayed straw hat around and around by the brim. "Yassuh, cap'm . . . You ain't got a quarter you don't need, is you? Seem like we's plumb out o' salt and stuff. Ain't got no nails, neither, to mend de chicken house. . . ."

Dr. Saunders grunted and handed him fifty cents. "Here. But if you spend it on bay rum and get drunk this weekend, I'll tan your hide!"

"Naw*suh!*" Dody beamed, and guffawed his admiration of the bossman's unerring shot. "I ain't gwine do dat, cap'm! Does you want me for anything, jes' ring de bell. I'll send Clarabelle on up to look after de boys."

Dody shambled off, grinning. Cap'm Jim let out a baffled sigh.
He strode back toward the Place, well aware that Dody would be
drunk on dime-store bay rum by nightfall, and that the big rusty
plantation bell in the yard would clang in vain if he wanted any
chores performed. But he had laid the law down about the new
baby, and that order at least would be obeyed.

"A pure albino!" he told his wife later, at supper. "Poor little
mite; it's amazing how healthy she is on that treatment! They
won't even give her a name. They just call her Seven Sisters
. . . and cross their fool fingers every time she looks at 'em! I'll
have to say, myself, she is weird-looking with that paper-white
hair and skin. Oh, well—they'll get used to her. . . ."

Cap'm Jim laughed, shrugged and helped himself to some
more watermelon pickle.

Dody, with his fifty cents, rode mule-back to the nearest town
five miles away. In a fatherly moment, while buying his bay rum
at the five-and-ten, he bought a nickel's worth of peppermints
for the young-uns. He bought salt, soda, and some nails.

Plodding back home up the highway, he passed Aunt Fan's
cabin and hailed her with due solemnity.

"Us sho got a seb'm-sister, all right," he called over the sagging wire gate, after a moment of chitchat. "Cap'm Jim say she
ain't no woods-colt. He say she black, but she got pigmies in de
skin, what make her look so bright-colored. Do, my Savior! I bet
she got de blue-gum! I sho ain't gwine let her chaw on my
fingers like them other young-uns when she teethin'! I ain't
fixin' to git pizened!"

"Praise de Lawd!" Aunt Fan answered noncommittally, rocking and fanning herself on the front stoop. "Reckon what-all she
gwine be up to when she old enough to be noticin'? Whoo-ee!
Make my blood run cold to study 'bout it!"

Dody shivered, clutching his store-purchases as though their
prosaic touch could protect him from his own thoughts. If there
was any way to get rid of the baby, without violence. . . . But
Cap'm Jim had said his say, and there was nothing for him to do
but raise her along with the others.

It was a fearful cross to bear. For, Seven Sisters began to show signs of "the Power" at an early age. She could touch warts and they would disappear; if not at once, at least within a few weeks. She would cry, and almost every time, a bullbat would fly out of the dusk, to go circling and screeching about the cabin's field-stone chimney.

Then there was the time when she was three, playing quietly in the cabin's shade, her dead-white skin and hair in freakish contrast with those of her black brothers and sisters. The other pickaninnies were nearby—but not too near; keeping the eye on her demanded by Clarabelle without actually playing with her.

Willie T., five, was playing train with a row of bricks tied on a string. Booger and Gaynelle, twins of eight, were fishing for jackworms—poling a blade of grass down each hole, and jerking up the tiny dragonlike insects. Lula and Willene and Buzz, aged twelve, nine and thirteen, were engaged in a game of squat tag under the fig trees. They were not paying much attention to their queer-colored sister, though from time to time she glanced at them wistfully.

Willie T. it was who happened to look up and see the bird clumsily winging along overhead in the clear June sky. He pointed, not greatly interested.

"Look at dat ole shypoke!" Snatching up a stick, he aimed it at the flapping target, closed one eye and shouted: *"Bang! Bang! Babloom!"* in imitation of Cap'm Jim's rifle. The bird flew on.

The other children glanced up idly. Only the little albino, lonesome and longing for attention, feigned an interest in this byplay. Squinting eagerly up at the distant bird, she pointed the old chicken foot with which she was playing, and trebled in mimicry of her brother: *"Bang, bang! Boom!"*

And a weird, incredible thing happened.

The shypoke, flapping along, wavered suddenly, one wing drooping. With a lurching, fluttering motion it veered—then fell like a plummet, striking the ground not three yards from where the little girl sat.

Willie T. stared. The bird was dead. There was blood on its feathers.

In a stunned, silent, wide-eyed group, Mattie's other children backed away from their ghostly sister. She blinked at them, her pinkish eyes squinting painfully in the sunlight.

"*Bang-bang . . . ?*" Seven Sisters repeated in a hopeful undertone.

There was a shuffle of running feet. Her lower lip quivered when she saw that she had been left alone.

She was always alone after that, partly because the other children shunned her, and partly because she could not see well enough to run after them. She had developed a peculiar squint, holding her tow-head to one side, slit-eyed, upper lip drawn back to show her oddly pointed little teeth. For a "seven-sister" she tripped over things and hurt herself twice as often as her brothers and sisters who were not gifted with supernatural powers.

Cap'm Jim, on a flying visit to the plantation one Sunday, had noticed the way the child kept always to the shadowy places.

"Weak eyes," he pronounced. "Typical of albinos. Have to get her some special glasses. . . ." He sighed, mentally adding up his vanishing bank account. "Oh, well—time enough when she starts to school. Though, Lord help the little thing at recess!"

That preference for shadow was given another connotation by dark-skinned observers.

"Dah! Ain't I done tole you?" Aunt Fan was triumphant. "See jes' like a cat in de dark, but can't see hardly nothin' in de daytime. Yessirree—she a plain-out, hard-down conjure 'oman, and I knowed hit de first time I sot eyes on her!"

By this time, the lone screech-owl which had attracted Seven Sister's birth had become seven screech-owls, hovering in a ring around the cabin to demand Mattie's soul in return for the new baby's "Power."

This "Power" mystified Seven Sisters, though she did not doubt that she had it. Clarabelle and Dody had told her so, ever since she could understand words. Now a thin, too-quiet child of six, she accepted the fact as simply and sadly as one might accept having been born with an interesting club-foot. But, because it was the only way in which she could attract attention—half fear, half respect—the little albino drew on her imagination, and did not herself know where fact ended and fancy began.

The other children jeered at her but were frankly envious. The elders laughed and remarked that nobody but "ig'nant country niggers" believed in conjures any more.

Secretly they came to her by night, and hissed at her window, and proffered silver in return for her magic. Seven Sisters never saw any of the money, however, as the business was always transacted through Clarabelle or Dody.

Some of the things they wanted were incomprehensible to her at first. Mojoes—tiny bags of cloth that might contain anything at all, plus the one thing only she possessed: "the Power." In Atlanta, in Birmingham, and Memphis, especially in Harlem, a good one might sell for as much as ten dollars. These, according to whatever words the conjurer mumbled over them, were able to perform all sorts of miracles for the wearer—from restoring the affection of a bored mate to insuring luck in the numbers game.

Seven Sisters, with the precocity of all outcasts, caught the idea early. Like the little girls who started the witch-scare in Salem, she felt pains and saw apparitions for the bug-eyed approval of kin and neighbors. She made up words and mumbled them on every occasion, squinting weirdly and impressively. She hummed tuneless little chants, in the eerie rhythm of all darkies. She memorized the better-known household "conjures"; such as, burying three hairs from the end of a hound's tail under the front steps to keep him from straying. With a ready wit she invented new ones, then forgot them and supplied others on call.

True, most of these tricks had, at one time or another, been subtly suggested by Aunt Fan or Clarabelle as the proper procedure for a "seven-sister." But the little albino, pleased and excited by any substitute for affection, threw herself into the part —a pale wistful Shirley Temple in the role of Cybele.

She wanted to be admired, however. She did not want to be feared.

But even Clarabelle, who loved her in a skittish way one might grow to love a pet snake, gave her a wide berth after the incident of the stomachache.

It happened one sultry August day when Dody came stumbling into the cabin, drunker than usual and in a nasty mood.

"Whah dat low-down triflin' Seb'm-Sister?" he bellowed. "Whah she at? I gwine wear de hide off'n her back—takin' dat four-bit piece from Ole Man Wilson for a huntin' mojo. Hidin' it fum her po' ole pappy what feed her! Whah she at? . . . Young-un, you come out fum under dat table! I sees you!"

The other children, gnawing pork chop bones beside the fireplace—thanks to the sale of a "health mojo" purported to contain the infallible John the Conqueror root—stirred uneasily. In this mood Dody was apt to throw things at anyone within range. But it appeared that Seven Sisters, quaking under the table, was the main object of his wrath tonight.

"Come on out, you heah me?" Dody snarled, grabbing up a stick of lightwood from the hearth and advancing toward the culprit. "I'm gwine whup you good! Stealin' my four-bits. . . ."

"I . . . done lost it, pappy. . . ." Seven Sisters's childish treble was drowned out by his bellow of rage. "Don't whup me! I drapped it in de field. I couldn't see whereat I drapped it—I'll go git it. . . ."

"Now you's lyin' to me!" Dody roared, waving his club. "Come on out! I'll learn you. . . ."

The other pickaninnies, fascinated, stopped gnawing their chop bones for an instant to watch, their greasy black faces gleaming in the firelight. Dody jerked the table aside. Seven Sisters cringed. Then:

"Don't you hit me wid no stick!" the frightened child shrilled. "I'll put a hoodoo on you! I'll . . ."

Dody lunged, and fell over the table. His stick whistled dangerously close to the child's tow-head.

The next moment Dody was groaning with pain, doubled

over, hugging his stomach. Sweat stood out on his black face. He stared at his weirdly white daughter: backed away, thick lips trembling. Seven Sisters made a dive through the open door and out into the friendly night.

Cap'm Jim happened to be at the Place that day; it was a Sunday. He rushed Dody to the nearest city in his car. Appendicitis, Cap'm Jim called it, to the man at the hospital. He and Miss Ruth had a good laugh over Dody's version of the attack.

But after that, Clarabelle stopped giving her little albino sister a playful spank when she was naughty. No one would touch her, even in fun.

"I done tole you!" Aunt Fan intoned. "Do, Moses! Puttin' a hoodoo on she own pappy! Dat ole Seb'm-Sister, she jes' born to trouble! She *bad!*"

For more than a week thereafter, Seven Sisters hid in the woods, creeping out only to sneak food from the kitchen. She was deeply frightened. So frightened that when Cap'm Jim came to bring Dody back from the hospital, she ran from him like a wild creature. If she had not tripped over a log and knocked the breath from her slight body, he would never have caught her.

Dr. Saunders helped her up and held her gently by the shoulders, marveling anew at her Negroid features and cotton-white hair and skin. Her single garment, a faded dress which had not been changed for eight days, hung half-off one shoulder, torn and filthy. She was trembling all over, squinting up at him with white-lashed pinkish eyes dilated by terror.

"Now, now, child," the tall bossman was saying, in a tone as gentle as the grip of his hands. "What have those fools been telling you? That it's your fault about Dody's appendix? Well, Heaven help us!" He threw back his head, laughing, but stopped when he saw how it frightened his small captive. "Why, don't be scared. Cap'm Jim won't hurt you. Look here—I've got a present for you! Don't let the other young-uns get hold of it, you hear? Just hide it and play with it all by yourself, because it's yours."

The little albino stopped trembling. Gingerly she took the proffered box and gaped at the treasure inside. A doll-baby a foot high! With real hair, red hair, and eyes that opened and shut. When she turned it over, it gave a thin cry: *"Mama!"* Seven Sisters giggled.

The Cap'm chuckled. "Oh, I don't reckon you want this old doll-baby," he made a pretense of taking it back, eyes twinkling. The child clutched at it. "You do? Well, then, what do you say?"

Seven Sisters ducked her head shyly. "I don' care," she whispered—polite rural South for "Thank you!"

Dr. Saunders chuckled again. "That's a good girl." He stood up; gave her a careless pat. Then he strode off toward the Place, frowning over his own problems—not the least of which was mother-in-law trouble.

He and Ruth and their two boys had been so happy in their touch-and-go way. Then his wife's mother, a forthright lady from Oklahoma, had descended upon them and decided to run their lives with a new efficiency. With her customary dispatch she had found a buyer for the old Saunders plantation, and was now raging at her slipshod son's reluctance to sell.

Even Cap'm Jim had to admit that the price was half again as much as the property was worth. Besides, his practice in Chattanooga had been dwindling of late. A mother-in-law could point out such matters so vividly . . . !

Seven Sisters blinked after his retreating back. Keeping to the shade of the pine coppice, she followed the tall white man a little way, the doll squeezed tightly against her soiled blue-gingham dress. Cap'm Jim waved at someone, who met him in the orchard—a pretty redheaded woman. They went on to the house together, arms about each other's waists. Seven Sisters watched them until they were out of sight.

Thereafter she listened attentively whenever Dody or Clary spoke of cap'm. She grew to love anyone that he loved, and to hate anyone that he hated, with a doglike loyalty. In her child's mind, Good became personified as Dr. Saunders, and Evil as the sheriff or Old Miz Beecher.

It was common knowledge about the mother-in-law trouble. Clarabelle, who cooked all year round for the Saunderses now, had passed along every word of the quarrel.

"Us'll git turnt out like white-trash if'n de cap'm sell de Place," Dody mourned. "Dat old Miz Beecher! Do, Lawd! Dat old 'oman mean as a cottonmouth! She don't care what happen to us niggers, nor nobody. Miss Ruth sho don't take after her none. I wisht she'd fall down de steps and bus' her brains out, so she wouldn't plague de cap'm no more! If'n he don' sell come Thursday, Thanksgivin', she gwine jes' make his life mis'able!"

Seven Sisters listened, huddled apart from her black kin in a shadowy corner of the cabin. Her little heart began to beat rapidly as a mad idea crept into her tow-head. Without a sound, she slipped out into the frosty night of mid-November.

There was a thing Aunt Fan had hinted to her one day—or rather, to Clarabelle within her hearing, since no one ever spoke directly to a seven-sister in idle conversation. Something about a . . . a *graven image.* There was even, Aunt Fan said, a passage about it in the Good Book, warning all Christians to steer clear of the matter.

But Seven Sisters was not a Christian. She had never been baptized in the creek like the rest of Dody's brood. Nothing hindered the plan. And . . . it sounded remarkably simple.

". . . whatever you does to de image, you does to de one you names it!" Aunt Fan's solemn words came back to her clearly. "Jes' wrop somep'm around it what dey wears next to dey skin —don't make no never-mind what hit is. And dat's de conjure! Eh, Lawd, I seed a conjure man do dat when I was married up wid my first husband. And de 'oman he conjure drap daid as a doornail dat same winter. . . . And dey do say as how hit were a big black cat got in de room whah dey was settin' up wid de corp. Hit jump up on de bed and go to yowlin' like ole Satan hisse'f! Yessirree, dat's de Lawd's truth like I'm tellin' you!"

Seven Sisters, picking her way easily through the dark, slipped into the pine coppice. After a moment, heart pounding, she dug up something from under a pile of leaves. A faint sound issued from it, causing her to start violently—*"Mama!"*

Like a small white ghost, the child then ran through the peach orchard. The Place, dark now since Cap'm Jim had gone back to Chattanooga, loomed just ahead. Seven Sisters found what she was looking for, under the steps of the isolated kitchen—an old piece of silk nightgown that she had seen Miss Ruth's mother herself give Clarabelle as a polishing rag for the flat silver. The older girl had used it and flung it under the kitchen steps. Seven Sisters retrieved it now furtively, and padded swiftly back through the orchard.

Deep in the pine coppice, illumined only by the filtered light of a quarter moon, she sat down cross-legged. For a long time she stared at the lovely thing Cap'm Jim had given her, the only thing that had ever been truly her own. The hair was so soft, the glass eyes so friendly. But now the doll had taken on a new personality, a hated one. Seven Sisters glared at it, shivering a little.

Then, deftly, she tied the silk rag about its china neck, and stood up.

"Ole Miz Beecher—you's ole Miz Beecher!" she hissed with careful emphasis; then clarified, against all mistake, to whatever dark pointed ears might be listening: "Miss Ruth's mama. Cap'm Jim's wife's mama. Dat's who you is, doll; you heah me? Ole Miz Beecher . . . !"

With a fierce motion she banged the poppet hard against a tree trunk. The china head broke off and rolled at her bare feet.

"Mama!" wailed the headless body, accusingly.

Seven Sisters dropped it as though it were red-hot. She backed away, rubbing her hands on her dress like an infant Lady Macbeth, and shuddering in the Indian summer chill. Panting, shaken, she turned and ran back to the cabin.

But she paused in the half-open door.

Excited activity was going on inside. Aunt Fan was there, puffing with importance and fumbling for her box of snuff. Dody was shouting questions, wringing his big hands. Clarabelle, Ressie and the others were milling about like a flock of chickens, clucking and squawking in chorus.

". . . and de phome call say for you to clean up de fambly plot on de south hill," Aunt Fan made herself heard shrilly. "She gwine be buried fum de Place like Miss Addie. . . ."

"Oh, Lawsy! Ain't it awful?" This from Ressie.

"Sho is, honey," Aunt Fan agreed complacently. "I don't reckon the cap'm'll ever be de same, hit was so awful. I don't reckon he care what become of de Place, nor nothin', he so cut up about hit."

"Lawd he'p us!" Dody shouted for a fifth time. "When it happen? How come?"

"I done tole you," Aunt Fan repeated, relishing the drama of her words. "Truck run slap into 'em. She was plumb flang out'n de car. Cap'm want even scratched up. But it broke her pore neck. . . ."

The child in the doorway caught her breath sharply. The conjure had worked! So soon? A little knot of nausea gathered in her stomach, in memory of the china head rolling against her bare foot. Then an angry thought came.

"Aunt Fan—cap'm ain't gwine bury that old 'oman in de fambly plot, is he?" Seven Sisters piped above the chatter. "Not dat ole Miz Beecher . . . !"

The excited group barely glanced at her, impatient of the interruption.

"Miz Beecher?" Aunt Fan grunted. "Lawd, chile, hit ain't ole Miz Beecher what got killt. Hit was Miss Ruth. . . ." The aged Negress went on with her narrative, dwelling on the details with relish. "And de man tole Marse Joe Andrews over de phome. . . . Eh, Lawd; he say de cap'm jes' set dah by she bed and hold she hand. Don't cry nor nothin'. Jes' set dah and stare, like he daid, too. . . ."

Seven Sisters heard no more. A sound like falling timber roared in her ears. Through it, dimly, she thought she heard a screech-owl's quavering cry—eerie, mocking, malicious.

She turned and ran. Ran, blindly sobbing. Cap'm Jim's Miss Ruth! She had forgotten Miss Ruth's hair was red, exactly like the doll's. And . . . that soiled bit of nightgown might not have been ole Miz Beecher's at all, but Miss Ruth's. Cap'm Jim's Miss Ruth. . . .

Beyond the cornfield the black woods opened up to receive the small ghostly figure, running like an animal in pain; running nowhere, anywhere, into the chill autumn night.

Sawbriars tore dark scratches in her dead-white skin, but Seven Sisters did not feel them. She ran, careening into tree trunks and fighting through scuppernong vines, until the salt taste of blood came into her mouth. Twice she fell and lay in the damp leaves for a long time, her thin shoulders racked with sobs.

"Oh, cap'm! Cap'm Jim . . . I . . . I didn't go to do it!" she whimpered aloud once. "I didn't mean to! I didn'—hones' I didn'. . . ."

At that moment she heard the dogs baying.

Tense as a fox, she sat up and listened. Was it only Old Man Wilson, hunting with his pack along the north ridge? Or was it . . . the Law? A posse, with guns, following the deputy sheriff and his two flop-eared bloodhounds through the canebrake. Following a trail of small bare feet. *Her* feet. . . .

The little albino sprang up, her features contorted with panic. Harrowing yarns crowded her memory. Of the time Aunt Fan's preacher husband had hid in the canebrake for eight days, with the dogs baying closer and closer. And Aunt Fan's husband had only cut a man with his razor, while *she*. . . .

Just then she heard the screech-owl, right over her head.

Seven Sisters was running again, goaded now by the spurs of terror. But now the very woods seemed hostile. Gnarled branches snatched at her cottony hair and tore a jagged flap in her gingham dress. Old spider webs clung to her face. The dogs sounded nearer. Once more she tripped and fell, panting, but sprang up again with a scream as something slithered out from beneath her arm.

The screech-owl tittered again, from somewhere above her. It seemed to be trailing the ghostly little fugitive, so white against the ground.

Seven Sisters ran on, blindly, staggering with exhaustion. Once she cried out in her terror—oddly, the very name of the one she was running from:

"Cap'm . . . ! Cap'm Jim. . . ."

Of a sudden the ground dropped from beneath her feet. She pitched forward, and felt herself falling into space. Dark icy water rushed up out of nowhere to meet and engulf her. . . .

Mist rose from the cornfield in front of Dody's cabin. Dry leaves rattled. The gourds of the martin pole swung in the wind.

Somewhere a screech-owl quavered again, far away, in the direction of the creek—whose muddy waters had washed away the sins of many a baptized little darky.

THE DEVIL DOLL

by BRYCE WALTON

Another of the many places where you'll find the practitioners of voodoo is New York City—and if you should happen to be as unfortunate as the Greenwich Village artist named Earl in this story, you might even discover that a voodoo devil doll is not always a wax or clay image, that in some cases it can come alive and take root and grow in your own flesh. Skeptical? So was Earl, until he realized that "you'll believe in anything, anywhere, even among the steel and concrete jungles of Manhattan—when it happens to you."

Like "Papa Benjamin," "The Devil Doll" was first published in Dime Mystery, *one of the leading "thrill" pulps; unlike the Woolrich story, however, it has been overlooked by fantasy/horror anthologists since that initial publication in 1947. Perhaps this is because its plot is somewhat reminiscent of Edward Lucas White's widely reprinted "Lukundoo" (but only somewhat); nevertheless, its eerie atmosphere, its surprises and abundant terrors invite comparisons to Woolrich and make its neglect insupportable. It is a pleasure to present it here.*

Bryce Walton was born in Missouri in 1918, headed West on a freight train after high school graduation, and held jobs as a placer miner, migrant fruit picker, sheepherder and sign painter before turning to the writing of short-shorts for newspaper syndicates. During World War II he was a combat correspondent for the Navy and, after being transferred to the Marine Corps, a staff correspondent for Leatherneck Magazine. *When the war ended he began to write extensively for the mystery/detective, science fiction and Western pulps; later, his work appeared in such magazines as* The Saturday Evening Post, Ellery Queen's Mystery Magazine *and* Alfred Hitchcock's Mystery Magazine *(which awarded his story "The Last Autopsy" first prize in its 1961 best story contest). He is also the author of seven novels, most of them juvenile adventure fiction, and has written and adapted TV scripts for* Captain Video *and* Alfred Hitchcock Presents. *He lives in Los Angeles, where he is at work on a new novel.*

JACK LONDON said it better than Earl could have said it. She was "fire in his blood and a thunder of trumpets." But no one could tell you of her laughter. It held undertones, suggestions of shadows and evil darkness.

Crita doesn't laugh any more, of course. Nor does Jean, though her laughter was never more than a thin cold smile. But Earl will always hear Crita's mocking laughter as long as he lives. And he will always remember the unspeakable little projection, with its soft, warm breath against his ear. The small, piping voice. The thing's laughter and its tiny fingers, fine and delicate and wet, that ran over his face like mice in the dark. . . .

He had been drinking heavily. He had never been able to drink well. But he had needed courage to tell Crita that it was quits. The courage gained was not in proportion to the bourbon consumed. His suit was wet and cold against his thin, quick-moving body as he edged up the stairs.

It was in the Village, on Grove Street. And he climbed the narrow stair slowly. Sweat was cold on his thin face. His heart was pounding pain against his ribs.

Why should he fear to tell Crita? They'd made the arrangement long in advance—when one tired of the other, the affair would be gracefully dissolved, no regrets, no fuss.

But he had learned since then that Crita never surrendered anything. And she had claimed him. He had been a promising artist until a few months ago, when he had met Jean Morris. Something had happened to his artistic ambitions. He had quit painting because of Jean. He had begun to play. Jean had money, more money than she had ever bothered to count. She was pretty but nothing like Crita.

Crita had been a singer in a Village night spot, with promise of getting into the big time. But Earl had been selfish. Too selfish, but he couldn't help it. She had quit singing. He'd wanted her all to himself, you understand.

She loved him with a strange, almost terrifying possessiveness. To him, she was a violent, roaring flame. He lived in the flood of her fire. But Jean had taken him away—from his painting, from the Village, from Crita. Jean was a traveler, a trotter of grotesque dogs along Park Avenue. She was small, delicate, white.

He had to tell Crita now. Jean was impatient with his dual role.

He shivered. He blinked hot burning eyes. Crita had given up everything, everything, for him. She had cooked, washed, done a thousand and one small things to make his meaningless life easier.

And he had to tell her that it was finished. He didn't want to. Money, the damned filthy compulsion. He hesitated outside the door. The narrow hall was confining, stuffy. He felt his breath suck in between tight lips. Then he opened the door.

The room was dark, the blinds drawn. A single candle burned in an onyx holder wound with red-eyed serpents, upon a small table. All the familiar things in the large, sky-lighted room were shadow-limned, distorted.

He saw her dark face framed by candlelight.

He backed away. Her eyes shone with a gleam of hateful understanding. Mingled with sudden horror in him was also relief, because now he wouldn't have to tell her. Crita knew about Jean. And she had already done something about it.

He didn't know that. There was much he didn't know.

Her skin was a deep bronze. He didn't know her origin, but her accent seemed subtly French. There was something primitive about her face, a beautiful savagery. Like an evil but beautiful jungle flower, hungry and unfolding.

Her lips were slightly parted, revealing strong teeth like white pearls. The deep brown of her eyes shone with that ineffable light of love that has frozen to hate and loathing.

Then he seemed to get the full implication of the props littering the shadowed room. They had always been there. But until now he had always considered them an affectation—"arty" stuff. He realized now that Crita's hobby of voodoo and black magic was more than a hobby. Maybe he had always known this, subconsciously. The voodoo drums on the walls. The "black magic" cult she belonged to.

Now the memory of these things came back. How strange she had seemed as she sometimes sat in the shadows, softly murmuring some alien chant, eyes closed, mouth lax, while her hands gently brought blood-throbbing rhythms from the drums.

She was familiar with Haiti. Maybe she came from Haiti. Haiti, dark island of voodoo, devil-devil. She made dolls, devil dolls, and also little packets which she called *ouangas.* Packets of carved bone, beads, potions.

That had been the thing about her songs at the clubs that made them different. Sultry, suggestive songs, half chanted, self-accompanied by the gentle, throbbing rhythm of a jungle drum.

"You're not going to leave me, Earl."

Her voice was low. The candle shuddered. Shadows swayed.

He moved toward her. He'd forgotten Jean for a moment. He had forgotten her delicate submissive slimness, the softness of her brown hair. Her wealth and her penthouse.

He stopped walking. The candlelight hurt his eyes. He was ill, very ill. He had been drinking much too much.

"How did you know about Jean and me?"

She laughed. Her eyes turned downward into the flame. He touched his wet lips. How had she known? A modern witch.

Strange contrast. A beautiful woman, compact and full and rounded with a penchant for black magic—in the heart of New York.

She got up, the candlelight flickering over her green evening gown. It clung to the roundness of her bronzed figure. She came to him slowly. His arms reached out. He felt the warmth of her body reaching out to him. His hands cupped her shoulder blades and she didn't move, just watched mutely. She was firm and warm in his arms.

Her head went back and she shut her eyes. He kissed her. The candle flame flickered, and he felt her arms about his neck as the kiss became deep. Lilac perfume closed around him.

"You can't leave me, Earl. No matter how you try."

He shook his head. His hands dropped. The way she had said that. As though she *knew* he couldn't leave. He looked up at the ceiling to escape her eyes. It was a Gothic ceiling with heavy rafters in squared angles. Like a row of gibbets strung across the room. A creeping knot of terror grew tighter and tighter around his waist.

He pushed her away. She stumbled. He fell back as she crashed into the wall. The voodoo drum fell from its hook. A dull dead *boommmmm* floated across the shadows.

Her eyes blazed as she climbed slowly to her feet and came toward him again. His hands were rubber fish against his sides. He had to get out of there, get a drink. He couldn't see or talk to Crita any more. He tried to move, but he seemed rooted there by old passions, memories, fears.

He watched her hand move to his right shoulder, a kind of lethargic terror dulling him, freezing him there.

Her hand moved quickly. His coat slid down over his right shoulder. The sound ripped in his ear as her fingers clawed his shirt open, baring his shoulder.

Then she kissed his shoulder. Her lips burned. A river of white-hot flame exploded in his head. She dropped back, laughing. Laughing. Always the laughter.

He looked at his shoulder. Nausea caused by pain thickened in his throat. Red on his shoulder where her lips had been. He was swearing as he rubbed at the red marks. But it wasn't lipstick; it wouldn't come off. He scrubbed frantically. She kept on laughing.

He stumbled back to the door and opened it. A draft of cool air was a shock to his sweating skin.

"You'll try, but you can't leave me, Earl. I won't let you go."

He ran. Down the dark stairs fast. And into the night.

He remembered drinking heavily that night. Straight shots in a dark booth where no one noticed him. But nothing could drown the fear. . . .

The fear, nor the pain that was growing in his right shoulder. He tried to ignore the pain later when he drove over to 61st Street to see Jean and tell her that he had gotten rid of Crita. Jean knew about Crita.

It wasn't that night that Jean died with his fingers around her thin white throat, throttling off her cries, her million dollars. It was later, maybe a week, maybe less. That isn't important to Earl. But he couldn't forget Crita that night when he was with Jean. The pain in his shoulder kept growing as they went walking in the park, threw popcorn to the ducks, watched the lights from the towers reflected on the water, watched other couples walking along the dark paths.

He got rid of Jean, left her at home and ran away to his own apartment. He ran frantically, sobbing. His shoulder was burning agony. And—*something was alive there. Something moved.*

He tore off his coat and shirt. He looked in the mirror. His face was a terrible image sculpted in wet, gray putty. His eyes bulged. . . .

A figure danced on his shoulder. A little, living, chortling marionette.

She's here . . . with me . . . on my shoulder. Crita. In a green dress. Only an inch high. But she's alive.

She is growing out of my shoulder.

There were familiars. You believed in them, you feared them in dark forbidden jungles and groveled in superstitious terror.

You'll believe in anything, anywhere, even among the steel and concrete jungles of Manhattan—*when it happens to you.*

"Go away!" he shrieked. He slapped at it. It slithered from the flat of his palm. "Get off me! Go away, damn you!"

The tiny swaying figure laughed.

Crita in miniature, growing out of his shoulder. A tiny, wispy body swaying to an invisible melody. And it leaned toward his ear. The laughter became high and shrill, then tiny, elfin.

He kept staring into the mirror. It was easier to see the thing there than to turn and see it directly, see it looking back at him from tiny pin-point eyes. Its little hands reaching for him, the elfin head tilted, and the shrill bleating laughter.

He reached up slowly with his left hand. But he couldn't grasp the devilish thing. He was afraid perhaps that he actually *could* touch it. And before his eyes, in the mirror, the ghastly miniature kept growing.

He stumbled about the apartment. It was hot, stuffy, damp. His clothes stuck to him. His right shoulder pained and twitched, and he felt its roots in his flesh.

He stumbled to the telephone and called Crita's apartment. He heard the phone ringing, over and over. But no answer. He dropped the receiver and groped his way to the bed, fell on it, shuddering.

From then on the thing on his shoulder talked to him. Talked and laughed.

"I'll not go way. I'll not go way. Not until you come back to Crita."

It was Crita's voice, only it was far away and tiny and silvery now. It mocked and laughed and swayed.

And through the hours, the laughter rose higher and more shrill in his ear. . . .

It was dark in the room. It was hot and sticky. Under his matted hair and through the stubble of beard, his eyes were depthless and terrified.

Suddenly, with a choking cry, he clutched at the thing on his shoulder. It squirmed in his grasp. He tore, wildly, gasping and gibbering. White-hot pain seared his arm, sizzled in his brain. He felt the warm lines of blood crawling down his chest as he slowly withdrew his hand.

The thing began to laugh again. He couldn't rid himself of it. Not that way. He staggered to the mirror. The thing was taller, more full-bodied now. It was four inches high. He knew he couldn't hurt it without hurting himself, and he couldn't stand pain.

He knew the thing laughing and growing from his shoulder was real. That Crita had sent it to him and was making it grow.

Voodoo. Witches in Manhattan. Black Mass on altars of chome and white walnut. He knew now. He believed now.

There was no sleep for Earl. There would never be sleep for him until he went back to Crita, back to her apartment in the Village, with the dusty paintings in the corner. . . .

Long nights, twisting and turning in a clammy shroud. The tiny laughter and the shrill voice mocking and beckoning as the Lorelei beckon.

He had called up Jean. He had tried to explain in a way she would believe. He formulated stories and none of them sounded credible. She kept calling him. He sat waiting for her calls while the thing in the green gown swayed from his shoulder. It was fat and sleek. Its voice was stronger now.

"Come back to Crita. Come back to Crita."

You can't leave me, Earl. The only way you can be free of me is to come back to me.

He phoned Crita's apartment again. He phoned many times. He couldn't remember now how many times. There was never any answer.

But Jean came to see him. She came unexpectedly, without phoning. The bell rang. He cried out, felt his muscles jerk with fear as he stumbled to the door, stood leaning against the wall.

The thing on his shoulder rubbed tiny fingers down his neck. He shivered.

"Let her in. It's Jean. Let her in."

He was muttering. Terror clawed and scrabbled in his heart. His lips felt wet and loose. The little voice whispered hoarsely, *"Let her in, Earl. Hurry. You'll never be able to come back to Crita until Jean's out of the way."*

His hand trembled as he managed to hook it around the knob of the door, and pull it open.

"Jean . . . don't. . . ."

She screamed in terror when she saw him.

"No, Jean. Don't. . . ."

"You've got to kill her, Earl—quick! You've got to stop that screaming!" the little voice whispered.

He slammed the door shut. His back was against it. He jumped. A sense of intense relief flowed through him, warmly, as her cries died between his hands. He kept his hands there, made them tighter and tighter.

"You . . . Jean, I was happy enough . . . things were nice . . . until you and your damned money . . . you . . . talking all the time about what we could do . . . where we could go . . . you laughed at my work. . . ."

He staggered back. He flattened against the wall. His breath was choked and heavy in his throat as he looked down at her. The little familiar on his shoulder twisted its head and looked at him. It laughed its shrill little laugh.

"Hurry, Earl. Come back to Crita. You haven't much time."

He taped the thing down. It shrieked and he tried to smother its cries, bind its lashing body. He put on a coat, then a topcoat. But he could still feel it squirming against him. He could hear its muffled cries as he drove blindly toward Crita's apartment in the Village. . . .

The hallway was still. A faint wind blew some white hall curtains gently. They floated faintly in the soggy darkness. A musty odor hung imprisoned by the flood of dim yellow light outside her door.

He listened. He couldn't hear anything from beyond the door. Only the muffled whispering of the thing on his shoulder, the familiar, the vicious little monster that had grown out of him.

He opened the door and edged into the room. It was very still and smothered in thick dusty shadows and hot breathless air. No songs now to ancient gods. No incantations to the monody of evil drums. There was an unfamiliar smell. Yet he should be able to recognize it—the unmistakable smell of death.

He lurched toward a window. Dead flies lay on the sill, dead flies and dust. He needed air. He cried out as he bumped into something, something that thudded hollowly against his face. Something that swayed back and forth now. There was a creaking sound overhead. The swaying form bumped him, slid around him, then twirled slowly around and around. . . .

Rafters strung across the darkened ceiling like gibbets. Crita! *Crita!* And a length of hemp squeaking on dry wood. Her body in its green gown hanging, stiff and cold and twisted.

He opened his mouth to scream, but nothing happened.

The miniature thing on his shoulder laughed.

We found him crouched in the dark corner of Crita Montez's apartment over a shattered pile of his dusty, abandoned paintings. He later admitted murdering Jean Morris. Crita had evidently committed suicide.

We found a doll in his hand. It was a very lifelike doll with a green dress. It was an amazing duplication of Crita Montez.

An odd case. There's a birthmark on his shoulder—a peculiar birthmark. It looks startlingly like the imprint of a woman's lips.

Police psychiatrist Dr. Joseph Wright says that as far as he can determine, Earl Gleason is sane.

KUNDU

by MORRIS WEST

The true evocation of a primitive culture is not easy for most writers to capture on paper; the sights, sounds, smells—and, of course, insights—are not often fully realized and the treatment is generally superficial. Morris West, however, is not "most writers," and when he sets out to portray a primitive society, as he does in regard to the New Guinean aborigines in Kundu, *the results are both vivid and electrifying.*

Kundu, *which was West's second novel and first to be published in the United States (in 1956, as a paperback original by Dell First Editions), deals in large part with voodoo magic. The excerpts offered here describe the mating ceremony known as* kunande *and the powers of such sorcerers as Kumo, who are able to turn themselves into cassowary birds and run like the wind; they also offer a superior character study of a man named Max Lansing, one of the Australians who have migrated to the area. In sum, as the Dell edition's back cover blurb says, accurately if somewhat flamboyantly, "Here is a story of New Guinea's fetid villages and wind-cooled valleys, of barbaric natives and over-civilized whites—all finally made one in desire and fear by the timeless beat of the great kundu drums."*

Although his first few novels achieved a certain success, it was the publication of The Devil's Advocate *in 1959 that brought Morris West widespread critical acclaim as one of this generation's major writers.*

Such subsequent titles as The Shoes of the Fisherman, Tower of Babel, The Salamander *and* Harlequin *enhanced that reputation and created a worldwide and ever-growing audience for his work. Born in Melbourne, Australia, in 1916, West now makes his home in Europe and is a fellow of the Royal Society of Literature and a member of the World Academy of Arts and Sciences.*

DOWN IN the village, they were making *kunande.*

There were perhaps a hundred of them, bucks and girls, squatting two by two around the little fires in the long, low hut. Behind them in the smoky shadows sat the drum-mers, crouching over the kundus, filling the fetid air with the deep insistent beat that changed from song to song, from verse to refrain, with never a pause and never a falter.

The couples around the fires leaned face to face and breast to breast, and sang low, murmurous, haunting songs that lapsed from time to time into a wordless passionate melody. And, as they sang, they rolled their faces and their breasts together, lip to lip, nipple to nipple, cheek to brown and painted cheek.

The small flames shone on their oiled bodies and glistened on the green armor of the beetles in their headdresses. Their plumes bobbed in the drifting smoke and their necklets of shell and beads made a small clattering like castanets as they turned and rolled to the rolling of the drums.

The air was full of the smell of sweat and oil and smoke and the pubic exhalation of bodies rising slowly to the pitch of passion. This was *kunande,* the public love-play of the unmarried, the courting time, the knowing time, when a man might tell from the responses of his singing partner whether she desired or disdained him. For this was the time of the women. The girl chose her partner for the *kunande,* left him when she chose, solicited him if she wished, or held herself cool and aloof in the formal cadence of the songs.

N'Daria was among them, but the man with her was not

Kumo. Kumo would come in his own time and when he came she would leave her partner and go to him. For the present, she was content to sing and sway and warm herself with the contact of other flesh and let the drum beats take slow possession of her blood.

A woman moved slowly down the line of singers. She was not adorned like the others. Her breasts were heavy with milk, her waist swollen with childbearing. Now she would throw fresh twigs on the fire, now she would part one couple and rearrange the partners. Now she would pour water in the open mouth of a drummer, as he bent back his head without slackening his beat on the black kundu. This was the mistress of ceremonies, the duenna, ordering the courtship to the desires of her younger sisters, dreaming of her own days of *kunande* when she, too, wore the cane belt of the unmarried.

The drum beats rose to a wild climax, then dropped suddenly to a low humming. The singing stopped. The singers opened their eyes and sat rigid, expectant. Distant at first, then closer and closer and closer, they heard the running of the cassowary bird. They heard the great clawed feet pounding the earth— *chuff-chuff-chuff-chuff*—down the mountain path, through the darkness of the rain forest, on to the flat places of the taro gardens and into the village itself. Tomorrow they would go out and see the footprints in the black earth. But now they waited, tense and silent, as the beat came closer and closer, louder than the drums, then stopped abruptly outside the hut.

A moment later, Kumo the Sorcerer stood in the doorway.

He did not enter as the others had done, stooping under the low lintel. He was there, erect and challenging as if he had walked through the wall. He wore a gold wig, fringed with green beetle shards. His forehead was painted green and the upper part of his face was red with ocher. His nose ornament was enormous, his feathered casque was scarlet and blue and orange. His pubic skirt was of woven bark and his belt was covered with cowrie shells. His whole body shone with pig fat.

The boy who had been singing with N'Daria rose and moved

back into the shadows. N'Daria sat waiting. Then Kumo gave a curt signal to the drummers and they swung into a wild loud beat as he moved down the hut and sat facing N'Daria. No word was spoken between them. They sang and moved their faces together as the others did, but N'Daria's body was on fire and the drums beat in her blood, pounding against her belly and her breasts and her closed eyelids.

Then, after a long time, slowly the drum beats died and the fires died with them. Quietly the couples dispersed, some to sleep, some to carry on the love-play in a girl's house, others to seek swift consummation in the shadows of the tangket trees.

Kumo and N'Daria left the hut with them and walked through the darkness to the house of N'Daria's sister. Here there was food and drink and a small fire; and when they had eaten, two of the drummers came in with two more girls and they sat in pairs, backed against the bamboo walls to make the greater love-play, called in pidgin "carry-leg."

Kumo sat with his legs stretched out toward the center of the hut. N'Daria sat beside him, her body half turned to him, her thighs thrown over his left leg. His right leg locked over hers so that he held her firmly, and with his left arm around her shoulders, he drew her close up to his breast. Then the fondling began, a long, slow ritual of excitement, tentative at first, then more and more intimate and urgent. At first, they sang a little, snatches of the *kunande* songs; then they laughed, telling stories of other lovers and scandalous doings in the village and on the jungle paths. They made laughing flatteries of one another's bodies and their skill in the arts of love. Then, gradually, their voices dropped and their whispers became fiercer and more desirous.

"Does the white man touch you like this?"

"No, no." She lied and half believed the lie in the warmth of the moment.

"Is the white man as great a man as I am?" His fingers pressed painfully into her flesh.

"He is not a man. Beside you, he is a lizard."

"If he touches you, I will kill him."

"I would want you to kill him."

"I will make his blood boil and his bones turn to water. I will put ants in his brain and a snake in his belly."

"And I will watch and laugh, Kumo."

He caught her to him, suddenly. His nails scored into her body so that she gasped with the sudden pain.

"What does he teach you there in the little hut?"

She buried her face in his shoulder to hide the small smile of triumph. Kumo was a great sorcerer, the greatest in the valleys. Kumo could change himself into a cassowary bird and travel fast as the wind. But even Kumo did not know the secrets she learned in Sonderfeld's laboratory.

"Tell me. What does he teach you?"

She giggled and clung to him, her hands searching his body.

"What will you give me if I tell you?"

"I will give you the charm that makes children and the charm that destroys them. I will make you desired of all men. I will give you the power to strike any woman barren and make any man a giant to embrace you."

"I want none of these things."

His mouth was pressed to her ear. He whispered urgently, so that the others could not hear, "What do you want? Tell me and I will give it to you. Am I not the greatest sorcerer in the valleys? Does not the Red Spirit speak to me in the thunder and in the wind? Ask me and I will give. What do you want for the secrets of the white man's room?"

"Only that you should take me—now!"

His body shuddered with the flattery and the triumph of it.

"And you will tell me, when?"

"Tomorrow or the day after, when I can come without being seen. But not now—not now!"

Kumo laughed. His plumes tossed. His teeth shone. He swept the girl to her feet and half ran, half carried her out of the hut.

The consummation was a wild, brief frenzy that left her bruised and crumpled and only half content, alone in the tall and trodden kunai grass.

In the warmth of the rich mountain morning, Max Lansing walked home to his village. It lay in a deep saucer-shaped depression between Père Louis's community and the Lahgi Valley. To reach it, he had to make a wide traverse westward of Sonderfeld's property and cross two steep saddles before he struck the path that led over the lip of the crater and downward into the taro plots and the banana groves and the dancing park. He would not reach it till the middle of the afternoon.

He had a water bottle hooked to his belt with a canvas knapsack filled with food from Gerda's kitchen and a bottle of Sonderfeld's best whisky. By midday he would have crossed the first saddle and he would rest and eat by the swift water that came singing down over the rocks from the high peaks. Then he would push on, with neither joy nor impatience, to the small bamboo hut on the outer edge of the village—his home for the years of his subsidized exile.

As he topped the rise that overlooked the plantation, he halted a moment and looked back. He saw the blaze of Gerda's garden, the nestling of the bungalow under its thatched roof, the long serried lines of the plantation trees. He saw the work boys moving about like leisurely ants and the white tall figure of Sonderfeld standing at the head of the first grove. He saw them all as a symbol of permanence and possession, a mockery of his own rootless, pointless existence.

Long, long ago he had been fired with zeal for knowledge— knowledge for its own sake, knowledge without thought of gain, profitless except in human dignity and spiritual enlargement. But the fire had burned out years since and he saw himself, not great among the solitary great ones, but a poor and tattered pedant, piling his dry facts like children's blocks, while the laughing, weeping, lusting, suffering world rolled heedless past his doorstep. Without faith in himself and in his work, he found himself without strength for dedication. He could no longer walk happily among the scholars and he had forgotten the speech of the marketplace. Even his love was a pedantry, dusty and dry beside the welling passion of Gerda.

When Sonderfeld had left the house, he had sat with her at

breakfast on the verandah and he had tried to recapture the brief warmth of their night's embrace. But Gerda refused to match this mood. She had talked cheerfully enough about the dinner party, the guests, the plantation, the news from Goroka. But when he had urged her to discussion of their own relationship, she refused gently, but with finality.

"No, Max. All that can be put into words has been said between us. I am here, whenever you care to come. I will be with you as I have always been. But I will not talk—talk—talk! Better to kiss or make love, or simply walk among the flowers together. But why rake our hearts with words that mean nothing?"

To which, of course, there was no answer. Take it or leave it. He had not the courage to leave it and he lacked the wisdom to take it without question. He must itch and scratch and itch and scratch again until the warm and willing heart was scarred into a running sore.

He had risen abruptly from the table and gathered his things to leave. She had come to him then and kissed him with that maddening maternal gentleness.

"Don't be angry with me, Max. I am as I am. I cannot change. But before you go, let me tell you one thing."

"Yes?"

Let her tell him she loved him, and he would be happy again. Let her give him one small hope, and ambition would soar again, mountains high.

"Be careful, Max, I beg of you. Be careful!"

"Careful of what?"

Her hands made a helpless fluttering gesture.

"I don't know. I wish I did. But after what you said last night, my husband—"

"To hell with your husband!"

He caught her to him, crushing his mouth brutally on hers. Then he released her, picked up his knapsack and without a backward glance strode off, a lost and angry man, storming up the hillside.

When he came to the river he was sweating and exhausted. It was a long walk at the best of times, but for a lonely and unhappy fellow, it was twice as tedious. He plunged down to the water, and felt the humid air close round him like a curtain. A cloud of insects enveloped him. He beat at them irritably with his handkerchief and by the time he reached the sandy hollow near the ford, he was free of them.

He slipped off his knapsack, took a long pull at the water bottle and flung himself down at the edge of the clear singing water. He was too tired to eat, so he lay sprawled on his back, head pillowed on the knapsack, looking up into the dappled green of the jungle overhang, through a cloud of bright blue butterflies. He saw the flash of brilliant scarlet as a bird of paradise made his mating dance on the branch of an albizzia tree. A tiny tree kangaroo peered cautiously between two broad purple leaves. A lizard sunned himself on the rock beside him, and in the undergrowth he heard the scurrying of small animals, rooting for food.

The thought struck him that in his four-hour walk he had seen not a single human being. This was unusual, for the mountain paths were the highways of the tribes. Since the white man's law had abolished war and killing raids, there was a modest traffic between the villages in canes and bird of paradise feathers and gum and galip nuts and pigs and produce of the gardens.

This traffic had been increased of late by the movement of the tribes for the approaching pig festival. Yet today he had seen no one. Because he was tired, the thought nagged at him uneasily. He fumbled for a cigarette, lit it and watched the blue smoke spiral up toward the green canopy.

Then he heard it, distant but distinct—*chuff-chuff-chuff*—the unmistakable beat of a running cassowary. The sound was unusual enough to interest him. The cassowary bird was native to the high valleys, but the breed was being thinned out by killing and the survivors were retreating into the less populated mountains.

The footsteps came closer, thudding like the muffled beat of a train on steel rails. Lansing sat up. The bird was coming down the same path that he had followed. He wondered if it would break out on to the beach.. He was not afraid, only interested.

The big ungainly bird is easily frightened and will not attack a human being unless it is angered or cornered. The footsteps came closer and closer. Then they stopped.

He judged the bird was probably a dozen yards away, hidden by the dense screen of undergrowth. He could hear its rustling among the leaves and low branches. Then the rustling stopped, and after a moment Lansing lay back drowsily against the knapsack. He thought he would sleep a little, then eat before he continued his walk. He worked a hollow for his hip in the warm sand and turned comfortably on his side.

Suddenly, a yard from his face, he saw a small white snake, dappled with black spots. In the suspended moment of shock he saw the trail of its body in the white sand. It had come from the bush at his back, the deadliest reptile in the whole island. If it struck him, he would die, paralyzed and beyond help, within two hours. Cautiously, he moved his hand to get purchase on the sand, then, with a single movement, he thrust himself to his feet. In that same moment the snake moved, fast as a flicker of light to the spot where his head had lain. Its jaws opened and it struck at the stiff canvas of the knapsack. Before Lansing had time to snatch up a stick or stone it was gone again, a dappled death, slithering into the fallen leaves at the fringe of the bush.

Sick with terror, he stood looking down at the knapsack and the tiny dark stain of the ejected poison. Then he shivered, snatched up the bag and plunged across the ford, heedless of the water that swirled about his knees and the hidden stones that sent him half-sprawling into the icy current.

Gerda's parting words beat in his brain. "Be careful, Max. I beg of you, be careful."

Breathless, he scrambled up the steep bank and looked back at the small white beach. It was bare and empty of life. The jungle was like a painted backdrop, motionless in the heavy air.

Then he heard it again—*chuff-chuff-chuff*—the running feet of the cassowary, retreating into the stillness.

Suddenly he remembered the cassowary men. They were an old story in the valleys, an old fear among the tribes. They were sorcerers who, by common repute, had power to change themselves into cassowary birds and run faster than the wind. They were the Territory counterpart of the Carpathian werewolves and the jackal-men of Africa. The tribes believed in them implicitly and for proof pointed to the claw marks on the soft ground after a nocturnal visit from one of the sorcerers. Newcomers to the mountains scoffed at such rank superstition, but the old hands—traders, missionaries, senior men in the District services —were less skeptical. Each had his own stories to tell of phenomena apparently beyond physical explanation. But all had one thing in common: a healthy respect and a prickling fear of the dim borderlands of primitive mysticism.

At first Lansing had rejected the manifestations as pure charlatanry. But the more he studied, the less certain he became; and now, in the eerie solitude of the upland paths, he, too, was gripped by the cold, uncanny fear of the bird man.

It was late in the afternoon when he came to the village. The mountain shadows were lengthening and the first faint chill was creeping down the valley. He was hungry and tired and trembling as if with the onset of fever. He paid no heed to the curious stares of the villagers, but went straight to his hut, crammed a couple of suppressant tablets in his mouth, stripped himself naked and sponged himself with water from the canvas bucket.

When he was clean and dressed in fresh clothes, he poured himself a noggin of Sonderfeld's whisky and tossed it off at a gulp. He poured another, tempered it with water and stood in his doorway with the glass in his hand, looking out on the village.

The women were coming up from the taro gardens, naked except for the pubic belt, their thick bodies bowed under the weight of string baskets full of sweet potatoes which they carried suspended from their broad foreheads and supported on the small of their backs. In the far corner of the compound a young girl was feeding the pigs. They were blinded so that they could not run away and tethered to stakes of casuarina wood. They grunted and snuffled and squealed as she passed among them with fruit rinds and bananas and taro pulp.

The pigs and the gardens and the children, these were the

charges of the women—and in that order. A woman would suckle a child at one breast and a piglet at the other. The men would make the gardens, laying them out, breaking the first soil, marking each patch with the small blunt mound of the phallic symbol crossed with the cut that represented the female principle. But it was the women who tilled them and dug the big ripe tubers that were the staple diet of the tribe.

As for the men, they sat as they sat now: one making a ceremonial wig of fiber and gum and flaring feathers and green beetle shards; another plaiting a cane socket for his obsidian axe; this one chipping a round stone for the head of his club; that, stringing the short cane bow which would bring down birds and possums and the furry cuscus whose tail made armlets for the bucks and the unmarried girls.

Looking at them there, bent over their small tasks, Lansing thought how like children they were—intent, mistrustful, jealous of their trivial possessions. The second thought came hard on the heels of the first. They were not children. They were adults, intelligent within the limits of their knowledge, bound by sanctions older than the Pentateuch, preoccupied with the problems of birth and death—and survival for the years between.

To the outsider their tasks were trivial, but in the small stringent world of the tribal unit, they were of major importance. Let a blight come on the taro patch, the whole village must move to new territory. If the pigs should be stricken with swine fever, they would have no protein in their diet—the ancient island of New Guinea is poor in all but the smallest animal life.

They went naked because there were no furs to give them warmth. They practiced abortion and birth control because there was a limit to the crops that could be raised in the narrow gardens and because the pigs were decimated at festival after festival by a meat-hungry people, bound, moreover, by the primal need to propitiate a hostile Pig God in whom lay the principle of fertility. They had no written language. They had never made a wheel. Their traditions were buried in ancient words and phrases that even the elders could not translate.

In their narrow uncertain world, love, as the white man knew it, did not exist. The girl who made the love-play in the *kunande* would be raped on her wedding night and her husband would scowl if she wore any but the simplest ornament. In certain villages a man chose his bride by firing an arrow into her thigh —an act of hostility and enslavement.

In this climate of fear, behind the closed frontiers of the razorbacks, superstition flourished like a rank growth and the old magical practices of the dawn people were the straws to which the simple clung for security and the clubs which the ambitious used to bludgeon them into submission.

As he sipped his whisky and watched the small but complex pattern unfold itself, Lansing was conscious of his own inadequacy. Two years now he had lived among these people. His notebooks were full of careful observations on every aspect of their life pattern, yet he was as far from understanding them as he had been on the day of his arrival. It was as if there were a curtain drawn between him and the arcana of their secret life and unless he could penetrate the curtain, his work would be without significance.

The missionaries did better. The old ones, like Père Louis, did best of all. They came unabashed to make commerce in souls and spirits. They had secrets of their own to trade. They offered protection against the sorcerers, an answer to the ambient mystery of creation.

But when you didn't believe in the soul, when you were committed by birth and training to the pragmatic materialism of the twentieth century, what then? You were shut out from the sanctuary, condemned to walk in the courts of the strangers, denied access to the mysteries and the sacrifice.

He tossed off the dregs of his whisky, rinsed the glass carefully and set it on the table. Then he walked out into the compound.

There was a girl in the village whom he had trained to look after him, to wash his clothes and tidy his hut and prepare his food with moderate cleanliness. He had not seen her since his arrival; he was going to look for her.

First, he went to her father's hut. The girl was not there. The old man was sitting outside the door sharpening a set of cane

arrows. When Lansing questioned him, he gave him a sidelong
look, shrugged indifferently and bent over his work. Accustomed to the moodiness of the mountain folk, Lansing made no
comment but walked over to a group of women bending over a
fire pit.

They giggled and simpered and exchanged smiles of secret
amusement, but they would tell him nothing. He was irritated,
but he dared not show it for fear of losing face. He hailed the
women coming up from the taro gardens. They shook their
heads. They had not set eyes on the girl. He tried the children,
but they drew away from him and ran to hide their faces behind
the buttocks of their mothers.

Then, suddenly, he became aware that the whole village was
watching him. They had not paused for a moment in their work,
but they were following his every movement, eyes slanting and
secret, their smiles a silent mockery. They were not hostile, they
were simply amused. They were watching a dancing doll, jerked
this way and that by forces beyond his control.

Anger rose in him, sour and acid from the pit of his belly. He
wanted to shout at them, curse them, strike them at least into
recognition of his presence. He knew he could not do it. The
loss of face would be final and irrecoverable.

He turned on his heel and with elaborate slowness walked
back to his hut. He closed the door and lit the lamp. His hands
were trembling and his palms were clammy with sweat. This
concerted mockery was new in his experience. Sullenness he had
met and had learned to ignore. Suspicion had been rasped and
honed away by the daily familiar intercourse. This was something different. It was like . . . he fumbled for a tag to identify
the strangeness . . . like being sent to Coventry. But for what?

He knew enough of ritual and custom to make him careful of
their observance. He had crossed no one of the elders. He was
aloof from village scandal. There was no reason why they should
turn against him. Then, he thought of Sonderfeld and of Kumo
and of Gerda's cryptic warning; and he was suddenly afraid.

He thought of Père Louis and the dappled snake and the
sound of the unseen cassowary bird and his fear was a wild,

screaming terror. He was alone and naked and defenseless among the secret people in the darkening valley.

Desperately he struggled for control. At all costs he must show a brave face to the village mockery, must maintain the simple order of his studious existence.

He broke out Gerda's package of food and tried to eat. The cold food gagged him and he thrust it away. He lit the spirit lamp and tried to work over his notes, but the letters danced confusedly before his eyes and his trembling fingers could not control the pencil.

Then, with the abrupt coming of darkness, the kundus began their maddening climactic rhythm. He felt as though they were throbbing inside his skull case, thudding and pounding till his brain must burst into wild incurable madness.

Then he knew what he must do if he were to get through the night. He set the whisky bottle and the water canteen on the table in front of him, broke out a fresh pack of cigarettes, pushed the lamp to a safe distance from his elbow and began carefully and methodically to get himself drunk.

He drank slowly at first lest his empty stomach revolt and cheat him of relief. Then, as the liquor warmed and relaxed him, he poured larger tots and used less water, until finally he was drinking neat spirits and the level of the bottle was below the halfway mark.

Long before the drums were silent, long before the singers were dumb, Max Lansing was slumped across his table, with his head pillowed on his unfinished manuscript, one nerveless hand lying on an overturned bottle, the other dangling over a broken glass and a pool of liquor that soaked slowly into the earthen floor.

Then Kumo came in.

All through the solitary orgy he had been squatting outside the hut watching Lansing's slow collapse into insensibility. He was dressed in the ceremonial costume with the tossing plumes and the clattering ornaments of pearl shell. His long, crescent nose ornament gave him the look of a tusked animal. Tucked in his fur armband he carried a small closed tube of bamboo.

For a long moment he stood over the unconscious man, then with a sudden gesture he lifted Max's head by the hair and let it fall with a thump on the table. Lansing made no sound. His head lolled into equilibrium on one cheek and one ear. Kumo grunted with satisfaction, and took the bamboo tube in his hands.

First he rolled it rapidly between his fingers, then tapped it rapidly on the edge of the desk, making a dry, drumming sound. Finally, he held it a long time against the hot glass of the lamp, so that the warmth soaked through the pithy wood and into the hollow center.

Now he was ready.

Carefully he took up his position between the edge of the table and the open door of the hut. Then he bent over Lansing, holding the butt of the tube in one hand and its cap in the other, the cap end pointing downwards, six inches from Lansing's face. With a sharp movement, he pulled off the cap and stepped backwards. There was a soft *plop* and a small dappled snake fell onto the desk.

Maddened by the noise and the movement and the heat, the snake struck and struck again at Lansing's cheek. Then it slithered off the table and disappeared in the shadows of the hut.

Anesthetized by the liquor, Lansing felt no pain and made no movement. Kumo stood a moment looking down at his victim and at the twin punctures just below his cheekbone. Then, silently as the snake, he, too, went out into the darkness and soon, over the beat of the drums, the villagers heard the thudding feet of the cassowary bird.

PART III
THE "ULTIMATE" VOODOO

THE CANDIDATE

by HENRY SLESAR

The plot of this "ultimate" voodoo story is doubly intriguing: not only is it a brilliant and unique fiction idea, it may also be "an idea whose time has come" for practical application. There are a lot of people in this world who have harmed others—dozens or hundreds or thousands of others—and who would make the good Earth a happier place by departing it. Just think of the politicians alone who fall into that category. . . .

Could it work, this unique idea, this "ultimate" voodoo? Could an organization such as the Society for United Action be formed and achieve the results postulated herein? Perhaps. After all, we know that almost anything is possible these days. Almost anything at all.

One thing is certain: no one would want to be in Burton Grunzer's shoes.

Since he began writing in 1956, while in his late twenties, Henry Slesar has accumulated a list of credits that any ten average authors would be hard-pressed to equal in a lifetime: some five hundred and fifty short stories in periodicals ranging from Ellery Queen's Mystery Magazine *to* Playboy; *two collections; five novels, the first of which,* The Gray Flannel Shroud, *received the Mystery Writers of America Edgar Award as Best First Mystery of 1959; twenty radio plays for* CBS Radio Mystery Theatre; *well over a hundred teleplays for such shows as* Alfred Hitchcock Presents *(which alone produced sixty of his scripts),* Run for Your

Life, Batman, *and* The Man from U.N.C.L.E.; *and, last but by no means least, all the scripts for the much-acclaimed daytime TV serial* The Edge of Night, *which won the National Academy of Television Arts and Sciences Emmy Award in 1973. (At the same time, for two years, he was head writer for another daytime serial,* Somerset.*) TV Guide *once called him "the writer with the largest audience in America." Little wonder. At present he lives in New York City, not all that far from his Brooklyn birthplace.*

A MAN'S worth can be judged by the calibre of his enemies. Burton Grunzer, encountering the phrase in a pocket-sized biography he had purchased at a newsstand, put the book in his lap and stared reflectively from the murky window of the commuter train. Darkness silvered the glass and gave him nothing to look at but his own image, but it seemed appropriate to his line of thought. How many people were enemies of that face, of the eyes narrowed by a myopic squint denied by vanity the correction of spectacles, of the nose he secretly called patrician, of the mouth that was soft in relaxation and hard when animated by speech or smiles or frowns? How many enemies? Grunzer mused. A few he could name, others he could guess. But it was their calibre that was important. Men like Whitman Hayes, for instance; there was a 24-carat opponent for you. Grunzer smiled, darting a sidelong glance at the seat-sharer beside him, not wanting to be caught indulging in a secret thought. Grunzer was thirty-four; Hayes was twice as old, his white hairs synonymous with experience, an enemy to be proud of. Hayes knew the food business, all right, knew it from every angle: he'd been a wagon jobber for six years, a broker for ten, a food company executive for twenty before the old man had brought him into the organization to sit on his right hand. Pinning Hayes to the mat wasn't easy, and that made Grunzer's small but increasing triumphs all the sweeter. He congratulated himself. He had twisted Hayes's advantages into drawbacks, had made his long years seem tantamount to senility and outlived usefulness; in meetings, he had concentrated his questions on the new supermarket and suburbia phenomena to demonstrate to the old man that times had changed, that the past was dead, that new merchandising tactics were needed, and that only a younger man could supply them. . . .

Suddenly, he was depressed. His enjoyment of remembered victories seemed tasteless. Yes, he'd won a minor battle or two in the company conference room; he'd made Hayes's ruddy face go crimson, and seen the old man's parchment skin wrinkle in a sly grin. But what had been accomplished? Hayes seemed more self-assured than ever, and the old man more dependent upon his advice. . . .

When he arrived home, later than usual, his wife Jean didn't ask questions. After eight years of a marriage in which, childless, she knew her husband almost too well, she wisely offered nothing more than a quiet greeting, a hot meal, and the day's mail. Grunzer flipped through the bills and circulars, and found an unmarked letter. He slipped it into his hip pocket, reserving it for private perusal, and finished the meal in silence.

After dinner, Jean suggested a movie and he agreed; he had a passion for violent action movies. But first, he locked himself in the bathroom and opened the letter. Its heading was cryptic: *Society for United Action.* The return address was a post office box. It read:

> *Dear Mr. Grunzer:*
> *Your name has been suggested to us by a mutual acquaintance. Our organization has an unusual mission which cannot be described in this letter, but which you may find of exceeding interest. We would be gratified by a private discussion at your earliest convenience. If I do not hear from you to the contrary in the next few days, I will take the liberty of calling you at your office.*

It was signed, *Carl Tucker, Secretary.* A thin line at the bottom of the page read: *A Nonprofit Organization.*

His first reaction was a defensive one; he suspected an oblique attack on his pocketbook. His second was curiosity: he went to the bedroom and located the telephone directory, but found no organization listed by the letterhead name. *Okay, Mr. Tucker,* he thought wryly, *I'll bite.*

When no call came in the next three days, his curiosity was increased. But when Friday arrived, he forgot the letter's promise in the crush of office affairs. The old man called a meeting with the bakery products division. Grunzer sat opposite Whitman Hayes at the conference table, poised to pounce on fallacies in his statements. He almost had him once, but Eckhardt, the bakery products manager, spoke up in defense of Hayes's views. Eckhardt had only been with the company a year, but he had evidently chosen sides already. Grunzer glared at him, and reserved a place for Eckhardt in the hate chamber of his mind.

At three o'clock, Carl Tucker called.

"Mr. Grunzer?" The voice was friendly, even cheery. "I haven't heard from you, so I assume you don't mind my calling today. Is there a chance we can get together sometime?"

"Well, if you could give me some idea, Mr. Tucker—"

The chuckle was resonant. "We're not a charity organization, Mr. Grunzer, in case you got that notion. Nor do we sell anything. We're more or less a voluntary service group: our membership is over a thousand at present."

"To tell you the truth," Grunzer frowned, "I never heard of you."

"No, you haven't, and that's one of the assets. I think you'll understand when I tell you about us. I can be over at your office in fifteen minutes, unless you want to make it another day."

Grunzer glanced at his calendar. "Okay, Mr. Tucker. Best time for me is right now."

"Fine! I'll be right over."

Tucker was prompt. When he walked into the office, Grunzer's eyes went dismayed at the officious briefcase in the man's right hand. But he felt better when Tucker, a florid man in his early sixties with small, pleasant features, began talking.

"Nice of you to take the time, Mr. Grunzer. And believe me,

I'm not here to sell you insurance or razor blades. Couldn't if I tried; I'm a semi-retired broker. However, the subject I want to discuss is rather—intimate, so I'll have to ask you to bear with me on a certain point. May I close the door?"

"Sure," Grunzer said, mystified.

Tucker closed it, hitched his chair closer and said:

"The point is this. What I have to say must remain in the strictest confidence. If you betray that confidence, if you publicize our society in any way, the consequences could be most unpleasant. Is that agreeable?"

Grunzer, frowning, nodded.

"Fine!" The visitor snapped open the briefcase and produced a stapled manuscript. "Now, the society has prepared this little spiel about our basic philosophy, but I'm not going to bore you with it. I'm going to go straight to the heart of our argument. You may not agree with our first principle at all, and I'd like to know that now."

"How do you mean, first principle?"

"Well . . ." Tucker flushed slightly. "Put in the crudest form, Mr. Grunzer, the Society for United Action believes that—*some* people are just not fit to live." He looked up quickly, as if anxious to gauge the immediate reaction. "There, I've said it," he laughed, somewhat in relief. "Some of our members don't believe in my direct approach; they feel the argument has to be broached more discreetly. But frankly, I've gotten excellent results in this rather crude manner. How do you feel about what I've said, Mr. Grunzer?"

"I don't know. Guess I never thought about it much."

"Were you in the war, Mr. Grunzer?"

"Yes. Navy." Grunzer rubbed his jaw. "I suppose I didn't think the Japs were fit to live, back then. I guess maybe there are other cases. I mean, you take capital punishment, I believe in that. Murderers, rape-artists, perverts, hell, I certainly don't think *they're* fit to live."

"Ah," Tucker said. "So you really accept our first principle. It's a question of category, isn't it?"

"I guess you could say that."

"Good. So now I'll try another blunt question. Have you—personally—ever wished someone dead? Oh, I don't mean those casual, fleeting wishes everybody has. I mean a real, deep-down, uncomplicated wish for the death of someone *you* thought was unfit to live. Have you?"

"Sure," Grunzer said frankly. "I guess I have."

"There are times, in your opinion, when the removal of someone from this earth would be beneficial?"

Grunzer smiled. "Hey, what is this? You from Murder, Incorporated or something?"

Tucker grinned back. "Hardly, Mr. Grunzer, hardly. There is absolutely no criminal aspect to our aims or our methods. I'll admit we're a 'secret' society, but we're no Black Hand. You'd be amazed at the quality of our membership; it even includes members of the legal profession. But suppose I tell you how the society came into being?

"It began with two men; I can't reveal their names just now. The year was 1949, and one of these men was a lawyer attached to the district attorney's office. The other man was a state psychiatrist. Both of them were involved in a rather sensational trial, concerning a man accused of a hideous crime against two small boys. In their opinion, the man was unquestionably guilty, but an unusually persuasive defense counsel, and a highly suggestible jury, gave him his freedom. When the shocking verdict was announced, these two, who were personal friends as well as colleagues, were thunderstruck and furious. They felt a great wrong had been committed, and they were helpless to right it. . . .

"But I should explain something about this psychiatrist. For some years, he had made studies in a field which might be called anthropological psychiatry. One of these researches related to the voodoo practice of certain groups, the Haitian in particular. You've probably heard a great deal about voodoo, or Obeah as they call it in Jamaica, but I won't dwell on the subject lest you think we hold tribal rites and stick pins in dolls. . . . But the chief feature of his study was the uncanny *success* of certain strange practices. Naturally, as a scientist, he rejected the supernatural explanation and sought the rational one. And of course, there was only one answer. When the *vodun* priest decreed the punishment or death of a malefactor, it was the malefactor's own convictions concerning the efficacy of the death wish, his own faith in the voodoo power, that eventually made the wish come true. Sometimes, the process was organic—his body reacted psychosomatically to the voodoo curse, and he would sicken and die. Sometimes, he would die by 'accident'—an accident prompted by the secret belief that once cursed, he *must* die. Eerie, isn't it?"

"No doubt," Grunzer said, dry-lipped.

"Anyway, our friend, the psychiatrist, began wondering aloud if *any* of us have advanced so far along the civilized path that we couldn't be subject to this same sort of 'suggested' punishment. He proposed that they experiment on this choice subject, just to see.

"How they did it was simple," he said. "They went to see this man, and they announced their intentions. They told him they were going to *wish him dead.* They explained how and why the wish would become reality, and while he laughed at their proposal, they could see the look of superstitious fear cross his face. They promised him that regularly, every day, they would be wishing for his death, until he could no longer stop the mystic juggernaut that would make the wish come true."

Grunzer shivered suddenly, and clenched his fist. "That's pretty silly," he said softly.

"The man died of a heart attack two months later."

"Of course. I knew you'd say that. But there's such a thing as coincidence."

"Naturally. And our friends, while intrigued, weren't satisfied. *So they tried it again."*

"Again?"

"Yes, again. I won't recount who the victim was, but I will tell you that this time they enlisted the aid of four associates. This little band of pioneers was the nucleus of the society I represent today."

Grunzer shook his head. "And you mean to tell me there's a *thousand* now?"

"Yes, a thousand and more, all over the country. A society whose one function is to *wish people dead.* At first, membership was purely voluntary, but now we have a system. Each new member of the Society for United Action joins on the basis of submitting one potential victim. Naturally, the society investigates to determine whether the victim is deserving of his fate. If the case is a good one, the *entire* membership then sets about to *wish him dead.* Once the task has been accomplished, naturally, the new member must take part in all future concerted action. That and a small yearly fee, is the price of membership."

Carl Tucker grinned.

"And in case you think I'm not serious, Mr. Grunzer—" He dipped into the briefcase again, this time producing a blue-bound volume of telephone directory thickness. "Here are the facts. To date, two hundred and twenty-nine victims were named by our selection committee. Of those, *one hundred and four* are no longer alive. Coincidence, Mr. Grunzer?

"As for the remaining one hundred and twenty-five—perhaps that indicates that our method is not infallible. We're the first to admit that. But new techniques are being developed all the time. I assure you, Mr. Grunzer, *we will get them all.*"

He flipped through the blue-bound book.

"Our members are listed in this book, Mr. Grunzer. I'm going to give you the option to call one, ten or a hundred of them. Call them and see if I'm not telling the truth."

He flipped the manuscript toward Grunzer's desk. It landed on the blotter with a thud. Grunzer picked it up.

"Well?" Tucker said. "Want to call them?"

"No." He licked his lips. "I'm willing to take your word for it, Mr. Tucker. It's incredible, but I can see how it works. Just *knowing* that a thousand people are wishing you dead is enough to shake hell out of you." His eyes narrowed. "But there's one question. You talked about a 'small' fee—"

"It's fifty dollars, Mr. Grunzer."

"Fifty, huh? Fifty times a thousand, that's pretty good money, isn't it?"

"I assure you, the organization is not motivated by profit. Not the kind you mean. The dues merely cover expenses, committee work, research and the like. Surely you can understand that?"

"I guess so," he grunted.

"Then you find it interesting?"

Grunzer swiveled his chair about to face the window.

God! he thought.

God! if it *really* worked!

But how could it? If wishes became deeds, he would have slaughtered dozens in his lifetime. Yet, that was different. His wishes were always secret things, hidden where no man could know them. But this method was different, more practical, more terrifying. Yes, he could see how it might work. He could visualize a thousand minds burning with the single wish of death, see the victim sneering in disbelief at first, and then slowly, gradually, surely succumbing to the tightening, constricting chain of fear that it *might* work, that so many deadly thoughts could indeed emit a mystical, malevolent ray that destroyed life.

Suddenly, ghostlike, he saw the ruddy face of Whitman Hayes before him.

He wheeled about and said:

"But the victim has to *know* all this, of course? He has to know the society exists, and has succeeded, and is wishing for *his* death? That's essential, isn't it?"

"Absolutely essential," Tucker said, replacing the manuscripts in his briefcase. "You've touched on the vital point, Mr. Grunzer. The victim must be informed, and that, precisely, is what I have done." He looked at his watch. "Your death wish began at noon today. The society has begun to work. I'm very sorry."

At the doorway, he turned and lifted both hat and briefcase in one departing salute.

"Goodbye, Mr. Grunzer," he said.

Book Two

MUMMY!

A Chrestomathy
of Crypt·ology

INTRODUCTION

Death will slay with his wings
whoever disturbs the peace of the pharaoh
    —Inscription on a tablet
       found in the tomb of
       Tutankhamun

YOU ARE standing in the main chamber of an ancient Egyptian tomb.

You have just broken through the wall from the antechamber, after applying candle tests for toxic gases. The air is hot, musty, thick with dust; the oppressive odors of the dust mingled with spices and decay assail your nostrils. Panting for breath, you use one hand to rub sweat from your eyes and the other to extend your flickering torch into the darkness. The yellowish dust begins to settle, and as it does you can finally see what surrounds you within the tomb—a sight that no other living human has beheld in more than three thousand years.

The walls of the chamber are covered with intricate paintings and hieroglyphic inscriptions from the Book of the Dead. Arranged along the floor are *ushabtiu* figures of the god Osiris, gold and bronze statues of Horus, Isis, and Amen-Ra, canopic jars in which the principal intestines of the mummy would have been placed, scarabs and amulets, sepulchral boxes and tablets, lidded pottery vessels, tables and couches inlaid with squares of colored glass, life-sized figures kilted in gold and armed with mace and staff. Across the far wall is a gilt shrine, with folding doors closed and bolted. Behind those doors, you are certain, there will be another shrine and another set of doors, and behind the second set you will find the sarcophagus and the mummy of the pharaoh whose burial chamber this is.

Again you rub sweat from your eyes; your hand around the torch trembles slightly, causing the light to quiver and cast dancing shadows over the walls. You cross in slow steps to the shrine, each one stirring up more dust of the centuries. The closed doors are bolted but not locked, and you draw the bolts and swing the doors open and pass through. The second set of doors is also closed and bolted, but on this set there is a seal. This tells you that the pharaoh's resting place has never been disturbed by thieves; his sarcophagus and his mummy are just as they were when the priests laid them here three and a half millenia ago.

You breathe a relieved sigh, prepare to break the seal and unbolt the doors. But something stays your hand and gives you pause. Then you realize that above the cartouche there is an odd inscription in hieroglyphs. You shine your torchlight on it. You're familiar with ancient Egyptian writing and you study these hieroglyphs for some time, trying to decipher the message. It seems to say something about tomb robbers, but you can't be sure without much more intensive study in better light. It also seems to say something about death coming to anyone who disturbs the sleep of the pharaoh.

An ancient curse?

You do not believe in curses, of course; only fools and superstitious natives believe in such nonsense. So you put it out of your mind without dwelling on it. And proceed to break the seal on the second set of doors.

It is not long before you are standing before a delicately carved sarcophagus of fine rose granite, crafted in the image of Osiris. Within it, you know from past experience, you will find a wooden coffin, and within that a second coffin made of pure gold. The mummy will lie within this second coffin, its head perhaps protected by a gold and jewel-encrusted mask, its body wrapped in linen bandages in which will be hidden more precious stones.

Your hands are still trembling; you can't wait to open the sarcophagus and the two coffins, to remove the mask and the linen head-wrappings. To feast your eyes on the mummy of the pharaoh. But you know that you cannot do these things alone: the lids of the sarcophagus and the golden coffin are too heavy for one person to move. You must leave the tomb immediately, bring back others to help you.

And yet something stays you again, keeps you standing motionless above the sarcophagus. A sound? Movement among the shadows behind you? You twist your head, shine your torch back through the doorways into the main chamber. Undulant particles of dust, the cold gleam of gold; nothing more. You look back at the mummy case. The air in the tomb seems to have grown hotter, closer; you feel yourself starting to pant for breath again. The silence has taken on an eerie quality. The odor of decay seems stronger, almost suffocating. Suddenly you remember the inscription above the cartouche, and an irrational urge forms inside you to turn and flee this place, out into the light of the hot desert sun. You fight it down. And chide yourself about imagination and the power of suggestion.

But you are still unable to leave the presence of the sarcophagus. It is as if the sculpture of Osiris, or perhaps the mummy that lies within, has rendered you incapable of movement. You can do nothing except to stand listening to the eerie silence.

And to the whispers in your mind.

From the dead and crumbling past . . . whispers.

You know the penalty, they seem to say. For the inscription, the curse, speaks truly. The wrath of the gods awaits all those who desecrate the tomb of the pharaoh.

You know the penalty . . . .

The Egyptian practice of entombing the dead began in the Third Dynasty, about 2650 B.C., and was the logical culmination of a series of burial methods devised to protect the remains from marauding animals. Early graves were dug in a cultivated strip of land west of the Nile (the Egyptians believed that the entrance to the underworld was located where the sun sank behind the desert sands); the dead were placed on their left side in fetal positions and covered with fiber mats. These primitive ditches evolved into rectangular pits, then into chambers, with side chambers eventually added as storerooms for gifts and worldly possessions. The last stage of development was to build an outer wall around the tomb, forming a monument shaped like a long-ish rectangle with its four walls symmetrically inclined toward their common center; this monument was called a mastaba. By placing narrow mastabs one on top of another, the first step-pyramids were created.

Such tombs, it was believed, also served as a home for the *ka*, the spirit that protected the dead. Early on, false doors were constructed with the name of the deceased and various prayers and magical inscriptions emblazoned on them; these doors were always placed on the east side, facing west. Later, rooms and labyrinthian passages were built behind the doors, often to dis-courage grave robbers.

It was not until 2400 B.C. that the art of embalming was per-fected by Egyptian priests. (The oldest mummy in the world, however, dates from eight hundred years prior to this time: Seker-em-sa-f, son of Pepi I, found in 1881 at Saqqara.) So complex and innovative were these mummification techniques that modern science, with all its knowledge and apparatus, has not yet uncovered the entire list of details. Herodotus, the Greek historian, is the first to have witnessed (on a journey to Egypt in the fifth century B.C.) and written about the essential meth-ods:

> There are persons who are appointed as professional em-balmers. They, when the dead body is brought to them, show to the bearers wooden models of corpses made exactly life-like by painting. And they show that which they say is the most expensive manner of embalming next to that of the gods themselves, the name of which [Osiris] I do not think

it right to mention on such an occasion; they then show the second, which is inferior and less expensive; and then the third, which is the cheapest. Having explained them all, they learn from them in what way they wish the body to be prepared; then the relations, when they have agreed on the price, depart; but the embalmers remaining in the workshops thus proceed to embalm in the most expensive manner.

First they draw out the brains through the nostrils with an iron hook, taking part of it out in this manner, the rest by the infusion of drugs. Then with a sharp Ethiopian stone they make an incision in the side, and take out all the bowels; and having cleansed the abdomen and rinsed it with palm wine, they next sprinkle it with pounded perfumes. Then having filled the belly with pure myrrh pounded, and cassia, and other perfumes, frankincense excepted, they sew it up again; and when they have done this, they steep it in natron, leaving it under for seventy days; for a longer time than this it is not lawful to steep it. At the expiration of the seventy days they wash the corpse, and wrap the whole body in bandages of flaxen cloth, smearing it with gum, which the Egyptians commonly use instead of glue. After this the body is returned to the relations, who make a wooden case in the shape of a man [actually Osiris], and having made it, enclose the body; and thus, having fastened it, they store it in a sepulchral chamber, setting it upright against the wall.

Those who, avoiding great expense, desire the middle way, they prepare in the following manner. When they have charged their syringes with oil made from cedar, they fill the abdomen of the corpse without making any incision or taking out the bowels, but inject it at the anus; and having prevented the injection from escaping, they steep the body in natron for the prescribed number of days, and on the last day they let out from the abdomen the oil of cedar which they had before injected, and it has such power that it brings away the intestines and vitals in a state of dissolution; the natron dissolves the flesh, and nothing of the body remains but the skin and the bones. When they have done this they return the body without any further operation.

The third method of embalming is this, which is used only

for the poorer sort. Having thoroughly rinsed the abdomen in syrmaea [a laxative], and having salted it, they steep it in natron for seventy days and then deliver it to be carried away.

Four centuries later, Diodorus Siculus provided more details following his own visit to Egypt:

> Once the corpse has been laid down, a man known as the demonstrator puts a mark on the left side of the body where the incision is to be made. Then the man who is called the dissecter takes a knife of Ethiopian stone and cuts through the abdominal wall, precisely according to the instructions. Then he runs away, and those present pursue him, throw stones after him, and curse him for what he has done. For in Egypt anyone is hated who injures or wounds or does some other damage to another. On the other hand, the embalmers enjoy dignity and honor. They are on the same level as the priests and are allowed into the temple as holy men without anyone hindering them.
>
> When the embalmers have gathered to prepare the opened body, one of them puts his hand through the wound into the chest and takes out heart and kidney. Another cleans the organs and makes them fragrant with palm wine and incense. After the corpse has been washed, it is treated for thirty days with cedar oil, later with myrrh and cinnamon.
>
> The dead are then returned to their relatives. So carefully have the bodies been prepared that even eyelashes and brows are intact. The body exterior does not change and even facial expressions are recognizable.

Modern Egyptologists have noted that brains were first removed from the skull during the Eighteenth Dynasty (from 1570 B.C.). The nasal septum was cut through by chisel and hammer, after which the brain was drawn out through the nose with an iron fire hook. The heart, believed to be the seat of spirit and emotion, was not treated as were other organs, since it would be weighed during the last judgment. On some occasions it was left inside the body; on others it was replaced by a holy scarab. Also, the dead were stuffed during the drying process with herbs and straw, or with desert sand, to prevent shrinkage and/or malformation. Milk, mastic, wine, and cedar oil were used to give the skin color; cheeks and eye sockets were prepared with linen balls; the nostrils were sealed with resin. Incense and myrrh were placed inside the mouth because the Egyptians believed these aromatic resins possessed such great powers that they could overcome even the *ka* of the gods. Other spices and drugs used in mummification include balsam, laudanum, storax, and galbanum.

Historians estimate that by the time the practice died out among the Egyptians in A.D. 700, they had embalmed some 730 million corpses. Many of these mummies were destroyed by grave robbers, or disintegrated in the desert heat, but large numbers were nonetheless preserved; archeologists believe that several million remain undiscovered in hidden tombs and burial places.

The Egyptian embalming methods spread to other ancient peoples, including the Assyrians, Jews and Persians (the Assyrians used honey as part of their procedure, the Persians wax, the Jews spices and aloes). In other parts of the world, mummification was a much more primitive process. Many tribes sought to double the untreated corpse into the smallest possible area, with the chin resting on the knees; this custom of "packing the body" was practiced by the ancient Peruvian civilizations, for example, which used a strong rope to draw the limbs into place and bind them fast. Embalming and burial techniques of other cultures vary widely. Some, such as those of the Indians of the western plains of North America, used a natural process whereby the arid climate dessicates the flesh. The one universal custom appears to be the interment of such items as household goods, weapons, and jewelry with the dead.

Over the centuries the plundering of burial tombs has been a common, and often lucrative, practice. This is true of all cultures, in all lands, but nowhere has the practice been so widespread as in Egypt, where it continues to this day (in 1973 an estimated five thousand graves were looted near Beni Suef alone, on the west bank of the Nile). The preponderance of these burial sites are those of common people and have little or no historical importance; but an Egyptian law requiring all such finds to be reported to the authorities, and a heavy tourist trade in mummies and artifacts, helped create a flourishing and ongoing black market. Mummified heads fetch as much as one hundred dollars today; certain artifacts bring considerably more. The result, of course, has been the establishment of a constant "plunder watch"—thousands of Egyptian peasants and underworld figures involved in the search for new tombs and new spoils.

(The actual forgery of mummies has also become a lucrative undertaking in modern Egypt. In Cairo in the early 1950s, a doctor named Ali Schukri Benam was arrested for operating a "mummy factory": several of the city's grave diggers would bring him fresh corpses, which he would make over into the likenesses of ancient mummies, using anatomical textbooks from Cairo University as guides. So skilled were these forgeries that a staff member of Cairo's Egyptian Museum estimated that 70 percent of all mummies exported from Egypt in the previous decade had been fakes.)

Although there have been grave robbers for thousands of years, it was not until Napoleon's discovery of the land along the Nile that western adventurers such as Richard Pococke, who unearthed fourteen grave sites in the Valley of the Kings in 1745, took an interest in the tombs of the ancients. A flood of others followed, including Giovanni Belzoni, an Italian explorer, in the early 1800s, and Victor Loret, who discovered the tomb of Amenhotep II in 1898. Loret's discovery is of particular interest. In the tomb were thirteen mummies, including that of the pharaoh, which had lain undisturbed for three thousand years; Loret removed all to Cairo, except that of Amenhotep II, which was left in its sarcophagus with armed guards posted outside the tomb. But the guards were attacked by thieves late in 1901 and routed; the grave robbers subsequently tore the mummy apart and stole a treasure of jewels and amulets. The robbery enraged Howard Carter, one half of the famous Carnarvon-Carter team, who was at that time inspector-in-chief for the Monuments of Upper Egypt and Nubia; he managed to round up all suspects, force the return of the stolen treasure, and bring the culprits to trial. Despite being proven guilty, however (and after several threats against Carter's life), they were allowed to go free by a native judge.

Carter was a British painter and archeologist who had been in Egypt since 1890 and who had discovered two tombs in the Valley of the Kings for a wealthy American financier named Theodore Davis. In 1906 he teamed for the first time with Lord Carnarvon, a British earl who was also a race-car driver, horseman, playboy, and amateur Egyptologist. Carnarvon, after a near-fatal racing accident had robbed him of his good health, first began traveling to Egypt for winter convalescence in 1903 and developed his interest in archeology as a result of these yearly trips. Carter and Carnarvon made modest findings between 1907 and 1911, which they chronicled in their book *Five Years' Exploration at Thebes* (1912). But it was not until 1914, when they purchased Davis's digging concession, that their central quest began—and not until 1917, after a three-year interruption as a result of the First World War, that they commenced in earnest their search for the tomb of Tutankhamun.

During the season of 1907–1908, workers employed by Davis had uncovered several large baked clay jars containing funerary equipment; the seal impressions in the closures of the jars contained the name of Tutankhamun, a minor young king of the Eighteenth Dynasty (1358–1349 B.C.). This discovery convinced Carter and Carnarvon that the royal tomb must be somewhere in the vicinity. It took them six years of measuring the area foot by foot, of removing tons of debris from earlier diggings, to find it.

The discovery was made in November of 1922, below the tomb of Rameses VI; the seals on the entrance were broken on the twenty-fifth of that month and the outer passageway entered on the twenty-sixth. In the antechamber they found statues, lotiform cups of translucent alabaster, overturned chariots glistening with gold and inlay, and other wonders. They also found an ordinary clay tablet with a hieroglyphic inscription on it; deciphered, the inscription read: *Death will slay with his wings whoever disturbs the peace of the pharaoh.* A second version of the curse was later discovered on the back of a statue: *It is I who drive back the robbers of the tomb with the flames of the desert. I am the protector of Tutankhamun's grave.*

In ancient Egypt curses were somewhat rare, for they could only be uttered by one man, the pharaoh, who spoke with divine power. Curse tablets, such as the one found in Tutankhamun's tomb, were believed to strip the accursed of divine protection and stamp them as enemies of the gods. It was the gods who originated such curses—that of Osiris-Sokaris, the great god, master of Abydos; that of Isis, the great goddess. One tablet, found in a tomb near the Medum pyramid, bore the inscription: *The spirit of the dead will wring the neck of a grave robber as if it were that of a goose.* Only one dead person was supposed to occupy the tomb, but two corpses were found—one mummified, the second that of a grave robber killed by a falling stone just as he was about to steal the mummy's jewelry.

The curse of King Tut made a few of those involved in the Carter-Carnarvon team nervous, but most, including the two principals, neither feared it nor took it seriously. On February 17, 1923, the main chamber of the tomb was opened, revealing a vast wall of gold and a great gilt shrine containing the mummy of Tutankhamun. After the first wave of celebrating and publicity, Carnarvon drove back to Cairo, where he rented a hotel suite, while Carter remained at the tomb site.

Two months later Lord Carnarvon was dead, having succumbed to a strangely undiagnosed illness symptomized by high fever and wracking chills. And at almost the same hour, thousands of miles away in London, Carnarvon's fox terrier suddenly began to howl, sat up on her hind legs, and toppled over dead.

Other men involved with the Tutankhamun excavations began to die under mysterious circumstances. Arthur Mace, the American archeologist who had helped Carter open the tomb, complained of exhaustion after Carnarvon's death, fell into a coma, and died of an unexplained disease. George Jay Gould, son of the American financier, who had visited the tomb, was stricken with a high fever and died soon afterward; the same fate befell another visitor, British industrialist Joel Wool. Archibald Douglas Reid, the radiologist who was the first to cut the wrappings around Tutankhamun's mummy in order to x-ray the body, suffered strange attacks of debilitating feebleness and died not long after his return to England.

By 1929 twenty-two people who had been directly or indirectly involved with King Tut and his tomb had died premature deaths. (The startling total number is more than three dozen.) Thirteen of the twenty-two had taken part in the actual opening of the grave. These included professors Winlock and Foucrat, archeologists Davies, Harkness, and Derry, and assistants Astor and Callender. In the year 1929 Lord Carnarvon's wife, Lady Almina, died of an alleged insect bite, and Carter's secretary, Richard Bethell, was found dead in bed of a circulatory collapse. To add a further bizarre note, Bethell's father, Lord Westbury, jumped from the seventh story of his London house upon receiving word of his son's death; and the hearse containing Bethell's remains ran over and killed a little boy on its way to the cemetery.

These mysterious deaths have been explained variously as radiation from rare chemical elements or metals found by Egyptian scientists; as forgotten poisons or disease-producing organisms which somehow managed to retain their potency over the centuries; as massive coincidence with elements of subconscious death wish and superstitious fear—the same sort of phenomenon that causes victims of voodoo curses to take sick, wither, and die. It is the last of these which is the most probable explanation, of course. The theories involving radiation or obscure poisons or deadly germs have been scientifically disproven. And antiquated Egyptian curses, after all, have no power in the enlightened world of today; the desecration of the tombs of kings and queens cannot call forth the wrath of ancient gods.

Can they?

There have been literally hundreds of nonfiction works, beginning with Giovanni Belzoni's *Narrative of the Operations and Recent Discoveries in Egypt and Nubia* (1820), which deal with the mysteries (and modern man's quest for knowledge) of ancient Egypt. The smaller percentage of these is concerned with Egyptian society, hieroglyphics, mummification, and other practices and ceremonies. The preponderance, all written over the past six decades, is concerned with Tutankhamun—the discovery, the curse, the treasure, or a combination of all three.

In the former category the most informative books are those of Sir E.A. Wallis Budge, former keeper of the Department of Egyptian and Assyrian Antiquities, British Museum. They include *The Mummy* and *The Book of the Dead,* which explain the secrets of ancient Egypt's funereal amulets and scarabs, idols and mummy-making, and offer capsule courses in the deciphering of hieroglyphics; and *Egyptian Magic,* which contains material on tomb curses such as that of King Tut. Also good is *Tombs, Temples and Ancient Art* (1956), edited by Corinna Lindon Smith.

Of all the books on Tutankhamun, the definitive is certainly co-discoverer Howard Carter's three-volume *The Tomb of Tutankh-Amen,* co-written by A. C. Mace, which details all facets of the search and the tragic aftermath. The work that best outlines and attempts to explain the curse itself is Philipp Vandenberg's *The Curse of the Pharaohs* (1975)—a fascinating and meticulously researched study which also encompasses other curses, mummies, grave robbing, and related matters, and which reads like an occult thriller. Other recent books of interest on the subject include Arnold Brackman's *The Search for the Gold of Tutankhamun* (1976) and Thomas Hoving's *Tutankhamun: The Untold Story* (1978).

Works on mummies of other cultures are quite a bit scarcer, and primarily devoted to Central and South American peoples. Among the most informative is *Masks, Mummies, and Magicians: A Voyage of Exploration in Pre-Inca Peru,* by Simone and Roger Waisbard. Another interesting book is *The Mummies of Guanajuato,* a fine photographic study by Archie Leiberman (accompanied by the text of Ray Bradbury's short story "The Next in Line") of the famed mummies of Guanajuato, Mexico.

Perhaps the first fantasy novel to make use of the mummy theme is French writer Théophile Gautier's *Romance of a Mummy* (1856); but the book is not available in a modern edition and is virtually unknown to today's reader. (A superior short story by Gautier, "The Mummy's Foot," appears later in these pages.) The most well-known mummy novel is no doubt *The Jewel of Seven Stars,* by the creator of Dracula, Bram Stoker, which was first published in England in 1903. Among its several classic fantasy/horror elements are a strange mummified cat, a magic jewel, and a fearful curse (it also contains elements of gothic romance and the detective story). If its style is somewhat dated by modern standards, it remains both readable and interesting and has been deservedly reprinted in a contemporary paperback edition.

A second novel of interest is Burton Stevenson's *A King in Babylon* (1917), which deals with a Hollywood production company that travels to Egypt to film a silent movie and runs afoul of an ancient curse. Though its style, too, is dated, and it contains glaring archeological misinformation, its blend of horror and a vivid Egyptian background make it worth seeking out and reading.

A number of detective novels in the twenties and thirties utilized the mummy theme, either as a nonfantastic mystery element or as a touch of pure fantasy. Some of the better hybrids include Dermot Morrah's *The Mummy Case,* which has a British academic background (Oxford) and is a first-rate detective story; John Dickson Carr's excellent "impossible crime" novel, *The Lost Gallows;* and S.S. Van Dine's *The Scarab Murder Case,* starring Philo Vance.

Sax Rohmer, creator of the villainous Fu Manchu, wrote several novels and short stories during the first half of this century involving mummies and Egyptian magic. *Brood of the Witch Queen* (1924) and *The Green Eyes of Bast* (1920) are two of the best longer works; *Tales of Secret Egypt* (1919) and *Tales of East and West* (1933) offer a variety of entertaining shorter pieces.

Although mummies and Egyptian curses have not been in vogue in recent years, two novels published in 1979 indicate that they may be making a welcome comeback. The first of these is Robin Cook's lavish suspense thriller, *Sphinx,* which mixes murder, intrigue in modern-day Egypt, an archeological quest, and an ancient curse—ingredients which made it a modest bestseller. The second novel is a maiden effort by T.W. Hard about a resurrected mummy named *Sum VII;* the handling here is science fictional rather than fantastic, with sound scientific basis for the central premise.

There has been one other anthology of short fiction about mummies: *The Mummy Walks Among Us* (1971), edited by Vic Ghidalia. But it was published by a small paperback house and was not widely distributed; copies are scarce and have already become collectors' items. Each of its seven stories deals with Egyptian mummies and the range is above-average to excellent.

The first mummy film was a silent entitled *The Mummy of the King of Ramsee,* made in 1909. Other silents followed, including *The Eyes of the Mummy* (1918), which starred Pola Negri and Emil Jannings, two well-known actors of the period, and which was directed by Ernst Lubitsch. The first talking mummy movie is one of the two best made to date—Boris Karloff's classic *The Mummy* (1932), in which he portrays Imhotep, an ancient Egyptian priest, and Ardath Bey, a modern scholar connected with the Cairo Museum. His performance is masterful, and there are several scenes, such as the one in which he rises from Imhotep's sarcophagus before the horrified eyes of a young archeologist, which can raise the hackles on the neck of any horror-film fan.

The second of the two topflight mummy movies is *The Mummy's Hand* (1940), starring Dick Foran and George Zucco, with a minor cowboy actor, Tom Tyler, surprisingly good as the mummy. This film, in which a high priest (Zucco) uses tana leaves to keep the mummy Karis alive, and which makes disguised use of the Carnarvon-Carter expedition and the King Tut curse, is the first to depict the monster trailing his wrappings on missions of murder and mayhem. Three sequels, all starring Lon Chaney, Jr. as the monster—*The Mummy's Tomb* (1942), *The Mummy's Ghost* (1944), and *The Mummy's Curse* (1945), followed the same pattern, though with much weaker scripting, and helped solidify the popular mummy image.

Three Mexican films of the 1960s, *The Aztec Mummy, Attack of the Mayan Mummy,* and the rather incredibly titled *Wrestling Women Versus the Aztec Mummy,* are not only the worst mummy movies ever made but are unintentionally funnier than 90 percent of all intentional comedies. They give new meaning to the word "camp" (and no doubt have caused a few genuine Mayan mummies to turn over in their graves). Serious students of the macabre as an art form should avoid them at all costs.

After a hiatus of some thirteen years—the last film in the subgenre, the disappointing British production titled *The Mummy's Shroud,* was made in 1967—filmmakers have indicated a revival of interest in mummies and ancient curses. At the time of this writing two new movies are scheduled for appearance in 1980: *The Curse of King Tut's Tomb,* starring Raymond Burr and Eva Marie Saint, which purports to offer the inside story of the Carnarvon-Carter tragedy (one actor was forced to withdraw from the production after breaking his leg in a freak accident, which may or may not be significant); and *Macabra,* with Samantha Eggar and Roy Jenson, about an exploration of the mummy caves of Mexico. Whether either one will be of sufficient quality and interest to be accorded a place of honor alongside *The Mummy* and *The Mummy's Hand* remains to be seen.

Almost all of the short mummy fiction is of the Egyptian variety. The best of these stories explore the theme in unusual ways, sometimes as exercises in pure horror and sometimes with satirical humor; they include "Lot No. 249" by Sir Arthur Conan Doyle, "Some Words with a Mummy" by Edgar Allan Poe, E.F. Benson's "Monkeys" and Donald A. Wollheim's "Bones," "The Mummy's Foot" by Théophile Gautier, "The Eyes of the Mummy" by Robert Bloch, and "The Vengeance of Nitocris" by famed playwright Tennessee Williams. All seven of these stories, whose settings range from the Valley of the Kings to Paris, England, and New York, are presented here.

Stories involving mummies of other cultures and other lands are much harder to find. As a result, Part II contains five original tales especially written for this anthology: "Charlie" by Talmage

Powell (the Mayan culture in Guatemala); "The Weekend Magus" by Edward D. Hoch (mummies in Scotland); Joe R. Lansdale's "The Princess" (the mummy of a Danish sorceress); Ardath Mayhar's "The Eagle-Claw Rattle" (an American Indian mummy); and "The Other Room" by Charles L. Grant. The final story in the book, Barry N. Malzberg's "Revelation in Seven Stages," is an extrapolative look at the fate of Egyptian mummies in the far future.

These thirteen stories, therefore, not only offer considerable chills and entertainment, but cover every facet of the mummy theme.

You might even say that they have it all wrapped up . . . .

And now you're ready to view the first of many odd and fearful mummies, in and out of their tombs. Or *are* you truly ready? Not everyone is as equipped as he or she might believe, you know, to handle such frightening experiences. On an upper floor in the Egyptian Museum of Cairo there are twenty male and female mummies exhibited in glass caskets, all of them smiling with bared teeth; some visitors have found that they cannot bear the sight, and have broken into cold sweats and run screaming from the room. So be careful before you proceed. Be very careful.

Don't let the same thing happen to you . . . .

—Bill Pronzini

PART I
EGYPTIAN MUMMIES

LOT NO. 249

by SIR ARTHUR CONAN DOYLE

The popular image of the mummy as a hulking, prune-faced monster, sent out trailing his wrappings on murderous errands by evil Egyptian cultists, is due in large part to the horror films of the thirties and forties. But where, one wonders, did the authors of those films get their inspiration? Bram Stoker's The Jewel of Seven Stars *and the curse of King Tut are two obvious answers—but another possible source might be this relatively little-known but admirable story by Sir Arthur Conan Doyle.*

First published in the 1880s, early in Doyle's literary career, "Lot No. 249" relates the curious tale of Edward Bellingham, a young Egyptologist at Oxford, and a couple of collegians named Abercrombie Smith and Monkhouse Lee. The mummy featured in these pages is not of the Lon Chaney ilk; rather, it is "a horrid, black, withered thing, like a charred head on a gnarled bush." The fact that it is every bit as murderous as Chaney in The Mummy's Curse *and other films, however, is unquestionable. And for some of the same reasons. Similar cinematic chills abound as well.*

Although Sir Arthur Conan Doyle (1859–1930) is justifiably famous as the creator of Sherlock Holmes, he was also a writer of macabre fiction (as well as historical romances, popular history, science fiction, and adventure fiction) of some renown. Some of the best of his weird stories, among them "The Terror of Blue John Gap," "The Horror on the Heights," and "The Nightmare Room," can be found in a recent collection, Tales of Terror and Mystery *(1977). A few of the Sherlock Holmes stories—* The Hound of the Baskervilles, *"The Adventure of the Devil's Foot," "The Adventure of the Sussex Vampire"—also have macabre elements. Doyle's interest in the bizarre and unexplained led him, later in life following the death of his eldest son in World War I, to write six books on spiritualism and psychical research, including the two-volume* History of Spiritualism *(1926).*

OF THE dealings of Edward Bellingham with William Monkhouse Lee, and of the cause of the great terror of Abercrombie Smith, it may be that no absolute and final judgment will ever be delivered. It is true that we have the full and clear narrative of Smith himself, and such corroboration as he could look for from Thomas Styles the servant, from the Reverend Plumptree Peterson, Fellow of Old's, and from such other people as chanced to gain some passing glance at this or that incident in a singular chain of events. Yet, in the main, the story must rest upon Smith alone, and the most will think that it is more likely that one brain, however outwardly sane, has some subtle warp in its texture, some strange flaw in its workings, than that the path of Nature has been overstepped in open day in so famed a center of learning and light as the University of Oxford. Yet when we think how narrow and how devious this path of Nature is, how dimly we can trace it, for all our lamps of science, and how from the darkness that girds it round great and terrible possibilities loom ever shadowly upward, it is a bold and confident man who will put a limit to the strange bypaths into which the human spirit may wander.

In a certain wing of what we will call Old College in Oxford there is a corner turret of an exceeding great age. The heavy arch that spans the open door has bent downward in the center under the weight of its years, and the gray, lichen-blotched blocks of stone are bound and knitted together with withes and strands of ivy, as though the old mother had set herself to brace them up against wind and weather. From the door a stone stair curves upward spirally, passing two landings, and terminating in a third one, its steps all shapeless and hollowed by the tread of so many generations of the seekers after knowledge. Life has flowed like water down this winding stair, and, waterlike, has left these smooth-worn grooves behind it. From the long-gowned, pedantic scholars of Plantagenet days down to the young bloods of a later age, how full and strong had been that tide of young, English life. And what was left now of all those hopes, those strivings, those fiery energies, save here and there in some old world churchyard a few scratches upon a stone, and perchance a handful of dust in a moldering coffin? Yet here were the silent stair and the gray, old wall, with bend and saltire and many another heraldic device still to be read upon its surface, like grotesque shadows thrown back from the days that had passed.

In the month of May, in the year 1884, three young men occupied the sets of rooms which opened on to the separate landings of the old stair. Each set consisted simply of a sitting room and of a bedroom, while the two corresponding rooms upon the ground floor were used, the one as a coal cellar, and the other as the living room of the servant, or scout, Thomas Styles, whose duty it was to wait upon the three men above him. To right and to left was a line of lecture rooms and of offices, so that the dwellers in the old turret enjoyed a certain seclusion, which made the chambers popular among the more studious undergraduates. Such were the three who occupied them now —Abercrombie Smith above, Edward Bellingham beneath him, and William Monkhouse Lee upon the lowest story.

It was ten o'clock on a bright, spring night, and Abercrombie Smith lay back in his armchair, his feet upon the fender, and his brierroot pipe between his lips. In a similar chair, and equally at his ease, there lounged on the other side of the fireplace his old school friend Jephro Hastie. Both men were in flannels, for they had spent their evening upon the river, but apart from their dress no one could look at their hard-cut, alert faces without seeing that they were open-air men—men whose minds and tastes turned naturally to all that was manly and robust. Hastie, indeed, was stroke of his college boat, and Smith was an even better oar, but a coming examination had already cast its shadow over him and held him to his work, save for the few hours a week which health demanded. A litter of medical books upon the table, with scattered bones, models, and anatomical plates, pointed to the extent as well as the nature of his studies, while a couple of single sticks and a set of boxing gloves above the mantelpiece hinted at the means by which, with Hastie's help, he might take his exercise in its most compressed and least distant form. They knew each other very well—so well that they could sit now in that soothing silence which is the very highest development of companionship.

"Have some whisky," said Abercrombie Smith at last between two cloudbursts. "Scotch in the jug and Irish in the bottle."

"No, thanks. I'm in for the sculls. I don't liquor when I'm training. How about you?"

"I'm reading hard. I think it best to leave it alone."

Hastie nodded, and they relapsed into a contented silence.

"By the way, Smith," asked Hastie, presently, "have you made the acquaintance of either of the fellows on your stair yet?"

"Just a nod when we pass. Nothing more."

"Hum! I should be inclined to let it stand at that. I know something of them both. Not much, but as much as I want. I don't think I should take them to my bosom if I were you. Not that there's much amiss with Monkhouse Lee."

"Meaning the thin one?"

"Precisely. He is a gentlemanly little fellow. I don't think there is any vice in him. But then you can't know him without knowing Bellingham."

"Meaning the fat one?"

"Yes, the fat one. And he's a man whom I, for one, would rather not know."

Abercrombie Smith raised his eyebrows and glanced across at his companion.

"What's up, then?" he asked. "Drink? Cards? Cad? You used not to be censorious."

"Ah! you evidently don't know the man, or you wouldn't ask. There's something damnable about him—something reptilian. My gorge always rises at him. I should put him down as a man with secret vices—an evil liver. He's no fool, though. They say that he is one of the best men in his line that they have ever had in the college."

"Medicine or classics?"

"Eastern languages. He's a demon at them. Chillingworth met him somewhere above the second cataract last summer vacation, and he told me that he just prattled to the Arabs as if he had been born and nursed and weaned among them. He talked Coptic to the Copts, and Hebrew to the Jews, and Arabic to the Bedouins, and they were all ready to kiss the hem of his frock coat. There are some old hermit johnnies up in those parts who sit on rocks and scowl and spit at the casual stranger. Well, when they saw this chap Bellingham, before he had said five words they just lay down on their bellies and wriggled. Chillingworth said that he never saw anything like it. Bellingham seemed to take it as his right, too, and strutted about among them and talked down to them like a Dutch uncle. Pretty good for an undergrad of Old's, wasn't it?"

"Why do you say you can't know Lee without knowing Bellingham?"

"Because Bellingham is engaged to his sister Eveline. Such a bright little girl, Smith! I know the whole family well. It's disgusting to see that brute with her. A toad and a dove, that's what they always remind me of."

Abercrombie Smith grinned and knocked his ashes out against the side of the grate.

"You show every card in your hand, old chap," said he. "What a prejudiced, green-eyed, evil-thinking old man it is! You have really nothing against the fellow except that."

"Well, I've known her ever since she was as long as that cherrywood pipe, and I don't like to see her taking risks. And it is a risk. He looks beastly. And he has a beastly temper, a venomous temper. You remember his row with Long Norton?"

"No; you always forget that I am a freshman."

"Ah, it was last winter. Of course. Well, you know the towpath along by the river. There were several fellows going along it, Bellingham in front, when they came on an old market woman coming the other way. It had been raining—you know what those fields are like when it has rained—and the path ran between the river and a great puddle that was nearly as broad. Well, what does this swine do but keep the path, and push the old girl into the mud, where she and her marketings came to terrible grief. It was a blackguard thing to do, and Long Norton, who is as gentle a fellow as ever stepped, told him what he thought of it. One word led to another, and it ended in Norton laying his stick across the fellow's shoulders. There was the deuce of a fuss about it, and it's a treat to see the way in which Bellingham looks at Norton when they meet now. By Jove, Smith, it's nearly eleven o'clock!"

"No hurry. Light your pipe again."

"Not I. I'm supposed to be in training. Here I've been sitting gossiping when I ought to have been safely tucked up. I'll borrow your skull, if you can share it. Williams has had mine for a month. I'll take the little bones of your ear, too, if you are sure you won't need them. Thanks very much. Never mind a bag, I can carry them very well under my arm. Good night, my son, and take my tip as to your neighbor."

When Hastie, bearing his anatomical plunder, had clattered off down the winding stair, Abercrombie Smith hurled his pipe into the wastepaper basket, and drawing his chair nearer to the lamp, plunged into a formidable, green-covered volume, adorned with great, colored maps of that strange, internal kingdom of which we are the hapless and helpless monarchs. Though a freshman at Oxford, the student was not so in medicine, for he had worked for four years at Glasgow and at Berlin, and this coming examination would place him finally as a member of his profession. With his firm mouth, broad forehead, and clear-cut, somewhat hard-featured face, he was a man who, if he had no brilliant talent, was yet so dogged, so patient, and so strong that he might in the end overtop a more showy genius. A man who can hold his own among Scotchmen and North Germans is not a man to be easily set back. Smith had left a name at Glasgow and at Berlin, and he was bent upon doing as much at Oxford, if hard work and devotion could accomplish it.

He had sat reading for about an hour, and the hands of the noisy carriage clock upon the side table were rapidly closing together upon the twelve, when a sudden sound fell upon his student's ear—a sharp, rather shrill sound, like the hissing intake of a man's breath who gasps under some strong emotion. Smith laid down his book and slanted his ear to listen. There was no one on either side or above him, so that the interruption came certainly from the neighbor beneath—the same neighbor of whom Hastie had given so unsavory an account. Smith knew him only as a flabby, pale-faced man of silent and studious habits, a man whose lamp threw a golden bar from the old turret even after he had extinguished his own. This community in lateness had formed a certain silent bond between them. It was soothing to Smith when the hours stole on toward dawn to feel that there was another so close who set as small a value upon his sleep as he did. Even now, as his thoughts turned toward him, Smith's feelings were kindly. Hastie was a good fellow, but he was rough, strong-fibered, with no imagination or sympathy. He could not tolerate departures from what he looked upon as the model type of manliness. If a man could not be measured by a public school standard, then he was beyond the pale with Hastie. Like so many who are themselves robust, he was apt to confuse the constitution with the character, to ascribe to want of principle what was really a want of circulation. Smith, with his stronger mind, knew his friend's habit, and made allowance for it now as his thoughts turned toward the man beneath him.

There was no return of the singular sound, and Smith was about to turn to his work once more, when suddenly there broke out in the silence of the night a hoarse cry, a positive scream—the call of a man who is moved and shaken beyond all control. Smith sprang out of his chair and dropped his book. He was a man of fairly firm fiber, but there was something in this sudden,

uncontrollable shriek of horror that chilled his blood and prin-
gled in his skin. Coming in such a place and at such an hour, it
brought a thousand fantastic possibilities into his head. Should
he rush down, or was it better to wait? He had all the national
hatred of making a scene, and he knew so little of his neighbor
that he would not lightly intrude upon his affairs. For a moment
he stood in doubt and even as he balanced the matter there was
a quick rattle of footsteps upon the stairs, and young Monkhouse Lee, half dressed and as white as ashes, burst into his
room.

"Come down!" he gasped. "Bellingham's ill."

Abercrombie Smith followed him closely downstairs into the
sitting room which was beneath his own, and intent as he was
upon the matter in hand, he could not but take an amazed glance
around him as he crossed the threshold. It was such a chamber
as he had never seen before—a museum rather than a study.
Walls and ceiling were thickly covered with a thousand strange
relics from Egypt and the East. Tall, angular figures bearing
burdens or weapons stalked in an uncouth frieze round the
apartment. Above were bull-headed, stork-headed, cat-headed,
owl-headed statues, with viper-crowned, almond-eyed monarchs, and strange, beetlelike deities cut out of the blue Egyptian
lapis lazuli. Horus and Isis and Osiris peeped down from every
niche and shelf, while across the ceiling a true son of Old Nile,
a great, hanging-jawed crocodile, was slung in a double noose.

In the center of this singular chamber was a large, square
table, littered with papers, bottles, and the dried leaves of some
graceful, palmlike plant. These varied objects had all been
heaped together in order to make room for a mummy case,
which had been conveyed from the wall, as was evident from the
gap there, and laid across the front of the table. The mummy
itself, a horrid, black, withered thing, like a charred head on a
gnarled bush, was lying half out of the case, with its clawlike
hand and bony forearm resting upon the table. Propped up
against the sarcophagus was an old, yellow scroll of papyrus, and
in front of it, in a wooden armchair, sat the owner of the room,
his head thrown back, his widely opened eyes directed in a

horrified stare to the crocodile above him, and his blue, thick lips puffing loudly with every expiration.

"My God! He's dying!" cried Monkhouse Lee, distractedly.

He was a slim, handsome young fellow, olive-skinned and dark-eyed, of a Spanish rather than of an English type, with a Celtic intensity of manner which contrasted with the Saxon phlegm of Abercrombie Smith.

"Only a faint, I think," said the medical student. "Just give me a hand with him. You take his feet. Now onto the sofa. Can you kick all those little wooden devils off? What a litter it is! Now he will be all right if we undo his collar and give him some water. What has he been up to at all?"

"I don't know. I heard him cry out. I ran up. I know him pretty well, you know. It is very good of you to come down."

"His heart is going like a pair of castanets," said Smith, laying his hand on the breast of the unconscious man. "He seems to me to be frightened all to pieces. Chuck the water over him! What a face he has got on him!"

It was indeed a strange and most repellent face, for color and outline were equally unnatural. It was white, not with the ordinary pallor of fear, but with an absolutely bloodless white, like the underside of a sole. He was very fat, but gave the impression of having at some time been considerably fatter, for his skin hung loosely in creases and folds, and was shot with a meshwork of wrinkles. Short, stubby brown hair bristled up from his scalp, with a pair of thick, wrinkled ears protruding at the sides. His light gray eyes were still open, the pupils dilated and the balls projecting in a fixed and horrid stare. It seemed to Smith as he looked down upon him that he had never seen Nature's danger signals flying so plainly upon a man's countenance, and his thoughts turned more seriously to the warning which Hastie had given him an hour before.

"What the deuce can have frightened him so?" he asked.

"It's the mummy."

"The mummy? How, then?"

"I don't know. It's beastly and morbid. I wish he would drop it. It's the second fright he has given me. It was the same last winter. I found him just like this, with that horrid thing in front of him."

"What does he want with the mummy, then?"

"Oh, he's a crank, you know. It's his hobby. He knows more about these things than any man in England. But I wish he wouldn't! Ah, he's beginning to come to."

A faint tinge of color had begun to steal back into Bellingham's ghastly cheeks, and his eyelids shivered like a sail after a calm. He clasped and unclasped his hands, drew a long, thin breath between his teeth, and suddenly jerking up his head, threw a glance of recognition around him. As his eyes fell upon the mummy, he sprang off the sofa, seized the roll of papyrus, thrust it into a drawer, turned the key, and then staggered back onto the sofa.

"What's up?" he asked. "What do you chaps want?"

"You've been shrieking out and making no end of a fuss," said Monkhouse Lee. "If our neighbor here from above hadn't come down, I'm sure I don't know what I should have done with you."

"Ah, it's Abercrombie Smith," said Bellingham, glancing up at him. "How very good of you to come in! What a fool I am! Oh, my God, what a fool I am!"

He sank his head on to his hands, and burst into peal after peal of hysterical laughter.

"Look here! Drop it!" cried Smith, shaking him roughly by the shoulder.

"Your nerves are all in a jangle. You must drop these little midnight games with mummies, or you'll be going off your chump. You're all on wires now."

"I wonder," said Bellingham, "whether you would be as cool as I am if you had seen—"

"What then?"

"Oh, nothing. I meant that I wonder if you could sit up at night with a mummy without trying your nerves. I have no doubt that you are quite right. I dare say that I have been taking it out of myself too much lately. But I am all right now. Please don't go, though. Just wait for a few minutes until I am quite myself."

"The room is very close," remarked Lee, throwing open the

window and letting in the cool night air.

"It's balsamic resin," said Bellingham. He lifted up one of the dried palmate leaves from the table and frizzled it over the chimney of the lamp. It broke away into heavy smoke wreaths, and a pungent, biting odor filled the chamber. "It's the sacred plant—the plant of the priests," he remarked. "Do you know anything of Eastern languages, Smith?"

"Nothing at all. Not a word."

The answer seemed to lift a weight from the Egyptologist's mind.

"By the way," he continued, "how long was it from the time that you ran down, until I came to my senses?"

"Not long. Some four or five minutes."

"I thought it could not be very long," said he, drawing a long breath. "But what a strange thing unconsciousness is! There is no measurement to it. I could not tell from my own sensations if it were seconds or weeks. Now that gentleman on the table was packed up in the days of the Eleventh Dynasty, some forty centuries ago, and yet if he could find his tongue, he would tell us that this lapse of time has been but a closing of the eyes and a reopening of them. He is a singularly fine mummy, Smith."

Smith stepped over to the table and looked down with a professional eye at the black and twisted form in front of him. The features, though horribly discolored, were perfect, and two little nutlike eyes still lurked in the depths of the black, hollow sockets. The blotched skin was drawn tightly from bone to bone, and a tangled wrap of black, coarse hair fell over the ears. Two thin teeth, like those of a rat, overlay the shriveled lower lip. In its crouching position, with bent joints and craned head, there was a suggestion of energy about the horrid thing which made Smith's gorge rise. The gaunt ribs, with their parchmentlike covering, were exposed, and the sunken, leaden-hued abdomen, with the long slit where the embalmer had left his mark; but the lower limbs were wrapped round with coarse, yellow bandages. A number of little clovelike pieces of myrrh and of cassia were sprinkled over the body, and lay scattered on the inside of the case.

"I don't know his name," said Bellingham, passing his hand over the shriveled head. "You see the outer sarcophagus with the inscriptions is missing. Lot 249 is all the title he has now. You see it printed on his case. That was his number in the auction at which I picked him up."

"He has been a very pretty sort of fellow in his day," remarked Abercrombie Smith.

"He has been a giant. His mummy is six feet seven in length, and that would be a giant over there, for they were never a very robust race. Feel these great, knotted bones, too. He would be a nasty fellow to tackle."

"Perhaps these very hands helped to build the stones into the pyramids," suggested Monkhouse Lee, looking down with disgust in his eyes at the crooked, unclean talons.

"No fear. This fellow has been pickled in natron, and looked after in the most approved style. They did not serve hodsmen in that fashion. Salt or bitumen was enough for them. It has been calculated that this sort of thing cost about seven hundred and thirty pounds in our money. Our friend was a noble at the least. What do you make of that small inscription near his feet, Smith?"

"I told you that I know no Eastern tongue."

"Ah, so you did. It is the name of the embalmer, I take it. A very conscientious worker he must have been. I wonder how many modern works will survive four thousand years?"

He kept on speaking lightly and rapidly, but it was evident to Abercrombie Smith that he was still palpitating with fear. His hands shook, his lower lip trembled, and look where he would, his eye always came sliding round to his gruesome companion. Through all his fear, however, there was a suspicion of triumph in his tone and manner. His eyes shone, and his footstep, as he paced the room, was brisk and jaunty. He gave the impression of a man who has gone through an ordeal, the marks of which he still bears upon him, but which has helped him to his end.

"You're not going yet?" he cried, as Smith rose from the sofa.

At the prospect of solitude, his fears seemed to crowd back upon him, and he stretched out a hand to detain him.

"Yes, I must go. I have my work to do. You are all right now. I think that with your nervous system you should take up some less morbid study."

"Oh, I am not nervous as a rule; and I have unwrapped mummies before."

"You fainted last time," observed Monkhouse Lee.

"Ah, yes, so I did. Well, I must have a nerve tonic or a course of electricity. You are not going, Lee?"

"I'll do whatever you wish, Ned."

"Then I'll come down with you and have a shakedown on your sofa. Good night, Smith. I am so sorry to have disturbed you with my foolishness."

They shook hands, and as the medical student stumbled up the spiral and irregular stair he heard a key turn in a door, and the steps of his two new acquaintances as they descended to the lower floor.

In this strange way began the acquaintance between Edward Bellingham and Abercrombie Smith, an acquaintance which the latter, at least, had no desire to push further. Bellingham, however, appeared to have taken a fancy to his rough-spoken neighbor, and made his advances in such a way that he could hardly be repulsed without absolute brutality. Twice he called to thank Smith for his assistance, and many times afterward he looked in with books, papers, and such other civilities as two bachelor neighbors can offer each other. He was, as Smith soon found, a man of wide reading, with catholic tastes and an extraordinary memory. His manner, too, was so pleasing and suave that one came, after a time, to overlook his repellent appearance. For a jaded and wearied man he was no unpleasant companion, and Smith found himself, after a time, looking forward to his visits, and even returning them.

Clever as he undoubtedly was, however, the medical student seemed to detect a dash of insanity in the man. He broke out at times into a high, inflated style of talk which was in contrast with the simplicity of his life.

"It is a wonderful thing," he cried, "to feel that one can command powers of good and of evil—a ministering angel or a

demon of vengeance." And again, of Monkhouse Lee, he said
—"Lee is a good fellow, an honest fellow, but he is without
strength or ambition. He would not make a fit partner for a man
with a great enterprise. He would not make a fit partner for me."

At such hints and innuendoes stolid Smith, puffing solemnly
at his pipe, would simply raise his eyebrows and shake his head,
with little interjections of medical wisdom as to earlier hours and
fresher air.

One habit Bellingham had developed of late which Smith
knew to be a frequent herald of a weakening mind. He appeared
to be forever talking to himself. At late hours of the night, when
there could be no visitor with him, Smith could still hear his
voice beneath him in a low, muffled monologue, sunk almost to
a whisper, and yet very audible in the silence. This solitary
babbling annoyed and distracted the student, so that he spoke
more than once to his neighbor about it. Bellingham, however,
flushed up at the charge, and denied curtly that he had uttered
a sound; indeed, he showed more annoyance over the matter
than the occasion seemed to demand.

Had Abercrombie Smith had any doubt as to his own ears he
had not to go far to find corroboration. Tom Styles, the little
wrinkled manservant who had attended to the wants of the lodgers in the turret for a longer time than any man's memory could
carry him, was sorely put to it over the same matter.

"If you please, sir," said he, as he tidied down the top chamber one morning, "do you think Mr. Bellingham is all right, sir?"

"All right, Styles?"

"Yes, sir. Right in his head, sir."

"Why should he not be, then?"

"Well, I don't know, sir. His habits has changed of late. He's
not the same man he used to be, though I make free to say that
he was never quite one of my gentlemen, like Mr. Hastie or
yourself, sir. He's took to talkin' to himself something awful. I
wonder it don't disturb you. I don't know what to make of him,
sir."

"I don't know what business it is of yours, Styles."

"Well, I takes an interest, Mr. Smith. It may be forward of me, but I can't help it. I feel sometimes as if I was mother and father to my young gentlemen. It all falls on me when things go wrong and the relations come. But Mr. Bellingham, sir. I want to know what it is that walks about his room sometimes when he's out and when the door's locked on the outside."

"Eh? You're talking nonsense, Styles."

"Maybe so, sir; but I heard it more'n once with my own ears."

"Rubbish, Styles."

"Very good, sir. You'll ring the bell if you want me."

Abercrombie Smith gave little heed to the gossip of the old manservant, but a small incident occurred a few days later which left an unpleasant effect upon his mind, and brought the words of Styles forcibly to his memory.

Bellingham had come up to see him late one night, and was entertaining him with an interesting account of the rock tombs of Beni Hassan in Upper Egypt, when Smith, whose hearing was remarkably acute, distinctly heard the sound of a door opening on the landing below.

"There's some fellow gone in or out of your room," he remarked.

Bellingham sprang up and stood helpless for a moment, with the expression of a man who is half incredulous and half afraid.

"I surely locked it. I am almost positive that I locked it," he stammered. "No one could have opened it."

"Why, I hear someone coming up the steps now," said Smith.

Bellingham rushed out through the door, slammed it loudly behind him, and hurried down the stairs. About halfway down Smith heard him stop, and thought he caught the sound of whispering. A moment later the door beneath him shut, a key creaked in a lock, and Bellingham, with beads of moisture upon his pale face, ascended the stairs once more, and reentered the room.

"It's all right," he said, throwing himself down in a chair. "It was that fool of a dog. He had pushed the door open. I don't know how I came to forget to lock it."

"I didn't know you kept a dog," said Smith, looking very thoughtfully at the disturbed face of his companion.

"Yes, I haven't had him long. I must get rid of him. He's a great nuisance."

"He must be, if you find it so hard to shut him up. I should have thought that shutting the door would have been enough, without locking it."

"I want to prevent old Styles from letting him out. He's of some value, you know, and it would be awkward to lose him."

"I am a bit of a dog fancier myself," said Smith, still gazing hard at his companion from the corner of his eyes. "Perhaps you'll let me have a look at it."

"Certainly. But I am afraid it cannot be tonight; I have an appointment. Is that clock right? Then I am a quarter of an hour late already. You'll excuse me, I am sure."

He picked up his cap and hurried from the room. In spite of his appointment, Smith heard him reenter his own chamber and lock his door upon the inside.

This interview left a disagreeable impression upon the medical student's mind. Bellingham had lied to him, and lied so clumsily that it looked as if he had desperate reasons for concealing the truth. Smith knew that his neighbor had no dog. He knew, also, that the step which he had heard upon the stairs was not the step of an animal. But if it were not, then what could it be? There was old Styles's statement about the something that used to pace the room at times when the owner was absent. Could it be a woman? Smith rather inclined to the view. If so, it would mean disgrace and expulsion to Bellingham if it were discovered by the authorities, so that his anxiety and falsehoods might be accounted for. And yet it was inconceivable that an undergraduate could keep a woman in his rooms without being instantly detected. Be the explanation what it might, there was something ugly about it, and Smith determined, as he turned to his books, to discourage all further attempts at intimacy on the part of his soft-spoken and ill-favored neighbor.

But his work was destined to interruption that night. He had hardly caught up the broken threads when a firm, heavy footfall came three steps at a time from below, and Hastie, in blazer and flannels, burst into the room.

"Still at it!" said he, plumping down into his wonted armchair. "What a chap you are to stew! I believe an earthquake might come and knock Oxford into a cocked hat, and you would sit perfectly placid with your books among the ruins. However, I won't bore you long. Three whiffs of baccy, and I am off."

"What's the news, then?" asked Smith, cramming a plug of bird's-eye into his brier with his forefinger.

"Nothing very much. Wilson made seventy for the freshmen against the eleven. They say that they will play him instead of Buddicomb, for Buddicomb is clean off color. He used to be able to bowl a little, but it's nothing but half volleys and long hops now."

"Medium right," suggested Smith, with the intense gravity that comes upon a varsity man when he speaks of athletics.

"Inclining to fast, with a work from leg. Comes with the arm about three inches or so. He used to be nasty on a wet wicket. Oh, by the way, have you heard about Long Norton?"

"What's that?"

"He's been attacked."

"Attacked?"

"Yes, just as he was turning out of the High Street, and within a hundred yards of the gate of Old's."

"But who—"

"Ah, that's the rub! If you said 'what,' you would be more grammatical. Norton swears that it was not human, and, indeed, from the scratches on his throat, I should be inclined to agree with him."

"What, then? Have we come down to spooks?" Abercrombie Smith puffed his scientific contempt.

"Well, no; I don't think that is quite the idea, either. I am inclined to think that if any showman has lost a great ape lately, and the brute is in these parts, a jury would find a true bill against it. Norton passes that way every night, you know, about the same hour. There's a tree that hangs low over the path—the big elm from Rainy's garden. Norton thinks the thing dropped on him out of the tree. Anyhow, he was nearly strangled by two arms, which, he says, were as strong and as thin as steel bands.

He saw nothing; only those beastly arms that tightened and tightened on him. He yelled his head off, and a couple of chaps came running, and the thing went over the wall like a cat. He never got a fair sight of it the whole time. It gave Norton a shake up, I can tell you. I tell him it has been as good as a change at the seaside for him."

"A garroter, most likely," said Smith.

"Very possibly. Norton says not; but we don't mind what he says. The garroter has long nails, and was pretty smart at swinging himself over walls. By the way, your beautiful neighbor would be pleased if he heard about it. He had a grudge against Norton, and he's not a man, from what I know of him, to forget his little debts. But hallo, old chap, what have you got in your noddle?"

"Nothing," Smith answered curtly.

He had started in his chair, and the look had flashed over his face which comes upon a man who is struck suddenly by some unpleasant idea.

"You looked as if something I had said had taken you on the raw. By the way, you have made the acquaintance of Master B. since I looked in last, have you not? Young Monkhouse Lee told me something to that effect."

"Yes; I know him slightly. He has been up here once or twice."

"Well, you're big enough and ugly enough to take care of yourself. He's not what I should call exactly a healthy sort of johnny, though, no doubt, he's very clever, and all that. But you'll soon find out for yourself. Lee is all right; he's a very decent little fellow. Well, so long, old chap! I row Mullins for the vice chancellor's pot on Wednesday week, so mind you come down, in case I don't see you before."

Bovine Smith laid down his pipe and turned stolidly to his books once more. But with all the will in the world, he found it very hard to keep his mind upon his work. It would slip away to brood upon the man beneath him, and upon the little mystery which hung round his chambers. Then his thoughts turned to this singular attack of which Hastie had spoken, and to the grudge which Bellingham was said to owe the object of it. The two ideas would persist in rising together in his mind, as though there were some close and intimate connection between them. And yet the suspicion was so dim and vague that it could not be put down in words.

"Confound the chap!" cried Smith, as he shied his book on pathology across the room. "He has spoiled my night's reading, and that's reason enough, if there were no other, why I should steer clear of him in the future."

For ten days the medical student confined himself so closely to his studies that he neither saw nor heard anything of either of the men beneath him. At the hours when Bellingham had been accustomed to visit him, he took care to sport his oak, and though he more than once heard a knocking at his outer door, he resolutely refused to answer it. One afternoon, however, he was descending the stairs when, just as he was passing it, Bellingham's door flew open, and young Monkhouse Lee came out with his eyes sparkling and a dark flush of anger upon his olive cheeks. Close at his heels followed Bellingham, his fat, unhealthy face all quivering with malignant passion.

"You fool!" he hissed. "You'll be sorry."

"Very likely," cried the other. "Mind what I say. It's off! I won't hear of it!"

"You've promised, anyhow."

"Oh, I'll keep that! I won't speak. But I'd rather little Eva was in her grave. Once for all, it's off. She'll do what I say. We don't want to see you again."

So much Smith could not avoid hearing, but he hurried on, for he had no wish to be involved in their dispute. There had been a serious breach between them, that was clear enough, and Lee was going to cause the engagement with his sister to be broken off. Smith thought of Hastie's comparison of the toad and the dove, and was glad to think that the matter was at an end. Bellingham's face when he was in a passion was not pleasant to look upon. He was not a man to whom an innocent girl could be trusted for life. As he walked, Smith wondered lan-

guidly what could have caused the quarrel, and what the promise might be which Bellingham had been so anxious that Monkhouse Lee should keep.

It was the day of the sculling match between Hastie and Mullins, and a stream of men were making their way down to the
banks of the Isis. A May sun was shining brightly, and the yellow
path was barred with the black shadows of the tall elm trees. On
either side the gray colleges lay back from the road, the hoary
old mothers of minds looking out from their high, mullioned
windows at the tide of young life which swept so merrily past
them. Black-clad tutors, prim officials, pale, reading men,
brown-faced, straw-hatted young athletes in white sweaters or
many-colored blazers, all were hurrying toward the blue, winding river which curves through the Oxford meadows.

Abercrombie Smith, with the intuition of an old oarsman,
chose his position at the point where he knew that the struggle,
if there were a struggle, would come. Far off he heard the hum
that announced the start, the gathering roar of the approach, the
thunder of running feet, and the shouts of the men in the boats
beneath him. A spray of half-clad, deep-breathing runners shot
past him, and craning over their shoulders, he saw Hastie pulling a steady thirty-six, while his opponent, with a jerky forty, was
a good boat's length behind him. Smith gave a cheer for his
friend, and pulling out his watch, was starting off again for his
chambers, when he felt a touch upon his shoulder, and found
that young Monkhouse Lee was beside him.

"I saw you there," he said, in a timid, deprecating way. "I
wanted to speak to you, if you could spare me a half hour. This
cottage is mine. I share it with Harrington of King's. Come in
and have a cup of tea."

"I must be back presently," said Smith. "I am hard on the
grind at present. But I'll come in for a few minutes with pleasure. I wouldn't have come out only Hastie is a friend of mine."

"So he is of mine. Hasn't he a beautiful style? Mullins wasn't
in it. But come into the cottage. It's a little den of a place, but
it is pleasant to work in during the summer months."

It was a small, square, white building, with green doors and shutters, and a rustic trelliswork porch, standing back some fifty yards from the river's bank. Inside, the main room was roughly fitted up as a study—deal table, unpainted shelves with books, and a few cheap oleographs upon the wall. A kettle sang upon a spirit-stove, and there were tea things upon a tray on the table.

"Try that chair and have a cigarette," said Lee. "Let me pour you out a cup of tea. It's so good of you to come in, for I know that your time is a good deal taken up. I wanted to say to you that, if I were you, I should change my rooms at once."

"Eh?"

Smith sat staring with a lighted match in one hand and his unlit cigarette in the other.

"Yes; it must seem very extraordinary, and the worst of it is that I cannot give my reasons, for I am under a solemn promise —a very solemn promise. But I may go so far as to say that I don't think Bellingham is a very safe man to live near. I intend to camp out here as much as I can for a time."

"Not safe! What do you mean?"

"Ah, that's what I mustn't say. But do take my advice and move your rooms. We had a grand row today. You must have heard us, for you came down the stairs."

"I saw that you had fallen out."

"He's a horrible chap, Smith. That is the only word for him. I have had doubts about him ever since that night when he fainted—you remember, when you came down. I taxed him today, and he told me things that made my hair rise, and wanted me to stand in with him. I'm not straitlaced, but I am a clergyman's son, you know, and I think there are some things which are quite beyond the pale. I only thank God that I found him out before it was too late, for he was to have married into my family."

"This is all very fine, Lee," said Abercrombie Smith curtly. "But either you are saying a great deal too much or a great deal too little."

"I give you a warning."

"If there is real reason for warning, no promise can bind you. If I see a rascal about to blow a place up with dynamite no pledge will stand in my way of preventing him."

"Ah, but I cannot prevent him, and I can do nothing but warn you."

"Without saying what you warn me against."

"Against Bellingham."

"But that is childish. Why should I fear him, or any man?"

"I can't tell you. I can only entreat you to change your rooms. You are in danger where you are. I don't even say that Bellingham would wish to injure you. But it might happen, for he is a dangerous neighbor just now."

"Perhaps I know more than you think," said Smith, looking keenly at the young man's boyish, earnest face. "Suppose I tell you that someone else shares Bellingham's rooms."

Monkhouse Lee sprang from his chair in uncontrollable excitement.

"You know, then?" he gasped.

"A woman."

Lee dropped back again with a groan.

"My lips are sealed," he said. "I must not speak."

"Well, anyhow," said Smith, rising, "it is not likely that I should allow myself to be frightened out of rooms which suit me very nicely. It would be a little too feeble for me to move out all my goods and chattels because you say that Bellingham might in some unexplained way do me an injury. I think that I'll just take my chance, and stay where I am, and as I see that it's nearly five o'clock, I must ask you to excuse me."

He bade the young student adieu in a few curt words, and made his way homeward through the sweet spring evening, feeling half ruffled, half amused, as any other strong, unimaginative man might who has been menaced by a vague and shadowy danger.

There was one little indulgence which Abercrombie Smith always allowed himself, however closely his work might press upon him. Twice a week, on the Tuesday and the Friday, it was his invariable custom to walk over to Farlingford, the residence of Dr. Plumptree Peterson, situated about a mile and a half out of Oxford. Peterson had been a close friend of Smith's elder brother, Francis, and as he was a bachelor, fairly well-to-do, with a good cellar and a better library, his house was a pleasant goal for a man who was in need of a brisk walk. Twice a week, then, the medical student would swing out there along the dark country roads and spend a pleasant hour in Peterson's comfortable study, discussing, over a glass of old port, the gossip of the varsity or the latest developments of medicine or of surgery.

On the day that followed his interview with Monkhouse Lee, Smith shut up his books at a quarter past eight, the hour when he usually started for his friend's house. As he was leaving his room, however, his eyes chanced to fall upon one of the books which Bellingham had lent him, and his conscience pricked him for not having returned it. However repellent the man might be, he should not be treated with discourtesy. Taking the book, he walked downstairs and knocked at his neighbor's door. There was no answer; but on turning the handle he found that it was unlocked. Pleased at the thought of avoiding an interview, he stepped inside, and placed the book with his card upon the table.

The lamp was turned half down, but Smith could see the details of the room plainly enough. It was all much as he had seen it before—the frieze, the animal-headed gods, the hanging crocodile, and the table littered over with papers and dried leaves. The mummy case stood upright against the wall, but the mummy itself was missing. There was no sign of any second occupant of the room, and he felt as he withdrew that he had probably done Bellingham an injustice. Had he a guilty secret to preserve, he would hardly leave his door open so that all the world might enter.

The spiral stair was as black as pitch, and Smith was slowly making his way down its irregular steps, when he was suddenly conscious that something had passed him in the darkness. There was a faint sound, a whiff of air, a light brushing past his elbow, but so slight that he could scarcely be certain of it. He stopped and listened, but the wind was rustling among the ivy outside, and he could hear nothing else.

"Is that you, Styles?" he shouted.

There was no answer, and all was still behind him. It must have been a sudden gust of air, for there were crannies and cracks in the old turret. And yet he could almost have sworn that he heard a footfall by his very side. He had emerged into the quadrangle, still turning the matter over in his head, when a man came running swiftly across the smooth-cropped lawn.

"Is that you, Smith?"

"Hullo, Hastie!"

"For God's sake come at once! Young Lee is drowned! Here's Harrington of King's with the news. The doctor is out. You'll do, but come along at once. There may be life in him."

"Have you brandy?"

"No."

"I'll bring some. There's a flask on my table."

Smith bounded up the stairs, taking three at a time, seized the flask, and was rushing down with it, when, as he passed Bellingham's room, his eyes fell upon something which left him gasping and staring upon the landing.

The door, which he had closed behind him, was now open, and right in front of him, with the lamplight shining upon it, was the mummy case. Three minutes ago it had been empty. He could swear to that. Now it framed the lank body of its horrible occupant, who stood, grim and stark, with his black, shriveled face toward the door. The form was lifeless and inert, but it seemed to Smith as he gazed that there still lingered a lurid spark of vitality, some faint sign of consciousness in the little eyes which lurked in the depths of the hollow sockets. So astounded and shaken was he that he had forgotten his errand, and was still staring at the lean, sunken figure when the voice of his friend below recalled him to himself.

"Come on, Smith!" he shouted. "It's life and death, you know. Hurry up! Now, then," he added, as the medical student reappeared, "let us do a sprint. It is well under a mile, and we should do it in five minutes. A human life is better worth running for than a pot."

Neck and neck they dashed through the darkness, and did not pull up until, panting and spent, they had reached the little cottage by the river. Young Lee, limp and dripping like a broken water plant, was stretched upon the sofa, the green scum of the river upon his black hair, and a fringe of white foam upon his leaden-hued lips. Beside him knelt his fellow student, Harrington, endeavoring to chafe some warmth back into his rigid limbs.

"I think there's life in him," said Smith, with his hand to the lad's side. "Put your watch glass to his lips. Yes, there's dimming on it. You take one arm, Hastie. Now work it as I do, and we'll soon pull him round."

For ten minutes they worked in silence, inflating and depressing the chest of the unconscious man. At the end of that time a shiver ran through his body, his lips trembled, and he opened his eyes. The three students burst out into an irrepressible cheer.

"Wake up, old chap. You've frightened us quite enough."

"Have some brandy. Take a sip from the flask."

"He's all right now," said his companion Harrington. "Heavens, what a fright I got! I was reading here, and he had gone out for a stroll as far as the river, when I heard a scream and a splash. Out I ran, and by the time I could find him and fish him out, all life seemed to have gone. Then Simpson couldn't get a doctor, for he has a game leg, and I had to run, and I don't know what I'd have done without you fellows. That's right, old chap. Sit up."

Monkhouse Lee had raised himself on his hands, and looked wildly about him.

"What's up?" he asked. "I've been in the water. Ah, yes; I remember."

A look of fear came into his eyes, and he sank his face into his hands.

"How did you fall in?"

"I didn't fall in."

"How then?"

"I was thrown in. I was standing by the bank, and something from behind picked me up like a feather and hurled me in. I heard nothing, and I saw nothing. But I know what it was, for all that."

"And so do I," whispered Smith.

Lee looked up with a quick glance of surprise.

"You've learned, then?" he said. "You remember the advice I gave you?"

"Yes, and I begin to think that I shall take it."

"I don't know what the deuce you fellows are talking about," said Hastie, "but I think, if I were you, Harrington, I should get Lee to bed at once. It will be time enough to discuss the why and the wherefore when he is a little stronger. I think, Smith, you and I can leave him alone now. I am walking back to college; if you are coming in that direction, we can have a chat."

But it was little chat that they had upon their homeward path. Smith's mind was too full of the incidents of the evening, the absence of the mummy from his neighbor's rooms, the step that passed him on the stair, the reappearance—the extraordinary, inexplicable reappearance—of the grisly thing, and then this attack upon Lee, corresponding so closely to the previous outrage upon another man against whom Bellingham bore a grudge. All this settled in his thoughts, together with the many little incidents which had previously turned him against his neighbor, and the singular circumstances under which he was first called in to him. What had been a dim suspicion, a vague, fantastic conjecture, had suddenly taken form, and stood out in his mind as a grim fact, a thing not to be denied. And yet, how monstrous it was! how unheard of! how entirely beyond all bounds of human experience. An impartial judge, or even the friend who walked by his side, would simply tell him that his eyes had deceived him, that the mummy had been there all the time, that young Lee had tumbled into the river as any other man tumbles into a river, and the blue pill was the best thing for a disordered liver. He felt that he would have said as much if the positions had been reversed. And yet he could swear that Bellingham was a murderer at heart, and that he wielded a weapon such as no man had ever used in all the grim history of crime.

Hastie had branched off to his rooms with a few crisp and emphatic comments upon his friend's unsociability, and Abercrombie Smith crossed the quadrangle to his corner turret with a strong feeling of repulsion for his chambers and their associations. He would take Lee's advice, and move his quarters as soon as possible, for how could a man study when his ear was ever straining for every murmur or footstep in the room below? He observed, as he crossed over the lawn, that the light was still shining in Bellingham's window, and as he passed up the staircase the door opened, and the man himself looked out at him. With his fat, evil face he was like some bloated spider fresh from the weaving of his poisonous web.

"Good evening," said he. "Won't you come in?"

"No," cried Smith fiercely.

"No? You are as busy as ever? I wanted to ask you about Lee. I was sorry to hear that there was a rumor that something was amiss with him."

His features were grave, but there was the gleam of a hidden laugh in his eyes as he spoke. Smith saw it, and he could have knocked him down for it.

"You'll be sorrier still to hear that Monkhouse Lee is doing very well, and is out of all danger," he answered. "Your hellish tricks have not come off this time. Oh, you needn't try to brazen it out. I know all about it."

Bellingham took a step back from the angry student, and half closed the door as if to protect himself.

"You are mad," he said. "What do you mean? Do you assert that I had anything to do with Lee's accident?"

"Yes," thundered Smith. "You and that bag of bones behind you; you worked it between you. I tell you what it is, Master B., they have given up burning folk like you, but we still keep a hangman, and, by George! if any man in this college meets his death while you are here, I'll have you up, and if you don't swing for it, it won't be my fault. You'll find that your filthy Egyptian tricks won't answer in England."

"You're a raving lunatic," said Bellingham.

"All right. You just remember what I say, for you'll find that I'll be better than my word."

The door slammed, and Smith went fuming up to his chamber, where he locked the door upon the inside, and spent half the night in smoking his old brier, and brooding over the strange events of the evening.

Next morning Abercrombie Smith heard nothing of his neighbor, but Harrington called upon him in the afternoon to say that Lee was almost himself again. All day Smith stuck fast to his work, but in the evening he determined to pay the visit to his friend Dr. Peterson upon which he had started the night before. A good walk and a friendly chat would be welcome to his jangled nerves.

Bellingham's door was shut as he passed, but glancing back when he was some distance from the turret, he saw his neighbor's head at the window outlined against the lamplight, his face pressed apparently against the glass as he gazed out into the darkness. It was a blessing to be away from all contact with him, if but for a few hours, and Smith stepped out briskly, and breathed the soft spring air into his lungs. The half moon lay in the west between two Gothic pinnacles, and threw upon the silvered street a dark tracery from the stonework above. There was a brisk breeze, and light, fleecy clouds drifted swiftly across the sky. Old's was on the very border of the town, and in five minutes Smith found himself beyond the houses and between the hedges of a May-scented, Oxfordshire lane.

It was a lonely and little-frequented road which led to his friend's house. Early as it was, Smith did not meet a single soul upon his way. He walked briskly along until he came to the avenue gate, which opened into the long, gravel drive leading up to Farlingford. In front of him he could see the cozy, red light of the windows glimmering through the foliage. He stood with his hand upon the iron latch of the swinging gate, and he glanced back at the road along which he had come. Something was coming swiftly down it.

It moved in the shadow of the hedge, silently and furtively, a dark, crouching figure, dimly visible against the black background. Even as he gazed back at it, it had lessened its distance by twenty paces, and was fast closing upon him. Out of the darkness he had a glimpse of a scraggy neck, and of two eyes that will ever haunt him in his dreams. He turned, and with a cry of terror he ran for his life up the avenue. There were the red lights, the signals of safety, almost within a stone's throw of him. He was a famous runner, but never had he run as he ran that night.

The heavy gate had swung into place behind him but he heard it dash open again before his pursuer. As he rushed madly and wildly through the night, he could hear a swift, dry patter behind him, and could see, as he threw back a glance, that this horror was bounding like a tiger at his heels, with blazing eyes and one stringy arm outthrown. Thank God, the door was ajar. He could see the thin bar of light which shot from the lamp in the hall. Nearer yet sounded the clatter from behind. He heard a hoarse gurgling at his very shoulder. With a shriek he flung himself against the door, slammed and bolted it behind him, and sank half fainting on the hall chair.

"My goodness, Smith, what's the matter?" asked Peterson, appearing at the door of his study.

"Give me some brandy."

Peterson disappeared, and came rushing out again with a glass and a decanter.

"You need it," he said, as his visitor drank off what he poured out for him. "Why, man, you are as white as a cheese."

Smith laid down his glass, rose up, and took a deep breath.

"I am my own man again now," said he. "I was never so unmanned before. But, with your leave, Peterson, I will sleep here tonight, for I don't think I could face that road again except by daylight. It's weak, I know, but I can't help it."

Peterson looked at his visitor with a very questioning eye.

"Of course you shall sleep here if you wish. I'll tell Mrs. Burney to make up the spare bed. Where are you off to now?"

"Come up with me to the window that overlooks the door. I want you to see what I have seen."

They went up to the window of the upper hall whence they could look down upon the approach to the house. The drive and the fields on either side lay quiet and still, bathed in the peaceful moonlight.

"Well, really, Smith," remarked Peterson, "it is well that I know you to be an abstemious man. What in the world can have frightened you?"

"I'll tell you presently. But where can it have gone? Ah, now, look, look! See the curve of the road just beyond your gate."

"Yes, I see; you needn't pinch my arm off. I saw someone pass. I should say a man, rather thin, apparently, and tall, very tall. But what of him? And what of yourself? You are still shaking like an aspen leaf."

"I have been within handgrip of the devil, that's all. But come down to your study, and I shall tell you the whole story."

He did so. Under the cherry lamplight with a glass of wine on the table beside him, and the portly form and florid face of his friend in front, he narrated, in their order, all the events, great and small, which had formed so singular a chain, from the night on which he had found Bellingham fainting in front of the mummy case until this horried experience of an hour ago.

"There now," he said as he concluded, "that's the whole, black business. It is monstrous and incredible, but it is true."

Dr. Plumptree Peterson sat for some time in silence with a very puzzled expression upon his face.

"I never heard of such a thing in my life, never!" he said at last. "You have told me the facts. Now tell me your inferences."

"You can draw your own."

"But I should like to hear yours. You have thought over the matter, and I have not."

"Well, it must be a little vague in detail, but the main points seem to me to be clear enough. This fellow Bellingham, in his Eastern studies, has got hold of some infernal secret by which a mummy—or possibly only this particular mummy—can be temporarily brought to life. He was trying this disgusting business on the night when he fainted. No doubt the sight of the creature moving had shaken his nerve, even though he had expected it. You remember that almost the first words he said were to call out upon himself as a fool. Well, he got more hardened afterward, and carried the matter through without fainting. The vitality which he could put into it was evidently only a passing thing, for I have seen it continually in its case as dead as this table. He has some elaborate process, I fancy, by which he brings the thing to pass. Having done it, he naturally bethought him that he might use the creature as an agent. It has intelligence and it has strength. For some purpose he took Lee into his confidence; but Lee, like a decent Christian, would have nothing to do with such a business. Then they had a row, and Lee vowed that he would tell his sister of Bellingham's true character. Bellingham's game was to prevent him, and he nearly managed it, by setting this creature of his on his track. He had already tried its powers upon another man—Norton—toward whom he had a grudge. It is the merest chance that he has not two murders upon his soul. Then, when I taxed him with the matter, he had the strongest reasons for wishing to get me out of the way before I could convey my knowledge to anyone else. He got his chance when I went out, for he knew my habits and where I was bound for. I have had a narrow shave, Peterson, and it is mere luck you didn't find me on your doorstep in the morning. I'm not a nervous man as a rule, and I never thought to have the fear of death put upon me as it was tonight."

"My dear boy, you take the matter too seriously," said his companion. "Your nerves are out of order with your work, and you make too much of it. How could such a thing as this stride about the streets of Oxford, even at night, without being seen?"

"It has been seen. There is quite a scare in the town about an escaped ape, as they imagine the creature to be. It is the talk of the place."

"Well, it's a striking chain of events. And yet, my dear fellow, you must allow that each incident in itself is capable of a more natural explanation."

"What! even my adventure of tonight?"

"Certainly. You come out with your nerves all unstrung, and your head full of this theory of yours. Some gaunt, half famished tramp steals after you, and seeing you run, is emboldened to pursue you. Your fears and imagination do the rest."

"It won't do, Peterson; it won't do."

"And again, in the instance of your finding the mummy case empty, and then a few moments later with an occupant, you know that it was lamplight, that the lamp was half turned down, and that you had no special reason to look hard at the case. It is quite possible that you may have overlooked the creature in the first instance."

"No, no; it is out of the question."

"And then Lee may have fallen into the river, and Norton been garroted. It is certainly a formidable indictment that you have against Bellingham; but if you were to place it before a police magistrate, he would simply laugh in your face."

"I know he would. That is why I mean to take the matter into my own hands."

"Eh?"

"Yes; I feel that a public duty rests upon me, and, besides, I must do it for my own safety, unless I choose to allow myself to be hunted by this beast out of the college, and that would be a little too feeble. I have quite made up my mind what I shall do. And first of all, may I use your paper and pens for an hour?"

"Most certainly. You will find all that you want upon that side table."

Abercrombie Smith sat down before a sheet of foolscap, and for an hour, and then for a second hour, his pen traveled swiftly over it. Page after page was finished and tossed aside while his friend leaned back in his armchair, looking across at him with patient curiosity. At last, with an exclamation of satisfaction, Smith sprang to his feet, gathered his papers up into order, and laid the last one upon Peterson's desk.

"Kindly sign this as a witness," he said.

"A witness? Of what?"

"Of my signature, and of the date. The date is the most important. Why, Peterson, my life might hang upon it."

"My dear Smith, you are talking wildly. Let me beg you to go to bed."

"On the contrary, I never spoke so deliberately in my life. And I will promise to go to bed the moment you have signed it."

"But what is it?"

"It is a statement of all that I have been telling you tonight. I wish you to witness it."

"Certainly," said Peterson, signing his name under that of his companion. "There you are! But what is the idea?"

"You will kindly retain it, and produce it in case I am arrested."

"Arrested? For what?"

"For murder. It is quite on the cards. I wish to be ready for every event. There is only one course open to me, and I am determined to take it."

"For heaven's sake, don't do anything rash!"

"Believe me, it would be far more rash to adopt any other course. I hope that we won't need to bother you, but it will ease my mind to know that you have this statement of my motives. And now I am ready to take your advice and to go to roost, for I want to be at my best in the morning."

Abercrombie Smith was not an entirely pleasant man to have as an enemy. Slow and easy tempered, he was formidable when driven to action. He brought to every purpose in life the same deliberate resoluteness that had distinguished him as a scientific student. He had laid his studies aside for a day, but he intended that the day should not be wasted. Not a word did he say to his host as to his plans, but by nine o'clock he was well on his way to Oxford.

In the High Street he stopped at Clifford's, the gunmaker's, and bought a heavy revolver, with a box of center-fire cartridges. Six of them he slipped into the chambers, and half cocking the weapon, placed it in the pocket of his coat. He then made his way to Hastie's rooms, where the big oarsman was lounging over his breakfast, with the *Sporting Times* propped up against the coffeepot.

"Hullo! What's up?" he asked. "Have some coffee?"

"No, thank you. I want you to come with me, Hastie, and do what I ask you."

"Certainly, my boy."

"And bring a heavy stick with you."

"Hullo!" Hastie stared. "Here's a hunting crop that would fell an ox."

"One other thing. You have a box of amputating knives. Give me the longest of them."

"There you are. You seem to be fairly on the war trail. Anything else?"

"No; that will do." Smith placed the knife inside his coat, and led the way to the quadrangle. "We are neither of us chickens, Hastie," said he. "I think I can do this job alone, but I take you as a precaution. I am going to have a little talk with Bellingham. If I have only him to deal with, I won't, of course, need you. If I shout, however, up you come, and lam out with your whip as hard as you can lick. Do you understand?"

"All right. I'll come if I hear you bellow."

"Stay here, then. I may be a little time, but don't budge until I come down."

"I'm a fixture."

Smith ascended the stairs, opened Bellingham's door and stepped in. Bellingham was seated behind his table, writing. Beside him, among his litter of strange possessions, towered the mummy case, with its sale number 249 still stuck upon its front, and its hideous occupant stiff and stark within it. Smith looked very deliberately round him, closed the door, and then, stepping across to the fireplace, struck a match and set the fire alight. Bellingham sat staring, with amazement and rage upon his bloated face.

"Well, really now, you make yourself at home," he gasped.

Smith sat himself deliberately down, placing his watch upon the table, drew out his pistol, cocked it, and laid it in his lap. Then he took the long amputating knife from his bosom, and threw it down in front of Bellingham.

"Now, then," said he, "just get to work and cut up that mummy."

"Oh, is that it?" said Bellingham with a sneer.

"Yes, that is it. They tell me that the law can't touch you. But I have a law that will set matters straight. If in five minutes you have not set to work, I swear by the God who made me that I will put a bullet through your brain!"

"You would murder me?"

Bellingham had half risen, and his face was the color of putty.

"Yes."

"And for what?"

"To stop your mischief. One minute has gone."

"But what have I done?"

"I know and you know."

"This is mere bullying."

"Two minutes are gone."

"But you must give reasons. You are a madman—a dangerous madman. Why should I destroy my own property? It is a valuable mummy."

"You must cut it up, and you must burn it."

"I will do no such thing."

"Four minutes are gone."

Smith took up the pistol and he looked toward Bellingham with an inexorable face. As the second hand stole round, he raised his hand, and the finger twitched upon the trigger.

"There! there! I'll do it!" screamed Bellingham.

In frantic haste he caught up the knife and hacked at the figure of the mummy, ever glancing round to see the eye and the weapon of his terrible visitor bent upon him. The creature crackled and snapped under every stab of the keen blade. A thick, yellow dust rose up from it. Spices and dried essences rained down upon the floor. Suddenly, with a rending crack, its backbone snapped asunder, and it fell, a brown heap of sprawling limbs, upon the floor.

"Now into the fire!" said Smith.

The flames leaped and roared as the dried and tinderlike debris was piled upon it. The little room was like the stokehole of a steamer and the sweat ran down the faces of the two men; but still the one stooped and worked, while the other sat watching him with a set face. A thick, fat smoke oozed out from the fire, and a heavy smell of burned resin and singed hair filled the air. In a quarter of an hour a few charred and brittle sticks were all that was left of Lot No. 249.

"Perhaps that will satisfy you," snarled Bellingham, with hate and fear in his little gray eyes as he glanced back at his tormentor.

"No; I must make a clean sweep of all your materials. We must have no more devil's tricks. In with all these leaves! They may have something to do with it."

"And what now?" asked Bellingham, when the leaves also had been added to the blaze.

"Now the roll of papyrus which you had on the table that night. It is in that drawer, I think."

"No, no," shouted Bellingham. "Don't burn that! Why, man, you don't know what you do. It is unique; it contains wisdom which is nowhere else to be found."

"Out with it!"

"But look here, Smith, you can't really mean it. I'll share the knowledge with you. I'll teach you all that is in it. Or, stay, let me only copy it before you burn it!"

Smith stepped forward and turned the key in the drawer. Taking out the yellow, curled roll of paper, he threw it into the fire, and pressed it down with his heel. Bellingham screamed, and grabbed at it; but Smith pushed him back and stood over it until it was reduced to a formless, gray ash.

"Now, Master B.," said he, "I think I have pretty well drawn your teeth. You'll hear from me again, if you return to your old tricks. And now good morning, for I must go back to my studies."

And such is the narrative of Abercrombie Smith as to the singular events that occurred in Old College, Oxford, in the spring of '84. As Bellingham left the university immediately afterward, and was last heard of in the Sudan, there is no one who can contradict his statement. But the wisdom of men is small, and the ways of Nature are strange, and who shall put a bound to the dark things that may be found by those who seek for them?

SOME WORDS WITH A MUMMY

by EDGAR ALLAN POE

Edgar Allan Poe is best known, of course, as the father of the detective story and as the creator of some of the most terrifying tales of madness and the macabre ever committed to paper. But Poe wore many literary hats during his brief but prolific career, and perhaps the least recognized today is that of satirist. That he could write with tongue firmly planted in cheek, and create chuckles as well as chills, is nowhere better demonstrated than in the story (or, more properly, sketch) which follows.

"Some Words with a Mummy" is also a premier example of the flip side of the mummy theme. Horror takes a distant backseat to humor in this account of an Egyptian mummy named (ahem) Allamistakeo who is electrically revived by a group of "learned" individuals in Poe's 1840s New York. The rather heated confrontation which follows offers quite a few barbed and witty observations on ancient versus modern "civilization."

Born in Boston in 1809, Poe began writing in his teens and anonymously published his first book, Tamerlane and Other Poems, *in 1827. He began to write short stories in 1832 and was one of the first to develop the short story as a distinct literary form. His first detective story, "The Murders in the Rue Morgue," featuring C. Auguste Dupin, ap-*

peared in 1841. Much of his work dealt with death and madness, owing in part to Poe's own deteriorating mental condition (brought about by alcoholism, drug usage, and the illness and subsequent death of his young wife Virginia, whom he had married eleven years earlier, in 1847). In addition to short stories, he wrote verse and epic poetry, essays, sketches, and literary criticism—all of major importance in American letters; he also edited the Southern Literary Messenger, *a prestigious magazine of the time, from 1835 to 1837. He died as he lived, under tragic circumstances involving alcohol and drugs, in Baltimore in 1849.*

THE SYMPOSIUM of the preceding evening had been a little too much for my nerves. I had a wretched headache, and was desperately drowsy. Instead of going out, therefore, to spend the evening, as I had proposed, it occurred to me that I could not do a wiser thing than just eat a mouthful of supper and go immediately to bed.

A *light* supper, of course. I am exceedingly fond of Welsh rabbit. More than a pound at once, however, may not at all times be advisable. Still, there can be no material objection to two. And really between two and three, there is merely a single unit of difference. I ventured, perhaps, upon four. My wife will have it five—but, clearly, she has confounded two very distinct affairs. The abstract number, five, I am willing to admit; but, concretely, it has reference to bottles of Brown Stout, without which, in the way of condiment, Welsh rabbit is to be eschewed.

Having thus concluded a frugal meal, and donned my nightcap, with the sincere hope of enjoying it till noon the next day, I placed my head upon the pillow, and, through the aid of a capital conscience, fell into a profound slumber forthwith.

But when were the hopes of humanity fulfilled? I could not have completed my third snore when there came a furious ringing at the street-door bell, and then an impatient thumping at the knocker, which awakened me at once. In a minute afterward, and while I was still rubbing my eyes, my wife thrust in my face a note, from my old friend, Dr. Ponnonner. It ran thus:

Come to me, by all means, my dear good friend, as soon as you receive this. Come and help us to rejoice. At last, by long persevering diplomacy, I have gained the assent of the directors of the City Museum, to my examination of the mummy —you know the one I mean. I have permission to unswathe it and open it, if desirable. A few friends only will be present —you, of course. The mummy is now at my house, and we shall begin to unroll it at eleven tonight.

Yours, ever,

PONNONNER

By the time I had reached the "Ponnonner," it struck me that I was as wide awake as a man need be. I leaped out of bed in an ecstasy, overthrowing all in my way; dressed myself with a rapidity truly marvelous; and set off, at the top of my speed, for the doctor's.

There I found a very eager company assembled. They had been awaiting me with much impatience; the mummy was extended upon the dining table; and the moment I entered its examination was commenced.

It was one of a pair brought, several years previously, by Captain Arthur Sabretash, a cousin of Ponnonner's, from a tomb near Eleithias, in the Lybian mountains, a considerable distance above Thebes on the Nile. The grottoes at this point, although less magnificent than the Theban sepulchers, are of higher interest, on account of affording more numerous illustrations of the private life of the Egyptians. The chamber from which our specimen was taken, was said to be very rich in such illustrations—the walls being completely covered with fresco paintings and bas-reliefs, while statues, vases, and mosaic work of rich patterns indicated the vast wealth of the deceased.

The treasure had been deposited in the museum precisely in the same condition in which Captain Sabretash had found it—

that is to say, the coffin had not been disturbed. For eight years it had thus stood, subject only externally to public inspection. We had now, therefore, the complete mummy at our disposal; and to those who are aware how very rarely the unransacked antique reaches our shores, it will be evident at once that we had great reason to congratulate ourselves upon our good fortune.

Approaching the table, I saw on it a large box, or case, nearly seven feet long, and perhaps three feet wide, by two feet and a half deep. It was oblong—not coffin-shaped. The material was at first supposed to be the wood of the sycamore *(platanus),* but, upon cutting into it, we found it to be pasteboard, or, more properly, *papier-mâché,* composed of papyrus. It was thickly ornamented with paintings, representing funeral scenes, and other mournful subjects—interspersed among which, in every variety of position, were certain series of hieroglyphical characters, intended, no doubt, for the name of the departed. By good luck, Mr. Gliddon formed one of our party; and he had no difficulty in translating the letters, which were simply phonetic, and represented the word *"Allamistakeo."*

We had some difficulty in getting this case open without injury; but, having at length accomplished the task, we came to a second, coffin-shaped, and very considerably less in size than the exterior one, but resembling it precisely in every other respect. The interval between the two was filled with resin, which had, in some degree, defaced the colors of the interior box.

Upon opening this latter (which we did quite easily), we arrived at a third case, also coffin-shaped, and varying from the second one in no particular, except in that of its material, which was cedar, and still emitted the peculiar and highly aromatic odor of that wood. Between the second and the third case there was no interval—the one fitting accurately within the other.

Removing the third case, we discovered and took out the body itself. We had expected to find it, as usual, enveloped in frequent rolls, or bandages, of linen; but, in place of these, we found a sort of sheath, made of papyrus, and coated with a layer of plaster, thickly gilt and painted. The paintings represented subjects connected with the various supposed duties of the soul, and its presentation to different divinities, with numerous identical human figures, intended, very probably, as portraits of the persons embalmed. Extending from head to foot was a columnar, or perpendicular, inscription, in phonetic hieroglyphics, giving again his name and titles, and the names and titles of his relations.

Around the neck thus unsheathed, was a collar of cylindrical glass beads, diverse in color, and so arranged as to form images of deities, of the scarabaeus, etc., with the winged globe. Around the small of the waist was a similar collar or belt.

Stripping off the papyrus, we found the flesh in excellent preservation, with no perceptible odor. The color was reddish. The skin was hard, smooth, and glossy. The teeth and hair were in good condition. The eyes (it seemed) had been removed, and glass ones substituted, which were very beautiful and wonderfully lifelike, with the exception of somewhat too determined a stare. The fingers and the nails were brilliantly gilded.

Mr. Gliddon was of opinion, from the redness of the epidermis, that the embalmment had been effected altogether by asphaltum; but, on scraping the surface with a steel instrument, and throwing into the fire some of the powder thus obtained, the flavor of camphor and other sweet-scented gums became apparent.

We searched the corpse very carefully for the usual openings through which the entrails are extracted, but, to our surprise, we could discover none. No member of the party was at that period aware that entire or unopened mummies are not unfrequently met. The brain it was customary to withdraw through the nose; the intestines through an incision in the side; the body was then shaved, washed, and salted; then laid aside for several weeks, when the operation of embalming, properly so called, began.

As no trace of an opening could be found, Dr. Ponnonner was preparing his instruments for dissection, when I observed that it was then past two o'clock. Hereupon it was agreed to postpone the internal examination until the next evening; and we were about to separate for the present, when some one suggested an experiment or two with the voltaic pile.

The application of electricity to a mummy three or four thousand years old at the least, was an idea, if not very sage, still sufficiently original, and we all caught it at once. About one-tenth in earnest and nine-tenths in jest, we arranged a battery in the doctor's study, and conveyed thither the Egyptian.

It was only after much trouble that we succeeded in laying bare some portions of the temporal muscle which appeared of less stony rigidity than other parts of the frame, but which, as we had anticipated, of course, gave no indication of galvanic susceptibility when brought in contact with the wire. This, the first trial, indeed, seemed decisive, and, with a hearty laugh at our own absurdity, we were bidding each other good night, when my eyes, happening to fall upon those of the mummy, were there immediately riveted in amazement. My brief glance, in fact, had sufficed to assure me that the orbs which we had all supposed to be glass, and which were originally noticeable for a certain wild stare, were now so far covered by the lids, that only a small portion of the *tunica albuginea* remained visible.

With a shout I called attention to the fact, and it became immediately obvious to all.

I cannot say that I was *alarmed* at the phenomenon, because "alarmed" is, in my case, not exactly the word. It is possible however, that, but for the Brown Stout, I might have been a little nervous. As for the rest of the company, they really made no attempt at concealing the downright fright which possessed them. Dr. Ponnonner was a man to be pitied. Mr. Gliddon, by some peculiar process, rendered himself invisible. Mr. Silk Buckingham, I fancy, will scarcely be so bold as to deny that he made his way, upon all fours, under the table.

After the first shock of astonishment, however, we resolved, as a matter of course, upon further experiment forthwith. Our operations were now directed against the great toe of the right foot. We made an incision over the outside of the exterior *os sesamoideum pollicis pedis,* and thus got at the root of the abductor muscle. Readjusting the battery, we now applied the fluid to the bisected nerves—when, with a movement of exceeding life likeness, the mummy first drew up its right knee so as to bring it nearly in contact with the abdomen, and then, straightening the limb with inconceivable force, bestowed a kick upon Dr. Ponnonner, which had the effect of discharging that gentleman, like an arrow from a catapult, through a window into the street below.

We rushed out en masse to bring in the mangled remains of the victim, but had the happiness to meet him upon the staircase, coming up in an unaccountable hurry, brimful of the most ardent philosophy, and more than ever impressed with the necessity of prosecuting our experiment with vigor and with zeal.

It was by this advice, accordingly, that we made, upon the spot, a profound incision into the tip of the subject's nose, while the doctor himself, laying violent hands upon it, pulled it into vehement contact with the wire.

Morally and physically—figuratively and literally—was the effect electric. In the first place, the corpse opened its eyes and winked very rapidly for several minutes, as does Mr. Barnes in the pantomime; in the second place, it sneezed; in the third, it sat upon end; in the fourth, it shook its fist in Dr. Ponnonner's face; in the fifth, turning to Messrs. Gliddon and Buckingham, it addressed them, in very capital Egyptian, thus:

"I must say, gentlemen, that I am as much surprised as I am mortified at your behavior. Of Dr. Ponnonner nothing better was to be expected. He is a poor little fat fool who *knows* no better. I pity and forgive him. But you, Mr. Gliddon—and you, Silk—who have travelled and resided in Egypt until one might imagine you to the manor born—you, I say, who have been so much among us that you speak Egyptian fully as well, I think, as you write your mother tongue—you, whom I have always been led to regard as the firm friend of the mummies—I really did anticipate more gentlemanly conduct from *you.* What am I to think of your standing quietly by and seeing me thus unhandsomely used? What am I to suppose by your permitting Tom, Dick, and Harry to strip me of my coffins, and my clothes, in this wretchedly cold climate? In what light (to come to the point) am I to regard your aiding and abetting that little villain, Dr. Ponnonner, in pulling me by the nose?"

It will be taken for granted, no doubt, that upon hearing this speech under the circumstances, we all either made for the door, or fell into violent hysterics, or went off in a general swoon. One of these three things was, I say, to be expected. Indeed each and all of these lines of conduct might have been very plausibly pursued. And, upon my word, I am at a loss to know how or why it was that we pursued neither the one nor the other. But, perhaps, the true reason is to be sought in the spirit of the age, which proceeds by the rule of contraries altogether, and is now usually admitted as the solution of everything in the way of paradox and impossibility. Or, perhaps, after all, it was only the mummy's exceedingly natural and matter-of-course air that divested his words of the terrible. However this may be, the facts are clear, and no member of our party betrayed any very particular trepidation, or seemed to consider that anything had gone very especially wrong.

For my part I was convinced it was all right, and merely stepped aside, out of the range of the Egyptian's fist. Dr. Ponnonner thrust his hands into his breeches pockets, looked hard at the mummy, and grew excessively red in the face. Mr. Gliddon stroked his whiskers and drew up the collar of his shirt. Mr. Buckingham hung down his head, and put his right thumb into the left corner of his mouth.

The Egyptian regarded him with a severe countenance for some minutes and at length, with a sneer, said:

"Why don't you speak, Mr. Buckingham? Did you hear what I asked you, or not? *Do* take your thumb out of your mouth!"

Mr. Buckingham, hereupon, gave a slight start, took his right thumb out of the left corner of his mouth, and, by way of indemnification, inserted his left thumb in the right corner of the aperture above-mentioned.

Not being able to get an answer from Mr. B., the figure turned peevishly to Mr. Gliddon, and, in a peremptory tone, demanded in general terms what we all meant.

Mr. Gliddon replied at great length, in phonetics; and but for the deficiency of American printing offices in hieroglyphical type, it would afford me much pleasure to record here, in the original, the whole of his very excellent speech.

I may as well take this occasion to remark, that all the subsequent conversation in which the mummy took a part, was carried on in primitive Egyptian, through the medium (so far as concerned myself and other untraveled members of the company) —through the medium, I say, of Messrs. Gliddon and Buckingham, as interpreters. These gentlemen spoke the mother tongue of the mummy with inimitable fluency and grace; but I could not help observing that (owing, no doubt, to the introduction of images entirely modern, and, of course, entirely novel to the stranger) the two travelers were reduced, occasionally, to the employment of sensible forms for the purpose of conveying a particular meaning. Mr. Gliddon, at one period, for example, could not make the Egyptian comprehend the term "politics," until he sketched upon the wall, with a bit of charcoal, a little carbuncle-nosed gentleman, out at elbows, standing upon a stump, with his left leg drawn back, right arm thrown forward, with his fist shut, the eyes rolled up toward heaven, and the mouth open at an angle of ninety degrees. Just in the same way Mr. Buckingham failed to convey the absolutely modern idea "whig," until (at Dr. Ponnonner's suggestion) he grew very pale in the face, and consented to take off his own.

It will be readily understood that Mr. Gliddon's discourse turned chiefly upon the vast benefits accruing to science from the unrolling and disemboweling of mummies; apologizing, upon this score, for any disturbance that might have been occasioned *him,* in particular, the individual mummy called Allamistakeo; and concluding with a mere hint (for it could scarcely be considered more) that, as these little matters were now explained, it might be as well to proceed with the investigation intended. Here Dr. Ponnonner made ready his instruments.

In regard to the latter suggestions of the orator, it appears that Allamistakeo had certain scruples of conscience, the nature of which I did not distinctly learn; but he expressed himself satisfied with the apologies tendered, and, getting down from the table, shook hands with the company all round.

When this ceremony was at an end, we immediately busied

ourselves in repairing the damages which our subject had sustained from the scalpel. We sewed up the wound in his temple, bandaged his foot, and applied a square inch of black plaster to the tip of his nose.

It was now observed that the count (this was the title, it seems, of Allamistakeo) had a slight fit of shivering—no doubt from the cold. The doctor immediately repaired to his wardrobe, and soon returned with a black dress coat, made in Jennings's best manner, a pair of sky-blue plaid pantaloons with straps, a pink gingham chemise, a flapped vest of brocade, a white sack overcoat, a walking cane with a hook, a hat with no brim, patent leather boots, straw-colored kid gloves, an eyeglass, a pair of whiskers, and a waterfall cravat. Owing to the disparity of size between the count and the doctor (the proportion being as two to one), there was some little difficulty in adjusting these habiliments upon the person of the Egyptian; but when all was arranged, he might have been said to be dressed. Mr. Gliddon, therefore, gave him his arm, and led him to a comfortable chair by the fire, while the doctor rang the bell upon the spot and ordered a supply of cigars and wine.

The conversation soon grew animated. Much curiosity was, of course, expressed in regard to the somewhat remarkable fact of Allamistakeo's still remaining alive.

"I should have thought," observed Mr. Buckingham, "that it is high time you were dead."

"Why," replied the count, very much astonished, "I am little more than seven hundred years old! My father lived a thousand, and was by no means in his dotage when he died."

Here ensued a brisk series of questions and computations, by means of which it became evident that the antiquity of the mummy had been grossly misjudged. It had been five thousand and fifty years and some months since he had been consigned to the catacombs at Eleithias.

"But my remark," resumed Mr. Buckingham, "had no reference to your age at the period of interment (I am willing to grant, in fact, that you are still a young man), and my allusion was to the immensity of time during which, by your own showing, you must have been done up in asphaltum."

"In what?" said the count.

"In asphaltum," persisted Mr. B.

"Ah, yes; I have some faint notion of what you mean; it might be made to answer, no doubt—but in my time we employed scarcely anything else than the bichloride of mercury."

"But what we are especially at a loss to understand," said Dr. Ponnonner, "is how it happens that, having been dead and buried in Egypt five thousand years ago, you are here today all alive and looking so delightfully well."

"Had I been, as you say, *dead,*" replied the count, "it is more than probable that dead I should still be; for I perceive you are yet in the infancy of galvanism, and cannot accomplish with it what was a common thing among us in the old days. But the fact is, I fell into catalepsy, and it was considered by my best friends that I was either dead or should be; they accordingly embalmed me at once—I presume you are aware of the chief principle of the embalming process?"

"Why, not altogether."

"Ah, I perceive—a deplorable condition of ignorance! Well, I cannot enter into details just now: but it is necessary to explain that to embalm (properly speaking), in Egypt, was to arrest indefinitely *all* the animal functions subjected to the process. I used the word 'animal' in its widest sense, as including the physical not more than the moral and *vital* being. I repeat that the leading principle of embalming consisted, with us, in the immediately arresting, and holding in perpetual *abeyance, all* the animal functions subjected to the process. To be brief, in whatever condition the individual was, at the period of embalmment, in that condition he remained. Now, as it is my good fortune to be of the blood of the scarabaeus, I was embalmed *alive,* as you see me at present."

"The blood of the scarabaeus!" exclaimed Dr. Ponnonner.

"Yes. The scarabaeus was the *insignium,* or the 'arms,' of a very distinguished and very rare patrician family. To be 'of the blood of the scarabaeus,' is merely to be one of that family of which the scarabaeus is the *insignium.* I speak figuratively."

"But what has this to do with your being alive?"

"Why, it is the general custom in Egypt to deprive a corpse, before embalmment, of its bowels and brains; the race of the scarabaei alone did not coincide with the custom. Had I not been a scarabaeus, therefore, I should have been without bowels and brains; and without either it is inconvenient to live."

"I perceive that," said Mr. Buckingham, "and I presume that all the *entire* mummies that come to hand are of the race of scarabaei."

"Beyond doubt."

"I thought," said Mr. Gliddon, very meekly, "that the scarabaeus was one of the Egyptian gods."

"One of the Egyptian *what?*" exclaimed the mummy, starting to its feet.

"Gods!" repeated the traveler.

"Mr. Gliddon, I really am astonished to hear you talk in this style," said the count, resuming his chair. "No nation upon the face of the earth has ever acknowledged more than one *god.* The scarabaeus, the ibis, etc., were with us (as similar creatures have been with others) the symbols, or media, through which we offered worship to the Creator too august to be more directly approached."

There was here a pause. At length the colloquy was renewed by Dr. Ponnonner.

"It is not improbable, then, from what you have explained," said he, "that among the catacombs near the Nile there may exist other mummies of the scarabaeus tribe in a condition of vitality."

"There can be no question of it," replied the count; "all the scarabaei embalmed accidentally while alive, are alive. Even some of those *purposely* so embalmed, may have been overlooked by their executors, and still remain in the tomb."

"Will you be kind enough to explain," I said, "what you mean by 'purposely so embalmed'?"

"With great pleasure," answered the mummy, after surveying me leisurely through his eyeglass—for it was the first time I had ventured to address him a direct question.

"With great pleasure," he said. "The usual duration of man's life, in my time, was about eight hundred years. Few men died, unless by most extraordinary accident, before the age of six hundred; few lived longer than a decade of centuries; but eight were considered the natural term. After the discovery of the embalming principle, as I have already described it to you, it occurred to our philosophers that a laudable curiosity might be gratified, and, at the same time, the interests of science much advanced, by living this natural term in installments. In the case of history, indeed, experience demonstrated that something of this kind was indispensable. A historian, for example, having attained the age of five hundred, would write a book with great labor and then get himself carefully embalmed; leaving instructions to his executors pro tem., that they should cause him to be revivified after the lapse of a certain period—say five or six hundred years. Resuming existence at the expiration of this time, he would invariably find his great work converted into a species of haphazard notebook—that is to say, into a kind of literary arena for the conflicting guesses, riddles, and personal squabbles of whole herds of exasperated commentators. These guesses, etc., which passed under the name of annotations, or emendations, were found so completely to have enveloped, distorted, and overwhelmed the text, that the author had to go about with a lantern to discover his own book. When discovered, it was never worth the trouble of the search. After rewriting it throughout, it was regarded as the bounden duty of the historian to set himself to work immediately in correcting, from his own private knowledge and experience, the traditions of the day concerning the epoch at which he had originally lived. Now this process of rescription and personal rectification, pursued by various individual sages from time to time, had the effect of preventing our history from degenerating into absolute fable."

"I beg your pardon," said Dr. Ponnonner at this point, laying his hand gently upon the arm of the Egyptian—"I beg your pardon, sir, but may I presume to interrupt you for one moment?"

"By all means, *sir*," replied the count, drawing up.

"I merely wished to ask you a question," said the doctor. "You mentioned the historian's personal correction of *traditions* respecting his own epoch. Pray, sir, upon an average, what proportion of these kabbala were usually found to be right?"

"The kabbala, as you properly term them, sir, were generally discovered to be precisely on a par with the facts recorded in the unrewritten histories themselves—that is to say, not one individual iota of either was ever known, under any circumstances, to be not totally and radically wrong."

"But since it is clear," resumed the doctor, "that at least five thousand years have elapsed since your entombment, I take it for granted that your histories at that period, if not your traditions, were sufficiently explicit on that one topic of universal interest, the Creation, which took place, as I presume you are aware, only about ten centuries before."

"Sir!" said the Count Allamistakeo.

The doctor repeated his remarks, but it was only after much additional explanation that the foreigner could be made to comprehend them. The latter at length said, hesitatingly:

"The ideas you have suggested are to me, I confess, utterly novel. During my time I never knew anyone to entertain so singular a fancy as that the universe (or this world if you will have it so) ever had a beginning at all. I remember once, and once only, hearing something remotely hinted, by a man of many speculations, concerning the origin *of the human race;* and by this individual, the very word 'Adam' (or Red Earth), which you make use of, was employed. He employed it, however, in a generical sense, with reference to the spontaneous germination from rank soil (just as a thousand of the lower genera of creatures are germinated)—the spontaneous germination, I say, of five vast hordes of men, simultaneously upspringing in five distinct and nearly equal divisions of the globe."

Here, in general, the company shrugged their shoulders, and one or two of us touched our foreheads with a very significant air. Mr. Silk Buckingham, first glancing slightly at the occiput and then at the sinciput of Allamistakeo, spoke thus:

"The long duration of human life in your time, together with the occasional practice of passing it, as you have explained, in installments, must have had, indeed, a strong tendency to the general development and conglomeration of knowledge. I presume, therefore, that we are to attribute the marked inferiority of the old Egyptians in all particulars of science, when compared with the moderns, and more especially with the Yankees, altogether to the superior solidity of the Egyptian skull."

"I confess again," replied the count, with much suavity, "that I am somewhat at a loss to comprehend you; pray, to what particulars of science do you allude?"

Here our whole party, joining voices, detailed, at great length, the assumptions of phrenology and the marvels of animal magnetism.

Having heard us to an end, the count proceeded to relate a few anecdotes, which rendered it evident that prototypes of Gall and Spurzheim had flourished and faded in Egypt so long ago as to have been nearly forgotten, and that the maneuvers of Mesmer were really very contemptible tricks when put in collation with the positive miracles of the Theban *savans,* who created lice and a great many other similar things.

I here asked the count if his people were able to calculate eclipses. He smiled rather contemptuously, and said they were.

This put me a little out, but I began to make other inquiries in regard to his astronomical knowledge, when a member of the company, who had never as yet opened his mouth, whispered in my ear, that for information on this head, I had better consult Ptolemy (whoever Ptolemy is), as well as one Plutarch *de facie lunae.*

I then questioned the mummy about burning-glasses and lenses, and, in general, about the manufacture of glass; but I had not made an end of my queries before the silent member again touched me quietly on the elbow, and begged me for God's sake to take a peep at Diodorus Siculus. As for the count, he merely asked me, in the way of reply, if we moderns possessed any such microscopes as would enable us to cut cameos in the style of the

Egyptians. While I was thinking how I should answer this question, little Dr. Ponnonner committed himself in a very extraordinary way.

"Look at our architecture!" he exclaimed, greatly to the indignation of both the travelers, who pinched him black and blue to no purpose.

"Look," he cried with enthusiasm, "at the Bowling Green Fountain in New York! or if this be too vast a contemplation, regard for a moment the Capitol at Washington, D.C.!"—and the good little medical man went on to detail, very minutely, the proportions of the fabric to which he referred. He explained that the portico alone was adorned with no less than four and twenty columns, five feet in diameter, and ten feet apart.

The count said that he regretted not being able to remember, just at that moment, the precise dimensions of any one of the principal buildings of the city of Aznac, whose foundations were laid in the night of Time, but the ruins of which were still standing, at the epoch of his entombment, in a vast plain of sand to the westward of Thebes. He recollected, however (talking of the porticoes), that one affixed to an inferior palace in a kind of suburb called Carnac, consisted of a hundred and forty-four columns, thirty-seven feet in circumference, and twenty-five feet apart. The approach to this portico, from the Nile, was through an avenue two miles long, composed of sphinxes, statues, and obelisks, twenty, sixty, and a hundred feet in height. The palace itself (as well as he could remember) was, in one direction, two miles long, and might have been altogether about seven in circuit. Its walls were richly painted all over, within and without, with hieroglyphics. He would not pretend to *assert* that even fifty or sixty of the doctor's Capitols might have been built within these walls, but he was by no means sure that two or three hundred of them might not have been squeezed in with some trouble. That palace at Carnac was an insignificant little building after all. He (the count), however, could not conscientiously refuse to admit the ingenuity, magnificence, and superiority of the fountain at the Bowling Green, as described by the doctor. Nothing like it, he was forced to allow, had ever been seen in Egypt or elsewhere.

I here asked the count what he had to say to our railroads.

"Nothing," he replied, "in particular." They were rather slight, rather ill-conceived, and clumsily put together. They could not be compared, of course, with the vast, level, direct, iron-grooved causeways upon which the Egyptians conveyed entire temples and solid obelisks of a hundred and fifty feet in altitude.

I spoke of our gigantic mechanical forces.

He agreed that we knew something in that way, but inquired how I should have gone to work in getting up the imposts on the lintels of even the little palace at Carnac.

This question I concluded not to hear, and demanded if he had any idea of artesian wells; but he simply raised his eyebrows; while Mr. Gliddon winked at me very hard and said, in a low tone, that one had been recently discovered by the engineers employed to bore for water in the Great Oasis.

I then mentioned our steel; but the foreigner elevated his nose, and asked me if our steel could have executed the sharp carved work seen on the obelisks, and which was wrought altogether by edge-tools of copper.

This disconcerted us so greatly that we thought it advisable to vary the attack to metaphysics. We sent for a copy of a book called the "Dial," and read out of it a chapter or two about something which is not very clear, but which the Bostonians call the Great Movement of Progress.

The count merely said that great movements were awfully common things in his day, and as for progress, it was at one time quite a nuisance, but it never progressed.

We then spoke of the great beauty and importance of democracy, and were at much trouble in impressing the count with a due sense of the advantages we enjoyed in living where there was suffrage *ad libitum,* and no king.

He listened with marked interest, and in fact seemed not a little amused. When we had done, he said that, a great while ago, there had occurred something of a very similar sort. Thirteen Egyptian provinces determined all at once to be free, and to set a magnificent example to the rest of mankind. They assembled their wise men, and concocted the most ingenious constitution it is possible to conceive. For a while they managed remarkably well; only their habit of bragging was prodigious. The thing ended, however, in the consolidation of the thirteen states, with some fifteen or twenty others, in the most odious and insupportable despotism that was ever heard of upon the face of the earth.

I asked what was the name of the usurping tyrant.

As well as the count could recollect, it was *Mob*.

Not knowing what to say to this, I raised my voice, and deplored the Egyptian ignorance of steam.

The count looked at me with much astonishment, but made no answer. The silent gentleman, however, gave me a violent nudge in the ribs with his elbows—told me I had sufficiently exposed myself for once—and demanded if I was really such a fool as not to know that the modern steam engine is derived from the invention of Hero, through Solomon de Caus.

We were now in imminent danger of being discomfited; but, as good luck would have it, Dr. Ponnonner, having rallied, returned to our rescue, and inquired if the people of Egypt would seriously pretend to rival the moderns in the all-important particular of dress.

The count, at this, glanced downward to the straps of his pantaloons, and then taking hold of the end of one of his coat tails, held it up close to his eyes for some minutes. Letting it fall, at last, his mouth extended itself very gradually from ear to ear; but I do not remember that he said anything in the way of reply.

Hereupon we recovered our spirits, and the doctor, approaching the mummy with great dignity, desired it to say candidly, upon its honor as a gentleman, if the Egyptians had comprehended, at *any* period, the manufacture of either Ponnonner's lozenges or Brandreth's pills.

We looked, with profound anxiety, for an answer—but in vain. It was not forthcoming. The Egyptian blushed and hung down his head. Never was triumph more consummate; never was defeat borne with so ill a grace. Indeed, I could not endure the spectacle of the poor mummy's mortification. I reached my hat, bowed to him stiffly, and took leave.

Upon getting home I found it past four o'clock, and went immediately to bed. It is now 10 A.M. I have been up since seven, penning these memoranda for the benefit of my family and of mankind. The former I shall behold no more. My wife is a shrew. The truth is, I am heartily sick of this life and of the nineteenth century in general. I am convinced that everything is going wrong. Besides, I am anxious to know who will be president in 2045. As soon, therefore, as I shave and swallow a cup of coffee, I shall just step over to Ponnonner's and get embalmed for a couple of hundred years.

MONKEYS

by E. F. BENSON

The Egyptian curse theme, with or without ambulatory mummies, has been a favorite of fantasy writers throughout this century. (Some of the best variations, such as those in Bram Stoker's The Jewel of Seven Stars *and Burton Stevenson's* A King in Babylon, *predate the phenomenon of King Tut.) The classic treatment involves tombs and mummies protected by a terrible curse inscribed on tablets, on walls, on statues, on the mummy case itself, which provides an unpleasant fate for anyone who desecrates the tomb and/or disturbs the mummy's bones.*

"Monkeys" is just such a classic treatment, but with a unique difference: it also deals with a surgeon who believes in wholesale vivisection, notably of monkeys, to further medical science, and with early Egyptian surgical practices. The curse itself, which protects the body of a young woman, A-pen-ara, is a particularly nasty one: "A-pen-ara curses any who desecrates or meddles with her bones, and should anyone do so, the guardians of her sepulcher will see to him, and he shall die childless and in panic and agony; also the guardians of her sepulcher will tear the hair from his head and scoop his eyes from their sockets, and pluck the thumb from his right hand, as a man plucks the young blade of corn from its sheath." What transpires is the stuff of nightmares . . .

Edward Frederic Benson (1867–1940) was best known during his

356

lifetime as the author of British comedies of manners in the Wodehouse vein (Mammon & Co., Account Rendered, Paying Guests) *and of popular biographies* (Queen Victoria, Queen Victoria's Daughter). *Today, however, he is remembered primarily for his collections of uncanny tales*—The Room in the Tower *(1912),* Visible and Invisible *(1923),* Spook Stories *(1933), and* More Spook Stories *(1934). Most often reprinted of these stories are such small masterpieces as "The Thing in the Hall," "Negotium Perambulans," and "Caterpillars." Benson also wrote a number of macabre novels, among them* The Inheritor *(1930), which deals with a non-Egyptian curse.*

Dr. HUGH Morris, while still in the early thirties of his age, had justly earned for himself the reputation of being one of the most dexterous and daring surgeons in his profession, and both in his private practice and in his voluntary work at one of the great London hospitals his record of success as an operator was unparalleled among his colleagues. He believed that vivisection was the most fruitful means of progress in the science of surgery, holding, rightly or wrongly, that he was justified in causing suffering to animals, though sparing them all possible pain, if thereby he could reasonably hope to gain fresh knowledge about similar operations on human beings which would save life or mitigate suffering; the motive was good, and the gain already immense. But he had nothing but scorn for those who, for their own amusement, took out packs of hounds to run foxes to death, or matched two greyhounds to see which would give the death-grip to a single terrified hare: that, to him, was wanton torture, utterly unjustifiable. Year in and year out, he took no holiday at all, and for the most part he occupied his leisure, when the day's work was over, in study.

He and his friend Jack Madden were dining together one warm October night at his house looking onto Regent's Park. The windows of his drawing room on the ground floor were open, and they sat smoking, when dinner was done, on the broad window seat. Madden was starting next day for Egypt, where he was engaged in archeological work, and he had been vainly trying to persuade Morris to join him for a month up the Nile, where he would be engaged throughout the winter in the excavation of a newly discovered cemetery across the river from Luxor, near Medinet Habu. But it was no good.

"When my eye begins to fail and my fingers to falter," said Morris, "it will be time for me to think of taking my ease. What do I want with a holiday? I should be pining to get back to my work all the time. I like work better than loafing. Purely selfish."

"Well, be unselfish for once," said Madden. "Besides, your work would benefit. It can't be good for a man never to relax. Surely freshness is worth something."

"Precious little if you're as strong as I am. I believe in continual concentration if one wants to make progress. One may be tired, but why not? I'm not tired when I'm actually engaged on a dangerous operation, which is what matters. And time's so short. Twenty years from now I shall be past my best, and I'll have my holiday then, and when my holiday is over, I shall fold my hands and go to sleep for ever and ever. Thank God, I've got no fear that there's an afterlife. The spark of vitality that has animated us burns low and then goes out like a wind-blown candle, and as for my body, what do I care what happens to that when I have done with it? Nothing will survive of me except some small contribution I may have made to surgery, and in a few years' time that will be superseded. But for that I perish utterly."

Madden squirted some soda into his glass.

"Well, if you've quite settled that—" he began.

"I haven't settled it, science has," said Morris. "The body is transmuted into other forms, worms batten on it, it helps to feed the grass, and some animal consumes the grass. But as for the survival of the individual spirit of a man, show me one tittle of scientific evidence to support it. Besides, if it did survive, all the evil and malice in it must surely survive too. Why should the death of the body purge that away? It's a nightmare to contemplate such a thing, and oddly enough, unhinged people like spiritualists want to persuade us for our consolation that the nightmare is true. But odder still are those old Egyptians of yours, who thought that there was something sacred about their bodies, after they were quit of them. And didn't you tell me that they covered their coffins with curses on anyone who disturbed their bones?"

"Constantly," said Madden. "It's the general rule in fact. Marrowy curses written in hieroglyphics on the mummy case or carved on the sarcophagus."

"But that's not going to deter you this winter from opening as many tombs as you can find, and rifling from them any objects of interest or value."

Madden laughed.

"Certainly it isn't," he said. "I take out of the tombs all objects of art, and I unwind the mummies to find and annex their scarabs and jewelry. But I make an absolute rule always to bury the bodies again. I don't say that I believe in the power of those curses, but anyhow a mummy in a museum is an indecent object."

"But if you found some mummied body with an interesting malformation, wouldn't you send it to some anatomical institute?" asked Morris.

"It has never happened to me yet," said Madden, "but I'm pretty sure I shouldn't."

"Then you're a superstitious Goth and an antieducational Vandal," remarked Morris. . . . "Hullo, what's that?" He leaned out of the window as he spoke. The light from the room vividly illuminated the square of lawn outside, and across it was crawling the small twitching shape of some animal. Hugh Morris vaulted out of the window, and presently returned, carrying carefully in his spread hands a little gray monkey, evidently desperately injured. Its hind legs were stiff and outstretched as if it was partially paralyzed.

Morris ran his soft deft fingers over it.

"What's the matter with the little beggar, I wonder," he said. "Paralysis of the lower limbs: it looks like some lesion of the spine."

The monkey lay quite still, looking at him with anguished appealing eyes as he continued his manipulation.

"Yes, I thought so," he said. "Fracture of one of the lumbar vertebrae. What luck for me! It's a rare injury, but I've often wondered. . . . And perhaps luck for the monkey too, though that's not very probable. If he was a man and a patient of mine, I shouldn't dare to take the risk. But, as it is . . ."

Jack Madden started on his southward journey next day, and by the middle of November was at work on this newly discovered cemetery. He and another Englishman were in charge of the excavation, under the control of the Antiquity Department of the Egyptian government. In order to be close to their work and to avoid the daily ferrying across the Nile from Luxor, they hired a bare roomy native house in the adjoining village of Gurnah. A reef of low sandstone cliff ran northwards from here towards the temple and terraces of Deir-el-Bahari, and it was in the face of this and on the level below it that the ancient graveyard lay. There was much accumulation of sand to be cleared away before the actual exploration of the tombs could begin, but trenches cut below the foot of the sandstone ridge showed that there was an extensive area to investigate.

The more important sepulchers, they found, were hewn in the face of this small cliff: many of these had been rifled in ancient days, for the slabs forming the entrances into them had been split, and the mummies unwound, but now and then Madden unearthed some tomb that had escaped these marauders, and in one he found the sarcophagus of a priest of the Nineteenth Dynasty, and that alone repaid weeks of fruitless work. There were nearly a hundred *ushaptiu* figures of the finest blue glaze; there were four alabaster vessels in which had been placed the viscera of the dead man removed before embalming: there was a table of which the top was inalid with squares of variously colored glass, and the legs were of carved ivory and ebony: there were the priest's sandals adorned with exquisite silver filigree: there was his staff of office inlaid with a diaper-pattern of cornelian and gold, and on the head of it, forming the handle, was the figure of a squatting cat, carved in amethyst, and the mummy, when unwound, was found to be decked with a necklace of gold plaques and onyx beads. All these were sent down to the Gizeh Museum at Cairo, and Madden reinterred the mummy at the foot of the cliff below the tomb. He wrote to Hugh Morris describing this find, and laying stress on the unbroken splendor of these crystalline winter days, when from morning to night the sun cruised across the blue, and on the cool nights when the stars rose and set on the vaporless rim of the desert. If by chance Hugh should change his mind, there was ample room for him in this house at Gurnah, and he would be very welcome.

A fortnight later Madden received a telegram from his friend. It stated that he had been unwell and was starting at once by long sea to Port Said, and would come straight up to Luxor. In due course he announced his arrival at Cairo and Madden went across the river next day to meet him: it was reassuring to find him as vital and active as ever, the picture of bronzed health. The two were alone that night, for Madden's colleague had gone for a week's trip up the Nile, and they sat out, when dinner was done, in the enclosed courtyard adjoining the house. Till then Madden had shied off the subject of himself and his health.

"Now I may as well tell you what's been amiss with me," he said, "for I know I look a fearful fraud as an invalid, and physically I've never been better in my life. Every organ has been functioning perfectly except one, but something suddenly went wrong there just once. It was like this."

He paused a moment.

"After you left," he said, "I went on as usual for another month or so, very busy, very serene and, I may say, very successful. Then one morning I arrived at the hospital when there was one perfectly ordinary but major operation waiting for me. The patient, a man, was wheeled into the theater anesthetized, and I was just about to make the first incision into the abdomen, when I saw that there was sitting on his chest a little gray monkey. It was not looking at me, but at the fold of skin which I held between my thumb and finger. I knew, of course, that there was no monkey there, and that what I saw was a hallucination, and I think you'll agree that there was nothing much wrong with my nerves when I tell you that I went through the operation with clear eyes and an unshaking hand. I had to go on: there was no choice about the matter. I couldn't say: 'Please take that monkey away,' for I knew there was no monkey there. Nor could I say: 'Somebody else must do this, as I have a distressing hallucination that there is a monkey sitting on the patient's chest.' There would have been an end of me as a surgeon and no mistake. All the time I was at work it sat there absorbed for the most part in what I was doing and peering into the wound, but now and then it looked up at me, and chattered with rage. Once it fingered a spring-forceps which clipped a severed vein, and that was the worst moment of all. . . . At the end it was carried out still balancing itself on the man's chest. . . . I think I'll have a drink. Strongish, please. . . . Thanks.

"A beastly experience," he said when he had drunk. "Then I went straight away from the hospital to consult my old friend Robert Angus, the alienist and nerve specialist, and told him exactly what had happened to me. He made several tests, he examined my eyes, tried my reflexes, took my blood pressure: there was nothing wrong with any of them. Then he asked me questions about my general health and manner of life, and among these questions was one which I am sure has already occurred to you, namely, had anything occurred to me lately, or even remotely, which was likely to make me visualize a monkey. I told him that a few weeks ago a monkey with a broken lumbar vertebra had crawled on to my lawn, and that I had attempted an operation—binding the broken vertebra with wire—which had occurred to me before as a possibility. You remember the night, no doubt?"

"Perfectly," said Madden, "I started for Egypt next day. What happened to the monkey, by the way?"

"It lived for two days: I was pleased, because I had expected it would die under the anesthetic, or immediately afterwards from shock. To get back to what I was telling you. When Angus had asked all his questions, he gave me a good wigging. He said

that I had persistently overtaxed my brain for years, without
giving it any rest or change of occupation, and that if I wanted
to be of any further use in the world, I must drop my work at
once for a couple of months. He told me that my brain was tired
out and that I had persisted in stimulating it. A man like me, he
said, was no better than a confirmed drunkard, and that, as a
warning, I had had a touch of an appropriate delirium tremens.
The cure was to drop work, just as a drunkard must drop drink.
He laid it on hot and strong: he said I was on the verge of a
breakdown, entirely owing to my own foolishness, but that I had
wonderful physical health, and that if I did break down I should
be a disgrace. Above all—and this seemed to me awfully sound
advice—he told me not to attempt to avoid thinking about what
had happened to me. If I kept my mind off it, I should be
perhaps driving it into the subconscious, and then there might
be bad trouble. 'Rub it in: think what a fool you've been,' he said.
'Face it, dwell on it, make yourself thoroughly ashamed of yourself.' Monkeys, too: I wasn't to avoid the thought of monkeys.
In fact, he recommended me to go straight away to the Zoological Gardens, and spend an hour in the monkey house."

"Odd treatment," interrupted Madden.

"Brilliant treatment. My brain, he explained, had rebelled
against its slavery, and had hoisted a red flag with the device of
a monkey on it. I must show it that I wasn't frightened at its
bogus monkeys. I must retort on it by making myself look at
dozens of real ones which could bite and maul you savagely,
instead of one little sham monkey that had no existence at all.
At the same time I must take the red flag seriously, recognize
there was danger, and rest. And he promised me that sham
monkeys wouldn't trouble me again. Are there any real ones in
Egypt, by the way?"

"Not so far as I know," said Madden. "But there must have
been once, for there are many images of them in tombs and
temples."

"That's good. We'll keep their memory green and my brain
cool. Well, there's my story. What do you think of it?"

"Terrifying," said Madden. "But you must have got nerves of

iron to get through that operation with the monkey watching."

"A hellish hour. Out of some disordered slime in my brain there had crawled this unbidden thing, which showed itself, apparently substantial, to my eyes. It didn't come from outside: my eyes hadn't told my brain that there was a monkey sitting on the man's chest, but my brain had told my eyes so, making fools of them. I felt as if someone whom I absolutely trusted had played me false. Then again I have wondered whether some instinct in my subconscious mind revolted against vivisection. My reason says that it is justified, for it teaches us how pain can be relieved and death postponed for human beings. But what if my subconscious persuaded my brain to give me a good fright, and reproduce before my eyes the semblance of a monkey, just when I was putting into practice what I had learned from dealing out pain and death to animals?"

He got up suddenly.

"What about bed?" he said. "Five hours' sleep was enough for me when I was at work, but now I believe I could sleep the clock round every night."

Young Wilson, Madden's colleague in the excavations, returned next day and the work went steadily on. One of them was on the spot to start it soon after sunrise, and either one or both of them were superintending it, with an interval of a couple of hours at noon, until sunset. When the mere work of clearing the face of the sandstone cliff was in progress and of carting away the silted soil, the presence of one of them sufficed, for there was nothing to do but to see that the workmen shoveled industriously, and passed regularly with their baskets of earth and sand on their shoulders to the dumping grounds, which stretched away from the area to be excavated, in lengthening peninsulas of trodden soil. But, as they advanced along the sandstone ridge, there would now and then appear a chiseled smoothness in the cliff and then both must be alert. There was great excitement to see if, when they exposed the hewn slab that formed the door into the tomb, it had escaped ancient marauders, and still stood in place and intact for the modern to explore. But now for many days they came upon no sepulcher that had not already been opened. The mummy, in these cases, had been unwound in the search for necklaces and scarabs, and its scattered bones lay about. Madden was always at pains to reinter these.

At first Hugh Morris was assiduous in watching the excavations, but as day after day went by without anything of interest turning up, his attendance grew less frequent: it was too much of a holiday to watch the day-long removal of sand from one place to another. He visited the Tomb of the Kings, he went across the river and saw the temples at Karnak, but his appetite for antiquities was small. On other days he rode in the desert, or spent the day with friends at one of the Luxor hotels. He came home from there one evening in rare good spirits, for he had played lawn tennis with a woman on whom he had operated for malignant tumor six months before and she had skipped about the court like a two-year-old. "God, how I want to be at work again," he exclaimed. "I wonder whether I ought not to have stuck it out, and defied my brain to frighten me with bogies."

The weeks passed on, and now there were but two days left before his return to England, where he hoped to resume work at once: his tickets were taken and his berth booked. As he sat over breakfast that morning with Wilson, there came a workman from the excavation, with a note scribbled in hot haste by Madden, to say that they had just come upon a tomb which seemed to be unrifled, for the slab that closed it was in place and unbroken. To Wilson, the news was like the sight of a sail to a marooned mariner, and when, a quarter of an hour later, Morris followed him, he was just in time to see the slab prised away. There was no sarcophagus within, for the rock walls did duty for that, but there lay there, varnished and bright in hue as if painted yesterday, the mummy case roughly following the outline of the human form. By it stood the alabaster vases containing the entrails of the dead, and at each corner of the sepulcher there were carved out of the sandstone rock, forming, as it were, pillars to support the roof, thick set images of squatting apes. The mummy case was hoisted out and carried away by workmen on a bier of boards into the courtyard of the excavators' house at Gurnah, for the opening of it and the unwrapping of the dead.

They got to work that evening directly they had fed: the face painted on the lid was that of a girl or young woman, and presently deciphering the hieroglyphic inscription, Madden read out that within lay the body of A-pen-ara, daughter of the overseer of the cattle of Senmut.

"Then follow the usual formulas," he said. "Yes, yes . . . ah, you'll be interested in this, Hugh, for you asked me once about it. A-pen-ara curses any who desecrates or meddles with her bones, and should anyone do so, the guardians of her sepulcher will see to him, and he shall die childless and in panic and agony; also the guardians of her sepulcher will tear the hair from his head and scoop his eyes from their sockets, and pluck the thumb from his right hand, as a man plucks the young blade of corn from its sheath."

Morris laughed.

"Very pretty little attentions," he said. "And who are the guardians of this sweet young lady's sepulcher? Those four great apes carved at the corners?"

"No doubt. But we won't trouble them, for tomorrow I shall bury Miss A-pen-ara's bones again with all decency in the trench at the foot of her tomb. They'll be safer there, for if we put them back where we found them, there would be pieces of her hawked about by half the donkey-boys in Luxor in a few days. 'Buy a mummy hand, lady? . . . Foot of a gyppy queen, only ten piasters, gentlemen' . . . Now for the unwinding."

It was dark by now, and Wilson fetched out a paraffin lamp, which burned unwaveringly in the still air. The lid of the mummy case was easily detached, and within was the slim, swaddled body. The embalming had not been very thoroughly done, for all the skin and flesh had perished from the head, leaving only bones of the skull stained brown with bitumen. Round it was a mop of hair, which with the ingress of the air subsided like a belated soufflé, and crumbled into dust. The cloth that swathed the body was as brittle, but round the neck, still just holding together, was a collar of curious and rare workmanship: little ivory figures of squatting apes alternated with silver beads.

But again a touch broke the thread that strung them together, and each had to be picked out singly. A bracelet of scarabs and cornelians still clasped one of the fleshless wrists, and then they turned the body over in order to get at the members of the necklace which lay beneath the nape. The rotted mummy-cloth fell away altogether from the back, disclosing the shoulder blades and the spine down as far as the pelvis. Here the embalming had been better done, for the bones still held together with remnants of muscle and cartilage.

Hugh Morris suddenly sprang to his feet.

"My God, look there!" he cried, "one of the lumbar vertebrae, there at the base of the spine, has been broken and clamped together with a metal band. To hell with your antiquities: let me come and examine something much more modern than any of us!"

He pushed Jack Madden aside, and peered at this marvel of surgery.

"Put the lamp closer," he said, as if directing some nurse at an operation. "Yes: that vertebra has been broken right across and has been clamped together. No one has ever, as far as I know, attempted such an operation except myself, and I have only performed it on that little paralyzed monkey that crept into my garden one night. But some Egyptian surgeon, more than three thousand years ago, performed it on a woman. And look, look! She lived afterwards, for the broken vertebra put out that bony efflorescence of healing which has encroached over the metal band. That's a slow process, and it must have taken place during her lifetime, for there is no such energy in a corpse. The woman lived long: probably she recovered completely. And my wretched little monkey only lived two days and was dying all the time."

Those questing hawk-visioned fingers of the surgeon perceived more finely than actual sight, and now he closed his eyes as the tip of them felt their way about the fracture in the broken vertebra and the clamping metal band.

"The band doesn't encircle the bone," he said, "and there are no studs attaching it. There must have been a spring in it, which, when it was clasped there, kept it tight. It has been clamped round the bone itself: the surgeon must have scraped the vertebra clean of flesh before he attached it. I would give two years of my life to have looked on, like a student, at that masterpiece of skill, and it was worthwhile giving up two months of my work only to have seen the result. And the injury itself is so rare, this breaking of a spinal vertebra. To be sure, the hangman does something of the sort, but there's no mending that! Good Lord, my holiday has not been a waste of time!"

Madden settled that it was not worth while to send the mummy case to the museum at Gizeh, for it was of a very ordinary type, and when the examination was over they lifted the body back into it, for reinterment next day. It was now long after midnight and presently the house was dark.

Hugh Morris slept on the ground floor in a room adjoining the yard where the mummy case lay. He remained long awake marveling at that astonishing piece of surgical skill performed, according to Madden, some thirty-five centuries ago. So occupied had his mind been with homage that not till now did he realize that the tangible proof and witness of the operation would tomorrow be buried again and lost to science. He must persuade Madden to let him detach at least three of the vertebrae, the mended one and those immediately above and below it, and take them back to England as demonstration of what could be done: he would lecture on his exhibit and present it to the Royal College of Surgeons for example and incitement. Other trained eyes beside his own must see what had been successfully achieved by some unknown operator in the nineteenth dynasty. . . . But supposing Madden refused? He always made a point of scrupulously reburying these remains: it was a principle with him, and no doubt some superstition complex—the hardest of all to combat with because of its sheer unreasonableness—was involved. Briefly, it was impossible to risk the chance of his refusal.

He got out of bed, listened for a moment by his door, and then softly went out into the yard. The moon had risen, for the brightness of the stars was paled, and though no direct rays shone into the walled enclosure, the dusk was dispersed by the toneless luminosity of the sky, and he had no need of a lamp. He drew the lid off the coffin, and folded back the tattered cerements which Madden had replaced over the body. He had thought that those lower vertebrae of which he was determined to possess himself would be easily detached, so far perished were the muscle and cartilage which held them together, but they cohered as if they had been clamped, and it required the utmost force of his powerful fingers to snap the spine, and as he did so the severed bones cracked as with the noise of a pistol shot. But there was no sign that anyone in the house had heard it, there came no sound of steps, nor lights in the windows. One more fracture was needed, and then the relic was his. Before he replaced the ragged cloths he looked again at the stained flesh-less bones. Shadow dwelt in the empty eye sockets, as if black sunken eyes still lay there, fixedly regarding him, the lipless mouth snarled and grimaced. Even as he looked some change came over its aspect, and for one brief moment he fancied that there lay staring up at him the face of a great brown ape. But instantly that illusion vanished, and replacing the lid he went back to his room.

The mummy case was reinterred next day, and two evenings after Morris left Luxor by the night train for Cairo, to join a homeward-bound P. & O. at Port Said. There were some hours to spare before his ship sailed, and having deposited his luggage, including a locked leather dispatch case, on board, he lunched at the Café Tewfik near the quay. There was a garden in front of it with palm trees and trellises gaily clad in bougain-villeas: a low wooden rail separated it from the street, and Morris had a table close to this. As he ate he watched the poly-chromatic pageant of Eastern life passing by: there were Egyptian officials in broadcloth frock coats and red fezzes; bare-footed splaytoed fellahin in blue gabardines; veiled women in white making stealthy eyes at passers by; half-naked gutter snipe, one with a sprig of scarlet hibiscus behind his ear; travel-ers from India with solar topees and an air of aloof British superiority; disheveled sons of the Prophet in green turbans; a

stately sheik in a white burnous; French painted ladies of a
professional class with lace-rimmed parasols and provocative
glances; a wild-eyed dervish in an accordion-pleated skirt, chew-
ing betel nut and slightly foaming at the mouth. A Greek boot-
black with box adorned with brass plaques tapped his brushes
on it to encourage customers, an Egyptian girl squatted in the
gutter beside a gramophone, steamers passing into the canal
hooted on their sirens.

Then at the edge of the pavement there sauntered by a young
Italian harnessed to a barrel organ: with one hand he ground out
a popular air by Verdi, in the other he held out a tin can for the
tributes of music-lovers: a small monkey in a yellow jacket, tethered to his wrist, sat on the top of his instrument. The musician
had come opposite the table where Morris sat: Morris liked the
gay tinkling tune, and feeling in his pocket for a piaster, he
beckoned to him. The boy grinned and stepped up to the rail.

Then suddenly the melancholy-eyed monkey leaped from its
place on the organ and sprang on to the table by which Morris
sat. It alighted there, chattering with rage in a crash of broken
glass. A flower vase was upset, a plate clattered on to the floor.
Morris's coffee cup discharged its black contents on the table-
cloth. Next moment the Italian had twitched the frenzied little
beast back to him, and it fell head downwards on the pavement.
A shrill hubbub arose, the waiter at Morris's table hurried up
with voluble execrations, a policeman kicked out at the monkey
as it lay on the ground, the barrel organ tottered and crashed
on the roadway. Then all subsided again, and the Italian boy
picked up the little body from the pavement. He held it out in
his hands to Morris.

"*E morto,*" he said.

"Serve it right, too," retorted Morris. "Why did it fly at me
like that?"

He traveled back to London by long sea, and day after day that
tragic little incident, in which he had had no responsible part,
began to make a sort of coloring matter in his mind during those
hours of lazy leisure on shipboard, when a man gives about an
equal inattention to the book he reads and to what passes round

him. Sometimes if the shadow of a seagull overhead slid across the deck towards him, there leaped into his brain, before his eyes could reassure him, the ludicrous fancy that this shadow was a monkey springing at him. One day they ran into a gale from the west: there was a crash of glass at his elbow as a sudden lurch of the ship upset a laden steward, and Morris jumped from his seat thinking that a monkey had leaped onto his table again. There was a cinematograph show in the saloon one evening, in which some naturalist exhibited the films he had taken of wildlife in Indian jungles: when he put on the screen the picture of a company of monkeys swinging their way through the trees Morris involuntarily clutched the sides of his chair in hideous panic that lasted but a fraction of a second, until he recalled to himself that he was only looking at a film in the saloon of a steamer passing up the coast of Portugal. He came sleepy into his cabin one night and saw some animal crouching by the locked leather dispatch case. His breath caught in his throat before he perceived that this was a friendly cat which rose with gleaming eyes and arched its back. . . .

These fantastic unreasonable alarms were disquieting. He had as yet no repetition of the hallucination that he saw a monkey, but some deep-buried "idea," to cure which he had taken two months' holiday, was still unpurged from his mind. He must consult Robert Angus again when he got home, and seek further advice. Probably that incident at Port Said had rekindled the obscure trouble, and there was this added to it, that he knew he was now frightened of real monkeys: there was terror sprouting in the dark of his soul. But as for it having any connection with his pilfered treasure, so rank and childish a superstition deserved only the ridicule he gave it. Often he unlocked his leather case and sat poring over that miracle of surgery which made practical again long-forgotten dexterities.

But it was good to be back in England. For the last three days of the voyage no menace had flashed out on him from the unknown dusks, and surely he had been disquieting himself in vain. There was a light mist lying over Regent's Park on this warm March evening, and a drizzle of rain was falling. He made an appointment for the next morning with the specialist, he telephoned to the hospital that he had returned and hoped to resume work at once. He dined in very good spirits, talking to his manservant, and, as subsequently came out, he showed him his treasured bones, telling him that he had taken the relic from a mummy which he had seen unwrapped and that he meant to lecture on it. When he went up to bed he carried the leather case with him. Bed was comfortable after the ship's berth, and through his open window came the soft hissing of the rain on to the shrubs outside.

His servant slept in the room immediately over his. A little before dawn he woke with a start, roused by horrible cries from somewhere close at hand. Then came words yelled out in a voice that he knew:

"Help! Help!" it cried. "O my God, my God! Ah—h—" and it rose to a scream again.

The man hurried down and clicked on the light in his master's room as he entered. The cries had ceased: only a low moaning came from the bed. A huge ape with busy hands was bending over it; then taking up the body that lay there by the neck and the hips he bent it backwards and it cracked like a dry stick. Then it tore open the leather case that was on a table by the bedside, and with something that gleamed white in its dripping fingers it shambled to the window and disappeared.

A doctor arrived within half an hour, but too late. Handfuls of hair with flaps of skins attached had been torn from the head of the murdered man, both eyes were scooped out of their sockets, the right thumb had been plucked off the hand, and the back was broken across the lower vertebrae.

Nothing has since come to light which could rationally explain the tragedy. No large ape had escaped from the neighboring Zoological Gardens, or, as far as could be ascertained, from elsewhere, nor was the monstrous visitor of that night ever seen again. Morris's servant had only had the briefest sight of it, and his description of it at the inquest did not tally with that of any known simian type. And the sequel was even more mysterious, for Madden, returning to England at the close of the season in Egypt, had asked Morris's servant exactly what it was that his master had shown him the evening before as having been taken by him from a mummy which he had seen unwrapped, and had got from him a sufficiently conclusive account of it. Next autumn he continued his excavations in the cemetery at Gurnah, and he disinterred once more the mummy case of A-pen-ara and opened it. But the spinal vertebrae were all in place and complete: one had round it the silver clip which Morris had hailed as a unique achievement in surgery.

BONES

by DONALD A. WOLLHEIM

The central premise of "Bones" is both simple and unusual. As one of the Egyptologists in the story explains: "According to our painstaking translation of the hieroglyphics of the sarcophagus whence this body came, this marks an attempt of the priesthood of the Fourth Dynasty to send one of their number alive into the lands to come. The unique part of it, and that which occupies us tonight, is that this priest did not die, nor was his body in any way mutilated. Instead, according to the inscriptions, he was fed and bathed in certain compounds that would suspend, indefinitely, the actions of his body cells; he was then put to sleep and prepared for a slumber very like death, yet not true death. In this state he could remain for years, yet still be reawakened to walk again, a living man."

But the operative word here is unusual: *this is not an ordinary resurrection-of-a-mummy story. On the contrary, its pure horror derives not from a hulking monster in tattered wrappings but from something far more commonplace and, in this case, far more terrifying. The story's final paragraph just may be the most vivid and gruesome in all of macabre fiction.*

For more than four decades Donald A. Wollheim has been a writer, editor, and publisher of no small stature in the field of science fiction and fantasy. He began writing in the early 1930s, was appointed editor of two

374

pulp magazines, Stirring Science Stories *(where "Bones" first appeared) and* Cosmic Stories *in 1940, and in 1952 began a twenty-year tenure as editor-in-chief of Ace Books, which terminated in 1972 when he left to found his own paperback science fiction imprint, DAW Books. Among the large number of novels, anthologies, and collections to his credit is* Two Dozen Dragon's Eggs *(1969), a gathering of twenty-four stories as mordant, if not always as horrific, as "Bones."*

THE MUSEUM of Natural Sciences was not very far from the place where he was staying, so Severus found himself striding briskly through the dim, winding streets that night. He had come to Boston on a visit, renewed acquaintances with learned men with whom he had exchanged knowledge in years past; thus the letter he had received in this morning's mail inviting him to a private demonstration this night.

It was not a pleasant walk; already he was beginning to regret not having taken some other means of transportation. The buildings were old and loomed darkly over the narrow streets. Lights were few; for the most part, they came from flickering, dust-encrusted lampposts of last century's design. Large moths and other nocturnal insects fluttered over their surfaces, added their moving shadows to the air of desolation which hung about these ways.

The moon was behind clouds that had streaked across the autumn skies all day and now blocked out the stars. The night about him was warm with that touch of unexpected chill which comes in autumn. Severus shuddered more than once as a wandering breeze slithered across his face unexpectedly around some dreary corner. He increased his pace, looked more suspiciously about him.

Boston, the oldest section of the city. Antique brick buildings dating back to the Revolution, some much farther. Dwelling places of the best families of two centuries ago. Now steadily advancing progress and life had left them derelict as upon de-

serted shores. Old, three or four story structures, narrow tottering dirty red-bricked houses with yawning black windows that
now looked out through filth-encrusted panes upon streets and
byways that served to shelter only the poorest and most alien
section of the city's people. Forgotten, the district imparted its
despair and overhanging doom to the man who walked its ways
that night.

Half conquered by the smell of the antique houses, the subtle
vibrations of past generations still pervading his spirit, Severus
came at last out of the narrow streets into the open square where
stood the museum.

The change surprised him. Here all was open. The dark,
cloud-streaked sky loomed down overhead with a closeness that
appalled him for a moment. The white marble facade of the
structure glistened oddly in his view. It stood out, the cleanliness of it, as something exceedingly out of place, as something
too new, too recent to have any right here. Its neo-Grecian
designs were horribly modern and crude for the eighteenth
century blocks that surrounded it.

He walked swiftly across the open square, up the wide stone
steps to the entrance of the building. Quickly he thrust open the
small side door, hurried through as if to escape the thoughts of
forgotten streets outside.

How futile such hopes in a museum! He realized that, the
instant the door was closed. He stood in a dark hall, lit dimly by
one bulb above the entrance, another one at the opposite end
of the main passage. And at once his nostrils were assailed by
the inescapable odor of all such institutions—age!

The musty air rushed over his body, took him into its folds.
The silence assailed his ears with a suddenness that all but took
his breath away. He looked about, trying to catch his bearings.
Then he ventured a step, walked rapidly across the large chamber, down a wide corridor opening off it. Not a glance did he cast
from side to side. The looming shadows of indescribable things
were enough for him. His imagination supplied the rest. Unav-
oidable glimpses of shadowy sarcophagi and grotesquely carven

idols sent great cold chills thrilling down his spine, stirring up his heart.

Up a narrow staircase, a turn to the right. At last he was at the room set aside for the night's demonstration. He stood a moment trying to catch his breath and regain composure. Then he pushed the door open, stepped inside.

A bare room with scarcely any furnishings. About seven or eight other men were there. In low tones they greeted him, drew him over to their circle. All were standing; there were no chairs in the room. A couple of small instrument racks and the main object was all.

The room was dominated by a long, low table upon which rested a six-foot bundle of dull gray cloth like a giant cocoon. Severus stared at it a moment, then recognized it as an Egyptian mummy removed from its coffin case. It obviously awaited unwinding.

So this was what he'd been invited to, he thought, wishing he hadn't been so friendly to the Egyptologists attached to this particular museum.

Glancing around, Severus took note of the others present. He was surprised to recognize one as a medical doctor highly esteemed at a city hospital. The doctor indeed seemed to be one of the active participants in what was about to take place for he wore a white smock that indicated action.

Bantling, the Egyptologist, held up a hand for silence.

"Most of you know what is about to take place tonight, therefore I will merely outline it for your convenience and for the one or two who know nothing about it." He nodded to Severus and smiled.

"This object, as you have all surmised, is an Egyptian mummy. But it is, we hope, different from all other such mummies previously examined.

"According to our painstaking translation of the hieroglyphics of the sarcophagus whence this body came, this marks an attempt of the priesthood of the Fourth Dynasty to send one of their number alive into the lands to come. The unique part of it, and that which occupies us tonight, is that this priest did not die, nor was his body in any way mutilated. Instead, according to the inscriptions, he was fed and bathed in certain compounds that would suspend, indefinitely, the actions of his body cells; he was then put to sleep and prepared for a slumber very like death, yet not true death. In this state he could remain for years, yet still be reawakened to walk again, a living man.

"In brief, and using modern terminology, these people of what we call ancient times, claim to have solved the secret of suspended animation. Whether or not they did is for us to determine."

Severus felt himself grow cold as this knowledge penetrated his being. The past had indeed reached out to the present. He would witness this night the end of an experiment started thousands of years before. Perhaps he himself would yet speak to and hear speak an inhabitant of this lost age. Egypt, buried these hundreds of centuries, Egypt aged beyond belief—yet, a man of that time-lost empire lay here in this very room, in the North American city of Boston.

"3700 B.C.," he heard someone remark in answer to an unheard question.

Severus raised his eyes from the object on the table, let his gaze fall upon the window and what was revealed through it. Some of the clouds had cleared away and the cold, bright stars shone through. Far-off flickering spots of light that must surely have shone upon ancient Egypt as coldly. The very light just passing through his cornea may have originated in the time when this thing upon the table was about to be plunged into life-in-death.

Far off, the dull clanging of a church bell drifted into the room.

"Buck up, old man." A hand patted Severus's shoulder as an acquaintance came over to him. "It isn't as bad as it looks. Why that fellow will be as hale as any of us before the night is out. You'll think he's just a new immigrant."

Bantling and an assistant were even now engaged in unwrapping the mummy. Rolls and rolls of old, crumbling cloth were carefully being unwound from the figure on the table. Dust of death and ages now filled the air. Several coughs were heard; the door was opened on the dark passage outside to let the air change.

A gasp as at last the windings fell away. The body now lay entirely uncovered. Quickly, quietly, the wrappings were gathered together and piled in a receptacle while all crowded about to observe the Egyptian.

All in all, it was in a fine state of preservation. The skin was not brownish; it had not hardened. The arms and legs were still movable, had never stiffened in rigor mortis. Bantling seemed much pleased.

With horror Severus noted the several grayish blue patches on parts of the face and body which he recognized without asking as a kind of mold.

Dr. Zweig, the physician, bent over and carefully scraped off the fungoid growths. They left nasty reddish pitted scars in the body that made Severus feel sick. He wanted to rush out of the room, out of the building into the clean night air. But the fascination of the horrible kept his glance fixed in hypnosis on the gruesome object before him.

"We are ready," Dr. Zweig said in a low voice.

They began to bathe the body with a sharp-smelling antiseptic, taking off all remaining traces of the preservatives used.

"Remarkable how perfect this thing is," breathed the physician. "Remarkable!"

Now at last the way was open for the work of revival. Large electric pads were brought out, laid all over the body, face and legs. Current was switched into them; the body surface was slowly brought up to normal warmth.

Then arteries and veins were opened, tubes clamped to them running from apparatus under the table. Severus understood that warm artificial blood was being pumped into the body to warm up the internal organs and open up the flow of blood again.

Shortly Dr. Zweig announced himself ready to attempt the final work toward actually bringing the now pliant and vibrant corpse to life. Already the body seemed like that of a living man, the flush of red tinging its skin and cheeks. Severus was in a cold sweat.

"Blood flows again through his veins and arteries," whispered the Egyptologist. "It is time to turn off the mechanical heart and attempt to revive his own."

A needle was plunged into the chest, a substance injected into the dormant, thousands-year-old cardiac apparatus of the body. Adrenaline, Severus assumed.

Over the mouth and nostrils of the former mummy a bellows was placed, air forced into the lungs at regular periods. For a while there was no result. Severus began fervently to hope that there would be no result. The air was supercharged with tension, horror mixed with scientific zeal. Through the chamber, the wheeze of the bellows was the only sound.

"Look!"

Someone cried out the word, electrifying all in the room of resurrection. A hand pointed shakily at the chest of the thing on the table. There was more action now; the chest rose and fell more vigorously. Quietly the doctor reached over and pulled away the face mask and stopped the pumps.

And the chest of the Egyptian still moved. Up and down in a ghastly rhythm of its own. Now to their ears became noticeable an odd sound, a rattling soft wheezing sound as of air being sucked in and out of a sleeping man.

"He breathes." The doctor reached out and laid a finger on the body's wrist. "The heart beats."

"He lives again!"

Their eyes stared at what had been done. There, on the table, lay a man, a light brown-skinned, sharp Semitic-featured man, appearing to be in early middle age. He lay there as one quietly asleep.

"Who will waken him?" whispered Severus above the pounding of his heart.

"He will awaken soon," was the answer. "He will rise and walk as if nothing had happened."

Severus shook his head, disbelievingly. Then—

The Egyptian moved. His hand shook slightly; the eyes opened with a jerk.

Spellbound they stood, the eyes of Americans fixed upon the eyes of the ancient. In shocked silence they watched one another.

The Egyptian sat up slowly, as if painfully. His features moved not a bit; his body moved slowly and jerkily.

The ancient's eyes roved over the assembly. They caught Severus full in the face. For an instant they gazed at one another, the Vermont man looking into pain-swept ages, into grim depths of agony and sorrow, into the aeons of old past time itself.

The Egyptian suddenly wrinkled up his features, swept up an arm and opened his mouth to speak.

And Severus fled from the room in frightful terror, the others closely following. Behind them rang out a terrible, hoarse bellow, cut off by a gurgling which they barely heard. The entire company, to a man, fought each other like terrified animals, each struggling to be the first out of that museum, out the doors into the black streets and away.

For there are parts of the human body which, never having been alive, cannot be preserved in suspended life. They are the bones, the teeth—strong in death, but unable to defy the crushing millenia.

And when the Egyptian had moved his body and opened his mouth to speak, his face had fallen in like termite-infested wood, the splinters of fragile, age-crumbled bones tearing through the flesh. His whole body had shaken, and, with the swing of the arm, smashed itself into a shapeless mass of heaving flesh and blood through which projected innumerable jagged fragments of dark gray, pitted bones.

THE VENGEANCE OF NITOCRIS

by TENNESSEE WILLIAMS

While this story is not about mummies per se, it is about ancient Egypt and fiendish doings involving the waters of the Nile, a terrible sacrilege committed by the pharaoh in many-peopled Thebes, and the vengeance wreaked by the pharaoh's sister, Nitocris, after he is brutally slain by a priest-led mob. The manner in which Nitocris goes about her vendetta, as you'll discover, is particularly fiendish . . .

"The Vengeance of Nitocris" represents the first published work of renowned playwright Tennessee Williams, having appeared in the famed pulp Weird Tales *in 1928 when Williams was only sixteen years old. Although the story is his only publication in the fantasy field, and although it shows signs of youthful exuberance, it remains both readable and evocative a half century later. And makes your editor wonder what other macabre tales Williams might have written if he had set his considerable talents to the task.*

Thomas Lanier Williams was born in Columbus, Mississippi, attended the University of Iowa, and worked at several different jobs until his first play, Battle of Angels, *was produced by the New York Theatre Guild in 1940. A scant five years later* The Glass Menagerie *was awarded*

the New York Drama Critics Circle Award for the best American play of
the season; and in 1948 he received the first of his two Pulitzer Prizes for
A Streetcar Named Desire *(his second Pulitzer was awarded in 1955*
for Cat on a Hot Tin Roof*). He has also written the novel* The
Roman Spring of Mrs. Stone *(1950), poetry, and other short fiction.*

HUSHED WERE the streets of many-peopled Thebes. Those few
who passed through them moved with the shadowy fleetness of
bats near dawn, and bent their faces from the sky as if fearful of
seeing what in their fancies might be hovering there. Weird,
high-noted incantations of a wailing sound were audible
through the barred doors. On corners groups of naked and
bleeding priests cast themselves repeatedly and with loud cries
upon the rough stones of the walks. Even dogs and cats and
oxen seemed impressed by some strange menace and foreboding and cowered and slunk dejectedly. All Thebes was in dread.
And indeed there was cause for their dread and for their wails
of lamentation. A terrible sacrilege had been committed. In all
the annals of Egypt none more monstrous was recorded.

Five days had the altar fires of the god of gods, Osiris, been
left unburning. Even for one moment to allow darkness upon
the altars of the god was considered by the priests to be a great
offense against him. Whole years of dearth and famine had been
known to result from such an offense. But now the altar fires had
been deliberately extinguished, and left extinguished for five
days. It was an unspeakable sacrilege.

Hourly there was expectancy of some great calamity to befall. Perhaps within the approaching night a mighty earthquake
would shake the city to the ground, or a fire from heaven
would sweep upon them, or some monster from the desert,
where wild and terrible monsters were said to dwell, would
rush upon them and Osiris himself would rise up, as he had
done before, and swallow all Egypt in his wrath. Surely some
such dread catastrophe would befall them ere the week had

passed. Unless—unless the sacrilege were avenged.

But how might it be avenged? That was the question high lords and priests debated. Pharaoh alone had committed the sacrilege. It was he, angered because the bridge, which he had spent five years in constructing so that one day he might cross the Nile in his chariot as he had once boasted that he would do, had been swept away by the rising waters. Raging with anger, he had flogged the priests from the temple. He had barred the temple doors and with his own breath had blown out the sacred candles. He had defiled the hallowed altars with the carcasses of beasts. Even, it was said in low, shocked whispers, in a mock ceremony of worship he had burned the carrion of a hyena, most abhorrent of all beasts to Osiris, upon the holy altar of gold, which even the most high of priests forbore to lay naked hands upon!

Surely, even though he be pharaoh, ruler of all Egypt and holder of the golden eagle, he could not be permitted to commit such violent sacrileges without punishment from man. The god Osiris was waiting for them to inflict that punishment, and if they failed to do it, upon them would come a scourge from heaven.

Standing before the awed assembly of nobles, the high Kha Semblor made a gesture with his hands. A cry broke from those who watched. Sentence had been delivered. Death had been pronounced as doom for the pharaoh.

The heavy, barred doors were shoved open. The crowd came out, and within an hour a well-organized mob passed through the streets of Thebes, directed for the palace of the pharaoh. Mob justice was to be done.

Within the resplendent portals of the palace the pharaoh, ruler of all Egypt, watched with tightened brow the orderly but menacing approach of the mob. He divined their intent. But was he not their pharaoh? He could contend with gods, so why should he fear mere dogs of men?

A woman clung to his stiffened arm. She was tall and as majestically handsome as he. A garb of linen, as brilliantly golden as the sun, entwined her body closely and bands of jet were around

her throat and forehead. She was the fair and well-loved Nitocris, sister of the pharaoh.

"Brother, brother!" she cried, "light the fires! Pacify the
dogs! They come to kill you."

Only more stern grew the look of the pharaoh. He thrust aside
his pleading sister, and beckoned to the attendants.

"Open the doors!"

Startled, trembling, the man obeyed.

The haughty lord of Egypt drew his sword from its sheath. He
slashed the air with a stroke that would have severed stone. Out
on the steep steps leading between tall, colored pillars to the
doors of the palace he stepped. The people saw him. A howl
rose from their lips.

"Light the fires!"

The figure of the pharaoh stood inflexible as rock. Superbly
tall and muscular, his bare arms and limbs glittering like bur-
nished copper in the light of the brilliant sun, his body erect and
tense in his attitude of defiance, he looked indeed a mortal fit
almost to challenge gods.

The mob, led by the black-robed priests and nobles who had
arrived at the foot of the steps, now fell back before the stun-
ning, magnificent defiance of their giant ruler. They felt like
demons who had assailed the heavens and had been abashed
and shamed by the mere sight of that which they had assailed.
A hush fell over them. Their upraised arms faltered and sank
down. A moment more and they would have fallen to their
knees.

What happened then seemed nothing less than a miracle. In
his triumph and exultation, the pharaoh had been careless of the
crumbling edges of the steps. Centuries old, there were sections
of these steps which were falling apart. Upon such a section had
the gold-sandaled foot of the pharaoh descended, and it was not
strong enough to sustain his great weight. With a scuttling
sound it broke loose. A gasp came from the mob—the pharaoh
was about to fall. He was palpitating, wavering in the air, fighting
to retain his balance. He looked as if he were grappling with
some monstrous, invisible snake, coiled about his gleaming

body. A hoarse cry burst from his lips; his sword fell; and then his body thudded down the steps in a series of somersaults, and landed at the foot, sprawled out before the gasping mob. For a moment there was breathless silence. And then came the shout of a priest.

"A sign from the gods!"

That vibrant cry seemed to restore the mob to all of its wolf-like rage. They surged forward. The struggling body of the pharaoh was lifted up and torn to pieces by their clawing hands and weapons. Thus was the god Osiris avenged.

A week later another large assembly of persons confronted the brilliant-pillared palace. This time they were there to acknowledge a ruler, not to slay one. The week before they had rended the pharaoh and now they were proclaiming his sister empress. Priests had declared that it was the will of the gods that she should succeed her brother. She was famously beautiful, pious, and wise. The people were not reluctant to accept her.

When she was borne down the steps of the palace in her rich litter, after the elaborate ceremony of the coronation had been concluded, she responded to the cheers of the multitude with a smile which could not have appeared more amicable and gracious. None might know from that smile upon her beautiful carmined lips that within her heart she was thinking, "These are the people who slew my brother. Ah, god Isis, grant me power to avenge his death upon them!"

Not long after the beauteous Nitocris mounted the golden throne of Egypt, rumors were whispered of some vast, mysterious enterprise being conducted in secret. A large number of slaves were observed each dawn to embark upon barges and to be carried down the river to some unknown point, where they labored through the day, returning after dark. The slaves were Ethiopians, neither able to speak nor to understand the Egyptian language, and therefore no information could be got from them by the curious as to the object of their mysterious daily excursions. The general opinion, though, was that the pious queen was having a great temple constructed to the gods and that when it was finished, enormous public banquets would be held within it before its dedication. She meant it to be a surprise gift to the priests who were ever desirous of some new place of worship and were dissatisfied with their old altars, which they said were defiled.

Throughout the winter the slaves repeated daily their excursions. Traffic of all kinds plying down the river was restricted for several miles to within forty yards of one shore. Any craft seen to disregard that restriction was set upon by a galley of armed men and pursued back into bounds. All that could be learned was that a prodigious temple or hall of some sort was in construction.

It was late in the spring when the excursions of the workmen were finally discontinued. Restrictions upon the river traffic were withdrawn. The men who went eagerly to investigate the mysterious construction returned with tales of a magnificent new temple, surrounded by rich, green, tropical verdure, situated near the bank of the river. It was a temple to the god Osiris. It had been built by the queen probably that she might partly atone for the sacrilege of her brother and deliver him from some of the torture which he undoubtedly suffered. It was to be dedicated within the month by a great banquet. All the nobles and the high priests of Osiris, of which there were a tremendous number, were to be invited.

Never had the delighted priests been more extravagant in their praises of Queen Nitocris. When she passed through the streets in her open litter, bedazzling eyes by the glitter of her golden ornaments, the cries of the people were almost frantic in their exaltation of her.

True to the predictions of the gossipers, before the month had passed the banquet had been formally announced and to all the nobility and the priests of Osiris had been issued invitations to attend.

The day of the dedication, which was to be followed by the night of banqueting, was a gala holiday. At noon the guests of the empress formed a colorful assembly upon the bank of the river. Gaily draped barges floated at their moorings until preparations should be completed for the transportation of the guests to the temple. All anticipated a holiday of great merriment, and the lustful epicureans were warmed by visualizations of the delightful banquet of copious meats, fruit, luscious delicacies and other less innocent indulgences.

When the queen arrived, clamorous shouts rang deafeningly in her ears. She responded with charming smiles and gracious bows. The most discerning observer could not have detected anything but the greatest cordiality and kindliness reflected in her bearing towards those around her. No action, no fleeting expression upon her lovely face could have caused anyone to suspect anything except entire amicability in her feelings or her intentions. The rats, as they followed the Pied Piper of Hamelin through the streets, entranced by the notes of his magical pipe, could not have been less apprehensive of any great danger impending than were the guests of the empress as they followed her in gaily draped barges, singing and laughing down the sunglowing waters of the Nile.

The most vivid descriptions of those who had already seen the temple did not prepare the others for the spectacle of beauty and grandeur which it presented. Gasps of delight came from the priests. What a place in which to conduct their ceremonies! They began to feel that the sacrilege of the dead pharaoh was not, after all, to be so greatly regretted, since it was responsible for the building of this glorious new temple.

The columns were massive and painted with the greatest artistry. The temple itself was proportionately large. The center of it was unroofed. Above the entrance were carved the various symbols of the god Osiris, with splendid workmanship. The building was immensely big, and against the background of green foliage it presented a picture of almost breathtaking beauty. Ethopian attendants stood on each side of the doorway, their shining black bodies ornamented with bands of brilliant gold. On the interior the guests were inspired to even greater wonderment. The walls were hung with magnificent painted tapestries. The altars were more beautifully and elaborately carved than any seen before. Aromatic powders were burning upon them and sending up veils of scented smoke. The sacramental vessels were of the most exquisite and costly metals. Golden coffers and urns were piled high with perfect fruits of all kinds.

Ah, yes—a splendid place for the making of sacrifices, gloated the staring priests.

Ah, yes indeed, agreed the queen Nitocris, smiling with half-closed eyes, it was a splendid place for sacrifices—especially for the human sacrifice that had been planned. But all who observed that guileful smile interpreted it as gratification over the pleasure which her creation in honor of their god had brought to the priests of Osiris. Not the slightest shadow of portent was upon the hearts of the joyous guests.

The ceremony of dedication occupied the whole of the afternoon. And when it drew to its impressive conclusion, the large assembly, their nostrils quivering from the savory odor of the roasting meats, were fully ready and impatient for the banquet that awaited them. They gazed about them, observing that the whole building composed an unpartitioned amphitheater and wondering where might be the room of the banquet. However, when the concluding processional chant had been completed, the queen summoned a number of burly slaves, and by several iron rings attached to its outer edges they lifted up a large slab of flooring, disclosing to the astonished guests the fact that the scene of the banquet was to be an immense subterranean vault.

Such vaults were decidedly uncommon among the Egyptians. The idea of feasting in one was novel and appealing. Thrilled exclamations came from the eager, excited crowd and they pressed forward to gaze into the depths, now brightly illuminated. They saw a room beneath them almost as vast in size as the amphitheater in which they were standing. It was filled with banquet tables upon which were set the most delectable foods and rich, sparkling wines in an abundance that would satiate the banqueters of Bacchus. Luxurious, thick rugs covered the floors. Among the tables passed nymphlike maidens, and at one end of the room harpists and singers stood, making sublime music.

The air was cool with the dampness of under-earth, and it was delightfully fragrant by the perfumes of burning spices and the savory odors of the feast. If it had been heaven itself which the crowd of the queen's guests now gazed down upon they would not have considered the vision disappointing. Perhaps even if they had known the hideous menace that lurked in those gay-draped walls beneath them, they would still have found the allurement of the banquet scene difficult to resist.

Decorum and reserve were almost completely forgotten in the swiftness of the guests' descent. The stairs were not wide enough to afford room for all those who rushed upon them, and some tumbled over, landing unhurt upon the thick carpets. The priests themselves forgot their customary dignity and aloofness when they looked upon the beauty of the maiden attendants.

Immediately all of the guests gathered around the banquet tables, and the next hour was occupied in gluttonous feasting. Wine was unlimited and so was the thirst of the guests. Goblets were refilled as quickly as they were emptied by the capacious mouths of the drinkers. The singing and the laughter, the dancing and the wild frolicking grew less and less restrained until the banquet became a delirious orgy.

The queen alone, seated upon a cushioned dais from which she might overlook the whole room, remained aloof from the general hilarity. Her thick black brows twitched; her luminous black eyes shone strangely between their narrow painted lids. There was something peculiarly feline in the curl of her rich red lips. Now and again her eyes sought the section of wall to her left, where hung gorgeous braided tapestries from the East. But it seemed not the tapestries that she looked upon. Color would mount upon her brow and her slender fingers would dig still tighter into the cushions she reclined upon.

In her mind the queen Nitocris was seeing a ghastly picture. It was the picture of a room of orgy and feasting suddenly converted into a room of terror and horror; human beings one moment drunken and lustful, the next screaming in the seizure of sudden and awful death. If any of those present had been empowered to see also that picture of dire horror, they would have clambered wildly to make their escape. But none was so empowered.

With increasing wildness the banquet continued into the middle of the night. Some of the banqueters, disgustingly gluttonous, still gorged themselves at the greasy tables. Others lay in drunken stupor, or lolled amorously with the slave girls. But most of them, formed in a great, irregular circle, skipped about the room in a barbaric, joy-mad dance, dragging and tripping each other in uncouth merriment and making the hall ring with their ceaseless shouts, laughter and hoarse song.

When the hour had approached near to midnight, the queen, who had sat like one entranced, arose from the cushioned dais. One last intent survey she gave to the crowded room of banquet. It was a scene which she wished to imprint permanently upon her mind. Much pleasure might she derive in the future by recalling that picture, and the imagining what came afterwards —stark, searing terror rushing in upon barbaric joy!

She stepped down from the dais and walked swiftly to the steps. Her departure made no impression upon the revelers. When she arrived at the top of the stairs, she looked down and observed that no one had marked her exit.

Around the walls of the temple, dim-lit and fantastic-looking at night, with the cool wind from the river sweeping through and bending the flames of the tall candelabra, stalwart guardsmen were standing at their posts, and when the gold-cloaked figure of the queen arose from the aperture, they advanced towards her hurriedly. With a motion, she directed them to place the slab of rock in its tight-fitting socket. With a swift, noiseless hoist and lowering, they obeyed the command. The queen bent down. There was no change in the boisterous sounds from below. Nothing was yet suspected.

Drawing the soft and shimmering folds of her cloak about her with fingers that trembled with eagerness, excitement and the intense emotion which she felt, the queen passed swiftly across the stone floor of the temple towards the open front through which the night wind swept, blowing her cloak in sheenful waves about her tall and graceful figure. The slaves followed after in silent file, well aware of the monstrous deed about to be executed and without reluctance to play their parts.

Down the steps of the palace into the moon-white night passed the weird procession. Their way led them down an obviously secreted path through thick ranks of murmuring palms which in their low voices seemed to be whispering shocked remonstrances against what was about to be done. But in her stern purpose the queen was not susceptible to any discussion from god or man. Vengeance, strongest of passions, made her obdurate as stone.

Out upon a rough and apparently new-constructed stone pier the thin path led. Beneath, the cold, dark waters of the Nile surged silently by. Here the party came to a halt. Upon this stone pier would the object of their awful midnight errand be accomplished.

With a low-spoken word, the queen commanded her followers to hold back. With her own hand she would perform the act of vengeance.

In the foreground of the pier a number of fantastic, wand like levers extended upwards. Towards these the queen advanced, slowly and stiffly as an executioner mounts the steps of the scaffold. When she had come beside them, she grasped one upthrust bar, fiercely, as if it had been the throat of a hated antagonist. Then she lifted her face with a quick intake of breath towards the moon-lighted sky. This was to her a moment of supreme ecstasy. Grasped in her hand was an instrument which could release awful death upon those against whom she wished vengeance. Their lives were as securely in her grasp as was this bar of iron.

Slowly, lusting upon every triumph-filled second of this time of ecstasy, she turned her face down again to the formidable bar in her hand. Deliberately she drew it back to its limit. This was the lever that opened the wall in the banquet vault. It gave entrance to death. Only the other bar now intervened between the banqueters, probably still reveling undisturbed, and the dreadful fate which she had prepared for them. Upon this bar now her jeweled fingers clutched. Savagely this time she pulled it; then with the litheness of a tiger she sprang to the edge of the pier. She leaned over it and stared down into the inky rush of the river. A new sound she heard above the steady flow. It was the sound of waters suddenly diverted into a new channel—an eager, plunging sound. Down to the hall of revelry they were rushing—these savage waters—bringing terror and sudden death.

A cry of triumph, wild and terrible enough to make even the hearts of the brutish slaves turn cold, now broke from the lips of the queen. The pharaoh was avenged.

And even he must have considered his avenging adequate had he been able to witness it.

After the retiring of the queen, the banquet had gone on without interruption of gaiety. None noticed her absence. None noticed the silent replacing of the stone in its socket. No premonition of disaster was felt. The musicians, having been informed beforehand of the intended event of the evening, had made their withdrawal before the queen. The slaves, whose lives were of little value to the queen, were as ignorant of what was to happen as were the guests themselves.

Not until the wall opened up with a loud and startling crunch did even those most inclined towards suspicion feel the slightest uneasiness. Then it was that a few noticed the slab to have been replaced, shutting them in. This discovery, communicated throughout the hall in a moment, seemed to instill a sudden fear in the hearts of all. Laughter did not cease, but the ring of dancers were distracted from their wild jubilee. They all turned towards the mysteriously opened wall and gazed into its black depths.

A hush fell over them. And then became audible the mounting sound of rushing water. A shriek rose from the throat of a woman. And then terror took possession of all within the room. Panic like the burst of flames flared into their hearts. Of one accord, they rushed upon the stair. And it, being purposely made frail, collapsed before the foremost of the wildly screaming mob had reached its summit. Turbulently they piled over the tables, filling the room with a hideous clamor. But rising above their screams was the shrill roar of the rushing water, and no sound could be more provoking of dread and terror. Somewhere in its circuitous route from the pier to the chamber of its reception it must have met with temporary blockade, for it was several minutes after the sound of it was first detected that the first spray of that death bringing water leapt into the faces of the doomed occupants of the room.

With the ferocity of a lion springing into the arena of a Roman amphitheater to devour the gladiators set there for its delectation, the black water plunged in. Furiously it surged over the floor of the room, sweeping tables before it and sending its victims, now face to face with their harrowing doom, into a hysteria of terror. In a moment that icy, black water had risen to their knees, although the room was vast. Some fell instantly dead from the shock, or were trampled upon by the desperate rushing of the mob. Tables were clambered upon. Lamps and candles were extinguished. Brilliant light rapidly faded to twilight, and a ghastly dimness fell over the room as only the suspended lanterns remained lit. And what a scene of chaotic and hideous horror might a spectator have beheld! The gorgeous trumpery of banquet invaded by howling waters of death! Gaily dressed merrymakers caught suddenly in the grip of terror! Gasps and screams of the dying amid tumult and thickening dark!

What more horrible vengeance could Queen Nitocris have conceived than this banquet of death? Not Diablo himself could be capable of anything more fiendishly artistic. Here in the temple of Osiris those nobles and priests who had slain the pharaoh in expiation of his sacrilege against Osiris had now met their deaths. And it was in the waters of the Nile, material symbol of the god Osiris, that they had died. It was magnificent in its irony!

I would be content to end this story here if it were but a story. However, it is not merely a story, as you will have discerned before now if you have been a student of the history of Egypt. Queen Nitocris is not a fictitious personage. In the annals of ancient Egypt she is no inconspicuous figure. Principally re-

sponsible for her prominence is her monstrous revenge upon
the slayers of her brother, the narration of which I have just
concluded. Glad would I be to end this story here; for surely
anything following must be in the nature of an anticlimax. However, being not a mere storyteller here, but having upon me also
the responsibility of a historian, I feel obligated to continue the
account to the point where it was left off by Herodotus, the great
Greek historian. And, therefore, I add this postscript, anticlimax
though it be.

The morning of the day after the massacre in the temple, the
guests of the queen not having made their return, the citizens
of Thebes began to glower with dark suspicions. Rumors came
to them through divers channels that something of a most extraordinary and calamitous nature had occurred at the scene of
the banquet during the night. Some had it that the temple had
collapsed upon the revelers and all had been killed. However,
this theory was speedily dispelled when a voyager from down the
river reported having passed the temple in a perfectly firm condition but declared that he had seen no signs of life about the
place—only the brightly canopied boats, drifting at their moorings.

Uneasiness steadily increased throughout the day. Sage persons recalled the great devotion of the queen towards her dead
brother, and noted that the guests at the banquet of last night
had been composed almost entirely of those who had participated in his slaying.

When in the evening the queen arrived in the city, pale, silent,
and obviously nervous, threatening crowds blocked the path of
her chariot, demanding roughly an explanation of the disappearance of her guests. Haughtily she ignored them and lashed
forward the horses of her chariot, pushing aside the tight mass
of people. Well she knew, however, that her life would be
doomed as soon as they confirmed their suspicions. She resolved to meet her inevitable death in a way that befitted one of
her rank, not at the filthy hands of a mob.

Therefore, upon her entrance into the palace she ordered her
slaves to fill instantly her boudoir with hot and smoking ashes.

When this has been done, she went to the room, entered it, closed the door and locked it securely, and then flung herself down upon a couch in the center of the room. In a short time the scorching heat and the suffocating thick fumes of the smoke overpowered her. Only her beautiful dead body remained for the hands of the mob.

THE MUMMY'S FOOT

by THÉOPHILE GAUTIER

Can there be much of anything more intriguing than a little out-of-the-way shop which specializes in antiques, bric-à-brac, and just plain "things"? Such shops, like Egyptian curses, have been a favorite ploy of fantasy writers for many years, and almost always with success because their presence in a story is bound to stir the imagination. The unwary visitor might find any of an infinite number of items in such a shop, with an infinite number of possibilities connected to them. Jade idols, for example, or a two-handed sword, or abominable Mexican fetishes representing the god Witziliputzili. He might even find, if the shop happens to be that of a certain Parisian dealer in curiosities, the embalmed foot of an Egyptian mummy.

"The Mummy's Foot" not only takes the narrator (and the reader) on a fascinating tour of this dealer's abode, but on an even more fascinating tour of ancient Egypt in the company of the lovely Princess Hermonthis. There are chills along the way, to be sure, but there are also some chuckles and perhaps even a guffaw or two—an expert blending of bizarre fantasy and satirical humor.

Théophile Gautier (1811–1872) was a journalist, poet, and storyteller whose work was highly regarded in France in the middle nineteenth century. One of his early novels may well be the first piece of prose to make use of the mummy theme: Romance of a Mummy *(1856). Among aficionados of the macabre, his best-known novel is the vampire tale* Clarimonde. *Other fantastic works include* Spirite: A Fantasy, One of Cleopatra's Nights, Avatar, or The Double Transformation, *and* Jettatura.

HAVING NOTHING particular to do, I had entered the shop of one of those dealers in curiosities called bric-à-brac dealers in our Parisian slang, which is utterly unintelligible in other parts of France. No doubt you have sometimes glanced at the windows of some of these shops, which have multiplied since it has become fashionable to purchase old furniture, and every stockbroker thinks he must have a medieval room. They have at one and the same time something of the junk dealer, the upholsterer, the alchemist's laboratory, and the painter's studio. In these mysterious dens, through which a prudent half-light filters, what is most genuinely old is the dirt. The cobwebs there are more authentic than the lace, and old pear tree wood is younger than mahogany imported last week from America.

The shop of my bric-à-brac dealer was a regular lumber room; every age and every country appeared to be represented in it. A red clay Etruscan lamp rested upon a cabinet by Boule, with ebony panels austerely inlaid with brass; a half-lounge of the days of Louis XV carelessly extended its fawn feet under a thick Louis XIII table, with heavy oaken spirals and carved foliage and monsters. In one corner gleamed the wavy breastplate of a damascened suit of Milan armor. Parian porcelain cupids and nymphs, Chinese grotesques, vases of céladon and craquelé, cups of Dresden and old Sèvres china, covered the shelves and filled up the corners. On the denticulated shelves of the sideboards shone resplendently great Japanese dishes with red and blue ornaments, set off by gold hatchings, side by side with enamels by Bernard Palissy, representing adders, frogs, and lizards in relief. From wardrobes that burst open escaped cascades of silk damask, overlaid with silver, waves of brocatelle, which a sunbeam covered with luminous dots; while portraits of every period in more or less dull gold frames smiled through their yellow varnish.

The dealer carefully followed me along the narrow passage left open between the piles of furniture, keeping down the fluttering skirts of my coat, and watching my elbows, with the restless attention of an antiquarian and a usurer.

He had a curious face, that dealer; a big skull, polished like marble, with a thin aureole of white hair, brought out more strongly by the pale salmon color of his skin, giving him a sham look of patriarchal kindness, which was neutralized, however, by the sparkling of two little yellow eyes that shone in their orbs like two gold coins laid on mercury. The aquiline profile of his nose recalled the Oriental or Jewish type; his thin, slender hands, covered with veins and full of nerves standing out like the strings of a violin, and provided with nails like the claws at the end of a bat's wings, had a most unpleasant senile trembling; but when they lifted some precious object, an onyx cup, a Venetian glass, or a tray of Bohemian crystal, these trembling hands became stronger than steel pincers or lobster's claws. The old rascal had such a thoroughly rabbinical and cabalistic look that he would have burned at the stake three centuries ago merely on account of his appearance.

"Are you not going to buy anything today, sir? Here is a Malay creese, the blade of which is waved like a flame. Look at the grooves for the blood to run down; and at these teeth cut the reverse way to tear the entrails as you pull out the weapon. It is a ferocious arm, very characteristic, which would look uncommonly well on your wall. This two-handed sword is very handsome. It is by Joseph de la Hera. And this great dueling sword with openwork pearl handle is a superb piece of work."

"No, I have enough weapons and instruments of destruction.

I want a statuette, a trifle, for a paperweight, for I cannot bear those cheap bronzes sold by stationers, which are to be found on every writing table."

The old gnome, rummaging among his possessions, spread out before me antique bronzes—or at least claimed to be antique—pieces of malachite, small Hindu or Chinese jade idols, grotesque incarnations of Brahma or Vishnu, uncommonly well fitted to the not very divine purpose of keeping down newspapers and letters.

I was hesitating between a porcelain dragon covered with warts, its mouth adorned with fangs and tentacles, and a small abominable Mexican fetish representing the god Witziliputzili, when I noticed a lovely foot, which at first I thought must be a fragment of some antique Venus. It had the lovely tawny, ruddy tints that give to Florentine bronze its warm and living tints so preferable to the verdigrised tone of ordinary bronzes, which might easily be mistaken for statues in a state of putrefaction. Satiny gleams shimmered over its round forms, polished by the loving kisses of twenty centuries; for it unquestionably was of Corinthian brass, a piece of work of the best epoch, perhaps a casting by Lysippus.

"This foot will do for me," said I to the dealer, who looked at me with a sly, ironical glance, as he held it out to allow me to examine it more comfortably.

I was surprised at its lightness. It was not a foot of metal, but of flesh; an embalmed foot, a mummy's foot. On looking closely the grain of the skin and the almost imperceptible mark made by the bandages could be perceived. The toes were small and delicate, with perfect, pure nails, transparent as agate; the great toe, somewhat apart, after the fashion of antiquity, contrasted happily with the direction of the other toes, and gave it a free attitude, the neat aspect of a bird's foot. The sole, scarcely marked by a few faint lines, had evidently never come in contact with the ground, and had trodden only upon the finest matting of Nile reeds, and the softest carpets of panther's skins.

"Ha! ha! you want the foot of the princess Hermonthis," said the dealer, with a horrible chuckle, as he fixed upon me his owllike glance. "Ha! ha!—for a paperweight! That is a novel idea; that is an artist's idea. If old pharaoh had been told that his adored daughter's foot would be used as a paperweight he would have been astounded, considering that he was having a mountain of granite hollowed out in order to put inside the triple painted and gilded coffin, covered with hieroglyphs, with beautiful paintings representing the judgment of the soul," added the queer little dealer, in a low voice, as if speaking to himself.

"How much will you sell me this fragment of a mummy for?"

"As dear as I can, for it is quite a curiosity. If I had the companion to it, I would not let you have the pair for less than five hundred francs. Pharaoh's daughters are scarce, very scarce."

"I know it; I am aware that it is not very common; but how much do you want? To begin with, I must inform you that my whole wealth amounts to five louis. I shall buy whatever may cost five louis, but nothing more. You might search the back pockets of my vests, and my most secret drawers, you would not find another sou in them."

"Five louis for the foot of Princess Hermonthis! That is very little, very little indeed for an authentic foot," said the dealer, wagging his head and rolling his eyes. "Well, take it. I will give you the wrapper into the bargain," he added, as he rolled the foot in an old piece of damask. "It is very beautiful genuine Indian damask; never has been dyed; it is strong and sound," he muttered, as he rubbed with his fingers the worn tissue; the force of commercial habit making him praise an object of so little value that even he thought it might as well be given away.

He slipped the gold pieces into a sort of medieval purse hanging from his belt, repeating, "The foot of Princess Hermonthis for a paperweight!"

Then, fixing on me his flaming eyes, he said, in a voice as strident as the mewing of a cat that has just swallowed a fishbone: "Old pharaoh will not be very pleased; he was very fond of his daughter, the worthy man."

"You talk about him as if you were his contemporary. Old

though you are, you do not quite go back to the pyramids of Egypt," I replied laughingly, as I passed out of the shop.

I returned home, very well satisfied with my purchase, and in order to turn it to account at once, I placed the foot of the divine Princess Hermonthis upon a bundle of papers, drafts of verses, an undecipherable mosaic of corrections, beginnings of articles, forgotten letters which I had posted in the drawer—a mistake often committed by absentminded people. The effect the foot produced was charming, eccentric, and romantic.

Greatly pleased with this embellishment of my table, I went out into the street and walked along with the gravity and the pride that become a man who has over every passerby he elbows the ineffable advantage of possessing a portion of the princess Hermonthis, daughter of the pharaoh. I considered as beneath contempt all those who did not possess, as I did, so notoriously Egyptian a paperweight, and it appeared to me that the proper business in the life of a sensible man was to have a mummy's foot on his writing table. Happily, I met some friends, who drew me out of my infatuation. I went to dinner with them, for it would have been difficult for me to dine with myself.

When I returned at night, my head filled with a light, pearly gray vapor, a faint puff of Oriental perfume tickled my olfactory nerves. The warmth of the room had warmed up the natron, bitumen, and myrrh in which the embalmers had dipped the princess's body. It was a sweet and penetrating perfume that had not wholly evaporated during the lapse of four thousand years; for Egypt dreamed of eternity: its odors have the solidity of granite and last as long.

I soon drank deep of the black cup of sleep. For an hour or two everything remained a blank, and I sank in the somber waves of forgetfulness and nothingness. Then my intellectual darkness lightened, and dreams began to flutter silently around. The eyes of my soul were opened, and I saw my room such as it actually was. I might have thought myself awake. A strange feeling convinced me that I was asleep and that something curious was about to happen.

The odor of myrrh had grown stronger, and I felt a slight

headache, which I very naturally attributed to a number of glasses of champagne which we had drunk to the unknown gods and our future success. I looked round the room with a feeling of expectation that nothing justified. The furniture was in its place, the lamp burning on the table, pleasantly softened by the milky whiteness of the ground-glass globe; the water-colors shimmered under their Bohemian glass; the curtains hung languidly; everything looked serene and quiet.

But after a few moments this peaceful interior seemed to be disturbed. The woodwork cracked furtively, the log buried in the ashes suddenly shot out a jet of blue flame, and the disks of the coathooks looked like metal eyes, attentively watching, as I was, for whatever was about to happen.

By chance I glanced at the table on which I had placed the foot of the princess Hermonthis. Instead of resting quietly as became a foot embalmed for more than four thousand years, it was moving, contracting, and hopping about the papers like a frightened frog. I could have sworn it was in contact with a voltaic battery. I could quite distinctly hear the sharp sound made by its little heel, as hard as a gazelle's hoof.

I was not quite satisfied with my purchase, for I prefer sedentary paperweights, and it does not seem natural to me to see feet going about without limbs. Indeed, I began to experience something not unlike fear.

Suddenly I saw a fold of one of my curtains move, and I heard a sound like that made by a person hopping round on one foot. I must confess I turned cold and hot alternately; a strange chill ran up and down my back, and my hair stood up on my head.

The curtains opened, and I saw coming forward the strangest figure imaginable. It was that of a young girl of a very dark coffee-color, like Amani the bayadere, of perfect beauty, and recalling the purest Egyptian type. Her almond-shaped eyes were turned up at the corners, and her eyebrows were so black that they showed blue. Her nose was delicately shaped, almost Greek in its outline, and she might have been taken for a Corinthian bronze statue, but that the prominence of the cheekbones and the somewhat African size of the mouth showed plainly that she belonged to the hieroglyphic race of the banks of the Nile. Her well-shaped arms, slender like those of very young girls, were clasped by metal and glass bracelets; her hair was plaited into little tresses; and on her bosom hung an idol of green clay, which I recognized by the seven-tailed whip as Isis, the conductress of souls; on her brow shone a plate of gold, and some traces of rouge were visible on her copper-colored cheeks.

As for her costume, it was strange indeed. Imagine a loin cloth of narrow bands covered with black and red hieroglyphics, stiff with bitumen, which seemed to belong to a recently unrolled mummy.

By one of those sudden changes of thought which are so frequent in dreams, I heard the shrill, hoarse voice of the bric-à-brac dealer repeating like a monotonous refrain the remark he had made in his shop in so enigmatic a tone—

"Old pharaoh will not be very much pleased. He was very fond of his daughter, the worthy man."

There was one curious peculiarity which did not contribute to reassure me—the apparition had but one foot. The other leg was broken off at the ankle.

She went to the table, where the mummy's foot was jumping and quivering with greater rapidity. On reaching it, she leaned upon the edge, and I saw a tear grow in her eyes. Though she said not a word, I could clearly make out her thoughts. She looked at the foot, for it was hers, with an infinitely graceful expression of coquettish sadness, while the foot ran and leaped hither and thither as if moved by steel springs.

Twice or thrice she stretched out her hand to seize it, but failed to do so.

Then there took place between the princess Hermonthis and her foot, which appeared endowed with a life of its own, a very curious dialogue, in a very ancient Coptic dialect, such as was spoken some thirty centuries ago in the mummy pits of the country of Ser. Luckily that night I happened to know Coptic perfectly well.

Princess Hermonthis said in a sweet voice that vibrated like a crystal bell—

"Well, my dear little foot, so you are still fleeing from me, though I took good care of you. I washed you with scented water in an alabaster basin; I polished your heel with pumice stone dipped in palm oil; I cut your nails with golden scissors, and polished them with hippopotamus teeth; I took care to choose for you painted and embroidered sandals with turned-up points, that made every Egyptian girl envy us. I put on your toes rings representing the sacred scarabaeus, and you supported one of the daintiest bodies that a lazy foot could wish for."

The foot replied in a sulky tone—

"You know very well I do not belong to myself any more. I have been purchased and paid for. The old dealer knew what he was doing. He is still angry with you for refusing to marry him. It is a trick that he is playing upon you. The Arab that broke open your royal coffin in the subterranean well of the Theban Necropolis had been sent by him. He meant to prevent your going to the meeting of the people in darkness in the lower cities. Have you got five gold pieces to buy me back with?"

"Alas, I have not. My gems, my rings, my purses of gold and silver, everything has been stolen from me," replied Princess Hermonthis, with a sigh.

"Princess," I cried then, "I have never unjustly kept back anyone's foot. Although you have not got the five louis which I paid for it, I return it to you most willingly. I should be uncommonly sorry to cripple so lovely a person as Princess Hermonthis."

The beautiful Egyptian must have been surprised at the Regency manner and the troubadour tone in which I spoke this speech. She cast upon me a glance full of gratitude, and her eyes lighted up with blue flashes. She took her foot, which allowed itself to be caught this time, like a woman about to put on a shoe, and fitted it very skillfully to her leg, after which she took two or three steps through the room, as if to make certain that she was really no longer a cripple.

"How glad my father will be, for he was so troubled by the mutilation I suffered. The very day I was born he had set a whole nation to work to dig me a tomb deep enough to preserve me intact until the great day when souls are to be weighed in the balances of Amenthi. Come with me to him. He will welcome you, for you have restored my foot to me."

The proposal struck me as quite natural. I put on a dressing gown with a great flowered pattern, in which I looked most pharaohlike, hastily slipped my feet into a pair of Turkish slippers, and told Princess Hermonthis that I was ready to follow her.

Before leaving, she took from her neck the little figure in green china, and placed it upon the scattered papers that covered my table.

"It is only right," she said, "that I should give you something in place of your paperweight."

She held out her hand to me. It was soft and cold as a serpent's skin. We were off.

We sped for some time as swift as an arrow through a grayish fluid air in which faintly outlined forms passed to right and left. At one time nothing was visible but sky and water. Presently obelisks began to show up; pylons and long stairs, with sphinxes ranged all the way down, stood out against the horizon. We had arrived.

The princess led me to a mountain of rose granite, in which there was a low, narrow opening which it would have been difficult to distinguish from the cracks in the stone had not a couple of stelae covered with carvings made it recognizable.

Hermonthis lighted a torch and walked on before me.

We entered corridors cut in the living rock; the walls, covered with panels of hieroglyphs and allegorical processions, must have occupied thousands of men for thousands of years. These corridors, interminably long, ended in square halls, in the center of which were dug wells. We descended these by means of cramp-irons or of spiral staircases. The wells led into other chambers from which issued other corridors, also adorned with hawks, serpents biting their tails, representations of the mystic tau, pedum, and bari—a prodigious piece of work which no living eye was to see, endless legends in granite which the dead alone had time to read during eternity.

At last we entered so vast, so enormous, so immense a hall that its limits were invisible. As far as I could see stretched rows of monstrous pillars, between which gleamed limpid stars of yellow light. These brilliant points indicated incalculable depths.

Princess Hermonthis still held my hand, and bowed graciously to the mummies of her acquaintance.

My eyes becoming accustomed to the twilight, I began to discern objects. I saw seated upon thrones the kings of subterranean races. They were tall, dry old men, wrinkled, parchment-like, black with naphtha and bitumen, wearing the golden pschent, pectorals, and neckplates covered with gems, their eyes staring like those of sphinxes, and they wore long beards, whitened with the snow of centuries. Behind them stood their embalmed peoples, in the stiff, constrained attitudes of Egyptian art, preserving forever the pose prescribed by the hieratic code; behind the peoples, the cats, ibises, and crocodiles of those days, made more mysterious still by being swathed up in bands, mewed, flapped their wings, and chuckled.

Every pharaoh was there, Cheops, Chephrenes, Psammetichus, Sesostris, Amenoteph; all the swarthy lords of pyramids and pits. On a higher throne sat King Chronos, Xixouthros, who lived in the days of the deluge, and Tubal Cain, who preceded him.

King Xixouthros's beard had grown so much that it had already circled seven times the granite table on which he leaned, dreamy and sleepy.

Farther away, through a dusty vapor, through the mist of eternities, I managed to make out the seventy-two pre-Adamite kings, with their seventy-two peoples, vanished forever.

Princess Hermonthis, having allowed me to enjoy this marvelous spectacle for a few moments, presented me to the pharaoh, her father, who nodded to me most majestically.

"I have found my foot, I have found my foot!" cried the princess, clapping her little hands together, with every mark of mad joy. "It is this gentleman who gave it back to me."

The races of Keme, of Nahasi, all the black, bronze, and copper-colored nations, repeated together—

"The princess Hermonthis has found her foot again."

Xixouthros himself was interested. He raised his heavy lids, stroked his moustache, and let fall upon me his glance, laden with centuries.

"By Oms, the dog of Hades, and Tmei, daughter of the Sun and of Truth, you are a fine and worthy fellow," said the pharaoh, extending towards me his scepter, ending in a lotus flower. "What will you have for a reward?"

Bold as one is in dreams, in which nothing seems impossible, I asked for the hand of Hermonthis. It struck me that to get the hand in return for the foot was an antithetical reward in pretty good taste.

The pharaoh opened wide his glass eyes, amazed at my joke and my request.

"What is your country, and what is your age?"

"I am a Frenchman, and I am twenty-seven years old, venerable pharaoh."

"Twenty-seven years! and he proposes to wed Princess Hermonthis, who is thirty centuries old," cried out together all the thrones and all the circles of nations.

Hermonthis alone did not think my request at all improper.

"If you were only two thousand years old," answered the old king, "I would willingly give you the princess; but the disproportion is too great; and then, we must have for our daughters husbands that can last. You people do not know how to preserve yourselves. The last, brought here scarcely fifteen centuries ago, are now nothing but a handful of ashes. See, my own flesh is hard as basalt, my bones are like bars of steel. I shall see the last day of the world with the same body and the same face as I had when alive. My daughter Hermonthis will endure longer than a bronze statue. By that time the wind will have scattered the last grain of your dust, and Isis herself, who managed to find the pieces of Osiris, would be hard put to it to reconstruct your frame. See how vigorous I am yet, and how strong my arms are," said he, as he shook hands with me in English fashion, so that he cut my fingers with my rings.

He squeezed my hand so hard that I awoke, and perceived my friend Alfred, pulling me by the arm, and shaking me to make me get up.

"Look here, you confounded sleeper, shall I have to take you out into the street and to set off fireworks at your ears? It is past noon. Have you forgotten that you promised to call for me to go to see Aguado's Spanish paintings?"

"Good gracious, I had forgotten all about it," replied I, as I dressed. "We shall go at once. I have the invitation here on my table."

As I spoke, I stepped forward to take up the card; but judge of my astonishment when, instead of the mummy's foot which I had bought the night before, I saw the little figure of green clay put in its place by the princess Hermonthis.

THE EYES OF
THE MUMMY

by ROBERT BLOCH

*Egypt, as the narrator of "The Eyes of the Mummy" notes, is a land
of antique and mysterious secrets, an avatar of all strangeness. And of all
its secrets, there is perhaps none stranger or more terrible than that of
Sebek, the crocodile-headed god. For the crocodile cult was one which
worshiped evil, its priests invoking Sebek as a demon rather than a benignant deity, offering him sacrificial blood in their underground temples by
crushing maidens in the jaws of eidolons shaped as golden crocodiles. Evil
boons are said to have been granted to these priests of Sebek; in death they
and their mummified bodies are protected by the wrath of their ancient
patron, and by dark and fearful powers concentrated in great shining
jewels which replaced their eyes.*

*The narrator and his partner, Professor Weildan, dare to desecrate the
tomb of one such Sebekian votary, in an attempt to steal the mummy's
jeweled eyes. What happens to them makes for one of the most chilling horror
stories ever published in* Weird Tales—*a story which turns the "idol with
the jeweled eyes" ploy upside-down and, quite literally, inside out . . .*

*Robert Bloch's name has become a synonymn for quality macabre
fiction, and little wonder: he has been writing stories of this type for four*

and a half decades, ever since his first appeared in Weird Tales *in 1934 (at the tender age of seventeen), and has given us such classics of the form as* Psycho, The Scarf, *"Yours Truly, Jack the Ripper," "Enoch," and the recent* Strange Eons. *He has also penned numerous movie and television scripts in the realm of horror/fantasy, as well as other weird and psychological suspense novels and hundreds of short stories. The best of the latter may be found in his dozen or so collections, the latest of which is the aptly titled* Such Stuff As Screams Are Made Of.

EGYPT HAS always fascinated me; Egypt, land of antique and mysterious secrets. I had read of pyramids and kings; dreamed of vast, shadowy empires now dead as the empty eyes of the sphinx. It was of Egypt that I wrote in later years, for to me its weird faiths and cults made the land an avatar of all strangeness.

Not that I believed in the grotesque legends of olden times; I did not credit the faith in anthropomorphic gods with the heads and attributes of beasts. Still, I sensed behind the myths of Bast, Anubis, Set, and Thoth the allegorical implications of forgotten truths. Tales of beastmen are known the world over, in the racial lore of all climes. The werewolf legend is universal and unchanged since the furtive hintings of Pliny's days. Therefore to me, with my interest in the supernatural, Egypt provided a key to ancient knowledge.

But I did not believe in the actual existence of such beings or creatures in the days of Egypt's glory. The most I would admit to myself was that perhaps the legends of those days had come down from much remoter times when primal earth could hold such monstrosities due to evolutionary mutations.

Then, one evening in carnival New Orleans, I encountered a fearful substantiation of my theories. At the home of the eccentric Henricus Vanning I participated in a queer ceremony over the body of a priest of Sebek, the crocodile-headed god. Weildan, the archeologist, had smuggled it into this country, and we examined the mummy despite curse and warning. I was not myself at the time, and to this day I am not sure what occurred, exactly. There was a stranger present, wearing a crocodile mask, and events were precipitated in nightmare fashion. When I rushed from that house into the streets, Vanning was dead by the priest's hand—or fangs, set in the mask (if mask it was).

I cannot clarify the statement of the above facts; dare not. I told the story once, then determined to abandon writing of Egypt and its ancient ways forever.

This resolve I have adhered to, until tonight's dreadful experience has caused me to reveal what I feel must be told.

Hence this narrative. The preliminary facts are simple; yet they all seem to imply that I am linked to some awful chain of interlocking experiences, fashioned by a grim Egyptian god of fate. It is as though the old ones are jealous of my pryings into their ways, and are luring me onward to a final horror.

For after my New Orleans experience, after my return home with the resolution to abandon research into Egyptian mythology forever, I was again enmeshed.

Professor Weildan came to call on me. It was he who had smuggled in the mummy of Sebek's priest which I had seen in New Orleans; he had met me on that inexplicable evening when a jealous god or his emissary had seemed to walk the earth for vengeance. He knew of my interest, and had spoken to me quite seriously of the dangers involved when one pried into the past.

The gnomelike, bearded little man now came and greeted me with understanding eyes. I was reluctant to see him, I own, for his presence brought back memories of the very things I was endeavoring to forget forever. Despite my attempts to lead the conversation into more wholesome channels, he insisted on speaking of our first meeting. He told me how the death of the recluse Vanning had broken up the little group of occultists that had met over the body of the mummy that evening.

But he, Weildan, had not forsaken his pursuit of the Sebek legend. That, he informed me, was the reason he had taken this trip to see me. None of his former associates would aid him now in the project he had in mind. Perhaps I might be interested.

I flatly refused to have anything more to do with Egyptology. This I told him at once.

Weildan laughed. He understood my reasons for demurring, he said, but I must allow him to explain. This present project of his had nothing to do with sorcery, or mantic arts. It was, as he jovially explained, merely a chance to even the score with the powers of darkness, if I was so foolish as to term them such.

He explained. Briefly, he wanted me to go to Egypt with him, on a private expedition of our own. There would be no personal expense involved for me; he needed a young man as an assistant and did not care to trust any professional archeologists who might cause trouble.

His studies had always been directed in recent years toward the legends of the crocodile cult, and he had labored steadily in an effort to learn of the secret burial places of Sebek's priests. Now, from reputable sources—a native guide in his pay abroad —he had stumbled onto a new hiding place; a subterranean tomb which held a mummy of a Sebekian votary.

He would not waste words in giving me further details; the whole point of his story was that the mummy could be reached easily, with no need of labor or excavation, and there was absolutely no danger, no silly truck about curses or vengeance. We could therefore go there alone; the two of us, in utter secrecy. And our visit would be profitable. Not only could he secure the mummy without official intervention, but his source of information—on the authenticity of which he would stake his personal reputation—revealed that the mummy was interred with a hoard of sacred jewels. It was a safe, sure, secret opportunity for wealth he was offering me.

I must admit that this sounded attractive. Despite my unpleasant experience in the past, I would risk a great deal for the sake of suitable compensation. And then, too, although I was determined to eschew all dabblings in mysticism, there was a hint of the adventurous in this undertaking which allured me.

Weildan cunningly played upon my feelings; I realize that now. He talked with me for several hours, and returned the next day, until at last I agreed.

We sailed in March, landed in Cairo three weeks later after a brief stopover in London. The excitement of going abroad obscures my memory of personal contact with the professor; I know that he was very unctuous and reassuring at all times, and doing his best to convince me that our little expedition was entirely harmless. He wholly overrode my scruples as to the dishonesty of tomb-looting; attended to our visas, and fabricated some trumped-up tale to allow the officials to pass us through to the interior.

From Cairo we went by rail to Khartoum. It was there that Professor Weildan planned to meet his "source of information" —the native guide, who was now admittedly a spy in the archeologist's employ.

This revelation did not bother me nearly as much as it might have if it occurred midst more prosaic settings. The desert atmosphere seemed a fitting background for intrigue and conspiracy, and for the first time I understood the psychology of the wanderer and the adventurer.

It was thrilling to prowl through twisted streets of the Arab quarter on the evening we visited the spy's hovel. Weildan and I entered a dark, noisome courtyard and were admitted to a dim apartment by a tall, hawk-nosed Bedouin. The man greeted the professor warmly. Money changed hands. Then the Arab and my companion retired to an inner chamber. I heard the low whisper of their voices—Weildan's excited, questioning tones mingling with the guttural accented English of the native. I sat in the gloom and waited. The voices rose, as though in altercation. It seemed as though Weildan were attempting to placate or reassure, while the guide's voice assumed a note of warning and hesitant fear. Anger entered, as Weildan made an effort to shout down his companion.

Then I heard footsteps. The door to the inner chamber opened, and the native appeared on the threshold. His face seemed to hold a look of entreaty as he stared at me, and from his lips poured an incoherent babble, as though in his excited efforts to convey his warning to me he had relapsed into familiar Arabic speech. For warning me he was; that was unmistakable.

A second he stood there, and then Weildan's hand fell on his shoulder, wheeling him around. The door slammed shut as the Arab's voice rose high, almost to a scream. Weildan shouted something unintelligible; there was the sound of a scuffle, a muffled report, then silence.

Several minutes elapsed before the door opened and Weildan appeared, mopping his brow. His eyes avoided mine.

"Fellow kicked up a row about payments," he explained, speaking to the floor. "Got the information, though. Then he came out here to ask you for money. I had to put him out the back entrance, finally. Fired a shot to scare him off; these natives are so excitable."

I said nothing as we left the place, nor did I comment on the hurried furtiveness with which Weildan hastened our way through the black streets.

Nor did I appear to notice when he wiped his hands on his handkerchief and hastily thrust the cloth back into his pocket.

It might have embarrassed him to explain the presence of those red stains. . . .

I should have suspected then, should have abandoned the project at once. But I could not know, when Weildan proposed a ride into the desert the following morning, that our destination was to be the tomb.

It was so casually arranged. Two horses, bearing a light lunch in the saddlebags; a small tent "against the midday heat" Weildan said—and we cantered off, alone. No more fuss or preparation about it than if we were planning a picnic. Our hotel rooms were still engaged, and not a word was said to anyone.

We rode out of the gates into the calm, unrippled sands that stretched beneath a sky of bucolic blue. For an hour or so we jogged on through serene, if searing, sunlight. Weildan's manner was preoccupied, he continually scanned the monotonous horizon as though seeking some expected landmark; but there was nothing in his bearing to indicate his full intention.

We were almost upon the stones before I saw them; a great cluster of white boulders outcropping from the sandy sides of a little hillock. Their form seemed to indicate that the visible rocks formed an infinitesimal fragment of the stones concealed by the shifting sands; though there was nothing in the least unusual about their size, contour, or formation. They rested casually enough in the hillside, no differently than a dozen other small clusters we had previously passed.

Weildan said nothing beyond suggesting that we dismount, pitch the small tent, and lunch. He and I pegged in the stakes, lugged a few small, flat stones inside to serve as table and chairs; placing our pack-blankets as padding for the latter.

Then, as we ate, Weildan exploded his bombshell. The rocks before our tent, he averred, concealed the entrance to the tomb. Sand and wind and desert dust had done their work well, hidden the sanctuary from interlopers. His native accomplice, led by hints and rumors, had uncovered the spot in ways he did not seem anxious to mention.

But the tomb was there. Certain manuscripts and screeds bore testimony to the fact it would be unguarded. All we need do would be to roll away the few boulders blocking the entrance and descend. Once again he earnestly emphasized the fact that there would be no danger to me.

I played the fool no longer. I questioned him closely. Why would a priest of Sebek be buried in such a lonely spot?

Because, Weildan affirmed, he and his retinue were probably fleeing south at the time of his death. Perhaps he had been expelled from his temple by a new pharaoh; then, too, the priests were magic-workers and sorcerers in latter days, and often persecuted or driven out of the cities by irate citizenry. Fleeing, he had died and been interred here.

That, Weildan further explained, was the reason for the scarcity of such mummies. Ordinarily, the perverted cult of Sebek buried its priests only under the secret vaults of its city temples. These shrines had all been long destroyed. Therefore, it was only in rare circumstances like this that an expelled priest was laid away in some obscure spot where his mummy might still be found.

"But the jewels?" I persisted.

The priests were rich. A fleeing wizard would carry his wealth. And at death it would naturally be buried with him. It was a peculiarity of certain renegade sorcerous priests to be mummified with vital organs intact—they had some superstition about earthly resurrection. That was why the mummy would prove an unusual find. Probably the chamber was just a stone-walled hollow housing the mummy case; there would be no time to invoke or conjure any curses or other outlandish abracadabra such as I seemed to fear. We could enter freely, and secure the spoils. In the following of such a priest there surely were several expert temple craftsmen who would embalm the body properly; it needed skill to do a good job without removing the vital organs, and religious significance made this final operation imperative. Therefore we need not worry about finding the mummy in good condition.

Weildan was very glib. Too glib. He explained how easily we would smuggle the mummy case wrapped in our tent-folds; how he would arrange to smuggle both it and the jewels out of the country with the help of a native exporting firm.

He pooh-poohed each objection that I stated; and knowing that whatever his personal character as a man might be he was still a recognized archeologist, I was forced to concede his authority.

There was only one point which vaguely troubled me—his casual reference to some superstition concerning earthly resurrection. The burial of a mummy with organs intact sounded strange. Knowing what I did about the activities of the priests in connection with goetic and sorcerous rituals, I was leery of even the faintest possibility of mishap.

Still, he persuaded me at the last, and following lunch we left the tent. We found the boulders no great hindrance. They had been placed artfully, but we discovered their appearance of being firmly imbedded in rock to be deceptive. A few heavings and clearing away of minor debris enabled us to remove four great stones which formed a block before a black opening which slanted down into the earth.

We had found the tomb!

With the realization, with the sight of that gaping, gloomy pit before me, old horrors rose to mock and grin. I remembered all of the dark, perverted faith of Sebek; the minglings of myth, fable, and grimacing reality which should not be.

I thought of underground rites in temples now given to dust; of posturing worship before great idols of gold—man-shaped figures bearing the heads of crocodiles. I recalled the tales of darker parallel worships, bearing the same relationship as satanism now does to Christianity; of priests who invoked animal-headed gods as demons rather than as benignant deities. Sebek was such a dual god, and his priests had given him blood to drink. In some temples there were vaults, and in these vaults were eidolons of the god shaped as a golden crocodile. The beast had hinged and barbed jaws, into which maidens were flung. Then the maw was closed, and ivory fangs rended the sacrifice so that blood might trickle down the golden throat and the god be appeased. Strange powers were conferred by these offerings, evil boons granted the priests who thus sated beastlike lusts. It was small wonder that such men were driven from their temples, and that those sanctuaries of sin had been destroyed.

Such a priest had fled here, and died. Now he rested beneath, protected by the wrath of his ancient patron. This was my thought, and it did not comfort me.

Nor was I heartened by the noxious vaporing which now poured out from the opening in the rocks. It was not the reek of decay, but the almost palpable odor of unbelievable antiquity. A musty fetor, choking and biting, welled forth and coiled in strangling gusts about our throats.

Weildan bound a handkerchief over his nose and mouth, and I followed suit.

His pocket flashlight flicked on, and he led the way. His reassuring smile was drowned in the gloom as he descended the sloping rock floor which led into the interior passageway.

I followed. Let him be the first; should there be any falling rock traps, any devices of protection to assail interlopers, he would pay the penalty for temerity, not I. Besides, I could glance back at the reassuring spot of blue limned by the rocky opening.

But not for long. The way turned, wound as it descended. Soon we walked in shadows that clustered about the faint torch-beam which alone broke the nighted dimness of the tomb.

Weildan had been correct in his surmise; the place was merely a long rocky cavern leading to a hastily burrowed inner room. It was there that we found the slabs covering the mummy case. His face shone with triumph as he turned to me and pointed excitedly.

It was easy—much too easy, I realize now. But we suspected nothing. Even I was beginning to lose my initial qualms. After all, this was proving to be a very prosaic business; the only unnerving element was the gloom—and one would encounter such in any ordinary mining shaft.

I lost all fear, finally. Weildan and I tilted the rock slabs to the floor, stared at the handsome mummy case beneath. We eased it out and stood it against the wall. Eagerly the professor bent to examine the opening in the rocks which had held the sarco-phagus. It was empty.

"Strange!" he muttered. "No jewels! Must be in the case."

We laid the heavy wooden covering across the rocks. Then the professor went to work. He proceeded slowly, carefully, break-ing the seals, the outer waxing. The design on the mummy case was very elaborate, inlaid with gold leaf and silver patterns which highlighted the bronze patina of the painted face. There were many minute inscriptions and hieroglyphs which the ar-cheologist did not attempt to begin deciphering.

"That can wait," he said. "We must see what lies within."

It was some time before he succeeded in removing the first covering. Several hours must have elapsed, so delicately and carefully did he proceed. The torch was beginning to lose its power; the battery ran low.

The second layer was a smaller replica of the first, save that its pictured face was more exact as to detail. It seemed to be an attempt to duplicate conscientiously the true features of the priest within.

"Made in the temple," Weildan explained. "It was carried on the flight."

We stooped over, studying the countenance in the failing light. Abruptly, yet simultaneously, we made a strange discovery. The pictured face was eyeless!

"Blind," I commented.

Weildan nodded, then stared more closely. "No," he said. "The priest was not blind, if this portraiture is correct. His eyes were *plucked out!*"

I stared into torn sockets which confirmed this gruesome truth. Weildan pointed excitedly to a row of hieroglyphic figures which ornamented the side of the case. They showed the priest in the throes of death upon a couch. Two slaves with pincers hovered over him.

A second scene showed the slaves tearing his eyes from his head. In a third, the slaves were depicted in the act of inserting some shining objects into the now empty sockets. The rest of the series were scenes or funeral ceremonies, with an ominous corcodile-headed figure in the background—the god Sebek.

"Extraordinary," was Weildan's comment. "Do you understand the implication of those pictures? They were made *before* the priest died. They show that he *intended* to have his eyes removed before death, and those objects inserted in their place. Why would he willingly subject himself to such torture? What are those shining things?"

"The answer must be within," I answered.

Without a word, Weildan fell to work. The second covering was removed. The torch was flickering as it died. The third covering confronted us. In almost absolute blackness the professor worked, fingers moving deftly with knife and pryer as he broke the final seals. In the yellow half-light the lid swung up, open.

We saw the mummy.

A wave of vapor rose out of the case—a terrific odor of spice and gases which penetrated the handkerchiefs bound round nose and throat. The preservative power of those gaseous emanations was evidently enormous, for the mummy was not wrapped or shrouded. A naked, shriveled brown body lay before us, in a surprising state of preservation. But this we saw for only an instant. After that, we riveted our attention elsewhere—upon the eyes, or the place where they had been.

Two great yellow disks burned up at us through the darkness. Not diamonds or sapphires or opals were they, or any known stone; their enormous size precluded any thought of inclusion in a common category. They were not cut or faceted, yet they blinded with their brightness—a fierce flashing stabbed our retinas like naked fire.

These were the jewels we sought—and they had been worth seeking. I stooped to remove them, but Weildan's voice restrained me.

"Don't," he warned. "We'll get them later, without harming the mummy."

I heard his voice as though from afar. I was not conscious of again standing erect. Instead I remained stooped over those flaming stones. I stared at them.

They seemed to be growing into two yellow moons. It fascinated me to watch them—all my senses seemed to focus on their beauty. And they in turn focused their fire on me, bathing my brain in heat that soothed and numbed without scorching pain. My head was on fire.

I could not look away, but I did not wish to. These jewels were fascinating.

Dimly came Weildan's voice. I half felt him tugging at my shoulder.

"Don't look." His voice was absurd in its excited tones. "They aren't—natural stones. Gifts of the gods—that's why the priest had them replaced for eyes as he died. They're hypnotic . . . that theory of resurrection. . . ."

I half realized that I brushed the man off. But those jewels commanded my senses, compelled my surrender. Hypnotic? Of course they were—I could feel that warm yellow fire flooding my blood, pulsing at my temples, stealing toward my brain. The torch was out now, I knew, and yet the whole chamber was bathed in flashing yellow radiance from those dazzling eyes. Yellow radiance? No—a glowing red; a bright scarlet luminance in which I read a message.

The jewels were *thinking!* They had mind, or rather, a will—a will that sucked my senses away even as it flooded over me—a will that made me forget body and brain alike in an effort to lose myself in the red ecstasy of their burning beauty. I wanted to drown in the fire; it was leading me out of myself, so that I felt as though I were rushing toward the jewels—into them—into something else—

And then I was free. Free, and blind in darkness. With a start I realized that I must have fainted. At least I had fallen down, for I was now lying on my back against the stone floor of the cavern. Against stone? No—against wood.

That was strange. I could feel wood. The mummy lay in wood. I could not see. The mummy was blind.

I felt my dry, scaly, leprously peeling skin.

My mouth opened. A voice—a dust-choked voice that was my own but not my own—a voice that came from death shrieked, "Good God! *I'm in the mummy's body!*"

I heard a gasp, the sound of a falling shape striking the rocky floor. Weildan.

But what was that other rustling sound? *What wore my shape?*

That damned priest, enduring torture so that his dying eyes might hold hypnotic jewels god-given for the hope of eternal resurrection; buried with easy access to the tomb! Jeweled eyes had hypnotized me, we had changed forms, and now *he walked.*

The supreme ecstasy of horror was all that saved me. I raised myself blindly on shriveled limbs, and rotting arms clawed madly at my forehead, seeking what I knew must rest there. My dead fingers tore the jewels from my eyes.

Then I fainted.

The awakening was dreadful, for I knew not what I might find. I was afraid to be conscious of myself—of my body. But warm flesh housed my soul again, and my eyes peered through yellowed blackness. The mummy lay in its case, and it was hideous to note the empty eye sockets staring up; the dreadful confirmation afforded by the changed positions of its scabrous limbs.

Weildan rested where he had fallen, face empurpled in death.

The shock had done it, no doubt.

Near him were the sources of the yellow luminance—the evil, flaring fire of the twin jewels.

That was what saved me; tearing those monstrous instruments of transference from my temples. Without the thought of the mummy-mind behind them they evidently did not retain their permanent power. I shuddered to think of such a transference in open air, where the mummy body would immediately crumble into decay without being able to remove the jewels. Then would the soul of the priest of Sebek indeed arise to walk the earth, and resurrection be accomplished. It was a terrible thought.

I scooped up the jewels hastily and bound them into my handkerchief. Then I left, leaving Weildan and the mummy as they lay; groping my way to the surface with the aid of illumination afforded me by matches.

It was very good to see the nighted skies of Egypt, for dusk had fallen by this time.

When I saw this *clean* dark, the full nightmare force of my recent experience in the evil blackness of that tomb struck me anew, and I shrieked wildly as I ran across the sand toward the little tent that stood before the opening.

There was whisky in the saddle packs; I brought it out, and thanked heaven for the oil lamp I uncovered. I must have been delirious for a while, I fancy. I put a mirror up on the tent wall, and stared into it for a full three minutes to reassure myself as to identity. Then I brought out the portable typewriter and set it up on the table slab.

It was only then that I realized my subconscious intention to set down the truth. For a while I debated with myself—but sleep was impossible that evening, nor did I intend to return across the desert by night. At last, some elements of composure returned.

I typed this screed.

Now, then, the tale is told. I have returned to my tent to type these lines, and tomorrow I shall leave Egypt forever behind me

—leave that tomb, after sealing it again so that no one shall ever find the accursed entrance to those subterranean halls of horror.

As I write, I am grateful for the light which drives away the memory of noisome darkness and shadowed sound; grateful, too, for the mirror's reassuring image that erases the thought of that terrifying moment when the jeweled eyes of Sebek's priest stared out at me and I *changed.* Thank God I clawed them out in time!

I have a theory about those jewels—they were a definite trap. It is ghastly to think of the hypnosis of a dying brain three thousand years ago; hypnosis willing the urge to live as the suffering priest's eyes were torn out and the jewels placed in the sockets. Then the mind held but one thought—to live, and usurp flesh again. The dying thought, transmitted and held by the jewels, was retained by them through the centruies until the eyes of a discoverer would meet them. Then the thought would flash out, from the dead, rotted brain to the living jewels—the jewels that hypnotized the gazer and forced him into that terrible exchange of personality. The dead priest would assume man's form, and the man's consciousness be forced into the mummy's body. A demoniacally clever scheme—and to think that *I* came near to being that man!

I have the jewels; must examine them. Perhaps the museum authorities at Cairo can classify them; at any rate they're valuable enough. But Weildan's dead; I must never speak of the tomb—how can I explain the matter? Those two stones are so curious that they are bound to cause comment. There is something extraordinary about them, though poor Weildan's tale of the god bestowing them is too utterly preposterous. Still, that color change is most unusual; and the life, the hypnotic glow within them!

I have just made a startling discovery. I unwrapped the gems from my handkerchief just now and looked at them. They seem to be still alive!

Their glow is unchanged—they shine as luminously here under the electric torch as they did in the darkness; as they did in the ruined sockets of that shriveled mummy. Yellow they are, and looking at them I receive that same intuitive prescience of inner, alien life. Yellow? No—now they are reddening—coming to a point. I should not look; it's too reminiscent of that other time. But they are, they must be, hypnotic.

Deep red now, flaming furiously. Watching them I feel warmed, bathed in fire that does not burn so much as it caresses. I don't mind now; it's a pleasant sensation. No need to look away.

No need—unless . . . *Do those jewels retain their power even when they are not in the sockets of the mummy's eyes?*

I feel it again—they must—I don't want to go back into the body of the mummy—I cannot remove the stones and return to my own form now—removing them imprisoned the thought in the jewels.

I must look away. I can type, I can think—but those eyes before me, they swell and grow . . . look away.

I cannot! Redder—redder—I must fight them, keep from going under. Red thought now; I feel nothing—must fight. . . .

I can look away now. I've beaten the jewels. I'm all right.

I can look away—*but I cannot see.* I've gone blind! Blind—the jewels are gone from the sockets—*the mummy is blind.*

What has happened to me? I am sitting in the dark, typing blind. Blind, like the mummy! I feel as though something has happened; it's strange. My body seems lighter.

I know now.

I'm in the body of the mummy. I know it. The jewels—the thought they held—*and now, what is rising to walk from that open tomb?*

It is walking into the world of men. It will wear my body, and it will seek blood and prey for sacrifice in its rejoicing at resurrection.

And I am blind. Blind—and *crumbling!*

The air—it's causing disintegration. Vital organs intact, Weildan said, but I cannot breathe. I can't see. Must type—warn. Whoever sees this must know the truth. Warn.

Body going fast. Can't rise now. Cursed Egyptian magic. Those jewels! Someone must kill thing from the tomb.

Fingers—so hard to strike keys. Don't work properly. Air getting them. Brittle. Blind fumble. Slower. Must warn. Hard to pull carriage back.

Can't strike higher case letters anymore. can't capitalize. fingers going fast. crumbling away in air. in mummy now no air. crumbling to bits. dust fingers going must warn against thing magic sebek fingers grope stumps almost gone hard to strike.

damned sebek sebek sebek mind all dust sebek sebe seb seb seb se s sssssss s s s. . . .

PART II
OTHER LANDS, OTHER CULTURES

CHARLIE

by TALMAGE POWELL

The Mayan civilization, which flourished on the Yucatán peninsula a thousand years before Christ, was one of several in the Western Hemisphere which mummified its dead. Archeological expeditions in Mexico and Central America have uncovered pyramidal tombs in which mummies were placed on low stone biers sheeted with gold and surrounded with statues of feathered snakes, delicate pottery, and limestone jars of food. But no archeological expedition prior to that co-led by Marla Stone ever uncovered a mummy quite like the ugly little boy she calls "Charlie."

For Charlie, according to the legend handed down through a thousand generations of Kukulcanites in the primitive jungle of Guatemala, is Queaxtouxtl, the little prince from the seed of darkness. Both he and the sister who would be his wife, it is said, were fashioned by The Others— a race from beyond the stars which came in a black bubble that ate the light. A strange creation, Charlie; a terrifying creation whose eyes are "a blackness without bottom, a nothingness expression of anti-Life, anti-Light, anti-Spirit." Like Marla Stone, you may not soon forget him . . .

Talmage Powell has had a long and distinguished career as a professional writer, and has to his credit an enviable list of accomplishments. In his own words: "First sale in 1943, a mystery novelette that was cover-featured in a pulp. To date about five hundred short stories and novelettes,

429

various categories, in national magazines. Some two hundred of the total appeared in pulp magazines, mostly mystery and western. Sixteen books published; also ghosted four novels. Ten visual media credits, stories and/ or scripts to motion pictures and television. Stories and books reprinted in all languages of western Europe. About thirty-five short stories have been anthologized in soft- and hard-cover." It may be added that he is also an expert practitioner of the macabre story, as "Charlie" (and dozens of appearances in the best of the "shudder pulps," Dime Mystery) clearly demonstrates.

CHARLIE CAME up out of the depths of her sleep, a gray mist taking small human form in the langorous Guatemalan night. She herself was in the dream, sitting cross-legged in her tent, face uplifted, watching the shifting change in the heavy blackness and wondering at first what it was all about.

And there was Charlie, struggling up from the pit to stand before her. In her dream state, she felt not the slightest twinge of alarm. In dreams, little boy mummies who go bump in the night are perfectly acceptable. Mummification had accented all his features, bringing out an ebonized aspect even if originally there had been none. He was ugly . . . ugly . . . and yet she felt the strongest compulsion to stretch out the maternal warmth of her fingertips and touch him. She sensed that he'd had a devilish time getting through to her. He was, after all, only about four years old—three thousand years old—and rather forlorn in his clinging tatters of long-decayed mummy wrappings.

"We found you, Charlie. Dr. Pangborn and I."

"Be grateful for the privilege."

"We searched long and hard for you. Not really you. Actually we didn't expect to find a little boy and girl in the old minipyramid tomb."

"I know."

"The exquisite little carving of time-blackened limestone . . . the ancient amulet the Quinch woman was wearing about her neck . . . it was our first tangible clue after weeks of searching the mountains and valleys, the forgotten glens and forests of Guatemala, Charlie. We were about to give up and return to civilization when we came to the village. It was beside the muddy little river Patchutx. There we saw the woman wearing the amulet, the artifact from a civilization that flourished when my race were savages in Europe."

"Your race continues in the original state."

"Now is that nice, Charlie?"

"I don't have to be nice to anyone," Charlie said. "I am a prince."

"My! Aren't we the snotty little brat!"

"Would you like to lose your head with that kind of talk? But I choose to care not for your opinion. Only that you came. It was written, of course."

"The amulet? The woman? She said her man had found the trinket in the Valley of Chauxtl. He refused to speak to us, that man of hers, and drew her away. Never mind. Our blood sang. We came to the valley, certain in our sense of discovery. As if an unseen finger pointed the way, we found the mini-pyramid . . . all this was written?"

"On the scrolls of Cacacluthcin," Charlie said as if he were about to pat back a yawn.

"I have never heard of the scrolls, Charlie."

"Your ignorance is deplorable."

"The scrolls . . . you must tell me . . ."

"I am beginning to feel bored," Charlie said.

And with that, there was a confused blurring in the dream. Where was Dr. Pangborn? The tough old archeologist should be here. No . . . he was on his way to Guatemala City and medical attention. He'd tripped on rubble and fractured his right arm badly at the dig site yesterday. Bitterly disappointed, he would have to leave the site almost at the moment of discovery. He'd picked two of the Indian laborers to accompany him in one of the Land Rovers. He'd argued against Marla staying at the site in his absence. She had accepted none of that nonsense. She'd explored digs from Angkor Wat to the Indus. She was armed and could shoot as well as any professional guide. She had four of the labor crew remaining with her, recruits from the hardy Qhotan tribe. She had the second Land Rover and plenty of supplies. Abandon the site for even a precious hour? Never on your life! She would have the mini-pyramid half cleared and catalogued when Dr. Pangborn returned with his arm in a cast a few days from now.

She stirred. She would explain the situation. "Charlie . . ."

But he was gone.

A light slashed her eyes, a silence crashed against her ears, and Marla Stone reared up on her canvas cot fighting for a breath. She clutched the cot railing during the moment her mind was sorting dream from reality. . . .

For eleven days they had worked their way along a dim Indian trail that wound through the valley, at one point fording the shallow stream called Chauxtl.

"The fellow who found the amulet had to come down this trail," Dr. Pangborn had reasoned. "At some point he turned aside to forage for food—and found the artifact." He'd scanned the primeval terrain, stretches of lowland jungle broken here and there by volcanic outcroppings. "Thank heaven for the Land Rovers!"

The twelfth day, ranging south of the trail, Marla's experienced gaze had noted the unnatural contours of a viny tangle. She'd slammed the Land Rover to a halt, jumped from the seat, and, assisted by two of the Indian crew, parted the morass of dead and green vines. Then she was whipping out the walkie-talkie antenna and gasping into the mike, "Dr. Pangborn . . . quickly! I've found rubble, ruins . . ."

By nightfall, they'd dropped exhausted at the campsite cleared and readied by a pair of the Qhotans. "Hardly anything left," Dr. Pangborn had said. "The jungle has reclaimed the farmlands, the streets, but it must have been a bustling little community, about three thousand years ago."

Hardly anything left . . . little had he known, that first night. The next day, today . . . no, now it was yesterday, Marla had discovered the small pyramid, a weedy crown on a low promontory east of the ruins. In an unreal haze of excitement, their machetes had hacked, their shovels and pickaxes had clanged, their levers had pried. "Carefully now . . ." And when the weathered limestone slab slid away, opening the cramped smallness of the entrance, their electric torches had probed into a three-thousand-year-old darkness . . . fingering the rearing statue of a feathered snake, limestone jars of food, delicately wrought pottery—and a low stone bier, sheeted with beaten gold, wherea small boy and girl had lain side by side for three millenia.

It had been a moment beyond words, of simply staring and savoring a delicious giddiness. The immediate aftermath had been far less pleasant, Dr. Pangborn tripping, falling in the outside rubble as he'd rushed off for tools and camera. Sitting up with his creased, tough old face white from shock, cradling the broken arm with his left hand.

After his departure, Marla had worked inside the tomb, setting ranging poles, taking detailed pictures, calipering measurements, choosing samplings for carbon-14 dating. At day's end, she'd given the order for the removal of the little boy mummy. An obsessive desire to have him near had built within her. She ordered him placed on a low folding table in her tent.

Now, staring at the brightness of a new day that showed silver bands about the tent flap, her body steadied as the residue of the dream about Charlie faded.

She snapped her face about. Charlie of course was still there, right where they'd placed him. A tingling sensation began to crawl through her, unpleasantly. His sharp-visaged, blackened and saturnine little face was turned toward her, as if she was being studied by the black nothingness of the eyes. Charlie had moved during the night . . .

She sat stupefied, swallowing a dust-dryness. Am I losing my mind? She jerked her gaze away. In a froth, she thought: My imagination . . . whipped up to too fine an edge by the discovery of the tomb, Dr. Pangborn's accident, the sense of isolation after he was gone, the bone-rattling tiredness from too long a day, the dream. Cool it, Marla.

She swung her feet from the cot and reached for her hiking

boots. They were atop the footlocker at the head of the cot. She upended the chukkas and shook, making sure a scorpion hadn't taken up squatter's rights. She had slept in poplin walking shorts and shirt after a tired sponging in the eddies of a nearby pool, where a rock formation partially dammed the stream.

Bending to fasten her shoe straps, she began to feel the quietness of the day. Too quiet. No sounds of movement. No back-and-forth banter in the Qhotan dialect.

She flung back the tent flap. The clearing lay before her. Empty. The small, two-man sleeping tents crouched limply. The portable table and folding canvas chairs, the Coleman stove, the pair of lanterns, the tins of food and water canteens were all arranged neatly in the center of the clearing, like a parting message from the departed Qhotans. They had abandoned her, but stolen nothing.

She clung to the tent post. Why? What had caused the secretive slipping away of nonthieves in the night?

She took comfort from the sight of the remaining Land Rover and the gasoline cans lashed to its rear. She didn't relish the thought of the trip out alone, but she could manage. Rejoin Dr. Pangborn in Guatemala City. Recruit a fresh crew. Be back here in a matter of a few days.

And leave Charlie? Charlie and the little girl mummy who continued her eternal sleep in the small pyramid?

No way. The first passing native would help himself to everything at the deserted campsite. Including Charlie. Charlie would be passed from hand to hand, trader to trader, until he finally arrived at . . . where? Some tourist-trap curio shop?

Charlie and the little girl . . . archeological discovery of the century. Their pyramid, their embalming and wrapping reflected Egyptian influence. Here were first proofs at last of the theory Marla had long held, that Mayan civilization did not magically appear on the Yucatán peninsula a thousand years before Christ. Civilization was an inheritable, loanable, borrowable product of the human family. As in the case of Sumerian to Greek to Roman to northern European civilization of another cut had spread from Egypt to the western edges of Africa and across the Atlantic on the wings of the westerlies. Modern adventurers had reproduced the ancient boats of reed and wood and retraced long-forgotten routes across both major oceans. Perhaps the tales of Egyptian forebears had been told in Mayan writings. Who could say? The Spanish conquistadores had destroyed Mayan libraries as works of the devil, and the surviving remnants of Mayan literature had not yet been deciphered.

Marla turned, her mind zeroing on plans for loading the Land Rover. She wouldn't need much food. Little water. In the valleys between the towering volcanic peaks, Guatemala was verdant and well-watered. Lakes glittered in extinct volcanic craters. Streams spilled for miles down through thick green bowers to feed the lower-level jungles of hardwood, sapodilla, cacao, wild orchids, morasses of vines, wild bananas, underbrush, mangrove.

"Well, Charlie, I propose we take a ride, you and I and the little princess."

Standing over the gargoylean little mummy, she once more experienced the senseless sensation that he'd moved, was about to move.

Vagrant thoughts flicked, like impossible, out-of-season fireflies. Modern man . . . devotion to a materialism he called science. Ancient Egypt . . . far longer, through nearly forty dynasties, more than three thousand years devoted to the study of death, afterdeath, a nonmaterialism called science. . . . A person . . . lump of chemicals? . . . or the weightless force called Life?

Charlie, so small, so incredibly long in the tomb. Was he the repository of a power as unknown to Dr. Pangborn as electricity had been to Charlie's parents?

There were wheat kernels . . . yes, taken from an Egyptian tomb . . . that began to grow when exposed to fresh air and sunlight.

He's not a wheat kernel. He's a mummy.

And what is a mummy? We're making mummies right now in the good old U. S. of A. Not many. One now and then. Someone who believes and can afford the expenses of believing. Sufferers from incurable diseases frozen solid in tanks of liquid nitrogen to await the day of revival when the cures have been achieved. Mummies all, whether swathed in linen strips or nitrous ice. So what are the chances of it working? Maybe the secret doubters had asked the same question the day Charlie was sealed in total darkness to await his day.

" 'Allo!''

Marla gasped and slammed upright against the canvas slope of the tent.

Nothing. Silence.

"My God, have I started hearing voices?"

" 'Allo in there. Don't let me frighten you. It is I, a friend.''

She let out a breath, lifted the heavy thirty-ought-six repeating rifle from its tent-pole sling, and stepped outside. Framed against the tent, she was an attractive image, lithe, leggy, tanned. Nicely put together face. Tousled, short black hair. And capable looking. Even dangerous, with the rifle cradled in the crook of her elbow.

The man in the center of the clearing looked at the gun and stood cautiously, making no move. He was an Indian of about thirty-five, lean, fit, light-toned mahogony. He looked rather ordinary in rough white-gray blouse and pantaloon, huaraches, and straw hat with a wide, floppy brim. Rather commonplace—except for the black reflections in the large, almond-shaped eyes.

"I am Somato," he said. He moved his right hand in a small gesture. "Please . . . the gun . . .''

"The gun is no threat," Marla said, "to my friends.''

"I am that. Verdad! Your friend.'' He peeled the hat off the thick, coarse Indian hair and bent his body in a bow.

His movement dangled a fine golden neck chain. Marla's hands tightened on the gun. Sunlight caught in the swing of his neck chain amulet, the crest of the god Kukulcan. Older than three thousand years, Kukulcan was today's god in the hidden corners of Guatemala.

"I chanced upon one of your people," Somato said.

Liar, Marla thought; I'll bet you have watched us for days, priest of Kukulcan. And you came out of the night and spoke a word, and the Qhotans all ran away.

"The man I met," Somato ventured a step closer, "told me of your discoveries—and the accident. It is an evil place. Was his arm badly broken?"

"Yes."

"Too bad. All my wishes for his good health."

"Thank you. Now, I have a great deal to do."

"Is it not always so? I will be of help."

She shifted the gun an inch. "I can manage."

His intense gaze lifted from the gun barrel. "But I insist! You are the stranger, in my land. How can I be other than . . . how you say . . . hospitable?"

"You speak English quite well."

"I am in and out of Mazatenango where there are English speakers. I learn everything I can. I am interested in all things. Can I help being interested in your safety?" His face hovered, innocuous, foolish, except for the eyes.

His veiled threat brought a silence. Studying him, Marla knew he was here for a purpose and was not going to be easily discouraged. He appeared to be unarmed, even though men did not travel these remote pathways defenseless. He'd stashed machete or gun close by, wanting to allay quick fears or suspicions by making an unarmed appearance.

She felt the weight of the rifle for reassurance. Once the Land Rover was loaded, she would drive off and leave him, at gunpoint. No matter how tireless his legs, he could never overtake a motor vehicle.

Meanwhile, was he alone?

Somato had drawn several steps closer under her sharp, cold-eyed gaze. His perfect teeth flashed as he smiled.

"Please," he spread his hands, "you must accept my friendship. This is no place for a lone woman. You are surely self-reliant. But you are also—if I may say—very attractive. There are men without principles who would . . . well, you know what I mean. It would be my pleasure to help you secure the camp and drive you out in the Land Rover."

He flung up a palm as she started to speak. "Not so," he said amiably, "I will not hear any ladylike protests. Later, you and Dr. Pangborn can return with a fresh crew of diggers. Perhaps, then, you will have friendly thoughts of Somato."

Don't force the issue prematurely, she cautioned herself. Don't paint either yourself or him into a corner. You must have time to prepare for departure.

She seemed to relax. Her lips hinted a smile. "Have you had breakfast, Señor Somato? I haven't."

His friendly laugh rang out. He rushed to the camp table in the center of the clearing. "It is my pleasure!" His hands darted about the tinned goods. "Would you have some sausage? Flapjacks with honey?"

"I said I hadn't had breakfast. I didn't say I was very hungry."

"Ah, but coffee! By all means. I see you have Guatemalan coffee, the rich dark beans grown high on the mountain slopes." He began pumping up pressure in the small fuel tank of the Coleman stove.

She kept him in the periphery of her vision as she washed up from a tin basin outside her tent and brushed the night-tousle from the dark thickness of her hair.

The clearing filled with the pleasant aroma of coffee, and a tin cup was before her, steaming, as she sat down across the table from him.

"Must you keep the gun on your knees, señorita?"

"Yes," she said, "I must."

He rocked back, relaxed, good-natured, seemingly indolent. "So be it. I have no fears, although I am a gentle man and the sight of firearms I find unpleasant. You would use the gun only in—how you say—extreme circumstances. Against an enemy. And I am your friend."

He was, at least, another human presence, and the coffee warmed a chill that was in her despite the growing heat of the humid day.

He looked at her over the rim of his coffee cup. "You found the pyramid."

A quick alarm flicked through her. The artifacts still in the pyramid . . . the little girl mummy . . . had Somato already . . .

He read her thought in her eyes, and broke in: "I have touched nothing, señorita. I have not entered the tomb. You should not have done so. The tomb never should have been opened."

"Why not?"

He shrugged. "There are words best never spoken, deeds best left undone, dark places best without light."

"Perhaps, in some cases. But this time, Señor Somato, I'm sure you are wrong."

He studied her, a flicker of regret in his deep, glistening eyes. "How was it you came to this place, señorita?"

"In the course of my work."

"But the world is wide. There are so many places you could explore. Why the lowlands of Guatemala?"

"I've been interested in Mayan culture, at long range, for a long time," she said. "Dr. Pangborn of course is the authority on Mayan antiquities. I met him several years ago when he was in the United States on a lecture tour and I was doing postgrad work. We corresponded, reams of it, while I did a lot of work in various places. Finally, the opportunity . . . and I came to Guatemala. It's a lovely country, Señor Somato—the ancient volcanic cones that tower thirteen thousand feet, the lushness of the lowlands. Beauty and mystery everywhere, in the jungle wilderness, in the tucked-away tribes untouched by time. Much beauty—except for the poverty."

"The poor continue," he said. "The rich, the kings, the powerful, they come, they enjoy, they go. The poor are forever. You must be very rich, renting expensive Land Rovers, equipping an expedition."

"I wish I were. Truth is, I joined Dr. Pangborn through a complicated morass of red tape. There was some grant money available at the National Endowment. There was a board of trustees who might have access to some of the money. There was a blooming army of bureaucrats in Washington who had to be convinced that a dig in Guatemala would be worth the price tag. You have to hang in there, cut the tapes one at a time."

Somato lifted the pot from the Coleman burner and topped

off their cups. "Now you will be famous—if you succeed in making your revelation to the world."

He was begging her, and he was warning her. She must not take Charlie away. But, she thought, there will be a revelation only if I get Charlie out. Without hard evidence, Dr. Pangborn and I will have told only a wives' tale. And if I mess up this chance, there will never be another. Before another expedition can return there'll be no pyramid, no Charlie, no little girl mummy. Somato can bring in a crew and wipe away the evidence, the really important evidence, almost overnight.

"How do you call the little mummy?" he asked. "The Qhotan I met and talked with said you have named him Charlie."

"Why do you ask?"

"Curious. Is there a symbolism?"

He is attuned to symbolism, she thought, this priest of an ageless religion. His omens and portents are everywhere, in the brassiness of a sky before a storm, in the image of a feathered serpent, in the steaming entrails of a sacrificial animal.

She shifted uncomfortably, feeling the total, uncrossable gulf between herself and Somato. Aliens. Products of diametric culture patterns. They might have been beings from diverse planets meeting in this jungle clearing. Each thought of the other as a child of supersition. And what was superstition? Space and time were absolute—until Einstein dismissed the absurd superstition. Would the science of Einstein endure through a period of nearly forty dynasties? Where did one superstition end and another begin? Space was space, until a black hole was discovered in it.

"No symbolism," she answered his question at last. "I really don't know why I called the little fellow Charlie. There was a ventriloquist's dummy in the United States, very famous, named Charlie McCarthy. About the same size as the mummy. There, the resemblance stops. In the hands of his creator, Mr. Bergen, Charlie McCarthy was a happy, very nice little fellow . . ."

"I would like to see the mummy," Somato said, already on his feet. He started across the clearing toward Marla's tent.

She pushed up. "Señor Somato . . ."

Ignoring her, he stepped inside the tent. She ran across the short distance, hands firm on the rifle, and drew up in the inverted V of the tent opening. He had not touched Charlie. He was crouched over the mummy, fingering the amulet on his neck chain and murmuring soft and strange sounds under his breath. As their eyes locked and held, the eyes of Somato and the mummy, Marla caught her breath. It had to be a trick of the lighting, of her imagination. . . . The change in Charlie's eyes was not a glint of Life, not as she knew it. The expanding pupils were a blackness without bottom, a nothingness expression of anti-Life, anti-Light, anti-Spirit.

She backed off, holding the gun in desperately tight fingers, watching Somato. He haunched away from the mummy's side, tore his gaze away, and pushed to his feet. He slipped out into the sunlight and stood on spread, unsteady legs, wiping a hot, oily sheen from his brown face with a bandanna.

"He is Queaxtouxtl," he whispered.

"What?" she asked, keeping a safe distance between Somato and the rifle. "He is who?"

"The little prince from the seed of darkness. The Others . . . they fashioned him and the sister who would be his wife. The children grew like any children—until one day they drank of some water and sickened and died."

"Who were The Others?"

Somato pressed his wadded bandanna against his mouth for a moment. He lowered it slowly. "No one knows. It is said they came from beyond the stars. They came in a black bubble that ate the light. They had no shape or form. They made the two children in the image of our ancestors and went away in their black bubble. . . . It is our legend, handed down through a thousand generations of Kukulcanites."

So was Troy a legend, Marla thought, until somebody thought of digging at the site.

Easing back, she glanced at shafted sunlight in the green of the surrounding jungle. She heard the rustling of a soft breeze. Reassuring realities.

She let herself slip close to the tent flap on a strange compulsion to put herself between Somato and Charlie. "Sometime I'd like to hear the rest of the legend, the details. But right now I must get started."

Somato nodded. "I will start striking the tents."

She started to speak, but he was rushing across the clearing. She watched as he went to one knee and detached the rope anchor from a tent peg.

She had a sense of moving. She saw the loss of sunlight as the shadows within her tent flowed over her. She turned and looked at Charlie. Ugly . . . ugly . . . so ugly he was cute . . . strangely winsome . . . such a defenseless little fellow . . .

She was on her knees beside him. "Charlie . . ."

She imagined a faint stirring of a tattered end among the dessicated wrappings across his chest. She groped a hand backward without taking her eyes from Charlie, feeling through the clutter of a tool chest. She lifted out a calipers. Bit by bit she measured Charlie, repeating the procedure she'd effected yesterday when Charlie had been in his tomb. Fingers, toes, sole to ankle, ankle to knee, knee to hip, fibulal, tibial, femural, ulnal, humerusal.

The rifle lay forgotten. Her mind computerized figures, comparisons of minute variations of measurements. She crouched back on her haunches, hands worrying the calipers while she stared at Charlie.

Growing . . . was he actually beginning to *grow?*

A slight sound caught through her. Marla whirled her face about. Somato's shadow filled the tent opening.

"So you are beginning to understand?" he said in a tight voice. "You must give me the little fellow."

"Charlie? Let you destroy Charlie? You idiot! You don't realize the importance—"

As she snarled out the words, she was grasping for the gun, clutching it, rearing up to her feet. But the Indian was very fast. His shadow enveloped her. His fist caught her on the jaw. Her senses spun. Somato's sweating, set face went out of focus. He had caught hold of the gun. She clung to the weapon, wrestling backward.

Somato's fist crashed hard against her chin. And his face disappeared altogether.

The darkness held; then shards of pain knifed through, a throbbing in her jaw, a pounding in her head. A soft cry parted her lips. Gritty light pushed the darkness away. She pushed up, and a wave of nausea washed through her. She hung on, half risen, propped by stiffened, extended arms. She pulled her face about and looked at the emptiness where Charlie had lain. A wild urgency swept her mind to clarity. Adrenaline poured forth.

Where had Somato taken Charlie? Insane priest of an ancient heathen religion . . . superstition-ridden anachronism who hadn't the slightest idea of what he was doing . . .

She looked quickly about for the gun, and saw it. It was lying on the ground in the back part of the tent. She made a quick movement, then stopped. The gun was twisted, bent. Somato had smashed it across the edge of the foot locker.

Her lips thinned. Okay, pally. She ran outside to the Land Rover, flipped open the narrow metal carrier bolted to its side, and lifted out the one remaining gun. It, too, was a thirty-ought-six. She checked the load and stood scanning the empty campsite. The lowlands jungle about her was suddenly very vast. Colors sprang at her, splotches of yellows, reds, purples strewn through the density of green and brown vines, trellises, thickets and trees. Somato's territory. How could she ever find him?

She worked her way along the perimeter of the clearing, straining for the sight of any hint, a broken twig, a crushed wildflower.

Even in her sharp-eyed state, she almost missed it, almost passed it up. She backed a step, looked a second time, and her hand shot out. Her fingers touched the tiny fragment of decayed mummy-wrapping that clung to a thorn.

As her fingers lifted and ground the bit of decayed cloth to dust, her eyes studied the narrowness where the undergrowth seemed less dense. She shifted the rifle from shoulder strap to two-handed grip and plunged into the pathway.

The dim trail led north, away from the lazy little river, toward higher ground. At times there seemed to be no trail at all, only a burrow through slashing briars and trailing vines. Her breath began to cut into her lungs; she felt the weight of her sweat-blackened shirt with its smothering stickiness. Salty droplets stung the corners of her eyes.

Her vision began to fuzz. She stumbled now and then as she pushed her way through wall after wall of yielding greenery. A great mass of bright plumage on a tree limb far ahead screamed out her foolishness at her.

She half tripped and stayed on her knees, using the rifle as a prop, butt on the ground, her exhausted fingers grasping the end of the barrel near the front sight. Perhaps the screeching macaw was right. She was beaten. She would never see Charlie again. And before Somato let her leave the jungle the little girl mummy would have vanished also.

Ease down . . . just for a moment . . . close your eyes . . . let the touch of a green fern cool your cheek . . .

The macaw was suddenly silent.

Marla lifted her head. What was different? What had changed? She drew a shallow breath, then a deeper one. The air . . . the faintest taint of smoke-smell was in the air.

She pushed downward on the rifle, climbing to her feet. The cessation of the giant parrot's outcries had left an unreal silence, a stillness, a hush.

A twig snapped with a sharp, clear sound as Marla pressed forward. A hundred yards up a steepening slope, and the smoke-smell was stronger. She picked her way, stepping over vines and gnarled upcroppings of giant roots, ducking and brushing her way through twilight patches where the sunlight was shut out.

She saw the first red wink of flame through heavy foliage ahead, and dropped into a crouch, moving on carefully.

She parted a green and pink thicket that smelled of honey-suckle. The cautious movement revealed to her a rocky and volcanic-ash clearing where strata had buckled and thrust when the earth was young. Somato was there, facing away from Marla, backing away a few steps from the heat of his fire. Its first crackling had become a continuous roar. The flames were spewing up to a height equaling Somato's own.

He nodded, as if in satisfaction. He turned, and for a fractured moment it seemed that he looked directly at Marla's face as it hovered in the thicket.

But he was focusing elsewhere. And straining up and forward, Marla saw Charlie. She saw Somato close the distance in half a dozen strides. She saw Somato pick up Charlie. Somato turned once more toward the voracious fire, his face white beneath its brown, his lips moving in frantic supplication.

Legs spread, back arched, Somato slowly lifted Charlie overhead, higher, yet higher, to the full extension of his arms.

And through the roar of the flames Marla listened, as if to a whisper. She heard it, but did not hear it. She felt it, and it was no less real. Charlie was mewling a cry for help, a piteous plea for mercy, a broken note of terror of the flames.

"Somato!"

Somato spun about, holding Charlie high, seeing her tear her way through the brush at the edge of the clearing.

"You were about to throw Charlie into the fire! You heathen . . . you superstitious fool!"

Slightly crouched, she padded toward him. He stared at the gun in her hands, his tongue rimming his dry lips.

"I? I the fool? You know nothing, señorita, only what your microscopes tell you . . . but when you look at brain tissue do you see a thought?"

"Put him down, Somato."

"I will die first. We both may die anyway. He is of the black seed. That part of the legend you heard. The rest you did not. The blackness in him . . ."

"No more, Somato! I will not listen to any more of this nonsense!"

"Then watch as I do what must be done." He turned, for a moment a regal figure in his peon's rough, ill-fitting cotton clothing.

His arms tensed for the casting, the hurling of Charlie into the inferno.

The gun crashed.

Marla felt the sound split through her head. She felt the pressure of her finger on the trigger. She sensed the beating of wings and scurryings and slitherings that swept through the forest in the vane of the alien echoes.

She saw the puff of dust, almost between the shoulder blades, where the high velocity bullet entered Somato and ripped and shattered its way through.

He stumbled, twisting sideways under the impact. His arms broke under Charlie's slight weight. His knees folded. His mouth opened on an unspoken word. He broke at the middle, rolled forward and lay still.

Marla groped her way across the short, stony waste. "Charlie . . ."

She wouldn't look at Somato. She kneeled beside Charlie, turned him onto his back, brushed the smear of dust from his sunken little cheek.

"I'm here, Charlie. Right beside you."

She picked him up gently.

"It's okay, Charlie. Everything is fine now. We'll go back to camp, and no one will disturb us. It's obvious that Somato came alone."

She arose, holding him.

"We'll pretend that Somato never happened. And I'll bring her to you, out of the pyramid, the little girl who belongs at your side."

She turned in the direction of her campsite and walked across the clearing. As Charlie's black-hole eyes passed, the light dimmed faintly. So faintly that Marla's eyes didn't see. The shift in the spectrum was too slight for any human eyes to note.

She carried Charlie away in the maternal cradle of her arms, pressing him tightly to her breast. And his little black-claw hand was curled slightly, childishly, as if to grip her shoulder. But perhaps it was only her own walking motion that caused his hand to do that.

THE WEEKEND MAGUS

by EDWARD D. HOCH

"A mummy? In Scotland?" the narrator of this story asks his host, Sir Richard Forbish, with some amazement. But as Sir Richard, "The Weekend Magus," explains: "Hadrian's Wall was near the Scottish border, but the Wall of Antoninus was well into Scotland. And the Romans certainly ventured north of their walls, or they would not have realized the need for them . . . . I have found evidence that Egyptians accompanied the Romans this far. . . . Cleopatra lived in Rome as Caesar's mistress, and the ties between the two peoples were very great. I believe Egyptian specialists sometimes traveled with the Roman legions—specialists in astronomy, embalming, the building of pyramids."

The evidence found by Sir Richard, on the banks of Loch Awe north of Glasgow, is an earthen burial mound in the shape of a pyramid, containing the mummified remains of a man. It also contained a second mummy, that of a pet, for Egyptians often buried mummified dogs, cats and other animals with their dead rulers. This pet, however, known as Gavia, is quite different than the usual. Quite different.

There are mummies, to coin a phrase, and then there are mummies . . .

For at least a dozen years Edward D. Hoch has been widely recognized as the leading writer of mystery and detective short stories (he received a Mystery Writers of America Edgar Award for "The Oblong Room" in 1967; over the past eight years he has had at least one story, and sometimes two and three, in every issue of the monthly Ellery Queen's Mystery Magazine*). He has published some six hundred stories since he began writing a quarter of a century ago, most of them detective/suspense; but he is also adept in other fields, notably science fiction and horror/fantasy. In addition to his short work he has published four novels and four collections, two of the latter*—The Judges of Hades *and* City of Brass —*featuring his series character Simon Ark, a man who claims to be two thousand years old and who solves mysteries involving the macabre and the supernatural.*

"HE GOES up to Scotland every weekend," Sir Richard's secretary had told me. "Nobody knows what he does there."

I'd come to London to obtain an interview with Sir Richard Forbish for an American newsmagazine, and if I had to follow him to Scotland to get it, that was all right with me too. I flew up to Glasgow on the afternoon plane and rented a car at the airport, getting out just before the weekend rush.

Sir Richard's Scottish retreat was fifty miles northwest of Glasgow, on the banks of Loch Awe. The sun was low in the sky by the time I reached it, and my first impression was only of a country house of modest proportions. The bell was answered not by a gaunt mysterious butler but by a pert young blonde in a tennis tunic. I was beginning to learn what Sir Richard did with his weekends.

"Come in! You must be that American writer who's come to interview Rich."

"Guilty," I admitted. "Is Sir Richard about?"

"Oh, yes." Her accent wasn't quite British. "He's working downstairs. I'll call him." She paused and said, almost as an afterthought, "I'm Minerva Athens. Pleased to meet you." Glancing down at her short white tunic and bare legs she added,

"Rich and I had a game of tennis earlier."

"Charming," I remarked, leaving her to take it however she would.

She vanished through a door to the basement and when she reappeared after a moment she was followed by a tall, slender man who was both younger and handsomer than I'd expected him to look at forty-eight. "Good to see you here," he said, extending his hand.

"It's an honor, Sir Richard," I assured him.

"I don't usually receive journalists here on weekends, you know. I come up here with Minerva to get away from the pressures of London."

Minerva cleared her throat. "Let me slip into something else and I'll get us all a drink."

Sir Richard led me into a massive book-lined study in the best tradition of British manor houses. Seated behind his wide oak desk he seemed to assume the role of eminent man of science for the first time. "I was a bit baffled by your request for an interview," he said. "Is your publication doing a series on non-winners of the Nobel Prize?"

"You must know you're in line for that any year now."

"Perhaps."

"My editors in New York are mainly interested in your experiments with the radioactive dating of archeological sites."

"An interesting field," Sir Richard said. "We've made some astonishing discoveries right here in Scotland."

I reached for my briefcase. "Mind if I record this?"

"I wasn't aware the formal interview had begun. Let us relax with a drink first. Good Scotch always tastes best right here in Scotland."

In a moment Minerva Athens was back, wearing a gold lounging robe. While she went off to fix our drinks I asked Forbish, "Just as general background, what is your marital status?"

"My wife and I are separated. Minerva has been a great help to me in this trying time." His words seemed well rehearsed, as if he'd recited them many times in past months.

"She's a lovely young woman."

"She is that," he agreed.

Minerva returned with the Scotch and sat down to join us. Sir Richard left his desk and took one of the other chairs, reinforcing the informality of the session. "Are these weekends strictly for relaxation or do you manage to get some work in?" I asked.

"I'm working on something downstairs. A hobby of sorts."

"You've been especially successful in dating Egyptian artifacts."

Forbish warmed to his favorite subject. "My technique goes a step beyond carbon dating as practiced elsewhere. Interestingly enough, I've found some artifacts from Roman times right here in Scotland."

"This far north?"

Sir Richard smiled. "Hadrian's Wall was near the Scottish border, but the Wall of Antoninus was well into Scotland. And the Romans certainly ventured north of their walls, or they would not have realized the need for them."

"To keep out the barbarians from the north?"

He nodded and sipped his Scotch. "I have found evidence that Egyptians accompanied the Romans this far."

"What would Egyptians be doing here?"

He motioned toward the woman at his side. "Minerva is one-quarter Egyptian and she is here."

"But—"

"Seriously, Cleopatra lived in Rome as Caesar's mistress, and the ties between the two people were very great. I believe Egyptian specialists sometimes traveled with the Roman legions."

"Specialists in what?"

"Astronomy, embalming, the building of pyramids."

Minerva interrupted with a snort. "This solemn talk bores me. Do you play tennis?"

"Hardly at all," I answered.

"We have an indoor court around back. The house is much larger than it appears at first glance. I'll show you around tomorrow. You will be staying the weekend, won't you?"

"I hadn't planned—"

"Nonsense!" Sir Richard said. "Of course you'll stay!" He gave instructions for Minerva to prepare the guest room.

Later, after an excellent dinner of freshly killed pheasant, she showed me to the room. "He's pleased to have you here," she told me. "He has something very special to show you tomorrow."

In the morning after breakfast Sir Richard and I strolled down the hill to the edge of Loch Awe. I noticed that the rear of the large house overhung the hill, and big double doors provided a level access to the basement. "Is that a garage?" I asked.

"It was built as a boat house. The previous owner had a ramp running down to the water. I've put the space to other use."

"It's a fine clear lake for boating."

"All Scottish lochs are. That's why I love the country so much." He tossed a pebble far into the lake, and I watched the ripples break the calm mirrored surface.

"You're a weekend laird," I suggested.

"More of a weekend magus." His eyes twinkled at the words.

"Just what is it you're doing up here?"

Forbish stared out over the water. "Shortly after I purchased this house I made an amazing discovery. What I found was confirmation of an Egyptian presence here—confirmation in the most vivid manner. It was an earthen burial mound in the shape of a pyramid, containing the mummified remains of a man."

"A mummy? In Scotland?"

"Exactly."

"That's quite a discovery."

"There were the usual personal objects buried with him, and even what I took to be a pet. The Egyptians often buried mummified dogs and cats—even baboons—with their dead rulers."

"You found another tomb of King Tut!"

Sir Richard chuckled. "Hardly! There were no treasures of gold or precious gems. But my experiments with the mummified remains could make the Nobel Prize committee sit up and take notice."

I was beginning to see why this interview was so important to him. He would use it to make some important announcement. Before I could comment he hurried on. "Are you familiar with the experiments of the Americans Harris and Weeks in x-raying the mummies at the Cairo museum?"

"Vaguely."

"The work was carried out ten years ago by the University of Michigan School of Dentistry and yielded a wealth of new information. I attempted to carry the x-ray and radiation experiments a step further."

"With what result?"

He shrugged casually and tossed another pebble. "There is evidence of some reanimation in the bones of one of the subjects."

"What?" I couldn't believe my ears. "Are you talking about bringing a mummy back to life? Shades of Dr. Frankenstein!"

Forbish laughed. "Hardly anything like that. You won't encounter Boris Karloff lurching around the place trailing his wrappings."

"I hope not."

"Part of the Egyptian mummification technique involved the removal of brain matter, usually by metal hooks inserted through the nostrils. After such a procedure any resurrection would be quite impossible."

"Then what—?"

He held up a hand. "All in good time. Do you have a camera?"

"I have a small one in my briefcase, but my editor usually arranges to send a photographer if it's necessary."

"Never mind. Your camera will serve very well. And I've been teaching Minerva to operate my little movie camera."

"When will all this photography take place?"

Sir Richard smiled. "Perhaps this evening."

After lunch I watched them play tennis on the indoor court around the back of the house. Minerva was quite good, and more than a match for Sir Richard. While he disappeared downstairs I went for a stroll with her on the grounds of the estate, along the wooded hill that overlooked Loch Awe.

"What does he have in the basement?" I asked, coming right to the point.

She made a face. "Mummies. He'll show you tonight. That's what he lured you up here for."

"Mummies in Scotland! I can't get over it!"

"Neither can he. It's become an obsession with him—though only a weekend obsession, thank heavens!"

"He spoke of himself as a weekend magus."

"He is that, I suppose. A magus, a necromancer who would communicate with the dead."

"He wants to communicate?"

"Figuratively speaking."

"He mentioned reanimation."

"Yes."

"That implies a return to life."

"Sir Richard is a great man, a great scientist. You must know from your short time with him that he is no madman surrounded by bubbling test tubes and sparking generators."

"He seems quite sane," I agreed cautiously.

"The sanest man I've ever known. He has something here— a discovery whose very existence would be enough to make him famous around the world. And yet he's kept it secret for nearly a year while he's spent his weekends trying for the ultimate breakthrough. You see, he doesn't just want to be famous. He wants the recognition of his colleagues. He wants that prize."

"The Nobel. I gathered as much."

"Will you help him get it?"

"I'm only a poor journalist."

"But your magazine is one of the most important in America! This is not just any story he's giving you. It's the story of a lifetime!" She took a deep breath. "Can you get him a cover photograph?"

"If he can make a mummy walk, I'll get him his cover."

She turned to stare at me. "It will not walk, but I don't think you'll be disappointed."

We dined as we had the night before, by candlelight in the ornate dining room. Minerva proved to be a versatile cook, and this time the meal was French. As I finished my dessert and complimented her, Sir Richard pushed back his chair. "We must be about our business," he announced. "Let me show you to my laboratory."

Descending the basement steps reminded me of all the horror films of my youth, and only the light chatter of Forbish and Minerva relieved the tension. The basement room, behind the big double doors that led down to the water, was large enough to have accommodated several boats in its day. Now, however, it was given over to an array of electrical equipment. I recognized a large x-ray machine and some radiation gear of the sort sometimes found in hospitals for the treatment of tumors.

"This is expensive apparatus," I commented.

"But quite necessary." He led me to a table where a flat stone lay displayed beneath an overhead light. There was a line of hieroglyphics at the top, and beneath it a sentence in Latin. Forbish translated it for me. *"Here is entombed the remains of the Egyptian Satni along with his favorite Gavia who perished here together in the third summer of the reign of Antoninus Pius."*

"What date would that be?" I asked.

"Probably A.D. 141. Antoninus Pius was the adopted son of Hadrian, and like Hadrian he built a wall of his own across the country, quite close to here. He was attempting to extend Roman rule further into what is now Scotland, but he had little success. His own adopted son, Marcus Aurelius, was a much better emperor."

"So the mummies you uncovered belong to Satni and Gavia?"

"It would seem so." Sir Richard walked to another table and pulled away a sheet, revealing the traditional form of a wrapped mummy. "This is Satni. I uncovered a portion of the head for testing purposes. Carbon dating techniques confirm the date sometime in the middle of the second century."

"An Egyptian mummy in Scotland." There was a tone of wonder in my voice that I couldn't conceal. "It's quite a discovery."

"But only the beginning. After all, what's one more mummy in the world? Every big museum has a few on display."

"And this Gavia? Was it a woman?"

"More of a pet, I believe. The inscription speaks of his favorite. The word itself, 'Gavia,' is Latin for seagull—but it was loosely used here as a graceful name, a pet name, for a sea creature."

As he spoke he moved to the back of the large room and pulled aside a long drape.

And then I saw it, stretched across the basement floor for a distance of perhaps forty feet, its great scaled body intertwined with electric wires and the remains of the mummy-wrappings. "This," Sir Richard announced with a flourish, "is Gavia."

"It's some sort of giant serpent!" I exclaimed. "A python, perhaps?"

"Not at this size! Look again, sir—you are gazing upon a creature of the sea, an inhabitant of this very loch. I suspect it might be an ancestor of the one seen to the north of here, in Loch Ness."

"But—this is fantastic! You're telling me you've uncovered the mummy of some sea serpent that was buried along with an Egyptian in the second century? Why in heaven's name would they be buried together?"

Sir Richard was smiling at my bafflement. "The evidence indicates the Egyptian may have been riding on the back of Gavia when he died." He showed me another stone, and there upon it was a crude drawing of a man who seemed to be riding a serpent through the waves.

"I—I'm speechless!"

Minerva was at my elbow with a chuckle. "So was Rich when he first found this thing. I wanted him to phone the police, the government, anyone. I wanted to shout it from the rooftops what he'd discovered. But he was wise to wait."

"What are all these wires?" I asked.

"Naturally I was trying to date and x-ray the serpent as I'd done with the other mummy. In the process of administering a massive dose of radiation I detected some movement."

"You mean you've brought it back to life?"

"Hardly that! I mean the creature was never really dead. It

went into some sort of shock to its nervous system at the time Satni died. We'll never know exactly what happened, but I believe it's been in a state of suspended animation—a sort of prolonged hibernation—ever since. Naturally the embalmers did not use the same technique on this monster that they used on humans. As near as I can tell, its brain and internal organs are intact. The embalming and mummification process only served to keep it alive."

"How much movement has there been?"

"Only a bit of thrashing when the radiation is applied. If you'll get your camera I'll give a demonstration. And Minerva—the movie camera, please."

I took the camera from my briefcase with shaking hands, and brought out the tape recorder too. It was as near a moment to pure fantasy as I'd ever experienced, and I had to remind myself over and over that it was really happening. This was no pot-induced dream or movie shocker. It was happening, and to me.

"Go ahead," I said, moving as far back as I could to fit the sleeping monster in my lens. Minerva raised the movie camera and turned on her lights.

Sir Richard checked the wiring and then twisted his dials. There was a sudden thrashing of the serpent's tail that threatened to overturn a table. "Stop it!" Minerva warned. "You're giving him too much."

The old head lifted then from the floor, and the eyes seemed to stare into Sir Richard's eyes. He stepped backward and cut the power. I could see the little beads of sweat on his brow. "You see?" he asked me. "Everything I have told you is true."

Minerva took a sudden step forward. "It's still moving, Richard!"

"Of course. It's alive, after all."

"Let's go upstairs."

"Doesn't it need water?" I asked, still somewhat shaken by what I'd seen.

"The loch is its natural home, but it is an air-breathing creature." He turned out the lights and closed the drape over the serpent. Then we followed Minerva upstairs. "Is that worth a cover story?" he asked.

"I'll get you on the cover. I'll do better than that—I'll get you on the front page of every newspaper in the world!"

"Fine!"

"I'll phone our London office in the morning and have them send a photographic team up here. This is too big a story to handle by myself."

But when Sir Richard left us alone Minerva expressed misgivings. "I'm worried about him," she admitted. "And now I'm worried about that thing in the basement too. Richard is never satisfied. He's always striving to top himself. He found the earthen pyramid but that wasn't enough. He had to dig into it until he found the mummy, but that wasn't enough either. Then he found the coiled mummy of that sea serpent and I thought surely this would satisfy him. It did, for about a week. Then he was back up here on the weekend, talking about carbon dating and radiation doses. He brought the thing back to life, for God's sake, and I still don't think he's satisfied!"

"Well, the publicity he'll get should certainly satisfy him."

"I wonder."

Though I went to bed early I found I couldn't sleep. The excitement of the story I was about to break kept me tossing and turning in the big old bed, composing new leads and even picture captions. And through it all one question kept on bothering me. When the truth was out, when the world knew what Sir Richard Forbish had done on his weekends, would they give him the Nobel Prize or destroy him as a satanic sorcerer?

I must have finally dozed, because Minerva had to shake me awake. "Come quickly," she urged. "There are terrible noises from the basement."

I pulled on a robe and followed her downstairs, wishing I'd brought some sort of weapon. But when we reached the laboratory all was quiet, and it wasn't until I felt the cool night mist on my face that I realized the big double doors were standing open. The mummy of Satni still rested on its table, but there was no sign of the serpent Gavia. The wires which had coupled it to the various electrical devices lay in a tangle on the floor.

"Richard!" she cried out.

But there was no answer.

We searched through the darkness outside the doors and by the first light of dawn we could make out the track in the dirt where Gavia had slithered down the hill to the waiting waters of Loch Awe. "We have to face it," I told her finally. "The serpent must have attacked and killed Sir Richard, then carried his body into the loch. There's no other explanation."

She thought about it for a long time, and when we returned to the big house she said, "There is one other explanation. Remember that drawing he found in the pyramid? Rich was never satisfied. He was always trying for something more. I believe he might have urged the serpent down that hill to the water, making the noises I heard to frighten it. Certainly Gavia didn't open that double door by itself."

"But why—?"

"Don't you see? I think Richard wanted to ride it, just as Satni had done all those centuries ago."

We didn't find either of them, and though I still had the mummy of Satni for my story, somehow it wasn't enough—not with what I could have had. So I haven't written it yet, but I keep waiting. Sooner or later Sir Richard's body will wash up on the shore of Loch Awe, or Gavia will come to the surface once more.

I've gotten myself transferred to the magazine's London bureau, and every weekend I go up to Scotland and join Minerva at the big house. The police have given up trying to explain Sir Richard's disappearance, but the two of us still search. We know what we're looking for, and sooner or later we'll find it. Then I'll have the biggest news break of the century.

It should certainly bring me a Pulitzer Prize.

THE PRINCESS

by JOE R. LANSDALE

There have been mummies found in other parts of Europe, too, most notably those in the peat bogs near Bjaeldskov Dal, Denmark. Bog water, it has been speculated, has properties which act as a kind of natural embalming fluid, in that it prevents decay and can preserve corpses for thousands of years. The mummies of Bjaeldskov Dal are stranger than most for another reason, however: many of them appear to have been ritualistically strangled. Archeological experts have offered two possible explanations for this. The first is that these persons were sacrificed in order to insure abundant harvest; the second is that they were considered to be evil by the community, to be witches and warlocks endowed with dark powers, and were put to death in rites of exorcism.

But as Richard Dale learns in the pages which follow, "Evil, like energy, can transfer from one place or host to another. It seldom dies. It can also lie dormant for a very long time." As it has in the case of "The Princess," a sorceress whose own magic has kept her alive for a millenium, waiting for release, waiting for the chance to again practice her evil on an unsuspecting world . . .

Joe R. Lansdale is a talented and ambitious young writer who makes his home in his native Texas and who writes detective, suspense, Western and fantasy/horror fiction with equal ability. ("The Princess" is a story which would have found an enthusiastic home in the pages of Weird Tales.*) He has published several detective novelettes in* Mike Shayne Mystery Magazine, *short fiction in* Easy Rider *and* Dark Fantasy, *and some nonfiction as well. His first novel, as yet untitled, will be published some time next year.*

"There is a strange power in bog water which prevents decay. Bodies have been found which have lain in bogs for more than a thousand years, but which, though admittedly somewhat shrunken and brown, are in other respects unchanged."

—Danish
Almanac
1837

RICHARD DALE knew the roads that wound themselves among the foothills of the San Gabriel Mountains were much too dark and curving for the speed he was driving, but Dr. Olson's phone call had been so odd and urgent, he found it impossible to keep a light foot on the gas. He held the Scout's speed at close to sixty miles per hour.

"Come quick!" Dr. Olson had said. "It's Anna. We need your help." Perhaps a few more words had passed over the phone, but all Richard could remember was numbly agreeing and rushing out to his Scout. Anna was in trouble, and that was enough.

Besides, Dr. Olson's excitable phone call had made Richard think of the last disturbing letter he had received only this morning from his fiancée, mailed from Denmark. He was certain the two were connected.

It was bad enough that they had been separated all summer, but now for her to return and for something to be wrong, something as yet unnamed, was unbearable.

As he neared Mount Wilson he found himself easing the Scout up to seventy. It screamed around a narrow curve on two tires, tossed gravel to the night. Normally this area of the foothills was his favorite, and he often made nocturnal visits to the famous Mount Wilson Observatory just to see it outlined magnificently against the night sky. But tonight he hardly even noticed his location. His driving, though excellent, was rote. The bulk of his thoughts was elsewhere—those Danish bogs where Anna worked summers with her father.

What had happened there? Had that letter from her been fanciful, the results of a lonely, overtaxed mind? Perhaps, but why would this summer be different from the past two? Each summer she had worked with her father on his grant-financed expeditions to Denmark, and this summer, like the last two, had found her working in the peat bogs near Bjaeldskov Dal. Interesting finds had been made there in the last thirty years or so, and Dr. Olson was certain that there were others to be made, that they were patiently waiting for him, an American expert on Danish archeology, to make them.

As a graduate student in archeology, Richard shared Dr. Olson's enthusiasm, but his summer job was less romantic. He was reduced to cataloguing artifacts found on various digs throughout the world. It was not a job without interest, but the USC campus and southern California lacked the romance of the peat bogs of Denmark.

Richard would rather have spent the summers there doing fieldwork, and being near Anna. The Denmark bogs were one of archeology's most sensational finds. Certainly there had been bodies found preserved in peat before, but none quite so well preserved as those near Bjaeldskov Dal. These pits had been brought to the attention of the world May 8, 1950, when two farmers cutting their winter supply of peat from the bog found a dead man. So fresh was the body in appearance, they thought it a recent murder, but experts later verified the body as that of a man three thousand years old. Stranger yet, the experts agreed that he had been ritualistically strangled; probably as a sacrifice to insure abundant harvest. Some speculated that there were darker reasons for the strangulation. Reasons to match those of the Salem witch trials; the dismissing of evil from the community; the executions of humans endowed with the dark powers and design of the devil.

These facts and speculations were disturbing to Richard. They seemed linked with Anna's letter, and now with the phone call . . . Richard tried to shake off what he was thinking. It was crazy, absurd. But as he neared the Olson estate, parts of the letter came back to him in minute detail, as if the words had been branded white-hot on his brain.

"Dad still hasn't put together what this is all about. No archeologist has, but he did make one exceptional find yesterday. I think maybe I told you last letter that the peat in the bogs mummifies the corpses in a manner that rivals, perhaps even surpasses, Egyptian mummification. Well, the one we dug up yesterday was the body of a woman and the corpse was in near-perfect condition; all the flesh is on the bones and all internal organs are probably intact. She's suffered a bit of discoloration from the peat, which results in gray skin, and the flesh has shriveled a bit. Like a lot of the other mummies, she has been ritualistically strangled. The woven-hair cord that did the deed —with the help of strong hands, of course—is still around her neck, imbedded in the flesh.

"Her face, once beautiful, I think, is twisted from death, molded into a permanent, ugly, lopsided grin. Another interesting feature is that she was tied down after death and several sticks were placed across the body in cross formation. Stones were heaped on that. They sure didn't want her floating up. Guess it was some kind of sacrifice, or perhaps their method of capital punishment. Gruesome, anyway.

"Dad calls her the princess. Not because he really thinks she was one, but because she is dressed in really fine clothes for her day.

"Want to hear something odd? When we were draining the bog, and we had gone down there to work her free of the mess, I got a start. I was using a trowel to gently dig around her fingers, when I could have sworn they moved. I even jumped. It was probably due to the elasticity of her flesh, and when I freed her fingers they just naturally pulled in a bit.

"Later when the mummy was being photographed and crated up, I was putting some shipping labels on the crates, and when I came to the princess's crate, so help me, it moved. Not the crate, but something inside. I had Dr. Armond—you remember dad's assistant—look inside. Nothing. Just the princess in her packing foam, looking like she would probably look for all eternity."

But it was the postscript that had worried Richard the most.

"Last night I had a bad experience. It still seems very clear. There was a strong wind blowing, and chill. I fastened down the tent flaps and turned in early, had some awful nightmares. It's that damn crate, Rich. You know how dad mistrusts his workers, a fault of his I know, but because of that, it's in our tent.

"Anyway, there was this dream, if it was a dream. I remember first feeling a tightness in my throat, constricting to the point of suffocation. But for some reason I was frozen in the nightmare and couldn't wake up. I seemed to be standing by that infernal bog, only there was slushy water and tar in it now. It was jet black, reflecting orange-red lights—torch lights—that glowed all about me. Then came the pain in my throat. I couldn't breathe. I was no longer standing, but being held up. The odor of sweaty flesh was filling my nostrils. It was a man that held me up; he had a cord around my neck, and he was twisting and twisting. God how it hurt! And the torch lights were spinning, mixing, blurring out and fading into blackness. Pain. Terrible pain. I was aware of people, many people, holding the torches and chanting two words over and over. It was in a language I had never heard, yet I knew what they were saying. I can't remember the sound of those words now, but I remember their meaning clearly: 'Die, sorceress, die!'

"Then I awoke.

"I was out by the bog, standing on the edge of the drained pit where we had found the princess. It was cold and I was in my nightgown. Had I not awakened when I did, I might have fallen into the pit and broken my neck. It was the first time I had ever sleepwalked and the first time I had ever had a nightmare so real. I can't explain it, but suddenly I'm afraid. I'm afraid of the princess."

And now Richard was afraid. The letter, the Olsons' sudden return from Denmark, and the phone call. Too much coincidence.

The Olson residence lay in the beams of his headlights now, and the last words of Anna's letter would not melt away; they clung to his thoughts like bloated leeches. He shivered as he pulled into the drive.

The place was a mansion, set off from the highway by two acres of ground. It nestled comfortably and beautifully among dozens of imported trees, and though its location was not too far from Monrovia, it seemed set out of place and time. The Olsons' inherited money and mansion insulated them from the world outside; from the university where Dr. Olson sometimes taught, and from the gaudy "hipness" of southern California. But tonight, the house seemed more like a Gothic manor, or a funeral home. The moonless sky made it all the more forboding. As Richard hurried up to it, something Victor Hugo had once written came to him: "There is such a thing as the pressure of darkness." At that moment, looking at the night-shrouded house ahead, he knew exactly what Hugo had meant.

He was let into the house immediately by Dr. Olson's assistant and friend, Dr. Armond, and taken to the den. Armond's face was as pale as cigarette ash. His usually impeccable dark hair and Vandyke looked unkempt. Evident in his eyes was concern.

In the den, Dr. Olson paraded back and forth in front of his bookshelves, hands clasped behind his back. His thin figure, normally robust, seemed frail. His features seemed drawn and swallowed up in the bulk of his thick, gray beard.

"Is Anna all right?" Richard asked him. "You said to come quick."

"Yes," Olson said, "I did. I thought maybe her seeing you would help. She's resting at the moment."

"Help what?" Richard blurted. "Is she ill?"

"Our family doctor says no. At least not physically."

"You mean it's her mind?"

Olson and Armond exchanged looks. "She seems to be suffering from delusions," Olson said.

"The princess," Richard said grimly.

"You know about that?"

Richard unfolded Anna's letter from his pocket, gave it to Olson. Olson read it slowly, passed it to Armond. When Armond had finished reading, he said. "This adds weight to our suspicions."

"Yes," Olson said. He looked at Richard. "There's more to our inviting you here. We have a plan, more or less, and if it comes to that, we need your youth and your strength to accomplish it."

"Plan? What sort of plan?"

"I'll explain in a moment. First you should know about the night before we left the bogs. We were in my tent, having a late dinner. Suddenly Anna seemed to get something lodged in her throat. I stood up and went around the table to give her a slap on the back, you know how you do. So I went around behind her . . . and she turned into a tigress. I never even touched her. It was as if she were terrified of me."

"Or who she thought you were," Armond said.

"She jumped out of her chair, knocked it over and tried to stomp back on my shins, all the while tossing her head from side to side, clutching at her throat, struggling as if something were around her neck."

"I was sitting directly across from her," Armond said. "She never turned to face Dr. Olson. It was as if her head could not turn but an inch or two to either side and her body were rooted to the spot. Her face changed, became a gray face with twisted features, but not her face. Do you understand?"

"The princess's face," Richard said weakly.

Armond nodded. "We're afraid that Anna is being possessed by this dead woman, or rather by her spirit. If this mummy was in fact a sorceress in her lifetime, that would explain her execution and the sticks formed in the sign of the cross. You may know that the cross has considerable religious significance and power, and not just to Christians. Its symbol is ancient, magical. But if she were a sorceress, might not her own magic keep her spirit alive all these thousands of years, just waiting for release?"

"Are you trying to say all those mummified bodies from the peat are harboring witches and black magicians?" Richard asked.

"Hardly," Armond said. "Those bogs are full of plows, harness, bowls, tools of the harvest and the table. Most were probably nothing more than sacrifices to the goddess of fertility. Certainly they gave homage to such a goddess. Her image, a nude woman with outstretched arms, has been found many times in the bog, most often engraved on flat stones. But like our own country's ancestors, they must have surely had their witches. And in their own way they dealt with them. We hung them or used the dunking pool. They strangled them, placed them in the bog and held their evil intact with the sign of the cross. I know how it must sound, Richard, but we must face the facts."

"And to rid ourselves of this kind of evil," Olson said, "we must return it to its rest."

"You mean take it back to Denmark?"

"No," Dr. Olson said. "Our idea is to duplicate its former situation, but carry it one step farther. Ever read *The Golden Bough,* Richard? Well, to put it archaically, we must attempt to send it back to the regions from whence it came."

"Destroy it?"

"Perhaps. We will attempt exorcism by fire. P.V. Glob, who was the first to actually explore and chronicle the peat bogs, once quoted a saying of the Pacific Coast Indians. Went something like: 'Unless the body is burnt the soul will never reach the land of the dead . . . In the hot smoke it rises up to the shining sun to rejoice in its warmth and light; then it flies away to the happy land in the west.' Something like that. Most cultures mention such exorcism. It's the source for the practice of cremating bodies, or part of it anyway. *The Golden Bough* makes considerable mention of all this."

"Will it work?" Richard asked.

"Perhaps," Armond said. "Evil, like energy, can transfer from one place or host to another. It seldom dies. It can also lie dormant for a very long time. In the case of the princess, over three thousand years. It's possible, therefore, that we may fail. Our efforts may be totally useless or their effects only temporary. But if we do nothing, Anna is at its mercy. Perhaps even an unsuspecting world."

"Your plan?" Richard said, turning to Olson.

Olson outlined it. He told Richard of the Callahan Tar Pits, a recent discovery made while land-clearing near Irvine Lake in Orange County. Callahan, after whom the pits were named, was a colleague of Olson's. He had confided to Olson that the pits had proved of absolutely no archeological value, and that within the month they would be shut down, eventually turned over to the state to be made into a park, like the more famous tar pits in La Brea. Presently the place was fenced off and there were guards there, but Callahan owed Olson a favor.

"And I'm about ready to collect that favor," Olson said. "The pits are the closest thing we have to those in Denmark, other than La Brea, and there's no getting in there at night—"

At that moment Anna began to scream.

Anna's room was freezing and stank of decay.

Olson flipped on the lights.

Anna was standing upright in her bed, her baggy pajamas billowing out from her body as if blown by the wind. But there was no wind. Anna's face was twisted on the right side into a chilling grin, teeth exposed, eyes bulging like boiled eggs, no pupils showing. Something gray and ghostly moved behind her countenance like a wisp of smoke. It gathered into an image, a face. A gray, withered face with blazing eyes overlapping Anna's turned-up whites. For a moment it blended with Anna's features, then faded. Blue-black welts popped up on Anna's neck, stood out in crusty ridges, and then the flesh of her neck burst open and blood ran freely.

"Oh my God!" Olson said.

Suddenly Anna's hair went electric, stood straight out from her head. Her feet lifted from the bed. She floated six inches off the mattress, her face twisted horribly, her eyes bulging.

Then she collapsed, fell limply to the bed.

The mood of the room changed. The presence had departed, leaving only the sweet-sour stench of decay.

For a moment the trio stood as if paralyzed. Then Richard ran to Anna's bedside and examined her throat. There was no wound. No mark of any kind. He checked her pulse. Rapid, irregular. He looked up at Olson and Armond. His voice trembled when he said, "Jesus!"

"I hope He's listening," Armond said grimly. "I think we're going to need Him."

They weren't really surprised to find that the cellar lights would not work. They took flashlights and went down the dark stairs into a large room with the temperature of a refrigerator. Richard carried a crowbar tucked in his belt. Crates were everywhere, standing out in the gloom like ill-shaped terrors.

Their flashlights played feeble beams across the face of the darkness. Their breath puffed out in small, white clouds.

"It's the one in the corner," Olson said. "Over there," and he waved a beam in that direction.

For a moment Richard thought he saw movement, tried to dismiss it as his imagination. After all these years of petrification, there was no way that thing could move. Was there?

They weaved among several crates, all different sizes, until they came to the one in the corner. The cold seemed to originate there.

Richard handed Olson his flashlight, pried up the lid with the crowbar. The top of the crate was even with Richard's head. Ice dripped from its edges. Cold steam spewed out of the open crate. Richard tossed the crowbar aside, gripped the edge of the crate and pulled himself up. It was dark as the tomb inside.

"Flashlight," Richard said.

Olson passed it up to him and he shone it down into the crate.

Anna's face smiled back at him.

"Oh God!"

"What is it?" Olson said. "Richard, what's the matter?"

The thing seemed to be sleeping, a serene smile on its—Anna's—lips. The skin of its hands and exposed feet was gray . . . but the face . . . it was rosy with life and the peat-greased hair that surrounded it made it all the more obscene.

Then the princess opened her eyes.

Richard dropped the flashlight, but still he could see her eyes. Dark eyes. Black eyes, growing blacker yet, filling up the sockets with no room left for whites. They called his mind, and like a small child heeding its mother, he responded. Down, down, down, plunging into the twisting labyrinth of pure evil . . .

"Richard!"

Olson had hold of him, was slapping his face. Richard's mind cleared. He was lying on the cellar floor, Olson bending over him.

Almost crying, Richard said, "We haven't much time."

The horrible thing was very much alive. It seemed unable to move its body, but the head with Anna's face was mobile. The eyes, however, were not human. They were demoniac. The three men, chilled and feeling those eyes crawling across their spines, made no effort to look in her direction.

They took the princess out of the crate and built a cross from the plywood with a skill saw, a cross large enough to accommodate the mummy. Her feet were overlapped, her arms outstretched—Christ position. They bound her to the cross with crate wire and heavy chain. The princess lifted her head and watched with dark-eyed amusement. The thing's face was more like Anna's than ever, rosy, lovely. Richard tried not to wonder what Anna would look like when he saw her next.

When the living corpse was fastened securely to the cross, they lifted it out of the dark, cold cellar and carried it outside to Richard's Scout. They let down the back seats and put the cross and its burden inside, covered it with a tarp. Next they brought from the garage more chains, two sections of bamboo fishing pole, a can of gasoline, a flare pistol, and three flares. Richard was uncertain what it was all for, but he didn't ask.

"Anna's going with us," Olson said. "We don't dare leave her here alone. Please bring her, Richard, while I telephone Callahan."

Richard hurried upstairs, wrapped Anna's unconscious form in a blanket, and carried her down. He put her in the front seat of the Scout and sat beside her, held her up with one arm and peeled back the blanket for another look at her face. It was grotesque, worse than before. The teeth and gums on the right side were exposed. Her right eye bulged from its socket and there was no pupil. The welts on her throat were back, only this time they were solid with scabs that stood out in bold relief. They were cracking in spots, showing small beads of blood.

Olson returned. "We've got to hurry," he said.

The mummy laughed.

It was a hoarse and terrible laugh. It startled the men, sent jets of fear through Richard's body. Then, from beneath the tarp, the thing began to speak. The words were strangled and slurred, not in English.

"A bastard form of Danish," Olson said.

Armond nodded. "She's telling us it's useless."

Richard felt himself losing control. The next instant he started over the seat after the mummy. Armond grabbed him by the ankle and tugged him back. "Don't be a fool. There's only one way to destroy this kind of evil. Otherwise we'll lose Anna for sure. As is, Anna's will is fighting it."

The mummy laughed again.

No one spoke until they arrived at the tar pits. But from time to time, almost in turn, they glanced at Anna's comatose body bundled up between Richard and Dr. Olson who drove the Scout, and then at the tarp-covered princess. Richard feared most of all that Anna would open her eyes and reveal the black wells of the princess. Dead and cold like a fish, yet simultaneously burning with hideous life.

In the reflected green light of the dash, Richard thought Anna looked worse than ever. Was her skin turning gray? Or was it the light? The night? His mind?

They passed a dilapidated shack where an old man—equally

dilapidated-looking—sat on the sagging porch and comforted a wine bottle. Then they pulled off the blacktop and onto a hard, clay drive. There was a long chain-link fence at the end of the drive, rows of lights along the fence, and next to the gate a little metal building with a sign that read: GUARD.

Olson pulled up to the gate and honked his horn.

The princess moved. Shook violently for a moment, then was still.

"It knows," Armond whispered.

A uniformed guard of about thirty with a gun on his hip checked their credentials, verified that they were the ones Dr. Callahan had called him about, told him to expect. He let them proceed inside.

A narrow bridge made its way over a natural drainage ditch that connected to the tar pit; the tar in the ditch shone blackly in the moonless dark. Olson drove the Scout over the bridge and on up to the mouth of the tar pit.

When the Scout stopped the princess jumped and landed heavily.

"Hurry!" Armond said, and they climbed out of the Scout, opened up the back. Then they pulled the tarp-covered cross and its load out, carried it to the edge of the pit and put it down. Olson went back with Richard to the Scout. They brought out the two sections of bamboo, the gas can, the chains, the flare pistol and flares. Olson stuck the latter two items in his belt, put the bamboo lengths together.

"I'll use this fishing pole to push her out. That tar is like quicksand. Semi-solid. Here, Richard, wrap these chains around the thing."

Armond jerked off the tarp.

The face was Anna's. The hands and the arms were Anna's.

"Hurry!" Armond said again. With his help, Richard worked the heavy chains beneath and around the princess.

The mummy watched them, its eyes resting on them like weights.

"Stand back," Olson said. He tossed the bamboo aside, picked up the gas can and doused the princess from head to foot. The mummy shook its head, made a hissing sound like a goose.

"Hurry," Armond said.

The princess turned her head, looked at Richard. Blood suddenly flowed from the wound at her neck. "Richard," the mummy said. "Don't let them."

"That's Anna's voice," Richard moaned.

"Richard," the princess said, "don't let them kill me. Please, Richard. I love you."

Richard felt himself waver. His mind flashed to the last time Anna had held him in her arms. She had told him she loved him, in just that tone of voice. He clamped his hands to his ears.

Olson touched him urgently at the elbow. Richard nodded, licked his dry lips, and got a grip on himself. He bent down to help Armond lift the cross beam. Olson took the base end of the cross. When they lifted it the princess began her entreaties again.

"Richard, please."

"Shut up."

"Block it out, Richard," Armond said.

As they placed the tip of the cross in the tar, the voice changed to a strangled cry in old Danish. Olson used his pole to push the cross out farther. The chains and the tar made it a difficult job; the pole bent and would move the cross no more. The tar gathered around the cross and pulled it down. Olson drew the flare pistol from his belt, slipped in a flare, aimed.

The exploded flare lit up the pinched faces of the men for an instant, and the half-visible cross burst into flames. The princess began to scream, a hoarse, grating noise . . . like someone strangling. But the scream was never completed. Flames leaped up from the cross, enveloped the princess, ignited the tar pit. A wave of fire raced across the surface of the pit, and for a while the night was as bright as midday.

Richard ran to the Scout and opened the door, Olson and Armond behind him. He climbed in and cradled Anna's head in his lap, gingerly pulled back the blanket. Her face was smooth and soft as before. She opened her eyes—Anna's eyes.

Richard sighed. In the distance he could see the guard running toward them. A siren had gone off.

"Richard?"

"Yes, Anna. It's all over now, baby. It's all right."

Richard looked at Olson and Armond, outlined against the blazing tar pit. Then he turned back to Anna's face, saw that her eyes were closed again. She was smiling.

It's over, he thought. It's over.

The old man pulled his dirty trench coat off and settled down on the front porch of his shack to finish off the last of his early-morning bottle. And when he had done that he tossed the bottle away, watching with childlike fascination as it spun and fell shattering against the edge of the nearby ditch.

That was how he saw the charred thing lying there.

There was a pool of black stuff around it, dripping from it. Something had washed down during the night from those tar pits up above. Always one to investigate—for he who finds things to sell is he who drinks another bottle—he went over to the ditch, grasped the charred thing and pulled it out.

Reason finally worked its way through his wine-soaked brain and told him that what he was looking at was a body, a human body. The face was still there, burned considerably, with blackened teeth showing where the cheek had burned away, but recognizable as a face nonetheless. Fragments of what looked like charred wood dangled from its burned garments and the well-cooked flesh of its hands and feet.

The old man stumbled back a step. Suddenly afraid, wanting to get away from the dreadful thing.

And then the princess opened her eyes. . . .

THE EAGLE-CLAW RATTLE

by ARDATH MAYHAR

Although it is not exactly a well-known fact, there have been mummies discovered right here in the United States—American Indian mummies, in particular those of Sioux chiefs and medicine men in the Dakotas. In bygone years the Sioux erected burial scaffolds in private desert graveyards and placed the dead on them, wrapped in deer hide and festooned with eagle feathers, bundles of lances, and other wordly possessions, so that they would be closer to the Great Spirit. The dry desert air mummified the corpses until "they were just like old, stiff leather."

"The Eagle-Claw Rattle" is the story of one such Indian mummy, a powerful medicine man known as Thunder-on-the-Mountain, and what happens when a nineteenth century grave robber tries to steal his magic rattle. The result is an unusual blend of the horror story and the western, with several dandy shudders packed into slightly more than two thousand words.

Ardath Mayhar, like Joe Lansdale, is a talented and ambitious Texas native who is well on her way to making a name for herself in the fantasy field. Her first novel, How the Gods Wove in Kyrannon, *was published in 1978, and two more,* The Seekers of Shar-Nuhn *and* War-

lock's Gift, *have followed. Her short stories have appeared in* Alfred
Hitchcock Presents: Stories to Be Read with the Lights On,
Swords Against Darkness, Weirdbook, Dark Fantasy, Galaxy,
*and other publications. She is self-educated (six languages, philosophy,
theology, literature, logic, and more) and by her own testimony holds
entirely unorthodox views on almost every conceivable subject. She also
imparts the information that the word "anthology" is from the Greek
anthos legein, which means "to gather flowers"; i.e., a bouquet of stories.
Nice.*

IT WAS a shackledy old scaffold. You'd never catch a white man
doing such a sorry job, particularly if he was planning to stick
the body of one of his great men on top of it. The Sioux, though
. . . what can you expect from a bunch of heathen Injuns who
think that's the only proper way to do the dead? Closer to the
Great Spirit—hah! Any white man can tell you that the only
place to put a dead man is in the ground. This scaffold business
is just unsanitary, if not downright sinful.

Anyway, it was the devil and all to climb. Particularly in the
dark. Even out there in the back of beyond, you never knew if
one of those red-tailed varmints was there in the rocks, watching. A cautious man doesn't rob Injun graves, mind you, but of
those that do, the most wary live longest. I've been at it (and
other things) all over the Dakota Territory for a long time, and
I've still got my hair to prove it.

There was a tad of moon—just a toenail-trimming's worth. A
low and lonesome wind was whishing along the ground, stirring
up enough dust to fog up the landscape a bit, which suited me
fine. If it was also moaning and hissing around the scaffold and
its burden, well, that was fine, too. I figured that the day had
come and gone when old Thunder-on-the-Mountain could give
me any hassle.

I could see the dark, oblong shape against the stars, whenever
I'd look up. Mighty long and thin . . . of course, he'd been a big

cuss, from what I'd heard. Likely the desert air had dried the juices out of him and thinned him down. Even with all the bundled wraps they'd put around him, he looked mighty narrow. Still, I'd never seen one yet that'd rotted away to bones, not in this climate. When I first started taking orders for "Indian artifacts," I unwrapped one or two, just to see what I was dealing with. They were just like old, stiff leather. Not much different from what the really old 'uns look like when they're alive.

This one was the top of the line, though. The red devils think old Thunder helped hang the moon, from what you hear around the campfires at night. Said he could shake up storms out of the mountains with that painted rattle of his. Could make the ground shake so hard it split open and let whole rivers get lost and never come out again.

I laughed. Now here he hung, with the wind singing through his teeth, not even able to spit out a mouse-sized curse at the white man who was going to make off with his fourteen-karat, hundred-proof magic rattle. And sell it, what's more, to an Eastern fella who was fool enough to offer *two hundred dollars* for it.

The wind seemed to pick up, the higher I got. Or maybe I was going above the shelter of the ridge of rocks that curved away to the east. I could see eagle feathers fluttering, now, tied onto the scaffolding in untidy bunches. They were all but worn down to the nub by the wind and the dust, but they still spun round and round or else flittered away at the ends of thongs.

Funny, the way your imagination will rise to any occasion. I'd have sworn that I heard that corpse shift, just the way a man does when he's been lying down too long and needs to ease his bones. It was the wind moving the deer hide wrappings, of course, but it gave me an almighty start until I figured it out.

When I came out on the narrow platform, it seemed almost light, for the moon had pulled out from behind the thin mare's tails that were misted across the sky to the east. I could see the way the outer wrap was tied. It was buffalo hide, weathered to the toughness of wood, and the bindings had been knotted for so long that there was no way on God's green earth you could have untied them.

I got out my boot-knife and began cutting. I knocked down a couple of pots and what must have been a bundle of lances while I was moving around the edge of the platform, trying to get everything cut before I opened it up. They made a godawful clatter and crash, and I stopped for a minute and listened. Injuns have an unchancy habit of going out to forsaken places like this to sit and meditate and wait for their heathen gods to talk to them.

Still and all, if there'd been one around, I'd know it by now, I figured, and got busy again. Then the cutting was all done, and I carefully pulled back the buffalo robe. It cracked in a long split, and the section I'd lifted caught the wind and went sailing away. That left a shell shaped something like a long narrow boat, and in it was Thunder-on-the-Mountain, in person.

They'd tanned deer hide so fine that it was silky. Even in the dark I could see the beadwork twinkling in the moonlight, as I unfolded the top layer. Underneath that was a pair of dark hands. They were so well-preserved that they still looked strong enough to strangle a bear. Big, tough, long-fingered hands, they were, and they were clasped like grim death around the handle of a big gourd rattle.

And that was what I'd come for. A gourd that old, mind you, can be brittle as paper, so I tried to ease it out of those hands. It was as if they'd been glued together. I stood up for a minute to ease my back, and as I did, I looked up at the end where the face would have been, if it hadn't been covered with deerskin.

The wind fluttered the layer of hide just a bit. Just enough so it looked like somebody was breathing underneath it. And I felt like two hot black eyes were blazing away under there, fit to burn twin holes in the pale skin.

I shook my head and laughed. Robbing graveyards—even heathen graveyards—was no business for a man who let himself get fanciful. I laughed again and went back to work.

Now it's not that I'm squeamish. I've handled more than my share of dead bodies, both fresh and mummified, and I've never thought a thing of it. But those hands were another matter. First off, they looked alive. They looked as if, when I laid hand to them, they just might grab hold of my wrists and throw me down off the scaffold.

As I stood there considering, it suddenly dawned on me that he didn't *smell* right, either. All the others had had a faint, musty, nasty odor, not strong but mighty noticeable. This one didn't, and it wasn't just that the wind was carrying it off. The only smell there was was tanned deer hide and old buffalo robe. Not the best of stinks, but better than mummified Injun.

The moon was way up by now, and I wasn't done with my job, so I shook my head to get the foolishness out of it and went about my business. If the hands wouldn't turn loose of the rattle, then, by George, they'd just have to go along with it, at least until I could figure out a way to get them off without busting my two hundred dollars all to flinders.

My boot-knife was just the ticket, and I had them off at the wrists in no time. Even then, they held onto that rattle as if they'd grown to it. And I couldn't see that fella buying a pair of dead hands. Easterners have weak stomachs.

I cut off a bit of hide and tied it around the whole thing, rattle and all, making a loose bundle of it. As I lifted it, the eagle claws fastened to the rattle clicked sharply against its painted sides. It was shuddery—worse than a rattlesnake in a dark room.

I put things back as well as I could, for it's just as well to avoid any trouble you can. The piece of robe that had blown away was long gone, but I fixed the deer hide back together and tied some of the fringes to keep it in place. I'll admit that it was a relief to hide those dark wrist stumps, too.

I went back down with the bundle slung over my shoulder, the rattle clashing gently away at every move. The wind was picking up, too, whipping my coattails and pushing and prying at my bundle. As I reached the ground, the moon went under a cloud, and I looked up to see that the mare's tails had moved together into a black mat that covered half the sky.

My horse was dancing around, whinnying that wild way they do when a storm is coming, and it was all I could do to calm him down enough to get mounted. I hadn't more than got my feet settled into the stirrups when a pure wall of wind and dust and rain, all mixed up together, came whooping down on me.

I kneed Gray over against the rock outcrop to knock off part of the wind, and we just hunched down to wait it out. The lightning came, then, sizzling down so close that I could hear the little pop that comes before the big crack. Thunder rolled down over us like a giant walking on drums, and I glanced out from under my hatbrim to see if the rain was slacking off any.

It wasn't. It was, if anything, harder, and the continuous lightning lit it into silver sheets.

In the midst of it stood a big man. He was dressed in fine-tanned deerskin, and the rain hadn't wet an inch of it. He was standing four paces away, just looking at me, and his eyes were big dark holes in his face. The thunder boomed right above us, shaking the air and the ground and even the rock my elbow was touching.

The Injun didn't move. He stood there, waiting and watching, and I stared back, knowing what he wanted but still too stubborn to admit that I had to do it.

The rain got harder; the lightning danced around us like mad fireworks, and the thunder sounded fit to shake down the sky. In a little bit, that Injun stepped forward one pace. I shrunk down into my coat, wet as it was, but I couldn't look away.

He raised his head toward the sky, and he held up his arms. His hands were gone, but as if he had called on further powers, the storm got worse. A lot worse.

So I slowly got down from my shivering horse and tied him securely to a knob of rock. I took the bundle and put it over my shoulder again. Then I waited. I wasn't going a bit closer to that big Injun than I was, and he sensed it right off.

Between one wink of lightning and the next, he was gone.

I sighed; then I gritted my teeth. To think a white man, a Christian, could be maneuvered by a heathen Injun made my blood boil . . . but quietly.

I climbed the scaffold again, and the rain was ending as I reached the top. The long form lay there, and the wind hadn't stirred a fold of its wrappings. I untied the strings, then the bundle I carried. Carefully, I fitted the hands back to the stumps of the wrists. Before I could take my fingers away, I felt . . . I felt the damn things *flex*.

The lightning, dying away to westward, lit the place by flashes. The hands lay still and dark, grasping the rattle. I shook my head and looked at the bundled shape. Might as well do the thing right, I thought.

Sighing, I went down and got my buffalo robe from my bedroll. It was two jobs to get it back up, with the wind still blowing in gusts, but I managed. Then I lifted and shifted and maneuvered until I had it around old Thunder-on-the-Mountain, and I tied it down good and proper.

He lay there, quiet as death, but I still had the feeling that those eyes were wide open and seeing through to *my* bones. I went down the scaffold for the last time in one rush, got on my horse and lit out.

The lightning had stopped, now, but I could hear some sort of low, grumbling sound that hadn't any direction that I could fix. Then, over the rumbling and pounding of Gray's hooves, I could hear the sharp, clear sound of that eagle-claw rattle.

Gray screamed and shuddered, rearing and turning as the ground opened in front of us. It unseated me, and I fell, my boots sliding out of the stirrups as if they were greased. I seemed to fall forever, with the sound of that rattle clashing and laughing in my ears all the way down.

I felt bones snap all over me when I hit bottom. My teeth were full of grit, and I think my jaw was busted. I went out for a long time.

When I came to, old Thunder was sitting there beside me. The rattle was shushing away in a soft rhythm, and the old bastard was saying something long and complicated in his heathenish lingo. Now and again he'd stand up and shake his hands at the sky. They were back on, good and tight.

He's waiting for me to die. He's making Injun magic right now, and it'll trap me down here, with the walls of the crack already beginning to sag back together. As soon as I die, he's going to bury me, body, soul, and all, in all this rock and dirt, and I'll never get to heaven. I'll turn to old boot leather, just like he did, instead of rotting away like a Christian corpse to bones.

Damn him. He's going to make me a mummy, too.

THE OTHER ROOM

by CHARLES L. GRANT

Oxrun Station is a small town in New England where all sorts of strange things happen. On the surface it's an ordinary town, just like thousands of others across the country; the people who live there are ordinary people, with ordinary attitudes, drives and desires. But strange and extraordinary things happen to them nonetheless. Like the strange and extraordinary thing that happens to Gil and Else on a hot summer afternoon, when their teenage daughter accidentally uncovers a hidden room behind the fireplace of their Victorian house—a room that contains five mummies in five sarcophagi.

Where did the mummies come from? Were they Strangers, a sect which accompanied the Puritans on the Mayflower in 1620? Or, because of the curious "epitaph" on the wall of the room, Norse travelers? Or something else entirely, something far more bizarre and far more terrifying? "The Other Room" is quiet horror, the kind that sneaks up on you in daylight and everyday surroundings; the kind that builds and adds dimensions and puts chills on your neck at the climax—and keeps those chills there, like phantoms, for some time after you've read the final page.

Charles L. Grant has written a number of stories and several novels (The Hour of the Oxrun Dead, The Sound of Midnight, Nightmare Season) *featuring the inhabitants of Oxrun Station. All, like "The*

Other Room,'' are exercises in the type of quiet horror mentioned above. Grant is also recognized as one of the leading anthologists in the fantasy/- horror field, having edited three volumes of Shadows *(the first of which won a World Fantasy Award as the Best Anthology of 1978) and one of* Nightmares. *And he is an accomplished writer of science fiction as well, with several novels and short stories to his credit—two of the latter having earned him Nebula Awards from the Science Fiction Writers of America for Best Short Story of 1977 and Best Novelette of 1979.*

THE GATE on the new picket fence was slightly ajar, and a page from the *Station Herald* was caught in the gap. It fluttered in the late August breeze like a rare dove with a broken wing—at times frantically, at times weakly. And when the breeze finally died it slumped to the gray slate walk, bleached by a week's rain, a week's sodden heat. A match would have flared it, and a touch would have frightened it to dust.

Gil watched it from the top step of the front porch, wondering how long it would be before he found the energy to get up and fetch it, and dump it in the trash. The way he felt now, however, he wasn't going to move until September, if then. Breathing came hard, movement even harder, and he was barely able to lift a greeting hand when Else came out behind him, wiping her hands on a dish towel and squinting at the late afternoon sun's angry, sullen white.

"You look how I feel," she said. She was tall, buxom, her hair unsuccessfully pulled into a cooling bun at her nape. She wore a man's plaid shirt whose tails were tied below her breasts, and her jeans were snug, her feet bare.

"If you feel how I look, why aren't you dead?"

She smiled and sat beside him. Not touching. It was too hot. "If that bastard doesn't come for the air conditioning this afternoon, I'll kill him."

"Good," he said, "because I don't have the energy."

His left hand touched at his shirt pocket absently, and he

grunted when he realized he had no cigarettes. Just as well; it's too damned hot. And just as well he was trying to quit now, since smoking would only aggravate the searing in his lungs. "I thought," he said, "that Connecticut was supposed to be reasonably cool in summer. It was one of Rosen's selling points to get me up here."

"Relative to what, love? Hell?"

He pulled at his long thinning hair and grinned. Leave it to Else. When he complained about the cold, she reminded him about the Arctic; when he complained about supper, she reminded him about the army; and when he complained that his daughter didn't take him seriously, she reminded him that hardly anyone did . . . until it was too late. It was her calling, or her curse, to keep her world in perspective; and though he appreciated the effort there were times, like now, when he wished she would allow herself to be a little more fanciful, a little more unrestrained.

"I think I see a cloud," she said, a hand shading her eyes.

He glanced at the near hills, and the brown that covered them. "You're hallucinating."

A jay strutted across the lawn, jabbed at the ground once and flew off. Silently.

"The iced tea's almost done."

"Good. When you're ready, just jam the cubes into my mouth and pour."

She draped her hands over her knees and sighed. "You didn't tell me about classes today."

"What's to tell? Summer sessions are a bitch. They don't want to be there, I don't want to be there, and if it weren't for their having to pass and my paying the bills we could all be in the park, drowning in the pond."

"Poor baby."

"What's Jerri doing?"

"Cleaning."

"You're a heartless bitch."

She grinned. "Yeah. And when she goes off to college next

year you're going to be screaming because you have to do her work."

A car lumbered past, windows down, radio soft. They watched it vanish around the bend in the street, heading for the straight that would take it past the cemetery and into the village. The breeze kicked up again, cooler now, and he closed his eyes gratefully to its touch, was almost ready to fall into a doze when, suddenly, he heard a brief, panicked cry from inside. Instantly, he was on his feet before Else had a chance to move, was through the front door before the cry faded.

The house was a Victorian without the gingerbread that marked the others on the street, the rooms inside high-ceilinged, generally self-cooling, and of a mixture of styles both fascinating and disconcerting. At its core, so the agent had told them, was a massive block of stone, a cube nearly nine feet on a side; a custom, the man said, of earlier times when settlers in New England believed the native granite was a powerful symbol of their ability to survive. The original house had been constructed around this stone, and as owners changed so did the house until, now, only the firewall behind the hearth was left of the core. The rest, complete with odd-angled doorways and dark-beamed ceilings, had been enough to make Gil wonder early on if everyone who lived here before him had been somewhat, if not totally, mad.

But despite the history involved, it was in fact the fireplace that sold him on making a bid for the property. It was seven feet across at the mouth, four feet deep, spiked with flame-blackened iron bars from which Else had hung skittles, copper kettles, and anything else she could think of colonial. In the back wall, chest high, were recesses for baking bread, drying kindling, and keeping meals warm until the master returned. During the winter Gil hardly used the furnace at all for the ground floor, the stone heating so rapidly and uniformly that they had been forced on more than one occasion to sit back near the windows for a measure of comfort.

Now Jerri was standing back from the brick hearth, one hand

to her chest, the other tangled nervously in her chestnut hair. She turned when Gil raced in, accepted his hands on her shoulders with a quick, embarrassed smile.

"What?" he said, scanning the room for spiders, rats, or Jerri's hyperdrive imagination.

She's so much like you it's unnerving, Else had said.

Relax, he'd told her sourly, and maybe she'll grow out of it.

"What?" he said again.

"I don't know," the girl whispered. She puffed her cheeks and blew softly, moved away from her father's touch and reached out to the kettle. "I was kind of rearranging it, see, because it wasn't right. I, uh, thought it moved before I touched it."

He put hands on his hips and mock-scowled at her. "You've been chinning yourself on the pipes again."

She rubbed her palms guiltily over her hips, and shrugged. "Well . . . maybe once."

"You're going to pull it out of the wall, midget," he said. He took a step toward it. "You probably loosened it."

"A car went by," Else said. "There might have been vibrations."

The girl nodded. "Yeah, could be." She frowned. "Do you really think so?"

"Well, it wasn't a ghost, dear."

Gil ignored them both. His search for spiders had drawn his gaze to the hearth-and-wall juncture and slowly, as though afraid his bones might snap, he moved under the mantelpiece and eased the now-empty brass andirons to one side. Then he ran a hand along the base. "Hey," he said softly. Jerri was beside him immediately, oblivious to the dirt and her mother's half-hearted protest. "Look at this, folks."

Jerri touched where her father had.

"What?" Else said, drawn to them in spite of herself.

Gil pushed himself to his feet, glancing up toward the flue, then into the room. "It's separated, Else," he said.

"You're separated," she told him with a grin. "Come on, Jerri, I need help with the iced tea."

Gil moved to stop them, then turned away. He knew that any

settling this part of the house had done would have been over more than a century ago. And cracks don't show up in granite for no reason at all—it takes immense heat and sudden cooling, for example, or a mild earth tremor. However, neither had happened, and as he examined the back wall and found nothing out of place he began to think that the heat wave had finally gotten to him. Cursing the repairman's failure to show up, then, he was about to head back outside when he saw a gleaming, half-inch section of iron pipe pulled away from the firewall. Damn kid, he thought; a century or more yanked out for one lousy chin-up. He looked around, ready to scold, but the women were already out of the room; he looked back at the pipe, and told himself he was being ridiculous.

But it was tempting.

Very tempting.

And even as he reminded himself to buy some epoxy to reseal the break he reached out and gripped the bar with his left hand. His right. Sniffed, and pulled down. Pushed away. Pulled toward him. Shifted his feet and pushed up . . . gasping when stone suddenly and explosively grated against stone. He dropped his hands as though they'd been burned and rubbed them hard over his shirt.

Loose, of course. With kids climbing all over the place, why the hell shouldn't it be?

He took hold of the bar and pushed up again, this time keeping an eye on the meeting of floor and wall—the gap there widened.

"I'll be damned."

He looked to his right and noticed that instead of the pipe being set into the stone behind the mantel as the others were, it had been wedged into a narrow groove. He gnawed on his lower lip, bit at the inside of his cheek.

He called out for the others and, bracing himself for a possible spill, shoved as hard as he could toward the chimney.

His cheeks flushed, his arms bulged, perspiration broke along his forehead and spine . . . and the pipe, suddenly loosened, shrieked and snapped up. Gil released it just before it slammed against the firewall, stumbled backward and held up his arms to protect his face and head. Sooted dust fogged around him, making him cough, darkening his lips; the firewall grumbled like mountain-muffled thunder, shaking the hearth and the room, dropping him into a semi-crouch as it pivoted ponderously on a hidden axis.

Crumbled stone pattered like hail at his feet. The other pipes were torn loose from their moorings, scattering skillets and kettles onto the brick, onto the carpet. And he was driven backward by a sudden rush of fetid, musty air that escaped from the chamber beyond; pushed forward by a fresh wind that drove in to replace it. He tripped over an andiron and fell, hands outstretched to catch himself before his chin cracked against stone.

The dust settled; the stone stopped falling; and the brief windstorm was done so swiftly it might not have happened.

"Dad?"

He rose to his knees, his feet, made a show of brushing off the debris as he turned around, grinning foolishly. "Surprise," he said, and choked on a mouthful of grit.

"Are you all right, Gil?" Else said, keeping well away from the fireplace, her face pale, her hands folded tightly at her waist.

He nodded, even though he wasn't all that sure.

"Dad?" Jerri was trying not to cry in a maelstrom of fear and excitement, relief and amazement.

"I don't know," he said, leaning close to the opening without moving his feet. "Maybe a storeroom for fruit, things like that. Else, get me a flashlight, and those hurricane lamps at the top of the cellar steps."

"Hey," Jerri said, "maybe it's a place where they hid runaway slaves. You know, the Underground Railroad? They used to do that a lot up here. Professor Rosen said so."

"That . . . that man," Else declared, "never said anything about this when we bought it."

"I know, dear, just get me those lights. Jerri, call Howard Rosen at the college. I think he's still there. Tell him we've made the find of the century."

"No shit," Jerri said excitedly, then looked to her parents with a hand at her mouth, shrugged an apology and dashed for the telephone.

"Else," he said without turning around, "for God's sake, please!"

And fifteen minutes later he stood on the front porch, waiting for Rosen and wondering why the hell he wasn't more enthused about what he had uncovered. Jerri certainly was, and even Else was beginning to show some sparkle in her eyes; but there was something . . . *wrong* . . . about it all, something that didn't quite jibe with what he had seen.

The exposed chamber was barely five feet by five, a cube within a cube brushed by a thin layer of gray and fine dust. He had stood at its threshold for what seemed like hours, unsure despite his daughter's urgings that he wanted to be the first man inside since it had been sealed. One step was all he had taken, one long step behind the flashlight's dim yellow spear. The lanterns he placed at either side of the entrance, and the light all three gave made him take a deep breath he could not release.

Tomb was the first word that came to mind.

Propped upright against the far wall were five stone coffins, rounded at the top, squared and wide at the base. The lids of four of them had been carved into elaborate bas-relief similar to those he had seen in crypts under cathedrals during his walking tour of England. But these were not representations of those who were sealed within; his first impression had been that of gargoyles, his second one of people just on the generous side of hideously deformed. Their sharply slanted eyes beneath protruding brows were disturbingly blank, their hands—with talons for fingers—laced piously over their massive chests. It was impossible to tell what sort of clothing they wore because of the dust that still clung to them darkly, and he was not about to disturb any of it until Rosen had arrived.

The fifth coffin, in the center of the row and taller than the others by nearly two feet, was completely blank.

He had almost backed out when, in the moving, the flashlight caught indentations on the lefthand wall. Words. Epitaph, he thought, and read them before leaving.

If Stone to Earth
Air to Wind
Sky to Fire
Shed not a Tear for
   the Children of Hel

The temperature had begun to fall as the sun eased its white to a pale rose, and he rubbed his arms against the chill. He let his mind drift as he sought the key to the wrongness of what he felt, did not hear his wife when she came out to stand beside him.

"Fascinating," she said. "Don't you think it's fascinating?"

That, he thought sourly, was at least better than "creepy," which is what Jerri had called it when she realized she had been sleeping over five bodies for the past eight years.

"Hey," Else whispered, slipping an arm around his waist. "Hey, prof, what's the matter?"

He shook his head and smiled. "I don't know, to tell you the truth. It's a mystery. It bothers me."

She grunted. "I don't see it. We have a handful of people in there who were buried—"

"Sealed," he reminded her.

"All right, sealed. Sealed here instead of a graveyard. From that ditty on the wall, I suspect they were murderers or something, and they weren't allowed in hallowed ground. Maybe their people didn't think they did anything wrong and gave them a monument only they would appreciate. It wouldn't be the first time it's happened, you know. Howard probably knows a million of them."

"Yeah," he said, and said nothing more when a sleek roadster growled into the driveway, and a lank, sandy-haired man Gil's age climbed out and raced over the lawn. "Where?" he demanded, his tie askew and his sport jacket flapping behind his arms.

Gil pointed at the front door, listened as Jerri met Rosen in the foyer and began the guided tour.

"Gil?"

"You go ahead," he said, kissing her cheek. "I want to worry at something for a minute."

She stiffened and drew away from him. "That's getting to be a bad habit, love," she said, and left him before he could respond.

But it was true—whether it was ferreting through manuscripts at Yale or Harvard for a clue to Hawthorne or Melville, Poe or Whitman, or fretting over the bills that never seemed to quite get paid off before regenerating themselves, his life was dedicated to worrying. Howard told him he created worries just to keep in shape, and Else believed it was affecting his work.

She loved him, deeply and sincerely, but none of his other quirks bothered her nearly as much.

And suddenly he understood part of his problem—he was angry. Angry at Jerri for chinning herself on that bar, for loosening it and forcing his curiosity into a series of actions that resulted in the discovery of the chamber. Angry because it would mean publicity, sightseers and the like, and he had no intention of letting his life go public. And angry at . . . whoever the hell it was buried in there for making him angry at everything and everyone else.

He laughed suddenly, shortly, and took a series of deep breaths to calm himself as he watched the twilight settle over the valley that stretched behind Oxrun Station. Locusts, nightbirds, the sun finally dropping below the hills and shading the sky to indigo and black. Leaves whispering. Voices behind him trailing into the kitchen, and he turned to join them, paused in the foyer to glance into the living room. A shadeless lamp had been set up by the hearth to throw more light into the chamber. With not much strain he could see the first words of the epitaph, and he mulled them as he walked down the corridor.

Wrong.

Damnit, something was wrong!

They were all seated at the oval table, Rosen with a tall glass of iced tea cradled between his hands. His freckled face was bright with perspiration and excitement, his hair dusty, his eyes wide. Gil touched Else's shoulder lightly and took a chair opposite his friend.

"Well?"

Rosen grinned. "Among other things, pal, you are probably going to get rich."

"Yeah, I already thought of that."

Else looked at him strangely. "What's wrong with that, Gil?"

He shook the question off with a brusque wave of his hand, then told Rosen what he thought about the find, how those bodies came to be interred within the stone. Rosen nodded at each point, then leaned back in his seat.

"I would guess that's all pretty close, Gil. Without having any equipment here, of course, I can only make speculations, but by the manner of dress carved into the lids I think we can assume fairly accurately that those sarcophagi—not coffins, Gil—are pretty close to three hundred years old. And by the way those people have been disfigured, I would say your guess about crimes is damn near on the barrelhead."

"Oh, super!" Jerri said, ignoring the glares that came with the outburst. "Wow!"

"But who are they?" Else said.

"Don't look at me," Gil told her. "I'm English, remember? He's history."

Rosen brushed a hand over his shirt, through his hair. "If the dating is right, Else my love, they're probably Strangers."

"Well, I sure don't know them," Jerri muttered.

"God, child, haven't you learned anything?" Rosen demanded with a grin. "Strangers." He cleared this throat, a signal that Else was to pour him another glass of her tea. "When the Puritans came over here in 1620, they weren't alone. A large number of their company didn't belong to their religious sect—they were called Strangers. And though they all signed the Mayflower Compact, not all of them stuck around Plymouth Plantation. Now nobody knows for sure who settled Oxrun Station—not the first ones, at any rate—but rumor has it that our civic forebears weren't exactly the most savory of down-home folks.

I would guess what you have in that crypt is a handful of Strangers. Or descendants thereof."

"But mummies—"

Rosen lifted a cautious hand. "We don't know that for sure, Gil. We'll have to run dozens of tests, including x-rays, to see what we have. Then, with luck, we'll be able to open one of them and check the inside. It shouldn't be that hard; they're only sealed with lead as far as I can tell."

Gil tugged at his throat, and Else pulled a can of beer from the refrigerator. He drew it across his forehead before drinking, hoping the sudden chill would clear his mind. He knew Rosen suspected his nebulous doubts, but it maddened him to be unable as yet to put form to them, words to them. Instead, he asked about the epitaph.

"Beats me," Rosen admitted. "Usually they ask for some sort of forgiveness from the Almighty, or explain the crime, or just condemn them to hell. Weird, too, the way they misspelled it."

"No, they didn't," Jerri said, and winced when Gil spun around to stare at her. "Well, don't look at me, dad. I didn't do it."

"What do you mean, they didn't misspell it?"

She looked heavenward for a moment, her infinite patience noted, and spread her hands. "We had it in English, dad."

He was baffled.

"The Norse, silly. They called their netherworld Hel, and spelled it with one 'l.' Jeez, I thought you knew that."

Before he could say anything, Rosen nearly jumped from his seat. "Norse? My God, Gil, do you think it's possible we may have some evidence here of a . . ." He wiped a hand hard over his face. "I don't want to say it. I may jinx it." He pushed back his chair and paced to the sink, the stove, the table again and sat, heavily. "Think of it. Gil, just think of it."

He was; and though he did understand the potential importance of this new aspect of the discovery, there was something Jerri had left out, something none of them had—

"No, it was in English," he said, slapping a hand lightly to the table. He beckoned to the others and walked into the living room. As he stepped onto the hearth he felt a slight, knifelike chill that stopped him, had him turn to look at the windows—they were closed. Beautiful, he thought; now I'm spooking myself.

Jerri and Else did not come any closer than the edge of the brick flooring; Rosen, however, joined him immediately when he moved into the chamber.

Gray, in spite of the golden light from lanterns and lamp; musty, in spite of the fresh air; silent, without echoes.

He found it easier to look at the four smaller sarcophagi than the larger one. Somehow, its position contrived to keep it in shadow, its size doubling though the crypt's ceiling was too low for Gil to stand upright.

When Rosen touched his shoulder he almost shrieked.

Trying to keep his shadow from obscuring too much of the floor, he pointed at low mounds of what seemed like earth at the foot of each of the bases. "Dirt, right?"

Rosen nodded. "I think it might have been in wooden containers, but only an analysis of that stuff will tell me for sure."

"All right. But if Jerri's right, this here isn't right." He rubbed a hand across the back of his neck. "What I mean is, the Norse used to bury their dead with their weapons, worldly goods, things that were important to them. Much like the Egyptians, if it comes to that. But there isn't anything here, not even some kind of symbol to protect them in their crossing over to . . . wherever. No guardians, or companions, something like that."

"If they were criminals, as those depictions indicate, they wouldn't have them."

"I'm not so sure, Howard. Maybe."

They returned to the living room, and Gil felt the chill again. Rosen, however, seemed not to notice; he had moved to the side wall where he was staring enviously at Gil's small collection of rifles in a hanging, glass-door case.

"Always knew you had the Daniel Boone in you, Gil," he said, and lifted his glass to take a drink.

Gil turned back toward the crypt.

"Honey?" Else moved to his side. "Honey, you haven't eaten

all day. Do you want me to make up some sandwiches or something?"

The glass; the drink.

She hugged herself tightly. "Gil, are you going away again?"

"Jesus," Rosen said, "you've got enough ammunition here to fight off an army."

Drink.

"Gil?"

He smiled blankly and snatched up the flashlight from the coffee table. Back inside the chamber he stood in front of the epitaph, thinking.

Outside, he was dimly aware of a slow rising wind scratching leaves over the porch roof like rats' claws; of a white curtain fluttering in a draft; of a passing car; of Rosen chambering a round, pulling the bolt back and ejecting the shell.

Whatever was inside those coffins, or whatever the hell Howard called them, was probably mummified by now. An airless room, the intense heat held by the stone winter and summer— a mummy of . . . somebody in each. But why here? A pharaoh builds a pyramid not just to be buried in, but to point a regal finger that says *here I am!* Gravestones serve the same purpose. These weren't meant to be found by anyone, at any time . . . ever.

He reached out and traced a finger around *Earth.*

No. Correction. If that were so, the wall would not have been hinged.

Then . . .

He touched *Wind.*

Far enough in the future so that people would have forgotten why they were here in the first place? He nodded to himself. And why should they forget—so their discovery would yield only the fact that they lived, sometimes important enough for any man who doesn't want to die, to be forgotten; only that, and not their crimes.

He flashed the light over the gargoyles. Christ, what had they done to deserve memorials like this?

He stood away from the epitaph wall and shook his head. It

still wasn't right. It was the sound of ice cubes clinking in Rosen's glass that had reminded him of the words, and brought him the fact of the elements' mention: *earth, wind, fire . . . water.* So?

He grunted and stepped outside again, saw that the women had left, and heard them tinkering in the kitchen. Rosen was standing in the middle of the floor, a rifle cradled in his arms. He was smiling.

"I can't believe this, Gil," he said. "My God, this is going to make me, you know that."

Gil grinned back. "You wouldn't kid me, would you?"

"I mean, you deal with words, right? I'm the one who deals in facts, so I'm supposed to be the one who should have found this."

He laughed and punched at Rosen's shoulder. "Relax, pal, I don't want any of this rubbing off on me."

Rosen sobered. "What is it, Gil? You've been weird ever since I got here."

"I don't know. We've got all these theories down pat, with lots of nice supporting speculation that will probably be borne out once the experts get to work, and yet . . ."

"I . . . know what you mean."

Gil looked at him sharply.

"Jerri would say it's creepy. My mother would call it garbage. I say, though, that there's more to that place in there than I think I want to know."

"Like what?" He moved closer to his friend, searching his eyes for an answer.

"I watch a lot of old movies."

"So do I."

"There's always a little old woman who pops out of an alley and warns the hero not to—"

Gil clapped a hand to his forehead. "Damnit!" He looked around the room and found Rosen's glass. He grabbed it and returned to the crypt, pointing with it to the epitaph when Rosen followed him in.

"Okay . . . so?"

Gil felt the chill deepen, felt the shadows begin to writhe. He knew it was his imagination, but he couldn't help checking the door to see that it was still open.

"I'm supposed to be the one who works with words, you said." He lay the glass lightly against the epitaph's first word. "This is the operative thing here, Howard. If. If. *If* a combination of these things should occur over a period of time—or at one time, I don't know—*then* we're not supposed to cry. Water, get it? Water is a catalyst."

"For what?"

"Beats me. Animation? Bringing these things back to life? How the hell should I know?"

Rosen shifted the rifle from one hand to another. "Gil, sometimes you scare me, you know that?"

They turned, then, at a shout from the kitchen, a cry of pain, an exclamation of fright.

"Else burned herself again," Gil said. "She can't use a frying pan to save her life."

"You know something?" Rosen said, ignoring him. "If that's just dirt down there, and if we count the fireplace and what's there in winter—or maybe this heat wave, and that wind you said you felt when the chamber opened . . ." He grinned mischievously, took the glass from Gil's hand and swept his arm wide, dumping the contents across the five.

The chill became a cold.

Another cry, louder, from the kitchen.

The lanterns winked out.

They backed away to the hearth, not looking at each other, Gil suddenly wishing he were more like his wife so he could look at the matter with perspective, with practicality: there were no spells to be cast because spells did not exist; there were no creatures in there because the bodies inside the stone were decayed and dust; he had misinterpreted the epitaph because he had felt curious all day and his mind was simply looking for any explanation at all to calm itself.

He looked to the foyer; it was filling with smoke.

Within the crypt stone grated against stone.

To his left, orange light flickered in the dining room, giving a hellish life to the smoke boiling in.

A window smashed.

He could not move.

Jerri raced to the front door, a towel draped over her head. She yanked it open and screamed for her parents, plunging outside as Else ran out of a cloud of flame into the living room and grabbed Gil's arm. Shouting. Weeping. The sleeves of her shirt torn at the shoulder.

Stone against stone.

Gil yanked the rifle from Rosen's grip and pushed him and his wife toward the door. Rosen caught on immediately and pulled the shrieking woman through the smoke. Gil spun back to the fireplace, his eyes beginning to water, his throat growing parched, the skin on his hands and face drawing taut as the heat increased and the fire bellowed through the tinder-dry house.

Shapes drifted.

He snapped the rifle to his shoulder and began firing into the crypt. When the weapon was emptied he reloaded and fired again.

Shapes.

Again.

Then the carpet began to smolder and he threw the rifle aside, ran for the door and fell coughing into Else's arms while the front windows smashed outward, the elm tree took sparks, and the second floor windows had flames for a tongue.

They withdrew to the fence, to the sidewalk, as the first engine screamed to a halt at the curb. There was too much confusion, then, and hysterical giggling as Rosen suddenly remembered his roadster and fought through the growing crowd of onlookers and firemen to back it out of the drive.

Nobody asked him what he had seen through the smoke; nobody asked him why he was shooting in a fire.

But he watched his house transform itself into a torch, found himself following the thick grim hoses to the nozzles, to the futile streams of water that turned to steam on contact. Else was weeping, Jerri's teeth were chattering, and they did not argue when he guided them through the chaos to Rosen's car and made them get in. Howard looked to protest, changed his mind when he saw Gil's face.

"Where to?"

"Anywhere." He hesitated. "Fast."

"Gil?" He kissed Else's forehead and pulled her to his shoulder. Held her. Squeezed her. And finally, as they reached the bend that would take them to the village, he looked behind and knew what had been wrong. It hadn't been the epitaph, the spell, whatever it had been that had brought . . . something . . . from that granite; it was the chamber itself. The agent had said the core stone was easily nine feet on a side. The crypt was only five—and if the rest wasn't solid then the creatures were not, as he'd thought, what he was supposed to find. *They* were the guardians, the symbols, the trappings for the Beyond. There *was* another room.

"Gee," his daughter said at the fierce glow in the sky.

But Gil could only think of the fire, and the water . . . the heat, and the cold . . . and could only pray he was long gone before the core stone cracked open.

PART III
IN THE FAR FUTURE

REVELATION IN SEVEN STAGES

by BARRY N. MALZBERG

What role, one wonders, can yesterday's mummies possibly play in the far future? Are they doomed to extinction, along with other relics of the past, or is their destiny one of even greater importance than the museums and archeological digs of today? These questions were presented to Barry N. Malzberg, one of the finest of modern science fiction writers, and the strong extrapolative short-short which follows is his answer.

"Revelation in Seven Stages" postulates a postapocalyptic future in which the final war has devastated earth; its remaining inhabitants have fled to other worlds, leaving nothing for the Lyrans, a race of alien beings who belong to the Central Galactic Federation, to find when they arrive except thousands of undiscovered mummies buried under the old Egyptian valleys. The use to which the federation puts these mummies, in the year 7528, not only offers a fitting "afterword" to this anthology but perhaps the "last word" on the mummy theme.

In his dozen years of professional writing Barry N. Malzberg has published some eighty novels, two hundred fifty short stories and essays, eight collections, and ten co-edited anthologies, and managed in the bargain to enrage, bewilder, and delight any number of readers, editors, critics, and other writers. He is his own man and his own writer; his attitudes, like his fiction, are unique, idiosyncratic, and often misunderstood. Those who know him little or at all find him abrasive, puzzling, compulsive, and either depressing or exasperating. Those who know him well find him to be a human being, with all of the positive qualities that term conveys. (It should be noted that your editor is in the latter camp, having written four novels and some thirty short stories and co-edited four anthologies with Malzberg from 1972 to the time of this writing.) Among the best and best-known of his work are the novels Beyond Apollo, *for which he received the John W. Campbell Memorial Award as the Best Science Fiction Novel of 1972,* Herovit's World, Guernica Night, *and* Chorale, *and such outstanding collections as* Down Here in the Dream Quarter *and the recent* The Man Who Loved the Midnight Lady.

I

OBSERVERS AND crew of the great Lyran fleet come to an abandoned earth in A.D. 7528. Technologically adept portions of humanity had fled for the stars (and been lost) in the advent of the final war of 2033; the remainder of the race had perished. Five and a half millennia have long dispersed any trace of humanity or its artifacts; the Lyran expedition is only one stop on a routine survey which has been in progress since A.D. 853 and has arrived too late to be of any service to our barbarous and devastated race.

II

Carefully sweeping the terrain with sophisticated scanning devices, the Lyrans are led to mummies buried under the Egyptian valleys. It is the speculation of researchers that as many as seven and a half million undiscovered mummies might have existed after the fall of the empire; the survey team has come across what is left of this splendid cache. Needless to say, they

are astonished that on an otherwise violated and abandoned
planet there should exist corpses in such a remarkable state of
preservation. They chatter to one another in their birdlike way,
share thoughts with more intricate subvocalizations, and proceed to dissect the mummies so that they may understand as
much as possible of these phenomena.

III

The researchers, however, are puzzled. It seems impossible to
them that the decedents could have had intellectual or biologi-
cal function. Brain has been replaced by spice, viscera with wax
and herbs, the arteries of all design have been hardened to
glisten through embalming technique. The shells are well preserved: hairless bipeds, individually casketed, surrounded by
what appear to be their possessions. But the bipeds, according
to survey zoologists, could hardly have been motile, let alone
capable of evolving the very sophisticated and somewhat mysterious preservative technique.

"I do not fully understand this," the biochemist concedes to
his squad leader; "there seems no basis for such creatures to
have existed without nervous or circulatory systems, but they
did. Do you think this is some kind of elaborate joke?"

IV

The squad leader does not think that it is an elaborate joke
but decides to cable headquarters for further advice. Headquarters, temporarily established on Pluto in satellite orbit, comes in
to consider the situation and after a while transistors a verdict.

"These are not sentient beings or their remains," it advises.
"These are machines." Headquarters is pleased.

V

The mummies are unearthed, by the hundreds of thousands,
and laid in stacks in an area which was once the Kew Gardens

of Queens, New York. They present a fiery and disturbing aspect in daylight, were any of the Lyrans to pay them attention, but this aphidlike race has little poetic instinct and in any case lacks the cultural referent necessary for emotional response to mummies. They busy themselves with arrangement and spend their evenings in the survey colony using hastily constructed geodesic domes against the chill and counting the days to their flight.

VI

Great ships from the Central Galactic Federation arrive to take on the mummies. The mummies are valuable to the federation (and the Lyrans have done a major service by discovering them) because at this time of almost unbounded colonization, bodies are needed to fill the great ships that probe the undiscovered universe. A federation law, obscure in origin but regarded as based on sacred taboo, prohibits the use of probe ships without occupants; the ships must have aboard them figures which at least simulate the appearance of an intelligent race and the mummies are the best contribution to the solution of the problem ever found. Obviously duty on a probe ship would be risky or dull; only felons and lunatics could be induced previously to staff the probes.

But the mummies will solve this difficulty. Sentient in aspect, magnificent in form, they lack viscera to feed, circulation to nourish, brains to bore, emotions to feel pain. They provide all of the advantages of crew with none of its liabilities and since the probes are controlled by radio devices, they will never have to be brought back: no turnover, no murders or suicides aboard.

The federation expresses its thanks and promises rewards when the Lyrans return to the home worlds. The Lyrans acknowledge with humility. And the probes filled with mummies depart, one by one, from the Kew Gardens at several multiples of Planck's constant to seek the edges of possibility.

VII

What once were golden kings and queens, workers of the earth and tillers of the soil, advocates and doctors and princes of darkness lie in close steel as the dreaming universe whisks past. They will not know what has happened to them for a long time, but in due course the fabled reconstruction will begin. They will rise, they will rise and see again; their tongues will uncleave and their mouths speak homage; their eyes see and their hearts race . . . and who is to say at some incalculable distance in the divide of some incalculable star they will not apprehend all that has happened to them: Nefertiti's curse become a promise, their long sleep as a watch for morning? As a watch for morning.

Book Three

GHOUL!
A Chrestomathy
of Ogrery

INTRODUCTION

MIDNIGHT.

Inside the hushed graveyard, two men move stealthily among headstones and jutting tombs. Their clothing is dark, and in their hands are shovels, and they blend with the shadows that enwrap the night shapes of the cemetery. Each is watchful for only one thing—the freshly turned earth that marks a new grave.

These men are ghouls.

They have come here to desecrate and rob, to snatch away a body from its resting place and to sell it to a medical researcher for dissection. They are a latter-day Burke and Hare—a team of grave robbers.

There is no fear in them as they make their way through the darkness; these are men with little emotion of any kind. They know what time the caretaker makes his rounds, and that the man is old and hobbled and lives in a cottage on the far side of the burial ground. They are certain they will not be heard at their work, that they will not be discovered before it is completed. They have been here before, these men; they are ghouls of experience and guile. And so they are not afraid. What, after all, is there to be frightened of in a cemetery at midnight?

It does not take them long to find the new grave. They have a sixth sense about such things, and the faint smell of fresh earth draws them, radarlike, toward the bulky shape of a tomb nearby. The edge of a thin moon appears behind low scudding clouds;

the tomb's marble facing, and its statute of a winged angel, gleam palely in the darkness. And lying between it and a small tree they see the fresh grave.

But it is not quite what they expected to find, and they come to a standstill, staring, gripped by momentary confusion.

The grave is open, not closed, with earth scattered and mounded beside it. As if someone—or something—had dug into it in a frenzy. But not with shovels or other implements; with hands or feet. Or claws.

The first moment of confusion gives way to wariness, to pangs of unease. They are not totally without emotion, these men; they are not fearless. And what they see before them is the stuff of terror.

Their eyes probe the shadow shapes around them. But they see nothing. The wind makes low moanings as it skirls among the tombstones; there is nothing else to hear.

Or is there?

Both men move closer to the open grave, their shovels upraised. The moan of the wind lessens for a moment. The ghouls stop again; the hairs rise and prickle on their necks.

Sounds nearby.

Muted sounds, not quite discernible yet.

The wind repeats its lament, briefly. In the lull which follows, the two men identify the direction of the sounds: the heavy shadows alongside the nearest marble tomb. One of the ghouls takes a step toward it, but the other grasps his arm, restrains him. They stand rigid, listening, peering into the black.

And the sounds become louder, voracious—recognizable.

They are the sounds of *gnawing*.

Sudden primitive fear consumes the two men. They drop their shovels, screaming in whispers, and run away into the night.

For there are ghouls, and then there are ghouls. And the ones who rob graves for medical researchers are not at all the worst kind . . .

It is commonly believed that vampires and werewolves are the most dreaded of all mythical creatures in the superstition-rich countries of Eastern Europe. This is not so. The most feared of all is the *ghul*—the supernatural being who haunts graveyards and old ruins; who robs graves and feasts on the newly dead; who has the power to turn dead men into ghouls, forcing them to live inside their own graves and to periodically rise up and feed on other corpses or to commit acts of atrocity on the living.

Such demons do not really exist, of course. They, like the vampire and the werewolf, belong to the realm of superstition and fantasy, to a darker and more gullible age.

Yet there *are* ghouls in these modern and enlightened times: living men—not animated corpses or supernatural beings— grave robbers, body-snatchers, desecrators of the dead's domain. Their number is small, but perhaps not as small as one might think. And in some cases, the ghoulish acts they commit are even more terrible than any which could be perpetrated by mythical eaters of the dead.

Consider, for example; the case of Burke and Hare:

> *Up the close and doun the stair,*
> *But and ben wi' Burke and Hare.*
> *Burke's the butcher, Hare's the thief,*
> *Knox the boy that buys the beef.*

These lines are famous in the annals of crime and rascality, and so are the names William Burke and William Hare. That these two men were ghouls is beyond any doubt, as an account of their activities in the years 1827–1828 demonstrates.

Hare was the owner of a cheap doss-house called Log's Lodging, in a slum district of Edinburgh, Scotland; Burke, a cobbler, was one of his permanent lodgers. Both were native Irishmen who had immigrated to Scotland to work on the Union Canal.

Another of Hare's lodgers, an old army pensioner, died in November of 1827 owing three months' rent and leaving Hare no way in which to collect the debt. Until, that is, word reached the lodging-house owner that the Edinburgh medical school was in need of bodies for dissection in its new department of anatomy, since the number of bodies allocated by law for that purpose was inadequate. Some medical students had provided corpses themselves by stealing them from local graveyards; other suitable cadavers were supplied on a more businesslike basis by professional "Resurrection Men." But a demand still existed—and the school was willing to pay up to ten pounds sterling for a body in acceptable condition.

Hare, with Burke's help, removed the corpse of the army pensioner from its coffin, weighted down the coffin with timber, and resealed it. Then they placed the body in a sack and set out for the medical school. On the way, however, they were side-tracked by a friend of an anatomist named Dr. Knox, who was a professional rival of the school's owner. Knox paid Burke and Hare handsomely for the cadaver, taking them to be Resurrection Men, and allowed as how he would be delighted to see them again when they had another body to dispose of.

In the days that followed, Burke and Hare became ghoulish entrepreneurs. But instead of stealing bodies from graveyards after the fashion of Resurrection Men, they determined to create their own supply with considerably less effort. With the help of Mrs. Hare and Burke's mistress they murdered sixteen people over the next eleven months and sold the corpses to Dr. Knox. Their *modus operandi* was to single out friendless drifters, offer them bed-and-board, get them drunk, and smother them. They would then strip the body, place it in a tea chest, and send word to Dr. Knox that another subject was available.

The career of Burke and Hare came to an end in the summer of 1828 when, after quarreling over the division of money paid by Dr. Knox, they were careless with the disposal of one of their victims. An old woman named Mrs. Docherty had been stripped of her clothes and left under a heap of straw in the doss-house; one of the other lodgers became curious, had a look, and immediately went to the police. Burke and Hare and their women were arrested. Hare and Mrs. Hare turned King's Evidence (agreed to testify for the prosecution), thereby securing legal immunity for themselves. Burke was subsequently hanged. Hare did not get off without a fitting punishment, however: an enraged crowd tried to lynch him, and during his attempted escape he was hurled into a lime pit and blinded. He spent the rest of his days begging pennies along Oxford Street in London.

As for Dr. Knox, he escaped prosecution by claiming he had no knowledge of the source of the cadavers he purchased from Burke and Hare. But his medical career was ruined, and he died poor and broken in London in 1862.

A different, and much more monstrous case of ghoulism took place in Paris in 1848–1849, and had as its principal a sergeant-major in the French infantry named Françoise Bertrand. This individual rivals Gilles de Rais, the infamous lycanthropic child-murderer, in the perpetration of crimes so heinous that they boggle the mind.

The case began when graves in several Parisian cemeteries were discovered to have been desecrated. The corpses which had been interred in these graves were mutilated, disembow-eled, and in some instances even partially devoured. It was subsequently determined by medical experts that the teeth marks on the bodies were those of a human being.

Armed guards and dogs were placed on duty at all the city's burial grounds while police conducted a not very fruitful investi-gation. There were reports of a creature half-human and half-beast lurking around this or that graveyard, only to disappear when pursued, but these were largely the result of public hyste-ria. The atrocities ceased altogether; it seemed for a time that the ghoul had vanished.

But then, on the morning after the burial of an attractive young woman, the cycle began again. The young woman's grave was found to have been dug up, the coffin torn open, and the body mutilated and gnawed in the same fashion as the earlier cases. A wave of other barbarities followed, even though intense security measures were undertaken. Superstitious fear spread among the Parisian populace; there were tales of supernatural beings, of a plague of demons haunting the city's cemeteries.

The truth finally emerged as a result of detective work on the part of a policeman, who noted marks atop a wall at the grave-yard of St. Parnasse. A spring-gun loaded with nails and bits of iron was set upon this wall, and that night a squad of policemen hid in the area. In the dark hours toward morning, the spring-gun detonated. The converging police saw an apelike figure (or so they thought at the time) scaling the wall and fired several shots at it, but it managed to escape. Later investigation revealed bloodstains and pieces of a dark-colored fabric, which proved to have come from a French army uniform. This provided focus for the police manhunt, and it was only a matter of days before Sergeant-Major Bertrand, who claimed to have been accidentally wounded and was hospitalized on the night of the spring-gun explosion, was taken into custody.

Bertrand's confession revealed the tortured soul of the damned. He had had destructive impulses from an early age, he said, as well as bizarre desires toward women; his primary fantasy was of a roomful of women with whom he would engage in orgiastic relations and thereupon murder so he could mutilate their corpses. When these perverted cravings became too strong to withstand, he had committed atrocities on the bodies of animals in order to achieve sexual gratification. But it was human flesh he craved, and early in 1848 he had come upon a fresh grave in a Parisian cemetery.

"Horrible desires seized me," he is quoted as saying. "My head throbbed, my heart palpitated! I could not resist!"

Bertrand dug up the new-made grave, mutilated the body, and found such sadistic satisfaction in the act that he was compelled to repeat it again and again. He claimed to have committed necro-sexual acts on the remains of several women, beginning with the body of a sixteen-year-old girl in the summer of 1848. He further stated that he had violated at least eighteen corpses in this fashion during his two-year rampage.

Incredibly enough, psychiatrists of the time judged this human monster to be legally sane and capable of standing trial. Because Bertrand had not harmed a living person, and because the laws against the mutilation of corpses were uncertain, he was sentenced to a single year in prison. He disappeared soon after his release, and was not heard from for decades. Charles Fort, in the last of his books on strange phenomena, *Wild Talents* (1932), quotes an item from the June 27, 1874 issue of the *San*

Francisco Daily Evening Bulletin, which states that "Bertrand the Ghoul is still alive: he is cured of his hideous disease, and is cited as a model of gentleness and propriety." This may or may not be true. It also may or may not be true that Bertrand continued to sate his evil appetites for many years after his imprisonment; he was only twenty-five at the time of his arrest and trial.

So you see, ghouls do exist in reality as well as myth. Perhaps there is no such thing as a supernatural being who robs graves and feeds on corpses. Perhaps. But there *are* human beings who have done such things; there *are* ghouls who have run amok in the world as we know it.

We can only pray that we do not see or hear of their kind again . . . .

Nonfiction works dealing specifically with the phenomenon of the human ghoul have been few and far between. The only one of consequence is P.J. Murphy's *Ghouls: Studies and Case Histories of Necrophilia,* published in London in 1965. The subtitle aptly describes the contents, which is reading only for the strong of heart and stomach.

Two other interesting books are *The King and the Corpse* (1948), by Heinrich Zimmer, an account of the life and times of a medieval Teutonic king whose kingdom was toppled because of ghoulish acts performed on his dead wife's body, and Daniel Cohen's *The Body Snatchers,* a tongue-in-cheek look at the history of grave robbing.

A number of academic works on true crime and psychosexual aberration, as well as several popular texts dealing with these and related matters, mention Burke and Hare and Sergeant-Major Bertrand, among other case histories. One of the best of these books is R.L. Masters's *Perverse Crimes in History* (1963), which is subtitled *Sadism, Lust-Murder, Necrophilia—Ancient to Modern Times.* Again, not recommended for the faint of heart and stomach.

The list of novels based on ghoulish themes is somewhat longer and more varied, although none of those involving traditional ghouls—body-snatchers and eaters of the dead, both human and supernatural—is of any particular quality. Among these are Robert Tralins's *Ghoul Lover* (1972), and Michael McDowell's *Cold Moon Over Babylon* (1980).

One of the more interesting variations on the theme is Curt Siodmak's classic chiller, *Donovan's Brain* (1942), in which a doctor (a *sane* scientist, for a change) keeps the brain of a dead man alive in his desert laboratory. The brain gathers strength and eventually seizes control of the doctor, with terrifying results. Not a ghoulish story in the strict sense of the term, but powerful and effective nonetheless.

Jeff Rice's *The Night Strangler* (1974), the basis for the made-for-TV movie of the same title and a subsequent television series starring Darren McGavin *(The Night Stalker)*, is also a worthwhile tale of ghoulish goings-on. It deals with a supposedly long-dead medical man who strangles young women and taps their blood in order to manufacture an elixir that keeps him young and healthy. This gentleman also had a rather nasty penchant for keeping, wherever he went, and holding discussions with, the decaying bodies of his relatives.

Other recent novels of interest include John Russo's *Night of the Living Dead* (1974), based on the low-budget cult film about reanimated, flesh-eating corpses, and George Romero's and Susanna Sparrow's *Dawn of the Dead* (1978), based on the film sequel; Robin Cook's bestseller, *Coma* (1977), about doctors at a certain hospital who steal anatomical parts from patients and sell them to rich folks in need of transplants; and Gary Brandner's . . . *Walkers* (1980), which involves a woman who is supposed to die but doesn't, with the result that souls dwelling in the Beyond reanimate corpses to pursue and kill her—a far-fetched but still entertaining premise.

Ghoul-based films are much more prevalent than books. Among the notable are the famous "lost" film, *The Ghoul* (1933) —no known prints remain in existence—starring Boris Karloff and Sir Cedric Hardwicke; another fine Karloff vehicle, *The Body Snatcher* (1945), based on Robert Louis Stevenson's story which leads off this chrestomathy; still another Karloff shocker, *Corridors of Blood* (1962); *The Premature Burial* (1962), featuring Ray

Milland and loosely based on the classic Poe short story; and the British-made *The Ghoul* (1974), with Peter Cushing. All of these deal with ghouls of the traditional variety.

Worthwhile films employing variations on the theme include George Zucco as *The Mad Ghoul* (1943); *Donovan's Brain* (1953), with Lew Ayres; *Mr. Sardonicus* (1961), a William Castle production based on a Ray Russell novelette; and *Horror Express* (1972), starring the inimitable British team of Peter Cushing and Christopher Lee (with Telly Savalas thrown in for good measure), and effectively combining monsters and reanimated corpses aboard a speeding European train.

On the other side of the quality coin, there is a 1972 Spanish-Italian film with the more or less incredible title of *The Hunchback from the Morgue,* which deals with such topics as deformity, necrophilia, incineration, a mad scientist, a laboratory monster that breaks out of its dungeon and destroys several villains, and the love of a hunchback for a pretty girl. It has been reported that the main actor, one Paul Naschy, allowed himself to be attacked on film by half-starved rats, in the interest of authenticity; and that, for the same reason, he beheaded an actual corpse in front of the cameras, allegedly with permission from a local morgue!

There have been a few fantasy/horror anthologies devoted in part to ghouls; notable among them are Groff Conklin's *The Graveyard Reader* (1958) and Peter Haining's *The Unspeakable People* (1969). But the present volume is the first to bring together only those shorter works involving, directly or indirectly, matters ghoulish. In the pages which follow you will find such venerable classics of the horror genre as Robert Louis Stevenson's "The Body-Snatchers," C.M. Eddy's grim "The Loved Dead," Sir Hugh Clifford's "The Ghoul," and Henry S. Whitehead's "The Chadbourne Episode"; such neoclassics as Stephen King's "Gray Matter" and Barry N. Malzberg's "Indigestion"; such little-known chillers as Fredric Brown's "The Spherical Ghoul," Chelsea Quinn Yarbro's "Disturb Not My Slumbering Fair," Aubrey Davidson's "The Edinburgh Landlady" (verse), and this editor's "Memento Mori," and a superior original tale, "Quietly

Now," by Charles L. Grant.

Not all of these stories are as gruesome as the subject matter indicates: some are underplayed, some even have elements of humor. But each is, in its own way, an experience you will not soon forget, as well as a reminder that no matter how much we might like to believe otherwise, there *are* ghouls in reality as well as myth . . . .

Settle back, then. Turn the lights down and make yourself comfortable. And pay no attention to the moan of the wind outside; pay no attention to the darkness, or to the things that go bump in the night. For what you are holding in your hand is fiction. Only fiction.

Though there may be ghouls abroad in the world, none of them will be coming after *you*.

Not tonight, anyway . . . .

—Bill Pronzini

PART I
TRADITIONAL GHOULS

THE EDINBURGH LANDLADY

by AUBREY DAVIDSON

The saga of Burke and Hare is here revisited, in verse form and with a macabre new twist—an apt prologue to the ghoulish prose delights which follow.

Aubrey Davidson (born 1925) is a dental surgeon by profession—at present he is a dental adviser to the British government, in the Department of Health and Social Security—and a writer and poet by avocation. His short stories and verse have appeared in such American and British publications as Ellery Queen's Mystery Magazine, London Mystery Magazine, London Calling, Weekend, *and* The Countrymen. *He also published his own magazine for a short time, entitled* Mouthpiece. *Married and the father of two sons and a daughter, he makes his home in London.*

Now JENNY, bolt the outer door and trim the candle's light.
Outside the wind blows bitter and you *must* stay home tonight.
For just beyond the hospital, two killers idly lurk—

The name of one is Mr. Hare, the other Mr. Burke.
  Slung across their hand cart
  Rests a coffin box
  That carries pretty ladies
  Along to Dr. Knox.

Now Jenny, do as you are bidden for your own protection.
You know the Sawbones pays in gold for bodies for dissection.
The poor souls go to heaven from the house in Surgeons'
  Square
To buy a flask of gin for Mr. Burke and Mr. Hare.
  Remember Mary Haldane
  With her golden locks:
  A pretty lady till she went
  Along to Dr. Knox.

Now Jenny, close the shutters fast and do not leave your bed.
I hear the church gate creaking and they're bringing out the
  dead.
It means the body-snatchers are at their loathsome work,
And the best known of them all are Mr. Hare and Mr. Burke.
  One's a savage tiger
  And one's an artful fox,
  But both take pretty ladies
  Along to Dr. Knox.

Now Jenny's fast asleep and from the door I softly call.
I draw aside the bolt and let two shadows cross the hall.
My finger on my lips, I point the way toward the stair—
I get well paid for helping Mr. Burke and Mr. Hare.
  Such innocence and folly
  The Beast of Fortune mocks!
  For I send *all* my ladies
  Along to Dr. Knox.

THE BODY-SNATCHERS

by ROBERT LOUIS STEVENSON

As mentioned in the introduction, the human ghoul known as the Resurrection Man was not an uncommon figure in England and Scotland during the first half of the nineteenth century. Such an individual, Robert Louis Stevenson says, "was not to be deterred by any of the sanctities of customary piety. It was part of his trade to despise and desecrate the scrolls and trumpets of old tombs, the paths worn by the feet of worshipers and mourners . . . To bodies that had been laid in earth, in joyful expectation of a far different awakening, there came that hasty, lamplit, terror-haunted resurrection of the spade and mattock. The coffin was forced, the cerements torn, and the melancholy relics, clad in sackcloth, after being rattled for hours on moonless byways, were at length exposed to uttermost indignities before a class of gaping boys."

The body-snatchers in question here, like the infamous Burke and Hare (who are incidental characters in the tale), work for an Edinburgh anatomist named Mr. K——. And the ghostly fate which befalls them as a result of their crimes is, in its own way, even more fitting and terrible than the actual fates of Mr. Burke and Mr. Hare. Stevenson's personal name for the horror story was "crawler"; that he penned one of the great crawlers

*of all time in "The Body-Snatchers" is indisputable, as you'll no doubt
agree when you reach its final, chilling lines.*

*A native of Edinburgh, where he was born in 1850, Robert Louis
Stevenson was one of the most prolific (despite a premature death of
tuberculosis in 1894) and diversified writers of his time. In addition to
such romantic adventure novels as* Treasure Island, Kidnapped, *and*
David Balfour, *he wrote autobiographical travel books, essays and critical studies, poetry, collaborative novels with his American stepson, Lloyd
Osbourne* (The Wrong Box, The Wrecker), *and, of course, tales of
horror and the supernatural. Such short novels as* The Strange Case
of Dr. Jekyll and Mr. Hyde, The Beach of Falesa, *and* The Tale
of Tod Lapraik, *and such short stories as "The Body-Snatchers,"
"Markheim," "The Isle of Voices" (see* Voodoo!), *"Olalla," and
"Thrawn Janet" have earned him a richly deserved reputation as a master
of the macabre.*

EVERY NIGHT in the year, four of us sat in the small parlor of the
George at Debenham—the undertaker, and the landlord, and
Fettes, and myself. Sometimes there would be more; but blow
high, blow low, come rain or snow or frost, we four would be
each planted in his own particular armchair. Fettes was an old
drunken Scotsman, a man of education obviously, and a man of
some property, since he lived in idleness. He had come to
Debenham years ago, while still young, and by a mere continu-
ance of living had grown to be an adopted townsman. His blue
camlet cloak was a local antiquity, like the church spire. His
place in the parlor at the George, his absence from church, his
old, crapulous, disreputable vices, were all things of course in
Debenham. He had some vague radical opinions and some fleeting infidelities, which he would now and again set forth and
emphasize with tottering slaps upon the table. He drank rum—
five glasses regularly every evening; and for the greater portion
of his nightly visit to the George sat, with his glass in his right
hand, in a state of melancholy alcoholic saturation. We called

him the doctor, for he was supposed to have some special knowledge of medicine, and had been known, upon a pinch, to set a fracture or reduce a dislocation; but, beyond these slight particulars, we had no knowledge of his character and antecedents.

One dark winter night—it had struck nine some time before the landlord joined us—there was a sick man in the George, a great neighboring proprietor suddenly struck down with apoplexy on his way to Parliament; and the great man's still greater London doctor had been telegraphed to his bedside. It was the first time that such a thing had happened in Debenham, for the railway was but newly open, and we were all proportionately moved by the occurrence.

"He's come," said the landlord, after he had filled and lighted his pipe.

"He?" said I. "Who?—not the doctor?"

"Himself," replied our host.

"What is his name?"

"Dr. Macfarlane," said the landlord.

Fettes was far through his third tumbler, stupidly fuddled, now nodding over, now staring mazily around him; but at the last word he seemed to awaken, and repeated the name "Macfarlane" twice, quietly enough the first time, but with sudden emotion at the second.

"Yes," said the landlord, "that's his name, Dr. Wolfe Macfarlane."

Fettes became instantly sober; his eyes awoke, his voice became clear, loud and steady, his language forcible and earnest. We were all startled by the transformation, as if a man had risen from the dead.

"I beg your pardon," he said; "I am afraid I have not been paying much attention to your talk. Who is this Wolfe Macfarlane?" And then, when he had heard the landlord out, "It cannot be, it cannot be," he added; "and yet I would like well to see him face to face."

"Do you know him, doctor?" asked the undertaker, with a gasp.

"God forbid!" was the reply. "And yet the name is a strange

one; it were too much to fancy two. Tell me, landlord, is he old?"

"Well," said the host, "he's not a young man, to be sure, and his hair is white; but he looks younger than you."

"He is older, though; years older. But," with a slap upon the table, "it's the rum you see in my face—rum and sin. This man, perhaps, may have an easy conscience and a good digestion. Conscience! Hear me speak. You would think I was some good, old, decent Christian, would you not? But no, not I; I never canted. Voltaire might have canted if he'd stood in my shoes; but the brains"—with a rattling fillip on his bald head—"the brains were clear and active, and I saw and made no deductions."

"If you know this doctor," I ventured to remark, after a somewhat awful pause, "I should gather that you do not share the landlord's good opinion."

Fettes paid no regard to me.

"Yes," he said, with sudden decision, "I must see him face to face."

There was another pause, and then a door was closed rather sharply on the first floor, and a step was heard upon the stair.

"That's the doctor," cried the landlord. "Look sharp, and you can catch him."

It was but two steps from the small parlor to the door of the old George Inn; the wide oak staircase landed almost in the street; there was room for a Turkey rug and nothing more between the threshold and the last round of the descent; but this little space was every evening brilliantly lit up, not only by the light upon the stair and the great signal-lamp below the sign, but by the warm radiance of the barroom window. The George thus brightly advertised itself to passers-by in the cold street. Fettes walked steadily to the spot, and we, who were hanging behind, beheld the two men meet, as one of them had phrased it, face to face. Dr. Macfarlane was alert and vigorous. His white hair set off his pale and placid, although energetic countenance. He was richly dressed in the finest of broadcloth and the whitest of linen, with a great gold watch-chain, and studs and spectacles of the same precious material. He wore a broad folded tie, white and speckled with lilac, and he carried on his arm a comfortable driving coat of fur. There was no doubt but he became his years, breathing, as he did, of wealth and consideration; and it was a surprising contrast to see our parlor sot—bald, dirty, pimpled, and robed in his old camlet cloak—confront him at the bottom of the stairs.

"Macfarlane!" he said somewhat loudly, more like a herald than a friend.

The great doctor pulled up short on the fourth step, as though the familiarity of the address surprised and somewhat shocked his dignity.

"Toddy Macfarlane!" repeated Fettes.

The London man almost staggered. He stared for the swiftest of seconds at the man before him, glanced behind him with a sort of scare, and then in a startled whisper, "Fettes!" he said, "you!"

"Ay," said the other, "me! Did you think I was dead, too? We are not so easy shut of our acquaintance."

"Hush, hush!" exclaimed the doctor. "Hush, hush! this meeting is so unexpected—I can see you are unmanned. I hardly knew you, I confess, at first; but I am overjoyed—overjoyed to have this opportunity. For the present it must be how-d'ye-do and good-bye in one, for my fly is waiting, and I must not fail the train; but you shall—let me see—yes—you shall give me your address, and you can count on early news of me. We must do something for you, Fettes. I fear you are out at elbows; but we must see to that for auld lang syne, as once we sang at suppers."

"Money!" cried Fettes; "money from you! The money that I had from you is lying where I cast it in the rain."

Dr. Macfarlane had talked himself into some measure of superiority and confidence, but the uncommon energy of this refusal cast him back into his first confusion.

A horrible, ugly look came and went across his almost venerable countenance, "My dear fellow," he said, "be it as you please; my last thought is to offend you. I would intrude on none. I will leave you my address, however—"

"I do not wish it—I do not wish to know the roof that shelters you," interrupted the other. "I heard your name; I feared it might be you; I wished to know if, after all, there were a God; I know now that there is none. Begone!"

He still stood in the middle of the rug, between the stair and doorway; and the great London physician, in order to escape, would be forced to step to one side. It was plain that he hesitated before the thought of this humiliation. White as he was, there was a dangerous glitter in his spectacles; but, while he still paused uncertain, he became aware that the driver of his fly was peering in from the street at this unusual scene, and caught a glimpse at the same time of our little body from the parlor, huddled by the corner of the bar. The presence of so many witnesses decided him at once to flee. He crouched together, brushing on the wainscot, and made a dart like a serpent, striking for the door. But his tribulation was not yet entirely at an end, for even as he was passing Fettes clutched him by the arm and these words came in a whisper, and yet painfully distinct, "Have you seen it again?"

The great rich London doctor cried out aloud with a sharp, throttling cry; he dashed his questioner across the open space, and, with his hands over his head, fled out of the door like a detected thief. Before it had occurred to one of us to make a movement the fly was already rattling toward the station. The scene was over like a dream, but the dream had left proofs and traces of its passage. Next day the servant found the fine gold spectacles broken on the threshold, and that very night we were all standing breathless by the barroom window, and Fettes at our side, sober, pale, and resolute in look.

"God protect us, Mr. Fettes!" said the landlord, coming first into possession of his customary senses. "What in the universe is all this? These are strange things you have been saying."

Fettes turned toward us; he looked us each in succession in the face. "See if you can hold your tongues," said he. "That man Macfarlane is not safe to cross; those that have done so already have repented it too late."

And then, without so much as finishing his third glass, far less waiting for the other two, he bade us good-bye and went forth, under the lamp of the hotel, into the black night.

We three turned to our places in the parlor, with the big red fire and four clear candles; and, as we recapitulated what had passed, the first chill of our surprise soon changed into a glow of curiosity. We sat late; it was the latest session I have known in the old George. Each man, before we parted, had his theory that he was bound to prove; and none of us had any nearer business in this world than to track out the past of our condemned companion, and surprise the secret that he shared with the great London doctor. It is no great boast, but I believe I was a better hand at worming out a story than either of my fellows at the George; and perhaps there is now no other man alive who could narrate to you the following foul and unnatural events.

In his young days Fettes studied medicine in the schools of Edinburgh. He had talent of a kind, the talent that picks up swiftly what it hears and readily retains it for its own. He worked little at home; but he was civil, attentive, and intelligent in the presence of his masters. They soon picked him out as a lad who listened closely and remembered well; nay, strange as it seemed to me when I first heard it, he was in those days well-favored, and pleased by his exterior. There was, at that period, a certain extramural teacher of anatomy, whom I shall here designate by the letter K. His name was subsequently too well-known. The man who bore it skulked through the streets of Edinburgh in disguise, while the mob that applauded at the execution of Burke called loudly for the blood of his employer. But Mr. K—— was then at the top of his vogue; he enjoyed the popularity due partly to his own talent and address, partly to the incapacity of his rival, the university professor. The students, at least, swore by his name, and Fettes believed himself, and was believed by others, to have laid the foundations of success when he had acquired the favor of this meteorically famous man. Mr. K—— was a *bon vivant* as well as an accomplished teacher; he liked a sly illusion no less than a careful preparation. In both capacities Fettes enjoyed and deserved his notice, and by the second year of his attendance he held the half-regular position of second demonstrator or subassistant in his class.

In this capacity the charge of the theater and lecture room

devolved in particular upon his shoulders. He had to answer for the cleanliness of the premises and the conduct of the other students, and it was a part of his duty to supply, receive and divide the various subjects. It was with a view to this last—at that time very delicate—affair that he was lodged by Mr. K—— in the same wynd, and at last in the same building, with the dissecting rooms. Here, after a night of turbulent pleasures, his hand still tottering, his sight still misty and confused, he would be called out of bed in the black hours before the winter dawn by the unclean and desperate interlopers who supplied the table. He would open the door to these men, since infamous throughout the land. He would help them with their tragic burden, pay them their sordid price, and remain alone, when they were gone, with the unfriendly relics of humanity. From such a scene he would return to snatch another hour or two of slumber, to repair the abuses of the night, and refresh himself for the labors of the day.

Few lads could have been more insensible to the impressions of a life thus passed among the ensigns of morality. His mind was closed against all general considerations. He was incapable of interest in the fate and fortunes of another, the slave of his own desires and low ambitions. Cold, light and selfish in the last resort, he had that modicum of prudence, miscalled morality, which keeps a man from inconvenient drunkenness or punishable theft. He coveted, besides, a measure of consideration from his masters and his fellow pupils, and he had no desire to fail conspicuously in the external parts of life. Thus he made it his pleasure to gain some distinction in his studies, and day after day rendered unimpeachable eye-service to his employer, Mr. K——. For his day of work he indemnified himself by nights of roaring, blackguardly enjoyment; and when that balance had been struck, the organ that he called his conscience declared itself content.

The supply of subjects was a continual trouble to him as well as to his master. In that large and busy class, the raw material of the anatomists kept perpetually running out; and the business thus rendered necessary was not only unpleasant in itself, but threatened dangerous consequences to all who were concerned.

It was the policy of Mr. K—— to ask no questions in his dealings with the trade. "They bring the body, and we pay the price," he used to say, dwelling on the alliteration—*"quid pro quo."* And, again, and somewhat profanely, "Ask no questions," he would tell his assistants, "for conscience sake." There was no understanding that the subjects were provided by the crime of murder. Had that idea been broached to him in words, he would have recoiled in horror; but the lightness of his speech upon so grave a matter was, in itself, an offense against good manners, and a temptation to the men with whom he dealt. Fettes, for instance, had often remarked to himself upon the singular freshness of the bodies. He had been struck again and again by the hangdog, abominable looks of the ruffians who came to him before the dawn; and, putting things together clearly in his private thoughts, he perhaps attributed a meaning too immoral and too categorical to the unguarded councils of his master. He understood his duty, in short, to have three branches; to take what was brought, to pay the price, and to avert the eye from any evidence of crime.

One November morning this policy of silence was put sharply to the test. He had been awake all night with a racking toothache —pacing his room like a caged beast or throwing himself in fury on his bed—and had fallen at last into that profound, uneasy slumber that so often follows on a night of pain, when he was awakened by the third or fourth angry repetition of the concerted signal. There was a thin, bright moonshine; it was bitter cold, windy and frosty; the town had not yet awakened, but an indefinable stir already preluded the noise and business of the day. The ghouls had come later than usual, and they seemed more than usually eager to be gone. Fettes, sick with sleep, lighted them upstairs. He heard their grumbling Irish voices through a dream; and as they stripped the sack from their sad merchandise he leaned dozing, with his shoulder propped against the wall; he had to shake himself to find the men their money. As he did so his eyes lighted on the dead face. He started; he took two steps nearer, with the candle raised.

"God Almighty!" he cried. "That is Jane Galbraith!"

The men answered nothing, but they shuffled nearer the door.

"I know her, I tell you," he continued. "She was alive and hearty yesterday. It's impossible she can be dead; it's impossible you should have got this body fairly."

"Sure, sir, you're mistaken entirely," said one of the men.

But the other looked Fettes darkly in the eyes, and demanded the money on the spot.

It was impossible to misconceive the threat or to exaggerate the danger. The lad's heart failed him. He stammered some excuse, counted out the sum, and saw his hateful visitors depart. No sooner were they gone than he hastened to confirm his doubts. By a dozen unquestionable marks he identified the girl he had jested with the day before. He saw, with horror, marks upon her body that might well be taken as violence. A panic seized him, and he took refuge in his room. There he reflected at length over the discovery that he had made; considered soberly the bearing of Mr. K——'s instructions and the danger to himself of interference in so serious a business, and at last, in sore perplexity, determined to wait for the advice of his immediate superior, the class assistant.

This was a young doctor, Wolfe Macfarlane, a high favorite among the reckless students, clever, dissipated, and unscrupulous to the last degree. He had traveled and studied abroad. His manners were agreeable and a little forward. He was an authority on the stage, skillful on the ice or the links with skate or golf club; he dressed with nice audacity, and, to put the finishing touch upon his glory, he kept a gig and a strong trotting horse. With Fettes he was on terms of intimacy; indeed, their relative positions called for some community of life; and when subjects were scarce the pair would drive far into the country in Macfarlane's gig, visit and desecrate some lonely graveyard, and return before dawn with their booty to the door of the dissecting room.

On that particular morning Macfarlane arrived somewhat earlier than his wont. Fettes heard him, and met him on the stairs, told him his story, and showed him the cause of his alarm. Macfarlane examined the marks on her body.

"Yes," he said with a nod, "it looks fishy."

"Well, what should I do?" asked Fettes.

"Do?" repeated the other. "Do you want to do anything? Least said sooner mended, I should say."

"Someone else might recognize her," objected Fettes. "She was as well-known at the Castle Rock."

"We'll hope not," said Macfarlane, "and if anybody does—well, you didn't, don't you see, and there's an end. The fact is, this has been going on too long. Stir up the mud, and you'll get K—— into the most unholy trouble; you'll be in a shocking box yourself. So will I, if you come to that. I should like to know how anyone of us would look, or what the devil we should have to say ourselves, in any Christian witness box. For me, you know, there's one thing certain—that, practically speaking, all our subjects have been murdered."

"Macfarlane!" cried Fettes.

"Come now!" sneered the other. "As if you hadn't suspected it yourself!"

"Suspecting is one thing—"

"And proof another. Yes, I know; and I'm as sorry as you are this should have come here," tapping the body with his cane. "The next best thing for me is not to recognize it; and," he added coolly, "I don't. You may, if you please. I don't dictate, but I think a man of the world would do as I do; and, I may add, I fancy that is what K—— would look for at our hands. The question is, Why did he choose us two for his assistants? And I answer, Because he didn't want old wives."

This was the tone of all others to affect the mind of a lad like Fettes. He agreed to imitate Macfarlane. The body of the unfortunate girl was duly dissected, and no one remarked or appeared to recognize her.

One afternoon, when his day's work was over, Fettes dropped into a popular tavern and found Macfarlane sitting with a stranger. This was a small man, very pale and dark, with coal-black eyes. The cut of his features gave a promise of intellect and refinement which was but feebly realized in his manners, for he proved, upon a nearer acquaintance, coarse, vulgar and stupid.

He exercised, however, a very remarkable control over Macfarlane; issued orders like the Great Bashaw; became inflamed at the least discussion or delay, and commented rudely on the servility with which he was obeyed. This most offensive person took a fancy to Fettes on the spot, plied him with drinks, and honored him with unusual confidences on his past career. If a tenth of what he confessed were true, he was a very loathsome rogue; and the lad's vanity was tickled by the attention of so experienced a man.

"I'm a pretty bad fellow myself," the stranger remarked, "but Macfarlane is the boy—Toddy Macfarlane I call him. Toddy, order your friend another glass. Or it might be, Toddy, you jump up and shut the door. Toddy hates me," he said again. "Oh, yes, Toddy, you do!"

"Don't you call me that confounded name," growled Macfarlane.

"Hear him! Did you ever see the lads play knife? He would like to do that all over my body," remarked the stranger.

"We medicals have a better way than that," said Fettes. "When we dislike a dead friend of ours, we dissect him."

Macfarlane looked up sharply, as thought this jest were scarcely to his mind.

The afternoon passed. Gray, for that was the stranger's name, invited Fettes to join them at dinner, ordered a feast so sumptuous that the tavern was thrown into commotion, and when all was done commanded Macfarlane to settle the bill. It was late before they separated; the man Gray was incapably drunk. Macfarlane, sobered by his fury, chewed the cud of the money he had been forced to squander and the slights he had been obliged to swallow. Fettes, with various liquors singing in his head, returned home with devious footsteps and a mind entirely in abeyance. Next day Macfarlane was absent from the class, and Fettes smiled to himself as he imagined him still squiring the intolerable Gray from tavern to tavern. As soon as the hour of liberty had struck, he posted from place to place in quest of his last night's companions. He could find them, however, nowhere; so returned early to his rooms, went early to bed, and slept the sleep of the just.

At four in the morning he was awakened by the well-known signal. Descending to the door, he was filled with astonishment to find Macfarlane with his gig, and in the gig one of those long and ghastly packages with which he was so well-acquainted.

"What?" he cried. "Have you been out alone? How did you manage?"

But Macfarlane silenced him roughly, bidding him turn to business. When they had got the body upstairs and laid it on the table, Macfarlane made at first as if he were going away. Then he paused and seemed to hesitate; and then, "You had better look at the face," said he, in tones of some constraint. "You had better," he repeated, as Fettes only stared at him in wonder.

"But where, and how, and when did you come by it?" cried the other.

"Look at the face," was the only answer.

Fettes was staggered; strange doubts assailed him. He looked from the young doctor to the body, and then back again. At last, with a start, he did as he was bidden. He had almost expected the sight that met his eyes, and yet the shock was cruel. To see, fixed in the rigidity of death and naked on that coarse layer of sackcloth, the man whom he had left well-clad and full of meat and sin upon the threshold of a tavern, awoke, even in the thoughtless Fettes, some of the terrors of the conscience. It was a *cras tibi* which reechoed in his soul, that two whom he had known should have come to lie upon these icy tables. Yet these were only secondary thoughts. His first concern regarded Wolfe. Unprepared for a challenge so momentous, he knew not how to look his comrade in the face. He durst not meet his eye, and he had neither words nor voice at his command.

It was Macfarlane himself who made the first advance. He came up quietly behind and laid his hand gently but firmly on the other's shoulder.

"Richardson," said he, "may have the head."

Now, Richardson was a student who had long been anxious

for that portion of the human subject to dissect. There was no answer, and the murderer resumed: "Talking of business, you must pay me; your accounts, you see, must tally."

Fettes found a voice, the ghost of his own: "Pay you!" he cried. "Pay you for that?"

"Why, yes, of course you must. By all means and on every possible account, you must," returned the other. "I dare not give it for nothing, you dare not take it for nothing; it would compromise us both. This is another case like Jane Galbraith's. The more things are wrong, the more we must act as if all were right. Where does old K—— keep his money?"

"There," answered Fettes hoarsely, pointing to a cupboard in the corner.

"Give me the key, then," said the other calmly, holding out his hand.

There was an instant's hesitation, and the die was cast. Macfarlane could not suppress a nervous twitch, the infinitesimal mark of an immense relief, as he felt the key between his fingers. He opened the cupboard, brought out pen and ink and a paper book that stood in one compartment, and separated from the funds in a drawer a sum suitable to the occasion.

"Now; look here," he said, "there is the payment made—first proof of your good faith: first step to your security. You have now to clinch it by a second. Enter the payment in your book, and then you for your part may defy the devil."

The next few seconds were for Fettes an agony of thought; but in balancing his terrors it was the most immediate that triumphed. Any future difficulty seemed almost welcome if he could avoid a present quarrel with Macfarlane. He set down the candle which he had been carrying all this time, and with a steady hand entered the date, the nature and the amount of the transaction.

"And now," said Macfarlane, "it's only fair that you should pocket the lucre. I've had my share already. By the by, when a man of the world falls into a bit of luck, has a few extra shillings in his pocket—I'm ashamed to speak of it, but there's a rule of conduct in the case. No treating, no purchase of expensive class books, no squaring of old debts; borrow, don't lend."

"Macfarlane," began Fettes, still somewhat hoarsely, "I have put my neck in a halter to oblige you."

"To oblige me?" cried Wolfe. "Oh, come! You did, as near as I can see the matter, what you downright had to do in self-defense. Suppose I got into trouble, where would you be? This second little matter flows clearly from the first. Mr. Gray is the continuation of Miss Galbraith. You can't begin and then stop. If you begin, you must keep on beginning; that's the truth. No rest for the wicked."

A horrible sense of blackness and the treachery of fate seized hold upon the soul of the unhappy student.

"My God!" he cried, "but what have I done?" And when did I begin? To be made a class assistant—in the name of reason, where's the harm in that? Service wanted the position; Service might have got it. Would *he* have been where *I* am now?"

"My dear fellow," said Macfarlane, "what a boy you are! What harm *has* come to you? What harm *can* come to you if you hold your tongue? Why, man, do you know what this life is? There are two squads of us—the lions and the lambs. If you're a lamb, you'll come to lie upon these tables like Gray or Jane Galbraith; if you're a lion, you'll live and drive a horse like me, like K——, like all the world with any wit or courage. You're staggered at the first. But look at K——! My dear fellow, you're clever, you have pluck. I like you, and K—— likes you. You were born to lead the hunt; and I tell you, on my honor and my experience of life, three days from now you'll laugh at all these scarecrows like a high school boy at a farce."

And with that Macfarlane took his departure and drove off up the wynd in his gig to get under cover before daylight. Fettes was thus left alone with his regrets. He saw the miserable peril in which he stood involved. He saw, with inexpressible dismay, that there was no limit to his weakness, and that, from concession to concession, he had fallen from the arbiter of Macfarlane's destiny to his paid and helpless accomplice. He would have given the world to have been a little braver at the time, but it did not occur to him that he might still be brave. The secret of Jane

Galbraith and the cursed entry in the day book closed his mouth.

Hours passed; the class began to arrive; the members of the unhappy Gray were dealt out to one and to another, and received without remark. Richardson was made happy with the head; and, before the hour of freedom rang, Fettes trembled with exultation to perceive how far they had already gone toward safety.

For two days he continued to watch, with an increasing joy, the dreadful process of disguise.

On the third day Macfarlane made his appearance. He had been ill, he said; but he made up for lost time by the energy with which he directed the students. To Richardson in particular he extended the most valuable assistance and advice, and that student, encouraged by the praise of the demonstrator, burned high with ambitious hopes, and saw the medal already in his grasp.

Before the week was out Macfarlane's prophecy had been fulfilled. Fettes had outlived his terrors and had forgotten his baseness. He began to plume himself upon his courage, and had so arranged the story in his mind that he could look back on these events with an unhealthy pride. Of his accomplice he saw but little. They met, of course, in the business of the class; they received their orders together from Mr. K——. At times they had a word or two in private, and Macfarlane was from first to last particularly kind and jovial. But it was plain that he avoided any reference to their common secret; and even when Fettes whispered to him that he had cast in his lot with the lions and forsworn the lambs, he only signed to him smilingly to hold his peace.

At length an occasion arose which threw the pair once more into a closer union. Mr. K—— was again short of subjects; pupils were eager, and it was a part of this teacher's pretensions to be always well-supplied. At the same time there came the news of a burial in the rustic graveyard of Glencorse. Time has little changed the place in question. It stood then, as now, upon a crossroad, out of call of human habitations, and buried fathom deep in the foliage of six cedar trees. The cries of the sheep upon the neighboring hills, the streamlets upon either hand, one loudly singing among pebbles, the other dripping furtively from pond to pond, the stir of the wind in mountainous old flowering chestnuts, and once in seven days the voice of the bell and the old tunes of the precentor, were the only sounds that disturbed the silence around the rural church. The Resurrection Man—to use a byname of the period—was not to be deterred by any of the sanctities of customary piety. It was part of his trade to despise and desecrate the scrolls and trumpets of old tombs, the paths worn by the feet of worshipers and mourners, and the offerings and the inscriptions of bereaved affection. To rustic neighborhoods where love is more than commonly tenacious, and where some bonds of blood or fellowship unite the entire society of a parish, the body-snatcher, far from being repelled by natural respect, was attracted by the ease and safety of the task. To bodies that had been laid in earth, in joyful expectation of a far different awakening, there came that hasty, lamplit, terror-haunted resurrection of the spade and mattock. The coffin was forced, the cerements torn, and the melancholy relics, clad in sackcloth, after being rattled for hours on moonless byways, were at length exposed to uttermost indignities before a class of gaping boys.

Somewhat as two vultures may swoop upon a dying lamb, Fettes and Macfarlane were to be let loose upon a grave in that green and quiet resting place. The wife of a farmer, a woman who had lived for sixty years, and been known for nothing but good butter and a godly conversation, was to be rooted from her grave at midnight and carried, dead and naked, to that faraway city that she had always honored with her Sunday's best; the place beside her family was to be empty till the crack of doom; her innocent and always venerable members to be exposed to that last curiosity of the anatomist.

Late one afternoon the pair set forth, well-wrapped in cloaks and furnished with a formidable bottle. It rained without remission—a cold, dense, lashing rain. Now and again there blew a puff of wind, but these sheets of falling water kept it down. Bottle and all, it was a sad and silent drive as far as Penicuik, where they were to spend the evening. They stopped once, to hide their implements in a thick bush not far from the church-yard, and once again at the Fisher's Tryst, to have a toast before the kitchen fire and vary their nips of whisky with a glass of ale. When they reached their journey's end the gig was housed, the horse was fed and comforted, and the two young doctors in a private room sat down to the best dinner and the best wine the house afforded. The lights, the fire, the beating rain upon the window, the cold, incongruous work that lay before them, added zest to their enjoyment of the meal. With every glass their cordiality increased. Soon Macfarlane handed a little pile of gold to his companion.

"A compliment," he said. "Between friends these little damned accommodations ought to fly like pipelights."

Fettes pocketed the money, and applauded the sentiment to the echo. "You are a philosopher," he cried. "I was an ass till I knew you. You and K—— between you, by the Lord Harry! But you'll make a man of me."

"Of course we shall," applauded Macfarlane. "A man? I tell you, it required a man to back me up the other morning. There are some big, brawling, forty-year-old cowards who would have turned sick at the look of the damned thing; but not you—you kept your head. I watched you."

"Well, and why not?" Fettes thus vaunted himself. "It was no affair of mine. There was nothing to gain on the one side but disturbance, and on the other I could count on your gratitude, don't you see?" And he slapped his pocket till the gold pieces rang.

Macfarlane somehow felt a certain touch of alarm at these unpleasant words. He may have regretted that he had taught his young companion so successfully, but he had no time to interfere, for the other noisily continued in this boastful strain:

"The great thing is not to be afraid. No, between you and me, I don't want to hang—that's practical; but for all cant, Macfarlane, I was born with a contempt. Hell, God, devil, right, wrong, sin, crime and all the old gallery of curiosities—they may frighten boys, but men of the world, like you and me, despise them. Here's to the memory of Gray!"

It was by this time growing somewhat late. The gig, according to order, was brought round to the door with both lamps brightly shining, and the young men had to pay their bill and take the road. They announced that they were bound for Peebles, and drove in that direction till they were clear of the last houses of the town; then, extinguishing the lamps, returned upon their course, and followed a byroad toward Glencorse. There was no sound but that of their own passage, and the incessant, strident pouring of the rain. It was pitch dark; here and there a white gate or a white stone in the wall guided them for a short space across the night; but for the most part it was at a foot pace, and almost groping, that they picked their way through that resonant blackness to their solemn and isolated destination. In the sunken woods that traverse the neighborhood of the burying ground the last glimmer failed them, and it became necessary to kindle a match and reillumine one of the lanterns of the gig. Thus, under the dripping trees, and environed by huge and moving shadows, they reached the scene of their inhallowed labors.

They were both experienced in such affairs, and powerful with the spade; and they had scarce been twenty minutes at their task before they were rewarded by a dull rattle on the coffin lid. At the same moment, Macfarlane, having hurt his hand upon a stone, flung it carelessly above his head. The grave, in which they now stood almost to the shoulders, was close to the edge of the platform of the graveyard; and the gig lamp had been propped, the better to illuminate their labors, against a tree, and on the immediate verge of the steep bank descending to the stream. Chance had taken a sure aim with the stone. Then came a clang of broken glass; night fell upon them; sounds alternately dull and ringing announced the bounding of the lantern down the bank, and its occasional collision with the trees. A stone or two, which it had dislodged in its descent, rattled behind it into the profundities of the glen; and then silence, like night, resumed its sway; and they might bend their hearing to its utmost pitch, but naught was to be heard except the rain, now marching to the wind, now steadily falling over miles of open country.

They were so nearly at an end of their abhorred task that they judged it wisest to complete it in the dark. The coffin was exhumed and broken open; the body inserted in the dripping sack and carried between them to the gig; one mounted to keep it in its place, and the other, taking the horse by the mouth, groped along by wall and bush until they reached the wider road by the Fisher's Tryst. Here was a faint, diffused radiancy, which they hailed like daylight; by that they pushed the horse to a good pace and began to rattle along merrily in the direction of the town.

They had both been wetted to the skin during their operations, and now, as the gig jumped among the deep ruts, the thing that stood propped between them fell now upon one and now upon the other. At every repetition of the horrid contact each instinctively repelled it with the greater haste; and the process, natural although it was, began to tell upon the nerves of the companions. Macfarlane made some ill-favored jest about the farmer's wife, but it came hollowly from his lips, and was allowed to drop in silence. Still their unnatural burden bumped from side to side; and now the head would be laid, as if in confidence, upon their shoulders, and now the drenching sackcloth would flap icily about their faces. A creeping chill began to possess the soul of Fettes. He peered at the bundle, and it seemed somehow larger than at first. All over the countryside, and from every degree of distance, the farm dogs accompanied their passage with tragic ululations; and it grew and grew upon his mind that some unnatural miracle had been accomplished, that some nameless change had befallen the dead body, and that it was in fear of their unholy burden that the dogs were howling.

"For God's sake," said he, making a great effort to arrive at speech, "for God's sake, let's have a light!"

Seemingly Macfarlane was affected in the same direction; for, though he made no reply, he stopped the horse, passed the reins to his companion, got down, and proceeded to kindle the remaining lamp. They had by that time got no farther than the crossroad down to Auchenclinny. The rain still poured as though the deluge were returning, and it was no easy matter to make a light in such a world of wet and darkness. When at last the flickering blue flame had been transferred to the wick and began to expand and clarify, and shed a wide circle of misty brightness round the gig, it became possible for the two young men to see each other and the thing they had along with them. The rain had molded the rough sacking to the outlines of the body underneath, the head was distinct from the trunk, the shoulders plainly modeled; something at once spectral and human riveted their eyes upon the ghastly comrade of their drive.

For some time Macfarlane stood motionless, holding up the lamp. A nameless dread was swathed, like a wet sheet, about the body, and tightened the white skin upon the face of Fettes; a fear that was meaningless, a horror of what could not be, kept mounting to his brain; another beat of the watch, and he had spoken. But his comrade forestalled him.

"That is not a woman," said Macfarlane, in a hushed voice.

"It was a woman when we put her in," whispered Fettes.

"Hold that lamp," said the other. "I must see her face."

And as Fettes took the lamp his companion untied the fastenings of the sack and drew down the cover from the head. The light fell very clear upon the dark, well-molded features and smooth-shaven cheeks of a too familiar countenance, often beheld in dreams of both of these young men. A wild yell rang up into the night; each leaped from his own side into the roadway: the lamp fell, broke, and was extinguished; and the horse, terrified by this unusual commotion, bounded and went off toward Edinburgh at a gallop, bearing along with it, the sole occupant of the gig, the body of the dead and long-dissected Gray.

THE LOVED DEAD

by C.M. EDDY

The first thing that needs to be said about "The Loved Dead" is that it is not a story for the squeamish or delicate-minded.

This is a claim that has been made many times before about any number of stories, but in no case is it more appropriate than with this little exercise in madness and cauld grue. *When it first appeared in* Weird Tales *for May-June-July 1924, there was an immediate and rather vociferous public reaction. Several citizens and religious groups clamored for the withdrawal of the issue from newsstands, and complaints from outraged readers poured into the offices of* Weird Tales' *editor Farnsworth Wright —so many complaints, in fact, that Wright was inhibited from buying similarly graphic works for years to come.*

Despite what is stated above, it should also be noted that "The Loved Dead" is not all that horrible by today's gore-streaked standards. Any reader who has sat through such stomach-churning films as The Texas Chainsaw Massacre *and* Friday the 13th *would probably find it tame in comparison. Its inspiration (although there is no internal evidence to corroborate this, except by inference) seems to have been the real-life case of Sergeant-Major Bertrand, the Parisian ghoul whose story is recounted in the introduction; certainly the nameless narrator of "The Loved Dead" displays cannibalistic and necrophiliac appetites quite similar to those of*

Bertrand. It may be read, then, as a simple fictional study of psychosexual aberration, and also as a landmark tale in the horror genre. But only if you are not prone to queasiness and nightmares . . .

C.M. Eddy, Jr. (1896–1967) was primarily a songwriter who contributed occasional short fiction to detective and weird pulp magazines in the 1920s, and who also did some ghostwriting for Harry Houdini. (At the time of Houdini's death, Eddy and H.P. Lovecraft were working on "The Cancer of Superstition" for the illusionist.) Eddy was also a proofreader for Oxford Press, a theatrical agent, and president of the Rhode Island Writer's Guild. He and his wife were close friends of Lovecraft, also a Rhode Island resident, and it has been claimed that Lovecraft rewrote portions of "The Loved Dead" before its submission to Weird Tales.

IT'S MIDNIGHT. Before dawn they will find me and take me to a black cell where I shall languish interminably, while insatiable desires gnaw at my vitals and wither up my heart, till at last I become one with the dead that I love.

My seat is the fetid hollow of an aged grave; my desk is the back of a fallen tombstone worn smooth by devastating centuries; my only light is that of the stars and a thin-edged moon, yet I can see as clearly as though it were midday. Around me on every side, sepulchral sentinels guarding unkempt graves, the tilting, decrepit headstones lie half-hidden in masses of nauseous, rotting vegetation. Above the rest, silhouetted against the living sky, an august monument lifts its austere, tapering spire like the spectral chieftain of a lemurian horde. The air is heavy with the noxious odors of fungi and the scent of damp, moldy earth, but to me it is the aroma of Elysium. It is still—terrifyingly still—with a silence whose very profundity bespeaks the solemn and the hideous. Could I choose my habitation it would be in the heart of some such city of putrefying flesh and crumbling bones; for that nearness sends ecstatic thrills through my soul, causing the stagnant blood to race through my veins and my torpid heart to pound with delirious joy—for the presence of death is life to me!

My early childhood was one long, prosaic and monotonous apathy. Strictly ascetic, wan, pallid, undersized, and subject to protracted spells of morbid moroseness, I was ostracized by the healthy, normal youngsters of my own age. They dubbed me a spoilsport, and "old woman," because I had no interest in the rough, childish games they played, nor any stamina to participate in them, had I so desired.

Like all rural villages, Fenham had its quota of poison-tongued gossips. Their prying imaginations hailed my lethargic temperament as some abhorrent abnormality; they compared me with my parents and shook their heads in ominous doubt at the vast difference. Some of the more superstitious openly pronounced me a changeling while others who knew something of my ancestry called attention to the vague mysterious rumors concerning a great-great-grand-uncle who had been burned at the stake as a necromancer.

Had I lived in some larger town, with greater opportunities for congenial companionship, perhaps I could have overcome this early tendency to be a recluse. As I reached my teens I grew even more sullen, morbid, and apathetic. My life lacked motivation. I seemed in the grip of something that dulled my senses, stunted my development, retarded my activities, and left me unaccountably dissatisfied.

I was sixteen when I attended my first funeral. A funeral in Fenham was a preeminent social event, for our town was noted for the longevity of its inhabitants. When, moreover, the funeral was that of such a well-known character as my grandfather, it was safe to assume that the townspeople would turn out *en masse* to pay due homage to his memory. Yet I did not view the approaching ceremony with even latent interest. Anything that tended to lift me out of my habitual inertia held for me only the promise of physical and mental disquietude. In deference to my parents' importunings, mainly to give myself relief from their caustic condemnations of what they chose to call my unfilial attitude, I agreed to accompany them.

There was nothing out of the ordinary about my grandfather's funeral unless it was the voluminous array of floral tributes; but this, remember, was my first initiation to the solemn rites of such an occasion. Something about the darkened room, the oblong coffin with its somber drapings, the banked masses of fragrant blooms, the dolorous manifestations of the assembled villagers, stirred me from my normal listlessness and arrested my attention. Roused from my momentary reverie by a nudge from my mother's sharp elbow, I followed her across the room to the casket where the body of my grandparent lay.

For the first time I was face to face with Death. I looked down upon the calm placid face lined with its multitudinous wrinkles, and saw nothing to cause so much of sorrow. Instead, it seemed to me that grandfather was immeasurably content, blandly satisfied. I felt swayed by some strange discordant sense of elation. So slowly, so stealthily had it crept over me, that I could scarcely define its coming. As I mentally review that portentous hour it seems that it must have originated with my first glimpse of that funeral scene, silently strengthening its grip with subtle insidiousness. A baleful malignant influence that seemed to emanate from the corpse itself held me with magnetic fascination. My whole being seemed charged with some ecstatic electrifying force, and I felt my form straighten without conscious volition. My eyes were trying to burn beneath the closed lids of the dead man's and read some secret message they concealed. My heart gave a sudden leap of unholy glee, and pounded against my ribs with demoniacal force as if to free itself from the confining walls of my frail frame. Wild, wanton, soul-satisfying sensuality engulfed me. Once more the vigorous prod of a maternal elbow jarred me into activity. I had made my way to the sable-shrouded coffin with leaden tread; I walked away with newfound animation.

I accompanied the cortege to the cemetery, my whole physical being permeated with this mystic enlivening influence. It was as if I had quaffed deep draughts of some exotic elixir—some abominable concoction brewed from blasphemous formulas in the archives of Belial.

The townsfolk were so intent upon the ceremony that the

radical change in my demeanor passed unnoticed by all save my father and my mother, but in the fortnight that followed, the village busybodies found fresh material for their vitriolic tongues in my altered bearing. At the end of the fortnight, however, the potency of the stimulus began to lose its effectiveness. Another day or two and I had completely reverted to my old-time languor, though not to the complete and engulfing insipidity of the past. Before, there had been an utter lack of desire to emerge from the enervation; now vague and indefinable unrest disturbed me. Outwardly I have become myself again, and the scandal-mongers turned to some more engrossing subject. Had they even so much as dreamed the true cause of my exhilaration they would have shunned me as if I were a filthy, leprous thing. Had I visioned the execrable power behind my brief period of elation I would have locked myself forever from the rest of the world and spent my remaining years in penitent solitude.

Tragedy often runs in trilogies, hence despite the proverbial longevity of our townspeople the next five years brought the death of both parents. My mother went first, in an accident of the most unexpected nature; and so genuine was my grief that I was honestly surprised to find its poignancy mocked and contradicted by that almost forgotten feeling of supreme and diabolical ecstasy. Once more my heart leaped wildly within me, once more it pounded at trip-hammer speed and sent the hot blood coursing through my veins with meteoric fervor. I shook from my shoulders the harassing cloak of stagnation only to replace it with the infinitely more horrible burden of loathsome, unhallowed desire. I haunted the death chamber where the body of my mother lay, my soul athirst for the devilish nectar that seemed to saturate the air of the darkened room. Every breath strengthened me, lifted me to towering heights of seraphic satisfaction. I knew, now, that it was but a sort of drugged delirium which must soon pass and leave me correspondingly weakened by its malign power, yet I could no more control my longing than I could untwist the Gordian knots in the already tangled skein of my destiny.

I knew, too, that through some strange satanic curse my life depended upon the dead for its motive force; that there was a singularity in my make-up which responded only to the awesome presence of some lifeless clod. A few days later, frantic for the bestial intoxicant on which the fullness of my existence depended, I interviewed Fenham's sole undertaker and talked him into taking me on as a sort of apprentice.

The shock of my mother's demise had visibly affected my father. I think that if I had broached the idea of such *outré* employment at any other time he would have been emphatic in his refusal. As it was he nodded acquiescence after a moment's sober thought. How little did I dream that he would be the object of my first practical lesson!

He, too, died suddenly; developing some hitherto unsuspected heart affliction. My octogenarian employer tried his best to dissuade me from the unthinkable task of embalming his body, nor did he detect the rapturous glint in my eyes as I finally won him over to my damnable point of view. I cannot hope to express the reprehensible, the unutterable thoughts that swept in tumultuous waves of passion through my racing heart as I labored over the lifeless clay. Unsurpassed love was the keynote of these concepts, a love greater—far greater—than any I had ever borne him while he was alive.

My father was not a rich man, but he had possessed enough of worldly goods to make him comfortably independent. As his sole heir I found myself in rather a paradoxical position. My early youth had totally failed to fit me for contact with the modern world, yet the primitive life of Fenham with its attendant isolation palled upon me. Indeed, the longevity of the inhabitants defeated my sole motive in arranging my indenture.

After settling the estate it proved an easy matter to secure my release and I headed for Bayboro, a city some fifty miles away. Here my year of apprenticeship stood me in good stead. I had no trouble in establishing a favorable connection as an assistant with the Gresham Corporation, a concern that maintained the largest funeral parlors in the city. I even prevailed upon them to let me sleep upon the premises—for already the proximity of the dead was becoming an obsession.

I applied myself to my task with unwonted zeal. No case was too gruesome for my impious sensibilities, and I soon became master of my chosen vocation. Every fresh corpse brought into the establishment meant a fulfilled promise of ungodly gladness, of irreverent gratification; a return of that rapturous tumult of the arteries which transformed my grisly task into one of beloved devotion—yet every carnal satiation exacted its toll. I came to dread the days that brought no dead for me to gloat over, and prayed to all the obscene gods of the nethermost abysses to bring swift, sure death upon the residents of the city.

Then came the nights when a skulking figure stole surreptitiously through the shadowy streets of the suburbs; pitch-dark nights when the midnight moon was obscured by heavy lowering clouds. It was a furtive figure that blended with the trees and cast fugitive glances over its shoulder; a figure bent on some malignant mission. After one of these prowlings the morning papers would scream to their sensation-mad clientele the details of some nightmare crime; column on column of lurid gloating over abominable atrocities; paragraph on paragraph of impossible solutions and extravagant, conflicting suspicions. Through it all I felt a supreme sense of security, for who would for a moment suspect an employee in an undertaking establishment, where Death was supposedly an everyday affair, of seeking surcease from unnameable urgings in the cold-blooded slaughter of his fellow beings? I planned each crime with maniacal cunning, varying the manner of my murders so that no one would even dream that all were the work of one blood-stained pair of hands. The aftermath of each nocturnal venture was an ecstatic hour of pleasure, pernicious and unalloyed; a pleasure always heightened by the chance that its delicious source might later be assigned to my gloating administrations in the course of my regular occupation. Sometimes that double and ultimate pleasure did occur—Oh rare and delicious memory!

During long nights when I clung close to the shelter of my sanctuary, I was prompted by the mausoleum silence to devise new and unspeakable ways of lavishing my affections upon the dead that I loved—the dead that gave me life!

One morning Mr. Gresham came much earlier than usual—came to find me stretched out upon a cold slab deep in ghoulish slumber, my arms wrapped about the stark, naked body of a fetid corpse! He roused me from my salacious dreams, his eyes filled with mingled detestation and pity. Gently but firmly he told me that I must go, that my nerves were unstrung, that I needed a long rest from the repellent tasks my vocation required, that my impressionable youth was too deeply affected by the dismal atmosphere of my environment. How little did he know of the demoniacal desires that spurred me on in my disgusting infirmities! I was wise enough to see that argument would only strengthen his belief in my potential madness—it was far better to leave than to invite discovery of the motive underlying my actions.

After this I dared not stay long in one place for fear some overt act would bare my secret to an unsympathetic world. I drifted from city to city, from town to town. I worked in morgues, around cemeteries, once in a crematory—anywhere that afforded me an opportunity to be near the dead that I so craved.

Then came the World War. I was one of the first to go across, one of the last to return. Four years of blood-red charnel hell . . . sickening slime of rain and rotten trenches . . . deafening bursting of hysterical shells . . . monotonous droning of sardonic bullets . . . smoking frenzies of Phlegethon's fountains . . . stifling fumes of murderous gases . . . grotesque remnants of smashed and shredded bodies . . . four years of transcendent satisfaction.

In every wanderer there is a latent urge to return to the scenes of his childhood. A few months later found me making my way through the familiar byways of Fenham. Vacant dilapidated farmhouses lined the adjacent roadsides, while the years had brought equal retrogression to the town itself. A mere handful of the houses were occupied, but among those was the one I had once called home. The tangled, weed-choked driveway, the broken windowpanes, the uncared-for acres that stretched behind, all bore mute confirmation of the tales that guarded inquiries had elicited—that it now sheltered a dissolute drunkard who eked out a meager existence from the chores his few neighbors gave him out of sympathy for the mistreated wife and under-nourished child who shared his lot. All in all, the glamour surrounding my youthful environment was entirely dispelled; so, prompted by some errant foolhardy thought, I next turned my steps towards Bayboro.

Here, too, the years had brought changes, but in reverse order. The small city I remembered had almost doubled in size despite its wartime depopulation. Instinctively I sought my former place of employment, finding it still there but with an unfamiliar name and "Successor to" above the door, for the influenza epidemic had claimed Mr. Gresham, while the boys were overseas. Some fateful mood impelled me to ask for work. I referred to my tutelage under Mr. Gresham with some trepidation, but my fears were groundless—my late employer had carried the secret of my unethical conduct with him to the grave. An opportune vacancy insured my immediate reinstallation.

Then came vagrant haunting memories of scarlet nights of impious pilgrimages, and an uncontrollable desire to renew those illicit joys. I cast caution to the winds and launched upon another series of damnable debaucheries. Once more the yellow sheets found welcome material in the devilish details of my crimes, comparing them to the red weeks of horror that had appalled the city years before. Once more the police sent out their dragnet and drew into its enmeshing folds—nothing!

My thirst for the noxious nectar of the dead grew to a consuming fire, and I began to shorten the periods between my odious exploits. I realized that I was treading on dangerous ground, but demoniac desire gripped me in its torturing tentacles and urged me on.

All this time my mind was becoming more and more benumbed to any influence except the satiation of my insane longings. Little details vitally important to one bent on such evil escapades escaped me. Somehow, somewhere, I left a vague trace, an elusive clue, behind—not enough to warrant my arrest, but sufficient to turn the tide of suspicion in my direction. I sensed this espionage, yet was helpless to stem the surging demand for more dead to quicken my enervated soul.

Then came the night when the shrill whistle of the police roused me from my fiendish gloating over the body of my latest victim, a gory razor still clutched tightly in my hand. With one dexterous motion I closed the blade and thrust it into the pocket of the coat I wore. Truncheons beat a lusty tattoo upon the door. I crashed the window with a chair, thanking Fate I had chosen one of the cheaper tenement districts for my locale. I dropped into a dingy alley as blue-coated forms burst through the shattered door. Over shaky fences, through filthy back yards, past squalid ramshackle houses, down dimly lighted narrow streets I fled. I thought at once of the wooden marshes that lay beyond the city and stretched for half a hundred miles till they touched the outskirts of Fenham. If I could reach this goal I would be temporarily safe. Before dawn I was plunging headlong through the foreboding wasteland, stumbling over the rotting roots of half-dead trees whose naked branches stretched out like grotesque arms striving to encumber me with mocking embraces.

The imps of the nefarious gods to whom I offered my idolatrous prayers must have guided my footsteps through that menacing morass. A week later—wan, bedraggled, and emaciated, I lurked in the woods a mile from Fenham. So far I had eluded my pursuers, yet I dared not show myself, for I knew that the alarm must have been broadcast. I vaguely hoped I had thrown them off the trail. After that first frenetic night I had heard no sound of alien voices, no crashing of heavy bodies through the underbrush. Perhaps they had concluded that my body lay hidden in some stagnant pool or had vanished forever in the tenacious quagmire.

Hunger gnawed at my vitals with poignant pangs, thirst left my throat parched and dry. Yet far worse was the unbearable hunger of my starving soul for the stimulus I found only in the nearness of the dead. My nostrils quivered in sweet recollection.

No longer could I delude myself with the thought that this desire was a mere whim of the heated imagination. I knew now that it was an integral part of life itself; that without it I should burn out like an empty lamp. I summoned all my remaining energy to fit me for the task of satisfying my accursed appetite. Despite the peril attending my move I set out to reconnoiter, skirting the sheltering shadows like an obscene wraith. Once more I felt that strange sensation of being led by some unseen satellite of Satan. Yet even my sin-steeped soul revolted for a moment when I found myself before my native abode, a scene of my youthful hermitage.

Then these disquieting memories faded. In their place came overwhelming lustful desire. Behind the rotting walls of this old house lay my prey. A moment later I had raised one of the shattered windows and climbed over the sill. I listened for a moment, every sense alert, every muscle tensed for action. The silence reassured me. With catlike tread I stole through the familiar rooms until stertorous snores indicated the place where I was to find surcease from my sufferings. I allowed myself a sigh of anticipated ecstasy as I pushed open the door of the bed-chamber. Pantherlike I made my way to the supine form stretched out in drunken stupor. The wife and child—where were they?—well, they could wait. My clutching fingers groped for his throat.

Hours later I was again the fugitive, but a newfound stolen strength was mine. Three silent forms slept to wake no more. It was not until the garish light of day penetrated my hiding place that I visualized the certain consequences of my rashly purchased relief. By this time the bodies must have been discovered. Even the most obtuse of the rural police must surely link the tragedy with my flight from the nearby city. Besides, for the first time I had been careless enough to leave some tangible proof of my identity—my fingerprints on the throats of the newly dead. All day I shivered in nervous apprehension. The mere crackling of a dry twig beneath my feet conjured mental images that appalled me. That night, under cover of the protecting darness, I skirted Fenham and made for the woods that lay beyond. Before dawn came the first definite hint of renewed pursuit—the distant baying of hounds.

Through the long night I pressed on, but by morning I could feel my artificial strength ebbing. Noon brought once more the insistent call of the contaminating curse, and I knew I must fall by the way unless I could once more experience that exotic intoxication that came only with the proximity of the loved dead. I had traveled in a wide semicircle. If I pushed steadily ahead, midnight would bring me to the cemetery where I had laid away my parents years before. My only hope, I felt certain, lay in reaching this goal before I was overtaken. With silent prayer to the devils that dominated my destiny I turned leaden feet in the direction of my last stronghold.

God! Can it be that a scant twelve hours have passed since I started for my ghostly sanctuary? I have lived an eternity in each leaden hour. But I have reached a rich reward. The noxious odors of this neglected spot are frankincense to my suffering soul!

The first streaks of dawn are graying the horizon. They are coming! My sharp ears can catch the far-off howling of the dogs! It is but a matter of minutes before they find me and shut me away forever from the rest of the world, to spend my days in ravaging yearnings till at least I join the dead I love!

They shall not take me! A way of escape is open! A coward's choice, perhaps, but better—far better—than endless months of nameless misery. I will leave this record behind me that some soul may perhaps understand why I make this choice.

The razor! It has nestled forgotten in my pocket since my flight from Bayboro. Its blood-stained blade gleams oddly in the waning light of the thin-edged moon. One slashing stroke across my left wrist and deliverance is assured. . . .

Warm, fresh blood spatters grotesque patterns on dingy, decrepit slabs . . . phantasmal hordes swarm over the rotting graves . . . spectral fingers beckon me . . . ethereal fragments of unwritten melodies rise in celestial crescendo . . . distant stars dance drunkenly in demoniac accompaniment . . . a thousand tiny hammers beat hideous dissonances on anvils inside my chaotic brain . . . gray ghosts of slaughtered spirits parade in mocking silence before me . . . scorched tongues of invisible flame sear the brand of hell upon my sickened soul . . . I can—write—no —more. . . .

INDIGESTION

by BARRY N. MALZBERG

The narrator of "Indigestion," like that of the Eddy story, is a madman with unholy appetites. But he is much more than that. He is literate, even erudite; he is philosophical, even metaphysical; and he is a professional man of some stature in his community. Just what sort of profession he practices, while at the same time sating his lust for human carrion, is for you to discover. And, no doubt, to shudder at.

As alluded to above, there is a deeper message here than a cautionary study of the psychotic aberration of one man. The Other, the beast who lives within Henry, the narrator, and with whom he holds dialogues, is not one man's private demon; it is a universal demon, the imp of the perverse who has the power to make murderers of the meek, lunatics of the sane, ghouls of the righteous. The Other dwells in all of us, and we spend our lives struggling to contain his nascent influence. Most of us succeed. But some, the scattered few, lose the struggle and allow the Other to gain control. And that is when the terror begins.

Born in Brooklyn in 1939, Barry N. Malzberg has carved a somewhat polemical niche for himself in the literary world during the past fifteen years —most notably in the field of science fiction, where the bulk of his eighty novels and two hundred fifty short stories and essays has been published. His work is idiosyncratic, highly literate, mystical, unsettling, powerful, and demanding. Not everyone can penetrate it, but those who can find it an exhilarating experience. Among his novels are Beyond Apollo, Herovit's World, Underlay, Guernica Night, The Destruction of the Temple, Scop, Chorale, *and four collaborations with this editor, including* The Running of Beasts *and* Acts of Mercy. *He has also published six fictional collections, and has written a collection of essays on the nature of science fiction entitled* The Engines of the Night, *scheduled for publication at about the same time as this volume.*

AH WELL. Then again I sometimes wonder how it might have been if instead of the anonymous and forlorn I had ingested instead the bodies of the famous. The cells of Spinoza swimming to mingle with my own bright and burbling blood, the obsessions of Beethoven, the clear and cunning visions of W. J. Bryan taken unto me and merged with my glutinous bloodstream . . . why, I might have been anything. Anything at all! I would have been a congregation, a celebration unto myself, not Henry of this common nature (which for all the ecstasy of my activities is what I am; I know my limitations) but Henry Transmogrified, carrying within himself the seeds and decomposition of hundreds of the best.

If the ingestion of a corpse enables one (as I humbly do believe your honor) to take on many of the intellectual qualities of the deceased, then it is clear that I am limited only by the limitations of those within me. Still, that is absolute.

Still. I frequent bleak graveyards located far from the fashionable suburbs; I content myself with fresh grave sites unattended —which can only mean that the deceased left as little of a mark in the departure from life as in the partaking—I observe the amenities of my cruel and inexplicable trade by working as much as I can on the periphery of feeling. Not for me the leap into the still-open grave surrounded by mourning relatives and creditors, not for me either an attempt to insinuate myself nearer the deceased by obtaining a job in the trade: mortician, laboratory attendant, morgue custodian, and so on. For me there is an appreciation of the amenities of feeling. I observe them. I do what I must not without a bright thread of shame. I admit that I am a fiend.

Spinoza and Beethoven, the Kennedys or the cellular decomposition of Nobel Prize winners revolve with me not; I suit myself with simpler game, not a little of it (I will admit this, too) gathered from the potter's fields. I own a shortwave radio and keep up with the latest police reports; if a derelict is delivered anonymously DOA to a hospital I want to be prepared to call upon him tomorrow. But it is not me, it is Henry no longer, it is (as I have said) a congregation that now takes itself upon these tours; the dead feed upon the dead and all two hundred and fifty-five of us, the original Henry and parts of the two hundred and fifty-four he has consumed, prowl about their obsessive errands. I am more than a congregation, I am a civilization, an urban culture (or at least a medium-sized village) to myself. At the end of all of this, I am sure, lies a knowledge so absolute that only the amorphous outlines of the goal, rosy in their radiance, are there to tantalize me. I do not know what I (what we) am (are), I only know that I must go forward. Besides, the dead are very tasty. Eating parts of decomposed corpses is exciting, not only a bizarre gourmet treat but, as a meal taken on the run, heightened by a sense of mortality, of imminent capture. One can enjoy the task for its own sake. I enjoy eating the dead. (I already warned you that I was a fiend.)

So much for exposition and all of this in the persona of the original Henry, the corpse-eating Henry who began his journey just three and a half years ago. But Henry, now thirty-seven, can hardly be said to exist anymore, his fragile, mean soul has been overtaken by the souls of the two hundred and fifty-four ingested so that the congregation clangs and bangs against itself nervously within the confines of the tenement that is Henry's persona. Each of the two hundred and fifty-four would have its tale to tell; each of them could make its own case. They have found their immortality within Henry; this is firmly believed and each of them (as are all the living, too) is an individual, but the stories would remit to a common banality, a reiteration of the germinal act of *having been eaten;* this would be rather repetitious and thus Henry, the true and final narrator of these adventures, Henry will suppress the other two hundred and fifty-four in the interests of economy and fictional imperative, dealing only with the present instances as they refract into the past, as they summon up the future. It is he, after all, who has devised for the two hundred and fifty-four their immortality.

Into his rooms at some careful hour of the dawn Henry comes, his congregation chanting within him. Fluids roil murkily; Henry has spent the hours of the night at a cemetery in Forest Hills (Forest Hills!) where he has eaten richly of parts of an old woman buried not sixteen hours before. From his careful reading of the obituaries, from his tennis shoes and alert stalk, from his gloved hands, strong shoulders, and wood-cutting devices, from his energy and ambition Henry has derived rich proceeds; not only has he gorged himself with a hand, a foot, and an eyeball but (in a festival of gluttony) Henry has also eaten part of the chin and a weary, crushed-in nose, these last two superfluities sickening him, but Henry could not stop. Sometimes he is unable to control himself. Tossing over the dirt with shaking hands, replacing the marker guiltily, Henry stumbled away from the graveyard and onto a Queens Boulevard bus at the end of the line, his appearance bringing only desultory attention from the three inhabitants of the bus: a workman, a driver, a drug addict who sat nodding secretly in the back. Looking at Henry, it is impossible to know what they might have made of his appearance, the dirt on his shoes, the dirt on his nostrils, his flushed and yet pallid demeanor, but Henry knew what to make of them: looking at them, it was as if he regarded not people but metaphors, metaphors for the corpses that they would be. Shyly and tentatively, yet with increasing boldness, Henry and his congregation regarded these three, wondering what it might be like at some date in the indefinite future to eat them, what their personalities might be like added to the two hundred and fifty-four already in his bloodstream, and the two hundred and fifty-fifth making sliding entrance through gullet and bowels, and they in turn looked back. Did they judge his thoughts? Regarding his shovel, the valise in which he held his cutter, did these three have any inkling of that secret buzzing greedily in Henry's brain and throat like a demented insect? Or did they simply think nothing at all; were their minds as clean and darkly paneled as the minds of the dead? Henry looked between his feet and thought nothing at all, afflicted with an indigestion so severe that it drove metaphysical speculation clear from the pulpit of his consciousness, from the church of his interior, from the congregation of his choice. He returned to his rooms.

Not unaware that he was a fiend, Henry took the usual precautions when he had emerged from the 102 Queens Boulevard bus at the intersection of two numbered avenues. At one wastebasket he disposed of his gloves, at another the woolen hat which he had worn for customary disguise and which had become smeared in a somewhat implicatory fashion; at a third (Henry, staggering from his indigestion, reeling down the length of Queens Boulevard, pausing at wastebaskets to hurl objects, might have had a riotous aspect to anyone who was watching; Henry is not unaware of his appearance or how his activities might strike an appalled and unreasoning world; for this reason he takes more than the usual precautions over his activities and tries to write about himself in the third person as much as possible so that anyone stumbling across these well-secreted notes posthumously might well think that I was talking about someone *else,* which is more than a few senses is the case) Henry paused to retch, his insides convulsing as certain displacements took effect (he should not have had that eyeball), and then, somewhat eased in the flesh if not in the murmurings of the spirit, he returned to his rooms where he found the Other waiting for him as the Other so often does after these expeditions.

It might be necessary, by laws of fictional imperative already referred to, to discuss the Other, to talk about the background of the beast, to explain what it was doing in the rooms and why it and Henry have such undue familiarity, but if it is all the same to everyone, Henry will refuse this task. Henry will not discuss this anymore, being quite familiar with the appearance of the

Other and the Other's reasons for being there and having discussed this at length in previous narratives. Besides, there are
certain things which lie, perhaps, outside of any decent opinion
of mankind, outside of any normal range of human behavior,
and which, when written about, when even *hinted* about, can
cause only the most unusual disgust and revulsion, open up
emotions and responses that are archaic and long since buried.
Let them stay buried. There will be no discussion of the Other
here other than to state that it was there again and that Henry
felt the old twisting fear in his vitals. He had never gotten over
his terror of the Other. Try as he had to supersede that terror,
to realize that much of it was imaginary, that all of it could be
overcome, he could not stop that feeling but indeed found himself in its thrall. Very much as did his congregation, which
squirmed, trembled in place, murmured warnings and impreca-
tions. Half a congregation, three-quarters Henry, four-fifths
what he had most recently consumed, Henry faced the Other as
bravely as he could and said, "I thought I told you that I didn't
want you here anymore. I thought that we settled that last time.
Come on. Get out of here."

The Other took a slightly different posture and said, "Come
now, Henry, enough of this." It eyed him, saw the look on his
face which must have told him everything, not that a ringing,
foaming belch from Henry did not tell him more; small specks
of blood that were not his then pouring from Henry's mouth to
the corners of his lips. Henry wiped them slowly, trying not to
call attention to this disaster, but it was already too late. The face
of the Other congealed. It licked its horrid lips.

"You've been doing it again," it said.

"That's none of your business. That's none of your affair."

"But I'm afraid that it is my affair, Henry. It's very much my
responsibility; I'm implicated in this up to the hilt. Haven't I
warned you?"

"Warn away," Henry said rather sullenly. He was terrified but
still sullen; sullen but yet terrified; part of this having to do with
the reactions of his congregation. Some of them were sullen but
then again others of them were terrified. His reactions were

never consistent because his congregation was inconsistent. It involved a cross section. If Henry had partaken of a better class of person, if Henry had determined unto himself that he would seek only the best and the most consistent of personality traits, then things might have been quite different, but then again Henry could not control himself. Gluttony predominated, and the urge to multiply. If one cannot multiply in one way then one must do it in another, but this is a line of speculation that Henry finds very arcane and *he will not pursue it under any circumstances.* "Get out of here," he said again sullenly and with terror. "Get out now."

"You've been eating people," the Other said flatly. "You've been going to graves and tearing them open and you've been taking out corpses and eating them. A finger here, an eyeball there, sometimes a whole hand, occasionally even an arm. I know what you're doing, Henry. Do you think I'm a fool? You've been warned again and again."

"It's none of your business," Henry said. He put down the valise with a clatter, walked then into the second of the two rooms of his two-room furnished apartment, in which second room he walked to the window, looked down the clear pipe of the air shaft to the sheer drop, three stories below, the implacable stones of the courtyard assuming to him, in the first intimations of the dawn, the aspect of a kind of destiny. "None of your business," he repeated, hearing the footsteps of the Other as it came through the doorway and closed distance between them. There was no way to keep the horrid creature out.

"You've been warned and warned, Henry," the Other said, somewhat repetitiously. "You've been warned nicely and you've been warned harshly. You've been begged and you've been threatened. You've been reasoned with and once we even looked at pictures together while I tried to explain to you nicely why you can't go around eating corpses. Every time I thought you got the point but you're hopeless, Henry. You just keep on doing it. It's got to stop."

Henry shook his head, standing against the window. "What I do is my business," he said. "Besides," he added, "I've got not only myself to consider now. I'm eating for two hundred and fifty-six."

"That is lunacy, Henry. There are no two hundred and fifty-six. There is only you. Your personality does not increase through the personalities of those you ingest. The soul is ephemeral; it flies away at the moment of death. There is nothing but flesh. You lust to eat flesh, Henry. There is no congregation. It is only yourself and the rest is rationalization."

"Get out of here," Henry said severely. His stomach roiled at the thought that he might not be two hundred and fifty-six but only himself. Alone, alone: always alone; the suggestion was obscene. It could not be. He knew if nothing else that ingestion had given him *companionship.* He put the thought away. "Get out or I'll strike you."

The Other giggled in a rather feminine way. It has a rather high voice when under stress, very much as Henry does although Henry can control himself better. "Don't be ridiculous," it said, "I can't get out. I won't get out. You can't get rid of me. This has got to stop."

"I mean it," Henry said, turning from the window, raising his hand in a threatening way. "I've had quite enough of this now. Be gone with you."

The Other paused, looming, hanging just beyond Henry's reach. Its horrid little eyes turned meditative, its green scales prickled. It shook its beaked head. "I'm sorry," it said, "I'm sorry, Henry. This has gone too far. You're quite dangerous and you won't be held back. I've tried reasoning and threatening, begging and explanations. Still you go on looting graves, desecrating the friendless dead. This is hopeless. It has got to stop." It nodded solemnly, in a sudden and decisive way. "Yes," it said, "this has got to stop."

It closed upon Henry and a claw came out; suddenly Henry felt himself held within a tremendous and beckoning claw, yanked up against the scales of the creature. They exuded a foul odor; Henry felt the strength and conviction of the Other pouring into him and regrets suddenly spun the tumblers of his mind. Why hadn't he listened? Why hadn't he heeded the warnings? Why had he not understood that the Other was merely, as it had oft repeated, doing this for his own good in lieu of more horrid actions? But it was too late for any of this, of course. Henry knew how late it was. The Other had indeed threatened him and Henry had not thought that the threats would come to pass but now they had, and as he clung to the horrid green of the creature, a slimy ooze coming from little pores like abcesses in the scales of the Other, Henry's whole life seemed to flick before his eyes, right up to his thirty-fifth year when these activities (and the Other) had entered his life. Why had he done it? Why had he found it necessary to look to the dead for sustenance when there were so many of the living? Insight like a belch exploded and expanded his consciousness, but of course it was too late for any of this. With little peeps and cries his congregation fled the temple of his insides, plunged gabbling into the vestry of his unconscious, and Henry realized that he was indeed alone, always to be alone.

"I'm afraid that I'm going to have to kill you now," the Other said. It inclined its tentacled head in a gesture gracious and somehow touching, something humanoid in the aspect. "It's for your own good, Henry," it pointed out, "this would just go on and on and eventually you'd wind up doing something really dangerous and stupid like frequenting funeral homes, looking around open coffins. This has got to be brought to an end."

And Henry said, "Yes, yes, I see what you mean," his breath cut off by that suffocating embrace, his body arched in a spasm of agreement, for he did see, he truly saw what the Other was saying; he saw too that the Other, all along, had merely been trying to help him, to educate him into a better way of life, and like all of the other opportunities offered him Henry had mocked and lost this last of them but too late, too late for any of this. "I'm sorry," the Other said, "Henry, I'm truly sorry but there must come an end to this," and guided him toward the windows, centered Henry against it and then with one terrific thrust sent Henry arching and vaulting through the glass; for one instant hanging high in the air, his skin severed by a thousand cuts, his body at dreadful stillness, looking at the Other,

Henry thought that he understood everything up to the Other's identity . . . but in the next instant as he began that long, expiring fall to the courtyard beneath he realized that he understood nothing at all and that all of it must be, as it had always been, a mystery.

His last thought before his body explodes is not for himself but his congregation as truly befits the minister he has tried to be . . . but his congregation is out of touch, no time for benediction, and all two hundred and fifty-six of them slant to the stones before rebounding, the organs of his dismembered body spokes. The impact fire.

The impact fire.

THE CHADBOURNE EPISODE

by HENRY S. WHITEHEAD

The ghouls you have met thus far have been of the human variety; those who inhabit "The Chadbourne Episode," however, are decidedly not human. Nor, for that matter, are they supernatural. Rather, they are a race of beings unto themselves, "semimythical dwellers among the half-forgotten crypts of ancient burial grounds, eaters of the dead, which yet preferred the bodies of the living, furtive shapes shot down when glimpsed —in ancient, mysterious Persia. . . ."

What happens when these creatures surface in the New England village of Chadbourne is frightening indeed. For these ghouls have special preferences among the living—a taste, as it were, for the young and tender. Once you have visited their lair and witnessed the things they do, you will not soon forget them; nor will you forget, as narrator Gerald Canevin will not forget, those little bones, those pitiful little bones they leave behind . . .

Henry St. Clair Whitehead (1882–1932) was an Episcopalian minister who, after graduating from Harvard and then from divinity school, spent his early years in missionary work in the West Indies. Much of his substantial output of short fiction—macabre, adventure, juvenile—has Caribbean settings, and much of it also deals with various aspects of the

569

voodoo religion. (See his piratical novelette "Seven Turns in a Hangman's Rope" in Voodoo!*) Although he wrote no novels during his lifetime, he did publish a number of religious nonfiction books. And his finest "weird tales," from the magazine of that name and from such other periodicals as* Strange Tales *and* Adventure, *many of which also feature Gerald Canevin as narrator, were preserved in two posthumous Arkham House collections:* Jumbee and Other Uncanny Tales *(1944) and* West India Lights *(1946).*

PERHAPS THE most fortunate circumstance of the well-nigh incredible Chadbourne affair is that little Abby Chandler was not yet quite seven years of age on the evening when she came back home and told her mother her story about the old sow and the little pigs. It was July, and Abby with her big tin pail had been up on the high ridge near the Old Churchyard after low-bush blueberries. She had not even been especially frightened, her mother had said. That is what I mean by the fortunate aspect of it. Little Abby was altogether too young to be devastated, her sweet little soul permanently blasted, her mentality wrenched and twisted away from normality even by seeing with her round, China-blue eyes what she said she had seen up there on the steep hillside.

Little Abby had not noticed particularly the row of eight or nine pushing, squeaking, grunting little pigs at their early evening meal because her attention had been entirely concentrated on the curious appearance, as it seemed to her, of the source of that meal. That old sow, little Abby had told her mother, had had "a lady's head. . . ."

There was, of course, a *raison d'être*—a solution—back of this reported marvel. That solution occurred to Mrs. Chandler almost at once. Abby must have heard something, in the course of her six and three-quarter years of life here in Chadbourne among the little town's permanent inhabitants, some old-wives' gossip for choice, about "marked" people; whispered "cases" of people born with some strange anatomical characteristics of a domestic animal—freaks—or even farm animals "marked" with some human streak—a calf with a finger growing out of its left hind fetlock—things like that; animals quickly destroyed and buried out of sight. Such statements can be heard in many old New England rural settlements which have never wholly let go the oddments in tradition brought over from Cornwall and the West Country of Old England. Everybody has heard them.

Chadbourne would be no exception to anything like this. The old town lies nestling among the granite-bouldered ridges and dimpling hills of deep, rural, eastern Connecticut. In any such old New England town the older people talk much about all such affairs as Black Sabbaths, and Charmed Cattle, and Marked People.

All of that Mrs. Chandler knew and sensed in her blood and bones. She had been a Grantham before she had married Silas Chandler, and the Grantham family had been quietly shrinking and deteriorating for nine generations in Chadbourne along with the process of the old town's gradual dry-rotting, despite the efforts of such of the old-time gentry as may have survived in such places.

For gentry there are, deeply imbedded in New England, people who have never forgotten the meaning of the old *noblesse oblige,* people who have never allowed their fine sense of duty and obligation to lapse. In Chadbourne we had such a family, the Merritts; *Mayflower* passengers to Plymouth in the Massachusetts Colony in 1620; officers and trustees for generations of Dartmouth College in New Hampshire and of Trinity College, Hartford, Connecticut. We Canevins, Virginians, were not, of course, of this stock. My father, Alexander Canevin, had bought up an abandoned farm on a Chadbourne ridge-top about the time of the Spanish War. In that high air, among those rugged hills and to the intoxicating summer scents of bayberry blossoms and sweet fern—which the Connecticut farmers named appropriately, "hardhack"—I had sojourned summers since my early boyhood.

Tom Merritt and I had grown up together, and he, following

the family tradition, had gone to Dartmouth, thence to the Harvard Medical School. At the time of little Abby's adventure he was serving his community well as the Chadbourne general practitioner. But for the four years previous to his coming back and settling down to this useful if humdrum professional career, Thomas Bradford Merritt, M.D., had been in the diplomatic service as a career consul, chiefly in Persia where, before his attachment as a step up to our legation in Teheran, he had held consular posts at Jask, a town in the far south on the Gulf of Oman; at Kut-el-Amara in the west, just south of Baghdad; and finally at Shiraz, where he had collected some magnificent rugs.

The autumn before little Abby Chandler's blueberrying expedition Tom, who acted as my agent, had rented my Chadbourne farmhouse just as I was leaving New York for my customary winter's sojourn in the West Indies. That my tenants were Persians had, it appeared, no connection at all with Tom's long residence in that land. They had been surprised, Tom told me, when they found out that the New England gentleman whose advertisement of my place they had answered from New York City was familiar with their country, had resided there, and even spoke its language passably.

In spite of this inducement to some sort of sociability, the Persian family, according to Tom, had comported themselves, toward him and everybody else in Chadbourne, with a high degree of reticence and reserve. The womenfolk had kept themselves altogether secluded, rarely leaving the house that winter. When they did venture forth they were always heavily muffled up—actually veiled, Tom thought—and only the edges, so to speak, of the mother and two daughters were ever to be observed by any inhabitant of Chadbourne curious to know how Persian ladies might look through the windows of Mr. Rustum Dadh's big limousine.

Besides the stout mother and the two stout, "yellowish-complected," sloe-eyed daughters, there was Mr. Rustum Dadh himself, and two servants. These were the chauffeur, a square-built, tight-lipped, rather grim-looking fellow, who made all his own repairs to the big car and drove wrapped up in a fur-lined livery overcoat; and a woman, presumably the wife of the chauffeur, who never appeared outside at all, even on Friday nights when there was movies in Chadbourne's Palace Opera House.

All that I knew about my tenants Tom Merritt told me. I never saw any of the Rustum Dadh family from first to last. I had, in fact, completely forgotten all about them until I arrived in Chadbourne the following June some time after their departure and learned from Tom the bare facts I have set out here.

On a certain night in July that summer the Rustum Dadhs were farthest from my thoughts. It was nine o'clock, and I was sitting in the living room reading. My telephone rang insistently. I laid down my book with a sigh at being interrupted. I found Thomas Bradford Merritt, M.D., on the other end of the wire.

"Come on down here as soon as you can, Gerald," said Tom without any preliminaries, and there was a certain unusual urgency in his voice.

"What's happened?" I inquired.

"It may be—ah—something in your line, so to speak," said Dr. Merritt; "something—well—out of the ordinary. Bring that Männlicher rifle of yours!"

"I'll be right down," said I, snapped up the receiver, got the Männlicher out of my case in the hall where it is in with my shotguns, and raced out to the garage. Here, of a certainty, was something quite strange and new for Chadbourne, where the nearest thing to anything like excitement from year's end to year's end would be an altercation between a couple of robins over a simultaneously discovered worm! "Bring your rifle!" On the way down to the village I did not try to imagine what could possibly lie behind such a summons—from conservative Tom Merritt. I concentrated upon my driving, down the winding country road from my rugged hilltop into town, speeding on the short stretches, easing around treacherous turns at great speed. . . .

I dashed into Tom's house eight minutes after hanging up the receiver. There was a light I had observed, in the library as well as in the office, and I went straight in there and found Tom sitting on the edge of a stiff chair, plainly waiting for my arrival.

"Here I am," said I, and laid my rifle on the library table. Tom plunged into his story. . . .

"I'm tied up—a confinement case. They'll be calling me now any minute. Listen to this, Gerald—this is probably a new one on you—what I've got to tell you—even in the face of all the queer things you know—your West Indian experiences; *vodu;* all the rest of it; something *I* know, and—have always kept my mouth shut about! That is—if this is what I'm afraid it is. You'll have to take my word for it. I haven't lost my mind or anything of the sort—you'll probably think that if it turns out to be what I think it is—get this, now:

"Dan Curtiss's little boy, Truman, disappeared, late this afternoon, about sundown. Truman is five years old, a little fellow. He was last seen by some older kids coming back to town with berries from the Ridge, about suppertime. Little Truman, they said, was 'with a lady,' just outside the Old Cemetery.

"Two lambs and a calf have disappeared within the last week. Traced up there. A bone or two and a wisp of wool or so—the calf's ears, in different places, but both up there, and part of its tail; found 'em scattered around when they got up there to look.

"Some are saying 'a cattymaount.' Most of 'em say dogs.

"But—it isn't dogs, Gerald. 'Sheep-killers' tear up their victims on the spot. They don't drag 'em three miles up a steep hill before they eat 'em. They run in a pack, too. Everybody knows that. Nothing like that has been seen—no pack, no evidences of a pack. Those lost animals have all disappeared singly—more evidence that it isn't 'dogs.' They've been taken up and, presumably, eaten, up on top of the Cemetery Ridge. Sheep-killing dogs don't take calves, either, and there's that calf to be accounted for. You see—I've been thinking it all out, pretty carefully. As for the catamount, well, catamounts don't, commonly, live—and eat—out in the open. A catamount would drag off a stolen animal far into the deep woods."

I nodded.

"I've heard something about animals disappearing; only the way I heard it was that it's been going on for quite a long time, and somewhat more intensively during the past month or so."

Tom Merritt nodded at that. "Right," said he. "It's been going on ever since those Persians left, Gerald. All the time they were here—six months it was—they always bought their house supply of meat and poultry alive, 'on the hoof.' Presumably they preferred to kill and dress their meat themselves. I don't know, for a fact, of course. Anyhow, that was one of the peculiarities of the 'foreigners up at the Canevin Place,' and it got plenty of comment in the town, as you may well imagine. And—since they left—it hasn't been only lambs and calves. I know of at least four dogs. Cats, maybe, too! Nobody would keep much account of lost cats in Chadbourne."

This, somehow, surprised me. I had failed to hear about the dogs and possible cats.

"Dogs, too, eh?" I remarked.

Then Tom Merritt got up abruptly, off his stiff chair, and came over and stood close behind me and spoke low and intensively, and very convincingly, directly into my ear.

"And now—it's a child, Gerald. That's too much—for this, or any other decent town. You've never lived in Persia. I have. I'm going to tell you in plain words what I think is going on. Try to believe me, Gerald. Literally, I mean. You've got to believe me —trust me—to do what you've got to do tonight because I can't come right now. It's going to be an ordeal for you. It would be for anybody. Listen to this, now:

"This situation only came to me, clearly, just before I called you up, Gerald. I'd been sitting here, after supper, tied up on this Grantham case—waiting for them to call me. It was little Truman Curtiss's disappearance that brought the thing to a head, of course. The whole town's buzzing with it, naturally. No such thing has ever happened here before. A child has always been perfectly safe in Chadbourne since they killed off the last Indian a hundred and fifty years ago. I hadn't seen the connection before. I've been worked to death for one thing. I naturally hadn't been very much steamed up about a few lambs and dogs dropping out of sight.

"That might mean a camp of tramps somewhere. But—tramps don't steal five-year-old kids. It isn't tramps that do kidnaping for ransom.

"It all fitted together as soon as I really put my mind on it. Those Rustum Dadhs and their unaccountable reticence—the live animals that went up to that house of yours all winter—what I'd heard, and even seen a glimpse of—out there in Kut and Shiraz—that grim-jawed, tight-lipped chauffeur of theirs, with the wife that nobody ever got a glimpse of—finally that story of little Abby Chandler—"

And the incredible remainder of what Dr. Thomas Merritt had to tell me was said literally in my ear, in a tense whisper, as though the teller were actually reluctant that the walls and chairs and books of that mellow old New England library should over-hear the utterly monstrous thing he had to tell. . . .

I was shaken when he had finished. I looked long into my lifelong friend Tom Merritt's honest eyes as he stood before me when he had finished, his two firm, capable hands resting on my two shoulders. There was conviction, certainty, in his look. There was no slightest doubt in my mind but that he believed what he had been telling me. But—could he, or any one, by any possible chance, be right on the facts? Here, in Chadbourne, of all places on top of the globe!

"I've read about—them—in the *Arabian Nights,*" I managed to murmur.

Tom Merritt nodded decisively. "I've seen—two," he said, quietly. "Get going, Gerald," he added; "it's action from now on."

I stepped over to the table and picked up my rifle.

"And remember," he added, as we walked across the room to the door, "what I've told you about them. Shoot them down. Shoot to kill—if you see them. Don't hesitate. Don't wait. Don't —er—talk! No hesitation. That's the rule—in Persia. And re-member how to prove it—*remember the marks!* You may have to prove it—to anybody who may be up there still, hunting for poor little Truman Curtiss."

The office telephone rang.

Dr. Merritt opened the library door and looked out into the wide hallway. Then he shouted in the direction of the kitchen.

"Answer it, Mehitabel. Tell 'em I've left. It'll be Seymour Grantham, for his wife." Then, to me: "There are two search parties up there, Gerald."

And as we ran down the path from the front door to where our two cars were standing in the road I heard Dr. Merritt's elderly housekeeper at the telephone explaining in her high, nasal twang of the born Yankee, imparting the information that the doctor was on his way to the agitated Grantham family.

I drove up to the old cemetery on the Ridge even faster than I had come down from my own hill fifteen minutes earlier that evening.

The late July moon, one night away from full, bathed the fragrant hills in her clear, serene light. Halfway up the hill road to the Ridge I passed one search party returning. I encountered the other coming out of the cemetery gate as I stopped my steaming engine and set my brakes in front of the entrance. The three men of this party, armed with a lantern, a rifle, and two sizable clubs, gathered around me. The youngest, Jed Peters, was the first to speak. It was precisely in the spirit of Chadbourne that this first remark should have no direct reference to the pressing affair motivating all of us. Jed had pointed to my rifle, interest registered plainly in his heavy, honest countenance.

"Some weepon—thet-thar, I'd reckon, Mr. Canevin."

I have had a long experience with my Chadbourne neighbors.

"It's a Männlicher," said I, "What is called 'a weapon of precision.' It is accurate to the point of nicking the head off a pin up to about fourteen hundred yards."

These three fellows, one of them the uncle of the missing child, had discovered nothing. They turned back with me, however, without being asked. I could have excused them very gladly. After what Tom Merritt had told me, I should have preferred being left alone to deal with the situation unaided. There was no avoiding it, however. I suggested splitting up the party and had the satisfaction of seeing this suggestion put into effect. The three of them walked off slowly to the left while I waited, standing inside the cemetery gate, until I could just hear their voices.

Then I took up my stand with my back against the inside of the cemetery wall, directly opposite the big Merritt family mausoleum.

The strong moonlight made it stand out clearly. I leaned against the stone wall, my rifle cuddled in my arms, and waited. I made no attempt to watch the mausoleum continuously, but ranged with my eyes over the major portion of the cemetery, an area which, being only slightly shrubbed, and sloping upward gently from the entrance, was plainly visible. From time to time as I stood there, ready, I would catch a faint snatch of the continuous conversation going on among the three searchers, as they walked along on a long course which I had suggested to them, all the way around the cemetery, designed to cover territory which, in the local phraseology, ran "down through," "up across," and "over around." I had been waiting, and the three searchers had been meandering, for perhaps twenty minutes— the ancient town clock in the Congregational church tower had boomed ten about five minutes before—when I heard a soft, grating sound in the direction of the Merritt mausoleum. My eyes came back to it sharply.

There, directly before the now half-open bronze door, stood a strange, even a grotesque, figure. It was short, squat, thickset. Upon it, I might say accurately, hung—as though pulled on in the most hurried and slack fashion imaginable—a coat and trousers. The moonlight showed it up clearly and it was plain, even in such a light, that these two were the only garments in use. The trousers hung slackly, bagging thickly over a pair of large bare feet. The coat, unbuttoned, sagged and slithered lopsidedly. The coat and trousers were the standardized, unmistakable, diagonal gray material of a chauffeur's livery. The head was bare and on it a heavy, bristlelike crop of unkempt hair stood out absurdly. The face was covered with an equally bristlelike growth, unshaven for a month by the appearance. About the tight-shut, menacing mouth which divided a pair of square, iron-like broad jaws, the facial hairs were merged or blended in what seemed from my viewpoint a kind of vague smear, as though the hair were there heavily matted.

From this sinister figure there then emerged a thick, guttural, repressed voice, as though the speaker were trying to express himself in words without opening his lips:

"Come—come he-ar. Come—I will show you what you look for."

Through my head went everything that Tom Merritt had whispered in my ear. This was my test—my test, with a very great deal at stake—of my trust in what he had said—in him—in the rightness of his information; and it had been information, based on his deduction, such as few men have had to decide upon. I said a brief prayer in that space of a few instants. I observed that the figure was slowly approaching me.

"Come," it repeated—*"come now—I show you—what you, a-seek—here."*

I pulled myself together. I placed my confidence, and my future, in Tom Merritt's hands.

I raised my Männlicher, took careful aim, pulled the trigger. I repeated the shot. Two sharp cracks rang out on that still summer air, and then I lowered the deadly little weapon and watched while the figure crumpled and sagged down, two little holes one beside the other in its forehead, from which a dark stain was spreading over the bristly face, matting it all together the way the region of the mouth had looked even before it lay quiet and crumpled up on the ground halfway between the mausoleum and where I stood.

I had done it. I had done what Tom Merritt had told me to do, ruthlessly, without any hesitation, the way Tom had said they did it in Persia around Teheran, the capital, and Shiraz, and in Kut-el-Amara, and down south in Jask.

And then, having burned my bridges, and, for all I knew positively, made myself eligible for a noose at Wethersfield, I walked across to the mausoleum, and straight up to the opened bronze door, and looked inside.

A frightful smell—a smell like all the decayed meat in the world all together in one place—took me by the throat. A wave of quick nausea invaded me. But I stood my ground, and forced myself to envisage what was inside; and when I had seen, despite my short retchings and coughings I resolutely raised my Männlicher and shot and shot and shot at moving, scampering targets; shot again and again and again, until nothing moved inside there. I had seen, besides those moving targets, something else; some things that I will not attempt to describe beyond using the word "fragments." Poor little five-year-old Truman Curtiss who had last been seen just outside the cemetery gate "with a lady" would never climb that hill again, never pick any more blueberries in Chadbourne or any other place. . . .

I looked without regret on the shambles I had wrought within the old Merritt tomb. The Männlicher is a weapon of precision. . . .

I was brought to a sense of things going on outside the tomb by the sound of running feet, the insistent, clipping drawl of three excited voices asking questions. The three searchers, snapped out of their leisurely walk around the cemetery, and quite nearby at the time my shooting had begun, had arrived on the scene of action.

"What's it all about, Mr. Canevin?"

"We heard ye a-shootin' away."

"Good cripes! Gerald's shot a *man!*"

I blew the smoke out of the barrel of my Männlicher, withdrew the clip. I walked toward the group bending now over the crumpled figure on the ground halfway to the cemetery gate.

"Who's this man you shot, Gerald? Good cripes! It's the fella that druv the car for them-there Persians. Good cripes, Gerald —are ye crazy? You can't shoot down a man like that!"

"It's not a man," said I, coming up to them and looking down on the figure.

There was a joint explosion at that. I waited, standing quietly by, until they had exhausted themselves. They were, plainly, more concerned with what consequences I should have to suffer than with the fate of the chauffeur.

"You say it ain't no man! Are ye crazy, Gerald?"

"It's not a man," I repeated. "Reach down and press his jaws together so that he opens his mouth, and you'll see what I mean."

Then, as they naturally enough I suppose hesitated to fill this order, I stooped down, pressed together the buccinator muscles in the middle of the broad Mongollike cheeks. The mouth came open, and thereat there was another chorus from the three. It was just as Tom Merritt had described it! The teeth were the teeth of one of the great carnivores, only flat, fanglike, like a shark's teeth. No mortal man ever wore such a set within his mouth, or ever needed such a set, the fangs of a tearer of flesh. . . .

"Roll him over," said I, "and loosen that coat so you can see his back."

To this task young Jed addressed himself.

"Good cripes!" This from the Curtiss fellow, the lost child's uncle. Along the back, sewn thickly in the dark brown skin, ran a band of three-inch, coal-black bristles, longer and stiffer than those of any prize hog. We gazed down in silence for a long moment. Then:

"Come," said I, "and look inside the Merritt tomb—but—brace yourselves! It won't be any pleasant sight."

I turned, led the way, the others falling in behind me. Then, from young Jed Peters:

"You say this-here ain't no man—an'—I believe ye, Mr. Canevin! But—cripes almighty!—ef this'n hain't no man, what, a-God's name, is it?"

"It is a ghoul," said I over my shoulder, "and inside the tomb there are ten more of them—the dam and nine whelps. And what is left of the poor little Curtiss child. . . ."

Looking into the mausoleum that second time, in cold blood, so to speak, was a tough experience even for me who had wrought that havoc in there. As for the others—Eli Curtiss, the oldest of the three, was very sick. Bert Blatchford buried his face in his arms against the door's lintel, and when I shook him by the shoulder in fear lest he collapse, the face he turned to me was blank and ghastly, and his ruddy cheeks had gone the color of lead.

Only young Jed Peters really stood up to it. He simply swore roundly, repeating his "Good cripes!" over and over again—an articulate youth.

The whelps, with their flattish, humanlike faces and heads, equipped with those same punishing, overmuscled jaws like their sire's—like the jaws of a fighting bulldog—their short, thick legs and arms, and their narrow, bristly backs, resembled young pigs more nearly than human infants. All, being of one litter, were of about the same size; all were sickeningly bloody-mouthed from their recent feast. These things lay scattered about the large, circular, marble-walled chamber where they had dropped under the merciless impacts of my bullets.

Near the entrance lay sprawled the repulsive, heavy carcass of the dam, her dreadful, fanged mouth open, her sowlike double row of dugs uppermost, these dragged flaccid and purplish and horrible from the recent nursing of that lately weaned litter. All these unearthly looking carcasses were naked. The frightful stench still prevailed, still poured out through the open door-way. Heaps and mounds of nauseous offal cluttered the place.

It was young Jed who grasped first and most firmly my sugges-tion that these horrors be buried out of sight, that a curtain of silence should be drawn down tight by the four of us, fastened permanently against any utterance of the dreadful things we had seen that night. It was young Jed who organized the three into a digging party, who fetched the grave tools from the unfastened cemetery shed.

We worked in a complete silence, as fast as we could. It was not until we were hastily throwing back the loose earth over what we had placed in the sizable pit we had made that the sound of a car's engine, coming up the hill, caused our first pause. We listened.

"It's Dr. Merritt's car," I said, somewhat relieved. I looked at my wristwatch. It was a quarter past midnight.

To the four of us, leaning there on our spades, Dr. Merritt repeated something of the history of the Persian tombs, a little of what he had come to know of those mysterious, semimythical dwellers among the half-forgotten crypts of ancient burial grounds, eaters of the dead, which yet preferred the bodies of the living, furtive shapes shot down when glimpsed—in ancient, mysterious Persia. . . .

I left my own car for the three fellows to get home in, young Jed promising to have it back in my garage later in the morning, and drove home with Dr. Merritt.

"There was another thing which I didn't take the time to tell you," said Tom, as we slipped down the winding hill road under the pouring moonlight. "That was that the Rustum Dadh's servants were never seen to leave Chadbourne; although, of course, it was assumed that they had done so. The family went by train. I went down to the station to see them off and I found old Rustum Dadh even less communicative than usual.

" 'I suppose your man is driving your car down to New York,' I said. It had arrived, six months before, when they came to Chadbourne, with both the servants in it, and the inside all piled up with the family's belongings. The old boy merely grunted unintelligibly, in a way he had.

"That afternoon, when I went up to your place to see that everything was shipshape, there stood the car in the garage, empty. And, while I was wondering what had become of the chauffeur and his wife, and why they hadn't been sent off in the car the way they came, up drives Bartholomew Wade from his garage, and he has the car key and a letter from Rustum Dadh with directions, and a check for ten dollars and his carfare back from New York. His instructions were to drive the car to New York and leave it there. He did so that afternoon."

"What was the New York address?" I inquired. "That might take some looking into, if you think—"

"I don't know what to think—about Rustum Dadh's connection with it all, Gerald," said Tom. "The address was merely the Cunard Line Docks. Whether Rustum Dadh and his family were —the same—there's simply no telling. There's the evidence of the live animals sent up to the house. That live meat may have been for the chauffeur and his wife—seems unlikely, somehow. There was a rumor around town about some dispute or argument between the old man and his chauffeur, over their leaving all together—just a rumor, something picked up or overheard by some busybody. You can take that for what it's worth, of course. The two of 'em, desirous to break away from civilization, revert, here in Chadbourne—that, I imagine, is the probability. There are many times the number of people below ground in the three old cemeteries than going about their affairs—and other people's!—here in Chadbourne. But, whatever Rustum Dadh's connection with—what we know—whatever share of guilt rests on him—he's gone, Gerald, and we can make any one of the three or four possible guesses; but it won't get us anywhere." Then, a little weariness showing in his voice, for Tom Merritt, too, had had a pretty strenuous evening, he added:

"I hired young Jed Peters to spend tomorrow cleaning out the old tombhouse of the ancestors!"

I cleaned my rifle before turning in that night. When I had got this job done and had taken a boiling hot shower bath, it was close to two o'clock A.M. before I rolled in between the sheets. I had been dreading a sleepless night with the edge of my mind, after that experience up there on the Old Cemetery Ridge. I lay in bed for a while, wakeful, going over snatches of it in my mind. Young Jed! No deterioration there at any rate. There was a fellow who would stand by you in a pinch. The old yeoman stock had not run down appreciably in young Jed.

I fell asleep at last after assuring myself all over again that I had done a thorough job up there on the hill. Ghouls! Not merely *Arabian Nights* creatures, like the Afreets and the Djinn. No. Real—those jaws! They shot them down, on sight, over there in Persia when they were descried coming out of their holes among the old tomb places. . . .

Little, reddish, half-gnawed bones, scattered about that fetid shambles—little bones that had never been torn out of the bodies of calves or lambs—little bones that had been—

I wonder if I shall ever be able to forget those little bones, those little, pitiful bones. . . .

I awoke to the purr of an automobile engine in second speed, coming up the steep hill to my farmhouse, and it was a glorious

late-summer New England morning. Young Jed Peters was arriving with my returned car.

I jumped out of bed, pulled on a bathrobe, stepped into a pair
of slippers. It was seven-thirty. I went out to the garage and
brought young Jed back inside with me for a cup of coffee. It
started that new day propitiously to see the boy eat three fried
eggs and seven pieces of breakfast bacon. . . .

DISTURB NOT MY SLUMBERING FAIR

by CHELSEA QUINN YARBRO

And then there are the ghouls who were once human beings; those who, after death and burial, are possessed by the demon known as the ghul, *who are doomed to spend eternity (unless someone seals them in stone and thus starves them) sleeping in their graves and foraging from time to time for their sustenance. Diedre, the protagonist of "Disturb Not My Slumbering Fair," is such a ghoul—a sixteen-year-old female monster capable of wreaking the most awful havoc imaginable. And some that may be unimaginable . . .*

Does the concept of a teenybopper ghoul strike you as odd? It shouldn't. As the author herself has pointed out, "Ghosts come in all shapes, sizes, ages, and dispositions. Demons and other possessive spirits are as apt to pick a kid as a grandmother for their uses." It might be added that the demon who picked Diedre knew, in its hellish cunning, exactly what it was doing.

Chelsea Quinn Yarbro (born 1942) has also stated in print that she has "a certain sneaky sympathy" for various supernatural beings. This is evidenced by a quintet of successful and critically well-received historical horror novels about a unique (read sympathetic) vampire named le Comte

586

de Saint Germain: Hotel Transylvania, The Palace, Blood Games, Path of the Eclipse, *and* Tempting Fate. *She has also published science fiction* (Time of the Fourth Horseman), *mysteries* (Ogilvie, Tallant and Moon; Music When Sweet Voices Die), *occult nonfiction* (Messages from Michael), *a collection of speculative stories* (Cautionary Tales), *and an excellent novelization of a ghoulish film* (Dead and Buried). *A native Californian, she makes her home in the San Francisco Bay Area.*

IT WAS already Thursday when Diedre left her grave. The rain had made the soil soft and the loam clung to her cerements like a distracted lover. It was so late, the night so sodden, that there was no one to see her as she left the manicured lawns and chaste marble stones behind her for the enticing litter of the city.

"Pardon me, miss." The night watchman was old, white-haired under his battered hat. He held the flashlight aimed at her face, seeing only a disheveled young woman with mud in her hair, a wild look about her eyes, a livid cast to her face like a bruise. He wondered if she had been attacked; there was so much of that happening these days. "You all right, miss?"

Diedre chuckled, but she had not done it for some time and it came out badly. The watchman went pale and his mouth tightened. Whatever happened to her must have been very bad. "Don't you worry, miss. I'll call the cops. They'll catch the guy. You stay calm. He can't get you while I'm around."

"Cops?" she asked, managing the sounds better now. "It's not necessary."

"You look here, miss," said the night watchman, beginning to enjoy himself, to feel important once more. "You can't let him get away with it. You lean on me: I'll get you inside where it's warm. I'll take care of everything."

Diedre studied the old man, weighing up the risk. She was hungry and tired. The old man was alone. Making a mental shrug she sighed as she went to the old man, noting with amusement that he drew back as he got a whiff of her. She could almost see him recoil. "It was in the graveyard," she said.

"Christ, miss." The night watchman was shocked.

"Yes," she went on, warming to her subject. "There was a new grave . . . the earth hadn't settled yet . . . And the smell . . ." *was delicious.* she thought.

He was very upset, chafing her hand as he led her into the little building at the factory entrance. "Never you mind," he muttered. "I'll take care of you. Fine thing, when a man can . . . can . . . and in a graveyard, too . . ."

"Yes," she agreed, her tongue showing pink between her teeth.

He opened the door for her, standing aside with old-fashioned gallantry until the last of her train had slithered through before coming into the room himself. "Now, you sit down here." He pointed to an ancient armchair that sagged on bowed legs. "I'm going to call the cops."

Diedre wasn't quite ready for that. "Oh," she said faintly, "will you wait a bit? You've been so kind . . . and understanding. But sometimes the police think . . ." She left the sentence hanging as she huddled into the chair.

The night watchman frowned. Obviously the poor girl didn't know what she looked like. There could be no doubt about her case. "You won't get trouble from them," he promised her.

She shivered picturesquely. "Perhaps you're right. But wait a while, please. Let me collect myself a little more."

The night watchman was touched. He could see that she was close to breaking down, that only her courage was keeping her from collapsing. "Sure, miss. I'll hold off a bit. You don't want to wait too long, though. The cops are funny about that." He reached over to give her a reassuring pat but drew away from her when he saw the look in her eyes. Poor soul was scared to death, he could tell.

"Uh, sir," Diedre said after a moment, realizing that she didn't know his name. "I was wondering . . . I don't want you to get into trouble, after you've been so kind, but . . ."

He looked at her eagerly. "But what, miss?"

She contrived to look confused. "I just realized . . . I seem to have lost my ring." She held up both hands to show him. "It was valuable. An heirloom. My mother . . ." Her averted eyes were full of mischief.

"Oh, dear," said the night watchman solicitously. "Do you think you lost it back there?" He looked worried.

She nodded slowly. "Back at the grave," she whispered.

"Well, miss, as soon as the cops get here, we'll tell them and they'll get it for you." He paused awkwardly. "Thing is, miss. It might not still be there. Could have been taken, you know." He wanted to be gentle with her, to reassure her.

"Taken?" She stared at him through widened eyes. "My ring? Why?" Slowly she allowed comprehension to show in her face. "Oh! You think that he . . . that when he . . . that he took it?"

The night watchman looked away, mumbling, "He could have, miss. That's a fact. A man who'd do a thing like this, he'd steal. That's certain."

Diedre leaped up, distraction showing in every line of her sinuous body. "Then I've got to check! Now!" She rushed to the door and pulled on the knob. "It can't be gone. Oh, you've got to help me find it!" Pulling the door wide she ran into the night and listened with satisfaction as the old man came after her.

"Miss! Miss! Don't go back there! What if he hasn't gone? Let me call the cops, miss!" His breath grew short as he stumbled after her.

"Oh, no. No. I've got to be sure. If it's gone, I don't know what I'll do." She let herself stumble so that the old man could catch up with her; if he fell too far behind, Diedre knew she would lose him. This way it was so easy to lead him where she wanted him. Ahead she saw the cemetery gates gleaming faintly in the wan light.

"You don't want to go back in there, miss," said the night watchman between jagged breaths. His face was slippery with cold sweat that Diedre saw with a secret, predatory smile. "Oh, I can't . . ." It was the right sound, the right moment. He automatically put out his arm. Pretending to lean against him, she felt for his heart and was delighted at the panic-stricken way it battered at his ribs.

"But I've got to find it. I've got to." She broke away from him once more and ran toward the grave she had so recently left. "Over here," she cried, and watched as he staggered toward her, trying to speak.

Then his legs gave way and he fell against the feet of a marble angel. His skull made a pulpy noise when it cracked.

With a shriek of delight Diedre was upon him, her eager teeth sinking into the flesh greedily, although the body was still unpleasantly warm. Blood oozed down her chin and after a while she wiped it away.

Toward the end of the night she made a half-hearted attempt to bury the litter from her meal. It was useless; she knew that the body would be discovered in a little while, and there would be speculation on the state of it: the gnawed bones and the torn flesh. As an afterthought, she broke one of the gnawed arms against a pristinely white vault, just to confuse the issue. Then she gathered up a thigh and left, walking back into the city, filled, satisfied.

By the time the last of the night watchman was discovered, Diedre was miles away, sleeping off her feast in the cool damp of a dockside warehouse. Her face, if anyone had seen it, was soft and faintly smiling, the cyanose pallor of the grave fading away to be replaced with a rosy blush. She didn't look like a ghoul at all.

That night, when she left the warehouse, she saw the first headlines:

NIGHT WATCHMAN FOUND DEAD
IN GRAVEYARD
GRISLY SLAYING AT CEMETERY

Diedre giggled as she read the reports. Apparently there was some hot dispute in the police department about the teeth marks. There was also a plan to open the grave where the old

man had been killed. This made Diedre frown. If the grave were
opened, they would find it empty, and there would be more
questions asked. She bit her lip as she thought. And when the
solution came to her, she laughed almost merrily.

It was close to midnight when she spotted her quarry, a young
woman about her own height and build. Diedre followed her
away from the theater and into the many-tiered parking lot.

When the woman had opened the car door and was sliding
into the seat, Diedre came up beside her. "Excuse me," she said,
knowing that the old jacket and workmen's trousers she had
found in the warehouse made her look suspicious. "I saw you
come up, and maybe you can help me?"

The woman looked at her, her nose wrinkling as she looked
Diedre over. "What is the matter?" There was obvious condemnation in her words. Diedre had not made a good impression.

"It's my car," Diedre explained, pointing to a respectable
Toyota. "I've been trying to get it open, but the key doesn't
work. I've tried everything." She made a helpless gesture with
her hands, then added a deprecating smile.

"I don't think I can help you," said the woman stiffly. She was
seated now and had her hand on the door.

"Well, look," said Diedre quickly, holding the door open by
force. "If you'd give me a ride down, maybe there's a mechanic
still on duty. Or maybe I could phone the Auto Club . . ."

The woman in the car gave her another disapproving look,
then sighed and opened the door opposite her. "All right. Get
in."

"Gee, thank you," Diedre said and slipped around the car, slid
into the seat, and closed the door. "This is really awfully good
of you. You don't know how much I appreciate it."

The woman turned the key with an annoyed snap and the car
surged forward. "That's quite all right." The tone was glacial.

She was even more upset when they reached the ground level.
The attendant who took her money told the woman that there
was no mechanic on duty after ten and that it would take over
an hour for the Auto Club to get there, and the locksmith would
have to make a new key, and that would take time as well. Diedre

couldn't have painted a more depressing picture of her plight if she tried.

"I guess I'll have to wait," she said wistfully, looking out at the attendant.

"Well," the man answered, "there's a problem. We close up at two, and there's no way you'll be out of here by then. Why don't you come back in the morning?"

This was better than Diedre had hoped. "Well, if that's all I can do . . ." She shrugged. "Where can I catch a bus around here?"

"The nearest is six blocks down. What part of town you going to, lady?" the attendant asked Diedre.

"Serra Heights," she said, choosing a neighborhood near the cemetery, middle income, city-suburban. Altogether a safe address.

Reluctantly the woman driving the car said, "That's on my way. I'll drop you if you like." Each of the words came out of her like pulled teeth.

Diedre turned grateful eyes on her. "Oh, would you? Really? Oh, thanks. I don't mean to be a bother, but . . . well, you know." She added, as the inspiration struck her, "Jamie was so worried. This'll help. Really."

The woman's face softened a little. "I'll be glad to drive you." She turned to the attendant. "Perhaps you'll be good enough to leave a note for the mechanic so that there'll be no delay in the morning?" She was making up for her previously frosty behavior and gave Diedre a wide smile.

"Oh, thanks a lot for telling him that," Diedre said as the car sped out into the night. "I wouldn't have thought of it. I guess I'm more upset than I thought."

The conversation was occasional as they drove, Diedre keeping her mind on the imaginary Jamie, building the other woman a picture of two struggling young people, trying to establish themselves in the world. The woman listened, wearing a curious half-smile. "You know," she said as she swung off the freeway toward the Serra Valley district, "I've often thought things would be better with Grant and me if we'd had to work a little harder. It was too easy, always too easy."

"Oh," said Diedre at her most ingenuous, "did I say something wrong?"

"No," the woman sighed. "You didn't say anything wrong." She shook her head, as if shaking clouds away and glanced around. "Which way?"

"Umm. Left onto Harrison and then up Camino Alto." Camino Alto was the last street in the district, and it followed the boundary of the cemetery.

"Do you live on Camino Alto?" the woman asked.

"No. In Ponce de Leon Place. Up at the top of the hill." Behind that hill was open country, covered in brush. By the time the woman's body was found, the police would stop wondering about the missing one from Diedre's grave.

The car swung onto Harrison. "Doesn't it bother you, having that gruesome murder so close to home?"

Diedre smiled. "A little. You never know what might happen next."

They drove up the hill in silence, the woman glancing toward the thick shrubs that masked the cemetery. There was concern in her face and a lack of animation in her eyes. Diedre knew she would freeze when frightened.

"This is where I get out," she said at last, looking at the woman covertly. As the car came to a halt, Diedre reached over and grabbed the keys. "Thanks for the lift," she grinned.

"My keys . . ." the woman began.

Diedre shook her head. "Don't worry about them. I'll take care of them. Now, if you'll step out with me."

"Where are we going?" the woman quavered. "Not in there?"

"No," Diedre assured her. "Get out."

In the end she had to club the woman and drag her unconscious body from the car. It was awkward managing her limp form, but eventually she wrestled the woman from the car and into the brush. Branches tore at her and blackberry vines left claw marks on her arms and legs as she plunged farther down the hill. The woman moaned and then was silent.

It was almost an hour later when Diedre climbed up the hill

again, scratched, bruised, and happy. Tied to her belt by the hair, the woman's head banged on her legs with every step she took.

Taking the car, Diedre drove to the coast and down the old treacherous stretch of highway that twisted along the cliffs. Gunning the motor at the most dangerous curve, she rode the car down to its flaming destruction on the rocks where breakers hissed over it, steaming from the flames that licked upward as the gas tank exploded.

It was a nuisance, climbing up the cliff with a broken arm: the ulna had snapped, a greenstick fracture making the hand below it useless. Here and there Diedre's skin was scorched off, leaving black patches. But the job was done. The police would find the head in the wreck, along with one of the night watchman's leg bones, and would assume that the rest of the body had been washed out to sea: the headless woman back on the hillside would not be connected with this wreck, and she was clear.

But she was hungry. The night watchman was used up and she hadn't been able to use any part of the woman. Now Diedre knew she would have to be careful, for the police were checking cemeteries for vandals. And in her present condition the only place she wouldn't attract attention was the morgue.

The morgue!

Her broken arm was firmly splinted under her heavy sweater, her face carefully and unobviously made up as Diedre walked into the cold tile office outside the room where the bodies lay. The burned patches on her face had taken on the look of old acne and she used her lithe body with deliberate awkwardness.

"I'm Watson, the one who called?" she announced uncertainly to the colorless man at the desk.

He looked up at her and grunted. "Watson?"

Mentally she ground her teeth. What if this man had changed his mind; where would she go for food then? "Yes," she said, shuffling from one foot to the other. "I'm going to be a pathologist, and I thought . . . It's expensive, sir. Medical school is very expensive." Her eyes pleaded with him.

"I remember," he said measuredly. "Nothing like a little practical experience." He handed her a form. "I'll need your name and address and the usual information. Just fill this out and hand it in. I'll show you the place when you're done."

She took the form and started to work. The Social Security number stumped her and then she decided to use her old one. By the time it could be checked, she'd be long gone.

"No phone?" he asked as she handed the form back.

"Well, I'm at school so much . . . and it's kind of a luxury . . ."

"You'll make up for it when you get into practice," he said flatly. He knew doctors well.

As he filed her card away, Diedre glared at his back, wishing she could indulge herself long enough to make a meal of him. It would be so good to sip the marrow from his bones, to nibble the butter-soft convolutions of his brain.

"Okay, Watson. Come with me. If you get sick, out you go." He opened the door to the cold room and pointed out the silent drawers that waited for their cargo. "That's where we keep 'em. If they aren't identified, the county takes 'em over. We do autopsies on some of 'em, if it's ordered. Some of these stiffs are pretty messed up, some of 'em are real neat. Depends on how they go. Poison now," he said, warming to the topic, "poison can leave the outsides as neat as a pin and only part of the insides are ruined. Cars, well, cars make 'em pretty awful. Guns—that depends on what and where. Had a guy in here once, he'd put a shotgun in his mouth and fired both barrels. Well, I can tell you, he didn't look good." As he talked he strolled to one of the drawers and pulled it out. "Take this one," he went on.

Diedre ran her tongue over her lips and made a coughing noise. "What happened?"

"This one," said the man, "Had a run-in with some gasoline. We had to get identification from his teeth, and even part of his jaw was wrecked. Explosions do that." He glanced at her to see how she was taking it.

"I'm fine," she assured him.

"Huh." He closed the drawer and went on to the next. "This

one's drowned. In the water a long time." He wrinkled his nose. "Had to get the shrimps off him. Water really wrecks the tissues."

Five drawers later Diedre found what she had been looking for.

"This one," the man was saying, "well, it's murder, of course, and we haven't found all of him yet, but there's enough here to make some kind of identification, so he's our job."

"When did it happen?" Diedre asked.

"A week or so ago, I guess. Found him out in the Serra Heights cemetery. A big number in the papers about it."

Diedre stared at the bits of the night watchman. Something had shared her feast; she'd left more than this behind. It would be simple to take a bit more of him, here and there. No one would notice. But it paid to be careful. "Can I study this?" she said, doing her best to sound timorous.

"Why?" asked the man.

"To get used to it," she replied.

"If you help me out with ID, you can." He closed the night watchman away into his cold file cabinet. "In fact, you can do a work-up on the one we just got in. Get blood type and all those things. This one hasn't got a head, so it's gonna be fun, running her kin to earth."

"Hasn't got a head?" Diedre echoed, remembering the woman left on the hillside. "What happened?"

"Found her out by the cemetery where they got the other. Probably connected. The grave she was found on was new and it was empty. Could be she's the missing one."

"Oh," said Diedre, to fill in the silence that followed before the man closed the drawer. She stared at the body, watching it critically. She hadn't done too bad a job with it.

"Any of this getting to you?" the man asked as he showed her the last of the corpses. Only about half of the shelves were filled, and Diedre wondered at this. "I'm okay," she said, then added, as if it had just occurred to her. "Why are there so many shelves?"

"Right now things are a little slow. But if we get a good fire or quake or a six-car pile-up, we'll be filled up, all right." He gave her a shadowed, cynical smile. In the harsh light his skin had a dead-white cast to it, as if he had taken on the color of his charges.

Nodding, Diedre asked, "What do you want me to do first? Where do I work?"

The man showed her and she began.

It was hard getting food at first, but then she caught on and found that if she took a finger or two from a burn victim or some of the pulpy flesh from a water-logged drowner it was easy. Accident victims were best because, by the time the metal and fire were through with them, it was too hard to get all of a body together and a few unaccounted-for bits were never missed.

She was lipping just such an accident case one night when the door to her workroom shot open.

"Tisk, tisk, tisk, Watson," said the man she worked with.

Diedre froze, her mouth half-open and her face shocked.

The man strolled into the room. "You're an amateur, my girl. I've been keeping an eye on you. I know." He walked over to her and looked down. "First of all, don't eat where you work. It's too easy to get caught. Bring a couple of plastic bags with you and take the stuff home."

She decided to bluff. "I don't know what you're talking about."

He gave a harsh laugh. "Do you think you're the only ghoul in this morgue? I'm not interested in competition, and that's final. One of us has to go." He glared at her, fingering her scalpel.

It was quiet in the room for a moment, then Diedre put far more panic than she was feeling. "What are you going to do to me? What is going to happen?"

The man sniggered. "Oh, no. Not that way, Watson. You're going to have to wait until I've got everything ready. There's going to be another accident victim here, and there won't be any questions asked." He spun away from her and rushed to the door. "It won't be long; a day or two, perhaps. . . . Then it will be over and done with, Watson." He closed the door and in a moment she heard the lock click.

For some time she sat quietly, nibbling at the carrion in her hands. Her rosy face betrayed no fear, her slender fingers did not shake. And when she was through with her meal, she had a plan.

The telephone was easy to get to, and the number she wanted was on it. Quickly she dialed, then said in a breathless voice, "Police? This is Watson at the morgue. Something's wrong. The guy in charge here? He's trying to kill me." She waited while the officer on the other end expressed polite disbelief. "No. You don't understand. He's crazy. He thinks I'm a ghoul. He says he's going to beat me into a pulp and then hide me in drawer forty-seven until he can get rid of me. I'm scared. I'm so scared. He's locked me in. I can't get out. And he's coming back. . . ." She let her tone rise to a shriek and then hung up. So much for that.

When she unwrapped her broken arm, she saw that the ulna was still shattered and she twisted it to bring the shards out through the skin again. Next she banged her head into a cabinet, not hard enough to break the skull, but enough to bring a dark bruise to her temples. And finally she tore her clothes and dislocated her jaw before going into the file room and slipping herself into number forty-seven. It was all she could do to keep from smiling.

Somewhat later she heard the door open and the sound of voices reached her. The man she worked with was protesting to the police that there was nothing wrong here, and that his assistant seemed to be out for the night. The officer didn't believe him.

"But number forty-seven is empty," she heard the man protest as the voices came nearer.

"Be a sport and open it anyway," said the officer.

"I don't understand. This is all ridiculous." Amid his protests, he pulled the drawer back.

Diedre lay there, serene and ivory chill.

The man stopped talking and slammed the door shut. The officer opened it again. "Looks like you worked her over pretty good," he remarked, pulling the cloth away from her arm and touching the bruises on her face.

"But I didn't. . . ." Then he changed his voice. "Officer, you don't understand. She's a ghoul. She lives on the dead. That's why she was working here, so she could eat the dead. . . ."

"She said you were crazy," the officer said wearily. "Look at her, man," he went on in a choked tone. "That's a girl—a girl; not a ghoul. You've been working here too long, mister. Things get to a guy after a while." He turned to the men with him. "We'll need some pix of this. Get to work."

As the flashes glared, the officer asked for Diedre's work card, and when he saw it, "No relatives. Too bad. It'll have to be a county grave then."

But the man who ran the morgue cried out. "No! She's got to be buried in stone. In a vault with a lock on the door. Otherwise she'll get out. She'll get out and she'll be after people again. Don't you understand?" He rushed at the drawer Diedre lay in. "This isn't real. It doesn't matter if ghouls break bones or get burned. They're not like people! The only thing you can do is starve them. . . . You have to bury them in stone, locked in stone. . . ."

It was then that the police took the man away.

Diedre lay back and waited.

And this time, it was a full ten days before she left her grave.

QUIETLY NOW

by CHARLES L. GRANT

This is a tale of a somnolent village in northwestern New Jersey, of some of its inhabitants, and of ghoulish doings at the time of the darkmoon—those nights, "poets' nights, when the stars are perfect against a backdrop of perfect black, and the air is cool and the streams are running, and vision seems unlimited except for the moon. It could be crescent, it could be full, waxing or waning, yet darkened by a haze not born of a cloud." The darkmoon is legend, a Halloween tale, and yet people die during its time. The spring-thaw corpse huddled in a small cave, the partially devoured woman beneath a tree, the fleshless family unprotected in their tents, sleeping bags slashed and clothes rent at the seams—these are all victims of past darkmoons. During the time of the present darkmoon there will be more victims—many, many more . . .

"Quietly Now," in more ways than one, is an appropriate title. Like most of Charles L. Grant's work, it is an excursion into quiet horror—a story which unfolds slowly, layering its effects until the tension becomes acute, and which then achieves a climax of such dread that it remains in the mind long after reading, just like the unsettling afterimages of a particularly vivid nightmare.

Charles L. Grant (born 1943) sold his first short story in 1968 and has followed it with close to one hundred more, as well as several award-

winning novels of fantasy/horror and science fiction. He has received widespread acclaim for his series of novels and stories about a strange New England town called Oxrun Station (The Hour of the Oxrun Dead, Nightmare Season; *"The Other Room," which appears in* Mummy!), *and also for several excellent horror anthologies (five volumes of* Shadows, *one each of* Nightmares *and* Horrors). *Arkham House will shortly publish a collection of his finest macabre tales, both reprint and original, with an introduction by Stephen King.*

THE HILLS of northwestern New Jersey are low and ancient, densely forested and, for the most part, state protected. In those areas, however, which the state has kept clear there are children's camps and winter resorts, lakes natural and manmade, villages where only a radio tells them the year—and sufficient distances to exclude them all from New York City's commuting umbrella. Scarcely a wilderness by the Far West's standards, yet wilderness enough to make the ordinary tourist somewhat cautious after dark. And wilderness enough to spawn midnight stories of travelers wandering into the woodland and seldom returning.

Stories resurrected during the time of the darkmoon.

There are nights, poets' nights, when the stars are perfect against a backdrop of perfect black, and the air is cool and the streams are running, and vision seems unlimited except for the moon. It could be crescent, it could be full, waxing or waning, yet darkened by a haze not born of a cloud. Silverlight becomes gray, shadows lose definition, and old-timers head for the nearest tavern or hearth.

And travelers take walks, and the stories begin.

And like everyone else who lived there year-round, Keith Prior read the inevitable news with a slow-shaking head and a continuing wonderment that city people could be so eternally foolhardy, so infernally stupid. The darkmoon was legend, a Halloween tale, but it didn't change the fact that people sometimes died. He thought it would have been sufficient for them to see one two-column photo of a spring-thaw corpse huddled in a small cave, of a partially devoured woman huddled beneath a tree, of a fleshless family unprotected in their tents, sleeping bags slashed and clothes rent at the seams. But at least once a year someone refused to heed common-sense warnings, and once a year the stories returned.

Not, he thought, that he himself dwelled in a rustic log cabin and chopped wood for heat and hunted his meals and fashioned his wrappings from the pelts of the wild. That was a fancy he left to the movies, and his New York friends who thought he lived like a hermit.

The Greenwitch Arms Apartments complex was much more a place to foster a recluse's nightmares.

It had been constructed a decade before on a deserted farm just below a two-lane highway, sixty miles west of the Hudson River. Seventy-two two-story buildings of varicolored brick shaded by oaks still reaching for the eaves; a dozen units to a building—the upstairs with a narrow slatted balcony, the downstairs with a concrete slab that masked as a patio. Nearly two thousand people who thought they lived in the country.

It was May now, and warm, and the sky was of a blue better suited to a lover's eyes. He sat in his living room—a desk, two chairs, white walls buried behind unfinished bookcases—waiting for inspiration to lure him back to work.

Outside, on the twenty-yard patch of grass and shrubs between his building and the next, was a large, red plastic wading pool currently invaded by an army of young children. They splashed and complained and laughed so loudly he was unable to concentrate on the research he was doing—reading for an article on the fantasy whims of poets and prophets, for a magazine he'd never heard of, but which paid fifteen cents a word.

He sighed, and wondered if perhaps he shouldn't try calling Jane to apologize, though he had no idea if one was really necessary. It would be nice if he had to, because that would imply he might have another chance. But he doubted it. The affair had slowed to stasis during winter, had not thawed with spring. They were friends, they had drinks, he even visited now and then, but instinct warned him momentum had died. Probably, he thought sourly, he'd been preempted by Carl Andrews.

Another sigh, mockingly melodramatic, and he rose to stand at the sliding screen door to watch the kids playing. He counted eight, all of them trying to wedge into the pool without touching the ground now muddy with spillage. Suddenly, two of them—a carrot-top and a white-blond—broke away in disgust and wandered listlessly toward him. They looked up and waved before he could back off. He slid the door aside, stepped out, and rested his forearms on the railing.

"Hi, Uncle Keith!" A chorus high-pitched and pleasant. The title was honorary but he didn't mind it a bit.

"Gentlemen," he said solemnly, and nodded toward the others. "Too crowded at the beach?"

They scowled. They wore identical pairs of blue jogging shorts with gold piping. Chest, legs, arms bare and tanned. They seemed ill at ease, as if they missed having pockets in which their hands could hide.

"Did you guys have a good time yesterday?" he said. "See any neat freaks in the city?"

"No," said Peter, the carrot-top and older. "There wasn't anything but a bunch of dead animals. Bones and a lot of pictures. Nuts. Who wants to see bones?" And with a grimace of disgust he headed home, the first-floor apartment one over from Keith's.

"Hey, don't worry about him," Keith said when Philip looked stricken at his brother's desertion. "It's hard being ten these days. He'll grow up, I promise."

Philip considered, then shrugged with a rueful smile. "He still doesn't like it that Danny went away."

Keith only nodded. Euphemisms for death irritated him without exception, and when they were used by children he felt annoyingly helpless. Especially in this case. Danny Ramera had been found in the woodland tract behind the schoolhouse across the highway. He'd been missing for five days, and the police medical team had judged death by exposure. No matter the temperature hadn't dropped below sixty-five for a week or more, and no matter the body had been discovered less than eighty yards from the school; the boy had been playing, had fallen, had struck his head on a rock, and Nature was blamed for doing the rest.

That was the word circulated through the township, and that was the word accepted by the local paper.

"Mrs. German," Philip said suddenly, "thinks all those animals are damned or something because they're not human."

"What?" Keith blinked slowly and leaned farther over the railing.

The boy repeated himself, and Keith wondered what kind of teachers they were turning out these days. Jane, on the other hand—

"I think she's crazy," Philip declared.

"Well . . . she is rather strange."

"No, she's not," the boy said. "She's a vampire."

"So was my third mother-in-law, but I don't brag about it."

"No, I mean it," Philip said, moving closer, craning his neck and squinting against the sun. "She's a real vampire."

"No kidding."

"Really! She keeps the shades down in her room all the time. She *says* she doesn't want us looking outside, but I know it's because vampires can't take the sun. And you know something else?"

"No," he said. "What?"

"She never leaves the school!"

"That's because you don't see her," he said. "You leave before she does."

The boy shook his head vigorously. "No, I mean it! She doesn't have a car and she never leaves. Really. I'm not lying."

He smiled gentle tolerance for a boy who often seemed so much older than his years, and rubbed his chin thoughtfully against his forearm. "Listen, Phil, do you really think Mr. Bonachek would allow one of his teachers to—"

"He's right, you know."

He scowled and rolled his eyes, a tongue-in-cheek indication that a Great Truth had been interrupted. Phil dashed away, avoiding his mother's outstretched arm to duck into his home. Moira Leary was short, slim for bearing two children a year apart, and wore oversized sunglasses that made her eyes too wide, too innocent for the dark lips glistening in the afternoon's heat. She was almost Jane's twin, though she seemed years older. He saluted her silently.

"German's a vampire, right?"

A hand lifted to shade her eyes. "If not that, something else again, believe me. She knows her stuff, don't get me wrong, but there are times when she acts like she's right out of the Dark Ages."

"I would commiserate," he said, "but you'd only tell me that bachelors—especially ones three times divorced—don't know anything about raising children so what do I know anyway, right?"

She laughed. "What're you working on now, Hemingway?"

Several decidedly lecherous responses came to mind, but he discarded them reluctantly. Though he'd never met her sales-man husband in the two years he'd been here, and though he was positive she'd made a pass at him more than once, he didn't dare consider her more than a friend—though it hadn't stopped him from sneaking a sex-starved glance once in a while. He grinned, she grinned back knowingly, and he told her about the article. She laughed again, brightly, brushed the bangs from her forehead and waved him a farewell.

He waited until she was gone, then returned to his desk. A bored glance at his calendar made him realize with a start he'd promised Mike Bonachek he'd talk this Monday to the fourth graders about a book of his they were using, on astronomy and NASA. My God, he thought, me and my big mouth.

But it wasn't that bad, he admitted when it was over. The book had been read, and he'd been asked intelligent questions. The only argument he'd suffered centered on his refusal to believe in flying saucers; the classes—two jammed into a single room—had seen too much television, and they knew better.

Five minutes before the talk ended, however, the room

abruptly stilled. He turned automatically to the door, and just managed not to gape.

Mrs. German stood on the threshold. She was nearly six feet tall, slightly overweight, wearing a shapeless print dress whose colors had faded. Her hair was black and flat, her features sharp to the point of emaciation. Her shoes were brown, sturdy and laced, and he bet himself her dark stockings ended just above the knee with a darker band of elastic that left a red belt around her thighs.

He couldn't help it; he glanced at Philip who grinned an *I told you so*.

Jane Disanza smiled politely. "Yes, Mrs. German?"

The older woman did not turn. She kept her heavily veined hands clasped at her waist and stared at the class. "I am visiting all the rooms at Mr. Bonachek's request. I'm sorry for the interruption. It seems someone had been prying at the basement lock." Her gaze was stern, condemnation without trial. "It is not permitted."

The children said nothing; Jane said nothing; and Keith merely pursed his lips in a silent whistle and stared at the floor.

"Not permitted," she repeated, and nodded once before leaving. There was a rustling quelled by a sharp word from Jane. A bee droning against a pane. A fussing with books until the bell finally rang and he found himself surrounded. He grinned, shook a few hands, and stood with a groan once the last child was gone.

Jane had slumped into her desk chair, fluffed idly at the hair curling darkly to her shoulders. "Bitch," she said. "She's been here so long she thinks she owns the place. Hell, Keith, nobody *wants* to go into the stupid basement anyway, for God's sake."

He wanted to stand behind her then, massage her shoulders and bring back the days when they could laugh without strain. And the worst of it was, he understood all too well why their relationship had ended. Three times married, four years each time, and she had every right to be skeptical whenever he protested *but this time it's different, it isn't like the others*. She'd reasoned rightly he had said it (and had meant it) twice before, and at thirty-two (to his forty) a four-year contract was hardly a promise of security and heaven.

He shoved his hands into his pockets and leaned against the blackboard. "She sure looks old enough to have been here forever. As a matter of fact, your nephew thinks she's a vampire."

"That would be Philip. Peter's the one with the better command of street language." She shuffled paper for a moment, and stood. "How are you?"

"Hanging in," he said quietly.

She picked up a pencil and tapped it hard against her blotter. "Carl thinks we should get together, a double date or something."

He nodded. Death knell. Finishing touch. "Sure, why not?"

She reached for her purse in the desk's bottom drawer. "I'm supposed to feed you lunch."

"Fine," he said. "I never carp a free meal."

The cafeteria was midway along the central corridor—white wooden walls and green slippery tiles—and they tagged the end of a softly babbling line. Students giggled and gossiped, faculty feigning extreme patience. Keith played the stoic, smiling automatically while he wondered why he didn't feel more devastated than disappointed. But before he could consider further, a grizzled winter-bent man in grayed coveralls and carrying a stiff broom sidled up to him and tugged on his jacket.

"Mac, you gotta light?"

"You been drinking?" he said from the corner of his mouth.

Jane turned around briefly, pursed her lips and turned back.

"Not a drop, mac. Not since German found my whisky and curdled it with a look."

Keith barked a laugh and jabbed Stan Linkholm's scrawny arm with a loose fist. The man was three weeks away from retirement as the school's custodian, and was looking forward to spending the rest of his life watching dirt join him in his house. They had met at the Deer Head, the only bar on the highway within walking distance that didn't feature country music six nights out of seven. And it had been there Keith had heard the stories of the darkmoon, of the dogs tourists left behind in summer to run wild in the hills.

"Well, you gonna help my cancer or what?"

He pulled matches from his pocket and Linkholm nodded thanks, peered into the cafeteria with a sneer and grunted as he left—back bent, head down, a deceptively frail man tracking wisps of dust.

"You like him?" Jane asked innocently as the line finally drifted forward.

He shrugged. "He tells great jokes, he buys me a drink now and then, and he speaks his mind."

"Ah," she said, grinning, "he's mentioned his skirmishes with sweet Mrs. German."

Skirmishes, Keith thought, was hardly the word for what sounded like all-out warfare. It was Stan's contention that he should be permitted into the basement once in a while, just to see if the foundations were still holding the place up; the math teacher, however, informed him that his utensils and the boiler were in a different section of the building, and nothing in the records kept below the steepled core should have the slightest interest for a man who shaved only once or twice a month.

It was an impasse Stan was determined to break before he retired.

Jane then spent the next twenty minutes avoiding Keith's questions about her life with Carl Andrews. And finally, when he felt self-pity beginning to well, he excused himself with a blown kiss to her cheek and walked outside to let the fresh air calm him. He stood in front, just below the once-belled steeple, and directly ahead the ground sloped gently toward the highway; beyond, a steeper incline, and behind a row of thick-boled elms the apartments began, rising and falling on the gentle swells of the old farm until the woodland reasserted itself, dark with noon shadows.

He lit a cigarette and turned around to look at the school. It was an oddity, he thought—originally one room, it had been added to here and there, modernized, bloated and extended around the central building, which seemed now beneath flanking willows like a dwarfed New England church. He didn't like it. Innocent and white and crawling with children, and he didn't like it. It was, he thought, as if contemporary builders had known something everyone else hadn't, and had tried to hide it by disguising it, badly.

He tossed the cigarette away without finishing it, angry with the way his mood had soured, blame in equal parts on himself and Jane. He walked slowly, a conscious effort to clear his mind, and by the time he reached home he was at least ready to smile.

And he did when he saw Peter waiting there for him.

The entrance to his apartment was recessed beneath a slate roof, the door on the right his downstairs neighbors', the one on the left belonging to him. Peter was standing on the concrete stoop, his red hair awry, faint shadows over his eyes.

"Hi, Uncle Keith." Desultory, uncomfortable.

Keith leaned against the door frame. "You cut out of school early, m'boy. Does your mother know you're home yet?"

Peter shook his head, staring with a scowl at the building across the way. "Mrs. German wants to suspend me."

"What? For God's sake, you're only in fifth grade!"

There was almost a grin. "Well . . . I put a tack on her chair."

He couldn't help it—he laughed. Unoriginal and stupid and demeaning to the teacher, but he laughed and slipped an arm around the boy's shoulders, cool here in the shade, almost cold. "I don't believe it. Of all the people in the world . . . my God, don't tell your mother I think I approve."

"She's gonna kill me."

"You want me to talk to her?"

Peter pulled away instantly, brightening and smiling. "No kidding, you will?"

"Sure, why not. But you have to tell her first. Then I'll come over later to talk."

"But we're going to grandma's for dinner."

"You're always going to grandma's for dinner. She must be a hell of a cook. Nope. You first, then me, or no deal." He waited. "How high did she jump?"

"That's the dumb part. She didn't feel a thing. Elsie Franks snitched."

He was gone before Keith could make further comment. Great, he thought; I think I've just been conned. He shrugged and reached for the doorknob, stopped when he saw deep scratch marks around the lock. The door wasn't closed.

He glanced around, looked for Peter, then gently nudged the door with his shoe. It swung open slowly. Immediately to the right were the stairs, carpeted in dim gold and badly needing a vacuum. He listened and heard nothing, but took the steps cautiously, his gaze on the dim light that blocked the room above. His arms were stiff, the breath caught in his lungs spilling over to cold. He blinked rapidly, swallowed, told himself to go back down and call the cops from Moira's. For all he knew the robbers, the vandals, the murderers were still up there, hiding behind the recliner, in the bedroom, in the kitchen, behind the plastic shower curtain in the bath. For all he knew the whole place had been stripped and he was left with nothing but the clothes on his back.

He reached the top and paused.

The room was twenty-five feet from front to balcony, twelve feet wide in the living room area. It was dark, the drapes drawn and all the other doors closed. Darker than it should have been on a May afternoon. And colder. Much colder. He felt his breath pluming between lips growing chapped. He shivered, and clenched his left hand before reaching for the light switch. Clicked it and waited, but the lights wouldn't flare on.

Fuse, he thought; the circuit breaker's busted.

His vision adjusted, and he could see nothing wrong. All the books were on their shelves, his desk undisturbed, the manuscript by the typewriter still stacked in disarray.

But the cold persisted, and he hugged himself tightly.

Go away, he thought then; go away and leave me alone. But he wasn't at all sure whether he was talking to himself or the intruder.

He backed down one step, and the cold began to leave.

The lights winked on.

And when he looked across the room he saw the drapes hadn't been drawn at all, that there was sun out there spilling onto the carpet.

He sat suddenly and hard, his hands gripping his knees and his gaze fixed on the open door below. He knew there was an explanation for everything that had happened. He was tired. He was self-admittedly overworked. He was reacting to losing another woman from his life. It would be natural for his mind to overload, to punish him for the abuse and teach him a lesson. That was the logical path to pursue, and pursue it he did—sitting in the stairwell until just before sunset, then rising and going down, pulling the door closed, glancing at the lock and not seeing any scratches.

He walked away quickly. Away from the apartment, up the hill to the highway. His fingers were trembling and he hid them in his pockets, jumping to one side when the white-globed street-lamps reacted to their times and filled the complex with soft light. There were low hills below the sky, their ragged western edges shading from gray to brilliant rose. And as he walked along the verge gusts from passing buses and trucks kept his eyes in a squint. A few headlights were on, and dusk gave the air a black-spotted complexion.

At Frazier's—a mom-and-pop luncheonette and grocery—he ate a tasteless sandwich, drank four cups of coffee, and bought a carton of cigarettes he tucked swagger-stick under his arm. He felt better for the food and the quiet company the Fraziers gave him, and he'd just stepped outside when he remembered his promise to Peter.

"Great," he muttered, and stepped out in a hurry.

The scent of rain, a rising wind, tires on the blacktop already hissing wetly. He'd almost broken into a guilt-prodded run when an aborted siren's wail stopped and turned him. With his free hand screening the side of his face against the wind he looked toward the school. On the curved drive in front was a patrol car with blue lights swirling, and a rescue squad van whose rear doors were open, whose attendants were lifting a white-covered stretcher into the back. He checked the traffic quickly, then sprinted across and stood at the base of the grassy slope while Carl Andrews walked toward him.

"Carl," he said, as neutrally as he could while he eyed the van.

"How's it going, Keith?" He was tall, brawny and dark-haired. His left palm rested on his revolver's wooden stock, in his right hand a clipboard.

"Could be better, I suppose. You got trouble it seems."

"We can handle it."

"Yeah. Anybody I know? Jesus, not another kid, is it?"

Andrews didn't move.

"Dead?"

"Yeah. Dead." Andrews licked at his lips. "Very. It's Stan Linkholm."

"Ah . . . Christ." Keith looked back to the highway and shook his head slowly. "Heart attack, something like that?"

"Something like that."

Keith frowned slight irritation. "Carl, look, if you're going to tell me, then tell me. I mean, I knew him and I'd like to know. But if you're not going to tell me, then don't. I've got work to do."

Carl Andrews turned away.

He spent the next two days finishing the article, keeping his door locked and the phone off the hook. No one bothered him. No mail was delivered. He worked until his fingers cramped, ate and worked again. He slept badly. There were dreams, and there was a lingering memory of the cold he'd discovered after talking to Peter. The cold that had him lying under two layers of blankets.

On Thursday morning the weekly paper was shoved through the door's mail slot and he hurried down to grab it, sitting on the bottom step and snapping it open to the front page. A short piece about Stan, about a cardiac arrest, about his years with the school and a long quote from Bonachek. A grainy photograph. A story on page three about a New York couple who'd been missing since Monday from their campsite in the hills. An editorial demanding action, citing the tourism the county needed to survive.

It was spring, and it was business as usual, and he threw the paper into the corner and didn't believe it.

Stan's heart was as sound as his broomstick, and if Danny Ramera died of exposure he'd turn in his typewriter and dig ditches instead.

But it wasn't the stories that had finally convinced him, it was the memory of the cold, of the vanished scratches on the lock, of the way the children cowered when Mrs. German walked by.

He knew it was stupid. He knew he was driving himself out of the Jane-induced depression by grasping at whatever straws the wind carried his way. Mrs. German was odd, but no odder than the teachers he'd had himself as a child; and people who weren't used to the hills were always disappearing, always turning up, always changing their minds and heading for home without notification.

But the cold . . . it was the cold.

As soon as he dressed he drove to the hospital eight miles away, and was refused permission to check the medical records. The police stalled him, Andrews wouldn't meet with him, and when he talked to Philip after school he was given nothing more than bits of gossip about Jack the Ripper and Godzilla the Monster and everybody knew it was Mrs. German anyway so why don't we just get some stakes and catch her in the basement.

He punched at his typewriter, so hard his knuckles burned. There was a murderer out there, dammit, and no one was helping!

Another hour to stoke courage, and he grabbed his windbreaker and hurried to stand beside one of the highway's guardian elms. He was a hundred yards from the school, watching as the lights in each room died, as the faculty left in pairs and alone to vanish into an evening beginning too soon.

Five cigarettes. A handful of patrol cars that passed him, slowed, recognized him and moved on. The wind again, and the clouds, and the stars died before rising.

He tried to grin. Silliness is what it was. He understood that, and he approved. His early panic, his dreams, a combination of nonsense that produced further nonsense. But it was working, at least—he realized with a start not at all guilty that he hadn't thought of Jane in more than three days. Nevertheless, he was here, playing a country-boy Humphrey Bogart against a prickling at his nape that would not scratch away.

And just before seven he straightened and inched behind the tree. Mrs. German, tall even at this distance, stepped around the corner of the school, walking slowly and holding a deep-blue shawl closed at her throat. She seemed to be checking the windows, the front door, searching the grass for items dropped by the students. She disappeared. Reappeared with purse in hand and made her way briskly through the playground and into the trees.

Stupid, Keith thought as he raced across the road; stupid, he repeated as he cut between the swings and found the narrow path between two cages of birch.

Light faded, slipping swiftly through twilight to full dark as the foliage closed like lacing clouds overhead. His footfalls were muffled, but the slap and scrape of twigs against his trousers had him holding his breath, brought a hand to his forehead to wipe away the perspiration. Road sounds died. The day's warmth hung in patches of humid mist to the branches, to the hollowed ground, to the linings of his lungs. He gulped to breathe. He pulled at his shirt, his belt. His socks felt wet. He scolded himself impatiently when he glanced up through a leafy gap and saw the darkmoon hanging.

Ten minutes, and he wondered if he'd already passed the spot where Danny had been found. Where Stan had been found.

Another ten minutes and he stopped. Listened. Shadowswift whispers of wind through an elm, the scurrying of something small to his right, the lumbering of something large to his left.

He moved on, his sense of direction skewed, the silliness buried beneath a blanket of sour regret.

And when time finally blurred and his watch was unreadable, the trees thinned, the underbrush cleared, and he was staring at the backs of several clapboard houses. A street beyond. Fences around the yards. He felt his jaw lowering, and he snapped it shut with a curse. Mopped his face with a sleeve, and saw the kitchen light in the house directly ahead switch on to reveal Mrs. German at the window. She was holding a tea kettle close to her eyes, shaking it slowly.

A tea kettle. A goddamned copper tea kettle.

"Jesus," he whispered. "God . . . damn!" And he walked away with a gesture condemning the tract to hell, berating himself for almost believing she might be living in a coffin. "Idiot!" It sounded right. "Idiot!"

And all because he'd listened to the children.

He shivered, then, and slowed. It was cold. December had become dislodged and slipped down around him, tightening his cheeks and knifing through his chest. His nose began to run, his ears began to ache, and it took him several moments to hear the walking in the woods.

It was off to his left, deep in the black, at one point sounding furtive, at another perfectly calm. And as far as he knew he was on the only trail. He smothered a cough—God, it was cold!—and hurried on, left hand out in a wavering semaphore to keep the branches from his face, right hand clasping the windbreaker's collar tight to his neck.

It kept pace, then fell slowly behind.

He tried to stare through the dark, and succeeded only in making the boles twist, the brush climb, the leaves reach out to ensnare him. He faced forward, searching for the highway's lights. Nearer, then; he was positive the sounds were nearer. He tried to whistle; his mouth was too dry. He tried reciting all the lines of memorized verse, but the first line that came was from Bryant's "Thanatopsis."

The cold deepened. Dry, ancient, crackling as he passed through it, snapping as his shoes slapped against the ground.

Deathcold, and black, and digging through his scalp like the claws of an angry cat.

The shrubbery gave way behind him; whatever it was had broken from the trees.

And despite the fact he knew he wouldn't die, that he was like

all men immortal, that he was only a writer who lived just over
the low rise ahead and beyond the old school . . . he ran. He
jumped as if working from a starting gun and he ran, heedless
now of the twigs and the branches, leaping whenever he thought
he saw a root, swerving whenever he thought he saw a boulder.

He ran until he reached the playground, falling against one of
the canted iron legs (cold; it was cold) supporting the swings,
grasping it and gasping, sliding down to his knees as his gaze
fixed on a car's headlights speeding west to east.

The school was dark, its white turned to shadow. Lights from
the complex were trapped by the sky, a glow not quite white, not
quite gray, that shimmered like a storm cloud uncertain of its
power. He stared at it, shivering, until he heard the steps behind
him. Then he broke from the swings and loped across the grass,
slid down the slope and stumbled like a drunk until he reached
his doorway. Keys jumped and jangled while he cursed them;
the doorknob was curiously slick in his hand.

One step inside, and something poked him in the back.

"You ever do that again," he said to Carl Andrews, who was
on the stoop and laughing, "I don't care if I give away ten years
and a hundred pounds, I'll break your goddamned neck."

It was fifteen minutes before he stopped shaking, before he
felt warm again. By that time drinks had been poured and Andrews was in the recliner, while Keith, pacing through a narration loudly defensive and belligerently shamefaced, told him
where he'd gone, though he couldn't explain exactly why.

"I just did, that's all," he said, finally allowing his legs to fold
him to the floor. "It seemed like a good idea at the time." But
he didn't tell him about the dark, about the cold.

"I believe it," Carl said. "That old broad's been around for
damn ever. Easy to see why you'd think she—"

"I did not say she killed anybody," he snapped. "I just . . .
hell, I don't know. I just did, and that's all there is to it." Thinking: first thing in the morning he was going to borrow Moira's
car and take the boys around to German's house, to show them
where she lived before he broke both their necks.

Carl emptied his glass and placed it on the floor beside him. "Let's talk about Stan."

"Why? We saw each other a few times, had a few drinks, and I mostly listened to his war stories, that's all."

Andrews seemed disappointed. "He never talked about school?"

Keith shook his head, then caught himself. "Well, hardly a word. If he'd had a bad day he'd bitch, but nothing more than that." He looked up. "Good Lord, Carl, you're not suggesting . . ." He laughed nervously. "No, I see you're not. I guess they aren't nasty enough."

Andrews squirmed slightly. "You didn't see Stan. And you didn't see the kid."

"Bad?"

"Worse. Thought for a while we had wild dogs. They were done like that. Not all over. Just in . . . pieces."

Keith stared at his hands, pondering. "Rabies maybe. Animals don't eat even though they want to. You might—"

"We did. All over the damned place."

"The paper sure keeps quiet about it."

"The paper gets read by tourists."

A pause while Keith pulled at the side of his neck. "So, what do you think?"

"If I knew I'd be out there."

They talked a few minutes more, saying little, getting nowhere. Then Andrews thanked him for the drink and left, leaving Keith on the floor to decide finally that he had to see the school's basement. He wasn't sure why, but he knew if he didn't he wouldn't sleep for days.

The following morning he broached Bonachek, arming himself with an article premise he'd thought up on the way over. The principal refused politely.

"But those records," Keith protested gently. "I mean, they'd be invaluable."

"I understand," the man said, "but I'm afraid my hands are tied. It's school board property. You'll have to fill out a request, and they meet in two weeks."

Keith shrugged and left, stood in the corridor for a moment fuming over bureaucrats even in country schools, then checked for watchers before hurrying toward the back. Steps led down to the rear double doors. A sharp right, and another staircase leading to a thick-planked door bolted and padlocked. And though he knew he was no expert, he also knew by looking that neither bolt nor padlock was stiff from disuse.

Somebody, he thought, is lying through his teeth, and when he said as much to Jane when he stopped her before lunch, she turned to him, scowled, and told him to mind his own business.

"You're crazy," she said, and he had to trot up keep up as she hastened outside. "There's nothing down there but dust."

"Then what's the harm?" he said softly, taking hold of her arm. "Come on, Jane. You know where Checkie keeps the keys. Show a little leg or something. I'll wait for your call after school." He kissed her cheek before she could refuse, almost ran home, and almost collided with Moira, who was standing by his door. Her blouse was unbuttoned midway down her chest, her sunglasses off, and her jeans snugly inviting. Moira, whose husband he hadn't seen in over two years. A shadow behind the window, a just-closed door. Whenever he went over for lunch or dinner the man was gone on a trip, and small wonder the boys had taken him for an uncle.

Moira. Jane. How much of a lecher are you, he wondered as he pushed in the door, though remained outside.

"The kids again, right?" he said.

She shook her head. "It's Jane. I'm worried about her."

"No kidding?"

A finger touched his hand, cool and demanding. Standing with her was like lying in shade, and it didn't take him long to make up his mind her husband was a fool, and fools deserve fooling.

"Have you seen her today?"

"Can you keep a secret?" And before she could answer he told her about the keys, Mrs. German, and the scare he'd given himself. When he was done, she shook her head and looked pointedly up the staircase. "You're crazy," she told him. "No wonder the boys love you."

Not like. Love.

He swallowed. "I . . ." A hand to her shoulder. "I've got some work, Moira."

"That's all right," she said brightly. "I just wanted to invite you to dinner."

"Deal. And afterward I'll tell you all about my adventures."

She leaned into him suddenly, kissed him lightly on the chin. "It's Jane's loss," she whispered, and was gone.

He had no idea how long he'd stood there, gaping at the image she'd left in her wake, but the next thing he knew Peter and Philip were standing there, grinning. "He's a Greek god," Peter said solemnly to his brother.

"Nope, he's one of those dinosaur things we saw in the city. All stuffed and stuff."

Keith roused himself with a mock scowl. "Beat it, punks, or I won't give you dinner."

"We don't care," Peter said. "We're going to grandma's."

Keith almost contradicted him, but the telephone was ringing. He waved and ran up, snatched at the receiver on the fifth harsh summons. It was Carl, demanding to know where the hell Jane was. Keith explained what he knew—which wasn't much—and Carl complained she hadn't answered any of his messages, complained a moment longer before suddenly hanging up.

So what am I, Keith thought sourly, your girl friend's keeper?

But the call bothered him. It wasn't like Jane to ignore messages; nor, he remembered as he aimed a finger toward the dial, does she like personal calls at school.

He dropped into his chair and stared at the telephone, willing it to ring. Willing, squirming, rising once to fetch a beer and returning at a run.

Moira called at six, and he told her he'd be late.

Twice he called the school, and received no response.

At seven Carl called back, worried and angry and warning him not to go off on one of his half-assed explorations.

Seven-thirty, and he stood. Wavered. Then he took a look at

the sky and grabbed his raincoat from the closet, a flashlight from the desk drawer, and whispered an apology to Moira before he ran outside.

All he could think of was Mrs. German, and the cold.

The air was a curious shade of dim gray-green, and the leaves were turning belly up to the keening damp wind. Mutters of thunder. No traffic at all.

By the time he reached the school he was gasping for breath, and cursing the cigarettes he could feel in his pocket. The clouds were shifting rapidly, the steeple that once housed the morning bell seeming to topple when he approached the front steps. He glanced to either side, took the six steps two at a time and yanked at the door. It rattled but didn't give. He tried again, fighting panic, then swung off the porch and walked quickly around the side. All the shades had been drawn halfway, eyelids drowsing, but the sills were too high for him to see if the windows were unlocked.

He pulled the flashlight from his coat pocket and tapped it impatiently against a palm.

It darkened.

There was lightning.

He bunched his shoulders in frustration and turned a circle against the wind. She must have changed her mind, he decided, and had finally gone to Carl's. Or gone for a drive. Or gone through the woods to Mrs. German's for a cup of her damned tea. The wind gusted, and he ducked, stopped when he saw the playground in a flash of blue-white.

Slides. Swings. A sandbox. An iron horse.

He held his breath and began to walk slowly over the wet trampled grass.

Swings.

At one end there was a bench with a plank floor, two seats facing each other. Jane was sitting with her back to the school, her legs too long, her feet touching the ground. He didn't call out, and he didn't break into a run. He vaguely heard the rear doors slamming open with the wind, vaguely heard the rain pattering on his shoulders.

Blue-white again, and he saw without blinking the red gleaming in her hair.

He stopped directly behind her, reached out a hand and dropped it as if he'd been burned. The blood had trailed down the back of the seat and had gathered blackly on the ground. He swallowed. He whispered her name. He took a step to one side, and spun down to his knees.

Her face. It was gone.

The rain, then, and the lightning, and the darkmoon above the storm, and he rocked back to his heels and screamed at the thunder. Staggered to his feet and lurched toward the school. The door. He remembered the door, saw it now waiting through sheets of cold water. There was no time to think, no time for grand designs; he stumbled over the threshold and down the steps to the basement. Then he looked to his hands; the flashlight was gone. A slap to his sides and the feel of a matchbox crammed into his pocket.

A tearing shriek of lightning, and he saw his shadow slip through the open basement door.

He walked quickly, then, and down four more steps, pulled out a match and struck it on the railing, a quick sound that made him wince, the simultaneous hiss of burning sulphur that flared to lighten the dark and narrow his eyes. But there was nothing else. No breathing. No footfalls. No creaks of rotting planks or sighs of storm wind sneaking down behind him; only the light that wavered a curious blue-yellow above his pinched fingers.

He waited for a moment, then moved away from the stairs.

The basement was large, a disturbingly silent cave that extended beneath the entire central core of the school building above. On the left, along a rough-stone wall mottled by dampness, were rows of crates that seemed as if they would disintegrate at a touch; on the right, the same. Along the uneven stone flooring were aisles created by warped shelving atop crumbling brick, four tiers of them, with more cartons, mildewed books, papers wrapped with string or faded yarn—all of it nibbled at, eaten, littered with droppings like tiny black pebbles.

Beams hung low from the sagging stone ceiling, and there were no windows. There was only the silence and the mausoleum cold.

He hissed suddenly as the flame scorched his fingers, dropped the match and fumbled with a heel to crush it. He lit another quickly, and wished he hadn't lost the flashlight. But Jane . . . Jane . . . he felt the bile rising and swallowed hard and often.

When he felt dizziness slip by him, then, he stepped into the center aisle, shivering now with a cold that hadn't come with the storm. Shadows writhing, wind soughing, the weight of the building blackly descending. Toward the front he shuffled, cursing the children and all their foolish talk about vampires, cursing the stories about the travelers and the darkmoon.

At aisle's end he stopped, and waited.

For the first time since entering he knew he wasn't alone.

And for the first time since it started he knew who was with him.

Overhead and behind him a bare lightbulb flickered, painting his image darkly against the sweating blocks of stone. He would not move. He would not give his company the satisfaction of his fear. Instead, with movement so slow he wanted to scream, he slipped his hands into his pockets and bunched them to fists.

Remembered a time, too much time ago, when his father had brought him out at twilight onto a lake's shore and they'd waited for the bats to come out for their feeding. "Quietly now," the old man had told him. "Quietly now, you don't want him to hear."

Quietly now.

Don't let him hear you.

He turned to face the staircase, and the figure waiting by the railing. He glanced up at the ceiling. "Has . . . anyone guessed?"

"Danny," a voice said, made sexless by thunder and by the dead time in the basement. "Stan broke in. A few others over the years."

"Those people from New York?"

"One gets hungry, you know. I can't do anything about that."

"I don't believe it."

"You don't believe I get hungry, or you don't believe what I am."

"I don't believe in vampires, no matter what the children say."

A laugh slipped through the darkness. "To them everything monstrous is a vampire. Surely you can forgive them that."

I'm afraid, he thought; I'm afraid and I can't run. But he knew it wasn't the fear that held him; it was worse, much worse—he wanted to know. There was a good chance of his dying, but he wanted to know.

"Werewolf," he said then. "Or are you a ghoul."

A pause, more a hesitation, and he closed his eyes briefly, grunting silently as he fought against the loosening of his bowels.

The voice, then, and the cold.

"I'm too old to remember exactly how it began. But it did. One moment I was normal, the next . . ." An invisible shrug. "And living out here has made it very easy. Here, and places like here, all over the country. You move on when you're suspected, before someone can kill you. A nibble here"—a giggle—"a nibble there. It all adds up, Keith. It all adds up."

"You bitch! You killed Jane."

The cold was on the outside, but there was a heated rage working through the marrow, through the blood. His head was spinning, his eyes fighting a squint.

"You didn't have to, you know, Moira. You could've let her live. But then, you've known her for so long she must have suspected, must have wondered what wonder drugs you were taking."

A noise. Rumbling, snarling, cut off as if bitten. The figure shifted, and he shaded his eyes, glancing from side to side as he tried to make her out, tried to find something he could throw while escaping. She wouldn't follow; she couldn't. She knew he'd called Carl, he'd be here soon to hunt for his lover. All he had to do was keep talking, and make his way to the stairs. The door was still open, and he could hear the rain on the landing.

"How did you manage the children?" he said, moving an inch at a time back up the aisle.

"What children?" the voice said, and he stopped when she moved directly under the bulb.

Her face was moon pale, her lips dark and gleaming, her teeth when she smiled coated with saliva.

The cold. He could feel the cold now, could hear the yellowed papers rustling as they crumpled, could hear the orange crates creaking as they buckled.

The cold in his apartment.

He put a hand to his forehead, trying to think. It was important he keep on using his mind, to prevent its collapse in the face of her smiling.

Cold. A signal, perhaps, that portends her feeding, and the longer she's denied it, the colder she gets.

Moira touched a long finger to her chin. "The children," she said as though the thought amused her. "No, Keith, we're just one tiny family, kindred spirits if you will. It doesn't matter where we came from; we just came, that's all. Back there in the hills, and we decided to stick together. Strength in numbers, my love."

He heard the boys shifting quietly behind him.

Danny, Stan, Jane: *We're going to grandma's for dinner tonight.*

He bolted. Whatever he believed, whatever madness he was facing, it shrieked through his enforced calm and sent him charging toward the doorway. Moira yelled when he shoved her aside, clawed at his arm, and he was halfway to the door when the boys each snared a leg. He kicked frantically, punched wildly, slipped to the floor and was stunned when his skull cracked against the bottom step.

"No," he whispered. "No, please, Moira."

Philip sat on his stomach, Peter on his thighs. Moira loomed behind them, the light from the ceiling turning her face black and giving her hair an umbra of stark white.

"You don't know what it's like," she said then, reaching between the boys and coldly stroking his cheek. "To have to fake a husband. A man who's never home. Leaving yourself open to every damned horny bastard who comes to your door, and you're not even hungry."

His mind faded from a whimpering to a daze; there was only the cold, and the sound of her voice.

"I've had enough," she said wearily. "I've had quite enough."

Maneuvered, he thought; all this time I've been maneuvered. He swallowed. He sobbed once.

"Hey, don't worry," Peter told him. So old. So old.

Moira nodded. "You're not going to die, love. At least not for long."

He closed his eyes, opened them. Wide, and staring.

"Yes, dear, Jane is our meal. Little Jane is our meal. We brought you down here because I'm tired of all the deceptions. And besides, the boys need a father they can point to with pride."

Peter nodded quickly, his eyes bright and eager.

"Just a little pain," Moira whispered, dead wind over velvet. "Don't worry, just a little pain, a little dying. Then I'll say the words, the incantation, and you'll be just as good as new."

Philip leaned closer, his breath fetid and iced. "And then I can call you daddy. Boy, won't that be great?"

PART II
VARIATIONS ON THE THEME

THE GHOUL

by SIR HUGH CLIFFORD

*Among the aborigines of the Malay Peninsula there are a number of
legendary evil beings. The* pěnanggal, *for example, the "Undone One,"
a woman who has died in childbirth and who torments and preys upon
small children with a comet's tail of blood-stained entrails in her wake.
And the* mâti-ânak, *the weird little white animal which makes beast noises
round the graves of children and is supposed to have absorbed their souls.
And the* pôlong, *which men bind to their service by raising them up from
the corpses of babies that have been stillborn, the tips of whose tongues they
bite off and swallow after the infant has been brought to life by magical
agencies.*

It is the pôlong—*the aboriginal version of the ghoul—with which this
fearful little shocker is concerned. And a particularly nasty* pôlong *it is,
too: an "abominable old beldam capering uncleanly in the moonlight,"
with restless lips calling noiselessly "upon all the devils in hell." The things
"The Ghoul" does should never be witnessed firsthand, for they are enough
to drive sane men mad . . .*

*Sir Hugh Clifford (1866–?) was both an author and a member of the
British Foreign Service in the latter half of the nineteenth century and in
the early years of the twentieth. He was governor of Ceylon, Nigeria, and
Straits Settlements (Malaysia), and an acknowledged expert on the Far*

629

East of his time. In addition to short stories of mystery and the macabre,
he authored several nonfiction works on his Asiatic experiences, including
The Further Side of Silence *and* Bush Whacking and Other
Asiatic Tales *and* Memories.

WE HAD been sitting late upon the verandah of my bungalow at
Kuâla Lîpis, which, from the top of a low hill covered with coarse
grass, overlooked the long, narrow reach formed by the combined waters of the Lîpis and the Jĕelai. The moon had risen
some hours earlier, and the river ran white between the black
masses of forest, which seemed to shut it in on all sides, giving
to it the appearance of an isolated tarn. The roughly cleared
compound, with the tennis ground which had never got beyond
the stage of being dug over and weeded, and the rank growths
beyond the bamboo fence, were flooded by the soft light, every
tattered detail of their ugliness standing revealed as relentlessly
as though it were noon. The night was very still, but the heavy,
scented air was cool after the fierce heat of the day.

I had been holding forth to the handful of men who had been
dining with me on the subject of Malay superstitions, while they
manfully stifled their yawns. When a man has a working knowledge of anything which is not commonly known to his neighbors, he is apt to presuppose their interest in it when a chance
to descant upon it occurs, and in those days it was only at long
intervals that I had an opportunity of foregathering with other
white men. Therefore, I had made the most of it, and looking
back, I fear that I had occupied the rostrum during the greater
part of that evening. I had told my audience of the *pĕnanggal*—
the "Undone One"—that horrible wraith of a woman who has
died in childbirth, who comes to torment and prey upon small
children in the guise of a ghastly face and bust, with a comet's
tail of blood-stained entrails flying in her wake; of the *mâti-ânak,*
the weird little white animal which makes beast noises round the
graves of children, and is supposed to have absorbed their souls;

and of the *pôlong,* or familiar spirits, which men bind to their service by raising them up from the corpses of babies that have been stillborn, the tips of whose tongues they bite off and swallow after the infant has been brought to life by magic agencies. It was at this point that young Middleton began to pluck up his ears; and I, finding that one of my hearers was at last showing signs of being interested, launched out with renewed vigor, until my sorely tried companions, one by one, went off to bed, each to his own quarters.

Middleton was staying with me at the time, and he and I sat for a while in silence, after the others had gone, looking at the moonlight on the river. Middleton was the first to speak.

"That was a curious myth you were telling us about the *pôlong,"* he said. "There is an incident connected with it which I have never spoken of before, and have always sworn that I would keep to myself; but I have a good mind to tell you about it, because you are the only man I know who will not write me down a liar if I do."

"That's all right. Fire away," I said.

"Well," said Middleton. "It was like this. You remember Juggins, of course? He was a naturalist, you know, dead nuts upon becoming an F.R.S. and all that sort of thing, and he came to stay with me during the close season* last year. He was hunting for bugs and orchids and things, and spoke of himself as an anthropologist and a botanist and a zoologist, and heaven knows what besides; and he used to fill his bedroom with all sorts of creeping, crawling things, kept in very indifferent custody, and my verandah with all kinds of trash and rotting green trade that he brought in from the jungle. He stopped with me for about ten days, and when he heard that duty was taking me upriver into the Sâkai country, he asked me to let him come, too. I was rather bored, for the tribesmen are mighty shy of strangers and were only just getting used to me; but he was awfully keen, and

---

*"Close season," *i.e.* from the beginning of November to the end of February, during which time the rivers on the eastern seaboard of the Malay Peninsula used to be closed to traffic on account of the North-East Monsoon.

East of his time. In addition to short stories of mystery and the macabre, he authored several nonfiction works on his Asiatic experiences, including The Further Side of Silence *and* Bush Whacking and Other Asiatic Tales *and* Memories.

WE HAD been sitting late upon the verandah of my bungalow at Kuâla Lîpis, which, from the top of a low hill covered with coarse grass, overlooked the long, narrow reach formed by the combined waters of the Lîpis and the Jĕlai. The moon had risen some hours earlier, and the river ran white between the black masses of forest, which seemed to shut it in on all sides, giving to it the appearance of an isolated tarn. The roughly cleared compound, with the tennis ground which had never got beyond the stage of being dug over and weeded, and the rank growths beyond the bamboo fence, were flooded by the soft light, every tattered detail of their ugliness standing revealed as relentlessly as though it were noon. The night was very still, but the heavy, scented air was cool after the fierce heat of the day.

I had been holding forth to the handful of men who had been dining with me on the subject of Malay superstitions, while they manfully stifled their yawns. When a man has a working knowledge of anything which is not commonly known to his neighbors, he is apt to presuppose their interest in it when a chance to descant upon it occurs, and in those days it was only at long intervals that I had an opportunity of foregathering with other white men. Therefore, I had made the most of it, and looking back, I fear that I had occupied the rostrum during the greater part of that evening. I had told my audience of the *pĕnanggal*— the "Undone One"—that horrible wraith of a woman who has died in childbirth, who comes to torment and prey upon small children in the guise of a ghastly face and bust, with a comet's tail of blood-stained entrails flying in her wake; of the *mâti-ânak*, the weird little white animal which makes beast noises round the graves of children, and is supposed to have absorbed their souls;

"Presently, when the beggars who had run away found out that I was the intruder, they began to come back again. You know their way. First a couple of men came and peeped at us, and vanished as soon as they saw they were observed. Then they came a trifle nearer, bobbed up suddenly, and peeped at us again. I called to them in Sĕ-noi,* which always reassures them, and when they at last summoned up courage to approach, gave them each a handful of tobacco. Then they went back into the jungle and fetched the others, and very soon the place was crawling with Sâkai of both sexes and all ages.

"We got a meal of sorts, and settled down for the night as best we could; but it wasn't a restful business. Juggins swore with eloquence at the uneven flooring, made of very roughly trimmed boughs, which is an infernally uncomfortable thing to lie down upon, and makes one's bones ache as though they were coming out at the joints, and the Sâkai are abominably restless bedfellows as you know. I suppose one ought to realize that they have as yet only partially emerged from the animal, and that, like the beasts, they are still naturally nocturnal. Anyway, they never sleep for long at a stretch, though from time to time they snuggle down and snore among the piles of warm wood ashes round the central fireplace, and whenever you wake, you will always see half a dozen of them squatting near the blazing logs, half-hidden by the smoke, and jabbering like monkeys. It is a marvel to me what they find to yarn about: food, or rather the patent impossibility of ever getting enough to eat, and the stony-heartedness of Providence and of the neighboring Malays must furnish the principal topics, I should fancy, with an occasional respectful mention of beasts of prey and forest demons. That night they were more than ordinarily restless. The dead baby was enough to make them uneasy, and besides, they had got wet while hiding in the jungle after our arrival, and that always sets the skin disease, with which all Sâkai are smothered, itching like mad.

---

*Sĕ-noi—one of the two main branches into which the Sâkai are divided. The other is called Tĭ-mi-au by the Sĕ-noi. All the Sâkai dialects are variants of the languages spoken by these two principal tribes, which, though they have many words in common, differ from one another almost as much as, say, Italian from Spanish.

Whenever I woke I could hear their nails going on their dirty hides; but I had had a hard day and was used to my hosts' little ways, so I contrived to sleep fairly sound. Juggins told me next morning that he had had *une nuit blanche,* and he nearly caused another stampede among the Sâkai by trying to get a specimen of the fungus or bacillus, or whatever it is, that occasions the skin disease. I do not know whether he succeeded. For my own part, I think it is probably due to chronic anemia—the poor devils have never had more than a very occasional full meal for hundreds of generations. I have seen little brats, hardly able to stand, white with it, the skin peeling off in flakes, and I used to frighten Juggins out of his senses by telling him he had contracted it when his nose was flayed by the sun.

"Next morning I woke just in time to see the stillborn baby put into a hole in the ground. They fitted its body into a piece of bark, and stuck it in the grave they had dug for it at the edge of the clearing. They buried a flint and steel and a wood-knife and some food, and a few other things with it, though no living baby could have had any use for most of them, let alone a dead one. Then the old medicine man of the tribe recited the ritual over the grave. I took the trouble to translate it once. It goes something like this:

" 'Oh thou, who hast gone forth from among those who dwell upon the surface of the earth, and hast taken for thy dwelling place the land which is beneath the earth, flint and steel have we given thee to kindle thy fire, raiment to clothe thy nakedness, food to fill thy belly, and a wood-knife to clear thy path. Go, then, and make unto thyself friends among those who dwell beneath the earth, and come back no more to trouble or molest those who dwell upon the surface of the earth.'

"It was short and to the point; and then they trampled down the soil, while the mother, who had got upon her feet by now, whimpered about the place like a cat that had lost its kittens. A mangy, half-starved dog came and smelt hungrily about the grave, until it was sent howling away by kicks from every human animal that could reach it; and a poor little brat, who chanced to set up a piping song a few minutes later, was kicked and cuffed and knocked about by all who could conveniently get at him with foot, hand, or missile. Abstinence from song and dance for a period of nine days is the Sâkai way of mourning the dead, and any breach of this is held to give great offense to the spirit of the departed and to bring bad luck upon the tribe. It was considered necessary, therefore, to give the urchin who had done the wrong a fairly bad time of it in order to propitiate the implacable dead baby.

"Next the Sâkai set to work to pack all their household goods —not a very laborious business; and in about half an hour the last of the laden women, who was carrying so many cooking pots and babies and rattan bags and carved bamboo boxes and things, that she looked like the outside of a gypsy's cart at home, had filed out of the clearing and disappeared in the forest. The Sâkai always shift camp, like that, when a death occurs, because they think the ghost of the dead haunts the place where the body died. When an epidemic breaks out among them they are so busy changing quarters, building new huts, and planting fresh catch crops that they have not time to procure proper food, and half those who are not used up by the disease die of semistarvation. They are a queer lot.

"Well, Juggins and I were left alone, but my men needed a rest, so I decided to trek no farther that day, and Juggins and I spent our time trying to get a shot at a *sêlâdang,* * but though we came upon great plowed-up runs, which the herds had made going down to water, we saw neither hoof nor horn, and returned at night to the deserted Sâkai camp, two of my Malays fairly staggering under the piles of rubbish which Juggins called his botanical specimens. The men we had left behind had contrived to catch some fish, and with that and yams we got a pretty decent meal, and I was lying on my mat reading by the aid of a *dâmar* torch, and thinking how lucky it was that the Sâkai had cleared out, when suddenly old Juggins sat up, with his eyes fairly snapping at me through his gig-lamps in his excitement.

---

*Sêlâdang. The gaur or wild buffalo. It is the same as the Indian variety but in the Malay Peninsula attains to a greater size than in any other part of Asia.

" 'I say,' he said. 'I must have that baby. It would make a unique and invaluable ethnological specimen.'

" 'Rot,' I said. 'Go to sleep, old man. I want to read.'

" 'No, but I'm serious,' said Juggins. 'You do not realize the unprecedented character of the opportunity. The Sâkai have gone away, so their susceptibilities would not be outraged. The potential gain to science is immense—simply immense. It would be criminal to neglect such a chance. I regard the thing in the light of a duty which I owe to human knowledge. I tell you straight, I mean to have that baby whether you like it or not, and that is flat.'

"Juggins was forever talking about human knowledge, as though he and it were partners in a business firm.

" 'It is not only the Sâkai one has to consider,' I said. 'My Malays are sensitive about body-snatching, too. One has to think about the effect upon them.'

" 'I can't help that,' said Juggins resolutely. 'I am going out to dig it up now.'

"He had already put his boots on, and was sorting out his botanical tools in search of a trowel. I saw that there was no holding him.

" 'Juggins,' I said sharply. 'Sit down. You are a lunatic, of course, but I was another when I allowed you to come up here with me, knowing as I did that you are the particular species of crank you are. However, I've done you as well as circumstances permitted, and as a mere matter of gratitude and decency, I think you might do what I wish.'

" 'I am sorry,' said Juggins stiffly. 'I am extremely sorry not to be able to oblige you. My duty as a man of science, however, compels me to avail myself of this God-sent opportunity of enlarging our ethnological knowledge of a little-known people.'

" 'I thought you did not believe in God,' I said sourly; for Juggins added a militant agnosticism to his other attractive qualities.

" 'I believe in my duty to human knowledge,' he replied sententiously. 'And if you will not help me to perform it, I must discharge it unaided.'

"He had found his trowel, and again rose to his feet.

" 'Don't be an ass, Juggins,' I said. 'Listen to me. I have forgotten more about the people and the country here than you will ever learn. If you go and dig up that dead baby, and my Malays see you, there will be the devil to pay. They do not hold with exhumed corpses, and have no liking for or sympathy with people who go fooling about with such things. They have not yet been educated up to the pitch of interest in the secrets of science which has made of you a potential criminal, and if they could understand our talk, they would be convinced that you needed the kid's body for some devilry or witchcraft business, and ten to one they would clear out and leave us in the lurch. Then who would carry your precious botanical specimens back to the boats for you, and just think how the loss of them would knock the bottom out of human knowledge for good and all.'

" 'The skeleton of the child is more valuable still,' replied Juggins. 'It is well that you should understand that in this matter —which for me is a question of my duty—I am not to be moved from my purpose either by arguments or threats.'

"He was as obstinate as a mule, and I was pretty sick with him; but I saw that if I left him to himself he would do the thing so clumsily that my fellows would get wind of it, and if that happened I was afraid that they might desert us. The tracks in that Sâkai country are abominably confusing, and quite apart from the fear of losing all our camp-kit, which we could not hump for ourselves, I was by no means certain that I could find my own way back to civilization unaided. Making a virtue of necessity, there, I decided that I would let Juggins have his beastly specimen, provided that he would consent to be guided entirely by me in all details connected with the exhumation.

" 'You are a rotter of the first water,' I said frankly. 'And if I ever get you back to my station, I'll have nothing more to do with you as long as I live. All the same, I am to blame for having brought you up here, and I suppose I must see you through.'

" 'You're a brick,' said Juggins, quite unmoved by my insults. 'Come on.'

" 'Wait,' I replied repressively. 'This thing cannot be done until my people are all asleep. Lie down on your mat and keep quiet. When it is safe, I'll give you the word.'

"Juggins groaned, and tried to persuade me to let him go at once; but I swore that nothing would induce me to move before midnight, and with that I rolled over on my side and lay reading and smoking, while Juggins fumed and fretted as he watched the slow hands of his watch creeping round the dial.

"I always take books with me into the jungle, and the more completely incongruous they are to my immediate surroundings the more refreshing I find them. That evening, I remember, I happened to be rereading Miss Florence Montgomery's *Misunderstood* with the tears running down my nose; and by the time my Malays were all asleep, this incidental wallowing in sentimentality had made me more sick with Juggins and his disgusting project than ever.

"I never felt so like a criminal as I did that night, as Juggins and I gingerly picked our way out of the hut across the prostrate forms of my sleeping Malays; nor had I realized before what a difficult job it is to walk without noise on an openwork flooring of uneven boughs. We got out of the place and down the crazy stair-ladder at last, without waking any of my fellows, and we then began to creep along the edge of the jungle that hedged the clearing about. Why did we think it necessary to creep? I don't know. Partly we did not want to be seen by the Malays, if any of them happened to wake; and besides that, the long wait and the uncanny sort of work we were after had set our nerves going a bit, I expect.

"The night was as still as most nights are in real, *pukka* jungle. That is to say, that it was as full of noises—little, quiet, half-heard beast and tree noises—as an egg is full of meat; and every occasional louder sound made me jump almost out of my skin. There was not a breath astir in the clearing, but miles up above our heads the clouds were racing across the moon, which looked as though it were scudding through them in the opposite direction at a tremendous rate, like a great white fire balloon. It was pitch dark along the edge of the clearing, for the jungle threw a heavy shadow; and Juggins kept knocking those great clumsy feet of his against the stumps, and swearing softly under his breath.

"Just as we were getting near the child's grave the clouds obscuring the moon became a trifle thinner, and the slightly increased light showed me something that caused me to clutch Juggins by the arm.

" 'Hold hard!' I whispered, squatting down instinctively in the shadow, and dragging him after me. 'What's that on the grave?'

"Juggins hauled out his six-shooter with a tug, and looking at his face, I saw that he was as pale as death and more than a little shaky. He was pressing up against me, too, as he squatted, a bit closer, I fancied, than he would have thought necessary at any other time, and it seemed to me that he was trembling. I whispered to him, telling him not to shoot; and we sat there for nearly a minute, I should think, peering through the uncertain light, and trying to make out what the creature might be which was crouching above the grave and making a strange scratching noise.

"Then the moon came out suddenly into a patch of open sky, and we could see clearly at last, and what it revealed did not make me, for one, feel any better. The thing we had been looking at was kneeling on the grave, facing us. It, or rather she, was an old, old Sâkai hag. She was stark naked, and in the brilliant light of the moon I could see her long, pendulous breasts swaying about like an ox's dewlap, and the creases and wrinkles with which her withered hide was criss-crossed, and the discolored patches of foul skin disease. Her hair hung about her face in great matted locks, falling forward as she bent above the grave, and her eyes glinted through the tangle like those of some unclean and shaggy animal. Her long fingers, which had nails like claws, were tearing at the dirt of the grave, and her body was drenched with sweat, so that it glistened in the moonlight.

" 'It looks as though someone else wanted your precious baby for a specimen, Juggins,' I whispered; and a spirit of emulation set him floundering on to his feet, till I pulled him back. 'Keep still, man,' I added. 'Let us see what the old hag is up to. It isn't the brat's mother, is it?'

" 'No,' panted Juggins. 'This is a much older woman. Great God! What a ghoul it is!'

"Then we were silent again. Where we squatted we were hidden from the hag by a few tufts of rank *lâlang* grass, and the shadow of the jungle also covered us. Even if we had been in the open, however, I question whether the old woman would have seen us, she was so eagerly intent upon her work. For full five minutes, as near as I can guess, we squatted there watching her scrape and tear and scratch at the earth of the grave, with a sort of frenzy of energy; and all the while her lips kept going like a shivering man's teeth, though no sound that I could hear came from them.

"At length she got down to the corpse, and I saw her lift the bark wrapper out of the grave, and draw the baby's body from it. Then she sat back upon her heels, threw up her head, just like a dog, and bayed at the moon. She did this three times, and I do not know what there was about those long-drawn howls that jangled up one's nerves, but each time the sound became more insistent and intolerable, and as I listened, my hair fairly lifted. Then, very carefully, she laid the child's body down in a position that seemed to have some connection with the points of the compass, for she took a long time, and consulted the moon and the shadows repeatedly before she was satisfied with the orientation of the thing's head and feet.

"Then she got up, and began very slowly to dance round and round the grave. It was not a reassuring sight, out there in the awful loneliness of the night, miles away from everyone and everything, to watch that abominable old beldam capering uncleanly in the moonlight, while those restless lips of hers called noiselessly upon all the devils in hell, with words that we could not hear. Juggins pressed up against me harder than ever, and his hand on my arm gripped tighter and tighter. He was shaking like a leaf, and I do not fancy that I was much steadier. It does not sound very terrible, as I tell it to you here in comparatively civilized surroundings; but at the time, the sight of that obscure figure dancing silently in the moonlight with its ungainly shadow scared me badly.

"She capered like that for some minutes, setting to the dead baby as though she were inviting it to join her, and the intent purposefulness of her made me feel sick. If anybody had told me that morning that I was capable of being frightened out of my wits by an old woman, I should have laughed; but I saw nothing outlandish in the idea while that grotesque dancing lasted.

"Her movements, which had been very slow at first, became gradually faster and faster, till every atom of her was in violent motion, and her body and limbs were swaying this way and that, like the boughs of a tree in a tornado. Then, all of a sudden, she collapsed to the ground, with her back toward us, and seized the baby's body. She seemed to nurse it, as a mother might nurse her child, and as she swayed from side to side, I could see first the curve of the creature's head, resting on her thin left arm, and then its feet near the crook of her right elbow. And now she was crooning to it in a cracked falsetto chant that might have been a lullaby or perhaps some incantation.

"She rocked the child at first, but very rapidly the pace quickened, until her body was swaying to and fro from the hips, and from side to side, at such a rate that, to me, she looked as though she was falling all ways at once. And simultaneously her shrill chanting became faster and faster, and every instant more nerve-sawing.

"Next she suddenly changed the motion. She gripped the thing she was nursing by its arms, and began to dance it up and down, still moving with incredible agility, and crooning more damnably than ever. I could see the small, puckered face of the thing above her head every time she danced it up, and then, as she brought it down again, I lost sight of it for a second, until she danced it up once more. I kept my eyes fixed upon the thing's face every time it came into view, and I swear it was not an optical illusion—*it began to be alive.* Its eyes were open and moving, and its mouth was working, like that of a child which tries to laugh, but is too young to do it properly. Its face ceased to be like that of a newborn baby at all. It was distorted by a horrible animation. It was the most unearthly sight.

"Juggins saw it, too, for I could hear him drawing his breath harder and shorter than a healthy man should.

"Then, all in a moment, the hag did something. I did not see clearly precisely what it was, but it looked to me as though she bent forward and kissed it, and at that very instant a cry went up like the wail of a lost soul. It may have been something in the jungle, but I know my Malayan forests pretty thoroughly, and I have never heard any cry like it before or since. The next thing we knew was that the old hag had thrown the body back into the grave, and was dumping down the earth and jumping on it, while that strange cry grew fainter and fainter. It all happened so quickly that I had not had time to think or move before I was startled back into full consciousness by the sharp crack of Juggins's revolver fired close to my ear.

" 'She's burying it alive!' " he cried.

"It was a queer thing for a man to say, who had seen the child lying stark and dead more than thirty hours earlier, but the same thought was in my mind too, as we both started forward at a run. The hag had vanished into the jungle as silently as a shadow. Juggins had missed her, of course. He was always a rotten bad shot. However, we had no thought for her. We just flung ourselves upon the grave, and dug at the earth with our hands, until the baby lay in our arms. It was cold and stiff, and putrefaction had already begun its work. I forced open its mouth, and saw something that I had expected. The tip of its tongue was missing. It looked as though it had been bitten off by a set of shocking bad teeth, for the edge left behind was like a saw.

" 'The thing's quite dead,' I said to Juggins.

" 'But it cried—it cried!' whimpered Juggins. 'I can hear it now. To think that we let that horrible creature murder it.'

"He sat down with his head in his hands. He was utterly unmanned.

"Now that the fright was over, I was beginning to be quite brave again. It is a way I have.

" 'Rot,' I said. 'The thing's been dead for hours, and anyway, here's your precious specimen if you want it.'

"I had put it down, and now pointed at it from a distance. Its proximity was not pleasant. Juggins, however, only shuddered.

" 'Bury it, in heaven's name,' he said, his voice broken by sobs. 'I would not have it for the world. Besides, it *was* alive. I saw and heard it.'

"Well, I put it back in its grave, and next day we left the Sâkai country. Juggins had a whacking dose of fever, and anyway we had had about enough of the Sâkai and all of their engaging habits to last us for a bit.

"We swore one another to secrecy as Juggins, when he got his nerve back, said that the accuracy of our observations was not susceptible of scientific proof, which, I understand, was the rock his religion had gone to pieces on, and I did not fancy being told that I was drunk or that I was lying. You, however, know something of the uncanny things of the East, so tonight I have broken our vow. Now I'm going to turn in. Don't give me away."

Young Middleton died of fever and dysentery, somewhere up-country, a year or two later. His name was not Middleton, of course; so I am not really "giving him away," as he called it, even now. As for his companion, though when I last heard of him he was still alive and a shining light in the scientific world, I have named him Juggins, and as the family is a large one, he will run no great risk of being identified.

THE SPHERICAL GHOUL

by FREDRIC BROWN

"The Spherical Ghoul" is perhaps the strangest and most unusual ghoul in all of weird fiction. (In view of its activities in these pages, it is difficult to imagine any, natural or supernatural, which is more unusual.) Just what is the spherical ghoul? That is for you to discover, for this is a detective story—and a classic, locked-room detective story at that—as much as it is a tale of the bizarre and the terrifying.

First published in the "shudder pulp" Thrilling Mystery in 1942, and reprinted only once since (in a digest mystery magazine in 1962), "The Spherical Ghoul" is one of those gems which have inexplicably been neglected by anthologists. Considering its ingredients—a morgue at night, a horribly disfigured corpse, mayhem and mystery aplenty, and the cleverest of plot gimmicks—one can only marvel at such oversight. It is a pleasure to, um, resurrect it for a new generation of readers here.

For more than three decades Fredric Brown (1906–1972) was a much acclaimed writer in not one but two demanding genres: mystery/suspense and science fiction. His first mystery, The Fabulous Clipjoint, *featuring the detective team of Ed and Am Hunter, was accorded a Best First Novel Edgar by the Mystery Writers of America in 1947; it was followed by twenty-two other suspense novels, including such standouts as* Night of the Jabberwock, Murder Can Be Fun, Here Comes a Candle, *and* The Wench Is Dead. *In science fiction,* What Mad Universe? *is considered a cornerstone novel, and* Martians Go Home *and* The Lights in the Sky Are Stars *are considered minor classics. But Brown's real forte was the short story in general and the mordant short-short in particular. The best of his short works, many of which are in the macabre vein, may be found in such collections as* Nightmares *and* Geezenstacks *(the only single-author collection in any category comprising entirely short-shorts),* Mostly Murder, Honeymoon in Hell, The Shaggy Dog and Other Murders, *and* The Best of Fredric Brown.

I HAD no premonition of horror to come. When I reported to work that evening I had not the faintest inkling that I faced anything more startling than another quiet night on a snap job.

It was seven o'clock, just getting dark outside, when I went into the coroner's office. I stood looking out the window into the gray dusk for a few minutes.

Out there, I could see all the tall buildings of the college, and right across the way was Kane Dormitory, where Jerry Grant was supposed to sleep. The same Grant being myself.

Yes, "supposed to" is right. I was working my way through the last year of an ethnology course by holding down a night job for the city, and I hadn't slept more than a five-hour stretch for weeks.

But that night shift in the coroner's department *was* a snap, all right. A few hours' easy work, and the rest of the time left over for study and work on my thesis. I owed my chance to finish out that final year and get my doctor's degree despite the fact that dad had died, to the fact that I'd been able to get that job.

Behind me, I could hear Dr. Dwight Skibbine, the coroner, opening and closing drawers of his desk, getting ready to leave. I heard his swivel chair squeak as he shoved it back to stand up.

"Don't forget you're going to straighten out that card file tonight, Jerry," he said. "It's in a mess."

I turned away from the window and nodded. "Any customers around tonight?" I asked.

"Just one. In the display case, but I don't think you'll have anybody coming in to look at him. Keep an eye on that refrigeration unit, though. It's been acting up a bit."

"Thirty-two?" I asked just to make conversation, I guess, because we always keep the case at thirty-two degrees.

He nodded. "I'm going to be back later, for a little while. If Paton gets here before I get back, tell him to wait."

He went out, and I went over to the card file and started to straighten it out. It was a simple enough file—just a record of possessions found on bodies that were brought into the morgue, and their disposal after the body was either identified and claimed, or buried in potter's field—but the clerks on the day shift managed to get the file tangled up periodically.

It took me a little while to dope out what had gummed it up this time. Before I finished it, I decided to go downstairs to the basement—the morgue proper—and be sure the refrigerating unit was still holding down Old Man Fahrenheit.

It was. The thermometer in the showcase read thirty-two degrees on the head. The body in the case was that of a man of about forty, a heavy-set, ugly-looking customer. Even as dead as a doornail and under glass, he looked mean.

Maybe you don't know exactly how morgues are run. It's simple, if they are all handled the way the Springdale one was. We had accommodations for seven customers, and six of them were compartments built back into the walls, for all the world like the sliding drawers of a file cabinet. Those compartments were arranged for refrigeration.

But the showcase was where we put unidentified bodies, so they could be shown easily and quickly to anybody who came in to look at them for identification purposes. It was like a big coffin mounted on a bier, except that it was made of glass on all sides except the bottom.

That made it easy to show the body to prospective identifiers, especially as we could click a switch that threw on lights right inside the display case itself, focused on the face of the corpse.

Everything was okay, so I went back upstairs. I decided I would study a while before I resumed work on the file. The night went more quickly and I got more studying done if I alternated the two. I could have had all my routine work over with in three hours and had the rest of the night to study, but it had never worked as well that way.

I used the coroner's secretary's desk for studying and had just got some books and papers spread out when Mr. Paton came in. Harold Paton is superintendent of the zoological gardens, although you would never guess it to look at him. He looked like a man who would be unemployed eleven months of the year because department store Santa Clauses were hired for only one month out of twelve. True, he would need a little padding and a beard, but not a spot of make-up otherwise.

"Hello, Jerry," he said. "Dwight say when he was coming back?"

"Not exactly, Mr. Paton. Just said for you to wait."

The zoo director sighed and sat down.

"We're playing off the tie tonight," he said, "and I'm going to take him."

He was talking about chess, of course. Dr. Skibbine and Mr. Paton were both chess addicts of the first water, and about twice a week the coroner phoned his wife that he was going to be held up at the office, and the two men would play a game that sometimes lasted until well after midnight.

I picked up a volume of *The Golden Bough* and started to open it to my bookmark. I was interested in it, because *The Golden Bough* is the most complete account of the superstitions and early customs of mankind that has ever been compiled.

Mr. Paton's eyes twinkled a little as they took in the title of the volume in my hand.

"That part of the course you're taking?" he asked.

I shook my head. "I'm picking up data for my thesis from it. But I do think it ought to be in a course of ethnology."

"Jerry, Jerry," he said, "you take that thesis too seriously. Ghosts, ghouls, vampires, werewolves. If you ever find any, bring them around, and I'll have special cages built for them at the zoo. Or could you keep a werewolf in a cage?"

You couldn't get mad at Mr. Paton, no matter how he kidded you. That thesis was a bit of a sore point with me. I had taken considerable kidding because I had chosen as my subject, "The Origin and Partial Justification of Superstitions." When some people razzed me about it, I wanted to take a poke at them. But I grinned at Mr. Paton.

"You shouldn't have mentioned vampires in that category," I told him. "You've got them already. I saw a cageful the last time I was there."

"What? Oh, you mean the vampire bats."

"Sure, and you've got a unicorn too, or didn't you know that a rhinoceros is really a unicorn? Except that the medieval artists who drew pictures of it had never seen one and were guessing what it looked like."

"Of course, but—"

There were footsteps in the hallway, and he stopped talking as Dr. Skibbine came in.

"Hullo, Harold," he said to Mr. Paton, and to me: "Heard part of what you were saying, Jerry, and you're right. Don't let Paton kid you out of that thesis of yours."

He went over to his desk and got the chessmen out of the bottom drawer.

"I can't outtalk the two of you," Mr. Paton said. "But say, Jerry, how about ghouls? This ought to be a good place to catch them if there are any running loose around Springdale. Or is that one superstition you're not justifying?"

"Superstition?" I said. "What makes you think that's—"

Then the phone rang, and I went to answer it without finishing what I was going to say.

When I came away from the phone, the two men had the chess pieces set up. Dr. Skibbine had the whites and moved the pawn to king's fourth opening.

"Who was it, Jerry?" he asked.

"Just a man who wanted to know if he could come in to look at the body that was brought in this afternoon. His brother's late getting home."

Dr. Skibbine nodded and moved his king's knight in answer to Mr. Paton's opening move. Already both of them were completely lost in the game. Obviously, Mr. Paton had forgotten what he had asked me about ghouls, so I didn't butt in to finish what I had started to say.

I let *The Golden Bough* go, too, and went to look up the file folder on the unidentified body downstairs. If somebody was coming in to look at it, I wanted to have all the facts about it in mind.

There wasn't much in the folder. The man had been a tramp, judging from his clothes and the lack of money in his pockets and from the nature of the things he did have with him. There wasn't anything at all to indicate identification.

He had been killed on the Mill Road, presumably by a hit-run driver. A Mr. George Considine had found the body and he had also seen another car driving away. The other car had been too distant for him to get the license number or any description worth mentioning.

Of course, I thought, that car might or might not have been the car that had hit the man. Possibly the driver had seen and deliberately passed up the body, thinking it was a drunk.

But the former theory seemed more likely, because there was little traffic on the Mill Road. One end of it was blocked off for repairs, so the only people who used it were the few who lived along there, and there were not many of them. Probably only a few cars a day came along that particular stretch of the road.

Mr. Considine had got out of his car and found that the man was dead. He had driven on to the next house, half a mile beyond, and phoned the police from there, at four o'clock.

That's all there was in the files.

I had just finished reading it when Bill Drager came in. Bill is a lieutenant on the police force, and he and I had become pretty friendly during the time I had worked for the coroner. He was a pretty good friend of Dr. Skibbine too.

"Sorry to interrupt your game, doc," he said, "but I just wanted to ask something."

"What, Bill?"

"Look—the stiff you got in today. You've examined it already?"

"Of course, why?"

"Just wondering. I don't know what makes me think so, but —well, I'm not satisfied all the way. *Was* it just an auto accident?"

Dr. Skibbine had a bishop in his hand, ready to move it, but he put it down on the side of the board instead.

"Just a minute, Harold," he said to Mr. Paton, then turned his chair around to stare at Bill Drager. "Not an auto accident?" he inquired. "The car wheels ran across the man's neck, Bill. What more do you want?"

"I don't know. Was that the sole cause of death, or were there some other marks?"

Dr. Skibbine leaned back in the swivel chair.

"I don't think being hit was the cause of death, exactly. His forehead struck the road when he fell, and he was probably dead when the wheels ran over him. It could have been, for that matter, that he fell when there wasn't even a car around and the car ran over him later."

"In broad daylight?"

"Um—yes, that does sound unlikely. But he could have fallen into the path of the car. He had been drinking plenty. He reeked of liquor."

"Suppose he was hit by a car," Bill said. "How would you reconstruct it? How he fell, I mean, and stuff like that."

"Let's see. I'd say he fell first and was down when the car first touched him. Say he started across the road in front of the car. Horn honked and he tried to turn around and fell flat instead, and the motorist couldn't stop in time and ran over him."

I had not said anything yet, but I put in a protest at that.

"If the man was as obviously drunk as that," I said, "why would the motorist have kept on going? He couldn't have thought he would be blamed if a drunk staggered in front of his car and fell, even before he was hit."

Drager shrugged. "That could happen, Jerry," he said. "For one thing, he may not have any witnesses to prove that it happened that way. And some guys get panicky when they hit a pedestrian, even if the pedestrian is to blame. And then again, the driver of the car might have had a drink or two himself and been afraid to stop because of that."

Dr. Skibbine's swivel chair creaked.

"Sure," he said, "or he might have been afraid because he had a reckless driving count against him already. But, Bill, the cause of death was the blow he got on the forehead when he hit the road. Not that the tires' going over his neck wouldn't have finished him if the fall hadn't."

"We had a case like that here five years ago," said Bill. "Guy named Robbins. Remember?"

Dr. Skibbine grunted. "I wasn't here five years ago. Remember?"

"Yes, I forgot that," said Bill Drager.

I had forgotten it, too. Dr. Skibbine was a Springdale man, but he had spent several years in South American countries doing research work on tropical diseases. Then he had come back and had been elected coroner. Coroner was an easy job in Springdale and gave a man more time for things like research and chess than a private practice would.

"Go on down and look at him, if you want," Dr. Skibbine told Bill. Jerry'll take you down. It will get his mind off ghouls and goblins."

I took Bill Drager downstairs and flicked on the lights in the display case.

"I can take off the end and slide him out of there if you want me to," I said.

"I guess not," Drager said and leaned on the glass top to look closer at the body. The face was all you could see, of course, because a sheet covered the body up to the neck, and this time the sheet had been pulled a little higher than usual, probably to hide the unpleasant damage to the neck.

The face was bad enough. There was a big, ugly bruise on the forehead, and the lower part of the face was cut up a bit.

"The car ran over the back of his neck after he fell on his face, apparently," Bill Drager said. "Ground his face into the road a bit and took off skin. But—"

"But what?" I prompted when he lapsed into silence.

"I don't know," he said. "I was mostly wondering why he would have tried to cross the road at all out there. Right at that place there's nothing on one side of the road that isn't on the other."

He straightened up, and I switched off the showcase lights.

"Maybe you're just imagining things, Bill," I said. "How do you know he tried to cross at all? Doc said he'd been drinking, and maybe he just staggered from the edge of the road out toward the middle without any idea of crossing over."

"Yeah, there's that, of course. Come to think of it, you're probably right. When I got to wondering, I didn't know about the drinking part. Well, let's go back up."

We did, and I shut and locked the door at the head of the stairs. It is the only entrance to the morgue, and I don't know why it has to be kept locked, because it opens right into the coroner's office where I sit all night, and the key stays in the lock.

Anybody who could get past me could unlock it himself. But it's just one of those rules. Those stairs, incidentally, are absolutely the only way you can get down into the morgue which is walled off from the rest of the basement of the Municipal Building.

"Satisfied?" Dr. Skibbine asked Bill Drager, as we walked into the office.

"Guess so," said Drager. "Say, the guy looks vaguely familiar. I can't place him, but I think I've seen him somewhere. Nobody identified him yet?"

"Nope," said doc. "But if he's a local resident, somebody will. We'll have a lot of curiosity seekers in here tomorrow. Always get them after a violent death."

Bill Drager said he was going home and went out. His shift was over. He had just dropped in on his own time.

I stood around and watched the chess game for a few minutes. Mr. Paton was getting licked this time. He was two pieces down and on the defensive. Only a miracle could save him.

Then doc moved a knight and said, "Check," and it was all over but the shouting. Mr. Paton could move out of check all right, but the knight had forked his king and queen, and with the queen gone, as it would be after the next move, the situation was hopeless.

"You got me, Dwight," he said. "I'll resign. My mind must be fuzzy tonight. Didn't see that knight coming."

"Shall we start another game? It's early."

"You'd beat me. Let's bowl a quick game, instead, and get home early."

After they left, I finished up my work on the card file and then did my trigonometry. It was almost midnight then. I remembered the man who had phoned that he was coming in and decided he had changed his mind. Probably his brother had arrived home safely, after all.

I went downstairs to be sure the refrigerating unit was okay. Finding that it was, I came back up and locked the door again. Then I went out into the hall and locked the outer door. It's supposed to be kept locked, too, and I really should have locked it earlier.

After that, I read *The Golden Bough,* with a notebook in front of me so I could jot down anything I found that would fit into my thesis.

I must have become deeply engrossed in my reading because when the night bell rang, I jumped inches out of my chair. I looked at the clock and saw it was two in the morning.

Ordinarily, I don't mind the place where I work at all. Being near dead bodies gives some people the willies, but not me.

There isn't any nicer, quieter place for studying and reading than a morgue at night.

But I had a touch of the creeps then. I do get them once in a while. This time it was the result of being startled by the sudden ringing of that bell when I was so interested in something that I had forgotten where I was and why I was there.

I put down the book and went out into the long dark hallway. When I had put on the hall light, I felt a little better. I could see somebody standing outside the glass-paned door at the end of the hall. A tall thin man whom I didn't know. He wore glasses and was carrying a gold-headed cane.

"My name is Burke, Roger Burke," he said when I opened the door. "I phoned early this evening about my brother being missing. Uh—may I—"

"Of course," I told him. "Come this way. When you didn't come for so long, I thought you had located your brother."

"I thought I had," he said hesitantly. "A friend said he had seen him this evening, and I quit worrying for a while. But when it got after one o'clock and he wasn't home, I—"

We had reached the coroner's office by then, but I stopped and turned.

"There's only one unidentified body here," I told him, "and that was brought in this afternoon. If your brother was seen this evening, it couldn't be him."

The tall man said, "Oh," rather blankly and looked at me a moment. Then he said, "I hope that's right. But this friend said he saw him at a distance, on a crowded street. He could have been mistaken. So as long as I'm here—"

"I guess you might as well," I said, "now that you're here. Then you'll be sure."

I led the way through the office and unlocked the door.

I was glad, as we started down the stairs, that there seemed little likelihood of identification. I hate to be around when one is made. You always seem to share, vicariously, the emotion of the person who recognizes a friend or relative.

At the top of the stairs I pushed the button that put on the overhead lights downstairs in the morgue. The switch for the showcase was down below. I stopped to flick it as I reached the bottom of the stairs, and the tall man went on past me toward the case. Apparently he had been a visitor here before.

I had taken only a step or two after him when I heard him gasp. He stopped suddenly and took a step backward so quickly that I bumped into him and grabbed his arm to steady myself.

He turned around, and his face was a dull pasty gray that one seldom sees on the face of a living person.

"My God!" he said. "Why didn't you warn me that—"

It didn't make sense for him to say a thing like that. I've been with people before when they have identified relatives, but none of them had ever reacted just that way. Or had it been merely identification? He certainly looked as though he had seen something horrible.

I stepped a little to one side so that I could see past him. When I saw, it was as though a wave of cold started at the base of my spine and ran up along my body. I had never seen anything like it—and you get toughened when you work in a morgue.

The glass top of the display case had been broken in at the upper, the head, end, and the body inside was—well, I'll try to be as objective about it as I can. The best way to be objective is to put it bluntly. The flesh of the face had been eatenaway, eaten away as though acid had been poured on it, or as though—

I got hold of myself and stepped up to the edge of the display case and looked down.

It had not been acid. Acid does not leave the marks of teeth.

Nauseated, I closed my eyes for an instant until I got over it. Behind me, I heard sounds as though the tall man, who had been the first to see it, was being sick. I didn't blame him.

"I don't—" I said, and stepped back. "Something happened here."

Silly remark, but you can't think of the right thing to say in a spot like that.

"Come on," I told him. "I'll have to get the police."

The thought of the police steadied me. When the police got here, it would be all right. They would find out what had happened.

As I reached the bottom of the stairs my mind started to work logically again. I could picture Bill Drager up in the office firing questions at me, asking me, "When did it happen? You can judge by the temperature, can't you?"

The tall man stumbled up the stairs past me as I paused. Most decidedly I didn't want to be down there alone, but I yelled to him:

"Wait up there. I'll be with you in a minute."

He would have to wait, of course, because I would have to unlock the outer door to let him out.

I turned back and looked at the thermometer in the broken case, trying not to look at anything else. It read sixty-three degrees, and that was only about ten degrees under the temperature of the rest of the room.

The glass had been broken, then, for some time. An hour, I'd say offhand, or maybe a little less. Upstairs, with the heavy door closed, I wouldn't have heard it break. Anyway, I hadn't heard it break.

I left the lights on in the morgue, all of them, when I ran up the stairs.

The tall man was standing in the middle of the office, looking around as though he were in a daze. His face still had that grayish tinge, and I was just as glad that I didn't have to look in a mirror just then, because my own face was likely as bad.

I picked up the telephone and found myself giving Bill Drager's home telephone number instead of asking for the police. I don't know why my thoughts ran so strongly to Bill Drager, except that he had been the one who had suspected that something more than met the eye had been behind the hit-run case from the Mill Road.

"Can—will you let me out of here?" the tall man said. "I—I —that wasn't my—"

"I'm afraid not, I told him. "Until the police get here. You— uh—witnessed—"

It sounded screwy, even to me. Certainly he could not have preceded me into the morgue only by a second and hadn't even reached the case when I was beside him. But I knew what the police would say if I let him go before they had a chance to get his story.

Then Drager's voice was saying a sleepy, "Hullo," into my ear.

"Bill," I said, "you got to come down here. That corpse downstairs—it's—I—"

The sleepiness went out of Drager's voice.

"Calm down, Jerry," he said. "It can't be that bad. Now, what happened?"

I finally got it across.

"You phoned the department first, of course?" Drager asked.

"N-no. I thought of you first because—"

"Sit tight," he said. "I'll phone them and then come down. I'll have to dress first, so they'll get there ahead of me. Don't go down to the morgue again and don't touch anything."

He put the receiver on the hook, and I felt a little better. Somehow the worst seemed to be over, now that it was off my chest. Drager's offering to phone the police saved me from having to tell it again, over the phone.

The tall man—I remembered now that he had given the name Roger Burke—was leaning against the wall, weakly.

"Did—did I get from what you said on the phone that the body wasn't that way when—when you brought it in?" he asked.

I nodded. "It must have happened within the last hour," I said. "I was down there at midnight, and everything was all right then."

"But what—what happened?"

I opened my mouth and closed it again. Something had happened down there, but what? There wasn't any entrance to the morgue other than the ventilator and the door that opened at the top of the stairs. And nobody—nothing—had gone through that door since my trip of inspection.

I thought back and thought hard. No, I hadn't left this office for even a minute between midnight and the time the night bell had rung at two o'clock. I had left the office then of course, to answer the door. But whatever had happened had not happened then. The thermometer downstairs proved that.

Burke was fumbling cigarettes out of his pocket. He held out the package with a shaky hand, and I took one and managed to strike a match and light both cigarettes.

The first drag made me feel nearly human. Apparently he felt better too, because he said:

"I—I'm afraid I didn't make identification one way or the other. You couldn't—with—" He shuddered. "Say, my brother had a small anchor tattooed on his left forearm. I forgot it or I could have asked you over the phone. Was there—"

I thought back to the file and shook my head.

"No," I said definitely. "It would have been on the record, and there wasn't anything about it. They make a special point of noting down things like that."

"That's swell," Burke said. "I mean—Say, if I'm going to have to wait, I'm going to sit down. I still feel awful."

Then I remembered that I had better phone Dr. Skibbine, too, and give him the story firsthand before the police got here and called him. I went over to the phone.

The police got there first—Captain Quenlin and Sergeant Wilson and two other men I knew by sight but not by name. Bill Drager was only a few minutes later getting there, and around three o'clock Dr. Skibbine came.

By that time the police had questioned Burke and let him go, although one of them left to go home with him. They told him it was because they wanted to check on whether his brother had shown up yet, so the Missing Persons Bureau could handle it if he hadn't. But I guessed the real reason was that they wanted to check on his identity and place of residence.

Not that there seemed to be any way Burke could be involved in whatever had happened to the body, but when you don't know what has happened, you can't overlook any angle. After all, he was a material witness.

Bill Drager had spent most of the time since he had been there downstairs, but he came up now.

"The place is tighter than a drum down there, except for that ventilator," he said. "And I noticed something about it. One of the vanes in it is a little bent."

"How about rats?" Captain Quenlin asked.

Drager snorted. "Ever see rats break a sheet of glass?"

"The glass might have been broken some other way." Quenlin looked at me. "You're around here nights, Jerry Grant. Ever see any signs of rats or mice?"

I shook my head, and Bill Drager backed me up.

"I went over the whole place down there," he said. "There isn't a hole anywhere. Floor's tile set in cement. The walls are tile, in big close-set slabs, without a break. I went over them."

Dr. Skibbine was starting down the steps.

"Come on, Jerry," he said to me. "Show me where you and this Burke fellow were standing when he let out a yip."

I didn't much want to, but I followed him down. I showed him where I had been and where Burke had been and told him that Burke had not gone closer to the case than about five feet at any time. Also, I told him what I had already told the police about my looking at the thermometer in the case.

Dr. Skibbine went over and looked at it.

"Seventy-one now," he said. "I imagine that's as high as it's going. You say it was sixty-three when you saw it at two? Yes, I'd say the glass was broken between twelve-thirty and one-thirty."

Quenlin had followed us down the stairs. "When did you get home tonight, Dr. Skibbine?" he asked.

The coroner looked at him in surprise. "Around midnight. Good Lord, you don't think *I* had anything to do with this, do you, Quenlin?"

The captain shook his head. "Routine question. Look, doc, why would anybody or anything do that?"

"I wouldn't know," Skibbine said slowly, "unless it was to prevent identification of the corpse. That's possible. The body will never be identified now unless the man has a criminal record and his prints are on file. But making that 'anything' instead of 'anybody' makes it easier, cap. I'd say 'anything' was hungry, plenty hungry."

I leaned back against the wall at the bottom of the stairs, again fighting nausea that was almost worse than before.

Rats? Besides the fact that there weren't any rats, it would have taken a lot of them to do what had been done.

"Jerry," said Bill Drager, "you're sure you weren't out of the office up there for even a minute between midnight and two o'clock? Think hard. Didn't you maybe go to the washroom or something?"

"I'm positive," I told him.

Drager turned to the captain and pointed up to the ventilator.

"There are only two ways into this morgue, cap," he said. "One's through the door Jerry says he sat in front of, and the other's up there."

My eyes followed his pointing finger, and I studied the ventilator and its position. It was a round opening in the wall, twelve or maybe thirteen inches across, and there was a wheellike arrangement of vanes that revolved in it. It was turning slowly. It was set in the wall just under the high ceiling, maybe sixteen feet above the floor, and it was directly over the display case.

"Where's that open into?" Quenlin asked.

"Goes right through the wall," Dr. Skibbine told him. "Opens on the alley, just a foot or two above the ground. There's another wheel just like that one on the outside. A little electric motor turns them."

"Could the thing be dismantled from the outside?"

Dr. Skibbine shrugged. "Easiest way to find that out is to go out in the alley and try it. But nobody could get through there, even if you got the thing off. It's too narrow."

"A thin man might—"

"No, even a thin man is wider than twelve inches across the shoulders, and that's my guess on the width of that hole."

Quenlin shrugged.

"Got a flashlight, Drager?" he asked. "Go on out in the alley and take a look. Although if somebody did get that thing off, I don't see how the devil they could have—"

Then he looked down at the case and winced. "If everybody's through looking at this for the moment," he said, "for crying out loud put a sheet over it. It's giving me the willies. I'll dream about ghouls tonight."

The word hit me like a ton of bricks. Because it was then I remembered that we had talked about ghouls early that very evening. About—how had Mr. Paton put it?—"ghosts, ghouls, vampires, werewolves," and about a morgue being a good place for ghouls to hang around; and about—

Some of the others were looking at me, and I knew that Dr. Skibbine, at least, was remembering that conversation. Had he mentioned it to any of the others?

Sergeant Wilson was standing behind the other men and probably didn't know I could see him from where I stood, for he surreptitiously crossed himself.

"Ghouls, nuts!" he said in a voice a bit louder than necessary. "There ain't any such thing. Or is there?"

It was a weak but dramatic ending. Nobody answered him.

Me, I had had enough of that morgue for the moment. Nobody had put a sheet over the case because there was not one available downstairs.

"I'll get a sheet," I said and started up for the office. I stumbled on the bottom step.

"What's eating—" I heard Quenlin say, and then as though he regretted his choice of words, he started over again. "Something's wrong with the kid. Maybe you better send him home, doc."

He probably didn't realize I could hear him. But by that time I was most of the way up, so I didn't hear the coroner's answer.

From the cabinet I got a sheet, and the others were coming up the steps when I got back with it. Quenlin handed it to Wilson.

"You put it on, sarge," he said.

Wilson took it, and hesitated. I had seen his gesture downstairs and I knew he was scared stiff to go back down there alone. I was scared, too, but I did my Boy Scout act for the day and said:

"I'll go down with you, sergeant. I want to take a look at that ventilator."

While he put the sheet over the broken case, I stared up at the ventilator and saw the bent vane. As I watched, a hand reached through the slit between that vane and the next and bent it some more.

Then the hand, Bill Drager's hand, reached through the widened slit and groped for the nut on the center of the shaft on which the ventilator wheel revolved. Yes, the ventilator could be removed and replaced from the outside. The bent vane made it look as though that had been done.

But why? After the ventilator had been taken off, what then? The opening was too small for a man to get through and besides it was twelve feet above the glass display case.

Sergeant Wilson went past me up the stairs, and I followed him up. The conversation died abruptly as I went through the door, and I suspected that I had been the subject of the talk.

Dr. Skibbine was looking at me.

"The cap's right, Jerry," he said. "You don't look so well. We're going to be around here from now on, so you take the rest of the night off. Get some sleep."

Sleep, I thought. What's that? How could I sleep now? I felt dopey, I'll admit, from lack of it. But the mere thought of turning out a light and lying down alone in a dark room—huh-uh! I must have been a little lightheaded just then, for a goofy parody was running through my brain:

A ghoul hath murdered sleep, the innocent sleep, sleep that knits . . .

"Thanks, Dr. Skibbine," I said. "I—I guess it will do me good, at that."

It would get me out of here, somewhere where I could think without a lot of people talking. If I could get the unicorns and rhinoceros out of my mind, maybe I had the key. Maybe, but it didn't make sense yet.

I put on my hat and went outside and walked around the building into the dark alley.

Bill Drager's face was a dim patch in the light that came

through the circular hole in the wall where the ventilator had been.

He saw me coming and called out sharply, "Who's that?" and stood up. When he stood, he seemed to vanish, because it put him back in the darkness.

"It's me—Jerry Grant." I said. "Find out anything, Bill?"

"Just what you see. The ventilator comes out, from the outside. It was just about a foot in diameter. But it isn't a big enough hole for a man." He laughed a little off-key. "A ghoul, I don't know. How big is a ghoul, Jerry?"

"Can it, Bill," I said. "Did you do that in the dark? Didn't you bring a flashlight?"

"No. Look, whoever did it earlier in the night, if somebody did, wouldn't have dared use a light. They'd be too easy to see from either end of the alley. I wanted to see if it could be done in the dark."

"Yes," I said thoughtfully. "But the light from the inside shows."

"Was it on between midnight and two?"

"Um—no. I hadn't thought of that."

I stared at the hole in the wall. Large enough for a man to stick his head into, but not to crawl through.

Bill Drager was still standing back in the dark, but now that my eyes were used to the alley, I could make out the shadowy outline of his body.

"Jerry," he said, "you've been studying this superstition stuff. Just what is a ghoul?"

"Something in Eastern mythology, Bill. An imaginary creature that robs graves and feeds on corpses. The modern use of the word is confined to someone who robs graves, usually for jewelry that is sometimes interred with the bodies. Back in the early days of medicine, bodies were stolen and sold to the anatomists for purposes of disection, too."

"The modern ones don't—uh—"

"There have been psychopathic cases, a few of them. One

happened in Paris, in modern times. A man named Bertrand. Charles Fort tells about him in his book *Wild Talents*.

"*Wild Talents*, huh?" said Bill. "What happened?"

"Graves in a Paris cemetery were being dug up by something or someone who—" there in the dark alley, I couldn't say it plainly—"who—uh—acted like a ghoul. They couldn't catch him but they set a blunderbus trap. It got this man Bertrand, and he confessed."

Bill Drager didn't say anything, just stood there. Then, just as though I could read his mind, I got scared because I knew what he was thinking. If anything like that had happened here tonight, there was only one person it could possibly have been.

Me.

Bill Drager was standing there silently, staring at me, and wondering whether I—

Then I knew why the others had stopped talking when I had come up the stairs just a few minutes before, back at the morgue. No, there was not a shred of proof. But there had been a faint unspoken suspicion that somehow seemed a thousand times worse than an accusation I could deny.

I knew, then, that unless this case was solved suspicion would follow me the rest of my life. Something too absurd for open accusation. But people would look at me and wonder, and the mere possibility would make them shudder. Every word I spoke would be weighed to see whether it might indicate an unbalanced mind.

Even Bill Drager, one of my best friends, was wondering about me now.

"Bill," I said, "for God's sake, you don't think—"

"Of course not, Jerry."

But the fact that he knew what I meant before I had finished the sentence, proved I had been right about what he had been thinking.

There was something else in his voice, too, although he had tried to keep it out. Fear. He was alone with me in a dark alley, and I realized now why he had stepped back out of the light so quickly. Bill Drager was a little afraid of me.

But this was no time and place to talk about it. The atmosphere was wrong. Anything I could say would make things worse.

So I merely said, "Well, so long, Bill," as I turned and walked toward the street.

Half a block up the street on the other side was an all-night restaurant, and I headed for it. Not to eat, for I felt as though I would never want to eat again. The very thought of food was sickening. But a cup of coffee might take away some of the numbness in my mind.

Hank Perry was on duty behind the counter, and he was alone.

"Hi, Jerry," he said, as I sat down on a stool at the counter. "Off early tonight?"

I nodded and let it go at that.

"Just a cup of black coffee, Hank," I told him, and forestalled any salestalk by adding, "I'm not hungry. Just ate."

Silly thing to say, I realized the minute I had said it. Suppose someone asked Hank later what I had said when I came in. They all knew, back there, that I had not brought a lunch to work and hadn't eaten. Would I, from now on, have to watch every word I said to avoid slips like that?

But whatever significance Hank or others might read into my words later, there was nothing odd about them now, as long as Hank didn't know what had happened at the morgue.

He brought my coffee. I stirred in sugar and waited for it to cool enough to drink.

"Nice night out," Hank said.

I hadn't noticed, but I said, "Yeah."

To me it was one terrible night out, but I couldn't tell him that without spilling the rest of the story.

"How was business tonight, Hank?" I asked.

"Pretty slow."

"How many customers," I asked, "did you have between midnight and two o'clock?"

"Hardly any. Why?"

"Hank," I said, "something happened then. Look, I can't tell you about it now, honestly. I don't know whether or not it's going to be given out to the newspapers. If it isn't, it would lose me my job even to mention it. But will you think hard if you saw anybody or anything out of the ordinary between twelve and two?''

"Um," said Hank, leaning against the counter thoughtfully. "That's a couple of hours ago. Must have had several customers in here during that time. But all I can remember are regulars: people on night shifts that come in regularly."

"When you're standing at that grill in the window frying something, you can see out across the street," I said. "You ought to be able to see down as far as the alley, because this is a pretty wide street."

"Yeah, I can."

"Did you see anyone walk or drive in there?"

"Golly," said Hank. "Yeah, I did. I think it was around one o'clock. I happened to notice the guy on account of what he was carrying."

I felt my heart hammering with sudden excitement.

"What was he carrying? And what did he look like?"

"I didn't notice what he looked like," said Hank. "He was in shadow most of the time. But he was carrying a bowling ball."

"A bowling ball?"

Hank nodded. "That's what made me notice him. There aren't any alleys—I mean bowling alleys—right around here. I bowl myself so I wondered where this guy had been rolling."

"You mean he was carrying a bowling ball under his arm?"

I was still incredulous, even though Hank's voice showed me he was not kidding.

He looked at me contemptuously.

"No. Bowlers never carry 'em like that on the street. There's a sort of bag that's made for the purpose. A little bigger than the ball, some of them, so a guy can put in his bowling shoes and stuff."

I closed my eyes a moment to try to make sense out of it. Of all the things on this mad night; it seemed the maddest that a bowling ball had been carried into the alley by the morgue—or something the shape of a bowling ball. At just the right time, too. One o'clock.

It would be a devil of a coincidence if the man Hank had seen hadn't been the one.

"You're sure it was a bowling ball case?"

"Positive. I got one like it myself. And the way he carried it, it was just heavy enough to have the ball in it." He looked at me curiously. "Say, Jerry, I never thought of it before, but a case like that would be a handy thing to carry a bomb in. Did someone try to plant a bomb at the morgue?"

"No."

"Then if it wasn't a bowling ball—and you act like you think it wasn't—what would it have been?"

"I wish I knew," I told him. "I wish to high heaven I knew." I downed the rest of my coffee and stood up.

"Thanks a lot, Hank," I said. "Listen, you think it over and see if you can remember anything else about that case or the man who carried it. I'll see you later."

What I needed was some fresh air, so I started walking. I didn't pay any attention to where I was going; I just walked.

My feet didn't take me in circles, but my mind did. A bowling ball! Why would a bowling ball, or something shaped like it, be carried into the alley back of the morgue? A bowling ball would fit into that ventilator hole, all right, and a dropped bowling ball would have broken the glass of the case.

But a bowling ball wouldn't have done—the rest of it.

I vaguely remembered some mention of bowling earlier in the evening and thought back to what it was. Oh yes. Dr. Skibbine and Mr. Paton had been going to bowl a game instead of playing a second game of chess. But neither of them had bowling balls along. Anyway, if Dr. Skibbine had told the truth, they had both been home by midnight.

If not a bowling ball, then what? A ghoul? A spherical ghoul?

The thought was so incongruously horrible that I wanted to stop, right there in the middle of the sidewalk and laugh like a maniac. Maybe I was near hysteria.

I thought of going back to the morgue and telling them about it, and laughing. Watching Quenlin's face and Wilson's when I told them that our guest had been a man-eating bowling ball. A spherical—

Then I stopped walking, because all of a sudden I knew what the bowling ball had been, and I had the most important part of the answer.

Somewhere a clock was striking half-past three, and I looked around to see where I was. Oak Street, only a few doors from Grant Parkway. That meant I had come fifteen or sixteen blocks from the morgue and that I was only a block and a half from the zoo. At the zoo, I could find out if I was right.

So I started walking again. A block and a half later I was across the street from the zoo right in front of Mr. Paton's house. Strangely, there was a light in one of the downstairs rooms.

I went up onto the porch and rang the bell. Mr. Paton came to answer it. He was wearing a dressing gown, but I could see shoes and the bottoms of his trouser legs under it.

He didn't look surprised at all when he opened the door.

"Yes, Jerry?" he said, almost as though he had been expecting me.

"I'm glad you're still up, Mr. Paton," I said. "Could you walk across with me and get me past the guard at the gate? I'd like to look at one of the cages and verify—something."

"You guessed then, Jerry?"

"Yes, Mr. Paton," I told him. Then I had a sudden thought that scared me a little. "You were seen going into the alley," I added quickly, "and the man who saw you knows I came here. He saw you carrying—"

He held up his hand and smiled.

"You needn't worry, Jerry," he said. "I know it's over—the minute anybody is smart enough to guess. And—well, I murdered a man all right, but I'm not the type to murder another to try to cover up, because I can see where that would lead. The man I did kill deserved it, and I gambled on—well never mind all that."

"Who was he?" I asked.

"His name was Mark Leedom. He was my assistant four years ago. I was foolish at that time—I'd lost money speculating and I stole some zoo funds. They were supposed to be used for the purchase of—never mind the details. Mark Leedom found out and got proof.

"He made me turn over most of the money to him, and he—retired, and moved out of town. But he's been coming back periodically to keep shaking me down. He was a rat, Jerry, a worse crook than I ever thought of being. This time I couldn't pay so I killed him."

"You were going to make it look like an accident on the Mill Road?" I said. "You killed him here and took him—"

"Yes, I was going to have the car run over his head, so he wouldn't be identified. I missed by inches, but I couldn't try again because another car was coming, and I had to keep on driving away.

"Luckily, Doc Skibbine didn't know him. It was while doc was in South America that Leedom worked for me. But there are lots of people around who did know him. Some curiosity seeker would have identified him in the week they hold an unidentified body and—well, once they knew who he was and traced things back, they'd have got to me eventually for the old business four years ago if not the fact that I killed him."

"So that's why you had to make him unidentifiable," I said. "I see. He looked familiar to Bill Drager, but Bill couldn't place him."

He nodded. "Bill was just a patrolman then. He probably had seen Leedom only a few times, but someone else—well, Jerry, you go back and tell them about it. Tell them I'll be here."

"Gee, Mr. Paton, I'm sorry I got to," I said. "Isn't there anything—"

"No. Go and get them. I won't run away, I promise you. And tell doc he wouldn't have beat me that chess game tonight if I hadn't let him. With what I had to do, I wanted to get out of there early. Good night, Jerry."

He eased me out onto the porch again before I quite realized why he had never had a chance to tell Dr. Skibbine himself. Yes, he meant for them to find him here when they came, but not alive.

I almost turned to the door again, to break my way in and stop him. Then I realized that everything would be easier for him if he did it his way.

Yes, he was dead by the time they sent men out to bring him in. Even though I had expected it, I guess I had a case of the jitters when they phoned in the news, and I must have showed it, because Bill Drager threw an arm across my shoulders.

"Jerry," he said, "this has been the devil of a night for you. You need a drink. Come on."

The drink made me feel better and so did the frank admiration in Drager's eyes. It was so completely different from what I had seen there back in the alley.

"Jerry," he told me, "you ought to get on the force. Figuring out that—of all things—he had used an armadillo."

"But what else was possible? Look! All those ghoul legends trace back to beasts that are eaters of carrion. Like hyenas. A hyena could have done what was done back there in the morgue. But no one could have handled a hyena—pushed it through that ventilator hole with a rope on it to pull it up again.

"But an armadillo is an eater of corpses, too. It gets frightened when handled and curls up into a ball, like a bowling ball. It doesn't make any noise, and you could carry it in a bag like the one Hank described. It has an armored shell that would break the glass of the display case if Paton lowered it to within a few feet and let it drop the rest of the way. And of course he looked down with a flashlight to see—"

Bill Drager shuddered a little.

"Learning is a great thing if you like it," he said. "Studying origins of superstitions, I mean. But me, I want another drink. How about you?"

CORPUS DELECTABLE

by L. SPRAGUE DE CAMP AND FLETCHER PRATT

"Corpus Delectable" offers a wry, witty change of pace in which there are no ghouls as such. Or then again, maybe there are. Morticians populate these pages, and they can *be ghoulish on occasion, even if they don't engage in digging up and devouring some of the bodies they buried in the first place. So can members of a certain other brotherhood, the identity of which will become apparent. It all depends on your perspective, or to put it another way, on how you view the body . . .*

Gavagan's Bar, where "Corpus Delectable" takes place, is a watering hole wherein odd things happen and all manner of odd stories are told. A droll (and sometimes macabre) fantasy series of these stories was extremely popular in science fiction circles in the 1950s, and the best of them were gathered into a 1953 collection, Tales from Gavagan's Bar. *Modern readers can now enjoy them as well, since the book has recently been reissued.*

L. Sprague de Camp (born 1908) and Fletcher Pratt (1897–1957) collaborated on numerous other works of fantasy and science fiction, including The Incomplete Enchanter, The Castle of Iron, *and* The Carnelian Cube; *they were among the most popular of the writers who contributed to the great fantasy magazine of the 1940s,* Unknown.

*Individually, de Camp is the author of the definitive biography of re-
nowned horror writer H.P. Lovecraft, and of such novels as* Rogue
Queen *and* The Hand of Zei; *he has also edited several sword-and-
sorcery anthologies, and has helped to continue the Conan the Barbarian
series begun by Robert E. Howard. Pratt was the author of such science
fiction novels as* Well of the Unicorn, The Undying Fire, *and*
Double Jeopardy, *as well as nonfiction books on codes and ciphers, and
the Civil War.*

"THE LIGHT doesn't have the power of a regular flashbulb, but
it can be used over and over," said young Mr. Jeffers. He aimed
his camera at the stuffed owl over the bar. There was a bright,
noiseless flash, which caused the owl's eyes to light up yellowly
for an instant. A shutter clicked; Jeffers pressed a button and
there was a faint whirr as the little clockwork motor wound the
film through the next frame. "No double exposure," said Jeffers.

Mr. Gross looked up from his boilermaker. "I got a cousin by
marriage that got run in for that once," he said.

"What, making pictures of stuffed owls?" asked Mr. Keating
from the library.

"No, taking off his clothes in the theater. He done it twicet,
and the second time—"

Mr. Witherwax slid his glass across the bar and indicated his
desire for another martini by sign language. "Mr. Jeffers," he
said in a firm voice, "I noticed that when you were taking the
picture of that owl, it almost looked alive. Did you ever take a
picture of someone and almost make them look dead?"

"Yeah," said Jeffers, and indicated a man down the bar, one
with a rather handsome, but time-worn face under a mop of
white hair, who was drinking a double Scotch. "This one, now
—I'll bet when the picture is developed, he'll look as though he
just came out of a coffin." He lifted his camera and the flash went
off again.

The white-haired man started so violently that he only recov-

ered his drink with an effort. "What did you say?" he almost
shouted, taking two steps toward Jeffers.

"I'm sorry," said Jeffers. "I didn't mean to be offensive. I only
thought you'd make a good subject—"

The white-haired man gripped him fiercely by the arm. "What
business are you in?" he demanded.

"Now, now," said Mr. Cohan, from behind the bar. "In Gavagan's it's against the rule to have fights. When a man is drinking
good liquor, he should have no grudges against anyone."

"It was my fault, really," said Jeffers, laying down his camera,
and turned back to the white-haired man. "If it makes any difference to you, I work in a law office." He produced a card-case.
"May I buy you a drink and ask why?"

"Oh," said the other, with a gasp that might have been relief.
"I beg your pardon. Mr. Cohan, will you put both drinks on my
check? I thought—" He produced a card-case of his own.

"That's me, Frederick Moutier. Chevrolet agency; that is, I
work for it. I used to have my own business until I had to give
it up because of what you just did. In Indianapolis." He smiled
glassily.

"Do you mean taking pictures of you?" asked Jeffers, incredu-
lously.

"Just about. Don't you want something that has a little more
taste than that beer? Let me ask you this, my friend; how would
you like it if—oh, hell, you just won't get it. Nobody does, not
even the damn looney-doctor my wife sent me to."

(He buried his nose in his highball, and Jeffers, whose low
opinion of the psychiatric profession was frequently and force-
fully expressed at Gavagan's, encouraged him by remarking that
the only time a psychiatrist got anything was when he got it out
of somebody's pocket.)

"Ha, ha, ha, that's rich!" said Moutier. "Do you mind if I use
it sometime when I'm speaking before Rotary? That is, if I ever
do again. (His face assumed its former melancholy.) My friend,
they've got me on the skids; yes sir, royally on the skids. It
shouldn't happen to a dog, and certainly not to old Freddie
Moutier.

"Look, it all started with a man named Smith, Leroy Burlingame Smith. I wish I'd never met him. I did, though; we both bought houses in one of those new developments outside Indianapolis, and there we were, next-door neighbors. Well, of course the first thing that happened was the little woman got acquainted with Mrs. Smith, and the next was that we were going over there to play bridge. I'd rather have a little five-ten poker game myself, but you know how it is with women, and I never saw one anyway that had sense enough to lay off inside straights.

"Well, right away it developed that Smith was an undertaker. Now I know some people feel funny about undertakers, but I always say it's un-American to be prejudiced against a man because of his profession if he's a good citizen. Why, we even have some undertakers in Rotary. So we went over and played bridge, and when we got through they put out some beer and pretzels, and we sat around chatting for a while and getting acquainted. They seemed like a real nice, wholesome couple. He had his own business and I could tell from the way he talked that he probably had an A-1 credit rating. In my business you get so you can spot them every time.

"Well, the women liked each other all right, too, and it wasn't long before we got to be pretty good friends. If we didn't have anything else on, we'd get together in the evening and have some bridge, or maybe take in a movie and sit around a little afterward. But about the time I began to sort of measure him for a new Olds—ha, ha, I had the Oldsmobile agency out there— Leroy began acting kind of funny. I don't mean he was any less friendly. In fact, he was more so, and when I hinted that he might want to make his next car an Olds, he took me up so quick that I never even had a chance to explain the selling points.

"But when we were playing bridge, he'd sit there with the cards in his hand, and all of a sudden he'd be staring at me, kind of half-asleep, until his wife had to remind him that it was his turn to play. Then one evening he said he didn't feel like bridge at all, just wanted to listen to the radio. Well, golly, I could have understood it if there had been something special on, like Fred Allen or the Hit Parade, but he just tuned in on some classical

music for a whole hour and sat there all through it, staring at me
like I was some kind of Frankenstein.''

"You mean Frankenstein's monster," said Keating.

"Do I? I thought Dracula was the monster. Give me another
drink, Mr. Cohan. Well, anyway, that's what he did. I remember
talking to the little woman about it when we got home, asking
her if she heard anything from Elise Smith about Leroy maybe
being sick or things not going right in his business. But she said
no, she didn't know of anything, and she was pretty sure she
would, because Elise was always over there or they were going
out together.

"Well, it was the next morning after he was so funny about the
radio that old Leroy called me up at the agency. He said he was
ready for his demonstration on the Olds, and would I bring it
around and stop in at his shop. I got out the demonstrator and
went. The place was a big one with a couple of those potted
palms in front and more inside, very dignified. It made a good
presentation, you might say. I asked for Leroy and while I was
waiting for him, I stood talking to one of the other men in his
shop. He kept staring at me real hard, something like Leroy had
the night before, and I was just going to ask him what was the
matter with me when Leroy came in.

"He introduced me to his staff and showed me all around the
place. I thought it was an awful lot of trouble to take with
someone who was just there to demonstrate a car, but you don't
catch Fred Moutier telling another man how to run his business,
no sir. So I thanked him and we were just leaving when bingo!
A big flashlight went off right in my face. I jumped about three
feet and said 'What the hell!' but Leroy just said: 'Sorry I startled
you, old man. I thought I'd like a picture of you sometime, so
I got Hulberd to take one. He's pretty good with a camera.'

"Well, you can't get sore at someone that likes you so much
he wants your picture, especially when you're trying to sell him
a car, so I just laughed it off, and to make certain Leroy knew
I was taking it the right way, asked him to be my guest at Rotary
on Wednesday. I was giving a speech I had worked out on
'Salesmanship and American Ideals'; maybe you've heard of it,

I've given it at a lot of Rotaries and places around the country, about how America is built on the ideal of salesmanship service, and when the government spends a lot of money to give things away, we're getting to be like those socialistic Communists.

"Anyway, Leroy bought the car, and the little woman and me began playing bridge again with the Smiths, and even if he did keep up that funny habit of staring at me, it wasn't as bad as before. I forgot all about that picture until one evening we were over at his house, and he got up to go to the can or something, and the two women started gabbing about clothes, so I picked up a magazine that was laying there.

"It was an undertaker's trade journal, and when I opened it, right there smack in the middle of the book was a great big picture of myself, lying in a coffin with flowers piled all around me. Underneath it said: 'Arrangements by Leroy B. Smith, Funerary Director of Indianapolis.'

"Well, I got kind of sore. When Leroy came back, I told him what a hell of a trick I thought he'd pulled, and the little woman and I went home. Elise Smith tried to fix it up the next day by coming over and telling the little wife that it was intended as a compliment, and that Leroy thought I was the most perfect subject for an undertaker he had ever seen, but as far as I was concerned that only made it worse, if you get me. We cut out going over there for a while, but the two women kept on being friends, and you know how women are, I guess they might have fixed things up except for something else that happened.

"I went over to Columbus to give my speech about 'Salesmanship and American Ideals' to Rotary there, and afterwards I was in a bar with a couple of the boys from Columbus Rotary having a little drink before I had to hit the road again, when this fellow stepped up to me. He had on a blue serge suit and a white shirt with a polka-dot tie and he said: 'Pardon me, but I'm sure I've seen you before.'

"I said maybe he had at that, and told him who I was, and he said his name was Francis X. McKenna and bought a round of drinks. All the time he kept giving one look and then another, as though he had my name all right, but wondered who the hell

Fred Moutier was. Finally it seemed to hit him; he pulled me off
a little to one side and said: 'I remember now. You've the one
who posed for that wonderful presentation by Leroy Smith in
the *Living Mortician.* Look here, Mr. Moutier,' he said, 'I know
you have your own business and you're not a professional, but
if you'll spare half an hour of your time letting me build a
presentation around you, I'll make it well worth your while.' "

The white-haired man gloomily finished his drink and motioned for another.

"What did you do?" asked Witherwax.

"Do? I was so sore I could have let him have it right in the
puss, but I thought, no, that wouldn't be good for Rotary, so I
just walked away. Well, that was only the beginning of it. It
seemed I couldn't go anywhere or do anything without having
one of them show up, handing me his card and asking me to call
on him, or just sitting there staring at me. They used to come
to the agency sometimes, and I got so I could tell when a prospect wasn't listening to me at all, just standing there on the floor
looking at me, he wasn't interested in the Olds, he was just
another damn undertaker. I've even had them follow me on the
street. You know how you get a little prickly feeling in the back
of the neck when somebody's looking at you behind your back
like that? I know there are some people say it's a superstition,
but I'm telling you it happened to me. Anyone from Indianapolis will tell you that my reputation for telling the truth about
things like that is A-1. Absolutely A-1.

"Well, the worst of it was when I got an invitation to give my
speech at the Queen of Heaven Association in Chicago. I
thought it was some sort of religious group, so I went, but when
I got there, it was a whole roomful of these undertakers, sitting
around the lunch tables and staring at me, some of them taking
notes. It was so bad I couldn't even give the old speech. I had
to fake I had a bellyache and get the hell out of there."

"Wait a minute," said Keating. "It seems to me that you could
save yourself a lot of trouble with a thing like that by just relax-
ing. If you're so valuable to undertakers that they want to use
you as a model all the time, why don't you just have some

pictures taken and sell them to them. That's all they want, isn't it?"

"Yeah," said Moutier, "that's what the looney-doctor said when the little woman sent me to him. My friend, let me tell you there are a couple of difficulties about that program. In the first place it wouldn't look good for a member of Rotary to have his picture plastered all over every undertaker's shop in the country, looking as if he was dead and all laid out in a casket. The little woman wouldn't stand for it, and I wouldn't blame her.

"And in the second place it's a lot more serious being a—uh —subject for an undertaker than you might think. I told you I wasn't seeing Leroy B. Smith any more, but the little woman, she kind of kept up the connection with Elise Smith, and they used to gab at each other in the back yard. You know how women are. Well, about a month after this Queen of Heaven Association luncheon in Chicago, the little woman tells me at dinner one night that Elise has some news. She says Tony Passone has bought out the Weizmann undertaking shop over on Third Street.

"I said: 'What the hell do I care? The less I hear about undertakers the better.'

"She said: 'You needn't be rude. Elise was just trying to do you a favor.'

"I said I didn't want any favors from undertakers or their families, and maybe we had a little argument, but after she quieted down, she told me that this Tony Passone had been one of these gangsters in Chicago, but decided to go into the undertaking business—burying the stiffs other people made instead of making them himself, ha, ha. Only it wasn't very funny when I got to thinking that maybe this Tony Passone had been in the audience at the Queen of Heaven Association, if you get it.

"Well, I was right. This Passone hadn't been in town for more than a week before I got a circular from him, you know the kind undertakers put out, with photographs of tombs and stone angels. I didn't pay any attention to it. There was nobody dead in the family and I didn't want anybody to be. But about a week after that I got a phone call. The voice at the other end said this was Passone's Sympathetic Service, and Mr. Passone would like to have me call. I said I didn't want any service from Mr. Passone and hung up; but after I hung up, I got to worrying about it, so I went around to the police station and asked them for protection.

"When they asked me who I wanted to be protected against, and I told them, they just laughed and said that Tony was a legitimate businessman now and the only way to be protected against an undertaker was to stay alive. That's the way things are with this Raw Deal administration they have in Washington, and the next thing I knew, there was another call from this Passone, saying I better come around and see him.

"Well, I didn't go, but about three days after that, when I had finished demonstrating the Olds for a man who lived about twelve miles out and was coming back alone in the car, another car pulled up alongside me at a red light, with a couple of guys that had hats down over their faces, and somebody took a shot at me. If I hadn't been nervous about this undertaker business and seen his hand coming up, and if the Olds didn't have such wonderful pick-up, he might have hit me, too.

"Well, it didn't take me long to figure out that I'd be just as good to Tony Passone dead as I would be alive, and the police still wouldn't believe that he was after me, so I just said to myself, Fred Moutier, you're getting out of here, so I gave up the agency and sold my house and came here. And you can see why I get nervous when somebody says I'm a perfect subject . . ."

Moutier had been showing a tendency to run his sentences together. Now his words went down to a mumble, and as though the bones in his legs were melting, he folded gradually and gently to the floor.

"Ah, the poor felly, now," said Mr. Cohan. "I should never of given him that last one. But with him talking along and all, I thought he was all right."

Jeffers and Keating bent to help the prostrate figure but before they could get him upright, a voice said: "Let me assist him.

I assure you I will take very good care of him, very good."

They looked up and saw a man in a sober blue serge suit, with a white shirt and a polka-dot tie. He wore an expression in which eagerness combined with melancholy, and his fingers were twitching slightly.

MEMENTO MORI

by BILL PRONZINI

If you want to look at it a certain way, archeologists and anthropologists may be considered benevolent (usually) ghouls. They spend most of their time, after all, poking around in the graves of the long-dead—digging them up, desecrating them, robbing them of the bones they have contained for centuries. They do this in the interest of scientific knowledge, of course, and without malicious or unholy intent. And yet . . .

Philip Asher, the murder victim in this story, was an anthropologist and a ghoul—a distinction that will become apparent to you as it becomes apparent to the police officers investigating his bizarre demise. And it is a bizarre demise, for Asher was bludgeoned to death with a human skull which he kept in his study as a "Memento Mori," a reminder of mortality. The motive for his murder is equally bizarre; you might even say it is downright ghoulish . . .

Bill Pronzini was born in 1943, made his first professional sale in 1966, of a short story entitled "You Don't Know What It's Like," and became a full-time writer in 1969. Over the past fifteen years he has produced twenty-three novels, most of them mystery/suspense, among them the recent "novel of terror" from Arbor House, Masques, *and a mainstream collaboration with columnist Jack Anderson called* The Cambodia File; *some two hundred fifty short stories and articles; one forthcom-*

ing book of nonfiction, Gun in Cheek, *a humorous study of "alterna-
tive" (classically bad) mysteries; and thirteen fantasy/horror, mystery, and
science fiction anthologies. Like Agatha Christie, he gets most of his ideas
and does most of his plotting in the bathtub; unlike Mrs. Christie, he does
not eat apples while so engaged.*

THERE ARE murder weapons and there are murder weapons, but
the thing used to bludgeon Philip Asher to death was the grisli-
est I'd seen in more than two decades on the police force.

It was a skull—a human skull.

Ed Crane and I stood staring down at what was left of it, lying
splintered and gore-streaked to one side of the dead man. It had
apparently cracked like an eggshell on the first or second blow,
but that first or second blow had been enough to shatter Asher's
skull as well. Judging from the concavity of the wound, he had
been struck with considerable force.

I pulled my gaze away and let it move over the room, a large
masculine study. Well-used, leather-bound books covered two
walls, and a third was adorned with what appeared to be primitive Mexican or Central American art and craftwork: pottery,
statuary, wood carvings, weaponry. There were two teakwood
desks arranged so that they faced each other—one large and
ostentatious, the other small and functional—and several pieces
of teak-and-leather furniture. It should have been a comfortable
room, but for me it wasn't; there seemed to be a kind of cold,
impersonal quality to it, despite the books and art. Or maybe I
was just overreacting to the dead man's presence, and to the
presence of the broken and bloody skull.

Crane said, "If I wasn't seeing it for myself, I don't think I'd
believe it."

"Yeah."

He made a soft blowing sound between pursed lips, rubbed
at the bald spot on the crown of his head. "Well, I've had
enough in here if you have."

"More than enough," I agreed.

We crossed to the double entrance doors and went into the hallway beyond. At its far end was a large living room containing more of both teakwood furniture and primitive art. One of the two patrolmen who had preceded us on the scene stood stoically beside a long sofa; the other officer was waiting outside for the arrival of the lab crew and the coroner. Sitting stiff-backed in middle of the sofa was Douglas Falconer—hands flat on his knees, eyes blinking myopically behind thick-lensed glasses. He was about forty, with a thin, chinless face and sparse sand-colored hair, dressed in slacks and a navy blue shirt. He looked timid and harmless; but when he'd called headquarters a half-hour earlier, he had confessed to the murder of Philip Asher. The dried stains on his right shirt sleeve and on the back of his right hand confirmed his guilt well enough.

All we knew about Falconer and Asher was that the deceased owned this house, an expensive Spanish-style villa in one of the city's finer residential areas; that Falconer had been his male secretary; that no one else had been present at the time of the slaying; and that the crime had been committed, in Falconer's words, "during a moment of blind fury." We had no idea as to motive, and we hadn't been prepared at all for the nature of the murder weapon.

Falconer kept on blinking as Crane and I approached and stopped one on either side of him, but his eyes did not seem to be seeing anything in the room. I thought maybe he'd gone into delayed shock, but when I said his name, his head jerked up and the eyes focused on me. They, like the rest of his features, were expressionless.

I said, "You want to tell us about it, Falconer?" We'd already apprised him of his rights, and he had waived his privilege of presence of counsel during questioning.

"I murdered Asher," he said. His voice was soft, resigned. "I already told you that. At first I thought of trying to cover it up, make it look as though a burglar had done it. But I'm not a very good liar, even though I've had a lot of practice. Besides, I . . . I don't much care what happens to me from now on."

"Why did you kill him?" Crane asked.

Falconer shook his head—not so much a refusal to answer as a reluctance or inability to put voice to the reason. We would get it out of him sooner or later, so there was no point in trying to force it.

I said, "Why the skull, Mr. Falconer? Where did you get a thing like that?"

He closed his eyes, popped them open again. "Asher kept it on the shelf behind his desk. He was sitting at the desk when I . . . when I did it."

"He kept a human skull in full view in his study?" Crane's tone was incredulous. "What the hell for?"

"He had a macabre sense of humor. He claimed to enjoy the reactions of visitors when they saw it. It was his *memento mori*, he said."

"His what?"

"Reminder of death," Falconer said. "A thing that reminds us we're all mortal and all must die someday."

"That sounds pretty morbid to me."

"Philip Asher was a fearless, cold-blooded man. Death never bothered him in the least. In one sense, it was his life; he devoted his life to the dead."

Crane and I exchanged glances. "You'd better explain that," I said.

"He was an anthropologist, quite a renowned one," Falconer said. "He published several books on the Mayan and Aztec races, and was in great demand as a lecturer and as a consultant to various university anthropological departments specializing in pre-Columbian studies."

"You were his full-time secretary, is that right?"

"Yes. I helped him with research, accompanied him on his expeditions to the Yucatán and other parts of Mexico and Central America, correlated his notes, typed his book manuscripts and business correspondence."

"How long did you work for him?"

"Eight years."

"Do you live here?"

"Yes. I have a room in the south wing."

"Does anyone else live in this house?"

"No. Asher never remarried after his wife left him several years ago. He had no close relatives."

Crane said, "Did you premeditate his death?"

"I didn't plan to kill him today, if that's what you mean."

"The two of you had an argument, then?"

"No, there wasn't any argument."

"Then what triggered this murderous rage of yours?" I asked. "What happened this morning that made a killer out of you?"

He started to shake his head again, and then slumped backward bonelessly. His eyes seemed to be looking again at something not in the room.

At length he said, "It was a . . . revelation."

"Revelation?"

"Yes."

I traded another look with Crane. To Falconer I said, "Go ahead."

A heavy sigh. "I received a letter yesterday from another anthropologist I'd met through Asher," he said, "asking me to become his personal secretary at a substantial increase in salary. I considered the offer, and this morning decided that I couldn't afford to turn it down. But when I talked to Asher about it, he refused to accept my resignation. He said he couldn't be certain of my continued silence if I were no longer in his employ or in his house. He ordered me to remain. He said he would take steps against me if I didn't . . ."

"Wait a minute," I said. "Your continued silence about what?"

"Something that happened six years ago."

"What something?"

He didn't speak again for several seconds. Then he swallowed and said, "The death of his wife and her lover at Asher's summer lodge on Lake Pontrain."

We stared at him. Crane said, "You told us a couple of minutes ago that his wife had left him, not that she was dead."

"Did I? Yes, I suppose I did. I've told the same lie, in exactly the same way, so many times that it's an automatic response. Mildred and her lover died at Lake Pontrain; that is the truth."

"All right—how did they die?"

"By asphyxiation," he said. "It happened on a Saturday in September, six years ago. Early that morning Asher decided on the spur of the moment to spend a few days at the lodge; the book he was writing at the time was going badly and he thought a change of scenery might help. He drove up alone at eight; I had an errand to do and then followed in my own car about an hour later. When I reached the lodge I found Asher inside with the bodies. They were in bed—Mildred, who was supposed to have been visiting a friend in Los Angeles, and the man. I'd never seen him before; I found out later he was an itinerant musician." Pause. "They were both naked," he said.

"What did Asher say when you walked in?"

"That he'd found them just as they were. The lodge had been full of gas when he arrived, he said, and he'd aired it out. A tragic accident caused by a faulty gas heater in the bedroom."

"Did you believe that?" I asked.

"Yes. I was stunned. I'd always thought Mildred above such a thing as infidelity. She was beautiful, yes—but always so quiet, so dignified . . ."

"Was Asher also stunned?"

"He seemed to be," Falconer said. "But he was quite calm. When I suggested we contact the authorities he wouldn't hear of it. Think of the scandal, he said—the possible damage to his reputation and his career. I asked what else we could do. I wasn't prepared for his answer."

"Which was?"

"He suggested in that cold, calculating way of his that we dispose of the bodies, bury them somewhere at the lake. Then we could concoct a story to explain Mildred's disappearance, say that she had moved out and gone back to Boston, where she was born. He insisted no one would question this explanation, because he and Mildred had few close friends and because of his reputation. As it happened, he was right."

"So you went along with this coverup?"

"What choice did I have? I'm not a forceful man, and at the time I respected Asher and his judgment. And as I told you, I was stunned. Yes, I went along with it. I helped Asher transfer the bodies to a promontory a mile away, where we buried them beneath piles of rocks."

Crane said, "So for six years you kept this secret—until today, until something happened this morning."

"Yes."

"These 'steps' Asher told you he'd take if you tried to leave his employ—were they threats of bodily harm?"

Falconer nodded. "He said he would kill me."

"Pretty drastic just to insure your silence about two accidental deaths six years ago."

"Yes. I said the same thing to him."

"And?"

"He told me the truth," Falconer said.

What that truth was seemed obvious now. I said, "That his wife and her lover *didn't* die by accident? That he'd murdered them?"

"That's right. He found them in bed together, very much alive; his massive ego had been wounded, the sin was unforgivable and had to be punished—that was how Philip Asher was. He knocked them both out with his fists. I suppose I would have seen evidence of that if I'd looked closely at the bodies, but in my distraught state I noticed nothing. Then he suffocated them with a pillow. I arrived before he could remove the bodies by himself, and so he made up the story about the faulty gas heater. If I hadn't believed it, if I hadn't helped him, he would have killed me too, then and there."

"Did he tell you that too?"

"Yes."

"All of this is the revelation you were talking about, isn't it?" I said. "When you found out you'd been working for a murderer the past six years, that you'd helped cover up a cold-blooded double homicide, you lost control and picked up the skull and bashed his head in with it."

"No," Falconer said. "No, not exactly. I was sickened by his confession and by my part in the whole ugly affair; I loathed him and I wanted to strike back at him. But I'm not a violent man. It was his *second* revelation that made me do what I did."

"What was it, this second revelation?"

"Something else he'd done, a year after the murders. I don't know why he told me about it, but then he was quite mad. He had to have been mad, you see—a mad ghoul." Falconer laughed mirthlessly. "Mad ghoul. It sounds funny, doesn't it? Like an old Bela Lugosi film. But that's just what Asher was, always poking around among the dead."

"Mr. Falconer—"

He let out a shuddering breath. "Asher's *memento mori* didn't come from Mexico, as I always believed; it came from that promontory at Lake Pontrain. I killed him, using the one fitting weapon for his destruction, when he told me I'd been working in that study of his all these years, *all these years,* with the skull of the only woman I ever loved grinning at me over his shoulder . . ."

GRAY MATTER

by STEPHEN KING

There is a type of ghoul you have not as yet encountered, and it is only fitting that he be saved for the last entry in this book. He is the created *ghoul—that is, a living person who, through a natural (or unnatural, but not supernatural) agency, is transformed into a thing of unspeakable proportions. What sort of natural (or unnatural) agency, you may ask? Well, it could be anything. It could be something as simple as the kind of fungoid mildew—the gray matter—that collects around the edges of beer can tops. The unsuspecting victim pops the tab on the can without thinking to wipe it off first, and drinks some of the beer, and ingests the mildew along with the brew.*

That is what happens to poor Richie Grenadine in "Gray Matter." And what happens to him after that *is just about the most awful transformation in all of fiction. Not only does Richie begin to change shape and substance, but he develops certain insatiable appetites—such as a hunger for dead cats, among other things . . .*

It is beyond question that Stephen King was and is the literary phenomenon of the seventies and early eighties. Everything he has written, beginning with his first novel, Carrie, *in 1975, has turned to pure gold. Each new novel—*Salem's Lot, The Shining, The Stand, The Dead Zone, Firestarter—*became an instant bestseller, as did his first collec-*

tion, Night Shift, *and his recent nonfiction study of the horror genre,* Danse Macabre. Carrie, Salem's Lot, *and* The Shining *were made into successful films. His short stories are in constant demand by magazine editors and anthologists. He is the undisputed modern master of the weird tale, and his work is consistently fresh, literate and powerful. It may only be added that King is alive and well and still going strong; long live (and write) the King.*

THEY HAD been predicting a norther all week and along about Thursday we got it, a real screamer that piled up eight inches by four in the afternoon and showed no signs of slowing down. The usual five or six were gathered around the Reliable in Henry's Nite-Owl, which is the only little store on this side of Bangor that stays open right around the clock.

Henry don't do a huge business—mostly, it amounts to selling the college kids their beer and wine—but he gets by and it's a place for us old duffers on Social Security to get together and talk about who's died lately and how the world's going to hell.

This afternoon Henry was at the counter; Bill Pelham, Bertie Connors, Carl Littlefield, and me was tipped up by the stove. Outside, not a car was moving on Ohio Street, and the plows was having hard going. The wind was socking drifts across that looked like the backbone on a dinosaur.

Henry'd only had three customers all afternoon—that is, if you want to count in blind Eddie. Eddie's about seventy, and he ain't completely blind. Runs into things, mostly. He comes in once or twice a week and sticks a loaf of bread under his coat and walks out with an expression on his face like: *there, you stupid sonsabitches, fooled you again*

Bertie once asked Henry why he never put a stop to it.

"I'll tell you," Henry said. "A few years back the Air Force wanted twenty million dollars to rig up a flyin' model of an airplane they had planned out. Well, it cost them seventy-five million and then the damn thing wouldn't fly. That happened ten years ago, when blind Eddie and myself were considerable younger, and I voted for the woman who sponsored that bill. Blind Eddie voted against her. And since then I've been buyin' his bread."

Bertie didn't look like he quite followed all of that, but he sat back to muse over it.

Now the door opened again, letting in a blast of the cold gray air outside, and a young kid came in, stamping snow off his boots. I placed him after a second. He was Richie Grenadine's kid, and he looked like he'd just kissed the wrong end of the baby. His Adam's apple was going up and down and his face was the color of old oilcloth.

"Mr. Parmalee," he says to Henry, his eyeballs rolling around in his head like ball bearings, "you got to come. You got to take him his beer and come. I can't stand to go back there. I'm scared."

"Now slow down," Henry says, taking off his white butcher's apron and coming around the counter. "What's the matter? Your dad been on a drunk?"

I realized when he said that that Richie hadn't been in for quite some time. Usually he'd be by once a day to pick up a case of whatever beer was going cheapest at that time, a big fat man with jowls like pork butts and ham-hock arms. Richie always was a pig about his beer, but he handled it okay when he was working at the sawmill out in Clifton. Then something happened—a pulper piled a bad load, or maybe Richie just made it out that way—and Richie was off work, free an' easy, with the sawmill company paying him compensation. Something in his back. Anyway, he got awful fat. He hadn't been in lately, although once in a while I'd seen his boy come in for Richie's nightly case. Nice enough boy. Henry sold him the beer, for he knew it was only the boy doing as his father said.

"He's been on a drunk," the boy was saying now, "but that ain't the trouble. It's . . . it's . . . oh Lord, it's *awful!*"

Henry saw he was going to bawl, so he says real quick: "Carl, will you watch things for a minute?"

"Sure."

"Now, Timmy, you come back into the stockroom and tell me what's what."

He led the boy away, and Carl went around behind the counter and sat on Henry's stool. No one said anything for quite a while. We could hear 'em back there, Henry's deep, slow voice and then Timmy Grenadine's high one, speaking very fast. Then the boy commenced to cry, and Bill Pelham cleared his throat and started filling up his pipe.

"I ain't seen Richie for a couple months," I said.

Bill grunted. "No loss."

"He was in . . . oh, near the end of October," Carl said. "Near Halloween. Bought a case of Schlitz beer. He was gettin' awful meaty."

There wasn't much more to say. The boy was still crying, but he was talking at the same time. Outside the wind kept on whooping and yowling and the radio said we'd have another six inches or so by morning. It was mid-January and it made me wonder if anyone had seen Richie since October—besides his boy, that is.

The talking went on for quite a while, but finally Henry and the boy came back out. The boy had taken his coat off, but Henry had put his on. The boy was kinda hitching in his chest the way you do when the worst is past, but his eyes was red and when he glanced at you, he'd look down at the floor.

Henry looked worried. "I thought I'd send Timmy here upstairs an' have my wife cook him up a toasted cheese or somethin'. Maybe a couple of you fellas'd like to go around to Richie's place with me. Timmy says he wants some beer. He gave me the money." He tried to smile, but it was a pretty sick affair and he soon gave up.

"Sure," Bertie says. "What kind of beer? I'll go fetch her."

"Get Harrow's Supreme," Henry said. "We got some cutdown boxes back there."

I got up, too. It would have to be Bertie and me. Carl's arthritis gets something awful on days like this, and Billy Pelham don't have much use of his right arm anymore.

Bertie got four six-packs of Harrow's and I packed them into a box while Henry took the boy upstairs to the apartment, overhead.

Well, he straightened that out with his missus and came back down, looking over his shoulder once to make sure the upstairs door was closed. Billy spoke up, fairly busting: "What's up? Has Richie been workin' the kid over?"

"No," Henry said. "I'd just as soon not say anything just yet. It'd sound crazy. I will show you somethin', though. The money Timmy had to pay for the beer with." He shed four dollar bills out of his pocket, holding them by the corner, and I don't blame him. They was all covered with a gray, slimy stuff that looked like the scum on top of bad preserves. He laid them down on the counter with a funny smile and said to Carl; "Don't let anybody touch 'em. Not if what the kid says is even half-right!"

And he went around to the sink by the meat counter and washed his hands.

I got up, put on my pea coat and scarf and buttoned up. It was no good taking a car; Richie lived in an apartment building down on Curve Street, which is as close to straight up an' down as the law allows, and it's the last place the plows touch.

As we were going out, Bill Pelham called after us: "Watch out, now."

Henry just nodded and put the case of Harrow's on the little hand cart he keeps by the door, and out we trundled.

The wind hit us like a sawblade, and right away I pulled my scarf up over my ears. We paused in the doorway just for a second while Bertie pulled on his gloves. He had a pained sort of a wince on his face, and I knew how he felt. It's all well for younger fellows to go out skiing all day and running those goddamn wasp-wing snowmobiles half the night, but when you get up over seventy without an oil change, you feel that northeast wind around your heart.

"I don't want to scare you boys," Henry said, with that queer, sort of revolted smile still on his mouth, "but I'm goin' to show you this all the same. And I'm goin' to tell you what the boy told me while we walk up there . . . because I want you to know, you see!"

And he pulled a .45-caliber hogleg out of his coat pocket—the pistol he'd kept loaded and ready under the counter ever since he went to twenty-four hours a day back in 1958. I don't know where he got it, but I do know the one time he flashed it at a stickup guy, the fella just turned around and bolted right out the door. Henry was a cool one, all right. I saw him throw out a college kid that came in one time and gave him a hard time about cashing a check. That kid walked away like his ass was on sideways and he had to crap.

Well, I only tell you that because Henry wanted Bertie and me to know he meant business, and we did, too.

So we set out, bent into the wind like washerwomen, Henry trundling that cart and telling us what the boy had said. The wind was trying to rip the words away before we could hear 'em, but we got most of it—more'n we wanted to. I was damn glad Henry had his Frenchman's pecker stowed away in his coat pocket.

The kid said it must have been the beer—you know how you can get a bad can every now and again. Flat or smelly or green as the peestains in an Irishman's underwear. A fella once told me that all it takes is a tiny hole to let in bacteria that'll do some damn strange things. The hole can be so small that the beer won't hardly dribble out, but the bacteria can get in. And beer's good food for some of those bugs.

Anyway, the kid said Richie brought back a case of Golden Light just like always that night in October and sat down to polish it off while Timmy did his homework.

Timmy was just about ready for bed when he hears Richie say, "Christ Jesus, that ain't right."

And Timmy says, "What's that, pop?"

"That beer," Richie says. "God, that's the *worst* taste I ever had in my mouth."

Most people would wonder why in the name of God he drank it if it tasted so bad, but then, most people have never seen Richie Grenadine go to his beer. I was down in Wally's Spa one afternoon, and I saw him win the goddamnedest bet. He bet a fella he could drink twenty two-bit glasses of beer in one minute.

Nobody local would take him up, but this salesman from Montpelier laid down a twenty-dollar bill and Richie covered him. He drank all twenty with seven seconds to spare—although when he walked out he was more'n three sails into the wind. So I expect Richie had most of that bad can in his gut before his brain could warn him.

"I'm gonna puke," Richie says. "Look out!"

But by the time he got to the head it had passed off, and that was the end of it. The boy said he smelt the can, and it smelt like something crawled in there and died. There was a little gray dribble around the top, too.

Two days later the boy comes home from school and there's Richie sitting in front of the TV and watching the afternoon tearjerkers with every goddamn shade in the place pulled down.

"What's up?" Timmy asks, for Richie don't hardly ever roll in before nine.

"I'm watchin' the TV," Richie says. "I didn't seem to want to go out today."

Timmy turned on the light over the sink, and Richie yelled at him: "And turn off that friggin' light!"

So Timmy did, not asking how he's gonna do his homework in the dark. When Richie's in that mood, you don't ask him nothing.

"An' go out an' get me a case," Richie says. "Money's on the table."

When the kid gets back, his dad's still sitting in the dark, only now it's dark outside, too. And the TV's off. The kid starts getting the creeps—well, who wouldn't? Nothing but a dark flat and your daddy setting in the corner like a big lump.

So he puts the beer on the table, knowing that Richie don't like it so cold it spikes his forehead, and when he gets close to his old man he starts to notice a kind of rotten smell, like an old cheese someone left standing on the counter over the weekend. He don't say shit or go blind, though, as the old man was never what you'd call a cleanly soul. Instead he goes into his room and shuts the door and does his homework, and after a while he hears the TV start to go and Richie's popping the top in his first of the evening.

And for two weeks or so, that's the way things went. The kid got up in the morning and went to school an' when he got home Richie'd be in front of the television, and beer money on the table.

The flat was smelling ranker and ranker, too. Richie wouldn't have the shades up at all, and about the middle of November he made Timmy stop studying in his room. Said he couldn't abide the light under the door. So Timmy started going down the block to a friend's house after getting his dad the beer.

Then one day when Timmy came home from school—it was four o'clock and pretty near dark already—Richie says, "Turn on the light."

The kid turns on the light over the sink, and damn if Richie ain't all wrapped up in a blanket.

"Look," Richie says, and one hand creeps out from under the blanket. Only it ain't a hand at all. *Something gray,* is all the kid could tell Henry. *Didn't look like a hand at all. Just a gray lump.*

Well, Timmy Grenadine was scared bad. He says, "Pop, what's happening to you?"

And Richie says, "I dunno. But it don't hurt. It feels . . . kinda nice."

So, Timmy says, "I'm gonna call Dr. Westphail."

And the blanket starts to tremble all over, like something awful was shaking—*all over*—under there. And Richie says, "Don't you dare. If you do I'll touch ya and you'll end up just like this." And he slides the blanket down over his face for just a minute.

By then we were up to the corner of Harlow and Curve Street, and I was even colder than the temperature had been on Henry's Orange Crush thermometer when we came out. A person doesn't hardly want to believe such things, and yet there's still strange things in the world.

I once knew a fella named George Kelso, who worked for the Bangor Public Works Department. He spent fifteen years fixing water mains and mending electricity cables and all that, an' then one day he just up an' quit, not two years before his retirement. Frankie Haldeman, who knew him, said George went down into a sewer pipe on Essex laughing and joking just like always and came up fifteen minutes later with his hair just as white as snow and his eyes staring like he just looked through a window into hell. He walked straight down to the BPW garage and punched his clock and went down to Wally's Spa and started drinking. It killed him two years later. Frankie said he tried to talk to him about it and George said something one time, and that was when he was pretty well blotto. Turned around on his stool, George did, an' asked Frankie Haldeman if he'd ever seen a spider as big as a good-sized dog setting in a web full of kitties an' such all wrapped up in silk thread. Well, what could he say to that? I'm not saying there's any truth in it, but I am saying that there's things in the corners of the world that would drive a man insane to look 'em right in the face.

So we just stood on the corner a minute, in spite of the wind that was whooping up the street.

"What'd he see?" Bertie asked.

"He said he could still see his dad," Henry answered, "but he said it was like he was buried in gray jelly . . . and it was all kinda mashed together. He said his clothes were all stickin' in and out of his skin, like they was melted to his body."

"Holy Jesus," Bertie said.

"Then he covered right up again and started screaming at the kid to turn off the light."

"Like he was a fungus," I said.

"Yes," Henry said. "Sorta like that."

"You keep that pistol handy," Bertie said.

"Yes, I think I will." And with that, we started to trundle up Curve Street.

The apartment house where Richie Grenadine had his flat was almost at the top of the hill, one of those big Victorian monsters that were built by the pulp an' paper barons at the turn of the century. They've just about all been turned into apartment houses now. When Bertie got his breath he told us Richie lived on the third floor under that top gable that jutted out like an eyebrow. I took the chance to ask Henry what happened to the kid after that.

Along about the third week in November the kid came back one afternoon to find Richie had gone one further than just pulling the shades down. He'd taken and nailed blankets across every window in the place. It was starting to stink worse, too— kind of a mushy stink, the way fruit gets when it goes to ferment with yeast.

A week or so after that, Richie got the kid to start heating his beer on the stove. Can you feature that? The kid all by himself in that apartment with his dad turning into . . . well, into some-thing . . . an' heating his beer and then having to listen to him —it—drinking it with awful thick slurping sounds, the way an old man eats his chowder. Can you imagine it?

And that's the way things went on until today, when the kid's school let out early because of the storm.

"The boy says he went right home," Henry told us. "There's no light in the upstairs hall at all—the boy claims his dad musta snuck out some night and broke it—so he had to sort of creep down to his door.

"Well, he heard somethin' moving around in there, and it suddenly pops into his mind that he don't know what Richie does all day through the week. He ain't seen his dad stir out of that chair for almost a month, and a man's got to sleep and go to the bathroom sometime.

"There's a Judas hole in the middle of the door, and it's supposed to have a latch on the inside to fasten it shut, but it's been busted ever since they lived there. So the kid slides up to the door real easy and pushed it open a bit with his thumb and pokes his eye up to it."

By now we were at the foot of the steps and the house was looming over us like a high, ugly face, with those windows on the third floor for eyes. I looked up there and sure enough those two windows were just as black as pitch. Like somebody'd put blankets over 'em or painted 'em up.

"It took him a minute to get his eye adjusted to the gloom.

An' then he seen a great big gray lump, not like a man at all, slitherin' over the floor, leavin' a gray, slimy trail behind it. An' then it sort of snaked out an arm—or something like an arm— and pried a board off'n the wall. And took out a cat." Henry stopped for a second. Bertie was beating his hands together and it was godawful cold out there on the street, but none of us was ready to go up just yet. "A dead cat," Henry recommenced, "that had putrefacted. The boy said it looked all swole up stiff . . . and there was little white things crawlin' all over it . . ."

"Stop," Bertie said. "For Christ's sake."

"And then his dad ate it."

I tried to swallow and something tasted greasy in my throat.

"That's when Timmy closed the peephole." Henry finished softly. "And ran."

"I don't think I can go up there," Bertie said.

Henry didn't say nothing, just looked from Bertie to me and back again.

"I guess we better," I said. "We got Richie's beer."

Bertie didn't say anything to that, so we went up the steps and in through the front hall door. I smelled it right off.

Do you know how a cider house smells in summer? You never get the smell of apples out, but in the fall it's all right because it smells tangy and sharp enough to ream your nose right out. But in the summer, it just smells mean, this smell was like that, but a little bit worse.

There was one light on in the lower hall, a mean yellow thing in a frosted glass that threw a glow as thin as buttermilk. And those stairs that went up into the shadows.

Henry bumped the cart to a stop, and while he was lifting out the case of beer, I thumbed the button at the foot of the stairs that controlled the second-floor-landing bulb. But it was busted, just as the boy said.

Bertie quavered: "I'll lug the beer. You just take care of that pistol."

Henry didn't argue. He handed it over and we started up, Henry first, then me, then Bertie with the case in his arms. By the time we had fetched the second-floor landing, the stink was just that much worse. Rotted apples, all fermented, and under that an ever uglier stink.

When I lived out in Levant I had a dog one time—Rex, his name was—and he was a good mutt but not very wise about cars. He got hit a lick one afternoon while I was at work and he crawled under the house and died there. My Christ, what a stink. I finally had to go under and haul him out with a pole. That other stench was like that; flyblown and putrid and just as dirty as a borin' cob.

Up till then I had kept thinking that maybe it was some sort of joke, but I saw it wasn't. "Lord, why don't the neighbors kick up, Henry?" I asked.

"What neighbors?" Henry asked, and he was smiling that queer smile again.

I looked around and saw that the hall had a sort of dusty, unused look and the door of all three second-floor apartments was closed and locked up.

"Who's the landlord, I wonder?" Bertie asked, resting the case on the newel post and getting his breath. "Gaiteau? Surprised he don't kick 'im out."

"Who'd go up there and evict him?" Henry asked. "You?"

Bertie didn't say nothing.

Presently we started up the next flight, which was even narrower and steeper than the last. It was getting hotter, too. It sounded like every radiator in the place was clanking and hissing. The smell was awful, and I started to feel like someone was stirring my guts with a stick.

At the top was a short hall, and one door with a little Judas hole in the middle of it.

Bertie made a soft little cry an' whispered out: "Look what we're walkin' in!"

I looked down and saw all this slimy stuff on the hall floor, in little puddles. It looked like there'd been a carpet once, but the gray stuff had eaten it all away.

Henry walked down to the door, and we went after him. I

don't know about Bertie, but I was shaking in my shoes. Henry never hesitated, though; he raised up that gun and beat on the door with the butt of it.

"Richie?" he called, and his voice didn't sound a bit scared, although his face was deadly pale. "This is Henry Parmalee from down at the Nite-Owl. I brought your beer."

There wasn't any answer for p'raps a full minute, and then a voice said, "Where's Timmy? Where's my boy?"

I almost ran right then. That voice wasn't human at all. It was queer an' low an' bubbly, like someone talking through a mouthful of suet.

"He's at my store," Henry said, "havin' a decent meal. He's just as skinny as a slat cat, Richie."

There wasn't nothing for a while, and then some horrible squishing noises, like a man in rubber boots walking through mud. Then that decayed voice spoke right through the other side of the door.

"Open the door an' shove that beer through," it said. "Only you got to pull all the ring tabs first. I can't."

"In a minute," Henry said. "What kind of shape you in, Richie?"

"Never mind that," the voice said, and it was horribly eager. "Just push in the beer and go!"

"It ain't just dead cats anymore, is it?" Henry said, and he sounded sad. He wasn't holdin' the gun butt-up anymore; now it was business end first.

And suddenly, in a flash of light, I made the mental connection Henry had already made, perhaps even as Timmy was telling his story. The smell of decay and rot seemed to double in my nostrils when I remembered. Two young girls and some old Salvation Army wino had disappeared in town during the last three weeks or so—all after dark.

"Send it in or I'll come out an' get it," the voice said.

Henry gestured us back, and we went.

"I guess you better, Richie." He cocked his piece.

There was nothing then, not for a long time. To tell the truth, I began to feel as if it was all over. Then that door burst open, so sudden and so hard that it actually *bulged* before slamming out against the wall. And out came Richie.

It was just a second, just a second before Bertie and me was down those stairs like schoolkids, four an' five at a time, and out the door into the snow, slipping an' sliding.

Going down we heard Henry fire three times, the reports loud as grenades in the closed hallways of that empty, cursed house.

What we saw in that one or two seconds will last me a lifetime —or whatever's left of it. It was like a huge gray wave of jelly, jelly that looked like a man, and leaving a trail of slime behind it.

But that wasn't the worst. Its eyes were flat and yellow and wild, with no human soul in 'em. Only there wasn't two. There were four, an' right down the center of the thing, betwixt the two pairs of eyes, was a white, fibrous line with a kind of pulsing pink flesh showing through like a slit in a hog's belly.

It was dividing, you see. Dividing in two.

Bertie and I didn't say nothing to each other going back to the store. I don't know what was going through his mind, but I know well enough what was in mine: the multiplication table. Two times two is four, four times two is eight, eight times two is sixteen, sixteen times two is—

We got back. Carl and Bill Pelham jumped up and started asking questions right off. We wouldn't answer, neither of us. We just turned around and waited to see if Henry was gonna walk in outta the snow. I was up to 32,768 times two is the end of the human race and so we sat there cozied up to all that beer and waited to see which one was going to finally come back; and here we still sit.

I hope it's Henry. I surely do.

BIBLIOGRAPHY

BIBLIOGRAPHY

BOOK ONE: VOODOO!

NONFICTION:

Asbury, Herbert. *The French Quarter.* New York: Alfred A. Knopf, 1936. Chapter entitled "Voodoo."

Bach, Marcus. *Strange Altars.* New York: Bobbs-Merrill, 1952.

Cave, Hugh B. *Haiti: Highroad to Adventure.* New York: Henry Holt, 1952.

Deren, Maya. *Divine Horsemen: Voodoo Gods of Haiti.* New York: Delta Books, 1972.

Douglas, Drake. *Horror!* New York: Macmillan, 1966. Chapter entitled "The Walking Dead," which deals with voodoo and zombies in film and literature.

Dunham, Katherine. *Island Possessed.* New York: Doubleday, 1969.

Gonzalez-Wippler, Migene. *Santería: African Magic in Latin America.* New York: Julian Press, 1973.

Haskins, James. *Voodoo and Hoodoo.* New York: Stein & Day, 1978.

Herskovits, Melville J. *Life in a Haitian Valley.* New York: Alfred A. Knopf, 1937.

Hill, Douglas and Williams, Pat. *The Supernatural.* London: Aldus Books, Ltd., 1965. Chapter entitled "Land of Voodoo."

Hurston, Zora Neale. *Mules and Men.* Philadelphia: J.B. Lippincott, 1935.

Huxley, Francis. *The Invisibles.* New York: McGraw-Hill, 1969.

Kerboull, Jean. *Voodoo and Magic Practices.* London: Barrie & Jenkins, Ltd., 1978.

Kristos, Kyle. *Voodoo.* Philadelphia: J.B. Lippincott, 1976.

Langguth, A.J. *Macumba: White and Black Magic in Brazil.* New York: Harper, 1975.

Loederer, Richard A. *Voodoo Fire in Haiti.* New York: Doubleday Doran, 1935.

Martin, Kevin. *The Complete Book of Voodoo.* New York: G.P. Putnam's Sons, 1972.

Metraux, Alfred. *Voodoo in Haiti.* New York: Schocken Books, 1959.

Rigaud, Milo. *Secrets of Voodoo.* New York: Arco Books, 1970.

St. Clair, David. *Drum & Candle.* New York: Crown, 1971.

St. John, Spencer. *Hayti; or the Black Republic.* London: Smith, Elder & Company, 1884.

Seabrook, W.B. *The Magic Island.* New York: Harcourt Brace, 1929.

Tallant, Robert. *Voodoo in New Orleans.* New York: Macmillan, 1946.

Williams, Sheldon. *Voodoo and the Art of Haiti.* London: Morland Lee, Ltd., 1969.

FICTION:

Avallone, Michael. *The Voodoo Murders.* New York: Gold Medal, 1957.

Barrett, Monte. *Murder at Belle Camille.* New York: Bobbs-Merrill, 1943.

Bourne, Peter. *Drums of Destiny.* New York: G.P. Putnam's Sons, 1947.

Brandon, Michael. *Nonce.* New York: Coward-McCann, 1944.

Cave, Hugh B. *The Cross on the Drum.* New York: Doubleday, 1959.

————. *Legion of the Dead.* New York: Avon, 1979.

Chesnutt, Charles G. *The Conjure Woman.* Boston: Houghton-Mifflin, 1899. Collection of folkloric short stories.

Esteven, John. *Voodoo.* New York: Doubleday Crime Club, 1930.

Foran, W. Robert. *Drums of Sacrifice.* London: Hutchinson, 1934.

Gibson, Walter B. *Voodoo Death.* New York: Tempo Books, 1969.

Janson, Hank. *Voodoo Violence.* London: Roberts, 1964.

Lecale, Errol. *Zombie.* London: New English Library, 1975.

Meik, Vivian. *Devils' Drums.* London: Philip Allan, 1933. Collection of short stories.

Perkins, Kenneth. *Voodoo'd.* New York: Harper & Brothers, 1931.

Rohmer, Sax. *The Island of Fu Manchu.* New York: Doubleday Crime Club, 1941.

Tallant, Robert. *Voodoo Queen.* New York: G.P. Putnam's Sons, 1956.

Thoby-Marcelin, Philippe and Marcelin, Pierre. *Canapé Vert.* New York: Rinehart, 1944.

————. *The Beast of the Haitian Hills.* New York: Rinehart, 1946.

————. *The Pencil of God.* Boston: Houghton-Mifflin, 1951.

West, Morris. *Kundu.* New York: Dell Books, 1956.

Whitehead, Henry S. *Jumbee and Other Uncanny Tales.* Sauk City, Wisconsin: Arkham House, 1944. Collection of short stories.

————. *West India Lights.* Sauk City, Wisconsin: Arkham House, 1946. Collection of short stories.

PLAY:

St. Clair, Robert. *The Zombie.* Evanston, Illinois: Northwestern Press, 1941. Three acts.

FILMS:

Devil's Own, The (British, 1966). Joan Fontaine, Kay Walsh.

Disembodied, The (1957). Paul Burke, Allison Hayes.

Ghost Breakers, The (1940). Bob Hope, Paulette Goddard, Willie Best.

I Walked with a Zombie (1943). Frances Dee, Tom Conway, James Ellison. Written by Curt Siodmak and produced by Val Lewton; directed by Jacques Tourneur.

King of the Zombies (1941). John Archer, Henry Victor, Mantan Moreland.

Revenge of the Zombies (1943). John Carradine, Gale Storm, Mantan Moreland.

Revolt of the Zombies (1936). Dean Jagger, Dorothy Stone.

Voodoo Island (1957). Boris Karloff, Beverly Tyler, Murvyn Vye.

Voodoo Man, The (1944). Bela Lugosi, John Carradine.

Voodoo Tiger (1952). Johnny Weismuller, Jean Byron.

Voodoo Woman (1957). Marla English, Tom Conway.

White Zombie (1932). Bela Lugosi, Madge Bellamy, Robert Frazer.

Zombies of Mora Tau (1957). Gregg Palmer, Allison Hayes. (Also released as *The Dead That Walk.*)

Zombies on Broadway (1944). Bela Lugosi, Wally Brown, Alan Carney.

BOOK TWO: MUMMY!

NONFICTION:

Belzoni, Giovanni B. *Narrative of the Operations and Recent Discoveries in Egypt and Nubia.* London: 1820.

Brackman, Arnold C. *The Search for the Gold of Tutankhamun.* New York: Mason/Charter, 1976.

Bray, Warwick. *Everyday Life of the Aztecs.* New York: G.P. Putnam's Sons, 1968.

Brunton, Paul. *Search in Secret Egypt.* New York: 1936.

Budge, Sir E.A. Wallis. *Book of the Dead.* London: 1928.

————. *Egyptian Magic.* New York: University Books, 1958.

————. *The Mummy.* New York: Collier Books, 1972.

Carter, Howard and Mace, A.C. *The Tomb of Tut-ankh-Amen.* New York: Cooper Square Publishers, 1963. Reprint of three-volume work, 1923–1933.

Carter, Howard and the Earl of Carnarvon. *Five Years' Exploration at Thebes.* London: 1912.

Chapman, Francis W. *The Great Pyramid of Gizeh.* London: 1931.

Cottrell, Leonard. *The Secrets of Tutankhamun.* London: Evans Brothers, Ltd., 1965.

Dawson, Warren R. *Bibliography of Works Relating to Mummification in Egypt.* Cairo: 1929.

Disher, M. Willson. *Pharaoh's Fool.* London: Heinemann, 1957.

Douglas, Drake. *Horror!* New York: Macmillan, 1966. Chapter entitled "The Mummy," which deals with mummies in film and literature.

Fagan, Brian M. *The Rape of the Nile.* New York: Charles Scribner's Sons, 1975.

Garry, Thomas G. *Egypt: The Home of the Occult Sciences.* London: 1931.

Hoving, Thomas. *Tutankhamun: The Untold Story.* New York: Simon & Schuster, 1978.

Hurry, Jameison B. *Imhotep.* London: 1926.

McHargue, Georgess. *Mummies.* Philadelphia: J. B. Lippincott, 1972.

Mertz, Barbara. *Temples, Tombs and Hieroglyphs.* New York: Coward-McCann, 1964.

Noblecourt, C. Desroches. *Tutankhamun.* New York: New York Graphic Society, 1963.

Petrie, W.M. *Ten Years' Digging in Egypt, 1881–1891.* London: 1892.

Smith, Corinna Lindon (ed). *Tombs, Temples and Ancient Art.* Norman, Oklahoma: University of Oklahoma Press, 1956.

Tompkins, Peter. *Secrets of the Great Pyramid.* New York: Harper & Row, 1971.

Vandenberg, Philipp. *The Curse of the Pharaohs.* Philadelphia: J.B. Lippincott, 1975.

Von Hagen, Victor W. *World of the Maya.* New York: Signet Mentor, 1960.

Waisbard, Simone and Roger. *Masks, Mummies, and Magicians: A Voyage of Exploration in Pre-Inca Peru.* New York: Praeger, 1966.

Weigall, Arthur. *A History of the Pharaohs.* London: 1925.

FICTION

Bradbury, Ray (Photography by Archie Lieberman). *The Mummies of Guanajuato.* New York: Harry N. Abrams, 1978. Combination of photographs and text of Bradbury's story "The Next in Line."

Carr, John Dickson. *The Lost Gallows.* New York: Harper & Bros., 1931.

Cook, Robin. *Sphinx.* New York: G.P. Putnam's Sons, 1979.

Dreadstone, Carl. *The Mummy.* New York: Berkley Books, 1976. Novelization of 1932 Boris Karloff film of the same title.

Gaunt, Mary. *The Mummy Moves.* New York: Clode, 1925.

Gautier, Théophile. *Romance of a Mummy.* London: Spencer Blackett, 1856.

Ghidalia, Vic (ed.). *The Mummy Walks Among Us.* Middletown, Connecticut: American Education Publications, 1971. Anthology of mummy stories.

Griffith, George. *The Mummy and Miss Nitocris.* London: T. Werner Laurie, 1906.

Hard, T.W. *Sum VII.* New York: Harper & Row, 1979.

Kernahan, C. *The Mummy's Hand.* London: Mellifont, 1937.

King, T.S. *The Mummy's Curse.* London: Mellifont, 1933.

Lanse, John. *The Last Tomb.* New York: Bantam, 1974.

Morrah, Dermot. *The Mummy Case.* London: Faber & Faber, 1933.

Mundy, Talbot. *The Mystery of Khufu's Tomb.* New York: Appleton-Century, 1933.

Pettee, F.M. *The Palgrave Mummy.* London: Payson, 1929.

Pratt, Ambrose. *The Living Mummy.* London: Ward Lock, 1910.

Proctor, H.B. *The Mummy's Dream.* London: Simpkin, Marshall, 1898.

Rohmer, Sax. *The Bat Flies Low.* New York: Doubleday, 1935.

———. *Bat-Wing.* New York: Doubleday, 1921.

————. *Brood of the Witch Queen.* New York: Doubleday, 1924.

————. *The Green Eyes of Bast.* New York: McBride, 1920.

————. *Salute to Bazarada.* New York: Doubleday, 1939.

————. *Seven Sins.* New York: McBride, 1943.

————. *She Who Sleeps.* New York: Doubleday, 1928.

————. *Tales of East and West.* New York: Doubleday, 1933. Collection of short stories, some dealing with mummies and Egyptian mystery.

————. *Tales of Secret Egypt.* New York: McBride, 1919. Collection of short stories, all dealing with Egyptian mystery.

Sackville, Orme. *The Curse of Amen-Tah.* London: Modern Fiction, 1934.

Stephens, Riccardo. *The Mummy.* New York: Nash, 1912.

Stevenson, Burton. *A King in Babylon.* Boston: Small, Maynard, 1917.

Stoker, Bram. *The Jewel of Seven Stars.* London: Heinemann, 1903.

Thurston, E. Temple. *Mr. Bottleby Does Something.* New York: Doran, 1926.

Van Der Elst, Violet. *The Mummy Comes to Life.* London: Modern Fiction, 1946. Collection of short stories.

Van Dine, S.S. *The Scarab Murder Case.* New York: Charles Scribner's & Sons, 1930.

FILMS:

Abbott and Costello Meet the Mummy (1955). Bud Abbott, Lou Costello, Michael Ansara.

Attack of the Mayan Mummy (Mexican, 1963). Richard Webb, Nina Knight.

Aztec Mummy, The (Mexican, 1960). Ramon Gay, Steve Grant.

Blood from the Mummy's Tomb (British, 1972). Andrew Keir, Valerie Leon, George Coulouris.

Curse of King Tut's Tomb, The (Made-for-TV, 1980). Raymond Burr, Eva Marie Saint.

Curse of the Mummy's Tomb, The (British, 1965). Terence Morgan, Fred Clark.

Dust of Egypt, The (1915). Silent film.

Eyes of the Mummy, The (1918). Pola Negri, Emil Jannings. Directed by Ernst Lubitsch. Silent film.

Macabra (1980). Samantha Eggar, Roy Jenson.

Mummy, The (1911). Silent film.

Mummy, The (1932). Boris Karloff, Zita Johann, David Manners.

Mummy, The (British, 1959). Peter Cushing, Christopher Lee, Yvonne Furneaux.

Mummy of the King of Ramsee, The (1909). Silent film.

Mummy's Curse, The (1944). Lon Chaney, Jr., Virginia Christine.

Mummy's Ghost, The (1944). Lon Chaney, Jr., John Carradine, George Zucco.

Mummy's Hand, The (1940). Dick Foran, Peggy Moran, Wallace Ford, George Zucco, Tom Tyler.

Mummy's Shroud, The (British, 1967). Andre Morell, John Phillips.

Mummy's Tomb, The (1942). Lon Chaney, Jr., Dick Foran, Turhan Bey, George Zucco.

Wrestling Women Versus the Aztec Mummy (Mexican, 1965). Lorena Velasquez, Armand Sylvestre.

BOOK THREE: GHOUL!

NONFICTION

Ambler, Eric. *The Ability to Kill.* London: The Bodley Head, 1963.

Cohen, Daniel. *The Body Snatchers.* Philadelphia: Lippincott, 1975.

Fort, Charles. *Wild Talents.* New York: 1932

Hurwood, Bernhardt J. *Vampires, Werewolves and Ghouls.* New York: Ace Books, 1968.

Masters, R.L. *Perverse Crimes in History: Sadism, Lust-Murder, Necrophilia —Ancient to Modern Times.* New York: Julian Press, 1963.

Murphy, P.J. *Ghouls: Studies and Case Histories of Necrophilia.* London: J.R. Grant, 1965.

Zimmer, Heinrich. *The King and the Corpse.* New York: Pantheon Books, 1948.

FICTION

Brandner, Gary. . . . *Walkers.* New York: Fawcett Gold Medal, 1980.

Brooks, Collin. *The Body Snatchers.* London: Hutchinson, 1927.

Conklin, Groff (ed). *The Graveyard Reader.* New York: Ballantine Books, 1958. Collection of short stories, most of them ghoulish.

Cook, Robin. *Coma.* Boston: Little Brown, 1977.

Haining, Peter. *The Unspeakable People.* New York: Popular Library, 1969. Collection of short stories, most of them ghoulish.

King, Frank. *The Ghoul.* London: Bles, 1928.

Laumer, Keith. *Plague of Demons.* New York: Berkley Books, 1965.

Lem, Stanislaw. *The Investigation.* New York: 1974.

McDowell, Michael. *Cold Moon Over Babylon.* New York: Avon Books, 1980.

Ray, Jean. *Ghouls in My Grave.* New York: Berkley Books, 1965.

Rice, Jeff. *The Night Strangler.* New York: Pocket Books, 1974.

Romero, George, and Susanna Sparrow. *Dawn of the Dead.* New York: St. Martin's, 1978. Novelization of the film.

Russell, Ray. *Sardonicus.* New York: Ballantine Books, 1961. Collection of short stories, title novelette being ghoulish.

Russo, John. *Night of the Living Dead.* New York: Pocket Books, 1974. Novelization of the film.

Siodmak, Curt. *Donovan's Brain.* New York: Knopf, 1942.

Tralins, Robert. *Ghoul Lover.* New York: Popular Library, 1972.

Yarbro, Chelsea Quinn. *Dead and Buried.* New York: Warner Books, 1980. Novelization of the film.

FILMS

Body Snatcher, The (1945). Boris Karloff, Henry Daniell. Based on the story by Robert Louis Stevenson.

Coma (1978). Genevieve Bujold, Michael Douglas, Richard Widmark. Based on the novel by Robin Cook.

Corridors of Blood (1962). Boris Karloff, Betta St. John, Christopher Lee.

Dark, The (1978). William Devane, Cathy Lee Crosby.

Dawn of the Dead (1978). David Emge, Ken Foree.

Dead and Buried (1980). James Farentino, Jack Albertson.

Devil Commands, The (1941). Boris Karloff, Ann Revere.

Donovan's Brain (1953). Lew Ayres, Gene Evans. Based on the novel by Curt Siodmak.

Frozen Dead (1967). Dana Andrews.

Ghoul, The (1933). Boris Karloff, Sir Cedric Hardwicke, Ralph Richardson.

Ghoul, The (1974). Peter Cushing, John Hurt.

Horror Express (1972). Christopher Lee, Peter Cushing, Telly Savalas.

House of Wax (1953). Vincent Price, Frank Lovejoy, Carolyn Jones. Remake of *Mystery of the Wax Museum.*

Hunchback from the Morgue, The (Spanish-Italian, 1972). Paul Naschy.

Isle of the Dead (1945). Boris Karloff, Ellen Drew.

Mad Ghoul, The (1943). George Zucco, David Bruce.

Mr. Sardonicus (1961). Guy Rolfe, Oscar Homolka. Based on the novelette by Ray Russell.

Monster, The (1929). Lon Chaney, Sr.

Mystery of the Wax Museum (1933). Lionel Atwill, Fay Wray.

Night of the Living Dead (1968). Judith O'Dea, Russell Streiner.

Night Strangler, The (Made-for-TV, 1973). Darren McGavin, Simon Oakland, Jo Ann Pflug, John Carradine.

Oblong Box, The (1969). Vincent Price, Christopher Lee.

Premature Burial, The (1962). Ray Milland, Hazel Court. Based on the story by Edgar Allan Poe.

Tomb of Ligeia, The (1965). Vincent Price, Elizabeth Shepard.

Walking Dead, The (1936). Boris Karloff, Edmund Gwenn, Ricardo Cortez.